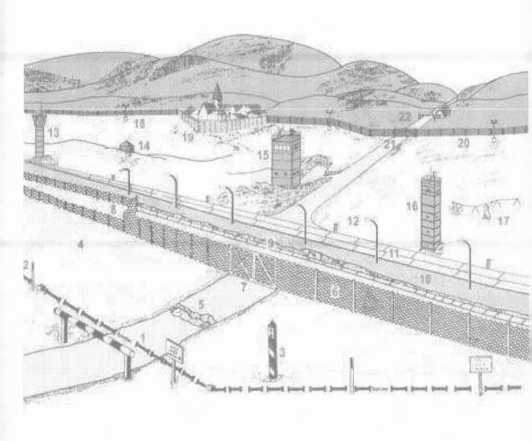

The First Sergeants

by
Richard E. Morgan, CSM (Ret)

DeRidder, Louisiana
2012

This publication is designed to provide accurate and authoritative information in regard to the subject matter covered. This book is sold with the understanding that the publisher is not engaged in rendering legal, accounting, or other professional services. If legal advice or other expert assistance is required, the services of a competent professional person should be sought.

First Printing, 2012
ISBN-10: 0615597564
ISBN-13: 978-0615597560 (Richard E Morgan)

Printed in the United States of America

Cover Design: Alan H. Anderson of Royal Atlantic E-Commerce, LLC
Front Cover Photo Credit: Jeff McCree
Back Cover Photo: Richard E. Morgan CSM (Ret)

DEDICATION

The First Sergeants is dedicated to the following:

To the Soldiers, Sailors, Marines, Airmen and Coast Guardsmen past and present who though they may need re-built, usually think they are just fine.

To the NCOs who do the job day in and day and know for sure the sitting President, whoever he may be, is in not in their Squad, but if he was, would chew his ass if he needed it, but he ain't.

To Officers who listen.

To Officers like David W. Dawson who teach and who back up their men.

To Linda and Leon Morgan, and Rhonda Brown who would not give up on me until I finished.

To Joe Nikruto whose brutal realism is always refreshing.

To Shonda Morales and Jason Swartz whose timely and incisive comments were a big help.

To Sergeant Major of the Army (Ret) Kenny Preston for his technical expertise and abiding friendship.

And finally, to the Renaissance man, LTG Daniel P. Bolger whose example, encouragement and deep insights made telling the story of re-building the peacetime Army worthwhile. May God or Allah, help our enemies when they go brain to brain against him and his troopers. They will need some form of salvation because they will be dead.

FORWARD

There are few things more American than the U. S. Cavalry. Think of John Ford's famous old western, *She Wore a Yellow Ribbon*, about the wars on the Great Plains. The film turns on the pending retirement of two veteran Cavalry Troopers, First Sergeant Timothy Quincannon, played by Victor MacLaglen, and Captain Nathan Brittles, played by John Wayne.

The First Sergeant stated: "The Army will never be the same when we retire, sir."

But the captain knew better. "The Army is always the same. The sun and the moon change, but the Army knows no seasons."

The Army is always the same. That movie had it right. Uniforms change. Faces change. Weapons and tactics change. But at its core, the Army is always the same. The Cavalry is always the same. And that is a result of a few men chosen to set and enforce the standards: the First Sergeants.

The essentials of Command Sergeant Major Dick Morgan's account would be very familiar to Timothy Quincannon or Nathan Brittles. But in the world of *The First Sergeants*, the enemies are not Plains warriors on swift ponies, but the armored regiments of the Soviet Russians over across the wire. Dick Morgan's Troopers do not ride the yellowing long grass of the Great Plains, but instead defend the rolling farmland of south central Germany. Their mounts are not big brown Federal horses, but great green snorting, clanking tanks capable of shooting a projectile the size of a fire extinguisher more than a mile away. And yet, from the Cavalry of the Plains Wars to the Cavalry of the Cold War, there is continuity. And that is embodied in the service and character of the men who make the Cavalry what it is—the First Sergeants.

For younger Americans, the dangerous stand-off between Americans and Russians in central Germany is as distant as the campaigning against the Sioux in the Dakota Territory. From today's vantage, it all seems very clear that the Soviets were doomed to collapse without initiating Armageddon, an outcome that to too many seems neatly preordained. But it was anything but inevitable to those who lived it, and indeed, made it so. For 46 years, from 1945 until 1991, men like Dick Morgan held the line, day and night, in heat and cold, in choking dust and driving rain. Their skill, discipline, determination—and guts—broke the will of the Russians, and ensured that the Cold War ended with a whimper, not a bang. This is their story.

Daniel P. Bolger
Lieutenant General, U.S. Army

PREFACE

Seventh Army was the centerpiece of the North Atlantic Treaty Organization (NATO). NATO was composed of the powers that won WW II. Though a political organization, the original NATO was organized for mutual defense. The primary foe of NATO was the Soviet Bloc led by the USSR consisting of the nations subjugated by the Soviets during their advance to Berlin. Each of these nation states was governed by off-shoots of the Communist Party. For all practical purposes, they were satellites of the USSR. As a bloc, they presented a strategic buffer between the USSR and its potential adversary, NATO. The USSR had an estimated 26 million casualties in WW II of a population of 99 million or nearly one in every four people of the nation. The surrogate states formed a barrier. If one draws a line from the 2d Squadron Border Camp to Moscow the following points are clear: It is 1,185 miles to Moscow; 600 miles to the Border of Belarus; and 214 miles to the Polish frontier. The nation states of Poland, Belarus, Hungary, Czechoslovakia and East Germany had some 98 million residents. Thus, the Russians were able to employ a strategy that enabled them to potentially fight to the last Pole or East German before any force penetrated the barrier to their homeland.

The forces of the United States Army Europe of the 1980's assigned to NATO were organized into an Army, the 7th Army, consisting of two Corps, Fifth Corps and Seventh Corps. The US provided the bulk of the forces of NATO. Each Corps was deployed in echelon with responsibility to defend West Germany from attack by the Russians from the East. The Corps were balanced as each was composed of an Infantry Division, an Armored Division, an Armored Cavalry Regiment and various units associated with the combat and combat service support of these forces. Each Corps area stretched approximately 200 kilometers or 120 miles north and south. It was defined and east and west from the westernmost border of East Germany to the easternmost border of France, Belgium, Luxembourg and to Holland. Both Corps were to be augmented by forces returning to Europe from the United States via a sea bridge of convoys of ships from America and a sky train of jet airliners flying soldiers from both the active duty force and reserve units to Europe. This plan, called REFORGER, was exercised by selected units on odd numbered years and by Command Post Exercises on even years.

The suppositions and assumptions contained in the REFORGER plan would not have sustained a hard look from any CGSC graduate. No submarines were employed against the ships and no fighters shot down any airliners during REFORGER. There was always a long workup period for the forces coming from America that may not have been present in a real world fight with the Soviets. But REFORGER was the best idea the hard pressed planners could devise that met the demands of Congress and the body politic to station the fewest possible forces in Europe and make some show of defending it.

This book is about a Cavalry (Cav) Troop and its parent units stationed on the East West German Border during the Cold War. The attitude of the soldiers of that era was, then, as it continues to be today, summarized by the phrase, "If it is to be, then it is up to me".

The average Cav Trooper in either the 2d or 11th Armored Cavalry Regiments had a rough idea about NATO and he certainly knew he was vastly outnumbered by the Russian hordes. He had no illusions about soldiers deploying in REFORGER being in time to save himself and his buddies.

If asked he would have probably just said, "Sheeit! By the time those assholes get recalled to Post at Fort Riley the Russians will be having a hot dog on Rhine Main Airbase in Frankfurt." However, the facts were that his Regiment had the latest and finest equipment, full staffing, the best officers and NCOs of the Armor Force, the finest training facilities and an over abundance of ammunition and resources. None of this was lost on Private Schmuckatelli. He knew he was there on the ground to fight his hardest for as long as possible to defeat the enemy. He also knew it was no accident that all of the Squadron Commanders were War College bound and every Regimental Commander in living memory had made Brigadier General. He knew because the rank-and-file kept score and his Sergeant had told him so.

The Cavalry Regiments were in a nearly ideal situation for peacetime development of their cadres. They had the latest equipment and an enemy they could see, evaluate and measure. More importantly, the East Germans routinely shot and killed their own citizens who tried to escape to the West. These incidents, observed by the soldiers of the cavalry units, became part of the lore of those units. Commanders throughout the history of the American Army have longed to have their soldiers hate the enemy of their day. With the East Germans, and by association the Russians, the commanders of this time frame saw their fondest wish come true. Their Cavalry soldiers deeply hated and would have, almost to a man, killed any East German or Russian without mercy or regret with the slightest provocation.

The pace of the 11th Cavalry was high speed and low drag in the argot of that era. The Regiment fielded no fewer than three major weapons systems in five years, the M60A3, the M1 tank as well as the M3 Bradley and the M1A1 tank. The Cavalry Troop rotated between; a Border Tour lasting a month three to four times per year, a gunnery training cycle of two 14-day periods, REFORGER, and a series of field exercises of eight to ten days duration. The field exercises conducted were to test and train each troop and squadron on tactics. There was little to no open or white space on the calendar. However, enterprising commanders have occasionally found the time to train and to take unit trips to ski resorts and sometimes to sunny Spain.

The pace of the unit and the demands of its leadership prevented shutting the unit down in the manner of a stateside unit of the period for training such as the Expert Infantry Badge, a worthy and noble event to be sure and the beau ideal for the Army. The climate was ripe for a training result of run, trip, and fall as opposed to crawl, walk and run. Units had to train in small groups and sustain their edge by adhering to high unit standards for daily life. The unit changed out its tanks so often the body of knowledge gained from long experience was not present.

The M1 series of tanks was brand new with systems that were mind boggling in their capabilities. The new equipment was billed as automatic and so simple to operate as to be dummy proof. It was not so but then, it never is.

Whatever shortcomings might have been present, the morale of the Cavalry units was sky high. The tanks of the unit had been changed so often that they were mostly new and rated at 90% ready to fight. The soldiers each generally had five pairs of boots and were well turned out for fatigue and dress uniforms. They were in good physical condition, were excellent map readers, navigators, appreciated terrain, could patrol both on foot and in vehicles, knew the rules of the Border, were deadly marksmen with personal weapons and were intimately familiar with their sectors of responsibility of the battle space. Many had continued to extend in Europe and to volunteer to remain in the Regiment, some for ten years or more.

They were a clannish lot and suffered fools not at all. All soldiers were judged on how well they could handle themselves at the Border and adapt to the rapid changes of Cavalry life. While badges of rank were respected, leaders who were "sorry" were despised and did not prosper. The Border Cavalry ate its runts, particularly its junior officers. The strong developed into remarkably good Company and Squadron Commanders and great Platoon Sergeants, First Sergeants and Sergeants Major.

The best leaders of Armies find ways and means to survive by training their soldiers to fight and win. It is only through training and tough testing in peacetime that forces can be forged to win the first time out in war. It does little good to have a tank that can out see, out range, out shoot and out kill their enemies if the soldiers cannot employ it to its fullest. Capability and intentions require skill and ability to bring them to full fruition.

Skill and ability are developed and nurtured in thorough training that combines the wisdom of academics with hands on training on the equipment. Amateurs train to get it right and professionals train so that they cannot do it wrong. Competence prevents confidence from becoming over-confidence.

As you read this book I ask you to remember that the means and structure used to lead and train the soldiers of that era was what was at hand and available, to include time. Leaders then as now, had to do the best they could with what they had. The results of the 1st Gulf War proved they learned their lessons well.

Today's soldiers carry on the proud traditions of the Army. Of their courage I have no doubt. I only can hope the political leadership and the nation remain worthy of their sacrifice. I agree with General Swartzkopf, and will paraphrase him by saying, "Retired CSM should never miss an opportunity to keep their mouths shut about current military operations."

INTRODUCTION

The time is coming when the US Army will need to regroup yet again after a valiant, long and arduous service in a difficult period of war followed by nation building made necessary by a strategic environment of neither their choice nor selection. The tactics, techniques and procedures of the last war rarely, if ever, work chapter and verse for the next one. This is particularly true when the period is one of almost total adaptation and development of new doctrine conceived and implemented on the wing. The lessons of preparation, troop leading procedures, combat integrity, marksmanship, planning and rehearsal and nation building are not lost, but will stand our troops in good stead.

Teaching only "How", though necessary and useful in hard times, presumes a one quart brain that need only worry about pint problems. "Why" requires in depth training of Soldiers by knowledgeable instructors. However, it is only in learning "why" and by developing one gallon brains to solve two quart problems through training of Soldiers that we will ensure future success. The courage of our Soldiers is not in doubt nor is their commitment and love of country. What we citizens, our leaders and old retired pukes can do is continue to be worthy of their efforts on our behalf.

The story of the M1 Abrams tank and the M2/3 Bradley and their impact on the Armored Forces of the 1980's is unique in the Army's history. The leadership of the Army coming out of the Vietnam War deliberately and carefully reflected on future operations. They realized the impacts of demographics, such as funding, education, patriotism, and computer technology as well the development of the third world could have on the Army and in particular, the Armor Force. They knew the Army would have to do more with less in terms of overhead even though the cost of the weapons systems would be greater initially.

To complete this vision, these far-sighted leaders made a number of very critical decisions that would have a tremendous impact on future events. Among these decisions were the development of a Unit conduct of fire Trainer or (UCOFT) for both the Abrams and the Bradley. It is a tribute to them how well their vision and their provision for the future of the Armor force worked. Again, they mastered the demographic rather than be enslaved by it. The ability to anticipate such trends and provide for them for those who follow is a rare leadership trait and is most admirable. Granted, it also helps to have a tank that kills from far outside the enemy's ability to either see or hit it, and if hit on the frontal arc of sixty degrees, to shrug off the missile as if it had missed. As for the Bradley, the ability of a scout and Infantry vehicle to not only keep up with the tanks but to actually be able to out kill them in a close fight as seen in 1991, was unheard of in modern Armored warfare. Between the two weapons systems, they may well have put themselves out of work. Among the industrialized nations, in the hands of our Soldiers and Marines, they have made devout pacifists out of many of the world's greediest and sinful folk.

Once weapons systems are invented, tested, fielded and employed, it falls to the leaders of the Army to teach, train and school Soldiers in their use to fight and win. It is believed by some that anyone with a high school diploma can easily master the M1 tank and its companion the M2/3. Many are certain anyone can fight these two weapons systems due to their technological superiority. Others are just as certain that although there is a lot of tiger in the tank, the most important tigers are the ones operating it. A rather erudite 1SG once assembled his cavalry troop and attempted to call an unmanned tank to attention and give it commands. The fallacy of the equipment argument was clear. The tank could not even remove and fold its own tarpaulin, the simplest of tasks.

For the civilian reader, the Army speaks a language all of its own. Part of this argot of technical speak is by design, some out of convention and because most of the time there is no one but another Soldier to hear them talk. The Army is organized to defend the nation against all enemies foreign and domestic. It performs these tasks by closing with and destroying enemies defined as such by Congress using by shock action, firepower and maneuver. The Army is not looking for a fair fight. It intends to bring every weapon and stratagem to bear to cause the greatest harm to our sworn enemies in the shortest time possible at the least cost to our nation's treasure. The greatest of any nation's treasure is its youth sent into harm's way by old men and young facile speakers who by dint of age, position in society and positions in the government life will cheer lustily from the sidelines.

It is a force organized and maintained for the sole purpose of causing the enemy to lose the fight. They will lose either from being beaten into submission or when they lose the will to continue the fight. Whatever reason a Soldier has for joining the Army, the Army has no other reason for being but to fight and win the nation's battles. To that end the Army is organized into forces of a size and shape to get the most return for the resources expended.

The Army is organized into a hierarchy as to generally result in one leader telling five folks what to do. This is as much as would be found in any publicly held manufacturing concern. While there are exceptions, they but prove the rule. Shown below is a simple chart showing how a maneuver Corps is often found to be organized. The ability to organize and shape forces to meet the mission at hand is an Army hallmark. The reader should know every Officer has a Sergeant and every Sergeant has an officer.

The United States Army Europe was organized into two Corps, the Fifth and the Seventh. Both Corps were responsible for portions of the East/West German Border. The Armored Cavalry Regiments from each of these Corps provided a force to watch the Soviets, act as early warning and serve as a force able to prevent Border incidents either from occurring at all, or to mitigate and contain them when they did. Any force used to prevent surprise and provide both early warning and the ability to blunt an attack is said to be acting as a covering force. Their job is to cover the forces stationed in the Corps area arrayed behind them to buy time to make forces ready and move to where they can fight to best advantage. It should be noted that additional units were assigned to be among those returning forces to Germany or REFORGER. These units were assigned to round out these two Corps or to serve under III Corps of Fort Hood, or the XVIII Airborne Corps, the first response force of the Army. Throughout recorded history borders have proven to be flash points for war. The depiction on the following page shows the array of forces typical of the era.

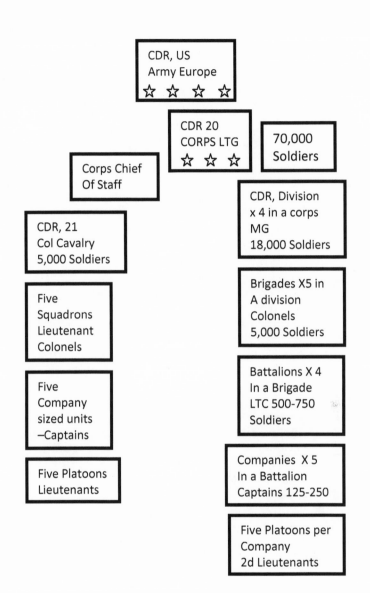

CDR, US
Army Europe
☆ ☆ ☆ ☆

CDR 20
CORPS LTG
☆ ☆ ☆

70,000
Soldiers

Corps Chief
Of Staff

CDR, Division
x 4 in a corps
MG
18,000 Soldiers

CDR, 21
Col Cavalry
5,000 Soldiers

Brigades X5 in
A division
Colonels
5,000 Soldiers

Five
Squadrons
Lieutenant
Colonels

Battalions X 4
In a Brigade
LTC 500-750
Soldiers

Five
Company
sized units
–Captains

Companies X 5
In a Battalion
Captains 125-250

Five Platoons
Lieutenants

Five Platoons per
Company
2d Lieutenants

The Cavalry of the period in both the Fifth and Seventh Corps maintained the tradition of their namesakes of old in that they moved on their equipment though it was now a horse of iron which eats JP-8 rather than a hay burning quadruped or horse. Life was about, centered on and occurred while, being mounted. The Cavalry life was one of almost constant activity. The Cavalry Trooper was in one of five places: The Border; A training area firing and or maneuvering; The Border Rights Area training area; At home station; On an organized trip or personal leave. It was not unusual for a Cavalry troop to drive off the railcars from a trip to a distant training area after an absence of 20 days or more, and drive past their living quarters enroute to the border camp, waving to wives and children as they drove by in a cloud of vehicle exhaust. Though statistics would be hard to come by, anyone who was there can tell you there were an untold number of children conceived in automobiles in the woods near the Border Camps of the 2d & 11th ACR.

Once at the Border Camp, a relief in place was conducted by the two units, the one being replaced and the one doing the replacing. The old unit had cleaned, prepared, re-fueled, swept, cut the grass, cleaned the kitchen, inventoried ammunition, replaced light bulbs and made ready any and every part and parcel of the border camp and its environs for the handover of responsibility. Their motivation was more than adequate to the task as they both wanted to depart, either to a training site or to home station, and because they were professional Soldiers with élan and pride in their unit. The cycle would then be repeated when the next border changeover was conducted.

The old unit left secure in the knowledge their Soldiers had been re-trained in those tasks critical to success in Cavalry operations by a month of repetition on the Border. The Border qualification was a formal process requiring each Soldier to qualify to be there. The process began with a written test, usually given at the home station. The test was extensive and covered the gamut of knowledge required to be an effective Soldier on the border. It was all about geography, a know your enemy tutorial on Soviet uniforms, rank insignia, equipment, US Reporting procedures, familiarity with enemy weapons, qualification with their assigned weapon and a review of first aid and the code of conduct. Also at home station, new Soldiers and those veterans new to the theater were trained and then licensed to drive the appropriate vehicles according to the traffic laws of West Germany. Novices were then taken on vehicle and foot patrols by veterans and took their places on remote Observation Posts where they watched the enemy and were in turn watched by them. Their food was a hot meal twice each day with the noon meal being field rations of the "C" ration variety and later the "Meals Ready to Eat" or MREs. MREs were also known as Meals Rejected by Ethiopians (starving) by the wags.

The Border Camps were noted for their great food as the cooks were permanently assigned. A number of the Border Cooks were graduates of a short course conducted in Frankfurt by Hotel Chefs. The Kitchen Police were German civilian ladies from the neighborhood around the camp, some of whom had worked there since the 1970's. Some Commanders will always elect the easy path and keep the same selected people in the same jobs until they drop over, are dead or leave the unit by employing the "good man" theory. Most camps had a beer hall and recreation room with pool table, ping pong table, fooseball, and a primitive sound system. The camps were enclosed by 11' tall hurricane fencing and were guarded at all times with controlled entry and exit.

Barracks were comfortable with tiled or linoleum floors, bathroom facilities, lights and central heating. For most of Germany, the summer season is neither long enough nor hot enough for air conditioning. It was not Club Med or Sandals with guests wearing fatigue uniforms by any measure. It was adequate for a down and out civilian and pure heaven for a Cavalry trooper just back from a training area. But it was not home and it was not Home Station. The day was long, often 24 hours, the duty was arduous with everyone on duty armed at all times. Patrols were conducted by foot, vehicle and helicopter at varied times of the day and into the night. For many years, patrol vehicles had no canvas or covering and were totally open to the elements. Sympathy in the Border Cavalry was known as a word in the dictionary located between shit and syphilis as that was the only place short of the bosom of his family a trooper was going to find it.

Passes and leave were not granted except under emergency conditions. Mail came and went most days. Normal actions to benefit Soldiers and to take care of their needs were accomplished on the cycle of the rear area, a five day week and an eight hour day. Holidays were noted and celebrated in an abbreviated or truncated fashion to include a full patrol schedule even on Christmas Day.

Most units could expect to spend 90 days per year on the Border. Those with hard core Commanders often spent 140 days annually there with another 100 days absent at distant training sites training for gunnery and maneuver. It was a marvelous learning laboratory for junior Officers and Noncommissioned Officers as they got to perform in concert with their level of responsibility and were employed with mission orders. For the most part, they were told what to do but not how to do it in every detail. They were also employed as the leader of their platoon each time the task could be made to fit. It is simpler to create an illusion of an elite unit in peace or war and achieve perfection by using the same folks over and over to do the tasks. It is a dumb thing to do. There is more pain, time and trouble involved to train and deploy Soldiers by platoon but it is more than worthwhile to give them a chance to learn and grow and the Army gets the dividend. Those who could learn and were motivated, thrived, the remainder who were merely spectators were eaten.

Most Cavalry units were/are consumed by the need to fill the white space on the calendar. When adapting to a new piece of equipment it is more cost effective to learn it well in all phases than to trust to luck and On the Job Training. A sophisticated, well trained, well led soldier equipped with the latest technology and trained to think will prevail.

Finally, when the 19D Scout transitioned to the M3 Cavalry Fighting Vehicle a very smart Cajun General asked me in 1986 what I thought the result was going to be. I told him the best simple comparison I could make was to imagine an Apache Indian who had ridden with Geronimo getting issued a Weatherby Custom Automatic rifle in .308 caliber with a Leupold day night scope with a bullet drop compensator fighting against a US Cavalry armed with single shot carbines with iron sights.

CHAPTER 1 – HOMECOMING

As the Delta Airliner landed at Rhine Main AFB, First Sergeant Ronald E. Martin felt as if he was returning home from a long leave. This feeling was in direct contrast to the mood of most of his fellow Soldiers on the military charter flight. The recruits were uncertain and apprehensive of their future service in a foreign land, the old Soldiers were resigned to making one more tour and the officers were looking forward to a five year tour with their families. First Sergeant Martin was leaving an unhappy home life behind and looking forward to service with the 11th Armored Cavalry Regiment, the Blackhorse, on an unaccompanied tour. He was a below the zone selection for both Sergeant First Class and First Sergeant, was enrolled in the Non-Resident Sergeant Major Course and had a bright future in the Army, personal life aside.

As the plane was taxiing to the terminal he reviewed what little he knew for certain about the famous, or infamous, Blackhorse. Outside of the XVIII Airborne Corps and the 73d Armor Battalion, the Blackhorse and the 2d ACR represented the toughest possible service for an Armor Soldier in the peacetime Army. He had previously served in a tank company of the 4/69 Armor Battalion where nine of his fifteen fellow NCOs were veterans of the Blackhorse who had served with the regiment in Vietnam. It was one of the best companies in the Division and a favorite of the Division Commander. Every officer and NCO he had ever encountered with a Blackhorse combat patch was an outstanding and thoroughly professional Soldier. While service in United States Army, either Europe or USAREUR, produced very good Soldiers, there was a special élan among those who were veterans of the Blackhorse. While serving as a Tank Gunnery Evaluator at Grafenwohr, the centralized training area for USARUER, he remembered watching Blackhorse NCOs gamble their car titles in high stakes poker games with little care for the morrow. They were great comrades with balls and brains and were utterly dependable. He suspected he would soon find out what made them special. He was also looking forward to being among the German populace, particularly among the ladies, making a special note to leave the married women alone.

First Sergeant Martin and Sergeant First Class Ruffino, an acquaintance from Fort Knox Drill Sergeant days who was also returning to Germany but as an Infantryman, made their way to the baggage claim area. On arrival, Martin noticed one man in particular looking at him in a very direct manner, as if he knew him. He recognized the man as Major General Miles Balznick, Martin had organized a last minute General Officer orientation for the Major General at Fort Knox to meet the guidance of the Commanding General of The Armor School and Fort Knox. The previous 3d Armored Division Commander was relieved for cause after he exerted command influence on a

Court Martial case. The Army wanted Major General Balznick to be given an orientation on the maintenance, tactics and gunnery issues he would face on assuming command of this prestigious outfit on Freedom's Frontier. Most of all, the job had to be done fast. It had been an unusual case. Martin was the Weapons Department Fireman. Not much was known about Major General Balznick at the NCO level except that he was a quick study and brave as a lion in war. The word on the NCO Street was to not underestimate the guy. The officer side of the street wanted the job done quickly without incident with the mercurial Major General on and off post with no fuss. As usual, the Armor Officer mafia wanted the impossible and knew they would get it from their NCOs.

The task was to familiarize the General on the M-60, M-60A3 and M-1 tank by way of firing a Tank Table VII and a mini-qualification Tank Table VIII for each. He was also to drive the M1 Tank, learn to use both the vehicle on board smoke generator and smoke grenade discharger systems. The exercise started at 0700 and the man had a plane to catch at 1530 at Standiford Field, one hour away in Louisville, KY. The exercise was to be conducted on the smallest range at Knox where a round fired in the wrong direction had a more than 80% chance of impacting on nearby Highway 31W, the notorious Dixie Die Way.

Fortunately, the Great Balznick was as advertised, a very, very quick study. He jumped out of his van into the wrong jeep, a raggedy ass target service vehicle full of Soldier gear instead of the Major General special model prepared for his use. Martin told the driver to hop in the back and then he explained the program of instruction to Major General Balzick as the jeep rocked through the mud to the first tank, the M-60A1. The General gave succinct guidance, "I know the M60 and I need a refresher on the bore sight procedures, prepare to fire checks for the Commander's Machinegun, and safety features important to a Division commander. On the M60A3, I need a tutorial on the thermal sight and I need to know everything about the M1 on all crew positions. Can we do all of that in the time we have available?"

Martin replied, "Sir, you will get what you need here today in the time allotted. If any point is not clear, we will repeat the training until we get it right. Everyone here is at your disposal. We will make it happen."

What followed was an orchestrated goat rope conducted at the speed of light. The M60 was prepared and seven engagements were fired. He did not miss a single target and all were well within the time limit. The M60A3 tutorial took a little longer and the General fired all of the day engagements and then used the thermal to fire all of the night engagements with the hatches closed. He hit them all and agreed it was a "no brainer" to fire the night tables off thermal in daylight.

The great fun came with the M1. Major General Balznick drove it after a short orientation at high speed around the gunnery course. He then bore sighted it, performed prepare to fire checks while the driver read the checklist, and fired a perfect score. Other than a small range fire from the red phosphorous generated by the smoke grenade systems, no harm was done.

He was very, very impressed with the range, his tutorial and his instructor. As he departed, he told Martin, "If I can ever do anything for you, let me know." Truthfully, Martin was just glad nothing went wrong and had never expected to see Major General Balznick again but the peacetime Armor Force can be pretty small.

"Martin, how are you? I see you are going to the Blackhorse or are you in it already?"

Martin replied, "No, Sir, the Blackhorse is a direct assignment from DA. I am doing very well and looking forward to serving in the Regiment. I had the patch sewn on at Fort Knox. How is the Division?"

"The 3d Armored Division is great and is bigger than any one person, even its Commanding General. Your tips are really working out well and I have some great NCOs there. If the Blackhorse does not treat you right, let me know. I will send a chopper for you and you can have a tank company in 3d AD any day. Play that card if you have to and I will back it up."

Not quite knowing what else to say, First Sergeant Martin merely said, "Thank you, General."

As the 3AD Commanding General departed, Sergeant First Class Ruffino immediately started to tease his fellow Drill Sergeant, "Wow, Ron, here you are still pissin' stateside water and you're already playing politics."

"Listen, Ruff Ruff, he started it and I have no intention of serving anywhere but the Blackhorse. I have been in 3 AD. I am going to the Blackhorse. Let's go get some breakfast and start the in processing circus," Martin said as he shouldered his duffle bag.

Sergeant First Class Ruffino was getting wound up as he opined, "Well you can go to the damn Blackhorse if you want to but I am going to the great 8th ID and the NCO academy. You can have that damn field duty 13 months out of twelve. The difference between us is you have a chance to be the Sergeant Major of the Army and I will be proud to retire as an Sergeant First Class and get a job at the Post Office, shit."

Martin found Ruffino's pithy summary profound in its simplicity but misguided. "Ruff, Ruff, I am too damn old to ever be the SMA. All I want is to be a Command Sergeant Major of a Cavalry Squadron. Right now, I would settle for a big breakfast and a cold Pepsi. What in the hell ever made you think I could ever be in the running for SMA?"

Ruffino regarded his friend with a benign smile saying, "Any NCO that takes a first aid kit, water and food to the field for trainees cutting wood in July for burning in winter fire barrels is SMA material. Any Drill Sergeant that hypnotizes trainees to pass the PT test and has 15 of 17 platoons win Honor Platoon is going places."

Martin replied, "No Ruff Ruff, the guy who makes SMA is the guy that sends bright eyed and bushy tailed dumb asses like me out to cut wood. Above Battalion, a Command Sergeant Major has little contact with Soldiers except his driver. He leads other Command Sergeants Major. If he remembers the Soldiers and where he came from when he gets past Battalion, he is a success. If not, he is just another kiss ass. Besides all that, can you see me testifying before Congress? Some Congresswoman who thinks we should take away the bayonet so we can pay for laser range finders asks me my opinion. Hell, I would set the Army back twenty years with my answers."

As they board the bus outside, the October air of Germany is crisp and cold. It takes no imagination to know winter is coming to the country. The bus is immaculate in the manner only a higher headquarters vehicle can be. There is a baggage truck, covered no less, with a detail to accept the bags. The Sergeant guide from the replacement company tactfully supervises the loading of bags and higher ranking passengers for the short trip to the replacement company. Even the newest soldiers were being well treated by the system of the replacement unit. It was not always so with "newbies" he remembered.

Sergeant First Class Denny of the Maintenance Department at Fort Knox knew Martin both from their service in Germany in the '70s and as a Drill Sergeant at Knox. Denny told Martin that the officers in the Armor Officer basic course were being cheated. The powers that be were not assigning the Second Lieutenants to the type of tank for training they would be manning in their next unit after their graduation from the Armor School. Sergeant First Class Denny asked Martin if he could help with the situation. He promised the NCOs of the Maintenance Department would close ranks with the Weapons Department and do whatever it took to set the situation right.

The Civilians and Mid-Level military NCOs and officers running the administrative part of the course showed no interest when Martin approached them but rather, displayed outright hostility when their territory was invaded.

Martin went back to Denny in his lab room and told him, "Those assholes do not care. We are going to have to fight a guerilla war to square away the Lieutenants. Are your guys prepared for that? It could get ugly!"

Denny gave him a withering stare saying, "Shit, the officers will never know what we did."

"Yeah, maybe, but we still have to the right thing for the right reason and benefit the AOB student or we will get our nuts crushed when it comes out. A Momma bear with cubs is more reasonable than a senior officer defending a wronged Second Lieutenant. And somehow it will come out. No good deed ever goes unpunished, Denny." The two NCOs parted to get their facts straight.

Sergeant First Class Denny went to the New Equipment Teams for the M1 and got the projected fielding schedule for the next twelve months. Martin went to work the people side of the equation and to find a way to put it all together once he got the fielding schedule from Denny.

When they met, Martin asked, "Did you have any problems at the NET Team?"

"No," said Denny, "I set it all up at Happy Hour at the Pig Pen (The Senior NCO Club adjacent to the BEQ frequented by fast women and amoral NCOs) last night and picked up the matrix this morning. The OIC was a little curious but I know him from Korea and I resorted to the oldest trick in the book with him."

"I'm not sure I want to know what that was but what was it?" asked Martin.

"I told the truth," said Denny.

"That is a novel approach for you Bud, think he will talk?"

"Hell no, he has too many troubles of his own with the team and all their trips and trying to stay married. Besides he is a twice passed over for Major with two tours to "Nam and a Silver Star. He knows the Army is hosed," snorted Denny.

Martin made ten calls before he got to the Specialist Fourth Class (SP4) at Department of the Army who did the actual work for accession of officers into the Army. He was surprised to learn Second Lieutenants were actually brought on active duty to be assigned to a specific unit vacancy. The system had great fidelity. That news from DA made the NCOs more determined to fix the problem.

The solution was quite simple but as with all direct NCO solutions to organization problems, Murphy's Law (If something could go wrong it would) was certain to appear at some point. Second Lieutenants may be seemingly abused and harshly led by senior officers but were also protected and nurtured by them. He knew his NCO group could fix the problem but must "do no harm" in the process or the concern of the senior officers for their juniors would land on them. Martin worked carefully to ensure he had all of his facts straight and a workable solution. He did a timeline depicting the month and year Armor units of the Regular Army were to be issued their M1 tanks for the next fiscal year. He then plotted each Armor Officer Basic Course onto the time line. Names of each Second Lieutenant accessed by DA for that unit were listed by their course number. The names received from the SP4 deep in bowels of DA, G1, once plotted on the timeline, revealed each class would have between 8 and 22 students who needed M1 training over the FY. Once Army NET was complete, the crisis would be over and the system might get it right.

Martin then assembled all of the manuals and pamphlets the students would need to navigate the Maintenance and Gunnery Departments. He worked a deal to get a special printing of a manual from General Dynamics printed as well. He then contacted a fellow conspirator, Sergeant First Class

Plowhaven, Tactics Instructor in the Command and Staff Department, in order to intercept the students before they made their appearance at Maintenance Department.

Sergeant First Class Plowhaven was one of Martin's Drill Sergeants from 14 years before who had made the mistake of running into the MP guard post after a night of over indulgence at the 19th Hole, the beer joint at the NCO Golf Course. Plowhaven was philosophical about his former trainee catching up and passing him in rank saying, "Yeah, you passed me up but you sure didn't have the good time I had."

In the class he was teaching, Sergeant First Class Plowhaven called the roster of Lieutenants who were going to M1 units and directed them to see the NCO in the parking lot at the Ford Pinto station wagon. He did not tell them why. Unexpectedly, he then gave the remainder of the class an extra ten minutes of break time. As in any service school, students soon learn to be flexible, not to volunteer and to ask questions sparingly. As the students approached, Martin told them to stand behind the pile of manuals with their name on it. He then addressed the group, "Gentlemen, I am Master Sergeant Martin. I am the NCOIC of the Gunnery Division of Weapons Department. Smoke 'em if you got 'em and if you don't have 'em, bum them off of Mac-Gregor, he used to be one of my trainees in 1980." He saluted Second Lieutenant MacGregor and shook his hand. "All of you are going to be assigned to M1 units in the near future. You are all going to be Armor and Cavalry Officers. Flexibility is the hallmark of an Armor officer so hear me out before you ask questions."

At this point Martin got truly flexible as the Commandant of the Armor School, Brigadier General Sullivan and a group of officers was approaching his little group from the rear. Ominously, they stopped at a point where they could hear everything but would not be noticed by the AOB students. None of the Lieutenants saw the senior officers, so Martin continued his briefing; glad none of the Lieutenants had called attention.

"The Army is a large, monolithic organization. It is capable of making mistakes. As the Lieutenants smiled with some snickers, Martin warmed to his audience, "No shit, the Army screws up." Now he had them, they were laughing. "You gentlemen are going to units that either have, or will soon have, M1 tanks. You may, or may not miss NET, or New Equipment Training, when your unit goes through it. You were scheduled to get either M60A1 or M60A3 training here at Knox. That changes right now. You are now all M1 students. These are your M1 manuals. There is no requirement to crash and burn to study them right now. I am here because this is the most convenient place in your schedule to issue you the correct manuals. Nothing you will do before you get to maintenance department requires you to use these books. Your training in Command and Staff is not tank specific until the field problem at the end of your course. The establishment of the Armor School has yet to recognize this situation. I am here because that is what NCOs do. They take care of their officers. Do not undergo training in Maintenance Dept on any tank but an M1. If anyone puts you on a tank that is not an M1, go see Sergeant First Class Washington, Sergeant First Class Denny, or Master Sergeant Holmes. Do not call DA and start sniveling about which unit you are going to be assigned. The unit listed on your piece of paper is the one to which you are assigned. Do not go back over to the scheduling office and try to correct this as a matter of honor and integrity. If those assholes at scheduling and at your company had any integrity, we would not be standing here having this conversation."

The laughter of the students was loud and long and it was a moment before he could continue. Holding up each manual from his control stack, Martin called them out one by one ensuring each officer had his issue, pausing as he held up a large thick book.

As he came to the last manual he paused, "Gentlemen, this last booklet is special. It connects the leg bone to the thigh bone for the M1 tank. It is from General Dynamics. There is a sign over the door at Skidgel Hall that states, 'The knowledge you gain here is not yours to keep.' Take this book with you to your unit. You will probably be the only soldier there that has one. Show it to your Platoon Sergeant and your Master Gunner. The Army is just beginning the effort to learn about this tank. We will all be learning about its quirks for years. If you lose this book or leave it on some coyote's dresser down in Louisville, I will give you another one. Noticing a puzzled look on a baby faced Lieutenant, Martin said, "Lieutenant Jones, a coyote is a woman so ugly that you will gnaw your arm off to get out of bed to keep from waking her up-okay. A good Christian lad, like you obviously must be, does not know about such things. Gentlemen, any questions on what we have covered?"

A skeptical Lieutenant Montgomery raised his hand and asked, "How do you of all people know where I am going, Sergeant?" Martin smiled and waved to silence the groaning from the ranks. The sound was obviously peer recognition marking Old Monty as the class Spring Butt. "Easy men, Lieutenant Montgomery has a good question. Lieutenant you were brought on active duty to go to that unit and I called DA to verify all of your unit assignments by name, for each AOB class for next year. I further matched the fielding dates and verified your follow on courses at Airborne and Ranger School. I did this individually for each and every officer slated for an M1 unit for the next year. Battalion Commanders do not want to hear excuses. You will be expected to lead immediately. The least we can do here is to make sure you are trained on the correct tank. Are there any other questions? Gentlemen, finish your break and return to the classroom."

As the Lieutenants departed, Brigadier General Sullivan summoned Martin. Martin reported and remained at attention until Brigadier General Sullivan gave him at ease. "Martin," he began, "You provided a fine illustration to this

7

class of PCC (Pre-Command Course) leaders on the principle of management by walking around. I knew when I saw a Weapons Department NCO stacking Maintenance and Gunnery manuals behind a Command and Staff building it was worth a look. I told these gentlemen we were going to exercise MBWA (Management By Walking Around) so I could figure out what was going on in my AO (Area of Operations). Summarize what this was all about for us if you please."

"Sir, and Gentlemen," Martin began, "These Lieutenants were incorrectly slated for training on tanks other than the M1, old tanks their unit would have already turned in after they arrived. All efforts to get their schedules changed officially came to naught. The Maintenance and Weapons NCOs fixed the problem. Colonel Harden, the Weapons Department and my boss, knows about it and felt our actions were well within your intent. We just could not let it slide."

Brigadier General Sullivan turned to the group of officers saying, "The fact that the NCOs of the Armor School detected a problem, researched the answer and executed the fix without telling me, or asking permission, has made my day. I will fix the institution policy." Turning to Martin he said, "Can you get a copy of that book for this PCC Class and a copy of your time-line for each officer and for me within the next hour?" Martin nodded yes. "Good, go do it," the General ordered.

So much for memory lane, First Sergeant Martin thought, that is behind me now. After a brief processing, a Soldier came up to Martin telling him, "First Sergeant Martin, I drove a van here from Fulda and the Blackhorse to pick you up. The Sergeant Major had to go V Corps Headquarters and we are going to go pick him up now and go back to Fulda. Are you ready to go?"

"As soon as I get my duffle bag and luggage I am, Specialist Myers" said Martin.

"Oh, I already loaded all of that stuff off of the baggage truck. We come up here a lot and I know everybody," said Meyers brightly.

Martin sought out Sergeant First Class Ruffino saying, "Well I'll see you on the trail, Ruff Ruff.

"Shit, you might see me somewhere but I doubt it. You ain't gonna' be seeing anything but diesel smoke and Kamerade's ass up on that Border, home boy," said the irrepressible Sergeant First Class.

The young Specialist handled the drive to V Corps Headquarters in the manner of a New York City cab driver hustling a fare to a meeting. The Sergeant Major was waiting at the front of the building smoking a cigarette. He was a familiar face.

"Well, I will be dipped in shit if it is not the man with the plan," said Sergeant Major Harris.

"Sergeant Major, how are you doing and are you going to be my Sergeant Major?" said Martin.

"You damn right I am. I told the Regimental Command Sergeant Major that I wanted you to put some starch in them damn aviators. You are going to an Air Cavalry Troop. It is a dream come true for a guy trying to finish his degree and work the Sergeants Major Academy Non-Resident Course," said Harris.

"Sergeant Major, I am surprised you are still in harness. I would have thought you would have pulled the pin by now. Are you still running?" asked Martin, thinking of the days when Harris was a moving black mountain of a Drill Sergeant at 6'5 and 280 pounds.

"I wished to hell I could still run. Runnin' all done for me. Wheels went bad, knee on the right and ankle on the left. Shit, I can barely limp straight. Damn Agent Orange will probably kill me before the Crown Royal can get it done. I am going to retire when Lieutenant Colonel Quigley, the Squadron Commander, changes command next 14 months. We do not have a Command Sergeant Major on the horizon. Another reason I need you. You can help me flex the S3 if it comes to it. There ain't enough people in an Aviation Cavalry Troop to sneeze at; we have both had twice as many in a basic training platoon. It is gonna' be great. What do you think?" asked Harris.

"That sounds great to me, Sergeant Major. I really expected to get assigned to an outfit with M1s but I will serve where I am sent. Forgive me if I sit here in shock for a minute. I mean, 26 people with all but 7 of them officers or warrant officers," as he shook his head in wonder. The visions of the Bachelor's degree were beginning to take shape.

"Are you still married to that older woman?" Harris asked.

"Yeah, but not for long," said Martin. "I'm not going to do anything stupid over here but I know how to fraternize quietly and when I get my shit together I am parting company with that one."

"Well," Harris said archly, "If you been wrong too long, you can get right tonight."

"Tell me about the unit and the mission," Martin requested.

Harris began a pitch that he had obviously given many times to a variety of audiences. He had been in the same unit, the 11th ACR for 12 years, his two years as a Drill Sergeant at Fort Knox aside. Soldiers like Harris, happily married to German women and owning homes in Germany did not regard two years in CONUS (Continental United States) as a PCS (Permanent Change of Station) to the US, but merely as Temporary Duty from the 11th ACR. CONUS service was a necessary evil that many Blackhorse NCOs had to suffer through every ten years or so. This was more than true for Harris. He and his wife had a home a Major General would be proud to own, on her ancestral land. She was a respected school teacher, a gifted musician and lovely blond Valkerie. Harris never intended to leave Fulda, dead or alive.

Harris began, "The Regiment is responsible for over 450 kilometers of the East/West German Border. There are about 5,300 soldiers assigned to the

Regiment. First Squadron, CSS and the Fourth Squadron are at Fulda. Most of the accompanied (read married with family coming with them to Germany) guys are assigned to Fulda. 2d Squadron is in Bad Kissingen and Third Squadron is at Bad Hershfeld. 2d ACR is to our south and their Headquarters is in Nuremberg. My squadron has Two Scout Troops, Two Attack Troops, a Transport Troop, a Maintenance Troop and naturally a Headquarters Troop."

"You are going to November Troop. It has a very good, but wild Commander. It has 4 Cobras (Attack Helicopters AH-1) and 6 '58s (Observation Helicopters OH-58). He needs all of the logistics help he can get. The best pilots in the world need fuel, food and the chance to clean up if they are going to stay effective. These guys know they are here to fight the Russians if need be. But they do not realize how much support they are going to need. They need ruthless bastards, guys like you to get it to them. Right now, they know airfield and clean sheets. I want them to see an old dog that can run their asses 'till their tongues hang out, use words of more than one syllable and read books with no pictures without moving his lips. You get my drift First Sergeant?"

Martin was taken aback. These were more words than he had ever heard Harris string together at one time.

"Damn, Sergeant Major. The Sergeants Major Academy got their money's worth out of you. How about the rest of the regiment?" he asked.

Satisfied his charge was paying attention, Harris continued, "The regiment is organized into five squadrons. They are in numerical order with each troop and Tank Company in the order of the alphabet. First Squadron has Cavalry Troops A, B, & C and the Tank Company is D. Second Squadron, is E, F & G, Tank Company is H and Third Squadron has I, K, L and Tank Company is M. Are you confused yet? See when you ask someone what unit they are in and they say Killer Troop, you know they are in Third Squadron. The Support Squadron is called Packhorse and they are organized by the service they provide. The Regimental Headquarters is under an HHT or a Detachment depending on what DA had for breakfast that day. Hell, it's easy once you see a CEOI (Command Electronic Operating Instructions)."

Sergeant Major Harris continued, "First stop for you is billeting. I got you a nice room in the BEQ/BOQ, got a small refrigerator, TV and bed with maid service. You can stay there while you are in processing Regiment and getting your briefings. It is a nice place and you have damn sure stayed in worse. We will get your stuff dropped off. As soon as you see the Regimental Command Sergeant Major, we will go look at your troop and you can meet the Squadron Commander. Say as little as possible to Regimental Command Sergeant Major and for Christ sakes, no cussin'. He is a Bible Thumper from way back. He don't drink, smoke, or chew and don't like them what do. Use your Chaplain manners."

"Damn Top, how does he square that attitude with the Regimental Commanding Officer? He is a hard drinking, skirt chasin' dude with women hangin' all over him," Martin said.

"You don't worry about it, bone head. The Regimental Command Sergeant Major ain't got shit to say to the Regimental Commanding Officer except yessir! He can and will say plenty to you. I been working this deal for weeks so I need you to be your charming self and hold the spoken curse word rate down to one per week with zero expended today, with him. Don't screw this up. I told him you would fit in fine, so fit in! Let's get a bratwurst; I know you are dying for something to eat and one of them damn Cokes you love. Pull over at our usual stop Meyer. Martin, you are uncivilized not drinking coffee. How in the hell did you ever get promoted, you don't drink coffee, or play pinochle and you ain't never been busted? Shit, I'll bet you haven't even gotten an Article 15, have you?" Harris concluded.

Martin replied, "Thanks for telling me about the Regimental Command Sergeant Major. I would have probably stepped on my crank with him. Should I carry my bible in there on my initial interview or will just crossing myself when he tells me he is blessed do the trick?"

Harris turned wide eyed in anger from the front seat to try to fix Martin with his famous 'stare of terror'. Martin stopped him short by saying, "Hey, I got marks in the states because I remembered what a tight ass you were so I can buy the damn bratwurst. I will even pay for that Rad Coke you are going to get with lemon in it."

"Hey Meyer, are you going to grow up like your Dad the Sergeant Major here, go native, drink Spatzee and marry a gorgeous German schoolteacher?" Martin asked the driver. Harris began to laugh deep down in his huge chest, almost shaking the vehicle. Meyer looked in the rear view mirror in complete confusion. He had never heard anyone even argue with the Sergeant Major before. Now, an NCO junior in rank to his Sergeant Major was being borderline disrespectful and his Sergeant Major was laughing.

"Meyer," said Harris, "That is First Sergeant Martin's way of telling me he is going to do exactly as I say but it ain't because he is scared of me but because he has decided it is best for the Army and for himself, in that order. He lives on the edge, Meyer. He likes hanging out there on a damn limb because he ain't got no sense. Do not grow up to be like him, you be like me, okay?"

"Shit Meyer, your Sergeant Major thinks I forgot about this town. I did not. I am going to enjoy stopping here for a bratwurst," said Martin.

"Yeah this is the place and that is why I am buying and you should just eat your bratwurst, dip your mustard and eat your brochen without ruining Meyer's vision of modern Germany," said Sergeant Major Harris.

The small bratwurst kiosk was located adjacent to a BP gas station. It was a bustling location on the cool October morning. Placing their order, the three Blackhorse Troopers were the only non-German customers present.

11

The passersby were some of the most attractive Aryan looking people one could ever hope to see anywhere. They were uniformly blond haired, blue eyed, well formed gorgeous folk who moved with fluid grace and athleticism. The lady running the Kiosk was pleasant enough as she, Martin and Sergeant Major Harris conversed in German as they ordered their snack. She gave First Sergeant Martin the bill and he deferentially told her the Sergeant Major would pay as he was merely a guest and under the orders of the large black man. She looked askance but took the hundred mark bill being tendered by the black mountain of a man in front of her. She then dutifully counted back the change to Sergeant Major Harris. Throughout the encounter, the Sergeant Major's expression never changed and he was unfailingly polite while speaking faultless German. First Sergeant Martin's face was that of a professional gambler, expressionless.

Meyer, having just listened to the two of them and their spirited banter in the van was at a loss to figure out what he had just seen. If he had not known differently, in the vehicle he would have thought they were both ready for mortal combat and now he was truly shocked. The two senior NCOs walked away from the window of the kiosk to a small table located at the side where the trio was out of sight of the lady who had served their snack. As they were eating their snack, Martin said, "I love being in this country again. I love it all, the food, the weather, most of the people. Damn this bratwurst is great. This little burg has not changed either. The super race is still here but I am sure it is getting diluted a bit here and there."

Sergeant Major Harris finished his wurst saying, "I always stop here to remind these assholes they lost the damn war and that some of us black folk will be here to keep their Nazi asses honest."

"Yeah, the Tuskegee airmen would be damn proud of you, Sergeant Major."

"Damn you, Martin, mount up," said Harris.

"Have you ever told Meyer the deal about this town?" asked Martin.

"You tell him if you think he needs to know, First Sergeant."

"Meyer, is there anything about that little place that bothers you or seems out of place?" asked the new First Sergeant. Specialist Fourth Class Meyer pondered the question as if it was a test that would give him an up or down check for a future appearance before the Sergeant promotion board.

"Meyer, that little burg was a R&R Center for the SS during WWII. The ladies there were encouraged to conceive and birth as many blue eyed, blond haired super kinder for the fatherland as possible. The SS troopers, in addition to being numerous, were hot blooded and did their best to help their Furher's future staffing by knocking up as many locals and imports as possible. The place was one of many Nazi nurseries. Sergeant Major Harris likes to rain on their Superman parade. Don't get confused Meyer, I'm white, he is black, and together we is YOU ESS Army and they are civilians. It is us against them Meyer. We will always win because they may have our ass in the Army but we have each other when the chips are down. All civilians have in a pinch is their VISA card."

The remaining ride to Fulda was somewhat subdued until it was necessary for Sergeant Major Harris to give Martin some guidance about the way to navigate the road to Fulda and the best way to travel to the Kaserne.

CHAPTER 2 – POLITICS

There is always politics in the Army. It is a lot like a minefield, you don't have to like the people that put it there. But you need to know it is there and how to get around it. Circa 1972 - Crazy Jack McDougal, First Sergeant A Battery, 2/52 ADA, 22 Years in Grade continuous service as a First Sergeant.

First Sergeant Martin got his room key and stowed his gear in his BEQ room, his new transit quarters until he could get his room on the economy. He had not told anyone he did not intend to get a civilian driver's license or buy a car on this tour. It was hard to get a DWI unless you were driving. Germany had strong drink and a lot of temptation for soldiers. The long periods of field duty enhanced a latent tendency for all soldiers to get a little crazy off duty here. He was going to play this whole tour by ear as he was too close to making E9 to screw it up now with some crazy stunt off duty. He did not plan on much recreation, if any at all. He was ready to be assigned to an outfit and get moving with the challenges of being a First Sergeant in USA-REUR.

The look of Downs Barracks was like many others in Germany. The buildings were leftover from WW II and were the former property of the Wehrmacht, Hitler's German Army. Their stucco finish was showing the fine patina of age and their large and wide windows were clearly of the age before central air conditioning. American units moved in barracks all over Germany as well as appropriating housing where they could find it. It was "to the victor go the spoils" in the manner of war since time began. The streets were cobblestone and named after regimental heroes or battles won. The Regimental Headquarters was facing what had once been a parade ground but was now typically American, a parking lot for POVs (Privately owned vehicles). Downs Barracks however, was guarded by armed troopers with a basic load of ammunition in their pouches. The buildings and grounds had the look of special care by soldiers with little funding and little to no capital investment in fixtures and equipment. All of the rolling stock and combat equipment was of the best and latest types available to the Army. Every soldier had a superior appearance with sharp, starched uniforms and highly polished boots sporting good haircuts and a uniformly good appearance. It had the look of an elite unit.

The Regimental Command Sergeant Major was very cordial to Martin. The office was typical with the usual I love me stuff up on the walls with some pictures of famous folks thrown in the game. It was also a reflection of the accomplishments of past black soldiers and why not Martin thought. The Regimental Command Sergeant Major inquired about his housing, his marital status and his length of tour plans. He asked him about his previous experience and what he had done in the Army prior to his assignment to Fulda.

14

"Sergeant Major, I entered the Army in 1969. I served at Fort Carson in 5th ID (Mech). I was an Air Defense guy in Miami, FL and served in 4/69 Armor in Mainz from 73-76. Drill Sergeant from 76-80 training support MOS Soldiers and Infantry. I moved to 3d AD, 1/33 Armor at Gelnhausen. Had a daughter killed in a traffic accident at Knox. As a result of a compassionate re-assignment, I spent three years in the Weapons Department as an Instructor on M551, M60, M60A3, and the M1. My last assignment was First Sergeant of H Co 2/6 Cav. I worked with the Regimental Commanding Officer on several projects at the Armor School and am at least on speaking terms with him. I am currently enrolled in the Sergeants Major Academy Non-Resident Course and I am on track to complete it by Jan or Feb 1986. I am very glad to be here and eager to begin my service with this great outfit." Throughout the monologue, the Regimental Command Sergeant Major took notes and Martin could see Sergeant Major Harris looking in as if to keep him on the straight and narrow.

Command Sergeant Major Naughton then told him, "First Sergeant Martin, you are to be assigned to November Troop as a First Sergeant. Sergeant Major Harris is a great Sergeant Major and a Command Sergeant Major for us now. We do not anticipate an Aviation Command Sergeant Major coming in any time soon to take his place. Welcome to the Regiment. He then proceeded to tell Martin what was expected of him in his job and none of the briefing was any different than he had ever heard before. He gave Martin a booklet that contained the Regimental standard for every soldier. It was a comprehensive small book. As he was walking Martin to his door, the Command Sergeant Major looked at him saying, "The Regimental Commanding Officer is out and is traveling today to Bad Hershfeld."

Martin replied, "That's fine with me Sergeant Major, I have no reason to see the Regimental Commanding Officer unless he wants to see me. I will stay within the Squadron Chain of Command. If I have to see the Regimental Commanding Officer, the road leads through you."

"Well, First Sergeant, I am glad to hear that. Sergeant Major Harris, here he is, put him to work." And with that, the Regimental Command Sergeant Major began to close his door.

"Yes, Sergeant Major, I will." said Harris.

Once outside, Harris asked, "What the hell was that all about with the Regimental Commanding Officer?"

"Beats me," Martin said, "I knew the RCO slightly at Knox, wrote some stuff for FM71-1-2-3 as the Weapons Department representative for a committee he chaired, and had my stuff in on time. He edited the hell out of it when it didn't need it but, shit, nobody writing for the Army has any pride of authorship. I doubt he remembers me at all."

"My ass," said Harris. "He knows you 'cause he prepped his Sergeant Major about you. The Sergeant Major was testing the water and you to make sure he was reading you right. What did you write for FM71-1-2-3?" Harris demanded.

"I wrote a lot of stuff, FM 17-12-1, the M1 Tank Gunnery manual, FM 71-1-2-3, Close Combat Heavy, some training device stuff and helped with the re-write of the bore sight policy. I also wrote some early work on converting training doctrine to Task, Condition and Standards. I proofed the Tank Gunnery Tables and did some other classified stuff to prep Marine tanks aboard ship and other M60A1 stuff on parallel bore sight," concluded Martin.

"Oh, that's all," said Harris, rolling his eyes in his expressive big black face. "For a minute there I thought you might have done something worth a shit that would get you sent to a line squadron with tanks."

"Sure you still want my high priced ass in your Aviation Squadron?" said Martin.

"We will do fine once we get away from here," Harris said. "We gonna' take a little tour to get you oriented to Fulda. Are you gonna' get a car?"

"Probably not, unless I have to," said Martin.

Sergeant Major Harris was shocked, "Shit, get a car. The airfield is too far to do without one and I'll bet your USAREUR driver's license is still good. Self-control means no DWI, not having a car is dumb."

"I'll see," said Martin, not wanting to share his financial situation with Harris.

As they came to the Airfield, they went into the 4/11 Command Sergeant Major office and sat down. Sergeant Major Harris told him to wait there and went to find the Squadron Commander. He was gone about 30 minutes and when he returned, he did not look happy. "Let's go get some lunch at this nice place I know. My wife will meet us. There is no school today. The only reason I came in was to pick you up and do some stuff at Corps. Besides, I want to show you my house on the way. We won't go in because the Frau ain't there and she never likes that."

Driven by the faithful and mostly silent Specialist Fourth Class Meyer, Sergeant Major Harris conducted the tour of the airfield. The Squadron Motor Pool looked like an aviation operation as it was immaculate and totally organized in every respect. The hangars, aircraft and all of the offices appeared ready for an IG inspection. It was a great looking unit and the environment was thoroughly professional.

Martin was very impressed.

"Well, what do you think?" asked Sergeant Major Harris.

"Damn fine looking outfit Sergeant Major. When do I start?" said Martin.

"Well, you need to get your in-processing straight because I really want you to be ready to go at it full bore," said Harris.

"Okay," Martin said, wondering why the rush to have him take over as a First Sergeant had slowed to a crawl. Martin had decided early in the process of being assigned to the Regiment to let it flow and not start out with the Regimental Commanding Officer. He truly wanted to be supportive of the Command Sergeant Major & Sergeant Major end of the Army.

"I know we're going to go someplace great to eat. Where and what is it?" Martin asked more to break the mood than anything.

"We are going to the Water Wheel. It is a great little place out near the LTA (Local Training Area) for First Squadron. It has great food. It is all good. There is not a bad dish on the menu. You look like you could use a good meal. How are you staying so skinny?" Harris asked.

"Well, running ten miles a day keeps me skinny and being married to that old bat who hates to cook helps," said Martin. "I am really looking forward to some great German food. There should be plenty of time to study and do extra PT as a Scout Troop First Sergeant."

The drive to the restaurant took a short detour past the Harris home. It was a single story ranch built with superior German craftsmanship. It had a three car garage and was faced in beautiful stone with a curved driveway that led to the home. The fence surrounding the property was wrought iron, about five feet in height. Stone columns matching the material used on the house supported the fence every eight feet. The yard was at least an acre of nice grass with flower beds along the fence. The gate was electric with a large "H" at the top. The windows were of the large German type and each had a Rollläden, a uniquely German window treatment consisting of a cylinder at the top that acted as a receiver or magazine for the metal cover when it was retracted into a roll during the day. The Rollläden could be lowered during the night, during inclement weather or during periods the family was absent from the home. The cover was noted for screening out light and noise and offering protection for the windows. It was also a clear indicator to the natives that the family in residence was no longer anticipating casual guests. Martin was chuckling as Harris asked him what he thought.

"It is beautiful. It's just like you said it would be back on the Drill Sergeant Trail at Knox when you were TDY," said Martin.

"So what's so funny?" glowered Harris.

"Well shit, Top, the house is Texas Cowboy meets Ricky the Rad. You transplanted all you love about living in American suburbia to here with the superior German workmanship. You planned your work and worked your plan and you probably don't owe a dime on it, do you?" stated Martin.

"Hell, no. No debt. You know you can send a German girl to town and she will buy $25 dollars worth of groceries and bring back $4 change from a $20 dollar bill," laughed Harris. "Go on to the Gaste Haus Meyer."

The Water Wheel Gasthaus was in a very beautiful setting. The parking lot was inside and below the highway. A large, functioning water wheel dominated the front of the building as a creek framed in concrete ran along its front. The soft rush of the water over the rocks soothed the spirit as one entered the building. The eatery was housed in a large white building trimmed in brown. Also of note were the large windows, common to Germany, which began on the left side of the building and continued around to the back. Once inside, the interior was all dark wood with a stone floor. The head waitress immediately recognized Harris and with a broad smile, greeted him in English, "Good day, Sergeant Major. Ushi is already here and I will take you to her. Hello, Meyer. And who is this, a new face?"

As Martin stepped forward to greet the waitress he caught the look from Harris, wordlessly telling him, 'Not here and not with her'.

"Nice to meet you, ma'am. I am Ron Martin."

"And you are Der Spiese," she said playfully, pointing to his collar rank and using the German Army term for First Sergeants, 'The Blade'.

"Jarwohl mine yungen frau," Martin replied in a Berlin dialect.

As the trio and waitress arrived at their table, Ursula Harris stood up to greet her husband with a kiss on the cheek and a squeeze of his hand. She was the quintessential German frau with long legs, long blonde hair, and translucent complexion with no noticeable make up. She was also endowed with full breasts and a smallish waist. Her smile was dazzling and her friendly eyes captivated the group. Turning to the head waitress she stated, "Danke, Heidi. Please, a wine for me, Spatze for my husband and whatever these gentlemen are going to have," serving notice she was in charge and probably buying the lunch. Martin and Meyer both ordered Cokes and sat down across from Sergeant Major Harris and his wife. It was clear Ushi was his beloved and he was her best friend.

"You are glad to be back in Germany First Sergeant?" asked Ursula.

"I am very, very glad to be back," answered Martin. "It is as if I have only been to the states on a long leave. My German will come back to me and I will be right at home here. This is a lovely place. It is a nice valley. Does the LTA butt right up to this land Sergeant Major?"

Meyer answered for the Sergeant Major, "Yes it does First Sergeant." Harris was looking at his wife and had not heard one word Martin had said.

Ushi patted her husband's hand and asked Martin, "Can you read the menu ok?"

"Yes," he replied, "I'm going to have the Jagerschnitzel with French fries, a salad and the chocolate pudding for dessert." Martin loved the dish consisting of a pork cutlet tenderized then cooked in batter in the manner of a chicken fried steak and smothered in onions, mushrooms with gravy. Meyer decided on the Venison stew with a fried egg on top.

Sergeant Major Harris duplicated Martin's selection but skipped the chocolate pudding saying, "I am too short to worry about my weight too much but I ain't buying no new Blues."

Martin then asked, "Where is the latrine in this place, downstairs?" When Harris nodded yes, Martin departed the group for the latrine. He was rehydrating from the long air trip over and his kidneys had not yet sorted out where he was. While going down the stairs he heard the sounds of a bowling alley. After using the immaculate facilities, he followed the sound of bowling alley. He was surprised to see a miniature bowling alley complete with small bowling balls, half sized pins and two lanes. A group of office workers were having a noon time beer either after, or instead of lunch, bowling and teasing each other unmercifully about their scores. Nice place to have a Troop Function Martin was thinking. As he turned to leave the happy scene, Martin felt the presence of Sergeant Major Harris approach.

"What do you think?" Harris asked.

"The place is nice, the bowling alley is great, it would be a nice place to bring the Troop. The waitress is cute, she is one of your wife's best friends, she just got screwed over by a senior NCO and you do not want me to be the next SOB she meets," Martin said with a friendly smile on his face.

"You are still a quick study," said Harris. "What else do you know?"

"There is a lot of underlying tension at Regiment. There is a connection with me and the Regimental Commanding Officer I have yet to make. I have yet to see my new Squadron Commander. You were gone long enough to settle the next war with him and you are still a nice guy. So let's go eat and whatever it is, can wait until I have had my schnitzel. Damn, Top, you act like you are missing me already!"

The meal came and everyone but Mrs. Harris fell to eating it like hungry wolves with manners. Ushi watched Martin eat in the exact manner of a German, knife in his right hand, fork in his left, never switching the two in the American style. She smiled as she realized he had immediately reverted to German table manners and style. She had almost decided to try to involve this First Sergeant with her friend Heidi the waitress and actual co-owner of the Water Wheel with her only brother, Stephon. But, as always, she would talk to her husband first as he knew this man and she did not. She knew they were Drill Sergeants together and were very friendly. She also knew her husband was momentarily very unsettled and she knew by the fact they were breaking bread together, their guest was not the cause of her husband's angst. He may eat people alive who made him mad but he did not eat with them, and he would certainly never introduce them to her. He always told her in due time.

Ursula insisted on paying for all of their meals. The new First Sergeant was part of the family and he was their guest. Meyer did a hundred small courtesies for her husband and was God's gift for taking care of him in the field. Though her husband was a very competent soldier and carried himself with the assurance of a gifted athlete, he had enough stress in his life. Specialist Fourth Class Meyer alleviated a lot of that stress and she was very grateful for Meyer's aid. Mrs. Heidi Harris knew what she wanted and a live husband for a long retirement was at the center of her life. She was very surprised when First Sergeant Martin left a tip once he figured out this was a country place and the gratuity was not figured into the final bill. She tried to leave the tip as well but Martin gave the tip directly to Heidi telling her, "Ursula is far too generous as it is and your service was far too good to be unrewarded. We will meet again, soon."

Ursula was quite surprised when she heard Heidi say, "I certainly hope we will First Sergeant Martin and thank you."

Ignorance is the bliss of the uninformed and the great German meal after a six years of an American diet left First Sergeant Martin feeling very content and happy. He had pep in his step and was cheerfully bantering Sergeant Major Harris and Specialist Fourth Class Meyer as they returned to Fulda.

"Well, what's next on the afternoon agenda, Sergeant Major?" Martin asked.

Surprisingly, Sergeant Major Harris replied, "Well, I thought you might want some time to get squared away in your room, go the PX and get some stuff and to see Sergeant Major Rankin in the S3 Shop at regiment. He asked me to have you drop by there while you were in processing. No need to go to Personnel just yet. Stop by and give a copy of your orders to the Regimental S1 and go see ACR. I'll come by and see you before I go home."

"Sounds great," said Martin, as he got out of the vehicle on their arrival at the BEQ.

As he went into his room, Martin looked out his window and saw the Sergeant Major's van again stop at the front of the Regiment and Sergeant Major Harris go inside. Martin thought it a bit odd that he did not continue his in processing. He unpacked his gear preparing for a stay of several weeks in the room until he got quarters on the German economy. Given his meager wardrobe and traveling gear this took but 45 minutes. He changed from Class A uniform into Battle Dress and put on his new boots to break them in gently.

Having the remainder of the day to and evening to wait, he decided to explore the Kaserne, visit the Post Exchange and look up Sergeant Major Arthur C. Rankin or ACR. Art Rankin was a former boss. They had been Drill Sergeants together and had a very good association. He was one the finest NCOs Martin had ever known. He did not want to interrupt him during the most productive part of the day and would see him about 1600 hours.

It did not take Martin long to make his way through the PX. It was typically USAREUR. The facility had the staples, some of the stock was old, the clothing sizes were goofy as they were either too small or too large for him. He contented himself with snack food, sodas, cigarettes and the Brasso, shoe polish and edge dressing the items soldiers need to maintain their appearance but that only a recruit packed in luggage for a PCS. He returned to his room put his purchases away and went to walk the Kaserne to see if some of the First Sergeants and Troop Commanders he knew from past service were assigned to First Squadron.

He was pleasantly surprised to see the sign for B Troop, 1/11 ACR proclaimed Douglas Drayton as the First Sergeant and Captain Wilson as the

Commander. As he entered the Troop, the Charge of Quarters Runner looked up and greeted him, "Good afternoon, First Sergeant, can I help you?"

"Just point me to the Orderly Room, Specialist Rathburne. I'm here to see your First Sergeant," said Martin.

Rathburne was taken aback, it was not often an NCO he did not know called him by his rank and his name and it never happened when a First Sergeant was involved. "It's right down the hall First Sergeant and First Sergeant Drayton is there working with the Training NCO."

"Thanks, Specialist Rathburne, I see it, you carry on," said Martin. As with all hallways of the Old German Barracks, the high ceilings, stone floors and the absence of any decorations or carpeting to deaden the sound caused Martin's loud, sonorous, and deep voice to echo.

First Sergeant Drayton came bounding out into the hallway, "I heard your crazy ass was coming to the Blackhorse but I just did not believe it. Welcome and come on into my office. We got Bucky as the Troop Commander and Abrams for an Squadron Commander and this place is shit hot. What troop are you going to? You did not get a Tank Company instead of me I hope? As far as I know, we do not have any openings for a First Sergeant. But if we did, you would love it here with Sergeant Major Fred Davenport and Abrams. Let me call Sergeant Major Davenport. Here sit down, move that shit. This is Fast Eddie Sutton, Master Gunner, Training NCO and Headquarters Platoon Sergeant and any other damn thing I need done." Thus concluding his rapid fire monologue, First Sergeant Drayton sat down to dial the Command Sergeant Major.

"Sergeant Major, Drayton here. Do we have any vacancies for a First Sergeant? One of my former Instructors from the Armor School is here and he would be great for gunnery but I don't know if we have any room. I know I am supposed to know everyone we have assigned Command Sergeant Major and I do, but I was hoping you had some way we could get him in First Squadron. He is that crazy guy I told you about that after we were notified we had made E-8, he went right on draining the chip collector. Yeah he is the guy you heard about. Well thanks, Sergeant Major, I'll tell him." As he hung up the phone, Doug Drayton told Martin, "No room at the Inn, Hoss. I guess they have stolen everyone they can as they came through here and they are full up. He can't even lie about it to get you and he sure don't need to fire anyone. First Squadron is at the flagpole and they usually get first pick. Sergeant Major Davenport is the best Command Sergeant Major I have ever seen. If he can't get you assigned here, no one can."

Martin smiled ruefully, "Well Doug, I hate to admit it but it looks like I lucked out and got an Air Cav Troop. I am enrolled in the SMA Non-Resident Course, trying to finish my BA and that should be the ticket." Seeing

21

the astonished look of his friend's face, Martin quickly added, "Hey, I didn't ask for it, Regimental Command Sergeant Major orders."

"Shit, an Air Cav Troop is not work for a self-respecting Armor First Sergeant. You have had bigger platoons. It is not enough of a challenge to keep you busy. You are too damn hyper to sit around listening to those pilots fly their hands and talk their shit."

"Hey, Sir," Drayton called to the Troop Commander. "Do you believe that shit? Mad Dog Martin is going to a damn Air Troop?"

"I thought I heard that crazy guy out there," said Captain Wilson.

"Good Afternoon, Sir," said Martin.

"What in hell are you doing by going to an Air Cav Troop?" exclaimed the Captain. "That is a total waste of resources. I don't give a damn what the TO&E says."

Spoken like an Army Blue Blood Martin thought, remembering his days under Major General Wilson, now a Lieutenant General, Captain Wilson's father. The elder Wilson was one of the best Division Commanders Martin had ever known. He was now a Corps Commander. Captain Wilson had irritated Martin as a student in the Advanced Course and he still did.

"What do you suggest I do about the assignment, Captain Wilson?" asked Martin.

"Go to the Regimental Commanding Officer and tell him you want a Tank Company or a ground Cavalry Troop," blustered the young Captain.

"Well, that might happen yet, you never know," said Martin.

"Wherever you go, your troop will never beat this one at Tank gunnery. Our Squadron Commander is so far ahead of the other guys they can't even see his dust cloud. We are the best," crowed the young Captain.

"Given that the Russians outnumber us five to one, you had better hope your flank units get smart quick or your perfect asses will be POWs or dead. Unless of course, First Squadron is going to kill them all and the rest of us are just here for police call," Martin stated.

"You'll see, welcome aboard," said Captain Wilson as he returned to his office.

"So how's Debbie and the little tyke?" Martin asked calmly.

"Damn, you could always shift gears quick couldn't you?" Drayton said with a smile.

"Shit, Doug, that guy has a load. He is carrying a whole family tree in his pack. Besides, everyone is supposed to feel that way about their outfit. His daddy is the finished product Doug - a three star. Bucky the Boy Wonder will be all right once he finds his way. It ain't as easy being an Army Blue Blood as it looks to us peasants," Martin concluded.

"Debbie is doing great. She has the wives organizing and hanging out with her. They are all going to Frankfurt to go Christmas shopping early. They go on tours to wineries, marketplaces, ski trips, you name it, and they do it. Let's walk through the troop, I want to show you the standard," Drayton said, leading Martin out the door. The two First Sergeants then went on a tour of the barracks, the bulletin board, supply room, several soldier rooms and ending at the arms room. It was a self-contained world with one other troop sharing the building. It looked nearly perfect to Martin's eye as it was clean and orderly, almost to NCO Academy standards.

At the Arms Room, First Sergeant Drayton introduced Martin to the Troop Armorer saying, "This is my registered NRA gun freak, PFC Carpenter from West By God Virginia who loves these weapons like only a Moonshiner's Kid could. Ask him anything you want, he has an answer for you," bragged Drayton.

"Well, First Sergeant, I'm sure he could answer any question I might ask," said Martin.

"No, I want you to ask him so we can both learn something, so ask okay?" said Drayton.

"So Carpenter, when were the machinegun barrels last gauged?" asked Martin. PFC Carpenter looked at his First Sergeant as if this were a trick question. "You see PFC Carpenter; each caliber of weapon the Army owns has a barrel life. The maintenance support units have specific instruments and gauges to determine how much life is remaining in the barrel. No amount of bore sighting, or praying for that matter, will put the first rounds fired from a worn out barrel on target. First Sergeant Drayton will show you how to make the request later this afternoon and get your machinegun barrels checked by higher headquarters maintenance."

Drayton spoke up quickly, "Sure, we will get right on that. See Carpenter, I told you we would both learn something today." At this point, the CQ Runner appeared telling First Sergeant Drayton he was to report to the Troop Commander immediately. Martin told him farewell, agreed to meet later in the week and walked to Regimental Hqs as it was approaching 1600 hours.

As Martin walked through the Hqs parking lot, he saw the smiling face of Master Sergeant (P) Rankin in an upstairs window of the building. Rankin opened the window and said, "I'll be right down." Rankin had always been an after duty hours runner and Martin knew he would be downstairs before he could even get across the space, and he was.

Rankin was happy to see Martin and the two shook hands and as old soldiers often do, talked to each louder than necessary in the effusive manner of good friends. Martin knew Rankin was a good friend and was certain he was about to learn just what the hell was going on in the Byzantine world of the Regiment. All afternoon he had puzzled over it and told Rankin, "Like the character in Alice in Wonderland, the situation gets 'curiouser and curiouser'."

Rankin laughed saying, "You can smell a rat a mile away but at least you are getting better about calling it a despicable rodent instead of a damn rat. How did you get so diplomatic, did the Armor School do that to you?"

"I'm not completely civilized. I am in unfamiliar territory so I am being cautious. Is this a military deal or is it personal toward me?" said Martin.

Rankin became the professor for his old subordinate Martin, "The TO & E for the regiment changes fast. They get the latest equipment in the Army up here on the border. Unlike the rest of the Army and even Europe, there is no institutional knowledge base to build on as the stuff is new, all of the time. The Commanders are so driven, they do not spend the time to fully train on new equipment but do it as OJT. It is the blind leading the blind or as you would call it, discovery learning. Units that undergo a lot of change get their timelines confused. The new TO&E has aviation E8s as First Sergeant and the old one, Treadheads like you. The 4/11 Squadron Commander wants Aviation guys, not Treadheads like you as his First Sergeants. They are kicking your assignment back and forth like a football. As far as I know it ain't personal but it will sure seem like it to you."

"Art, where are we walking?" said Martin.

"We're going to the mess hall. I missed breakfast and lunch and I'm getting an early supper," Rankin replied.

"Glad to see the S3 shop still has not changed. The Ammo NCO is probably fat as hell and the Ops Sergeant is starving to death," laughed Martin.

"You seem to be taking all of this lightly," said Rankin, as they neared the mess hall that they both thought of as the 'Dining Facility'.

Once inside, Martin went to the rear of the dining hall to the Officer/NCO section to wait for Rankin. Rankin cheerfully bantered with the cooks as they garnished his food and got him a special Spatze from the carbonated fountain. As he sat down at the table, Martin had to smile at the intensity radiated by his former platoon Sergeant. He knew ACR was working his butt off but that he was enjoying it. "So, it really doesn't piss you off, the football thing?" Rankin asked taking a bite of sandwich.

"Who should I be mad at, Art? The 4/11 Squadron Commander wants the best for his unit. Sergeant Major Harris wants a 'smoke bringer' back up at the end of his career. The Regimental Command Sergeant Major is following the book and assigning me as he thinks he must. However, the clock is ticking for my ass and I need to be a First Sergeant in the Blackhorse. If that is not to be in 4th Squadron, or 1st Squadron, there are two more. If there is no room, I will call on my friend the Commanding General of 3 AD and go there. He told me I had a job if the Blackhorse fumbled the ball. My intention is to brace the Command Sergeant Major mafia and go to 'Smokin' Joe' Bannister if I don't get an answer," Martin concluded.

"What will you tell 'Smokin Joe'?" asked ACR.

"Is his wife over here?" Martin asked.

24

"Yeah, she's here," replied Rankin. "I'll tell him I won't tell Madge about Bridget, the gorgeous blonde from the Knox O Club if he will just give me a real job in the Blackhorse," said Martin.

"Shit, you'd never rat him out. Did he really screw her?" Rankin asked incredulously. "She is as good looking as Marlene Dietrich!"

"If he didn't they were doing the best imitation of people screwing I ever saw or heard in the O'Club parking lot at 0200 when I was on Lightning Brigade Staff Duty," said Martin.

"But you're right, whatever I tell him, will be strictly military, short and to the point. I'll cogitate on it some and watch the 'mice' scramble when I press them for an answer. The source of Intell is safe with me, Art, they will never know we talked. I am okay anyway it goes but I do not want to waste two months while some old geezer field grades have a pissin' contest."

"Damn, you are skinnier than I knew you to be since Drill Sergeant days," declared Rankin.

"Running about ten miles a day and doing the daily dozen, drills one, two and three in the Florida Sun Art. I am 43 years old and their average age is 26. When they start to get the dry heaves and puke during the run, I'll be getting my second wind. Young guys hate big talkers who can't deliver physically. I demand a lot and you can only do that from the front, not wheezing in the rear," said Martin.

"Come on back to the S3 shop and I will show you how the Regiment is organized, the mission and who does what," volunteered Rankin.

Martin replied, "I think I know that stuff, Art, but I would appreciate a look at the calendar from up here and the Regimental Commanding Officer's training requirements."

Arriving at the S3 Shop, ACR took down his trusty 'New Guy' book and began to layout the requirements of the Regimental Commanding Officer and where each Squadron piece fit into the game.

"REFORGER (Return of Forces to Germany) dominates the whole training effort now and it is in late January and early February of next year. It is an every other year deal live one year, CPX the next. It is a big deal. It simulates the return of specific units to Germany and the fight against the Warsaw pact if Ivan ever gets froggy. In our real world mission, each squadron has its piece of the border. When we have a Regimental or larger exercise, such as Caravan Guard during off years for REFORGER, we have options. For the upcoming REFORGER, the option will be to use a composite force of diminished size under the control of the Border Officer to patrol the entire border. Instead of one troop sized element per squadron sector, we will use a platoon in each sector with borrowed radar elements from a Division of V Corps. Prior to REFORGER, each squadron will train up its units by giving each of them a week in the field and will culminate with a squadron exercise using a CPX to move units around with only minor aggressor unit play."

"Each of the squadrons train in maneuver rights areas they can use once the local harvests are complete. The Regimental Commanding Officer's training requirements are easy to state and to write but could be a bitch to do. Right now, you could lie about it and probably never get caught short of the first battle of the next war. I know you would not do that and that you will find a way to do the training. The Regimental Commanding Officer states the following are non-negotiable yard quarterly sticks for training with 90% of the unit certified:

- Marksmanship – Qualified, 40% Sharpshooter or Higher
- Physical Training – Pass – Average Score Noted,
- Gunnery All Weapons - Qualified – Grafenwohr or Wildflecken depending on range assigned, Tank Crew Proficiency Course, Mini-Tank Range
- NBC – Chamber quarterly
- Border – All higher headquarters drills and missions passed first time Special Emphasis - Handicap Black Messages
- All School Quotas for NCOES (Noncommissioned Officer Education System) filled and passed successfully
- Vehicle Operational Ready Rate – 85% minimum
- Drivers Licensing for assigned vehicles-85%
- Urinalysis Testing
- Tactics and maneuver Training- Platoon, Company Maneuver in Border Rights area or Squadron FTX, CPX."

"That is a full plate, Art. Do you have a copy of those requirements just in case? Those tasks could be a real challenge in the M1 units. When are we going to get the Bradleys?" asked Martin.

"Take the copy in the back of the book. I'll get another. The Bradley will not be fielded until later 1985 with the first gunnery in 1986," ACR said. "As far as the challenge goes, remember each squadron has its own small range complex complete with TCPC Course and sub-caliber weapons firing points. Wildflecken is also available and is close enough to be used by the entire Regiment in Squadron size iterations. This is an outfit that is both equipped and expected to move rapidly. If a Cavalry outfit cannot move 100 miles in a 12 hour day, it is not worth much. It can all be done. Unit Commanders need to be focused," he continued.

Rankin then asked Martin, "The question is, how long are going to wait before you make waves over your assignment?"

Martin smiled and said, "Art, I just got here. I think I should wait at least 48 hours or until I am sure I am pissing German water before I start telling Smokin' Joe how to run the Regiment. I need to see the Education Center guy, figure out how the promotion board system works, visit the commissary and visit the Training Aids Support Coordinator to see all of what is available here. Man Mountain Harris is supposed to come to my cage tonight and check in with me. I guess I better go back over there and be where he expects me to be. I'll see you before I go to a unit."

As Martin arrived at his BOQ/BEQ room, he noted that Sergeant Major Harris was in the room next door visiting a departing Major. He told Martin, "Standby First Sergeant, I'll be right over." Martin just nodded and opened his room. Leaving the door open, he turned on the TV where AFN or (Armed Forces Network) was showing a western movie and poured himself a coke with ice. He set out the Jack Daniels bottle but did not open it as it would be up to Sergeant Major Harris to pronounce duty hours. In an outfit such as the Blackhorse, duty hours were bound to be situational even for un-assigned folks like him.

Sergeant Major Harris came in, threw his hat on the dresser and said, "Yes, how generous of you to offer me a drink, Jack and Coke if you please - a double."

"Damn, ain't you driving?" said Martin.

"No, I am not, I am going to the Commissary with Ushi and she is driving me home. Meyer is picking me up at home in the morning on the way to Frankfort. I gotta' go back to Corps for a board."

"Ah duty, duty, duty," said Martin.

After a sip, Harris asked, "What does your intell spot report say Martin?"

"After Bravo Troop being the best outfit in the Army you mean. Every-body means well but I am a football being punted up and down the field be-tween the Regimental Command Sergeant Major and your Squadron Com-mander. I probably need to see the Squadron Commander early in the morn-ing to hear it from him. Then I will see how ignorant the Regimental Com-mand Sergeant Major is going to play it and I will go from there. How do you see it?" asked Martin.

Finishing his drink, Harris paused to gather his thoughts balancing what he could and could not say about the situation. "Same way. I knew I was screwed when the Squadron Commander said he wanted aviation guys in the slots as if the new TO & E was in effect. He does not realize that they may never have the same ability that you have right now and that having you there gives them a role model and a guide for development. I hate it we got led down the path," groused Harris.

"I gotta' go, take it easy on the sauce," Harris said as he moved his great bulk to the door.

Stopping at the door he said, "I will have the S1 vehicle here at 0700. The Colonel does not do morning PT. He will be doing paperwork to clear his desk as he is flying in the afternoon. I will call him tonight and tell him you have requested open door policy with him at 0730. He is a by the book guy and while he does not want to even meet with you, he will honor the re-quest."

"I appreciate it, Sergeant Major," said Martin. With no one to call, and not wanting to go out anywhere, Martin mixed a drink from his now used Jack Daniels bottle, made a sandwich and began work on a module of his course. He began to laugh as he thought of old Sam Cyrus telling then Sergeant First Class (P) Harris in response to an order to march their platoon back from the rifle range as Drill Sergeants while Harris went to recon a range. Sam was a master of the black falsetto saying "But Massa, you said I was going to Masta' Johnson's place to be a stud and cover bitches but all I does is chop sugar cane." Harris's response was classic, "Shit Sam, nobody said you had to like it, you just got to do it."

Promptly at 0500, Martin awoke and quickly found his smokes, had a glass of coke, took two aspirins and dressed for PT fully intending to be out the door by 0530. The October German morning was sure not Florida. The streets were dark and streetlights were few and far between. He decided to run down to the railhead and back up the long hill for a hard 30 minutes, do 2 minutes each of sit-ups and pushups, walk to cool down and get ready for the meeting with the Squadron Commander. He knew Sergeant Major Harris had carried out his end of the arrangement. Duty in USAREUR meant the leadership team got a response from those wearing the green tabs (a badge of green felt dating from the Revolution denoting combat leaders worn on the epaulets of the field jacket) any time, day or night, and if not, their second in command could, and would, answer for them. During his run he saw no one and encountered no other creature except a stray cat. He was surprised when a high speed German train zipped by on the Bundespost track running just outside the fence went by at an estimated 80 miles per hour. It was amazing how fast the trains traveled in Germany and how little noise they made-swift, silent, deadly. He made a note to include the point to his new soldiers to ensure they knew to never walk down the railroad track in Germany.

At 0600, he had made his way back to the BEQ and did his exercises in his room before showering and preparing for his meeting with Lieutenant Colonel Quigley. Promptly at 0700, the S1 driver was in front of the BEQ and Martin was standing there smoking a cigarette waiting for him. After verifying the purpose of the trip, Martin mounted and went to his meeting.

At the Squadron, Martin was surprised to see the Adjutant on duty and appearing to be waiting on him. He recognized the young Captain as a former AOAC (Armor Officer Advanced Course) student. They talked quietly and Martin told him the Squadron Commander was expecting him. The Captain told him many of the officers were happy he was there to be a First Sergeant and that he hoped everything would work out. The adjutant knocked on the Squadron Commander's door and told him, "Sir, First Sergeant Martin is here to see you. He then turned to Martin saying, "First Sergeant Martin, the Squadron Commander will see you now." Martin knocked on the door jam. Lieutenant Colonel Quigley looked up telling him, "Come in, First Sergeant."

Martin entered, coming to within a precise 30 inches of his desk, saluted and stated, "Sir, First Sergeant Martin reports."

"Stand At Ease, First Sergeant. I have opposed your assignment. It is not personal. I am sure you are a very good NCO based on your 2-1. I helped write the new TO & E to add aviation NCOs as First Sergeants to improve the promotion potential of the Sergeant First Class population in Aviation. The TO & E takes effect in less than sixty days. I have people on the promotion list and I know there are in bound Master Sergeants and Sergeant First Class promotables who will fill these slots. My opposition to you is not personal, it is professional. I am trying to fulfill the intent of the leadership of the Army. When the next generation of complex Army aircraft come on board, it is imperative that we provide a personnel pyramid to allow initiative, faithful service and potential to be recognized. I have heard you are very bright and very well regarded by the officers of this squadron and the regiment. Okay that is the official part of this conversation. This part is personal for you. I have no doubt you will be an outstanding First Sergeant. You just won't be a First Sergeant in my squadron and neither will any other 19Z as long as I command it. The Regimental Commanding Officer agrees with me on this or else I would not be saying it. Does this answer your question and put your mind at ease?"

"Yes, Sir. Thank you for seeing me and explaining the situation. I won't take up any more of your time." Martin saluted and on receiving a salute from the commander departed. The waiting adjutant who had overheard every word, told him the vehicle was waiting to outside to return him to his BEQ. He was in and out in less than ten minutes. *Leaders on firm ground need few words to explain their position, he mused.*

As the vehicle driver wound through the airfield streets in the thick morning fog avoiding formations of running soldiers, Martin knew now he needed to see the Regimental Command Sergeant Major and then see the Regimental Commanding Officer.

Martin had the S1 driver drop him at the consolidated dining facility. He was hoping it would be empty and he could have his breakfast in peace while he read the paper. The dining facility was bright, freshly painted, decorated with some nice prints and looked very up to date. The plates, silver, glasses and trays were in immaculate order. He got a full Army breakfast of eggs over easy, creamed beef on toast, fruit, cereal, milk, juice and a sweet roll before making his way to the NCO section. Breakfast was the cheapest meal of the day and the one he usually had the longest time available to eat so he meant to fully enjoy it. He was soon joined by two members of the Regimental S3 Shop, the Master Gunner whom he knew from Fort Knox as a student and the Ammunition & Schools NCO, a Corporal that looked familiar. Both NCOs were very friendly and had interesting personalities. Corporal Standiford spoke first, "So where are you going to be assigned, First Sergeant? Weren't you at the Weapons Department at Knox?"

"Yes, Corporal, I was. Have we met?" Martin asked.

"Well, you not many remember me, but I remember you from the Classified Ammunition Class and the Training Devices Briefings you gave the Armor Conference. I got to go back in May and represent the Regiment," said the Corporal.

"You must be one hot ticket for your rank Corporal, even if you did double up on the Color Guard to make the trip," said Martin, pleasing the Corporal that he remembered the Ceremony at the Blackhorse Monument. "I hope I do not get to know you professionally as all I want to know about ammo I want my master gunner to tell me," said Martin.

Sergeant Thornberg, the master Gunner spoke up, "We heard you were going to an Air Cav Troop. Is that true?"

"I don't know the answer to that just yet," Martin said.

"Do you remember where we met?" Thornberg asked.

"Yes," replied Martin, "I sat in on your presentation for your final training briefing for your Master Gunner Course. When they were short of instructors they would ask me to sit in as the third guy to receive the briefs and I had a vote. I never got to go to the course. You did a good job as I recall."

"Thanks," said Thornberg. "It was a close call and I was glad to see a friendly face. We were sure they had a failure quota at that school as we lost 19 of the 25 students that we started out with on Day 1."

"One thing schools ought to watch out for is getting into a corner of self-fulfilling prophecies on who is going to make it and who is not. Some of those guys think it adds to the aura of the Master Gunner to fail 85% of the class. If 85% of the best tankers in the Army fail a school, there is something wrong somewhere in the pipeline," Martin opined.

"Well, are you a Master Gunner, First Sergeant?" asked Thornberg.

"Nope," said Martin.

"Why not?" Thornberg asked.

"You see, Sergeant Thornberg, early in the life of the course, like 1976, an NCO could either be a Drill Sergeant, a Recruiter or a Master Gunner. He could not be more than one unless he was already a Drill Sergeant or former Recruiter when the Master Gunner course started. There were a number of professional Army Schoolboys from earlier days. The Army leadership wanted Master Gunners to be dedicated to improving Tank Gunnery. It was also about then that our Armor Officers began to get diverse assignments on their career path. The Army was changing to new equipment with rapid change just over the horizon. The Master Gunner was the easy way to keep Armor units on track."

"When I was a PFC, all of my officers who were Captains or above and were experts with all weapons in the unit. They led, taught the soldiers and set the standard on the tanks. At some point the Army leadership started career tracking and began training guys who were Captains to be qualified to be four star generals and they got to be dumber than dog shit about tanks, ergo, enter the Master Gunner. The Marines have the right idea with Limited Duty Officers or as they call them, LDOs. When the war starts, the Commandant breaks the glass around those smart gunnery sergeants with reserve commissions, and they have at least one instant Company Commander per Battalion, some Staff Officers and a few Battalion Executive Officers, with combat experience."

"Our officer corps is not about to ever let that happen, so they created the Master Gunner to establish and maintain technical expertise at all levels, leaving the officers free to command. Besides all of the philosophy, the guys running the Master Gunner Branch hated my guts for coaching the AOB students on the Tank Crew Gunnery Skills Test after Duty hours. The Master Gunner Instructors considered my coaching to be cheating. I could not care less, then or now. But, they would never have passed me in that course. I respect all of you that made it through. I have seen 25 of 25 students fail on at least two occasions and no one batted an eye. The key to passing the course is the TCGST and the key to the TCGST lies in the unit. You got to have absolute integrity and just re-test those that fail a station."

"Why on earth would they send you to an Aviation unit, First Sergeant?" asked Corporal Stadiford.

"Beats the hell out of me Corporal, I just work here," laughed Martin. "I ain't there yet fellows," Martin said as he gathered up his tray to turn it in to the window.

"Hey First Sergeant, the KPs do that here for this table," said Thornberg.

"Thanks Mike Gulf, but I hump my own rucksack and police up my own trash otherwise I get too high of an opinion about myself and it is high enough as it is. See you guys," Martin said with a smile.

As he walked to the BEQ, Martin realized he could just loaf and lay on his dead ass until someone made a decision. Hell, the power struggle between the Regimental Command Sergeant Major and an Lieutenant Colonel could take a month to solve. Meanwhile, his life would be in limbo, his additional housing allowance, assignment, mailing address, etc. Besides, too much leisure was not on his calendar. He knew his overall career was set up for his next and final promotion. His Maslow Needs Hierarchy was about to peak out at the self-actualization level. Some new PhD theory had left old Maslow in the dust by now but he was comfortable with the old "word" as it fit him and was ingrained in his thought process. He passed the Regimental Headquarters by continuing on to the BEQ, deciding to return there after 0900 when the mice re-entered their maze and mounted their centrifuge cages once again to begin their endless spinning that passed for progress.

31

What Martin could not know was the Regimental Commanding Officer was already aware of his 0700 meeting with the Squadron Commander of 4th Squadron as a result of a phone call before the duty vehicle taking him to main post had ever left the parking lot. The Regimental Commanding Officer wanted to give his Sergeant Major every opportunity to solve any assignment issues before he became involved. He knew his tasks, had very clear guidance from the Corps Commander and being the S1 or Regimental Command Sergeant Major was not part of the calculus. He knew First Sergeant Martin and wondered how long it would take the Regimental Command Sergeant Major to find out just how much wild cat he had treed when the "cat" made his next move. He smiled as he thought about the byplay that would ensue. He was very pleased Martin had not presumed on their previous working relationship to protest the initial assignment to the Air Cav. He was also pleased his request for First Sergeant Martin's assignment to the Regiment had worked so quickly after assuming command. He knew it would not be long before the First Sergeant was knocking on his door and he knew where he was going to assign him.

Jenny Johnson was the Regimental Commanding Officer's efficient secretary, keeping a million administrative details straight and keeping his schedule on track. She came to work early most days and today was no exception. After taking off her coat and setting up for the day, she always made his office her first stop. Jenny was married to one of the Warrant Officers at the Airfield and was a great addition to his staff. She had been a mid-level executive in a small plastics company in Indiana when she married Chief Warrant Officer 3 Johnson. Jenny's best friend had been Johnson's first wife and had passed away after a prolonged illness. After some time had passed, Jenny had married her best friend's widower. Career oriented, it was her first marriage. She had gotten a ready-made family of three pretty little girls when her best friend, Melinda Johnson died. It was never her intention to marry a soldier, but their relationship had blossomed during his compassionate re-assignment to Fort Campbell. The bond was made stronger by her nurturing of her best friend's daughters during the period following her friend's tragic death. When she looked at the girls, she saw Melinda. It had begun as duty and ended up as love and she was very happy.

"Good morning Colonel, how are you today?" Jenny asked.

"I'm fine JJ and how are all my girls today?" he asked.

"They are wonderful. We are lucky, they love school and cannot wait to go every day," said Jenny. She was not quite yet adjusted to the military nickname system of naming her JJ since she was Jenny Johnson. *It felt very good to be Mrs. Johnson and the 'JJ' confirmed her identity every time she heard it. 'Oh, Melinda I miss you,' she thought. 'And I am taking good care of the girls and Sam.'*

"JJ, have you seen the Command Sergeant Major yet today? If not, tell me his calendar for the day would you?" the Regimental Commanding Officer asked. He was careful to speak in a quiet and measured way as JJ was new to the Army.

"Sir, I have not seen him but then I just got here. His day planner reflects him to be in the office this morning and traveling to Bad Hershfeld this afternoon," JJ replied.

"As soon as you see him, ask him to come in if I do not see him first. Don't call him at home, it can wait until he comes in to the office. Give me a few minutes in order to finish this letter and then bring your folders and we'll get organized for the OER counseling before it gets crazy, okay?"

"Yes, Sir."

She did not know how the Regimental Commanding Officer juggled so many projects that were on-going at the same time. Just like a professional juggler, he managed to smoothly coordinate all items without dropping any of them. Actually, it seemed that many of the soldiers in her immediate sphere were amazing in the degree of organization that they possessed. All exhibited a singular superior talent with their ability to do so many varied tasks in any one given day.

Martin had gone back to his room and watched the AFN news for a short time before working on his course for the Academy. At about 0915, he made his way to the Regimental Hqs to see the Regimental Command Sergeant Major about his assignment. He said hello to the Regimental Commanding Officer's secretary and walked by her to the Regimental Command Sergeant Major's office. He saw the Regimental Command Sergeant Major was occupied on the phone and sat down to wait just outside the office out of earshot of the conversation.

It was an animated talk and Martin did not want to hear any of the details. Shortly, the Regimental Command Sergeant Major came to his door and motioned for Martin to come in and sit down.

"Sergeant Major, I went to see Lieutenant Colonel Quigley this morning on Open Door," Martin began.

"Open door," said the Regimental Command Sergeant Major. "What is that all about?"

"Well, Sergeant Major, he would not let me in process into his unit. He does not want me due to MOS mismatch with the new TO & E, citing DA and the Regimental Commanding Officer as his authority," replied Martin.

"That TO & E is not in effect. He does not have that authority. I assign all enlisted soldiers in the Regiment. He needs you. I assigned you there and that is where you are going to go, period," he stated.

Oh shit, Martin thought, the preachin' has started. The Sergeant Major has staked out his last fighting position and is about to fall on his bayonet.

"Sergeant Major I am just a simple old soldier looking for a home. If there is not a place here, I know there is a company for me in Third Armored Division. There is no harm done yet," said Martin.

"This is not over yet. Let me talk to him. Come back about 1100. You are not leavin' this Regiment for any other unit. Why would you say that?" he said glowering at Martin.

"Sergeant Major, I just want to get into the game. It is a two year tour and it is time to play me or trade me. The Squadron Commander is just as convinced he is right as you are and I promised you all roads to the Regimental Commanding Officer lead through your office. I'll see you at 1100," said Martin and as he departed to the lobby and Mrs. Johnson's area, the Regimental Command Sergeant Major's door was slammed behind him. Martin took care to go out the side door adjacent to the lobby so that he would not have to pass by the Regimental Commanding Officer. The time was not right to talk to Smokin' Joe just yet. Besides, he was probably enjoying the row between the two big dogs, measuring them and deciding who was doing the right thing. As far as Martin was concerned, the Regimental Commanding Officer was one of the best officers he had ever seen at getting tough jobs done with no fuss and was a genius at getting smart subordinates to do it for him. He was not in his high speed job by accident and would make a quick decision after the matter got to him.

Martin remembered the day a fat-ass Lieutenant Colonel told Smokin' Joe at Fort Knox that the contribution Martin had made for a manual they were working as a group to complete was not bad work for an NCO but was not good enough for the Army. He also sneered as he complained his department had to provide a Lieutenant Colonel while Weapons Department got by with sending a mere Sergeant. He would not soon forget the response from Smokin Joe. "Sergeant First Class Martin is the direct representative of an O-6, the Director of the Weapons Department. He wrote the largest part of the manual as it is now while teaching a full load of classes. Those changes went to you two weeks ago. It is too late now for any major re-writes. The last draft has been approved by General Sullivan. The Sergeant stays, the material stays as written. You can return to your duties in your department effective immediately." Dismissed, the outranked Lieutenant Colonel left in a huff and never came back to the group. Martin was in Smokin' Joe's camp from there forward. He also gained a new degree of respect for the ability of senior officers to deliver an ass chewing and to take one.

At 1100, Martin reappeared at Regimental HQs. Noticing that the door to the Regimental Command Sergeant Major's office was shut, he asked the secretary if the Regimental Command Sergeant Major was in his office.

She replied, "He is with the Regimental Executive Officer right now, you are welcome to sit and wait, First Sergeant."

"Thanks, Ma'am, I'll wait," Martin said. He took a seat and began to read the handout the Regimental Command Sergeant Major had given to him, making notes on the back page as he did so.

34

Engrossed, Martin did not notice the Regimental Commanding Officer come out of his office and walk over to him, saying "That book does not have any pictures in it, how can an old First Sergeant read it without moving his lips?"

"That's easy, Sir, I'm a ventriloquist," Martin said as he came to attention so quickly, Pavlov would have approved.

The Regimental Commanding Officer shook his hand and motioned him to come into his office, telling his secretary, "JJ, if they are not out of there in ten minutes, interrupt them and tell them to come to my office." On the phone, JJ nodded her assent and continued to take notes.

"So what do you think of the assignment?" the Regimental Commanding Officer asked.

"First, congratulations. The eagles look good on you. As for me, I could not be happier" said Martin. Continuing, he said, "It is great being back in Germany and great coming to the Blackhorse. I know it will be a challenge. Cavalry is new to me. I have already met folks I know."

"Is there anything we need to talk about, First Sergeant?" asked the Regimental Commanding Officer.

"Not yet, Sir, I promised the Sergeant Major the road to you led through him," said Martin reddening slightly. As he realized he was flushing a bit, the Sergeant Major and the Executive Officer knocked on the door frame and were waved into the office.

The Sergeant Major asked Martin, "What are you doing in here?"

Before Martin could reply, the Regimental Commanding Officer stated, "I invited him Sergeant Major. He declined to tell me if he was having any problems and told me you were handling any issues. So how did it go? Is Martin having any problems?"

"Sir, we need to talk," said the Sergeant Major gesturing to Martin to leave. Martin got up to leave and heard the Sergeant Major tell him, "Close the door, First Sergeant, and have a seat." Martin closed the door and resumed his seat.

The Sergeant Major then returned and asked Martin if he had a request.

Martin stated, "Sergeant Major, I would like to see the Regimental Commanding Officer on Open Door if I cannot be assigned to 4th Squadron."

"Go ahead," the Sergeant Major replied. "He is waiting for you. Report to the Regimental Commander."

Martin knocked on the door frame and the Regimental Commanding Officer formally stated, "Come in." Following formal protocol Martin was centered on the desk, saluted and reported. The Regimental Commanding Officer was unsmiling and stiffly formal, as he directed, "At Ease, First Sergeant. What is it I can do for you today?"

"Sir, play me or trade me. I would like the assignment to the worst Cavalry Troop in the Regiment as soon as you can get me there," Martin stated in a measured and respectful tone.

"First Sergeant Martin, I am assigning you to G Troop, 2d Squadron in Bad Kissingen. The last First Sergeant was relieved. The unit failed the Inspector General's Inspection, they failed Border Inspections, they have accidents and have a drug problem. They cannot do anything right. You have ninety days to straighten it out or I will relieve you. Do you have any questions?" the Regimental Commanding Officer concluded.

"No, Sir," Martin replied, saluting and departing the office after receiving what he thought was the best salute he ever saw Smokin' Joe give. He stood by at the Sergeant Major's office expecting a long counseling session.

Instead, the Sergeant Major shook his hand in his office and told him with a smile, "With that outfit there is only one way to go, up. Go pack. I will call your Command Sergeant Major. He will come to get you himself. I will be down there checking on you. Good luck and get ready for REFORGER. I do not want to see any cold injuries."

"Thanks, Sergeant Major," Martin said, amazed that the Sergeant Major had managed to make it appear that this was the intended outcome all along. "Will you square it away with Sergeant Major Harris?" Martin asked.

"I will," replied the Sergeant Major. "Go get ready to move to BK."

CHAPTER 3 – GATOR'S TAIL

"Always ask for the worst unit in the outfit. It only has one way to go, up." Circa 1969. Mad Marvin McDaniel First Sergeant, HHC, 3/70 Armor, 5 ID

Happy to be headed somewhere, First Sergeant Martin quickly packed the few things he had unpacked in his BEQ room, checked out with the clerk, Miss Sandy Norquist. Sandy insisted he keep the key and relax in the room until his ride arrived from Bad Kissingen. Wise in the ways of the Cavalry she had told Martin, "Things happen very quickly around here and sometimes they change even quicker. You just keep the room and turn in the key when it is final you are going to BK. We will clean it and get it ready for our next guest when you leave, if you leave, this afternoon." Martin thanked her and returned to his former room to change into Class A uniform and work on his course.

Before he realized it, it was almost noon. Command Sergeant Major Lonnie McCall stuck his head into his room saying, "I'm looking for First Sergeant Martin, is that you bud?"

"Yes, Sergeant Major, that's me," he said crossing the room to meet his new Squadron Command Sergeant Major. It was good to see a member of his new unit and gratifying to be picked up personally by the Command Sergeant Major.

"I drove my POV up to get you as a jeep just takes too long and the Colonel has the van tied up today," McCall said. "Are you ready to go? I have a Sergeant First Class Marshall, a new motor Sergeant out there as well."

"All set, Sergeant Major," Martin said as he lifted his suitcase, and garment bag. The Command Sergeant Major grabbed his duffle bag and they loaded the car. Martin retrieved his box of groceries and supplies and dropped off the key to the office, thanking Miss Norquist for her help. When he got outside everything else was loaded and McCall was behind the wheel obviously ready to go to BK. He appeared to be a man in a hurry.

Command Sergeant Major McCall not only appeared to be in a hurry, he drove like a man who had forgotten something important back at home. He drove like a German through the traffic toward the autobahn that led to Bad Kissingen. He was of medium height, had a good, if slightly heavy, appearance with a Combat Infantryman's Badge and a 1st Cavalry combat patch. His boots had a professional spit shine and his fatigues appeared to be new without blemish. He had black hair with silver gray temples and exuded a dynamic and nervous energy unlike any Command Sergeant Major in Martin's experience. Once the vehicle reached the autobahn, McCall kept the accelerator to the floor and relied on flashing his headlights to move cars out of the left lane. He rarely used his brakes. The performance as an autobahn warrior was accompanied by a non-stop monologue about the unit and his past service.

He had a disconcerting habit of looking at either Martin or in his rear view mirror at Marshall while driving 100 mph on the autobahn. Noting Martin's smile he slyly said, "I drive fast on the autobahn."

Martin replied, "If you can drive it, Sergeant Major McCall, I can ride it." Martin began to wonder if the guy's mood was enhanced by speed or some form of amphetamine but figured everybody at the unit was probably charged up like the Sergeant Major and if so, it was going to be a hell of a tour.

As the monologue continued, it turned to the unit and Martin's assignment. "There is nothing wrong with G Troop that a good First Sergeant will not fix immediately. These young leaders do not understand how good they have it. We have the best equipment, the best barracks, food and CIF anyone could want. The Border is a great training ground for people that take it seriously. The LTA has ranges and room to do training. I love it here. I was here as a Staff Sergeant in F Troop as a training NCO."

"I met my wife here after my second tour to Vietnam and it is a dream come true to come back as the Command Sergeant Major of a Cavalry Squadron as an Eleven Bang Bang. Our goals in the Squadron are the same as the Regimental Commanding Officer has for the Regiment."

"The Squadron Commander is a very smart guy, considerate of soldiers and who gives mission orders and the room to carry them out. Neither of us have a command philosophy. I have this card that I want you to use as guidelines. The Squadron Commander has some do's and don'ts on one sheet of paper. If you follow them and the Squadron SOPs you will be okay. I run the NCOs and the Squadron Commander runs the officers. I assign all enlisted men. We NCOs are responsible for all enlisted aspects of command as per AR 600-20. By the way, all NCOs are expected to have my card with them at all times. Monday is command maintenance day; one Thursday per month is a Squadron Run."

"Are you in shape First Sergeant?"

"Yes," said Martin.

"Can you run a marathon, because if you can, you can run with me in the Fulda Marathon in the spring? Do you want to run in it?" the monologue thus ending for a short period.

Martin qualified his answer by saying, "I could run 13 miles now, Sergeant Major, but 26 miles would take a training effort this outfit's schedule probably does not support, plus I am really too old to be running 26 miles."

"What the hell, the Greek soldiers did it," McCall said.

"Yes, one did, Sergeant Major, though he dropped dead at the finish line after delivering his message," Martin replied. "But ancient history aside, I will run any marathon with you that you want to run, Sergeant Major."

"No shit, he dropped dead," McCall said absorbing this factoid. "You will sign in at the S1 when we get to BK. You may want to let the Acting First Sergeant run the company while you in process. You can get it done in a half day. You will be waited on immediately in every office you visit and everything is located on Post except for the dental clinic. How is it all of the officers in the Squadron know who you are, is that the Armor school?"

"Yes, Sergeant Major. I was the Chief Instructor for the gunnery portion of AOAC, taught the Basic Course and was in overall charge of the ranges and testing. I just tried to ensure they all got a fair shake and that the classroom work and the practical exercises matched the test and all of the training reflected the reality of the field Army. I was a prick, so I guess that is what they remember," Martin concluded.

"First Sergeant, you might have been a prick, but those guys think you hung the moon and I hope you can live up to the expectations they have relayed to the Squadron Commander," McCall said. As they approached the gate of the kaserne, the arch over the gate identified it as Daley Barracks with the "e' missing. The sign and the post had clearly seen better days. The armed guard was of slightly less than perfect appearance but presentable. He was not wearing a Blackhorse patch.

The post reflected the rest of Germany and was more of the same with cobblestone streets, stucco buildings with seven very large four story barracks in a rectangle with an athletic field encircled by a hedge in the center on the quadrangle. Command Sergeant Major McCall parked in front of the Squadron Hqs in front of a parking sign marked 'CSM'.

"Leave your bags in my car. Come in and sign in and give the PSNCO copies of your orders. He has your in-processing checklist ready for you, at least he better have," said McCall moving at warp speed for the building, leaving Martin and Marshall in his wake.

McCall appeared in the S1 shop as both the new arrivals were finishing in-processing saying, "Your First Sergeants are in my office to pick you up and take you to your outfits. Your bags will be taken to your troop orderly rooms, so when you are ready, they are ready," as he again departed quickly.

Martin was not to be hurried, "Sergeant Adams, am I done here and have I satisfied all of your requirements?"

"It will be fine until tomorrow, First Sergeant."

"One last thing," Martin said, "Is the personal paperwork flowing correctly between G Troop and the S1? Are soldiers getting their just allowances and entitlements?"

Adams replied, "The Acting First Sergeant is doing the best he can under the circumstances, but we all know anything less than good service hurts morale. I will do anything I can to help the Troop get on its feet, First Sergeant."

"I'm glad to hear you testify Brother Adams because we are going to go to that same church together, do I hear an Amen?" Adams, a born again Christian was sure he had found a kindred soul and gave a fervent "Amen, First Sergeant."

39

It was at this point that Command Sergeant Major McCall appeared and stated emphatically, "First Sergeant, you are keeping everyone waiting." Martin thanked Adams and followed Command Sergeant Major McCall to his office. He could not help thinking the Squadron was akin to a convoy at sea. Convoys moved at the speed of the slowest ship in the group. He was probably hoping against hope the G Troop "ship" would be moving at the speed of the Squadron's slowest mind.

"First Sergeant Martin, how are you?" asked a slender First Sergeant with rather long hair. "I'm Joe James. I was Dino Messina's PSG in the 18th Battalion." Ruefully, Dino face came to mind as he was Martin's former son-in-law from what was now a failed marriage with Billie, his oldest stepdaughter.

"You got E Company?" asked Martin.

James looked at the Command Sergeant Major as if they were sharing a private joke then said, "You'll screw it up for a little while, all us Armor guys do. It is a troop. It is a big deal here in the Cav to call it that."

Martin was embarrassed but he knew it would not be last time these proud and clannish guys would correct him on Cavalry specific terms. It was a different tribe.

"Thanks, Joe, good to see you again."

"Hey, we're neighbors and in the same building. Come over tonight if you get a minute. I'll be there late," Joe said as he departed.

"This is the Acting First Sergeant of your Troop, Sergeant First Class Maldanado," said Command Sergeant Major McCall.

"Maldanado, good to meet you," said Martin.

Turning to McCall, Martin said, "With your permission, Sergeant Major, we'll be going to the Troop now." I appreciate your coming to Fulda to get me and thanks for the counsel and insight so far," Martin told his new Command Sergeant Major. He wasn't sure McCall accepted his thanks as he seemed puzzled at the courtesy. He merely waved to them saying, "Get out of here, you two."

Noting Maldanado's Drill Sergeant badge, and his excellent carriage, bearing and obvious faultless physical conditioning, Martin marked the man as a top notch NCO. The two began walking toward the Troop. While pointing at his Drill Sergeant badge indicating to Maldanado that their talk was going "out of school" and was not to be sugar coated, Martin began the conversation with, "Two questions; One - is Sergeant Major McCall a work-a-holic, so dedicated to his job that he hurries back from Fulda? Two - is the Troop really screwed up or is it just bad press?"

Pointing at his Drill Sergeant badge, Maldanado replied, "Answer number two first, it ain't no better or no worse than any other outfit. The last First Sergeant was screwed up and needed to be fired. He was the wrong guy in the wrong job. Answer number one, the Sergeant Major probably was in a hurry to take his wife to supper at the NCO Club where she works, play the slot machines and have a beer. He believes people who work late are inefficient and if it ain't done by 1630 it is better to do it the next day. What could you expect, he is an Earth Pig (local tanker speak for an 11B Infantryman)."

"Thanks, Sergeant First Class Maldanado. I've got a real soft spot for 11B's but the term is amusing," said Martin.

Sergeant First Class Maldanado gave Martin the distinct impression that he could not wait to give up the First Sergeant position of G Troop and everything he did underlined the perception. When the two NCOs entered the Troop, the Charge of Quarters (CQ) bellowed, "At Ease." Martin had noticed the guidon out front and asked the Acting First Sergeant, "What is with the 'At Ease'? It looks as if the Troop Commander is present."

"Well, that is an expression of respect for me and you as First Sergeants," came the reply from Maldanado.

"We need to correct that practice as it is a form of disrespect to the Troop Commander," said Martin. "You know the rule for the spot corrections Sergeant Maldanado. Once you walk by an on the spot correction and ignore it, you have set a new standard."

"Sergeant Matson, good afternoon, I'm First Sergeant Martin," he said, extending his hand to the CQ. As they shook hands, Martin asked, and "Who is your runner, Sergeant Matson, introduce us please." It was clear to Martin that Matson knew the name of his runner but that he also did not know him personally. This meant the man was not from Matson's crew, squad, or platoon. Thus the assigned duty was not doing anything toward fostering morale, esprit de corps or teamwork within the unit. "Specialist Fourth Class Bagwell, First Sergeant," the enlisted man said, extending his hand.

"Glad to meet you Specialist Fourth Class Bagwell, where do you stand on getting promoted to Sergeant," Martin asked.

"First Sergeant, I don't know anything about getting promoted," Bagwell replied.

"Well Bagwell, I don't know where you stand either, but we will both know before the next ten days go by," said Martin.

"Let's walk together a minute Sergeant Matson," Martin said, leading the CQ out of earshot of his runner. "There are senior NCOs, First Sergeants and Command Sergeant Major who have an exaggerated view of their importance. When a higher ranking person is already present and a lesser ranking NCO or officer is entering the unit, we do not call at ease in recognition of the arrival of the lesser ranking person. The Troop Commander is present. Do not call at ease for me or anyone else entering the troop when he is here. I don't care about the past. As of now, we do not do that, okay, Matson?" Martin concluded.

"Roger First Sergeant," Matson said.

Watching the new and acting First Sergeants go down stairs to the Headquarters area, Matson mused, it was about time they stopped that silly shit. Anyone who had gone through

41

basic training knew what 'At Ease' meant. The First Sergeant was right. He was glad it was all explained in a conversational tone. Best wait and see about the new First Sergeant. After what he had seen of First Sergeants in this outfit, they had not shown him much up to now. He wondered if he would be able to get his separate rations now, he could sure use the money.

As they entered the First Sergeant office, Martin was pleasantly surprised to see that it was a small room and shared space with the steam pipes for the hot water heating system. The floor was painted concrete and the walls were concrete without adornment. There were enough couches and chairs to hold a meeting with the eight or so NCO's making up the leadership team. It was also directly adjacent and connected by a door to the Troop Commander's office. The Troop Commander was not in his office although the light was on.

The Troop Commander was apparently a very organized, neat, almost fastidious leader. The Troop Guidon together with the US Colors was behind his desk. Nice chairs and furniture enough to seat all of the officers were present along with three wall lockers. There were no wall maps but there were several very nice Don Stivers prints in beautiful frames on the wall. There were several plaques indicating service in 2d ACR, the sister regiment to the Blackhorse stationed to the south with Headquarters in Nuremburg. After a brief look, Martin closed the connecting door and sat down on the settee in his new office, expecting Maldanado to sit behind the desk.

Maldanado, however, sat in one of the chairs across from the First Sergeant, steadfastly refusing to sit behind the desk. Maldnado smiled and said, "I am not the First Sergeant. I was just filling in as First Sergeant. You are here now. I will run things until you get in-processed. I am in full support of whatever you want done but I ain't the First Sergeant, you are, so please sit down at your desk."

Martin sat down at the desk and took everything out of the "In" box saying, "I am sure you have heard that I am unconventional, wild and like to disregard regulations. That is not really true. What I am is old style in regard to how I take care of soldiers and very modern on how I use new technology. Soldier care has not changed its basic form since Julius Caesar, Alexander the Great, and General Patton. The means of fighting may have changed but the principles of leadership remain. I do not intend to go home to a new BEQ room until every single request from or with an effect on any soldier has been acted on by me. Is everything in this box self explanatory?"

"It is, First Sergeant. I just did not get to a lot of that stuff as I was trying to run my platoon and the company. We had to do a lot of stuff when the old First Sergeant got fired and that is what I concentrated on doing," said Maldanado.

"Is the duty roster your product?" Martin asked.

"Yes, but we all know it is your prerogative to start a new one," said Maldanado.

"No, that would be unfair and a hardship on the wives and sweethearts who have already planned family stuff around the duty roster that is in effect. We will run the old one out without change. Listen Maldanado, everyone I have talked to says good things about what you have been able to do under very difficult circumstances. This is my third company, I mean Troop. The training NCO and I will take it from here, just like you had to do, okay?" Martin said.

"You mean it?" Maldanado said, doing a good imitation of a death row inmate receiving a commutation from the governor.

"Yes, I mean it. Get back to your platoon. If I need you, I'll call you," Martin said with a wave of his hand.

At this point, the training NCO, Staff Sergeant McKnight made his appearance. "Good afternoon, First Sergeant, I'm the Training NCO," he said.

"Glad to meet you, Sergeant McKnight, we have some work to do here but we won't try to get it all done in one day, regardless of what you may have heard about me," said Martin.

Sergeant McKnight looked at his new First Sergeant and then smiled. Martin thought he had seen few people that day that so resembled the animal kingdom as did the Training NCO. He appeared to be a ferret, though a tall one. He knew McKnight had a story; he just did not want to hear it right this minute. "Look, Sergeant McKnight, we will have time to talk later on after I get settled in a little bit. Right now, I am going to assume you are in the training NCO slot because you have a family issue the Army is not willing or able to solve. You have the motivation to do a good job, you know what to do, the troops trust you to keep their secrets and you have enough rank to tell me when I am pushing you too fast or too hard and keeping you from taking care of your situation at home. But I will listen right now if you think it needs to happen. Sit down, you obviously feel like you need to clear the air with me, sit down, but go close the door first," concluded Martin.

McKnight moved to close the door and regained his chair. "My wife left me and our ten year old daughter. She went back to Korea and got a divorce. I am a 19K and can be a tank commander anywhere. I have hurt my knee bad and have a brace. Everyone is content with me to be the training NCO. I have about ten months left before I go back to the states. My knee is responding to treatment and it should be okay when my physical therapy is over. I do the mail, personnel actions, training schedules, and run the unit as the rear detachment NCO when you guys are in the field, at the Border or gone to Gunnery, which is most of the time. My daughter comes here after school. I take her home and I have someone who stays with her in our quarters after we visit for a few minutes every day. I had a hard time getting paper back out of the First Sergeant and the Commanding Officer once I sent it across the hall. There is a lot to do and I want to do my part for the soldiers and their families. My situation will not be an issue. My daughter is very mature and very, very smart for her age. I do not want to go back to a tank platoon but will if I must. It is okay and sometimes even better for a First Sergeant to be a hard-ass and demanding leader. But troops have a hard time accepting a double standard and never give a hundred percent when the leaders do not follow the same regulations they cite and that is all I am going to say about days gone by. I have not heard anything about you one way or the other, First Sergeant. We can clear up almost everything that is not done in ten days work, at the most. Hard work is not an issue for me."

"Sounds great to me. If you will do your part, I will do mine. When I run into an issue that is historical, I will call you in to be my guide. You need to do a couple things for me right now. Get me a standard troop wall locker, a cot, a pillow and pillow case and a blanket. I intend to set up a wall locker in the office that is identical to the NCO Academy standard and I will be sleeping here a few nights until I get a handle on the administrative end of the unit," said Martin.

"First Sergeant, are you going to sleep in your office?" asked McKnight in disbelief.

"If I have too, I will. I do not want to be looking for a place to sleep if I do, so go get me the stuff, okay?" Martin said with a smile.

"Right away First Sergeant," said McKnight as he walked away. Unseen by the First Sergeant, the Troop Commander, Captain David W. Dawson had come into his office and had been listening to the exchange and he had heard the last orders First Sergeant Martin had given. He knew that voice and was elated as he opened the door.

After the painful relief of his first First Sergeant, Dawson was determined to assert his authority right from the first moment with his second First Sergeant. He controlled his initial excitement, went into the office and greeted his new First Sergeant. "First Sergeant Martin, welcome to G Troop. I am damn glad to see you," extending his hand in greeting.

Martin was trying to place the handsome young Captain in his memory of the Armor School and it came to him. "You were the LNO assigned to the Lieutenant Colonel from the Saudi National Guard who could not get the finer points of Tank Gunnery in AOAC! I certainly appreciated your candor then. It helped me and the Gunnery Division through a tough period."

While in AOAC, Dawson had quietly told Martin as he attempted to teach the doltish student an arcane point regarding the use of the M1 Gunner's quadrant, "Hey Top, he is an ignorant Sand Nigger who is a Prince at home and a spoiled idiot over here. Do not waste your time and effort and oh by the way, the class' time and effort. The stupid joker is going to pass anyway, so in the interest of efficiency and humanity, I suggest we move on down the road."

Martin then stated to the class, "Gentlemen, Captain Dawson has graciously consented to conduct after hours instruction as needed to rectify this issue." Martin then led the AOAC class in a subdued round of applause for Dawson who gave a mock bow and the review moved on to more meaningful study points. It was a welcome point of levity that lightened the mood of the entire class. Everyone save one very thick headed student passed the test, some with higher grades than others. Noteworthy was the fact an Infantryman achieved the highest score. All of the foreign students got a wave and a smile regardless of their score. As the academic review for the staff, led by the Commanding General, Martin and the Commanding General answered as one when the question arose as to why a grunt was the best student, "He had the least to unlearn."

Dawson's reply brought Martin back to the present when he stated, "Yeah, that test was a bitch, but since you probably wrote it, you know it was. But you never screwed us and everyone who studied, passed it. I still have my study guide right there on the shelf. Come on in and let me brief you on the Troop, what has happened and what we have to do."

"Are you bringing a wife and family over?" Dawson asked.

"No, Sir, it will be an unaccompanied tour of two years for me. I will be able to concentrate fully on the task at hand," Martin declared.

"First, I am very glad you are here. You were far and away the very best instructor we had at the Armor School. You were thoroughly prepared, technically proficient, and you had the students' best interests at heart. You were real, without bull shit or pretense and well, you just kept it real. We all said, 'Man how I hope I get a First Sergeant like that', and by God you are here and I got you. I have not had good luck with First Sergeants and some officers in the troop. I have had lots of problems I have had to deal with on my own."

"I relieved the last First Sergeant because he did not do his job. He did not do what I told him to do; he lied to me, drank on duty, lost equipment and could not hold up the logistics end of support for the troop. He was not where he was supposed to be and he did not do what he was supposed to do. I use this memo pad. It has carbons in it. When you get an original with a task, it is the first time I have asked you to do something. When I send you one of the carbons, that means you are late and have not done what I asked you to do. If you get more than one carbon copy for any task, you will know you are in trouble. I will relieve anybody that does not do their job and that includes you. Hell, my Dad was an Armor NCO. He served in a Sherman tank in WW II and had five different vehicles shot out from under him. I haven't got it in for NCOs." Dawson stated with the utmost aplomb.

"Captain, I have a lot to learn about Cavalry Tactics, Techniques, and Procedures. I will depend on you to tell me things and to give me some specific guidance, particularly when you see me going down the wrong road. It is your

45

privilege to relieve me any time you see fit. I have never been relieved for cause and I do not expect to be now. I got the same talk from the Regimental Commanding Officer and he gave me a ninety day time limit before re-inspection by the Regimental leadership with interim checks along the way."

"He said that?" Dawson asked.

"Captain, I will have no secrets from you although I know you will have some from me. It will take a little time for us to get a sense of trust and I can live with that. When I get to the point I can't, you will be the first to know. I go at this Army hard. We will have a great unit and a good time here, despite the bumps along the road," Martin said smiling.

Dawson then reached into the book case behind his desk and began handing Martin bound booklets. "This is the Troop SOP (Standard Operating Procedure), read it and tell me what you think. This book shows you the schedule and operations orders for upcoming events. This is the Border SOP. This is my map book for the border. If I were you, I would make up my own. We will all make map books for the upcoming troop and squadron FTXs coming up in a month or so. We have a Squadron Run on Thursday. We go on FTX, the following Monday as a Troop. The Squadron FTX follows the next Tuesday. At the conclusion of the Squadron FTX, there is a ten day break and we move to the Border for thirty days until 28 December and return here until early February when we go to Reforger. PT is five days per week. It starts at 0630 and ends at 0730 with a formation for work call at 0900. Lunch is from 1130 until 1300. 1300 is usually the last formation of the day. I do not want a retreat formation held unless I say so, any issues with that schedule?" he asked.

"No, Sir. Sounds fine to me. I intend to take charge of PT from Jump Street and run them into shape if they are not already there. I am taking the Sergeants Major Course Non-Resident Course. I will study it after duty hours and will need a day or so before exams to review the material prior to a two hour test. If you screw up the multiple guess, the first re-test test is essay. It ain't rocket science but it is tedious and I do not intend to screw it up," Martin said.

"Why on earth did you take the Non-Resident Course, doesn't it have an 80% failure rate?" Dawson asked.

"Sir, I have been either a student, Drill Sergeant or Instructor for seven years out of the last 14. I have had enough of TRADOC (Training and Doctrine Command). I surely do not want to go to Fort Bliss for a year with those stuffed shirts. It is also too close to Juarez and I have a terrible weakness for both Tequila and Senoritas. I would be busted for sure with a year to spend there. Not only that, they would surely ask me to instruct and that would be another year or two of exposure to Sodom on the Rio Grande. The temptation is just too great. The real point, is I like to be in TO & E units with soldiers. The school houses have taught me a lot and now it is my turn to give back. I am one of those weird guys who believes the sign on Skidgel Hall that says, 'The knowledge you gain here is not yours to keep.' I realize I have a lot to learn about Cav, but I am a quick study."

"Good, I am glad to hear you are a quick study. You are now the Urinalysis Control Officer. We have a drug problem in the troop that is confined to a small number of Soldiers. There have been irregularities in the past. The dopers always seem to find out ahead of time about the piss test. I want a 100% sample of the troop with detailed follow up. One of your first stops will be with the urinalysis people. I will back you up with whatever you decide to do. The damn dopers are embedded like ticks in a hound's ear and have great intelligence sources that are hard to track. Once you make your arrangements, make it a total surprise and do not tell anyone the details of a Troop or individual test, not even to me. I want it done within the next ten days. Is that clear?" the Troop Commander asked.

"Your orders are clear, Captain Dawson. Being the urinalysis officer is not a duty fit for a First Sergeant. However, I can understand why you are giving me the task. I will do it but would ask to be able to move the responsibility for the task to one of the Lieutenants once we break the present doper ring. Can we agree to that?" Martin asked.

"Yes, but first we break it open, then we will see," said Dawson. Martin had just made a snap decision, he could trust this Commander. He was a very handsome and attractive man, a definite lady killer. He knew what he wanted and was quietly ruthless in his approach. If he could keep the pieces in his head and move the troop, he would be very efficient in combat. He had spent years in Cavalry units and knew what he was doing and Martin did not know Cavalry. Martin was content to know his performance would have to do the selling with this guy, 'Show me, don't tell me was in effect'.

A knock on the hallway door followed with Dawson's order to come in, brought the Executive Officer and the four Platoon Leaders into the room. Then followed a boisterous reunion of the officers and one of their favorite instructors from the Armor School. Martin was a trifle embarrassed as he did not expect to be welcomed in a unit with such fanfare by former students. Each officer had a particular story with which to regale the others and after a period they all laughed loudly as Martin said, "Gentlemen, you all thought you were my favorite student. That is because you were all my favorite student."

"First Sergeant?" asked Second Lieutenant Rodney, the Aggie and rodeo cowboy of the group, "Can we come to PT with the soldiers in the morning?"

"Lieutenant, officers are not excluded from any training we will have in the troop except as directed by the Troop Commander. He prescribes where the officers will be, not me," Martin stated.

"We will all be at your first PT event, First Sergeant," said Captain Dawson. "Now we are going to have a formation inside the hallway and First Sergeant Martin is going to meet the Troop and tell them how it is going to be.

Everybody to the hallway. First Sergeant, wait here with me for a minute," Dawson concluded.

"Let me tell Sergeant First Class Maldanado to form the troop, Sir," Martin said, stepping toward his office.

"I already did that First Sergeant, this morning when we knew you were coming," said Dawson. "I want you to just be yourself and tell them where you stand. I will introduce you and then after I do so I want you to come up to the front with me. It echoes in there so they will hear every word we say so never try to say anything to me in the hallway you do not want them to hear, okay?" Dawson stated.

"Yes, Sir," said Martin wondering about the degree of caution in the Troop Commander. It approached paranoia. Dawson appeared to be a totally self-confident leader who was in full command of his environment. The doper shit must be deeply ingrained. But, these youngsters had not lived through the Army of the '70s when dope was really bad. Martin could tell by looking at the leaders that their experience did not include a brawl with the troops in the hallway slugging it out with privates high on Mandrax and beer. The leaders of the '70's would be very happy with these 80's soldiers.

As they left the office, they could hear the troop forming in the hallway and as they reached the CQ desk, the soldiers were standing at attention awaiting the arrival of the Troop Commander.

Captain Dawson arrived, stepped in front of Sergeant First Class Maldanado, received his salute and commanded, Post. The Platoon Leaders then assumed their Posts and the Platoon Sergeants moved to the rear of their platoon. Captain Dawson then Commanded, "Stand, At, Ease." This command resulted in the soldiers turning their head and eyes to their Troop Commander, with feet spread slightly less than shoulder width apart with their hands placed against the small of the back, palms facing outward.

Dawson directed the CQ to disconnect the telephone at his desk until the formation was concluded. "Men, we are very, very lucky to get one the best First Sergeants in the entire Army in G Troop today. Your officers and I were also lucky enough to be trained by First Sergeant Martin at Fort Knox during our time there. He knows the M1 Tank, Bradley, ITV and tank gunnery and ammunition inside and out. He is in great shape, likes soldiers and loves PT. I am very happy he is here. First Sergeant Martin come on up here and meet the Troop."

"Thank you, Captain Dawson, for those kind words. That is a lot to live up to here in the Blackhorse. I am here because our Regimental Headquarters thinks this troop is all screwed up. That is not true. There are no bad units, there are only bad leaders. The Regiment does know shit about this troop." Laughter began to come from the ranks. "They have a snap shot in time on incidents that are negative. When that occurs before you know it, everything you do, even some of those things that others get by with, are big black eyes.

That is bullshit. You know it and I know it. I was sent here to straighten your asses up and told I would be relieved if I did not get it done. I got news for those shit heads up at Regiment; I am not the main factor here. You are. You will be the same people whether or not I am judged to be a success. Hell, you survived the last First Sergeant getting fired didn't you?" More laughter.

"I did not come here to get fired. I also did not come here to get promoted. My promotion to Sergeant Major is in the bag. I did not make the list for E8 in thirteen years by being screwed up. What happens to me has very little to do with you but the end result for the troop means everything to you. You have dreams and aspirations."

"Some of you, like Freeman here have modest hopes, like going down to BK tonight and getting some mud for his duck. Now how do I know Freeman is a cock hound, I just got here?" Gales of laughter ensued. Captain Dawson, observing from the rear was enthralled and very pleased. In his mind, Martin's performance was "vintage" First Sergeant.

Martin continued. Placing his hand on Freeman's shoulder he said, "The boy is a dead ringer for Killer in Beetle Bailey. A blind man could see it in a minute. Don't worry Freeman, you won't be detained here in the hallway long enough for someone else to get the lucky fräulein drunk enough to take to bed, you will be there to do it yourself. Just stay with me for a few more minutes. Men, you have to be involved in something larger than yourself if you are ever going to have a life that is worth a shit. The Christians' Jesus said it best, 'If a man is to find himself, he must first lose himself.' When everyone thinks you are screwed up and they are all out to get you, it simplifies our task. Perception is reality. If they ain't in G Troop, they just do not damn count. If they ask you, tell 'em everything is great."

"Now listen up."

"Today is Tuesday. I have to in-process in the morning after PT. All of you stone shit heads, the folks that do not give a damn about the Army, their buddies or making their parents look like assholes by getting a less than honorable discharge, you are in luck. I will arrange for you to go home. Come and see me no later than Friday evening with a reason why you should get a workable discharge. You will be gone in 10 days without pain. You see, what we are going to have in this outfit, is everyone participating. This Army is a tough business. We have to have everyone's head in the game. I would rather have 85% of the people assigned who are 100% involved than have 15% who are always dragging the rest of us down. Men, serving with shit heads is like swimming with a damn anvil tied to your ankle. We are going to cut our anvils loose. After Friday, if you are a shit head and you want to go home and you do not want to be a good citizen, you will go to jail or get a general discharge."

"I strongly dislike chicken shit just to harass the troops. I do insist on doing what we do well. That is particularly true of drill and PT."

"When I first get assigned, I always like to know in an outfit who can call bullshit. You will find that you can call bullshit to me. I cannot tell you all the number of times PFC's have kept me from stepping on my crank. If you see something stupid and you have a better way, speak up to your Sergeants or to me. The life you save may be your own. This is my first time in a line Cavalry unit. Some of my very best friends, men who taught me and helped me learn about the Army, are Blackhorse veterans of peace and war. I owe them my best shot as I pass on some lessons to you. If I address you as 'COMPANY' instead of as 'TROOP' in a preparatory command, do not move. I will be embarrassed and get the idea that we are in a troop. My ego can stand the pain, if you can stand to teach me. I will not walk by a correction, do not take it personal, just fix it. Ass chewings are like bubble gum, they don't cost much and they don't last long."

"Some last points. If you have had a personnel action in and have not heard back for a result, stop by my office tonight and tell me about it. If you were due an award and it has not happened, a promotion or you have a problem you need to talk about I will be there. I do not care how long the line may be. Make sure you tell your Platoon Sergeant first unless he is the problem. I have a cot, a pillow and a blanket. I will not leave here on Friday night with any personnel action not forwarded to Squadron. Everything you have hanging will be caught up if at all possible tonight. If the load is too big, it may take a little longer. If an action has to do with your life, we are going to do all we can to do it right the first time."

"Next, if you have a problem with a spouse or girl friend, do not go off on them and beat their ass. It is wrong and you will have to answer to me and the Army. If the bitch is that screwed up, divorce her ass, it is cheaper by far than jail. Take care of each other down town. If I find out one of you has left a pal or fellow trooper in the lurch, I will have your ass. I realize some people cannot be helped."

"Drinking and driving, effective immediately, there is a 50 Deutsche Mark Bill in the CQ book. That is to pay the cab drivers. I will ensure the Polizei downtown know it is here. For your information, the Polizei drive most of the cabs after midnight in case you have been living in a cave. I need our best German speaker with the schlafzimmer (an ability to speak the German language gained in the bedroom(s) of German women) dictionary to see me in my office after this formation. You see folks, that is a big part of changing the image at Regiment. We, together, all of us, are going to change the conditions of our environment. The first step to presenting a new image is managing self-inflicted wounds. Drunks who do not drive do not get DUIs. You can pay me the 50 marks later, like the next day."

"Last point tonight, I will not have you here waiting for the word after duty hours. If something comes up we will use the recall roster. I will put notes in Platoon Sergeant Boxes. Waiting for the word up until 1800 is stupid. We will plan our work and work our plan. If the geniuses in charge of us cannot think up a task until after you go home at night, we will just start early in the morning and work like hell."

Martin then commanded, "Troop, Attention." Looking to Captain Dawson, who was shaking his head, Martin then told the Troop, "You will very rarely ever hear me give the command of 'Dismissed'. Rather it will be 'Fall Out'.

"FALL, OUT," Martin commanded.

A familiar, beaming face was then spied by Martin in the ranks. Staff Sergeant Gilberto Jesus Ramos approached Martin with a wide welcoming smile. "Ramos, what the hell are you doing trooper?" Martin asked.

"First Sergeant, you remember me?" Ramos asked.

"How the hell could I ever forget you Ramos? You and your famous, 'Me no talk' statement?" Martin said laughing.

"Hey those damn Drill Sergeants were busting my balls and that was the best I could do," exclaimed Ramos.

The Executive Officer, First Lieutenant John S. Brown was curious, "What was 'Me no talk'?"

"Ramos was a trainee when I was a Drill Sergeant. The Drill Sergeants were ganging up on him at a rifle range for dressing in the uniform I had prescribed. I had the Company put their overshoes turned soles up on the sides of his pack with their spare leather boots inside them. On arrival at the range, they changed and had dry feet. His Drill Sergeant was just letting them get on his ass. Ramos was just off the boat from Puerto Rico. He did not speak enough English to go through the chow line. So I got them off his ass and moved him to my platoon. The sneaky Drill Sergeants that set up the assignments in the company gave me all of the Warrant Officer Candidates and a contingent of 18 Puerto Ricans and 4 Filipinos who did not speak English to screw me up. It did not work."

"Do you speak Spanish? How did you do a whole cycle like that?" First Lieutenant Brown asked.

Staff Sergeant Ramos answered for him, "He got the former school teachers and us PRs to label everything in the barracks in Spanish and English. He got 'Dick and Jane' readers from the school and gave the clearest demonstrations of the stuff we could learn by imitation. Of course we taught each other to cuss first but it did us all a lot of good. I speak English good now, no, Ell Tee?" Ramos asked.

"So how did you make out as a Platoon, Ramos?" asked the Lieutenant.

"Shit, we won everything. We suffered together. We did everything so much smarter than everyone else. The First Sergeant is always about ten steps ahead of everybody else," Ramos said looking at the Executive Officer as if he were an oversized small child.

"Like you, huh, Ramos?" Brown said.

51

"Who you think I learn it from, Sir?" answered Ramos.

"Hey First Sergeant, we take my combat Bee Double U and go to the field and the run the Border condition shit for the alert. When you want to go?" asked Ramos.

"What do you recommend there 1st Platoon Sergeant Ramos?" asked Martin, prompting a big smile on both their faces.

"We go Saturday Morning about 0700 SP and get there at daylight. I have your map board ready with all of the shit plotted," Ramos stated.

"Fine," Martin said. "I got to go take care of the paperwork snarl now Ramos," Martin said. Martin noticed Ramos looked down at the precise moment he said the word snarl. "Hey, you got some shit snarled, Staff Sergeant Ramos?" asked Martin.

"Yes, First Sergeant," said Ramos. "Well you are the first man in line then," said Martin as they arrived at his office door.

"I don't want to buck the line," said Ramos. Martin surveyed the line that had at least 50 soldiers in it stretching down and around the supply room door.

"Anybody in line that was in one of my basic training platoons and is going to take me to the Border on Saturday Morning can cut in front of Staff Sergeant Ramos! What, no takers?! Well I guess then it is okay, huh, guys?" Martin said with a smile.

"Yes, First Sergeant" was the cheerful group response.

The CQ was in his office when Martin got to it. "We are sending out for chow First Sergeant, do you want something to eat?" he asked.

"Yes, give me a hamburger and a coke or a Pepsi," handing the CQ a five dollar bill.

Captain Dawson was working in his office on a writing assignment from the Squadron Commander as Martin was setting up to work. When he had seen the size of the line, he had been embarrassed at the scope of the problem. He had no idea the former First Sergeant had caused such havoc in the lives of his soldiers and of course, felt responsible. Martin came into his office before he began his work and closed the door.

"Captain, this is my third outfit. It is always this way for me. I never get to follow me. I learned from the finest First Sergeants from days long gone by. This is also pure Maslow's needs hierarchy but in my case it is not a trick. These guys need help. It is not your fault. You did your part. You had a lot going on with the Border violations, officer issues and the conduct of the past First Sergeant. You fixed it. You told me to fix this. I am."

"Hey, this is not bothering me, First Sergeant" said the Captain.

"My ass, you are still here ready to help and sign things aren't you, Troop Commander?" Martin asked. "You old softie," Martin said, closing his door.

With Staff Sergeant Ramos and his housing allowance paperwork as his first customer, First Sergeant and Staff Sergeant McKnight began to work the line. Many of the papers supporting the late and overdue actions, were either in the "In" box or stuffed in the bottom right hand drawer. After about 30 minutes, Martin organized the line by platoons taking all of the scouts first and deferring the others until the morning. All who wished to stay were allowed to do so, but most of the Troopers went on to their life and would return the next night. All, however, commented on the First Sergeant who reported to the Captain in greens at 1400 and stayed to work problems until 2300 hours on his first night in the unit.

What neither the First Sergeant nor Captain Dawson knew was what the ever efficient underground network of NCOs had been talking about since the identity of the new First Sergeant had been known. Sergeant First Class Victor Jackson had been with Martin at Fort Knox. He was slightly apprehensive about the assignment but as a relatively junior Sergeant First Class he was not eligible to become the Acting First Sergeant.

When asked about the new First Sergeant by his fellow NCOs, Jackson summarized his experience for the group. "Basically, Martin is a very, very smart lifer who will probably die in the Army before he gets out. He soldiers 24/7. He is in great shape, runs 5 miles with the troops and runs again at noon. He knows the M1 tank and Bradley inside out. He qualified a tank in the company. He filled in for a guy with quarters in my platoon, but funny, the guy went out instead of staying home and got a DUI in Radcliff. Martin had him busted to Corporal. He was able to qualify the tank because he did it right. He set up our TCGST (Tank Crew Gunnery Skills Test) at times when we were not supporting the Armor School. One time we did the machinegun portion at 0400, but you took it until you got it right, there were no gimmies, especially for him or the CO. He was fair, tough and smart. We got to do the complete gunnery tables in the field by using ammunition the officer students were not using. Basically, Martin stole the gunnery from spare parts. We did so well, the Commanding General used us to validate the M1 tank gunnery tables. Martin was well known and got a lot of the assets at Knox to support us. He re-did almost everything. He hates putting troops on detail worse than any First Sergeant I ever knew. It is always about training with him but he somehow still gets along with the Command Sergeant Major."

"That is what worries me," said Staff Sergeant Masterson, the Master Gunner. "The Earth Pig always bitches about rock painting projects."

Jackson replied, "He gave a kid in my platoon whose dad was a fire chief of a city in Virginia, a five day admin leave to go home, get 600 feet of fire hose and a hydrant wrench, with a booster pump to wash the motor pool so we would not have to sweep it. Before, we used to spend all friggin' day on Friday sweeping that huge St. Johns Motor Pool. Hell, that screwin' motor pool is bigger than the whole damn Border Camp. He had the extra duty and extra training guys do it. He figures out everything in advance. He will be way ahead of the Command Sergeant Major and the Squadron Commander on just about everything. You'll see - we will all be part of it. One bad thing, he tends to lead the troop as if it is a platoon, particularly for PT, but we will work on that, this ain't Knox and the focus is different."

Staff Sergeant Ramos said, "He was my basic Training Drill Sergeant. He had a platoon, was the Senior Drill Sergeant and the Acting First Sergeant. He moved me to his platoon when some Drill Sergeants were screwing with me hard. We beat the rest of the company at everything we did. We never cheated or failed to cooperate with the other platoons. He simply taught us everything we were going to learn in the next day's training, the short version, the night before. That way, when the classroom guys gave it, we're hearing for the second time. Hell, we had beer and soda after Phase testing in our barracks."

"So why were the Drill Sergeants on your ass, Jesus?" asked Maldanado, a former DS.

"DS Martin had us march to ranges in our leather boots in the snow, with no field jackets or long under wear. Shit it was cold, when we first started. We had our spare boots in our overshoes. They could not understand why my boots were where they were. My English was not so good and all I would say was 'Me no talk'. When we got to a range, we spread our ponchos, got naked, put on our long johns and dry boots. It was cold as hell, but he stood right in front of us and took his clothes off first. In the other companies, everybody else was freezing because they got sweating on the march out because they wore all of their stuff to stay warm. He marched us so fast, you stayed warm. Our morale was so high once we got re-dressed. Plus, we had lots of dry wood for the fire barrels 'cause he cut and stacked it in the summer."

"Why?" asked Maldanado.

"Simple, he never asked us to dress or wear anything he was not already doing himself. I never forget it when he say, Cold injuries happen when cold hearted leaders with warm asses are making decisions." Ramos replied.

"Is he crazy, Ramos?" Lieutenant Brown asked.

"Sheet, Sir, he ees crazy like a gray wolf, he is El Lobo," Ramos said with an exaggerated Spanish accent. The humor was not lost on the former West Point standout athlete Executive Officer who laughed heartily.

As he rode to the BOQ, Martin was lost in thought. His driver, PFC Staunton, a handsome Welsh lad from Virginia asked him if they were going to be late every night.

"Only until you trim your moustache, Staunton and if you keep your German girlfriend from getting pregnant," Martin said. Staunton was in shock as he replied.

"First Sergeant Tobias never worked late and he drove his own car everywhere," he said petulantly.

"Tom," Martin said, "I will only need you to carry me back and forth a few days. I am going to get a sleeping room within walking distance from

Post with a Bundespost telephone. I have no intention of using an official Army vehicle to get me back and forth to work. If getting the room drags on, I will run back and forth to the BEQ in the morning and evening. If you want, I will have the training NCO take me back on Thursday and Friday night."

"First Sergeant, I am not bitching. I am so glad to see everyone getting their personal problems fixed. You cannot believe how different everything is already. I can see the morale going up just tonight. Hell, waiting months for separate rations is bullshit and some of these guys have had a hell of a time paying their rent without the proper housing allowances. I just have a special date tomorrow night and I need to get off by 1800," the driver stated.

"You go ahead with your plans. There is no reason for you to stick around while I do paperwork. We will have the entire backlog that affects the Soldiers finances or family support done by Friday night. All that will be left is efficiency reports and end of tour awards. We will do those for those who have already departed and did not get an award first and then for those who are about to leave. Are you on separate rations, Tom?"

"No First Sergeant," Staunton replied.

"Do you want to be and can you manage your money so that you will be able to eat?" Martin asked bluntly, adding. "I know how hard it is for you to eat around our schedule."

"I would like that very much, First Sergeant," replied Staunton. "No one has ever asked me or thought about me like that, First Sergeant," he said.

"Leaders need to remember the soldiers closest to them are still soldiers. The circle of care needs to go outward from the leader's position. We will take care of it in the morning, Tom," the First Sergeant said directly as it was already tomorrow as it often would be in the Blackhorse.

"First Sergeant, do you have to do this in every unit you take over?" asked Staunton.

"Yes, Tom, I do. Or at least so far, I have," Martin replied.

"How can you do it without getting mad?" the hot tempered PFC asked.

"Tom, the soldier is not at fault. He generally does his best at everything he is told to do. He asks for very little. A lot of the time he does not know what he is entitled to get. The First Sergeant is the soul of the unit. The Commander is the unit face. He takes care of the brain and I take care of the body of the troop. The Germans say the Commander is the father and the First Sergeant is the mother of the company."

"My job is to give Captain Dawson a unit that is ready, willing and able to perform its tasks. His job is to lead it, maneuver it, fight it and die bravely leading it, if need be. He writes the letters to the next of kin. Congress put him in charge, not me. He is responsible to the nation with his brother officers. I am responsible to him."

"Yeah, Top, but Captain Dawson didn't tell you to do all of this, did he?" Staunton asked, adding, "The Old First Sergeant never did this stuff late at night."

"Tom, taking care of soldiers is just sound leadership. The primary need of a human being is personal safety followed closely by water, food and shelter. An organization that does not care enough about a soldier to see he is paid correctly and has his entitlements can never expect his loyal and willing cooperation. It is as simple as I am yours and you are mine. Rank is a badge of servitude not a mark of privilege."

"As for what the Captain expects, good First Sergeants give their officers what they need not just what they ask for. I am going to be asking a lot from the soldiers of the troop and the least I can do is to support them," Martin said, suddenly quite tired.

"How do you know what the officers need if they don't ever tell you?" Staunton asked.

"That is why they pay me the big bucks Tommy, to know the difference," Martin replied closing the discussion.

CHAPTER 4 – TRIBAL RITES

"If you are doing good you don't need your friends and if you're not, none of them can help you keep your job."- Bear Bryant

The driver was on time at the BEQ. It was 0500. Martin was ready with one other NCO who needed a ride to the barracks area. It was a cold German morning with serious frost in the air with a temperature of about 35 degrees and 50 percent humidity. The light at the entrance to the BEQ/Officers' Club cast an island of yellow while the surrounding area was black as midnight. Martin wore his fatigue uniform with boots and field jacket and carried his running shoes. The remainder of his gear had been stowed in his office in his wall locker. "Mornin' PFC Staunton," said Martin.

"Mornin' First Sergeant," Staunton answered without much enthusiasm.

"Fear not Staunton, I will be moved into a little apartment near the Kaserne shortly or I will be running back and forth to the BEQ, you young guys need your rest." Martin said.

"Damn, First Sergeant, it is about four or five miles to the Kaserne. Are you going to run ten miles every day until you get housing?" Staunton asked incredulously.

Martin answered, "No, I will probably just run in the morning and hold the troop run to less than five miles and walk to the BEQ at night, as soon as I learn the way. I try not to run more than ten miles every day unless I am training for something special."

"Well, no more PT than we have been doing, we are in deep shit if you are in charge of PT. Who is in charge of PT First Sergeant?" Staunton asked.

"I am in charge of PT and we will get the full bang for our buck. You sound like a man with a profile Staunton. What is it, a knee?" Martin asked.

"Yes, First Sergeant, I slipped on an oil spot in the motor pool. That is my real MOS; I am a 63C, Wheel Vehicle Mechanic. I am getting physical therapy for it in Schweinfurt and it is getting better. My German girlfriend is a nurse and she helps me a lot. I should be off profile by the end of November," opined Staunton.

Interesting thought Martin; he has just summarized everything quite nicely for me.

He is the First Sergeant's driver because he is a mechanic, leaving him able to work on the Hqs section vehicles, he keeps up my vehicle, he is sophisticated enough to have a German girl, a nurse no less, he skates on PT but has a date for re-entry to regular PT once his knee is healed. However, a mechanic that cannot kneel, squat and hunker is about as much use as a three legged dog. Wonder how many other folks are riding the system and have fallen into the cracks?

Martin knew Staunton was a loyal soldier and that something was troubling him beyond his inability to do PT. He told Staunton, "Tom, why don't you just spit it out? I know something is bothering you. What is it?"

Looking down at the dash board instruments, Staunton took a deep breath and said, "First Sergeant Tobias was not a bad guy and I liked him. I think he got screwed when he got relieved. I'm not so sure I can be your driver."

Martin smiled and said, "I told everyone last night. You were not there. I do not care to know what happened in the past. I am not interested in anyone's opinion of First Sergeant Tobias or in hearing gossip. Your lives are your own. We are all governed by the UCMJ (Uniform Code of Military Justice), Army Regulations and Title 10 US Code. Unless, and until, it is proven that someone knowingly has violated one of those regulations or laws, I am not worried about gossip. If First Sergeant Tobias was your friend and still is, that is fine with me. If you meet him off duty, that is also fine with me. Now if you feel you cannot drive for me after the first thirty days or when your physical profile is up, that is fine with me. I do not want anyone in a job where they are not happy. The other thing you need to know. A big part of my personal philosophy is, 'If it ain't broke, don't fix it.' I am not planning on changing the whole troop to prove I can. You guys who have been here already know your jobs. I am learning how to be a Cavalry First Sergeant. Once I know what you know about Cavalry, then we change things, not until. Clear?" Martin asked.

"Clear, First Sergeant."

As he went to the CQ desk, Martin thought, Staunton was a friend of Tobias, how interesting. The fact he stuck up for his old First Sergeant said more about Staunton than Tobias.

"Mornin', Sergeant Matson. Anything happen?" Martin asked.

"No First Sergeant, everything was quiet after you left. The troop is not used to a First Sergeant being here after 1630 so they tip-toed around here all night."

"Are the latrines straight and do they all have toilet paper in every stall with spare rolls?" Martin asked.

"Yes, First Sergeant," Matson said with a smile, adding, "I am in Sergeant First Class Jackson's platoon." They both smiled as they knew Sergeant First Class Jackson was one of First Sergeant Martin's platoon sergeants in his last outfit, H Company, 2/6 Cavalry at Fort Knox.

"Well Matson, you know what they say about Cavalry, if you ain't cheatin' you ain't tryin," Martin said, pausing to let Matson finish the quote.

Matson did not disappoint, saying, "And if you get caught, you ain't trying hard enough." Both NCOs laughed and Martin went on his way to his office.

"Sergeant Matson, does the new First Sergeant think cheating is okay?" the CQ runner asked.

Matson smiled saying, "No private, what he meant was, each soldier has to anticipate what needs to get done without being told every little detail. Sergeant Jackson told me First Sergeant thinks the barracks are the soldiers' home. They have a right to have the comforts of a home such as toilet paper,

58

light bulbs and cleaning supplies without begging for them. So before the supply sergeant went home, I made damn sure we had everything on hand last night. I do not want a brand new First Sergeant on my ass if I can help it and you don't either."

"He seems awful nice," PVT Martin said tentatively not quite sure how Matson would answer.

"Martin, the First Sergeant ain't nice, he ain't your buddy, he is civil. He is one hard-assed son-of-a-bitch. This is going to be one hard-ass outfit with him in charge of it. He sure as hell is not going to be relieved."

In quarters 4266 F, Debbie Jackson was pouring Sergeant First Class Victor L. Jackson's coffee as he sat in the kitchen watching her getting the family breakfast ready for the kids. Vic would not eat until after PT as he was fairly sure he would be puking it up if he did. He lit his third cigarette of the morning as he looked lovingly at his gorgeous wife. He was the luckiest man he knew.

Debbie looked up from her food preparations and asked him, "Did the First Sergeant remember you?"

"Oh yeah, we talked. It was good. He is a great First Sergeant. He will have some tricks up his sleeve for these guys. They are not going to know what hit 'em."

"Are you worried about him Vic?" Debbie asked.

"Nope, not at all. He is a straight up, down the line First Sergeant. He loves the Army and takes great care of soldiers," Vic answered.

"Well what is it you are worried about. I know you too well dear," she said with a smile as she came to him and pressed his balding head to her hip.

Vic thought a moment and said, "I am not sure I can hang with him physically. He has just got in from the states and a thirty day leave. He does not know how little we get a chance to do PT and I hope he is not going to try to smoke our asses too bad until he figures it out. This ain't Fort Knox and the only fixed thing in this schedule is the length of our tour and that is subject to change. I am going to go in a little early and talk to him."

"Vic, it is not even five thirty yet, do you think he will be there now?" Debbie asked, then laughed saying, "Excuse me, of course he will be there. Your thermos is ready. The kids will be off to school when you get done with PT and everything else will be ready here, including your breakfast." The implied invitation for a hot love making session got them both laughing. The Jacksons were the proud parents of three adopted children, two boys and a girl. The boys were siblings, now 10 and 9 and the girl was their new baby sister, 6 and in first grade. The Jacksons had 15 childless years of marriage to give them a solid financial base as well as a deep and abiding love and friendship. They both knew their lives were so much richer now with the children and in the manner of all great parents, could not remember a time without these wonderful kids.

"Is his wife coming over, Vic?" Debbie asked, adding, "I liked her, she was nice."

Vic grimaced, "Yeah she was nice to you, but she was not nice to him. She ain't coming. That is the main thing, he will have a lot of time on his hands and I hope he won't spend it all in the troops face bringing smoke on everyone. You remember how it was at Knox, all the extra things we had to do," said Vic. "Hell, we did the TCGST at 0300, Debbie."

"As I remember it Vic, you said it was a miracle you got to do tank gunnery in that chicken shit outfit and you all loved it," Debbie said with a smile. "Now go see Martin, get reacquainted and I will be here waiting for you after PT. Save a little strength for me big boy."

Vic made his way to the door, stopping to look into the kids rooms, each of them sleeping peacefully. Little Katie was in her pink and blue little girl's bedroom. Ryan was asleep in his Ninja pajamas that matched the Ninja Turtle poster on the wall of his bedroom. Vic noticed that Ryan had kicked his covers off and that Billy was sound asleep wearing the grownup plaid pajamas his mother had picked for him. Women and plaid never ceased to amaze Vic. He sure hoped none of these kids would ever see a rice paddy or a place like Vietnam - where the hell did that thought come from he wondered. As he reached the door, Debbie was there for her goodbye kiss. *'What a life,'* he thought to himself. Six more years and they could have this shit and he and Debbie would go home to Columbus, Georgia.

Arriving at his platoon area, Vic was glad to see his platoon up and moving, getting ready for PT with their areas reasonable straight. Hector Rodriguez, his hard driving Staff Sergeant was on the ball as usual. "Hector, I'll be downstairs with the new First Sergeant," Vic said.

"Are you going to set him straight, Sergeant Jackson?" Rodriguez asked with a smile.

"Shit, I am going to try to nudge him a little but he is going to go where he wants to run when he gets the lay of the land. He will be very good for us, if we can keep up," said Jackson leaving the upstairs hallway.

First Sergeant Martin looked up to see Vic Jackson knocking on his door. "Damn Vic, come on in, you don't need to knock, especially when there is no one in here. You PSGs run this outfit. You guys provide the perspiration and I just give the Captain hints of inspiration."

"What do you think First Sergeant?" Vic asked.

"Vic, I have to wonder when we have time to train. It looks like the unit goes 100 mph all of the time. It seems to me, we have to do what we do, well, when we do it. I am sure the Command Sergeant Major will be dogging us on the Infantry shit of uniformity, cleanliness, accountability, all of that 5 mph shit. I have a lot to learn about Cavalry tactics, re-supply and of course, the Border, the territory and the people. I am going to in-process this morning after PT. What is troubling you, if anything, about the outfit?" Martin asked.

"Not much but you," Vic said. "We do not get to do PT very much. The Troop Commander is young and a former College football player at Ole Miss, the Executive Officer is a former standout basketball and baseball varsity letterman at West Point. Lieutenant Robertson is a West Pointer, a wrestler and lacrosse player and one mean little sob. Red, Lieutenant Martin is an Aggie rodeo guy at the college level. My platoon leader is a champion 10,000 meter runner and Bevington is a former Staff Sergeant, Drill Sergeant who can run them all into the ground. It is the soldiers that are not getting the PT. Also, the Squadron Commander, Lieutenant Colonel Covington, does not want the troops to run more than the Army standard, two miles. Getting my drift," Vic concluded by saying, "This outfit is not in good physical condition because the leadership does not make the time for PT."

Resolved to keep his temper in check, Martin replied, "So what you are telling me, Vic, is that it would be best to concentrate on developing esprit de corps by doing what we can do rather than bringing smoke on the troops by showing them what they can't do and insulting them? Hell, I will probably be in the same shape after six months of the same schedule. Is that about it?"

"Can I close the door?" Jackson asked.

"Sure, Vic, close the door," Martin replied.

"Tobias was a sorry SOB. Most of the older soldiers know he was totally screwed up. They are all scared of the Troop Commander. Tobias could not carry your jock strap. I hope I get to be a First Sergeant before I get out but if I don't, it will be okay. I know you will not hold it against me to tell you the truth," Jackson said pausing for a sign of affirmation from Martin.

"You know I want the truth and further, you of all people should know I am not a messenger killer," Martin replied.

Jackson then continued, "The officers here want the impossible. They do not properly allocate the time to get things done. The Sergeant Major wants stupid shit done and does not take into account what the Squadron Commander has told the Troop Commanders to do. He just wants what he wants and thinks harder work will get it done. He is Infantry in a Cav outfit and the two do not mix. The Border eats us alive. Once you are up there, it is an all out drive every day just to get the minimum tasks done. I love it there but G Troop gets way more than their share of duty there at the Border. I have not been to gunnery with these guys yet. The M-1 gunnery they got at NET (New Equipment Training) probably sucked but they think it was great. They also think the tank does everything but wipe your ass for you. We know that is not true. The troop needs you more than you need it. Taking care of the paperwork that is behind has them all buzzing. I do not envy you and I do not see how you are going to do it all, but I know you will somehow get 90% of it perfect the first time. The only thing you should think about is taking it easy on them for PT for a few weeks. It is a shame but they are not in good shape and neither am I."

61

"Vic, thanks for your input. I will take it easy on PT until I figure out where we are on it. I suspect they may be in a little better shape than you think they are. I will put you PSGs in the front ranks until we can figure it out. You guys will pace the outfit and keep me from running everyone too fast too soon. After a few days of that, we will run by platoon in Company formation. Leaders fall in love with the formation run. We have to make sure we do timed runs to keep them ready for the PT test."

"You are right about me not knowing the best way to proceed. What I intend to do is to qualify myself for service in the troop by earning my spurs according to the troop SOP authored by Captain Dawson. That means leading every aspect of the Border, going on every field problem, being licensed to drive every vehicle, firing expert on every weapon, getting 300 on the PT test and so on. You get put in charge of the whole unit but you win the troops over, one soldier at a time. If I make me happy, they will respect my leadership. If you see me over reaching and working everyone harder than is necessary, tell me and I will back off. What I need from you is help during the critique process. I want you to find an occasion to disagree with me in public. That should not be too hard," Martin concluded laughing while Jackson joined in to the point of hilarity.

"That will serve several purposes, Vic. It will give them the idea that it is okay to disagree during the analysis of what happened after an exercise or an event and it sets you up to be the replacement First Sergeant if I am not present. I want them to look to you as my alter ego. That is what I need from you. Now you know why," Martin stated.

The last part of his statement unnerved Jackson slightly prompting him to say, "First Sergeant, I hope you are not going to bring up that old time shit from Vietnam. That was a dumb accident, it was nothing and I really do not want to even tell anybody about it."

"Vic, you are incorrect but I understand and I will not bring it up. But what you cannot avoid is the responsibility you have for leadership. Now you listen for a minute and hear me out. You are a great NCO and a fine leader. You have been through the wall of fire of Infantry close combat. You personally saved the life of one of the country's great writers, a Brigadier General and killed VC getting it done. Did your Battalion Commander make Bird Colonel? Yes, he did. Did your Brigade Commander make Brigadier General, yes. Did Abrams make Chief of Staff of the Army, yes. Would any of them got to go on without a whisper if that guy would have been killed? Maybe not, but because of you they did not have to find out."

"No, I have no desire to pump you up for getting a Silver Star and a Distinguished Service Cross because you are a modest man. I won't even do it because I don't have any war time medals. I will do it because one example is worth ten sermons. Your day to day devotion to your duty, your country and to your soldiers is beyond price. You, my friend, are more of a lifer than I am, you just do it in the manner of the 'aw shucks, twern't nothing' Vietnam era leader. The troops already know you are a hero without knowing about those two desperate days long ago. What I want is for more of them to become just like you are in your daily performance of duty. I do not yet know every detail about how I am going to re-shape this troop. But I know it won't be a bolt from the blue. This is peacetime. I do know you do not build a unit through parties and ski trips, though they help. Units are built through tough duty performed under field conditions so that everyone learns they can depend on the men on their right and their left. Nobody ever learned a lasting lesson from easy times. But, I will not tell anyone about how you got the medals, even if they ask, okay?"

"Okay, First Sergeant, I appreciate it," said Jackson.

"Open the door Vic, the others should be here any minute," Martin stated.

As if on cue the First Sergeant's office filled up with NCOs checking their boxes for orders, papers and details. Many were surprised to see a record number of personnel actions accomplished the night before. As they turned to look at the First Sergeant, he was trading his boots for his sneakers and getting set for PT formation while drinking a Coke and smoking a Marlboro. "So guys, how do you usually do PT? I see the uniform must be liberally interpreted as you are all wearing a rainbow of outfits."

Ramos replied, "First Sergeant, CIF don't got no uniforms for everybody. We wear civilian PT gear, old clothes, fatigues like you and those that have the whole outfit wear it. We do good at PT, we just don't look good doing it."

"Well and good there, Red." Using his call sign, Martin said, "Is everyone in the same shape across the squadron?"

"No, some people, like those suck asses in Fox Troop have their stuff," Ramos stated.

"And how do we know Fox sucks ass, Red?" Martin asked.

"Well the Commander walks the Squadron Commander's dog when he goes on leave and his wife baby sits the kids," Red said to the accompanying wise nods from the NCOs.

"Well, it don't look like we have any dog walkers in this outfit so we will have to come up with some other way to make the point," said Martin.

"So, who leads PT in this outfit?" Martin asked. All of the NCOs laughed at the same time though somewhat sheepishly. "Never mind," he said, "I understand. When I face the troop to the left, I will post the guidon and put the four line Platoon Sergeants in the front rank. Sergeant Hankinson, you will be the fall out NCO and kick ass in the rear as you are an 11C and a Ranger so you know how to do that very well. Sergeant Wintergreen, you will post the road guards and watch for traffic like a good motor sergeant. We are going to get our money's worth out of your ass before you get to be a warrant officer. Any questions?"

63

Wintergreen asked, "First Sergeant, I did not put in for Warrant Officer. What did you mean by that?"

"Wintergreen, when I come back to the Regiment in a couple of years as a Command Sergeant Major, you will already be a CW2 whether you know it now or not," Martin said.

Martin added, "Just look at you. Airborne, spit shined, starched, shaved, buzz cut, driving a BMW, a Mason, combat patch, shit, home style, you are ready."

"How you know all that First Sergeant? You just got here," Wintergreen asked plaintively.

"You are smart enough to know Wintergreen if you would just open your eyes. Your ring and car keys are clues and will get you started."

"Let's go out to PT guys. It is 0615. I intend to be the last one to formation, not the first, plus I am putting in a wrinkle for public relations purposes."

As Martin approached the formation, he saw the Platoon Sergeants had formed their elements. The guidon bearer was present and that the officers were in the rear acting like officers, engaged in some minor grab ass but ceasing it when they saw him. Engaging in the minor theater in the manner of First Sergeants time eternal, Martin arrived at his position and paused while looking over the unit, watching it become a living thing that stilled itself like a coiled spring. *He could not help thinking - shit, those dumb jacks at Regiment, this is one fine outfit and this is going to be too much fun.*

He commanded "Troop," waited for the Echo of the preparatory command of Platoon and commanded, "Attention," then gave the directive of "Receive the Report." When the Platoon Sergeants were all facing front again, he commanded, "Report." The Platoon Sergeants were professional and gave brisk reports of either all present, or "All Present or Accounted For." As Hankinson reported as the last element on the left side of the troop, Martin commanded, "Stand At, Ease," thus causing the unit to come to a modified position of Parade Rest with feet spread shoulder width apart, hands together, palms facing outward in the small of the back and head and eyes turned toward him.

"Men, the Cav is a busy place. We are going to do each thing we do when we do it, well. When you get a drill command, put snap into it, every time. Today, we will go over the Gator version of the hand salute. First two ranks, gently kneel, these cobblestones will kill you."

Once the men were in position he had just ordered, Martin continued on. "The first version of present arms is how everybody else does it." This was accompanied by Martin demonstrating the movement as he continued to talk. "Fingers extended and joined, elbow at a forty five degree angle and parallel to the ground, tip of the index finger at the corner of the eyebrow when without head gear. For order arms, the hand is sharply cut away and returned to the side resuming the position of attention. The difference for you is now and will always be while I am your First Sergeant; the hand salute is enhanced by tensing the muscles of the forearm as the hand stops its upward progression at the eyebrow so as to induce a quiver as it stops, in this manner." Martin demonstrated the salute accentuating the movement and exaggerating slightly for effect. "You will then cut away snappily making a fist and return your hand rapidly and silently to the position of attention, in this manner. Questions?"

"Platoon Sergeants face about and critique. Men, for the practice there will be no preparatory commands, all commands will come from me."

Martin then proceeded to drill the Troop in the enhanced method of present arms. Satisfied, he put the unit at Parade Rest and awaited Reveille.

The guidon bearer whispered to the First Sergeant, "Squadron Commander approaching from your right First Sergeant, coming in from his quarters." There appeared to be at least three minutes remaining before reveille. Martin faced about, called the troop to attention, faced about and saluted the Squadron Commander saying, "Good Morning, Sir."

The Squadron Commander appeared to be startled slightly as he saw the troop being called to attention but he recovered, smiled and returned the salute of the First Sergeant saying, "Good Morning First Sergeant."

Martin dropped his salute and kept the troop at attention awaiting the bugle call alerting the post for Reveille. He then faced about at its close and brought the troop to Present Arms. Each and every man popped the salute in a super sharp manner.

Well, little successes thought Martin as he faced about for Reveille.

After Reveille, Martin formed the troop and marched them to the Commissary Parking Lot for exercises in accordance with Army Conditioning Drill one, with 20 repetitions of each exercise at the proper cadence. At the conclusion of the exercises, Martin noted that some other units of the Squadron were already running in formation. Some were in platoon formation and others were in Company sized elements. He formed the troop in the manner he had described for the Platoon Sergeants in his office and began a two mile run at a slow pace intending to speed it up once the troops were sufficiently warmed up.

One of the more aggressive Sergeants fell out to call cadence. Martin let him do so as the troops expected it and responded to him very well. As the Sergeant's cadence ran down, Martin took over for him. The entire troop turned as one when he began because while the young Sergeant had a great voice, they just had to be certain that was really their First Sergeant calling cadence for a run. For many, it was a novel experience. Martin realized by their looks that not only had few if any of them ever heard any First Sergeant call cadence, even fewer had even seen a First Sergeant run with the troop. He smiled and shook his head in such a way that the most motivated of the soldiers had a good laugh. Immediately, another young Sergeant fell out and began the cadence of, "First Sergeant, First Sergeant can't you see, You can't bring no smoke on me!"

Martin let it go on and all were having a great time. He then made several other calls as it was plain the youngsters were running out of gas after one mile of running and singing. As an old Drill Sergeant, Martin never ran out of cadence calls and could call cadence and run for miles on end. The pace remained steady and in the last half mile Martin began the Amen Chorus. The young voices picked up the cadence and listened to him as he said, "Just the Brothers now, Tell your Sister," and just the black soldiers sang the chorus.

The effect was just as startling on the soldiers as Martin knew it would be when he called, "Everybody now," and the whole troop joined back in for the song.

Martin now continued to run the troop past the stopping point where all expected their ordeal to be over. He carefully noted which faces turned toward him when the expected terminal point of the run came and went. He cheerfully exhorted the troop to continue singing the Amen chorus and turned them up the next right turn to take them through the motor shop area of the kaserne. His intent was to run them for another quarter mile, come to quick time and cool them down. A quick look at his watch revealed it was past 0730 and would be later still when they arrived back at the formation area.

Martin then gave the troop quick time and drilled them enroute back to the formation area. Noting it was 0745, he set the recall formation for 0930 rather than 0900 while also excusing all who had conflicting appointments.

At the formation area Martin told the troop, "Men, we now train to standard, not to time. What just happened to you when we went by the formation area is life. So often, things do not go as we think they will. The definition of the word sophisticated is 'not easily surprised'. In the Army it is defined, 'don't sweat the small shit'. I ran you past where you normally stop to see who the wussies were. It is a curable disease; get tough in your mind. The pain you feel during PT is the weakness trying to get out of your body."

As he was walking back to the troop, a young officer came up to Martin and the platoon leaders.

"I am Chaplain Goodeux and that was a good run, First Sergeant."

"Chaplain, I hope the profanity did not offend you," Martin said as he saluted the Chaplain.

"What profanity, First Sergeant? I did not hear any profanity. I was an Infantry Platoon leader in Vietnam before I got my Divinity degree. I heard what you said about discharges. I am assuming you were serious."

Martin looked at the Chaplain hard while saying, "I was Chaplain. I do not intend to cast my pearls down before swine. And I will remember about the 'the least of these rule' while we are about it."

"How many takers do you think you will have, First Sergeant?" asked Goodeux.

"No more than three Chaplain and I hope to have them gone by next Friday," Martin replied.

"That is very optimistic First Sergeant. The paper moves very slowly here. No one ever gets it moving that fast. What is your secret?" the Chaplain asked, smiling.

"Simple Chaplain, I detail the very best NCO in the dud's platoon to out-process him. I give him one week and help him all I can. After one week, no one in the Platoon has a pass until the dud is a civilian. I also cut up his ID card and give him a paper application for one and confiscate his uniforms. You see Chaplain, it is a lot like re-enlistment. Units that have bars to re-enlistment applied have a higher re-enlistment rate than those who never bar anyone. The Army is very tribal. The genus of Army has within it various tribes, though conventional thinkers term them branches. Each tribe enforces its expectations and has written and unwritten rules for membership. Somewhat like 100 gallon Baptists and water sprinkling Presbyterians and saved and sanctified Pentecostals. It is only when a leader figure denies membership to those less than capable that the good Indians wake up. Chaplain, as you know, the truly self-motivated are very rare. For most of us, the wakeup call comes only after some degree of force is applied. In short, if anyone can get in a club, it must not amount to much."

"So First Sergeant, you are now going to give me a class on religion?" Goodeux asked, smiling.

"Shit no, Chaplain, I was using your branch, your Chaplain tribe vernacular to give you a frame of reference to show you the logic of my program, like the good Presbyterian I am. Now Chaplain, I would appreciate it if you did not spread it around that I use three syllable words and think in philosophical terms. I want these soldiers to think these hot ideas all spring forth like lesser Gods from Minerva, fully grown," Martin concluded, smiling.

"These troops are safe with you, First Sergeant. If you need my help or if you just want to come by and talk, I'll be here. I will not tell anyone you use big words in private nor that you know Greek and Roman mythology. Where is your Commander?" Goodeux asked.

"Where ever he wants to be Chaplain. I've got 161 soldiers to occupy my time. I don't supervise officers," said Martin.

Goodeaux could not help but see that throughout the conversation, Martin kept moving toward the barracks. He only stopped to prevent their conversation from being overheard. He was tactful and correct but this First Sergeant stuck to his timeline and advanced his own agenda in a very single minded way.

As Martin went into his office, he could hear Captain Dawson on the phone patiently explaining to his wife why she had to do a chore with their son and take him to the Doctor. So, that explained his absence from PT, family issues, Martin thought. Martin gathered up his gear and clothes intending to go upstairs to the troop area to shower and shave without disturbing the Commander, if possible.

"Hey First Sergeant, sorry to have missed PT, how did it go?" Dawson asked.

"No issues, Sir, I broke their hearts going by the Troop area but only the wussies seemed to mind. I am about to go upstairs, change, go eat and in-process the unit. Maldanado is going to take the work call," stated Martin.

"Where are you going to eat breakfast, the mess hall I suppose?" asked Dawson.

"Why, yes, Sir, I am. As I understand it, the cooks are still assigned to G Troop pending the change to the T O & E and we have some on the shift today. I found some leave and earnings statements and their checks when I inventoried the safe. I want to deliver them to the cooks. Until they get assigned to Headquarters Troop, there is always the chance their paperwork, pay and even paychecks are going to be screwed up. They live a shitty life and I want them to know they are part of us until the new organization comes into play," Martin concluded.

Dawson then observed, "You need to know the mess hall sucks. The officers and senior NCOs eat at the snack bar. The food is better, service is quicker and you can read the paper."

"That might all be, Sir. But I want to see what the mess hall is like for the troops. If it is screwed up, we will just have to make the corrections to make it right. If the mess daddy feels enough pain, it will get fixed," Martin said.

"Yeah, but don't forget that is the province of the Squadron Commander and Command Sergeant Major and the S4. You probably ought to go easy on fixing anything over there until you get the lay of the land," Dawson cautioned.

"Tell me, Sir, where do the Squadron Commander, the Squadron Executive Officer and the Command Sergeant Major eat breakfast?" Martin asked.

"Hell, they eat at home or the snack bar," Durston replied in a matter of fact manner. This last statement caused Martin to stop his trek to the shower and enter the Troop Commander's office.

"Captain Dawson. Thank you for your invitation to the snack bar for breakfast. I will join you there on another day. Today I am going to go to the mess hall. The mess hall is the center of unit life for the soldier. If it is good, it can be a priceless asset. If it is screwed up, it affects the whole unit. If it is screwed up, I will help get it fixed. My point is to let the cooks know I care about them and we will work from there. By the way, I kept the troops a little late so work call is at 0930, is that okay?" Martin concluded.

"Yeah, that's all right First Sergeant. Don't forget what I told you about the Urinalysis program. Get that on track today," Dawson stated bluntly.

"Yes, Sir, I will take care of it," Martin said, taking his leave.

"Hey, Top, are you really taking your shower here?" Dawson asked.

"Yes, Sir. That is how I intend to make sure everything works, drains, hot water heater, pipes, etc. Plus it's too convenient not to use it."

"Well, I never saw anybody do that, anywhere, ever, a First Sergeant showering in the troop billets, but I guess it's okay if that is what you want to do," Dawson said, shaking his head in silent disapproval.

Later, having dressed in his office, shower complete, Martin gathered up the pay statements and checks for the cooks from McKnight and went to the mess hall. It was a funky building and in poor overall repair. It looked bad, starting at the outside. Martin paid for his meal with the Headcount NCO with exact change. He then put on his hat and went behind the serving line to greet the Mess Sergeant and to make certain he knew the purpose of his visit.

The Mess Sergeant was very, very glad to see him and said so in the black brogue of his South Carolina heritage. "Are you here to eat, First Sergeant, after you deliver their paperwork?" Sergeant First Class Bartholomew asked.

"I sure am Mess Sergeant, if there is enough chow to feed me. I am here to see if you need some support and to make sure you are getting what you need to run an efficient mess hall. I know I just got here but that is good. A new broom sweeps clean, doesn't it?" Martin said with a smile.

Bartholomew was beaming when the G Troop cooks came over to meet their First Sergeant, get their paychecks and their pay statements. Two of the men also had mail which they were surprised to get hand delivered.

Staff Sergeant Nash asked, "First Sergeant is this going to be the standard service for us now that you is the First Sergeant?"

"Nash, what time did you guys get up this morning?" Martin asked.

"Bout 0330," Nash replied.

"That's right, 0330 wake up, on shift. On shift people get a break. I will have a key to the mail and if you make arrangements, I will have someone there to give it to you when you get off. You will not suffer because of your odd hours. Besides, only a fool pisses off the big three; the cook, the clerk, or finance, right?"

The whole kitchen crew laughed. One of the other cooks from another unit said, "First Sergeant, can you get me my check from Fox Troop?"

"Specialist Marshall, I can't tell your First Sergeant how to run his outfit, I can only run mine. But I will tell him about your situation," Martin replied.

"Hey, First Sergeant, time for your breakfast. What are you havin'?" Nash asked.

"That's easy," Martin said, "Everything with eggs over easy."

The first stop for the new First Sergeant after breakfast was the S1 shop as he already had his in-processing sheet from the ever efficient Staff Sergeant McKnight. He then proceeded through the rest of the stations.

He filed his paperwork with the buxom and charming lady at Housing. She told him it would be 7 to 10 days before they had an apartment for him. One that was within walking distance to kaserne. She also told him of the more than substantial allowance he would be getting to live off post. She cautioned him to pay his rent in the official German coinage, the Deutsche Mark, rather than trading liquor or cigarettes for his rent. She also displayed her ample German charms with a low cut blouse and a short skirt though she was about twenty years past her prime. He absolutely did not trust her as far as he could throw her, particularly when she told him she had been there for ten years. She was screwing someone other than her husband, that was for sure. Probably an officer he thought, uncharitably.

At the Central Issue Facility, he was surprised at the high quality of the field gear. He got no special treatment except he got two shelter halves. All of the gear was completely serviceable and everything worked.

The Staff Sergeant from S4 told him the reason for the snarl over the PT uniform. The Army was in the throes of changing out the banana suit to another style of PT uniform. The sizing and availability was just not there for the troops. Martin looked at what was available and agreed it was a bad situation. However, he scrounged through the selection and came up with two serviceable sets for himself. He felt that the right person could find the right button to push and get his troops the gear. Martin took the gear outside to PFC Staunton who took his gear back to the troop for him. Martin retained both his personal duffel bag and one that the CIF team had issued to him. He then told Staunton to meet him at the PX once he had dropped of the CIF gear in his office.

Martin was very pleasantly surprised at the Alcohol and Drug Center. He got a full briefing and was able to establish his program, albeit with a personal urinalysis, that very day. It made sense to test the tester first. Stranger things had happened than a First Sergeant being on drugs. He had seen First Sergeants and Sergeants Major on heroin. Martin surprised the center's staff when he set aside enough bottles to execute back to back mass urinalysis tests for the troop. One set was allocated for two days hence and the other set was for the end of the month. The end-of-month set had an on-call date option if he so decided.

Ms. McElvy, a Captain's wife from the Artillery unit on post asked, "Why are you setting up back to back testing, First Sergeant? That is a lot of resources to devote to one troop."

The Director of the facility and Ms. McElvy were both all ears as Martin answered, "Ladies, there are a lot of leaks in my organization. I am a newbie, a high ranking newbie, but still a newbie. If the doper intelligence service breaks the code on me either with some Danish drug that flushes it or some other strategy, I want the resources in my hip pocket to hit them again when they least expect it. If the initial test goes okay, I will return the extra kits to you unused and you will have them on hand for other units. If not, I will be able to strike at a time and place of my own choosing as I will have the logistics in place. Fair enough?" he concluded.

"You make it sound like a military operation," said the demure Ms. McElvy.

"Ma'am, the dopers have got to go, period. They are a clannish bunch and they think they are really cool. They think they are putting one over on the establishment. The use of dope is contrary to good order and discipline. It is also a clash between age groups and borders on cultural warfare with the young pitted against the old. We hope to hammer the ones responsible and save the rest for faithful service. We are going to make the "in crowd" to be the tough, smart and disciplined soldiers. They are going to be happy that they took the smart way. We can only do that by putting the dopers on the inside of the jail looking out. Remember what the smart man said ladies, 'All it takes for evil men to succeed is for good men and women to do nothing'," Martin finished.

Martin drew his urinalysis kits, placed them into the duffel bags as if they were TA-50 and took them back to his office.

He was very pleasantly surprised when Staff Sergeant McKnight had a stack of personnel actions ready for his review when he returned. "Except for efficiency reports and four awards, we are all caught up First Sergeant. If you will look at these, I will get them into the Troop Commander for approval, pronto," McKnight said, beaming with pride.

Martin was very surprised at the high quality of work and the very few minor typos on the forms. McKnight stated one small pen and ink change per form was all right and they would process through the personnel center without problems. The Squadron was supported by VII Corps even though it was a V Corps unit.

He opined, "The personnel guys are good troops. They want the soldiers to get everything they have coming. They know the flow was not right from this troop and they want to help. I coordinated each of the late actions and got advance approval from finance for the ones involving back pay for separate rations or allowance for quarters. These wives are going to want to kiss you, First Sergeant."

"A simple handshake will do fine, Mac," said Martin as he read through the stack of papers.

"Who is missing an EER? Never mind, get me the shells of those who need one and the names and the accomplishments for those needing an end of tour medal. I want to knock those out today. You can type them on Thursday unless they are so critical they have to be done today," Martin said.

"On second thought, get the soldiers down here one at a time who don't have an award. I will interview them and write them at the same time on the spare typewriter from the Supply Room," Martin continued.

"First Sergeant, you can type?" McKnight asked in amazement.

"Most First Sergeants can type faster than the Squadron Commander's secretary, Big Sarge," said Martin with a smile.

Using an interview technique, Martin pulled the vignettes from the soldiers to fill out the DA Form, 638, Recommendation for Award. He then wrote the citation draft and had the soldiers read both explaining to each one that the award would be presented at their next duty station or mailed to their home of record for those ending their service.

In response to hearing the soldiers express their gratitude at the level of trouble he was taking for them, the First Sergeant merely said, "This is the least we can do for the Border tours, Caravan Guard exercises and Grafenwohr and Wildflecken gunneries you went on and did well. Thanks for all you did."

Lunch hour had come and gone so McKinght and Martin had a C Ration meal from the orderly room stash. Martin was glad to see his old standby favorite, ham and eggs, was still available. Just as they were finishing lunch, McKnight's daughter came bouncing into the office. It was a delight to see her with her mixed Amerasian features and her sing song perfect English. Right on her heels, a statuesque, extremely attractive and fashionably dressed young woman came into the office. She bent over quickly and swooped up McKnight's daughter. When she stood back up, Martin could see the lady was also pregnant.

McKnight introduced her as Helga, Sergeant Bordelon's girlfriend. She was his daughter's sitter. In the course of the discussion, Martin put two and two together and came up with six. It was obvious Bordelon and his schatzi were living with McKnight in his government quarters. What a goat screw it was going to be to sort out, Martin thought to himself.

From his last unit, Martin remembered what a trial it was to counsel every soldier drawing Basic Allowance for Quarters and to verify his eligibility as he had 150 married soldiers and they were all over the post in support of the armor School on a daily basis. He decided to hold off on that task until the au pair had departed. He did not want to terrorize a Class B dependent. (Class B being soldier slang for a local national who was a wife in every way except by law.) She was a very beautiful Swabian woman with full breasts, nice legs, and translucent skin. She was one of the lucky ones, pregnancy enhanced her beauty. He hoped she had a future with her American Sergeant.

"Sergeant McKnight, I have looked at all of the paper I want to see today. I am going to walk up to the motor pool and smell some diesel fuel," Martin said.

"First Sergeant, the troops will be coming down from there real soon," McKnight said.

"That's okay Mac, I'm not going up there to see what they are doing so much as I am to see how much fuel they have in the vehicles. Friday is top

72

off day, right?" said Martin, smiling. "After they leave the motor pool, woulda', shoulda', coulda' won't mean much will it? See you in the morning."

As he walked out, Martin ran into Staff Sergeant Ramos. "Where you going, Red?" asked Martin using the platoon call sign instead of his name.

"I'm coming to see you, First Sergeant," Ramos said with a grin."Where you going, Top?"

"I am headed to the track park to check top off after I stop by the support platoon to see how much fuel we drew on Friday before I got here."

"Oh, sheet, First Sergeant, we did not top off on Friday. Nobody did I know of. We screwed up, huh?"

"Yeah, you did Gilberto. But it is early yet, it is only 1430. Come on, walk with me," Martin said.

As they walked toward the track park, Ramos had to know how Martin stayed so upbeat in the sub-standard conditions he was seeing everywhere, "How you do it, First Sergeant?"

"Do what, Red?"

"Stay so happy when everything is so screwed up," stated Ramos.

Martin smiled and put his hand on Ramos's shoulder, "In the first place, there is nothing wrong that attention to detail, discipline and a little old time leadership will not fix. In the next place, if the leader goes around with his head down, kicking rocks and muttering, the soldiers see his act and get down for no reason. When times are tough, great leaders lower their voices one octave, smile and reassure their troops. Screaming is okay sometimes but not when anything important is happening. If everything was perfect and NCOs had nothing to fix, some damn Congresswoman would make us all Spec Fours and appoint one General in charge of everybody. He would then just kiss her ass and hold her limo door open when he wasn't fighting, then where would we be?"

"Topping off the fuel tanks of a unit on Friday must be a religious rite, like confession on Thursday and communion on Sunday for you Catholics. The first one saves your ass and the second one your soul. From the President on down, everyone in the chain of command is certain all fuel tanks in the military are topped off at all times when the vehicles are parked up in the motor pool, the ship is docked or the airplane is tied down. Full fuel tanks are part of the national strategic petroleum reserve. Top off is a given, like honesty. Units that do not top off are fundamentally dishonest in the worst way, they are fooling themselves. Over confidence is a bad thing."

"This unit is in love with the Cavalry mystique. Dash, élan' and panache' are great if your fundamentals are sound but there ain't no Stetson in the world will make your track go forward without fuel. It is sorta' like the kid in the New York Italian neighborhood that tapes a 12 inch roll of small salami to his bare thigh inside his jeans. He looks great dancing in the bar but he is

73

shit outa' luck when he gets the girl back to the apartment and has to deliver a 12 inches of the real thing and all he has is the salami."

"Here is the great S4 and the Support Platoon. How about that, First Lieutenant Upton is the boss. I think I know that guy from Armor Officer Basic about two years ago."

"Hello Sergeant, is the Lieutenant around?" Martin asked as he opened the door.

"No, First Sergeant, can I help you?"

"Sergeant Gilbert, is it?"

"No, First Sergeant, I am Specialist Smith. I am wearing Sergeant Gilbert's coveralls cause mine got soaked yesterday during a de-fuel of a Howitzer," the well mannered but grubby looking soldier replied.

"Specialist Smith, could you tell me the last time G Troop drew fuel for top off?" Martin asked with a smile.

"I guess it was about three weeks ago when they came back from the Border. I know because I helped recover them," Smith said.

"How long would it take you to get DF-2 to G Troop motor pool if I asked you to do it?"

"First Sergeant, I would have to ask my platoon leader but we could probably have three of them up there in 15 minutes. They are just sitting right outside."

A sudden voice at the door caught everyone's attention, "Who wants fuel now? Oh no, not Deuteronomy P. Sabot!" shouted First Lieutenant Upton, referring to Martin by his Armor School nickname. "Good to see you, you old SOB. I saw you at PT do that heartbreaker shit and call out the wussies. We have been laughing all day about you being with the fabulous Gators, G Force, the F Troop of the Squadron."

"For your information, the Gators are on the way up. But then, that is the only direction available." Martin respectfully retorted.

"It is a little late in the day to take fuel to the track park. I suppose you want the gas pumps open as well for the wheels," the smiling support platoon leader opined.

"You know I do," said Martin. "Staff Sergeant Ramos, go tell the tread heads the good news, I'll bring the trucks up."

"Your faithful companion, Tonto?" the Lieutenant asked Martin as Ramos departed.

"He is the First Platoon Sergeant and doing very well. He was one of my basic trainees years ago," Martin said smiling.

"Where are you living, First Sergeant?" Upton asked.

"I am in the BEQ," said Martin. "You want to come over and eat tonight and we can have a beer or two, Lieutenant?"

"Hell, no. The club food sucks. I will take you to a nice place downtown. It's a Yugoslavian place called Zagreb's, besides I want to show you my Beamer," said Upton.

"Sounds great, I'll put some speed on this effort so we can get out of here at a decent hour," said Martin.

"Say, do you know something I don't know?" Upton asked with a smile.

"No, I don't even have a good rumor, this is just an every day, garden variety on the spot correction. The Gator does not even know where I am," said Martin.

"Put some speed on it, First Sergeant. I want to top off all of my vehicles before we go home tonight from the underground tanks. You make me nervous. You may not know if we are going on alert, but if you are twitching, I am too. But we are still going out tonight, right?" Upton asked.

"Hell yes," said Martin, "this won't take that long."

At five o'clock, the last of the tanks and track vehicle fuel tanks were finally filled to the brim. The corrective action had taken almost two full hours. Captain Dawson and First Lieutenant Brown had come to the track park and they were breathing fire. Everyone had reported their vehicles topped off to them, Brown explained to Martin.

"That might all be gentlemen, but the M1 is a fuel hog. These guys have been running their heaters. They have been to the wash rack and down for a squadron Technical Inspection. We need to help each other remember to top off on Friday. I would prefer if you let me chew their asses Captain. You have been the bad cop for too long," said Martin.

"You'll be too nice to 'em, First Sergeant," said Dawson.

"If I am too nice, Captain, you'll be here for the last word, won't you?" Martin asked calmly. Martin went to sit on the hood of his jeep and motioned the Platoon Sergeants to gather the troop around him. "Top off is life itself in an Armor or Armored Cavalry outfit. Today we got cut a break. Captain Dawson let us correct our error today using the trucks. Next time this happens, the violators will be using 5 gallon cans, two per man, from the bottom of the hill. That is fifty trips for an M1."

"What did Sergeant Stryker say in the Sands of Iwo Jima about stupid?" Martin asked while cupping his hand to his ear.

A wag in rear sounded off with, "Life is hard but it is harder when you are stupid!"

"You know men, that might be a psalm we should all sing together, 'Life is ….'. He smiled as they roared it in unison. Dawson was beaming but then Martin had no way of knowing John Wayne was his personal patron Saint of Celluloid.

"Platoon sergeants, stand by for a minute. Prepare to move by platoon back to the admin area." After the troops had departed to fall in Martin said, "I have a twitch. Verify the recall rosters, make sure the phone numbers are accurate so we can reach the off post folks. Tell the troops to be back in the barracks, sober, by midnight."

"What's up, Top?" asked Maldanado.

"Just a hunch," replied Martin. "If we get called for an alert, I will be more surprised than anyone. I just sense it, that's all. I don't mind looking like an idiot in front of you guys. I just don't want to be famous on Daley Barracks. I am going out tonight but will be back early. I am going out with some people to eat and will be in early and sober. I will be in my office early to work on some stuff for my course."

"How you going to get here?" Captain Dawson asked.

"I'll walk, it's only a couple of miles. It'll do me good." Martin replied.

"If you are walking to post in the morning, I am taking you to the BOQ tonight. It's on my way home," Dawson said.

"Who are you going to dinner with tonight, First Sergeant?" asked Dawson.

"Lieutenant Upton and some of the guys from his AOB class are meeting at Zagreb's tonight and they asked me to go," said Martin.

"That is a great place to eat. I had hoped to be the first one to take you there, "said Dawson.

"Sir, we will go anywhere you want anytime you want, socially," avowed Martin.

"That's all right First Sergeant. I have to go home tonight anyhow. We will have lots of time to get together, like Sunday at my house. I know you are going to the Border and to see our forward alert areas for Border Condition I on Saturday," said Durston.

"I will be here on Sunday by 0900. There is some stuff I need to read and I have to study for a test for my course. Any special time?" Martin asked.

"It will be after 1200, that's for sure," laughed Dawson. He added, "Angie cannot get enough sleep as she is expecting again. I am probably going to send her and the boy home for the holidays given our schedule."

The dinner at Zagreb's was wonderful. The atmosphere was strictly Middle-European. The white linen table cloths were accentuated by the richly dark furniture and trim though offset by large mirrors with gilded frames well placed by a decorator. The mirrors made the dining area appear larger and were tasteful. The service was superb. The food was served in four courses and was great. The combat arms carnivores each ordered from the wild game part of the menu. Any conversation was either over the salad or while waiting for desert. Lieutenant Bodenham from H Company remarked while waiting for desert, "That waiter is really quick, isn't he First Sergeant?"

"Yeah, he probably did not want to lose a hand by reaching for a plate at the wrong time. The folks at this table are serious eaters. An old Mexican Drill Sergeant once told me his daddy always said serious eaters move their fork toward them to eat and finicky eaters pick up their food on an away stroke. All of the wolves at this table but Brother Upton stroke it forward," said Martin.

"Yeah, that is probably that genteel education he got at the Citadel," Lieutenant Clark added.

"At least I got an education, unlike some Hudson High Grads," added Upton. "Besides who got the man to be the guest speaker at the Dining In? Me, that's who." The three officers growled their approval sounding more like unfed guard dogs than officers, thoroughly terrifying their Yugoslavian immigrant waiter.

"Hey, easy, you're scaring this kid" Martin said with mock seriousness. His sharp retort saved only to spook the youngster even more and he beat a hasty retreat to the kitchen. "What the hell is wrong with him? They have been killing each other for a thousand years in Yugoslavia," Martin said laughingly. "We will have to leave him a nice tip."

"So what is the scoop on the outfit guys?" Martin asked.

"Well it is probably nothing you don't already know. Dawson took over behind a marginally successful guy. I worked for him when he was the S4. He was okay as the S4. He did his job but was full of 2D ACR war stories and a control freak. His First Sergeant was out of place. He only cared about himself and was not worth a shit. Troops did not get fed, he got lost, fuel did not make it forward, he was AWOL from the border and he could not spell PT Test if you spotted him 2 of the 3 "T's," opined Upton. "Dawson gave him every chance. He had to go and the Regimental Commanding Officer relieved him. Don't let Dawson shit you. It takes the Regimental Commanding Officer to relieve a First Sergeant. If you don't get caught porking the Squadron Commander's cocker spaniel at the flag pole you ain't going to get relieved. Does anyone know how tight you are with the Regimental Commanding Officer?" Upton concluded.

"No one is tight enough with the Regimental Commanding Officer not to get fired. He would fire his momma if she stood between him and his first star. We know each other professionally, not personally. We are not tight. He may, at best, think I am good enough to turn G Troop around and you know, by God, he's right. How do I know? Because there ain't shit wrong with G Troop some good news can't fix," Martin said smiling.

"Do think Smokin Joe will get a star?" Bodenham asked.

"By getting this assignment, the star is his to lose," Upton said. "It will take a major screw up not to get it. Only the Cav guys destined to get a star get the Germany regiments."

"How are the units at gunnery?" Martin asked.

Bodenham leaned forward saying, "We think we are very good, I am not so sure I agree. The gunnery we got at Knox from you guys on the M60A1

77

was twice as tough as we got from the NET Team for the M1. The first big test will be in May when we go to Graf to do graded gunnery."

"Cav units do not seem to expect that much out of gunnery. It seems to me they treat it like a vacation from the border and feel it has no relation to their version of reality - which is the border," said Upton.

"What do you think, Lieutenant Miles? You are an old Marine. What is the Devil Dog outlook?" Martin asked.

"We are going to get our asses handed to us at Level I gunnery. In the Corps, everyone learns to fire their rifle in the same manner. Every Marine is a rifleman first. Everyone snaps in and practices for a full week before firing a live round. Here, we never seem to take the time to concentrate on a clear objective before rushing to the next event. People here have got the 'big head.' I just hope the Russians are just as screwed up as we are."

"Thank you, future Chairman of the Joint Chiefs," Upton said. "Are you suitably depressed yet, 'Dr. Sabot'?" he asked the only enlisted man present.

"Not at all, I am just happy you guys have learned your lessons so well and have developed so much as officers. It takes balls to know and admit your outfit is not as good as it thinks it is. The challenge will be to get it up to speed. Looking at the schedule, G Troop is definitely behind the power curve for training time. My challenge is to find the time to train on gunnery with the Troop FTX and the Squadron maneuver, followed by the Border, followed by Reforger, followed by the Border, concurrently with Wildflecken, followed by the Border, followed by Grafenwohr, followed by the Border, followed by Bradley Transition. We are some busy little beavers, all of us, but there must be some way to adequately train soldiers to fire the tanks and Bradleys" Martin concluded. With that, the group adjourned to the BOQ for a last drink and called it a night.

Arising to his alarm at 0300, Martin quickly dressed had a Coke and a Marlborough to review the plan of the day. This done, he resolved to walk through the town of Bad Kissingen to Daley Barracks. He knew full well the way around the town on the Ostring and the Nordring was quicker in a vehicle but he wanted to see the town again and had already discovered some short cuts on the tourist map and the military map Ramos had given him.

The Kurheim, or hotels with spas district lay below the BOQ. As usual, the town was spotlessly clean. He knew from long service in Germany that each citizen and by inference, each store owner, was responsible for the appearance of the street and sidewalk in front of their abode or business. He quickly walked through the area of hotels with their stylish lobbies and ornate furniture. Their efficient night clerks, doormen, and porters did not even give him a glance. All of the bars were long since closed. There were no hookers walking the street, why should they be, they had a state run whore house to ply their wares. There were no street people, no human flotsam and jetsam left by a capitalist tidal wave. It was a bare and somewhat antiseptic view of life.

The buildings were very nice and very solid. It looked to be a much cleaner town than either Mainz or Wiesbaden. He wondered how it had fared during WWII. He knew Mainz had been governed by fanatical Nazis suffering almost total destruction in house to house fighting with the Hitler Youth and Home Guard. In almost no time, he was through both the Kurheim district, the shopping area and was walking through the residential area leading to the kaserne. It was 0400. About a mile from the kaserne, walking up the long hill, he began to see heavy traffic with the US plates issued by US Army Europe whizzing by him enroute to post. Those shit heads will think I am psychic he thought. If they only knew how dumb he was about alerts. He had yet to even see the local alert area, let alone the Border area.

"Hey, First Sergeant, get in!" First Lieutenant Brown said as he stopped his BMW at the curb. "Man you are psychic. We are having a damn alert! How did you know?" Brown exclaimed.

"Lieutenant, I am a one legged man in an ass kicking contest on my first alert in this outfit," Martin said.

"Captain Dawson called and told me to tell you to lead the troop out to the local alert area. His wife is terribly ill this morning. He will come out to the alert area when he can get her feeling better. His driver will go out to his house to pick him up so he will come straight out there. Her car is also acting up. I will be taking the M577, the Command Post out. You take the troop out to the RP (Release Point) and go back to get breakfast to bring it out to the field. We will do assembly area activities, check load plans and stuff like that. We will also get a logistics report once we get there, but all of the Platoon Sergeants know what to do. You just need to get us out there, okay?" Brown stated.

"I got it, Lieutenant Brown, nothing to it," Martin said while thinking, *great, just damn great.*

"I see you took your time and cleaned out your car," Martin laughed seeing the pile of fast food wrappers, soda cans, and Chinese takeout boxes everywhere on the floor. "Your life is about like mine, pedal to the metal," he said.

Lieutenant Brown said, "Since I got here from Third Squadron, it has been non-stop with people getting fired, Lieutenants crossing the border and getting relieved, First Sergeant relieved. It is great training but hard on the social life. I sure have not had time to clear out my car, but I am going to get to it this weekend, First Sergeant," screaming out the last word as if at West Point and bracing as a cadet.

"See that you do, ELL TEE," Martin said smiling as they pulled up at the troop.

Martin stood outside for a moment and looked at the anthill of activity and listening to the cacophony of noise coming out of the barracks jointly occupied with E Troop. Alerts in Germany were brutal. Now, the M1 had three machine guns rather than the two of the M60 series tank and there were two duffel bags per man to be lugged and of course the clock was ticking.

Okay, let's work it backwards before we charge the whole Sioux nation he thought - Fuel, Green, Ammo, Green, probably not going to upload: machinegun ammo, TOW and Dragon missiles or mortars; maps were on board, orders will come later, food and water-have supply bring out later-better yet, have supply stay here and pick it up, go get your gear, find Tom, figure out the route to the LTA, assemble troop, move out. The words of his mentor, Sergeant First Class Werner Wienman's words in his German accent came to mind, "If it vas easy do you tink the Ahaamy would have made you a Staff Sergeant to command three men?" Thank you Herman the German, Sugar Bear Davis, Grim Reaper Thrift, Harvey the Hun Vick, and all you great old guys for all of your teachings and patience.

CHAPTER 5 – SPURS FOR THE NEWBIES

Spur qualification requires all aspirants to satisfy the following requirements to be awarded Spurs: Border Qualified; Qualified Sharp Shooter on assigned weapons; Tactically Proficient via exercises; No UCMJ; Recommended by his chain of command. Excerpt Squadron & Troop SOP, Spur Qualification.

Martin decided not to try to micro-manage the alert but to join in the effort making small corrections to help the troops get through it. It was obvious they were not capable of a cohesive effort that an organized rehearsal would have produced but that would soon change.

His own combat crew, PFC Staunton arrived at his office motivated but harried. "I got the vehicle outside, First Sergeant, and I got the trailer."

"Okay Tom, stand by," Martin said. "Come with me to the arms room."

Arriving at the arms room, Martin asked, "Armorer, have you started issuing the crew served weapons yet?"

"Some of them, First Sergeant," Specialist Betts replied.

"Well, stop issuing them. Issue personal weapons only along with M60s for the scouts. Have the tank, scout and mortar crews sign for their machineguns. My driver and I will then load them in my trailer and jeep and deliver them to the motor pool. We will take scout weapons first, and then tank and mortars last. Maintenance can get their own up there with the motor sergeant's jeep. Tell everyone the key points are vehicle prep, line up and prepare to fire followed by commo checks. Now what did I just tell you? Repeat it back."

Specialist Betts gave it right back to him verbatim. "Damn, Betts, maybe we will have to send you to OCS," Martin said patting him on the back.

"Let's go get our gear to the vehicle, Tom," Martin said.

"I'll get our stuff, First Sergeant," Staunton volunteered.

"No, Tom, I hump my own shit. Never, ever hump my gear. You are my driver, not my orderly. I want to feel the pain of the alert as much as any private. It will help later when we are sorting out who did what and why. But you can put it away once I hump it up the stairs. If we run out of room for weapons we will make two trips. No need to be in a hurry, they will be busy getting the vehicles ready to move," Martin stated and then added, "I need to go to supply."

"You'd better go there," Staunton said adding, "They are all screwed up."

Contrary to his driver's statement, Martin found the supply room an eye of calm in the alert storm. "Sergeant Webster, it is good to have a man who can keep his head when all around him are losing theirs," Martin said. "This is my first alert. I want you to pick up the A Breakfast if it is available and the C rations for the noon meal if they are available. Call me on the radio and I will tell you where to meet me. How many folks do you need to help?"

"None, First Sergeant. Three of the six platoons already sent me a man and I have four guys who have turned in their field gear who can help, so we will cheat a little. I am ready to play. I know you said you did not want to hear any gossip about the old First Sergeant, but he would not let me play logistics. He stayed back in the rear area with the other First Sergeants and the Sergeant Major," Webster said with some indignation. Martin listened to this statement without comment but was very pleased this great NCO knew he was not going to be hanging around in the rear by the stove.

"Webster, you look like a dream come true. Let's have a look at you, big knife, little knife, Leatherman, first aid pouch upside down, taped dog tags, compass, map case, secure communications key, and a portable radio for your supply truck. Shit, you are ready for war trooper. One thing, clear the barracks by picking up the big trash, emptying the trash cans, locking the rooms and set the rear detachment watch for me. Thanks. You got anything else for me?" Martin asked.

"Just one thing, First Sergeant. Be careful you don't do so much that the officers stack arms on you," Webster said taking a drink of coffee to preclude saying more.

"Are you sure you aren't a Ranger, Webster?" asked Martin.

Webster grew at least an inch of height saying proudly, "No, First Sergeant, I've got bad knees but I wish I was a Ranger. It will never happen."

"One more thing Staff Sergeant Webster, make sure you and PFC McMasters are at the critique. Keep an eye on everything and participate as we try to figure out who shot John after this is over," Martin said.

McMasters had to speak or bust and when he did he stuttered mightily, "Wwwwhat for you want me there Ffffirst Ssssergeant?"

Martin replied, "Well McMasters, your first name is what?"

"Billy Jean, but everybody calls me BJ," he replied with no trace of a stutter.

"Any man that already has the supply truck down here, with it loaded and drinking coffee, obviously has a lot to teach the tread heads. You are probably a Texan aren't you? From down near the border most likely. Where is it Tex?" he asked smiling.

"From near Corpus, First Sergeant," BJ stated.

"My ass BJ, you ain't from Corpus. You are too damn country. Where exactly?"

Putting his head down to concentrate, BJ manfully replied, "Fffrom Fffalfurias, Fffirst Sergeant."

"No shit, Falfurrias, King Ranch and all. Do you know the Hornsby family? Joe was a big time football star and his sister Crystal is a Majorette or Rangerette, five foot two eyes of blue and a real Texas heartbreaker?" asked Martin.

With no trace of a stutter BJ answered, "Yeah I know 'em and they are good people."

Knowing BJ had obviously been recently reduced in rank as the PFC stripe did not match his aging face and balding head, Martin knew BJ could use a boost so he said, "I think they are in good company with you and even though you are coming around again, most likely, you are good people too BJ. I want to hear your story BJ, but not right now, okay?"

"Okay, First Sergeant, I got another 14 months to tell it to you," BJ replied.

As he was walking from the Supply room BJ called, "Hey, First Sergeant?" causing Martin to turn and face him. BJ hung his head and scuffed his foot as he asked, "How you know so much about me, Texas and all?"

"Hell, BJ, you know there are only two kinds of people, those that are Texans and those that want to be," Martin said.

Thinking as he walked away, I hope the Command Sergeant Major does not see that Texas Longhorn belt buckle and that brown belt on old BJ before I can get that habit changed in the troop. BJ might be fat, bald, a smoker, drinker, and a whore chaser but he probably never fell out of a run and he was proud to be the front road guard. Martin sensed BJ's innate worth when as a new First Sergeant days before he hinted to BJ might not be up to the challenge of being the front road guard for long runs. His answer was classic, "First Sergeant, I am the front road guard. When I fall out or can't run, take the sign and the light from me as I fall over into the damn gutter, until then let me do it, okay?"

Martin did not know BJ's full story then or as yet, but he trusted the crusty old bastard and sensed he was a worthy soldier, warts and all.

Gear to the vehicle, Martin supervised the loading of the tank machine guns but noticed the mass of scout M2 Heavy Barrel guns in the trailer. It prompted him to ask, "Which tank platoon didn't choose to use our machine gun taxi service Tom? Maldanado I'll bet."

"How did you know First Sergeant?" Staunton said, adding, "He almost took my head off when I told him."

"The Drill Sergeant badge is a dead giveaway Tom. Most Drill Sergeants agree with Napoleon even though they never read what he said about making soldiers, "Poverty, privation and misery are the school of the soldier.""

"What do you say, First Sergeant?" Staunton asked.

"Wasted effort is the enemy of speed during an alert, Tom," Martin said. "Let's get these weapons to the track park. We'll go by the maintenance shop on the way."

A stop by the maintenance shop revealed Sergeant First Class Wintergreen had his outfit packing and chalking the word "destroyed" on a scout track missing a final drive assembly.

"Line up side by side so we do not clog the road way, Sergeant Wintergreen. As I bring the tracks by, fall in the rear of the Mortar Platoon. Do you know where to go in the LTA, Chief?" Martin asked.

"Nope, never been there," Wintergreen said.

"More good news," the First Sergeant said laughing. *Run, Trip, Fall was not an accident here, it was a damn institution.*

Once at the track park, PFC Staunton drove down the track line to issue weapons. The entire squadron less the unit at the border and those down for service, some 250 plus vehicles were all in the process of starting their engines, conducting preparation for combat checks and preparing to move. The noise was deafening, the smoke was thick and the smell would have been unbearable for an airborne or light infantry soldier. The tankers were the happiest men in the unit. Now the rest of the Squadron's soldiers were sharing their daily lot. They were dirty, deaf, smelly, and were jammed in 250,000 square feet or so of space with a high likelihood of getting squashed by a moving tank.

Martin was very pleasantly surprised to see the troop was about 90% ready to move with all vehicles running. All gear was on board, stowed and prepare to fire checks were being made. As the last of the automatic weapons disappeared from his trailer and vehicle, a very tall and powerfully built officer loomed up out of the darkness. His every move showed his athleticism and competence. Easily the biggest man in the unit, Major Oliver Braxton Bragg, had arrived.

The world was safe for democracy, Martin thought. The Squadron Executive Officer was here and on the job.

Saluting the Major with snap, Martin gave the greeting of the day, "Eaglehorse, Sir!"

The Squadron Executive Officer returned the salute just as smartly saying, "It is good to see a First Sergeant in the track park. Where is Captain Dawson? When can you move?"

Martin replied, "Sir, the Executive Officer and I are taking the troop to the LTA. The Commander's wife is deathly ill and he will join us there. I can move in ten minutes or less."

"It is a hell of a note when the new guy is ready to move ahead of the rest of the people who have been here for awhile. Start moving as soon as you can. Stop at the stop sign by the Chapel. Wait for the MPs and the German Police, the Polizei, to arrive at the front gate. Move when they get there. Stay off of the airstrip. Do not drive across the airstrip, do not drive on the airstrip. Move directly to your alert positions without stopping. Conduct prepare to fire checks, work on load plans and conduct crew drills with the NCOs giving classes. Do not draw ammo from the ASP; do not break into the machine gun ammunition in the shipping containers behind the tank line. Only the Operations Officer, me, or the Squadron Commander will visit your troop and can release you to return to the kaserne. Questions?"

"None, Sir," Martin replied.

"Good to have you with us. Come and see me as soon as you can. Upton says you are a good man, they need you. One more thing. Are you planning on coming back for Class I?" he asked with a trace of angst.

Martin smiled and said, "Sir, when G Troop is in the field, that is where I will be. The supply sergeant is picking up breakfast and one C Ration meal and bringing it forward with the supply room. He will then join the field trains. I will maintain the troop combat trains one hill behind the unit or further as directed."

"That's good to hear. Some First Sergeants can't spell forward," said Bragg with a smile.

As he turned back to his main task of leading the troop, Martin went to Sergeant First Class Jackson's tank with his map. Mounting the M1, Martin directed him, "So show me the LTA, Vic."

Vic started out yapping, obviously happy to be going to the field and very happy he was not leading the unit. "Gonna' be a long day for you ain't it, First Sergeant? Here we are, this is the gate to the kaserne. Go out the gate, turn left, go straight on out, turn up this hill. You will pass the wash rack on your left. When you get to this clearing, there will be the Hotel Soiftel on your right, visible over the trees. Bear to the left and stay on the large paved road. The airfield is on your right but it is way too foggy to see it. The release point for the troop to go to their positions is right past the airfield at the entrance to the TCPC course (Tank Crew Proficiency Course). Everyone should know where to go once you get them to the LTA."

"Thanks, Vic," Martin said. As an afterthought, he turned back to Jackson asking him, "Do all of the leaders know not to drive on the airstrip?"

"They do, damn right they do," Vic stated.

"Thanks, Vic, everything is okay and we will make it just fine. If I get hosed up, I will just stop the action until I can figure out my next move," Martin said.

"Yeah right, you will go high diddle, right up the middle and ask forgiveness later," laughed Jackson.

Martin's next stop was the command post. Lieutenant Brown had established communications with all of the platoons, had received all of their reports and his charts were in a semblance of order. He, too, was trying to make it all happen and was on his first alert in the unit. He gave Martin a somewhat sheepish smile saying, "Am I dumping on you, First Sergeant?"

Martin answered with a smile, "Executive Officer, my career is made. Yours is just starting. Anytime you can blame the little shit on me, go ahead. You keep doing your part. Once we get out there, we will travel around and do a PCI on everyone out there, together. That way we will have one standard for future ops and we will see our shortcomings together."

The scout platoon tracks of the troop began to move toward the gate and Martin proceeded to the Chapel stop sign. Glad to see his radios all worked,

85

Martin made a communications check with the platoon leaders. Shortly after he completed this check, the MPs and local police arrived and he moved the column forward. Martin was gratified to see the German Police guide the column past the airfield. He then took it on to the tank training course and pulled to the side. He announced to the leaders they were now past the release point and told them to proceed to their platoon areas and conduct training. He told them to take any further orders from the Executive Officer. He then called Staff Sergeant Webster to tell him where to bring the food. Martin reflected on the morning and thought it had gone far better than he expected for a maiden effort. He was wrong.

Captain Dawson arrived as the last of breakfast was being served. He hastily ate a bacon and scrambled egg sandwich while the First Sergeant and Executive Officer filled him on the conduct of the alert up to that point. Captain Dawson issued some instructions and made his way to report to Lieutenant Colonel Covington.

Other than dropping his beautiful and painstakingly constructed leader's notebook in the mud, Martin was having a good morning. As the NCOs watched him pick it up, they did not know for sure what to do. "So much for me getting into the Sergeant Morales Club, eh guys?" They all laughed uproariously.

The Sergeant Morales Club was an exclusive group sponsored by the USAREUR commander in the memory of the great NCOs who had raised him as a young officer. It was a good way to inspire NCOs to develop the best leadership traits possible. The NCOs of the units who personified leadership were selected by their First Sergeants and Command Sergeants Major. They then appeared before a series of boards subjected to minute scrutiny under the baleful eyes of Brigade, Division and Corps Command Sergeants Major. The survivors of the minute uniform inspection, about 50%, were then asked questions on their knowledge of skills, field craft and most of all, demonstrated a detailed knowledge on the contents of their leader's notebook. Numbers ruled with about 15% being selected.

The NCOs knew that they liked their new First Sergeant but they also knew there was no way he was Sergeant Morales material, he had too much sand in his craw for the Command Sergeants Major of the world. They also respected his ability to laugh off messing up a pretty notebook, a work of art, by getting it muddy and wiping it off with a towel in such a casual manner. "Now you jokers make sure your leader's notebook has some mud on it so I won't feel like such a klutz. And if you don't have one, have one before next Wednesday. You know I believe the Morales Club members are great NCOs, I just don't think much of the process that selects them."

As this message was concluding and the pre-combat inspection was about to begin, Captain Dawson returned with a long face. "The Squadron Commander said G Troop drove across the air strip with tanks. We have to go clean the mud off the air strip, right now. Why did you not tell everyone not to drive across the air strip, First Sergeant? You were in charge."

As Sergeant First Class Jackson and First Lieutenant Brown started to speak, Martin held up his hand to silence them, "I am responsible Captain Dawson. I will fix the problem." Martin then organized a detail to sweep the airfield, sent the supply truck to the area with brooms and went there to see which of his elements had driven across the airfield. He knew he had led the troop past the airfield to preclude such an occurrence. Someone has to be in charge and he was not going to snivel about who was wrong. As he suspected, Sergeant First Class Maldanado's platoon had become disoriented in the fog, drove in a circle on their way to their positions and had driven across the airfield, with Captain Dawson's tank crew driving nearly the length of the small strip. Other than the mud, there was no damage to the airstrip beyond the perception that G Troop could not follow orders. Martin started to use Lieutenant Colonel Covington's own words of "Perfection is not a reasonable standard," when the Squadron Commander came to oversee the cleanup, but decided against it. Martin knew he was a newbie and he needed to shut up and take it.

"First Sergeant, did the Executive Officer not tell you about the prohibition of no tanks on the airfield?"

"Yes, Sir, he did. No excuse, Sir," said Martin.

"If this airfield would have been damaged, your future in this squadron would be over right now. Do you understand that much First Sergeant?" snapped Covington.

"Yes, Sir," said Martin.

"Remember it. Your Commander's wife was ill. He trusted you to do the right things at the right time. Set an example or I will make you the example. That is all," dismissing Martin.

The Squadron Executive Officer motioned Martin to come to his vehicle when the Squadron Commander was finished. Martin walked to his vehicle, saluted, and reported.

Major Bragg gave him a wry smile, shook his head and asked, "Why did you take that ass chewing and not rat out your Executive Officer? I distinctly heard you turn over the troop to him after arrival. Those dumb shits drove across the air strip 25 minutes after that."

"Hey, Sir, you know the deal, we have to take care of the younguns'. I probably have at least one more serious offense before I get fired," Martin said.

"Do you want me to square it away with the Squadron Commander, First Sergeant?" asked Bragg.

"Did McCall know the truth and was he part of the fact finding?" asked Martin.

"Yes, but he passed," said Bragg.

87

"Well, it is always good to know where one stands with the power structure. I didn't think he had any balls," said Martin with a smile.

"Come to see me tonight when you get done," Bragg said.

Martin moved back from his leaning position on the jeep, saluted and said, "WILCO, Sir." He then moved to the airstrip, got a broom and started helping the detail pick up the mud. It was a long process but with lots of extra brooms, a snow shovel and the supply trailer, it went quickly. Martin was surprised to see the one of the NBC vehicles show up with a power pump and begin to hose off the runway with the water it carried on board. What a novel way to speed up the operation.

His surprise turned to respect as he saw his resident Wildman, Staff Sergeant Webster, running the hose with BJ McMasters driving the rig. "BJ, what the hell?" Martin asked.

"The supply room will be goddammed if you are sweeping no damn runway, First Sergeant. Your jeep is here. Go check on something, will you? We got this shit. Me and Sergeant Webster also lead your maneuver damage control team and this is maneuver damage. It may not be kamerade's damage but it is maneuver," BJ said without a trace of a stutter.

"Okay, BJ, you got it. See ya' in the rear," Martin said as he walked away.

"Let's go to the command track, Tom, and see how the PCI is coming along," he said to his driver. Sergeant First Class Maldanado was frantically waving at him and the driver looked questioningly at Martin. "Go on over there Tom," Martin said.

"First Sergeant, I am sorry. My lead tank got lost in the fog. I got me and my wing man stopped, but the Lieutenant, he is out here for the first time and his helmet connection cord came loose and he did not respond."

"Shit happens, Maldanado. The teaching point is for the Lieutenant to learn to listen to his crew. He and his crew must understand their Lieutenant is enrolled in the School of the Soldier and they are the instructors until he gets his shit together. It is okay to for a PFC to lightly hit him with a flag stick to get his attention. Today it is the airfield, next week it might be a minefield. Make sure those turds know what is expected of them." Martin said.

"Turds, First Sergeant?" questioned Maldanado.

"TURD is an acronym. It stands for Troopers Under Rapid Development for the 85% that are worth a shit and it means Trooper Under Rapid Deterioration for the 15% getting chaptered out of the Army for poor performance. You have not heard me cuss these kids yet and I suspect you never will. Mass ass-chewing is counterproductive. Did one ever do anything for you, Maldanado?" asked Martin.

"No, First Sergeant, never did, I just tuned it out."

"No shit, we all do."

"When we do the critique of the alert, think through the format we used to use for tank gunnery and particularly the one you were used to when you worked for Vilseck in the late 1970's. It is important for the troops to tell us what they saw and for us to get them to tell us what we all need to do to change. If we have a one way conversation it might as well be a mass chewing out with a smile for all they will learn. I want to get them on the right side and to make certain they have a stake in the outcome," Martin said.

"Do you think we can win, First Sergeant?" asked Maldanado.

"You mean against the East Germans and the Russians if the Cold War goes hot?" Martin asked.

"Yeah, the Soviet hordes," Maldanado said smiling.

"The real question is not can we win, but are they coming. My answer is, no, they are not coming. Three big reasons: 1. We are becoming alike. During WWII Molotov told Eddie Rickenbacker, the famous WWI pilot, our two systems were converging, or they would become more capitalist and we would become more socialist. I know, your face tells me you think I am some Commie Pinko fag Democrat, but those are the words of one of their smartest political people, a war hero. 2. There would not be a clear winner. They lost twice as many killed at Stalingrad, one battle, than we did in the whole war, six million people. We have quality, they have quantity. They know it and we know it. The Russians never choose to fight if the odds are not on their side. Unlike us, their leaders were in desperate fights in WW II. Reagan made training films. 3. We are no threat to them and they know it. Capability is not intention and they usually get what they want from us without a fight. Having said that, in two to three years, we will stomp the shit out of them, quantity aside. Their tanks are junk. The M1, the Bradley and the Apache along with the F-15, F-16 and A-10 will all come on strong. The new version of doctrine will mature past Close Combat Heavy and we will learn to maneuver against their weakness. Soon, information will be the key combat multiplier because we will own the night. A modern Cav Troop will be able to destroy a Soviet Battalion in minutes before the Russians can even see us in open terrain. If, and it is a big if, we can get to our second set of ammunition supplies, now, they will not win the war. I do not look forward to fighting the Russians. They are some terrible bad-asses amigo. Do I think I would personally live through a war with them, right now, no, I do not."

"I am surprised you know all of that shit. I never heard an NCO explain it like before," Maldanado said.

"Keep all of that Henry Kissinger shit to yourself big Sarge. As far as the soldiers are concerned, we will kill them by the bushel and we will win," Martin said as he drove to the next position.

The alert ended early. The entire troop was sitting in the hallway. The Cdr, First Sergeant and Executive Officer were conducting a critique of the alert. Martin was not surprised to see Major Bragg join them in the hallway for the soldier critique of the alert. Martin handed him a Diet Coke from a cooler as he arrived. Bragg was extremely happy to see the day's exercise being dissected in each of its phases by the Troop Commander and the First Sergeant.

The First Sergeant led off each phase by explaining what he had seen from his position and what his personal mistakes were during the alert. The candor was refreshing. Bragg knew it was deliberate. It was an Armor tradition dating back to George Patton and 2d Armored Division. Patton started his critiques in WW II by listing his mistakes first, in front of the field grade officers, in open forum. The First Sergeant's willingness to list his errors first, clearly showed the soldiers improvement was paramount. There was no right answer. Egos did not count and were not welcome.

Bragg wished he had written down the opening statement, "We are here to get better. Everybody's opinion counts in this discussion. A Private figured out how to make the Bocage Cutter to get us off of the dime during the Normandy invasion. Every time we do something we are going to talk through how it could have been better and how we are going to do it the next time. This is a combat game show and it is called 'You Bet Your Ass'."

The feedback from the troops filled pages of the chart paper. Every point, either wrong or right, produced a future course of action for future operations to either maintain, or change. He also noticed the soldiers were relaxed with boots off, sitting on the floor, drinking a beer or other beverage of their choice. It looked more like a Super Bowl party than a critique. Soldiers kept their seats when commenting but discipline was intact and military courtesy observed even though the discussion was at times very spirited. None of the other units had bothered to conduct such a review. Major Bragg was enjoying himself. Martin then flipped back to the recommendation page and went over every change, explaining each and what would happen if there was another alert that very night. At the end, Martin looked at him as if to ask if he wanted to speak. He nodded in the affirmative.

Stepping forward, Major Bragg immediately said, waving to the troops to remain seated, "Keep your seats. This is great to see the Gators working through the problems of the alert. Your First Sergeant is right to quote Eisenhower to you, so I will too. 'Once the soldier knows what he is supposed to and is taught how to do it, it will get done.' You guys are on the right track. Keep it up."

Captain Dawson then closed the session by stating, "Normal formation time for PT in the morning. I need to see all of the leadership in my office after this meeting to discuss the FTX and Reforger preparation. We all learned from the alert. The changes in our Troop SOP will be made in writing and they are all in effect as of now by verbal order. Thanks for your input. Good job. Fall Out.'

"First Sergeant, I want to see you in my office first, so Platoon Leaders get any other business done before you come down stairs, First Sergeant, shall we go?" Dawson asked while pointing the way.

On arrival at his office, Dawson closed the door and laughed, clouting his First Sergeant on the shoulder. "Damn, that was great. They are part of the solution. We are not going to have an alert anytime soon. That was only for the record. Covington is not fond of alerts. There is too much that can go wrong. He does not like exposing himself to failure when he does not have to do so. There is a lot that can go wrong with a Squadron alert on city streets. Great job overall. The Squadron Commander knows by now you covered for Brown and that your Sergeant Major screwed you. Bragg told him. Bragg loves what we are doing. Let me see your map of the border and the maneuver rights area where we are going for the FTX. Show the guys in now," Dawson concluded.

Martin opened the door and the leadership trooped into the office and found chairs. They brought chairs from the First Sergeant's office and Martin rolled in his own. Dawson reviewed the objectives of the upcoming maneuver stating it would begin with a troop alert but cautioned the group to keep that close hold. He reviewed the upcoming schedule to make certain the group knew they would be going to the Border area right after Thanksgiving and would remain there through Christmas returning before New Year's Eve. Dawson was very explicit as he made certain the Border reconnaissance by the First Sergeant and the 1st Platoon leader would take place on Saturday. Martin added they would be going to the first tactical assembly area on the tour as well.

Dawson then took this opportunity to remind everyone that the First Sergeant would be moving the troop tactically from the kaserne at every opportunity. Officers would accompany the Commanding Officer in an M-113 with sleeping bags departing on Sunday evening so that they could spend the day reviewing the maneuver area and rehearsing tactics. G Troop would be acting as the OPFOR (Opposition Force) for the Squadron FTX and would operate against each of the Cavalry troops and then against the Squadron minus and then finally, as part of the squadron before returning to home station.

Martin was gaining an appreciation for the pace of the unit just from hearing what was supposed to happen. Hell, he did not need an apartment, just two sleeping bags to rotate them through the cleaners.

After he made the finishing touches on his quick reference border map book, it was time to go to the BOQ for a quick meal and bed. The day was gone in a blur. Martin felt as if he had been in the unit for a year rather than three days.

Friday was a day of planning for the unit. Everything was packed for the upcoming trip to the field to enable an early morning departure. The entire day was spent in the effort. Captain Dawson would depart late on Sunday evening with the officers for the maneuver area and First Sergeant Martin would road march the unit about 15 miles to an assigned assembly area near Schweinfurt, Germany.

91

One of the consequences of losing a war for Germany was to suffer the indignity of having foreign troops stationed on their native soil, the partition of the nation, and maneuvers being held routinely. However, it was becoming increasingly difficult to see who had won the war as the American Army routinely bent over backwards to be the guests of West Germany, rather than its conquerors.

When the officers complained about the emphasis on respecting the property rights of the German civil population on the upcoming exercise, Martin pointed out to them why it had to be. "Now all of you gentlemen have been to college. You have studied the history of the world. Most of you had Latin in high school, complete with study on Julius Caesar. He was smart enough to know he did not have enough troops to fight all of the nations Rome conquered, all of the time. He made them allies and prospered."

"Churchill said it well, 'The Germans are either groveling at your feet or clawing at your throat.' It is a lot easier to cultivate them as their allies than it is to fight their asses every twenty years. Actions speak louder than words when troops are garrisoned in a nation. Words are for the politicians. The daily conduct of garrison troops is all that counts with the people being occupied. Rape, plunder, and pillage are great sport for the winner, particularly for those just passing through. Leaders that want a secure rear area with potentially firm allies, control their troops."

Martin got up early and walked to the kaserne on Saturday. He was comfortable with the route by now and enjoyed the walk. He was pleasantly surprised to see Ramos already there.

"Hey, Top, how 'bout we go to the Border to eat breakfast? I know this good backerei where we can get some cold cuts, rolls and sweet rolls and then go to OP Tennessee to eat breakfast."

Martin replied, "That will be great Gil, let me go get my stuff. I want my binoculars, map and boots in case we get into the mud." Retrieving his gear from where he had packed it and his maps, Martin soon reappeared and got into the nice looking Volkswagen that Ramos was driving.

Ramos proudly announced, "Don't worry about nothin', First Sergeant. This is a combat Bee Double You."

"Look Ramos, I do not want to spend the entire day at the Border, what is your plan?" Martin asked.

"We go the way we take the tanks first. We stop in Bad Neustadt for the chow, drive by Camp Lee and go to the OP to eat breakfast. Then we go down the south trace to the maneuver rights area we go to next week. After we find the Initial assembly area where we meet the CO, then we go back to BK, backwards of the road out. My English is good, no?" Ramos said with a big smile.

"Your English is great Gilberto, just great. Tell me everything, I am a sponge," Martin said with a smile.

92

"Did you queet smoking, First Sergeant?" Ramos asked.

"No, some folks do not like you smoking in their car," Martin replied.

"Sheet, give me one please, First Sergeant," Ramos replied, "I am the boss of my house and I do as I please. That is why I married a Korean, she don't give me no shit, but I treat her okay."

"Yeah, I bet you do or she will beat your ass when you are asleep," Martin replied.

"Oh, you know her too, huh?" Ramos said and both men laughed heartily.

Martin knew Ramos took care of his family like the treasures they were for him. "How did those PRs take to it when you brought a Korean girl home?" Martin asked.

"They ain't happy but Puerto Rican people do not look at race like, like..." Ramos sputtered.

"Gringos?" Martin offered.

"Si, Gringos," Ramos said with a broad smile accepting the input. He continued, "At home race is mixed up. Children, some come out black with an Afro, some Spanish. A little Korean ain't much of a stretch, besides, they don't pay my bills. I don't go back anyhow. I gonna' end up at some post in the states. I'll not go back to Puerto Rico. There is nothing there for me. We ain't got shit. I am best off in the whole family as a Staff Sergeant. I figure I do my twenty, get out, get a little business, go fishing, and hang out with the homies and my kids. I go back for visits."

As they drove, Martin followed the route on his military map. Ramos stopped frequently to describe choke points, scenes of past accidents and to give the new First Sergeant cautions about vehicle movement. It was at one of these intersections, Ramos stated, "That road to the right, leads to the border and comes out ten miles south of Observation Point Tennessee. It is almost all back roads and farm trails. It works real well for scouts, but tanks would have some issues with bridges. This highway we are on, B19, is a death trap if the Russians attacked with fighter jets and HIND helicopters while we were moving forward. The plan is bullsheet anyhow. We fight that way and we get our asses kicked for sure. They are just for show. I been all over up here, it is good maneuver country. We will kick everybody's ass if we are OP-FOR for Stallion Stakes (title of company level maneuvers)." With a brief pause at a gravel pit, Ramos described the area as the unit maintenance collection point designated by the Ground Defense Plan or GDP for the unit before moving on to the next large town on their route.

"Here in Bad Neustadt, make sure you stay to the left at this intersection and be prepared to change to the center lane about a mile ahead. This is the last town before we turn off to Camp Lee or Wollbach. Webster lives here and his wife works in the family business, a grocery store."

As the road continued east, the mist and fog were lifting from the countryside. The hills began to take on a gentler shape and Martin could see the country funneling down ahead to the centuries old high speed invasion route near Mellrichstadt.

"This is the road to the Border Camp. We don't want to go in there today. They will want to show you everything and take up all of our time with bull shit, damn tank company. They don't know sheet about the border anyhow," Ramos said, dismissively with the haughtiness of scouts everywhere for tankers. "Oh, oh, you was a tanker, First Sergeant. I did not mean you," Ramos said blushing under his tanned Spanish complexion.

"The hell you didn't, Ramos. You think I can't read a map, call for fire, recon a route, classify a bridge or remember where I just came from any better than any other tanker. I will have you know I am not a DAT (Dumb Ass Tanker). I am qualified on the M1 and the M3 and that makes me an EDAT," Martin said.

"First Sergeant," Ramos said respectfully, concentrating on driving, "What is an EDAT?"

"An EDAT my leetle scout friend, is an Electronic Dumb Ass Tanker," Martin laughed. "Our challenge, Gilberto, is to make our average tanker into as much of a scout as we can through classes, Spur Ride Military Stakes Training and lots of Border Patrols," said Martin.

As they drove to the gate of the border camp, Ramos pulled into the makeshift POV lot across the street and pointed out the salient features of the facility to Martin. As he did so, he conducted a running commentary of what usually went wrong and how to avoid various pitfalls and snares associated with Border duty.

As Martin knew it would, the information was coming to him in the manner of a man drinking from a fire hose. The briefing, Ramos style, was very, very informative. Martin was building his analysis method for conquering the border as that was the second of his challenges from the Regimental Commanding Officer. Ramos pointed out the gravel pit just behind the Border Camp. As he began to drive the road behind the camp that led back to the highway, Martin asked him to measure the distance the road covered from the camp. "PT test run route, huh, First Sergeant?" Ramos asked.

"Yes," replied Martin.

"First Sergeant, it is all downhill."

"Too Bad Gilberto. Those out of shape assholes at Regimental HQs that run our asses into the ground with no time for PT will just have to get over it, won't they?" Martin replied testily.

"This is a nice little town, Mellrichstadt. We go into the bakery here and get our stuff," Ramos said pulling into the parking lot of the German Bakery and delicatessen. The two NCOs loaded up on rolls, cold cuts and four German Cokes as well as some cheese and mustard in a tube.

As they were passing through the center of town, Martin noticed a curve in the road that led over a bridge spanning a small creek. He told Ramos, "That looks like a good spot to put a vehicle into that creek."

Ramos gave the First Sergeant a surprised look and replied, "That is where BJ made PFC. He was a Buck Sergeant E-5. They were enroute to OP Tennessee to assume the duty. Everybody was dead tired. He put a new guy in to drive the Hammer Head, you know, the ITV. The road was slick and it was snowing like a bitch. The new guy was going too fast for the turn. They flipped the ITV into the creek on its top. The driver broke his arm. BJ was in the back asleep. Got busted two ranks and sent to supply. The ITV was screwed up bad and had to go back to depot. It was bad, First Sergeant. I had just got here. He is a good guy but ain't no way the TC gets to sleep in the back when his track is moving."

"The OP is just outside of this town, First Sergeant. We go up there and then down below to a deer stand. We can see good from the stand and we eat there out of the mist, what you think? Top?" Ramos asked.

"Sounds good to me," Martin said. His thoughts however, were with the situation regarding McMasters that was just so succinctly described by Ramos. It was a man's whole life in three sentences. He continued to process all of the information. The Army was a cruel place when things went wrong. Somebody's head had to roll. It was almost always the guy in charge with something to lose. On that day, it was old BJ whose dick had gotten caught in the proverbial screen door. That, then, was the message behind the sardonic smile that he got from BJ. Then Martin asked Ramos, "How is BJ? Any issues there?"

Ramos thought before replying, "No, he does his job and always does more than his share. He is fat but he can run and do almost everything the skinny guys can do. He is a little nasty but Webster stays on his ass to take a shower. He would be good in combat, I theenk," this last said with a sly smile.

"BJ has a mean streak, huh?" Martin asked.

"If he gets you down, he ain't letting you get up and fight no more, if that is what you mean, First Sergeant," Ramos said. The he hastened to add, "But he don't never start nothing. Are you going to keep him in the troop, First Sergeant?"

"Hell, yes we are going to keep him. The Army still has room for a misanthrope or two as long as they are manageable," Martin replied.

"Is that like an antelope, First Sergeant?" Ramos asked, unfamiliar with the term.

"No, Gilberto, in the sense I used the word, a misanthrope is an asshole. It is a Greek word that means a person who hates or distrusts mankind. BJ can be charming. He is selective of who he hates. Plus he appears to know he is the source of his own troubles. The Army used to be full of them. They were called professional privates. They are soon going to be as 'out of date' as the buffalo. BJ will get a big kick out of straightening me out while I learn the ropes, and the troop commander as well, I suspect," Martin said laughing.

"Well, that is good, cause BJ sure ain't no antelope. An elephant, maybe, but not an antelope," Ramos answered.

Ramos then continued on with the tour commentary of the countryside. "First Sergeant, that is the Eussenhausen check point. It is manned on this side by the BGS (Bundesgrenzschutz). They do the border in this part of Germany. In 2d Cav sector it is the Bavarian Border Police. The other side is the DDR (Democratic Duetsche Republic) with East German Border guards. We do nothing at the checkpoint, it is all a West German deal. The Op is up this hill and to the right," Ramos said rapidly doing a u-turn and heading toward a farm road just below the hill mass. "OP Tennessee is up there. We go up after we eat. I am hungry as hell, you, First Sergeant?" asked Ramos.

"Me, too, I want to stretch. I love the combat bee double u but I need a break," Martin replied, gratified to see his exaggerated Spanish accent made Ramos smile. Martin knew Ramos was showing off a little. He also knew this trip personified the best of Army life, soldiers learning from Soldiers. He hoped it would always be so. Ramos was saying thank you for Martin's treatment of him when he was a scared trainee years before. He was entitled to be proud of what he had become and his ability to impart some knowledge to his old Drill Sergeant. Martin thought it was too bad no one could convey the sentiments the two of them felt today in a recruiting pitch. The learning between NCO leaders was one of the great things about the Army. Soldiers love to show their leaders what they know. He was going to soak it up. It had not always been so with him and he was grateful for the NCOs in his past that taught him to listen.

As they dismounted Ramos POV at the deer stand, the fog was rapidly burning off from the valley situated at their front. They took their breakfast to the upper level, sat on the bench and ate. The fare would not have appealed to many folks but they were men of simple and large appetites common to those who spend their lives outdoors. They were content to eat the plain but delicious food while watching East Germany appear as the fog rolled away.

In the manner of a professor, Ramos's lesson on the border continued as they ate. "The first marker you see, the small white one, is a KB stone. It stands for King of Bavaria put there by Ludwig, the damn fruitcake. Up north near the 1/11 sector the stones will have KP on them for the King of Prussia. The signs and the white stones are the last markers on the West German side. The taller one with red, yellow and black stripes is the one for East Germany. Americans cannot go in between the two stones, or even past the sign, legally. The only ones from their side who can come outside their fence are the GAKS (Grenze Auflarers). They are their best troops and trained like scouts.

Some of them defect but most have their families held over them as hostages. The fence and everything past the colored stones belongs to East Germany. The first fence is theirs. It is not wired for electric or mines here because of the gate. It is hard to keep our guys from helping escapees. I never see them shoot nobody. I hope I will not have to decide if I have to help those poor bastards trying to escape or not. The road is where they drive their vehicles on patrol and to check the border. We call that the control road. The dirt in between the control and the fence is mined. They also check it for foot prints and rake it down. The guys in the tower have rifles and machine guns. The ordinary soldiers ain't got no more than two magazines or fifty rounds, if that. The damn dogs are barking. They feed them about now. The dogs run on the dog run and can be turned loose on people trying to cross the border. The anti-tank ditch against the fence is designed to keep them in, not to keep us out. See how it slants with the high side up to the west. The second fence is their commo fence with phone lines."

"Past the control road, to the East, around that point, is a false checkpoint where they make the dumb people from deep inside East Germany think that they have made it home free to West Germany. They dress one guy in the West German uniform. They bull sheet those suckers and if they give themselves away, they drag them out of the car and beat their ass. By the time they figure it out they been scammed, it is too late. The locals and the higher ranking Communists guys know the deal and they cross legally."

"Way up the road, you can see it with a telescope like the one they use to look at the moon, is a tank range where they shoot T-55's, T-62's, BMPs and sometimes a PT-76. But it is hard to see. We came back here so the guys in the OP cannot see us and so we don't get them excited. We can be up here inside the 1 K zone, but the rest of USAREUR, like my brother-in-law in finance in Hanau, ist verboten! If unauthorized soldiers and dependents come up here we take them in custody and the BRO (Border Resident Office – an element of the Military Intelligence Battalion) comes to get them at Camp Lee."

"They got some neat guys in the BRO, First Sergeant. One of them is a Russian defector from Russian Special Forces. He is a warrant officer but he don't wear no uniform. I hear he laughed all the way through Ranger school and SF training. He is nuts. He wear short sleeves in winter, damn crazy. He dies in the summer heat and I tease him in Spanish when his ass be sweating like a pig. He is a good guy. He speak Russian, no shit, German, Italian, Spanish, Portuguese and English."

"How is his Spanish?" Martin asked.

"He got a Cuban accent so I figure he learn it from the Senoritas," Ramos replied.

"What are your questions, First Sergeant, about the border?" asked Ramos. Martin did not want to tell Ramos he had studied everything he could find about the border starting from the initial boundaries after WW II. He really appreciated everything the good Staff Sergeant was doing for him. He intended to keep his detailed knowledge about the history of the border to himself and soak up all of the local lore Ramos and the other NCOs had to tell him.

"Tell me about Handicap Black Messages," Martin asked, knowing full well representatives from higher headquarters dropped messages on the dumbest looking Private or NCO they could find. The response of these members of a unit then formed the basis for an evaluation. The results were also publicized to Army level.

Martin knew he could impact the unit response to Handicap Black messages and moreover had to do so, to succeed. It was a specified performance measure given to him by the Regimental Commander. What he did not yet understand were the sub-sets of the entire process of evaluation and how to deal with the obstacles. He knew the unit's inability to consistently deal with the messages was a symptom, not a disease. However noble his goal to train for war, rather than peacetime evaluation may be, his ninety day clock from Smokin' Joe was ticking. He would struggle to match long range strategy and short range goals. He knew his scruples would survive.

"These assholes come to the Border with papers that say a situation like, 'You are the leader of the reaction force. Mortar fire and RPG fire have been reported at grid 12345678. Execute your SOP (Standard Operating Procedures) and move to that location on the map. You have five minutes to begin your movement.' They can drop it on the gate guard or even somebody walking out of the front gate. They try to pick the dumbest guy they can find," Ramos replied.

Martin thought about his days in a Nike-Hercules missile unit and found the beginning of the solution. "So, the evaluator is usually some old Master Sergeant from Regiment or Corps who comes to the border without actually knowing what unit is up here, is that right Gilbert?" asked Martin.

"Oh no, First Sergeant, they know who is up here. That's reported up the chain of command when the transfer of authority takes place."

"So tell me about the Reaction force," Martin said.

"React is usually a scout section or a group of guys from a platoon acting as a section. They are on duty for 24 hours and park at the front of Camp Lee with all of their shit on board, with ammo, NODs (Night Observation Devices), Binos, maps, you know all their equipment. They are the first guys out of the gate. They are at the call of the Troop Commander or the Duty Officer," Ramos concluded.

"So, does the Lieutenant assume any responsibility to train the react crew? Does he make them practice? How do they train?" Martin asked.

"The Lieutenants screw with react when they get bored - they call them out to watch them jump. They are the only thing he can call out on his own.

If something happen, he can send them to the place or contact to get a report before he tell the Old Man," Ramos stated with some indignation.

"Are there some react squads who always get the message right the first time, Gilbert?" asked Martin.

"Si, First Sergeant, but the super guys are never on when the Inspectors get there. A new guy, or a screw up gets the message, screws it up, gets relieved and a good squad goes on react and stays there. But the Inspector, he no come back," Ramos said with some degree of mysticism.

No, thought Martin, smiling broadly, his work done, the Inspector can now return to Regiment or to Corps secure in the knowledge that Old G Troop is truly one of those piece of shit outfits that will never get it right.

"The shit ain't really funny, First Sergeant," Ramos said smiling broadly. "You are gonna' mess up those Inspectors, no?"

"Gilberto, I am going to 'mess up' those guys, yes. And guys like you are going to make sure I do."

"I know, I tell everybody, we are going to start winning all of our fights, big and small. I knew it," Ramos said with visible excitement. "How we going to do it, First Sergeant?" he asked with a broad smile.

"Very simply, Gilberto, the best are going to teach the rest," said Martin. He smiled again as he saw Ramos moving his lips while softly repeating the words Martin hoped would become a mantra.

The remainder of the morning was spent on the border trace. The two NCOs followed the obscene scar right across the heart of Germany. The area of no man's land, complete with its fences, machine gun towers, and dog runs, seemed to go on forever. Martin thought, the physical border has come to an end at the south end of Germany but the ache lives in the German heart forever. The WW II guys he had known in his youth from the American Legion, having fought the Germans, would not feel the first pang of remorse for any pain either the Nazi survivors, or their descendants, were feeling.

"So, tell me what about the duty at the Border pisses you off the worst as a Platoon Sergeant, Staff Sergeant Ramos," Martin asked formally as they stopped at Checkpoint 132.

"First Sergeant, I got a good platoon. My people have to report to run the Border Operations Cell, do gate guard, drive the Border jeeps and do the hard things that have to go right to support the Troop. I got no say in who does what except to verify if they can do a particular job," Ramos stated in a matter of fact way.

"So, that does not piss you off, amigo?" asked Martin smiling.

"Sure it does, First Sergeant, but hey, I am a Staff Sergeant Platoon Sergeant. Everybody got to pull their share. Then Ramos had a thought. "Hey, First Sergeant, what you doing?" asked Ramos. "Is everybody going to say Ramos spilled the beans to the First Sergeant?" he said with a sly grin.

"Ramos, everybody in the troop knows we are taking this trip today. It is Saturday. Who but a couple of lifer dogs would go to the Border, see the trace and the potential battle positions, ending up in the area of the next exercise. None of them volunteered to lead the trip. That means the officers know I am in good hands, the smart asses among the NCOs think I will trip up bad before I learn and the guys on the fence will have to be convinced. However it goes, it will all be your fault, you took the lead for the trip."

"Oh shit, First Sergeant. I do not care, you helped me and now I help you. But how you going to do it Top?" Ramos asked emphatically.

"You want to know what I am going to do and how I am going to do it. You give me far too much credit. I don't have the whole thing figured out. I do have some principles of management and of Army leadership to guide me and some common sense. What we will do after we come in from the field and before we go to the border is conduct an analysis of the mission with the key leaders, to include selected SP 4's. From that analysis, we will arrive at our methods. The most successful leaders are those that get their followers to do what they want done and make the followers think it was their idea. It is called buying in to the process. I have several big advantages over the Cavalry smart alecks who have been here for years and have Stetsons, like Staff Sergeant Masterson," Martin said.

"Yeah, you are smarter than them. Is that it?" asked Ramos.

"Not necessarily smarter Gilberto. The answers to the issues of the Border are all in plain sight. The present leaders just can't see the forest for the trees because they are too close to the problem and harried by a killer schedule. I am the new guy. I'm not married to any old solutions. What I am going to do is walk everyone through the critical positions at the Border in the order any Inspector will encounter the Troop. We will start at the Gate Guard, work through the React Squad, proceed to the Border Ops Office, work through the Duty Officer/Camp Commander, work the Arms Room and end up with the alert procedure for Border Condition I. Through it all, the best will train the rest."

"So you are going to put the best guys in spots at the start of the border and keep them there until the Inspectors come, First Sergeant, so we can pass and they will leave us be?" Ramos asked impatiently.

"Shit no Gilberto! That is the last thing I want to happen," said Martin. "We have a working model. It is old but it still works. It is the one Baron Von Stueben used at Valley Forge during the Revolutionary War. He took a picked group of men and taught them how to drill and perform the intricate tasks of how to load and fire a Revolutionary War musket and how to march as units to maneuver. There were fourteen separate tasks required to load and fire the weapons of that day. These movements had to be taught and practiced until they were automatic in order to sustain a rate of fire of 3 to 5 rounds per minute. He then dispersed this trained group back out into the Continental Army to teach their fellow soldiers."

"We are going to lead with our best people in key positions. Each platoon will then pick their best people to train right beside them in key jobs. My goal is to strengthen the whole troop using ranking leaders and peer leaders, not make it weaker by working our good horses to death. The elite Soldiers in units die quickly. With 10% fighting and 80% watching and 10% lost in a unit, once the elite get killed or wounded only the dumb and the lazy are left. For all practical purposes, the unit is destroyed. No, we will train the entire unit up to the standard of the trainers. Once we get that done, we will use platoon integrity to assign missions at the Border. We will then rotate responsibility for the key tasks among the platoons. Make no mistake, once we turn the Handicap Black situation around for the troop, the Inspectors will be back to make sure our success was not a onetime fluke. The real test will come on the second message we get on our border tour, not the first one."

"So the guys from Regiment are really going to come back," Ramos asked with visible disappointment.

"Gilberto, the guys that drop the message are not the enemy. The damn Russians are the enemy. It is a lot like MILES (Multiple Integrated Laser Evaluation System). When you are maneuvering with MILES gear and you get shot, who do you blame when the alarm goes off in your head gear?" Martin asked.

"Me, the alarm goes off 'cause I did something stupid and exposed myself or my crew," Ramos admitted.

"What do you do when the alarm gets re-keyed and you attempt your next maneuver during the exercise?" Martin asked.

"I be more careful next time when I attack," Ramos answered.

Martin laughed saying, "People change when the pain level gets high enough that making changes is in their best interest. The pain from MILES is to our self-respect. The guy that is delivering the Handicap Black Message may be an old guy that is fat and out of shape. Winners do not blame the mail man for delivering bad news. All of us want to play on a winning team. Winners never bitch about the officiating in a game, losers always do. Winning and losing are both habits. The two main differences between winners and losers are - Winners never quit and they accept constructive criticism, losers quit when the going gets a little tough - they are looking for a reason to fail - and they always find one. Losers cannot take criticism - it is all personal to them."

"You like this shit don't you, First Sergeant?" Ramos said smiling.

"Hell, yes, I like it. Where else do you have a clear mission, a hated enemy just feet away - that soldiers can see and even smell, new equipment, nearly unlimited maneuver space and great comrades? Thanks to you Brother Ramos, I will keep the bigger mission in perspective."

101

"Me, First Sergeant, what did I do?" asked Ramos, mystified.

"You are a competitive SOB, Gilberto. You are just like me when I was a Staff Sergeant. I always wanted to beat the guy in front of me, not just win, but beat his ass to a pulp in tactics or gunnery or PT, whatever. For you, that is the guy, or the headquarters, that brings the message. For me, the enemy has to be ignorance. It is training that will let the troop win the fight. If we do that the right way, it will matter very little what the Handicap Black Message says. Who brings it will not matter at all," Martin concluded.

"How will we know when we get to where you want to go, First Sergeant? When they quit screwin' with us?" asked Ramos.

"The big guys will leave us alone once they see the troop is functioning up and down the chain of command and laterally among the soldiers, Gilberto," said Martin. "We need the troop to receive the message, develop the mission, organize the effort in their head, issue orders, report their actions, and report giving the size, activity, location, enemy present, describe his actions and what we are doing to counter them."

"How you going to handle Masterson? He is a real smart-ass and he thinks he runs the troop as the Tank Master Gunner, First Sergeant." queried Ramos.

"He is the Commanding Officer's problem not mine, past setting a good example. Masterson has been here six years. Some soldiers that extend for more than two tours in Europe continue to contribute and some are just coasting. He has yet to reveal which he is but I will give him the benefit of the doubt. He is the tank master gunner, not me."

Stopping on a slight hill, Ramos pointed off to the South West saying, "First Sergeant, this is OP 13. We don't man it very often, maybe once during the border tour. The East Germans come up to the OP. They piss through the fence and get real brave. It sits right on the West German border line. The closest we come to shooting back happened right down there in that ravine where they shoot a guy and his boy some years ago. It was on their side. They shoot and drug them off, queek. The guys on the OP were still writing up the report when they went back across. They say they did not die but were wounded bad by AK-47 in their legs."

Martin looked at Ramos hard as he added, "That is what the local people say. They have relatives over here in Bad Konigshafen. That is what the BRO said anyway," Ramos said without a lot of conviction.

"I have no doubt people got shot on the border and that's too bad. It is hard to watch that kind of shit happen right in front of you. We all have to abide by the rules on this Border. I hope our people do not have to make the choice," Martin said.

"What would you do, First Sergeant?" Ramos asked.

"If they get across I would help them and return fire if those pricks shot into West Germany at our soldiers. I would not support any escape by fire

102

nor would I risk our soldiers' lives to save them. Borders are dangerous places. World history has too many examples of wars starting over border incidents, some real and some just made up. Our leaders depend on us not to do stupid shit that would lead to an international incident or war. If the Border was easy, they would not have a Cavalry Regiment up here doing the task."

"Tell me how we close out the border once it is time to turn it over to the next unit, Gilberto," Martin asked.

"It is hard First Sergeant. It is just like clearing Wildflecken or Grafenwohr. Everything has to be perfect, clean, topped off, policed and straight. We know how to do it, the NCOs just have to check and you have to check them. Many times the generator fuel tanks are not topped off, OPs are dirty, and mattress covers are not changed. But we have a bunch of new First Sergeants and if you all keep your word with each other, it should be better than in the past," Ramos replied.

Martin was very glad to see by his thought process that Ramos was ready for Sergeant First Class and to be a good First Sergeant when his turn came up.

"We are near our first assembly area for the trains, First Sergeant. It is about 20 kilometers to the south in this town, Sulzfeld. You get me there, okay?" asked Ramos with a sly smile.

"Okay, Ramos, you want to see if I can actually read this map. Take the combat Bee Double U east on B275 to Grabfeld and we will work it from there. Maybe we can find a place for lunch after we get there or would you prefer to go home and take your wife to the commissary?" Martin replied.

"We go home, First Sergeant," Ramos said.

In the small town of Alsleben, the initial assembly area for the Troop was far too congested to take the tanks. There was no way Martin was going to tear up a small German town just to reach a point on the map that some staff puke had picked without knowledge of the ground. He and Ramos picked another site with farm roads that formed a mile long rectangle with two outlets that led to a state highway, or priority road. Martin closed out the trip by saying, "We don't need to do anymore traveling today on Army business. I suspect the Gator is going to lead this trip himself. Once I tell him about the trouble we would encounter in that residential area, he will see the light. I will get a late lunch at the snack bar, do some paper work and walk back to the BEQ through town. What you think Ramos?"

"Sounds good to me, Top, if you have had enough briefing for today, I got stuff to do at home," Ramos said. "Top, are we having an alert on Monday morning for the troop?" Ramos asked.

"No, what made you ask that question Gilberto?" Martin replied.

"Well, one of the Mortar guys was getting his piss test stuff ready as an observer and the piss test starts with an alert. Everybody knows you are going to hunt for the dopers after you give them a chance to get a discharge," Ramos added.

"The details of the piss test are very close hold Ramos. Only the staff at the Drug and Alcohol place and I know when it is going to happen. From what you just told me, I suspect the process may be compromised. There is a good reason why the dopers in the troop have been able to dodge the test or have an impact on the results. They are always one step ahead of the lifers. However, one battle does not make a war. It is the war I intend to win. If I lose a skirmish or two, I can stand it, time is on my side, Brother Ramos," Martin concluded.

Ramos immediately began to laugh, saying, "The First Sergeant has an alternate fighting position. He will fire and maneuver. The enemy, they will think he is missing them with his fire. Then, when they are running down the trail, happy that the bullets missed, the First Sergeant blows the Claymore and poof, they are all screwed up. That is it, no, First Sergeant?"

Martin replied, "Sergeant Ramos, you are going to be a great First Sergeant provided you keep anything you might figure out to yourself."

Ramos was more right than he knew, Martin thought. It was almost a relief to learn the first test was compromised. Though disappointing, it was predictable. The ongoing fight between the dopers and the establishment was akin to guerilla warfare. The dopers were like the Viet Cong minus the political baggage. They were convinced drugs were good. The establishment was a bunch of old farts who did not know how to enjoy life and have fun. Like the VC, the dopers swam in the sea of the populace. Some of the indigenous population, or the troop as a whole, were social pot smokers, others were juicers, more interested in alcohol and still others wanted no part of the marijuana and hashish scene but would live and let live. The truly dangerous ones were those committed to the most wide spread use of drugs and were loosely organized along the lines of a Communist cell without the cutouts and security dead ends. Dopers were rather stupid. The Troop Commander had his rats. The dedicated dopers encouraged all to take part in drug binges and the "good times." Their motivation was to broaden their customer base enabling them to either smoke for free, make a profit, or some combination thereof. For the lifers like Martin and the Troop Commander, it was much simpler. Dope was illegal. It was prejudicial to good order and discipline and would not be tolerated, period. In G Troop, the dopers had been given their fair warning and a way out. However, he also knew any failure would reflect badly on him. The fact that he was a new guy and did not know the territory was just tough shit. He would work through it. He was amazed by the number of people who thought this was his first rodeo.

On Monday, there was an alert and a mass urinalysis. The doper intelligence network had functioned to perfection. The tests turned out totally negative. The dopers were euphoric. It appeared this First Sergeant was even dumber than the last guy. He did not even know one of the Staff Sergeants on the team, a trusted agent observer, warned the dopers and skewed the results. It was lucky for the Staff Sergeant that he was transferring to Fort Dix, NJ, before the results would be back, thus reducing the chances he would be

104

caught. Martin did not know of the Danish purgatives that flushed the system and when he was told, was skeptical of the story. The joy of the dopers completely overcame their survival instincts. They talked long and loud. Their smirks were plain even to the New Guy First Sergeant. They rejoiced in the breadth of the generation gap. The largest majority of the Troop, the straight arrows who never indulged in drugs, felt embarrassed for their new First Sergeant. He looked like a dumb ass, as he floundered in this, his first important task. This was confirmed by the rumor that both the Troop and Squadron Commanders were disappointed in the new First Sergeant. Both bluntly told him he screwed up the test.

Captain Dawson called First Sergeant Martin into his office and closed the door. "I guess you know that Staff Sergeant Faucett told the dopers the test was coming. I told you to keep it a secret."

Martin replied carefully, "Captain Dawson, I did keep it a secret. I told no one except the ladies at the Drug and Alcohol office. That is a requirement if you want any turn around at all from the test. One of them must have leaked it to Faucett. How good is your information that establishes Faucett as the leak?"

Dawson replied, "My information is good enough to court martial Faucett if I could get to him."

Dawson's entire manner had by this time convinced Martin that the Troop Commander did not trust him just yet. He probably had good reason since the last First Sergeant had been such a dud. Dawson's earlier life as a Deputy Sheriff had not included members of the force on drugs and he probably did not fully appreciate what a tough problem dope could be in a unit. Having lived through the 70's in line units and as a drill sergeant, Martin knew a lot more than the Troop Commander was giving him credit for, but that was okay. As Martin often told people that worked for him that were more talk than action, "Don't tell me what you are going to do, show me." It was now time to show his troop commander.

"Captain, it is never too late to screw an asshole like Faucett. Let me see what I can do. It is 1430 here so it is 0730 at Fort Dix. Any Post Command Sergeant Major worth his salt is at work by now. Let me put a hitch in Staff Sergeant Faucett's get along. Let me use your phone," Martin said. He then called the S3 office at squadron and got permission to use the Bundespost, or German Post Office Commercial telephone line. Martin then took a copy of Staff Sergeant Faucett's orders with him to Squadron Headquarters.

Fortunately, Martin had the phone number for the DA Operations center with him in his wallet from his days at Fort Knox. He placed a call there using the commercial line. He then asked the switchboard to connect him with Fort Dix Post Command Sergeant Major. Within seconds Martin was patched through to Command Sergeant Major Winston at Fort Dix.

"Command Sergeant Major Winston, this is First Sergeant Ron Martin, late of the Armor School at Fort Knox. We met on your trip with Command Sergeant Major Wren."

Winston replied, "Yeah, you are the guy they all wanted to kill when you said all Infantry and Scout Platoon Sergeants should be Bradley Master Gunners. Sergeant Major Wren and I were the only guys that agreed with you and since he was the TRADOC Command Sergeant Major and I was the Ops Guy, we were the only ones that counted. That was a damn good briefing, First Sergeant."

"Thank you, Sergeant Major, we tried to do our best for visitors at Knox. I am glad you remember me. I called because I need your help to kill a sheep eating dog. You know, Sergeant Major, when you have a dog that is supposed to be guarding the sheep and you find dead sheep, no signs of a fight with a wolf and wool in the sheep dog's teeth, it really pisses you off."

"Martin, who is this sheep eating dog I have got on my ranch here at Dix?"said Winston with a smile in his voice. He was thinking that Martin certainly knew how to tell the story in order to get maximum help.

Martin replied, "Sergeant Major, His name is Staff Sergeant Robert S. Faucett. He arrived on Sunday evening for out-processing but I am sure he will need a physical. He is intent on filing a disability claim with the VA. I am hoping you still have your hands on him, Sergeant Major. This guy told the dopers about a unit mass urinalysis. He got the info by posing as a trusted agent to the Drug and Alcohol Staff. The guilty got off the hook. I am going to fix that, but I would sure appreciate it if you guys could question him and deal the appropriate UCMJ."

"First Sergeant, you guys are doing a great job re-building the Army out there in the Blackhorse. I will see to it that we go over this guy with a fine tooth comb. The Commanding General will probably not be the guy that does the punishment, it will be a Colonel that is in charge of the Brigade of Headquarters Troops that runs the out-processing. Call me back and I will tell you what happened so you can brief your chain of command," Winston directed.

"Sergeant Major, what day do you want me to call you back?" Martin asked.

"Day?! What the hell is wrong with you, First Sergeant? Look Martin, I don't know how those Sergeants Major where you are operate, but I am taking care of this myself. Call me back about 1900, your time, for an update. I meant what I said about supporting you," Winston said gruffly.

"Thank you, Sergeant Major," Martin said as Winston grunted and hung up.

Martin walked back to his troop area and told Captain Dawson what had transpired. Dawson was incredulous, "Do really think the Post Command Sergeant Major of Fort Dix is going to help you First Sergeant?"

106

Martin quietly replied, "You know, Captain Dawson, I am beginning to think you had a very shitty Platoon Sergeant when you were a Second Lieutenant."

"How did you arrive at that conclusion, First Sergeant?" Dawson asked.

Martin replied, "It is obvious. You want to trust me, but your past experience with your PSG and the last First Sergeant tell you the result will be bad. You gave me all of the support one could hope for except to tell me everything you know and are doing about the dopers in the unit. That is the policeman in you protecting your informant. I am not worried. I will prove myself by my actions. Post Sergeants Major for the most part lack personal ambition. They are in the payback position, paying the Army back. Both Command Sergeant Major Winston and I are developing the Army as we have found it, not as we wish it were, but as it is."

"First Sergeant, I may give you the benefit of the doubt down the road but I believe all Sergeants Major past Battalion level are unnecessary. They assume the rank of their commander. They do not give a shit about the troops and only care about their privileges and their next assignment. Hell, they don't even talk to average soldiers unless they just have to. You work for me, not the Squadron Command Sergeant Major or any other Command Sergeant Major for that matter," Dawson replied with great feeling.

Martin replied, "I will let you know what happens after 1900 by calling you at home, Sir. It is payday and you probably have some things to do such as pay your land lord for the fuel oil bill you asked me to remind you about."

"Oh shit, I do have to see him about that. Get the troop together at 1630. After I talk with them, they will get the rest of the day off and the first formation tomorrow will be at 0900. PT is canceled. Cut a change to the Training Schedule and get it up to Squadron. I already cleared it with the Squadron Commander but the S3 needs the change. Thanks, First Sergeant," Dawson said, effectively dismissing Martin.

The very next day, Tuesday, the day after a riotous payday celebration marked by an orgy of smoke by the over confident doper crew and their followers, Martin sprang the trap using the reserve urinalysis cache. Over the next ten days, this test resulted in 17 positive urinalysis tests for members of the troop. Subsequent searches of automobiles, off post hang outs, the barracks, combat vehicles, soldiers and even paint sheds produced a large quantity of high quality marijuana and hashish. The street value of drugs came to nearly $80,000.

The entire chain of command greeted the surprise urinalysis and the subsequent actions as a win for the Army. There were no negative comments about the leadership. The dopers were crushed, the straight arrows were jubilant. Any soldiers on the fence showed the enthusiasm of recent converts and shunned all social contact with the dopers. The follow up investigations resulted in five special and one general of courts martial charges being preferred. Of the remaining positive test results: One was a testing anomaly, one due to prescription drug use, two were first offenders and the remaining nine were second offenders and were processed out of the Army in record time after appropriate punishment. Several of the soldiers awaiting court martial were defiant and unrepentant. The smug ignorance that caused these flower children in their BDUs to underestimate their First Sergeant also caused them to fail to maintain operational security. Captain Dawson maintained his direct line to his informants and knew their every move. The Post Sergeant Major from Fort Dix reported that the former Staff Sergeant Faucett was now Specialist Fourth Class Faucett and on his way out of the Army. To his credit, Captain Dawson acknowledged the fast and efficient action of the NCO Corps as he happily made the announcement to the unit. Even Dawson was quite surprised as the next act in the drama unfolded in a dramatic fashion.

The First Sergeant was at his desk working his Sergeant Major Course. Dawson was in his office with only his desk light on, his door only slightly ajar working on the operation order for the upcoming maneuver. Dawson could thus hear everything being said in the First Sergeant's office. To his pleasure, the First Sergeant spoke loudly in the self-assured way of his rank and because his hearing was failing after one too many tank main gun rounds going off in his ear. Specialist Bone had knocked on the First Sergeants door and asked to speak to him. Specialist Bone was "the" head man of the doper ring in the troop.

"Come in, Specialist Bone," Martin said. "Before you say anything Bone, let me tell you something. Stand at ease. You have such great qualities of leadership. You are a big, strong, handsome man. You are athletic, a great tanker in all crew positions, troops want to follow you. You could be anything in the Army you wanted be. You could possibly still turn this thing around if you wanted to do so. What do you say?" Martin asked finally.

"First Sergeant, why would you say such a thing to me? I am accused and under threat of court martial for distribution of drugs," Bone stated.

"That is true, Bone. In today's Army an Article 15 for non-judicial punishment is almost a death sentence for higher rank. However, there may be a chance. I would be willing to see if the chain of command would entertain a plea bargain. The very qualities that make you a good distributor are the qualities the Army will need in a desperate fight. Have you ever heard of the Yasotay Bone?" Martin asked.

"No, First Sergeant," Bone replied.

"The Yasotay were a select group of warriors who sought death. Genghis Khan combed them out from the ranks of his Mongol army. These soldiers gloried in the knowledge that they had conquered their fear. They were the best of the best. They sought death for death's sake. Now I do not know what the chain of command will say, but if you have any thought of trying to go on, you need to say so," Martin concluded.

108

"First Sergeant, why are you here so much?" Bone asked. "You never leave the troop," he finished.

"I am working on a course and I never leave unless everything that requires an action to help a soldier is analyzed and passed to the Captain for action," Martin said.

"But the Captain is not even here and it is 1900. He isn't here is he, First Sergeant?" Bone asked.

"No, Bone, he left earlier and has not returned," Martin replied, not knowing Captain Dawson had returned, as he so often did, by unlocking the front door to his office.

"I thought it may be because you have two households and are short of money. You never go downtown, you don't drink at the club, you even eat at the mess hall, all signs of an NCO who is conserving his cash," stated Bone with a half-smile.

Martin was puzzled by the turn of the conversation and asked, "So why this sudden interest in my financial condition, Specialist Bone?" Martin asked.

"First Sergeant, I have a big business deal going down Wednesday night. I need you to be gone. Will this do the trick?" asked Bone, tossing a wad of bills on the First Sergeant's desk bound by a large rubber band.

The next thing Dawson heard was the First Sergeant's shouting, "Bone, you jack-off!!" followed by the sound of a chair hitting the wall and breaking glass. Dawson quickly got up from his desk and hurried next door to rescue his First Sergeant. Bone was 4 inches taller, 50 pounds heavier, and twenty years younger than his First Sergeant. He fully expected Martin to be beaten to a pulp by the ultra strong and athletic Bone. He was astounded to see Martin slamming Bone's head repeatedly into the concrete floor with blood everywhere. It was soon clear to his experienced eye the blood being shed was all Bone's. His First Sergeant was obviously around the bend. What little brains Bone had were about to be visible. When shouting at the First Sergeant had no effect, Dawson put a choke hold on him until he passed out from lack of oxygen. Dawson then easily put him on the couch. Martin came to his senses rapidly, shaking his head.

"What did I ever do that made that guy think I could be bought?"

Dawson replied with a shy smile, "Well, Top, when he comes to, he probably will figure that out. What made you jump on such a big guy; he could have really hurt you and then what would I have done for a First Sergeant?"

"Size had nothing to do with it Captain. I was apprehending his ass and he resisted. It was only going to go one way. Let's clean his ass up and see what he is going to do next. I think he needs to go into pre-trial confinement at Mannheim, tonight," Martin stated with finality.

"That is not going to happen. He is not a flight risk, nor is he violent and is not a threat to the safety of his fellow soldiers. It looks like you are the most violent dude in the troop at the moment. He will probably still make his deal happen and I have a good idea what it is. Get an ammonia capsule, get him awake and we will see if he is just knocked out or has to go to the dispensary," Dawson said laughing. "Bone is one stupid ass to try to bribe you, First Sergeant, but you got to give him credit for threat analysis."

Regardless of their public face, both men were quite relieved to see the head pusher of the troop come to his senses and be little the worse for wear beyond a bloody nose. Little did the two leaders know just how far the doper clique would go to further their agenda of domination of their environment.

On Friday morning, the Executive Officer and Martin finished the pre-combat inspection of the combat vehicles in the motor pool prior to their road march to the training area.

"What do you think of the M-1's, First Sergeant?" First Lieutenant Brown asked.

"Our guys have a lot to learn about their mount, Sir," Martin replied. Seeing the confusion on the Executive Officer's face, Martin explained, "An old joke at the Armor School mocks an old time Sergeant introducing soldiers to Armor. The guy says, 'Men, this is the tank. Tank, this is the men'. That is about as far as their knowledge goes professionally, Sir. The exception is in Jackson's platoon but overall, they are still pitiful. That is to be expected. The tank is new and they are new to the tank. The whole Army is trying to absorb the technical and tactical applications of this wonderful piece of equipment."

"First Sergeant, I would like it if you, of all people, would have more confidence in our soldiers," Brown said with a hurt expression on his face.

"Lieutenant Brown, have you ever heard the phrase Crawl, Walk, Run, used to describe a training regimen?" Martin asked.

"Sure, Infantry uses that all of the time," Brown said.

"From what I see, the NET Team used a Run, Trip, Fall, method. These troops think the tank is automatic and will do everything but wipe their butts. It is not automatic. It is a very well designed piece of equipment that manages the accuracy error budget. It does this through environmental and physical inputs to the fire control through automatic and manual inputs. Simply stated, it is a tank designed by PhDs, engineered by Masters Degree Holders, supervised by College Graduate Officers, repaired by AA holders, prepared by High School Grads and crewed by grade school level intellects. At some point, the soldiers are going to have to know the tank inside and out. They are not at that point there yet, not by a damn sight. Hey, relax Lieutenant, ignorant can be fixed, but stupid is forever, okay?" Martin said laughing. "If the shit was perfect, we could all be Spec Fours and have one or two field grades, couldn't we, Lieutenant Brown?"

"Are you sure you are not too smart for this First Sergeant? How did you figure all of that out in thirty minutes?" Brown asked with a sheepish smile.

"Lucky for you, Lieutenant, I have forgotten more about that tank than most folks will ever know. When I ask a gunner if he has adjusted his thermal site to its optimum operational level, and he replies in the affirmative and if he then goes 'WOW' as he watches me adjust it, we have a problem. But it can be fixed and I expected to find it so," Martin said as his driver arrived. Martin was soon on the road march east to the maneuver rights area.

The trip to the field was an eye opener for First Sergeant Martin. The speed and distance covered by the Cavalry troop was much greater than in an Armor unit. The soldiers moved down the German highways at speeds of twenty five to thirty five miles per hour. The road march to the area of the maneuver was almost thirty miles. The speed and large area of the maneuver was so different from his earlier experience that he struggled to keep it all in perspective. At the maintenance halt, Captain Dawson called him to his position. "First Sergeant, what do you think of the Cavalry Troop on the march?" Dawson asked.

"It is fast. Faster than an armor unit. It is tough to keep up with the direction and the up to the minute location of the unit," Martin stated.

"Just concentrate on navigating by the road net work until we go across country, First Sergeant. The Troop is spread out for over a mile. You have to have great commo with the platoons and the command and control comes from subordinates taking charge of their elements. The radio is the key," Dawson stated in a professorial way. "First Sergeant, you keep giving me feedback and you will have all of this in your head in no time at all," Dawson said with a smile.

"I am going to go down into that small town and hit the bakery for the platoons. Do you and your driver want something?" Martin asked.

"You can go into the town but no one else. I do not want any drinking on this trip, First Sergeant, Dawson said.

"The only drinking will be Coca-Cola, Captain Dawson. It is sad you would have to tell me that Captain," Martin said.

"Be that as it may, First Sergeant, I said it and I meant it. I had a lot of trouble with the last First Sergeant and I mean to avoid it with you or fry your ass if you don't listen," Dawson said without a trace of regret. "Just bring us a sandwich of some kind, whatever you are getting is okay with us, right Poston?" Dawson concluded. Specialist Poston merely nodded and gave the First Sergeant a sheepish grin.

"What is on your mind Poston?" Martin asked.

"Have you thought about the football team practicing during PT time, First Sergeant?" Poston asked.

"With the Captain's permission Poston, we will excuse everybody on the football team that can score over 250 on the PT test from scheduled exercise to enable the football team to practice," Martin said.

"Shit, Top, most of those guys are big old dudes like Poston here who would not score 250 on their best day. What do you score, 300 I suppose, and at the 18 year old table?" Dawson asked with a wry smile.

111

"Sir, it is your troop. A score of 200 suits me with individual exceptions for guys like Sergeant Durston, your gunner," Martin stated.

"200 Hundred and Durston as an exception it is. Poston will tell the team. Good decision, First Sergeant, we might win a game or two," Dawson said. "What do you score, First Sergeant?" Dawson asked.

"300 at the old guy scale, Sir, 90, 90 and 12:40 minutes, whatever that totals out to be. At my age, not having a heart attack on the run equals a passing score," Martin replied.

As if he was recognizing some spark of humanity for the first time in his new First Sergeant, Dawson handed him a large and very black cigar, "Have a cigar, First Sergeant. It is an Al Capone, made in Brazil. Cubans are illegal you know."

"Why thank you, Captain, I'll smoke it later," Martin stated with obvious gratitude.

At the assembly area, a deli lunch was the order of the day. Martin was pleasantly surprised to see the soldiers of the troop seemed to have plenty of spending money. Their dress, appearance and personal equipment was quite good. However, once they dismounted from their vehicles they looked like gypsies with little or no regard for wearing the Regimental standard uniform.

During the actions at the assembly area, Captain Dawson gave Martin the standards for re-supply and told him to drill the troop in getting fuel, food and bullets very quickly. He patiently explained the methods of supply from tailgate to gas station and the occasions for the employment of each. He did this in the manner of a man who respected his new First Sergeant's ability to conduct the drill for re-supply in an Armor unit but who lacked experience in Cavalry. Martin absorbed the lessons and resolved to get the re-supply of the unit done in the most expeditious manner possible. He was somewhat surprised to hear how much value Captain Dawson placed on the timely turnaround of the supply teams from the Squadron Support Platoon.

Dawson explained, "The line units think they are the only true soldiers in the fight. They mess around with re-supply because it is not as important as tactics and the Commander does not get in their shit. Most First Sergeants hang out in the rear in the Squadron Field Trains. They take their time bringing up the logpaks (logistics packages containing fuel, food, spare parts, maintenance and repair assets, mail and replacements for those wounded or killed) and they baby the line platoons during re-supply. It is the only big thing First Sergeants in the field do all day so they think they have all day to do it. Get everybody involved so that we spend the least possible time on re-supply. We need to conserve those support platoon drivers because the driving distance between the supply drops of the regiment and our forward positions can be as much as 100 kilometers. It is your job and I will stay out of it as long as you do it right."

112

Martin paid attention and had the assembly area organized fairly well for an initial effort. It was easy, almost too easy, having the fuel tank trucks with the unit for the first three days of Troop practice. The unit became quite accomplished at re-supplying quickly. Martin was very pleased that his time spent learning the logistics big picture by writing manuals at Fort Knox was bearing fruit in the field. He knew the books did not cover the entire situation and was sure he had some painful lessons yet to learn. He was right.

CHAPTER 6 – TROOP FTX

The inability of the squadron to provide a correct location was very irritating. Martin wondered if he was the one who was wrong when he arrived in the empty field leading five diesel tankers and a gasoline truck. He patiently called the squadron logistics center on the radio to verify its location and read the grid location from his map to the radio operator. Lieutenant Upton monitored the conversation and answered the call on his vehicle radio, "Gator 7, this is Eaglehorse 44, the location you need is MB 489136, OVER."

"Eaglehorse 44, Gator 7, roger, OVER."

"Eaglehorse 44, out."

"Go to the LOC (logistics Operations Center), Private Howard," First Lieutenant Upton told his driver. Upton was going to find out why Martin was the second First Sergeant to go to an empty field to return his re-supply convoy.

Martin plotted the new location on his map and told his driver to get them to the new location by taking the farm road to the state highway. Martin had been carefully leading his convoy of fuel tankers by traveling at low speed to start his movements. For whatever reason, Staunton began driving at a high rate of speed toward the state road not realizing the route's twists and turns required just the opposite approach. By the time Martin got him slowed down, the accordion effect caused the convoy to stop suddenly causing a rear end collision of the last two trucks. One of the drivers complained of back pain, one bumper was damaged as well as a gasoline trailer. Luckily, there was no fuel spillage and all of the vehicles remained operable. Martin reported the accident to his Commander and then to the Squadron Headquarters.

While awaiting the Military Police to arrive from Schweinfurt, the nearest military post, Lieutenant Colonel Covington arrived and conducted his own investigation. His immediate thought was First Sergeant Martin had lost control of the movement and was the primary cause of the accident. As a result, he relieved First Sergeant Martin temporarily and sent for Captain Dawson. On Dawson's arrival he gave him his orders, "Dave, your First Sergeant is suspended from duty until after the investigation. You will personally conduct all troop convoy operations until you can assure me he is trained. We are about to enter REFORGER. If he cannot lead convoys in a unit FTX under the simplest of conditions, he will certainly fail to run them during two weeks of sub-zero temperature with snow and ice on the roads. If any of these fuel trucks are damaged beyond repair, he is going to buy it and be relieved. Any questions?"

Captain Dawson replied, "No questions about your immediate guidance, Sir. What did the MPs say and what did the fuel truck drivers say, Sir?"

Lieutenant Colonel Covington glared at Dawson saying, "There is no need to talk to any of them or wait for the MPs for temporary relief. I am sure my conclusion will be borne out. Send him back to the troop maneuver area and I will tell you when and if, he is to be reinstated. Is that clear?"

Dawson knew he was at the end of Lieutenant Colonel Covington's patience and discretion was more important than being right, he simply saluted saying, "Roger, Sir, I've got it."

Captain Dawson called his First Sergeant to him as he had been positioned out of ear shot of the officers' conversation. "Top, the old man is convinced you screwed up. He thinks you were doing a lot more than 25 MPH while leading the convoy and the sudden stop at the front caused the wreck. I know what you are going to say. If that is so, why did only the last vehicle of the seven trucks fail to stop? The reason is, there ain't no reason for it. He has been mad at you since you defended Staff Sergeant Hankinson and got him out of that bogus rape charge from his neighbor. It is payback time. The MPs will do thorough interviews and I am betting you will be okay. Everyone is new to the game and mistakes will happen. The trucks and the soldiers will come out okay. We will just engage Sergeant Webster in the process a little earlier than we planned. Go back to the troop and I will take the trucks to the LOC and see you back at the troop." Crestfallen, Martin dutifully complied.

Remembering, it had been at Dawson's insistence he ran interference for Hankinson on the Article 15. He was surprised the Squadron Commander would carry a grudge but he was human after all. He was in charge of the convoy and that made him responsible, period. He knew Dawson would do what he could. He hated anyone having to lay out their future for him-if only he had been more cautious-maybe he could have prevented it.

Just after midnight Martin was restored to duty and a very worrisome ten hours of cooling his heels. The MP investigation had cleared him. The last driver in the column, who was by his own admission speeding, had been trying to retrieve a Playboy magazine from the floor of the truck and failed to see the convoy was stopped ahead.

All convoy operations proceeded but at normal speed. Operations at the troop level continued to improve and the truck drivers attached to the troop were getting a full eight hours sleep per night back in their location. The coordination between the First Sergeant and Sergeant Webster had matured into a meeting of the minds after exercising the process twice per day for ten days. Martin formed the habit of meeting the re-supply column several miles from the location of the maneuver element.

Captain Dawson effortlessly moved the troop and maneuvered it with the greatest success against the other elements of the squadron and against the squadron as a whole. In two engagements, he forced the Squadron Commander into an attack on a narrow front, destroying two of his attacking troops due to piecemeal deployment. The error the Squadron Commander made was beginning the exercise with fixed positions for the fights but allowing freedom of maneuver for the opposing force commanded by Dawson. He soon realized, Dawson was taking all of his officers to the next series of locations and schooling them on his intent while the First Sergeant maneuvered the troop with the platoon sergeants leading their platoons.

The detachment left by Dawson to maintain contact with the attacking forces was led by Staff Sergeant Ramos. Ramos acted as the mouse to lure the cat into the ambush. He put up just enough fight to keep the attackers off balance and to maintain their interest in him as he moved to the next fighting position. If they made the slightest error, Ramos killed them with MILES. He killed the F Troop Commander so often, the Squadron Commander told Dawson to lay off the diminutive Captain Horace Filterbind.

Each time the Squadron was ready to attack, Dawson had the chance to brief his officers, organize his position and be fully prepared to put up a stiff fight. To Martin, Dawson was one of the rare ones. He had the gift of knowing where everyone was in time and space on the battlefield. Seemingly clairvoyant, he anticipated the next move of his opponent and was usually two moves ahead of everyone, including the Squadron Commander. The troop had no other accidents or incidents though there was an epidemic of them elsewhere. As the field problem ground to a close, G Troop was sent home to recover in preparation for the border mission. The Squadron Commander knew G Troop was highly organized and kept all of its assets focused on the mission. The ability of the Officers to reconnoiter, plan and rehearse with the Commander knowing the platoons would be where they were supposed to be, when they were required, fully ready to fight was a priceless asset.

Lieutenant Colonel Covington and Major Bragg both agreed G Troop logistics would prosper under the leadership of the First Sergeant. Neither of them wished to interfere with the management of the logistics of the other units. The squadron let the Gators be the only ones to keep their support tight behind the troop and move all elements together in a combat box. Both field grade officers disagreed with the arrangement of using the supply sergeant to move the squadron support element forward twice per day but for different reasons. Major Bragg hated the fact that none of the other units had invested the time and trouble to develop the re-supply procedure to an art form ala' G Troop. Lieutenant Colonel Covington attributed the G Troop system to a cover up of the inability of the First Sergeant to safely lead a convoy and the extra ordinary ability of Staff Sergeant Webster to pick up his slack. He thought both the First Sergeant and the Supply Sergeant from G Troop were exhausted at the end of the simple maneuver.

Neither found it hard to applaud the efficiency that Martin and Dawson demonstrated and the difference so readily apparent in the support platoon drivers. The headquarters drivers in support of G Troop appeared to be from a rear echelon unit as they were clean with well maintained vehicles. Most of all, they were well fed and well rested and happy. The drivers supporting the other units were zombies at the end of the third day and accidents and lost vehicles were the standard. Neither knew the G Troop always: met Lieutenant

Colonel Covington's standard of two hours for re-fuel/re-supply; included the support drivers on all briefings; demanded a complete safety inspection prior to movement; and arranged for the support drivers to have at least one meal at a nearby German restaurant. The response of the headquarters troops was predictable. They all wanted to transfer to G Troop permanently.

When both the field grades asked First Lieutenant Upton, now the S-4, why this was so, he credited the leadership of the First Sergeant and his willingness to train and to accept the risk of using Sergeant Webster as the guru of re-supply.

Upton was blunt, "Sir, G Troop has logistics re-supply solved. My drivers attached to G Troop look like they have been on leave compared to the other units. Martin has done everything you have asked. Granted, the traffic pattern of their race track during re-fueling ops looks like a demolition derby, but they know what they are doing and have had no further accidents. Meeting your requirement of two hours re-fuel/re-supply means tanks and tracks have to move very fast between stations. Anything less and it cannot be done in two hours."

"The reason the Gators are using more fuel is they are moving more and they consistently fill every fuel tank on the M1 at evening, not just the rears. Since day one, there have been no accidents. They know their shit. The other guys are screwed up and we will pay for it on REFORGER when the distances are greater, the days are shorter and the roads are slow go with snow and ice. The Gators will run wild. Dawson and Martin love this shit, they live for it."

Major Bragg listened to Upton and asked, "What do you recommend S-4?"

"Short of getting new First Sergeants, we better train the ones we have to meet the standard. I can set up a sand table before we go and we can draft some short time officers to be LNOs. They can run the convoys when units start to break down. I know I can depend on Martin to do an additional unit next to his own and I can handle the other two that fail by stove piping it forward. I know it will get unorganized toward the end of REFORGER. He is worth two ordinary First Sergeants. We will have the period of reset in the middle to re-group, find all of the lost, fix the broken and reorganize."

Both senior officers looked at First Lieutenant Upton with admiration as he had come to the same exact conclusions as they had the night before though his choice of First Sergeant Martin as a stalwart did not set that well with the Commander. However, both officers felt he was an unusually gifted First Lieutenant and would be fine when promoted to Captain in a few days. They knew they had the right guy as their S4. They also knew 14 days at 15 below zero was a long time and logistics was the key element of support for the exercise.

As he reflected on the Field Exercise, Lieutenant Colonel Covington was certain that the First Sergeant of G Troop caused the accident with the fuel trucks. He had said as much to the Regimental Commanding Officer but was told to abide by the MP investigation findings. The MP Master Sergeant exonerated the First Sergeant. That was more than enough for the Regimental Commanding Officer. Covington knew the Regimental Commanding Officer was troop leading him as he asked Covington penetrating questions: Did the Gators lose a fight during force on force; Did they quit when they were behind or in trouble; Did they lose a weapon, hurt anyone or have an accident; Did they miss a meal; Did they fuel by SOP or just when their vehicles were low on fuel; Did the other units pick up the Gator habit of twice daily bore sight of MILES. What was the percentage of their vehicles running at the end of the exercise; all of the answers were positive. However well they did, there was something about them that rankled Lieutenant Colonel Covington. He would rather be second than be first. When one came out first, an obligation to teach others and be responsible for their results came with the honors-he did not want that. The two Gator leaders were just too damn ruthless for his taste-too ruthless. They lacked humanity. Their humiliation of Horace was unnecessary. Can't tell that to the Regimental Commanding Officer, he is worse than they are in the ruthless department. There was a streak in Smokin' Joe that aligned perfectly with the Gators, a wildness that defied discipline and a willingness to take risks, nay, looking forward to risk for its own sake. They were like him. That is why the Regimental Commanding Officer liked them. We will see how they do on their Border Tour when their hero the Regimental Commanding Officer gets to screw with them directly. He really did not want to see them fail. A little humility would suffice.

CHAPTER 7 – BORDER CHRISTMAS

"You never learn anything while you are talking. When your mouth is open it blocks off your ears." 1969 Sergeant First Class Parks, DS A-11-4 Fort Knox, KY Veteran, 3 years RVN & Former French Foreign Legionairre

Sergeant First Class Maldanado had learned a great deal on the field exercise about Cavalry tactics, maneuver and the way Captain Dawson expected the troop to run. He realized his platoon leader, Second Lieutenant Chastain, still had a long way to go but he was learning. He took good care of his crew, didn't lose shit and after the first severe thrashing on the radio, had learned to be there when The Gator called. He smiled at the memory of it, but this was the second time in the Gator's pond for his Lieutenant.

"Blue, this is Six, OVER."

"Six, this is Blue 4, OVER."

"Negative Blue 4, I want your 1 element; get him up on the net, now, if you please." *Oh shit, that is his calm voice.*

"Six, Blue 4, roger, give me two mikes, OVER."

Dammit, pointing and waving is not going to get it, got to drive over there.

"Sczepanski, get over to the Lieutenant's track fast, gun it." The driver answered with a gathering whoosh of the M1's turbine as he moved to the Platoon Leader's tank. On arrival, Sczepanski expertly put the platoon sergeant's tank within inches where he needed to go. Thanks to his driver, Maldanado was able to step over to the other tank telling Lieutenant Chastain, "Sir, answer the Troop Commander." Looking at Chastain's face looked a lot like looking at a kid whose puppy had just got run over.

Seeing the Lieutenant's crestfallen expression, Maldanado asked, "What?" in the parent voice Platoon Sergeants often used to address their young Lieutenants.

"My tank is dead, we let the batteries run down - we all just woke up," Chastain stated.

Taking off his helmet and handing it to the dewy eyed officer he said, "Use my CVC to call the Troop Commander. You don't confess nothing - just take your ass chewin' and don't say nothin' about no dead batteries."

Hesitantly, Chastain put on his Sergeant's CVC (Combat Vehicle Crewman) helmet and called the Troop Cdr, "Six, this is Blue, OVER."

"Blue, this is Six. We have been out for nearly ten days. You need to understand that in Cavalry, commo is life itself. We are here to find and fix the enemy. Everything we do demands crisp, sharp reporting and the ability to call for and mass fires. A Cavalry leader who cannot stay up on the radio is worthless; he is a waste of time and energy. Get up on the net and stay up on the net. Do you understand? OVER."

119

Sczepanski, well trained by Sergeant Donovan, Maldanado's gunner, had passed the slave cable, the Army's version of civilian jumper cables, over to the Lieutenants driver as soon as he stopped beside the dead tank. Sczepanski knew the tank was dead because the heater was not working as no steam was visible and the driver was obviously very cold. The connection made, the Lieutenant's driver started the ignition sequence and the tank was soon running.

"Six, this is Blue, Acknowledged, OVER."

"Blue, are all of your vehicles up and running and are you prepared to move to home station immediately after chow? OVER."

Chastain looked at Maldanado who simply looked away as his hair ruffled in the wind and nodded. "Six, this is Blue, affirmative, all elements are running and prepared to move."

"Good, see me at breakfast, Six out."

Good old Maldanado, Dawson thought as he lowered his binoculars from his vantage point on the ridge line overlooking Chastain's platoon. He watched the NCO counseling of the officer continue. Maldanado was giving the boy 'down the road'. Guess Chastain never thought he would get his lessons from a Puerto Rican, who neither knew nor cared where Norwich University was and he damn sure did not care where Wharton was. Nor did Maldanado care what an MA in Economics stood for. Not much need out here for that shit.

As Chastain handed the platoon sergeant his helmet he said, "I feel less than honest giving that report."

"Sir, are you Catholic?" Maldanado asked.

"Why, yes, I am, you know I am. What does that have to do with it?" the puzzled Lieutenant asked.

"So you know suicide is against God's word. You go confessing shit to the Gator about falling asleep and draining your batteries, you're committing suicide. Your tank was running when you answered him. This is real shit Lieutenant. Can't tell the man the dog ate the homework. Fight through every situation - never, ever give up unless you are dead. We get paid to think and to lead."

Looking into the turret, he said addressing the Lieutenant's Sergeant Gunner, "Wilson, you sorry shit, you know better, you keep that shit up and you will be a Spec Four before you know it, you got me. I put you on this tank to help the Lieutenant, not to screw off and take advantage of him being a newbie. Was that trust misplaced?" Maldanado said.

"No, Sergeant, it won't happen again, Sergeant," Wilson answered.

"Good," Maldanado said smiling, "That is what I like, good Catholic boys, confession, contrition, repentance and traveling down the path of righteousness."

The Platoon Leader's crew knew Maldanado and NCOs of the troop did not hold a grudge. They were all smooth operators but very strict about oper-

120

ational stuff. Mistakes were made and corrected through counseling and training. The NCO would then move on to the next issue or Soldier who needed fixed. The NCOs had all been there and they only demanded performance, hated suck asses but never failed to end on an up note as Maldanado did now.

"Men, we are going in for recovery, Thanksgiving at the troop, followed by the border and REFORGER. I meant what I said about having day one of recovery done when we get in, you know the standard. Make it happen."

The Regiment had published recovery standards. Specific tasks were to be accomplished within five days of a unit's arrival back in a garrison environment. A large portion of the tasks enumerated for day one could be accomplished on the last day of most field exercises. All of the NCOs, led by the First Sergeant, were determined to perform as many actions of Days One and Two as possible in the field. The NCOs knew that they would have all of the assets and support they needed to get the tasks done with the new First Sergeant. He was demanding but was there every minute, was one of them and part of the solution.

Maldanado was going to tell the First Sergeant they were going to be forced to do PT in the field if they kept getting so much food. The Troop was not used to being fed regularly under past regimes. They had not missed a meal for ten days. He remained surprised the Gast Haus thing had worked. Not one Soldier had abused the one beer per day privilege and there had not been a single incident.

Martin had told them the strangest thing when he said, "I trust you implicitly. I never check up on platoon sergeants. I do check on the results. Until you show signs of failure, I am going to believe in you. Be where you need to be and do what you have to do to accomplish the business of the Army. Someone else will have to peek around corners. Your Soldiers are neon signs. A blind man could tell in two minutes if you are worth a shit just by looking at them."

Staff Sergeant Webster had taken the FTX to heart but was glad to be bringing the last meal, breakfast, to the troop this morning. He had been busy. He modified the supply truck by adding wooden racks to accommodate the insulated cans of food. He had ordered one large thermos per vehicle crew or squad in the entire troop plus several extra. The thermos silver bullets should be there on their return in time for issue for the Border tour and REFORGER. He took extra care to ensure the condiments were carried in weather proof containers and available on portable serving tables. Whenever possible, he or the First Sergeant had hot water for hand washing but at the speed the re-supply race track moved, there was seldom time for good sanitation. The best they could do was medical gloves for the headquarters crew handling the food.

The most significant change was the close coordination between him and the First Sergeant for re-supply. He brought the supplies forward meeting the

First Sergeant along the route. The First Sergeant organized the re-supply effort on the ground in a race track pattern based on the squares of farmer's fields which were surrounded by paved roads. Webster fed the troops in the infield of the race track as the armored vehicles were serviced. Just as when the Cavalry had horses, the mount still ate first. Oddly enough, the biggest effect Webster saw was the higher maintenance level of the troop. Keeping maintenance close by using the terrain had eliminated the "us" and "them" factor. They were all Cavalry troopers now.

Every Headquarters element now had a map. All leaders were forced to take turns leading. If the junior leader became lost, any other element commander sure of his location could call 'Gotcha' and assume the lead. The peer pressure made all leaders aware of where they were at all times. The mechanics now listened to the fight on the troop command radio net. When a vehicle Commander reported a maintenance issue, the maintenance crew sprang out of the tree line to provide service. The crew either fixed the broken vehicle on the spot or towed it away for repair.

The First Sergeant had the troop calling them the "Woods Brothers" pit crew after the innovative mechanics of NASCAR fame. The techniques and equipment had not changed. It was a change in spirit for the support guys that made the difference - they were part of the troop.

He smiled as he thought about the First Sergeant's comment to the Troop, "War is not a spectator sport. We have enough assholes watching and second guessing us in higher headquarters. Every last one of you is a Cavalry Trooper."

The new re-supply technique kept the First Sergeant close to site the weapons systems, let him relay commands and enabled him to provide technical expertise on the MILES and the tanks rather than spending hours on the road running convoys.

When Webster told the First Sergeant that the Command Sergeant Major was asking for him, the answer was predictable, "I am not the Sergeant Major's companion in the Field Trains. If those other First Sergeants want to stay there then that is up to them. My place is here, with the Troop, until the Commander says otherwise. I spent too long in units where we did not get fed in the field. Hell, for awhile as a Staff Sergeant, I thought it was part of the field problem to see how long the troops could go without a meal. If the Command Sergeant Major wants to see me, he can figure out where G Troop is by asking his Tactical Operations Center (TOC). Tell him we appreciate everything he is doing in the rear to push our supplies forward."

"Yeah, right, First Sergeant, that's him alright," Webster replied.

"Webster, don't be too hard on the Command Sergeant Major. He is at the end of the road. He is an Infantryman with a CIB in a Cav outfit. He has paid his dues and is doing what he knows; beans, bullets, boots, and tents along with uniformity. He knows he is ignorant about armor and does not really care. He has to make the Squadron Commander happy, not me and not you. We would do well to keep his standards. Don't be part of calling him the Earth Pig and shit like that - support him. In the Infantry, the Soldiers come first. In many Cavalry units, the vehicles come first," Martin said.

Staff Sergeant Webster did not always understand the new First Sergeant but he did appreciate the latitude to do his job. He felt very good about the tremendous feeling of esprit' de corps forming in the troop. Webster most enjoyed the "dopers" getting a knot jerked in their ass although he had yet to understand the lack of malice in the First Sergeant's attitude toward the law breakers. He smoked their ass unmercifully but he did not hate them. His mantra for the Troop was, "Save your anger for the enemy."

As he watched the troop setting up for re-supply for the last time in this field problem, Staff Sergeant Masterson, Master Gunner (MG), Troop Training NCO and six year veteran of the Regiment was still not a First Sergeant Martin fan. Martin was not a Master Gunner and Masterson did not buy his reason for this lapse. Martin said he knew his failure of the Master Gunner course would have been a foregone conclusion due to personal animosity of the NCOs in Master Gunner Branch toward him at Knox. He never gave them a chance to axe him. Masterson did not believe him when he said he was not interested in doing the Master Gunner's job.

He wondered how an old man like the First Sergeant was going to handle the Border Qualification. Martin had said, "For Border Qualification, pretend I am a Staff Sergeant and pour it on." Masterson sure wanted to see him do the foot patrol he had planned for him. At the training meeting, Masterson had tried to talk him out of becoming Border Qualified. He realized he had probably gone too far in rolling his eyes, telling him there was no way he could complete a 15 kilometer foot patrol in the winter at the Border. Masterson had further insulted the First Sergeant by saying they would be carrying him to the truck on a stretcher at the end of a nine mile march up and down the snowy and icy hills. He was going to make a fool of himself and the NCO Corps.

Neither Masterson, nor no one else would forget his reply, "Sergeant Masterson, I am going to give you the benefit of the doubt since I hardly know you. I am not going to assign any negative value to your being here in the Regiment for six years. It is a tough assignment. It is not the only tough assignment in the Army. The only way I know how to lead is from the front. If I cannot do everything I ask of a Soldier and let the unit's Soldiers teach me what I do not know about Cavalry and the Border, I should not a First Sergeant here."

"That is my point First Sergeant. If you have not been to the Border and are not Border qualified, how in the hell do you expect to change anything about how we do the mission? Who are you to tell us our job and criticize how we do the border?" Masterson was nearly hyperventilating when he finished his two questions.

"When we come back from the Field Exercise and get recovered, Sergeant Masterson, we will have a troop meeting of all the folks who are the smart guys on the Border. At the end of our session, the information to answer the questions of who, what, where, why, and how will be very clear to everyone. You will know all about it because you will be the recorder and thus be able to straighten us out when we go wrong. It will be leaders and selected personnel, not the whole troop. At the end of our session, I can assure you Sergeant Masterson, I will know everything I need to know about organizing for a Border tour and how to make the troop successful. This is not rocket science. The answers are already here in this great Cavalry Troop. It is just simply mission analysis, training, fixing responsibility, supervising critical points, and expecting to succeed. We have too much of everything to fail," Martin answered.

Masterson felt the First Sergeant would trust him to be loyal and to act professionally. He also knew he was not alone and that many NCOs in the unit felt the same way as he did about the First Sergeant but lacked the balls to say so. Either that or they had enough tact to wait and see.

What Masterson could not know was the First Sergeant was tolerant of him because he saw himself as a Staff Sergeant - confident and sometimes smug, and insufferable to any superior not fully committed to the Army.

Martin smiled to think of it, The kid tried to lead and dominate the troop from the middle of the dog team of the sled, when most of the time all he could see was the asshole of the sled dog to his immediate front. He was without a clue where the sled was headed right now. Nothing in his experience in the Blackhorse Regiment had prepared him for the latest in leadership techniques.

Martin smiled at the homily, prompting Masterson to ask "What's funny Top?"

"Sled Dogs, Mike Golf, Sled Dogs," the First Sergeant replied.

During the recovery, the Squadron Headquarters was shocked to see G Troop not in formation at 0630 on Day 2 of Recovery. When queried by as to the location of his unit at the Charge of Quarters Desk of the sleeping troop at 0630, First Sergeant Martin reported to Major Bannon, the S3, "Sir, the troop has accomplished Days 1 and Day 2 of recovery and will start on Day 3 today."

He further stated they would finish the effort in 3.5 days with a TA-50 Inspection on Thursday and a training holiday on Friday, all cited on the training schedule. The purpose of the late start that day was for Soldiers to get reacquainted with their wives after the kids had gone off to school and to give the single guys a chance to sleep in after a night on the town. Mollified, the S3 departed the Troop shaking his head in disbelief at the temerity of the First Sergeant in changing the guidance to fit his own needs.

124

On the conclusion of recovery, it was his intention to do the advance work for the leader's session on the border. He knew he was invited to the Commander's home for drinks and steaks this weekend and for Thanksgiving Dinner the next week. The Commander's wife had shared with him her plan to have each guest cook a part of the dinner while she baked the bird. Martin hated turkey, a hate made more intense after years of being married to a woman who was too fussy for words about every holiday, with Thanksgiving the most contentious. But he liked the Commander's company and enjoyed that of the Lieutenants as well.

The Platoon Leaders were all very idealistic and willing to learn. His three years of teaching student officers at the Weapons Department of the Armor School were among the most rewarding in his Army service. They were the future of the Army and he did not regard them as any more troublesome than his own children. They were young, dumb, and full of come. He regarded it as his job as an NCO to teach, guide, and protect them until they gained experience. Martin was also well aware that some Lieutenants grew up to be Colonels and Generals and woe unto the future generations of NCOs if their education were to be screwed up as Second Lieutenants. He knew the teacher always learned more than the student and he was grateful for the depth of the knowledge he had gained as an Armor School Instructor.

At the moment, Martin would be satisfied with a good breakfast at the snack bar and a quiet reading of the newspapers. He routinely read the German paper (zeitung) as well as the Stars and Stripes. He also read the Wall Street Journal albeit several days to a week later than it hit the street in America. He sat down at the back table with his huge breakfast of three eggs, ham steak, hash browns, toast, yoghurt, sweet roll, Coca Cola and Hot Chocolate. He was looking forward to his meal and some solitude. Martin was quite surprised to see all of the Master Gunners of unit come into the snack bar and line up at the grill. A fast eater since Drill Sergeant service, he felt that they would want to join him and he quickly began to finish his meal. As they got their orders filled, they did join him. Oddly, each asked permission with a sly smile before they sat down. Masterson was the last to appear. They obviously had something on their mind. Martin decided that offense was the best defense and said, "I am very glad to see all of you having breakfast together. That implies that you work together and communicate as brothers. I would hope you are all Franciscans but I suspect there is a Jesuit or two among you."

Masterson took the bait by asking, "What's the difference, Top?"

"Franciscans love and serve human kind and Jesuits tend to believe the end justifies the means, Bob," a smiling First Sergeant Martin replied.

Staff Sergeant Jester from the Tank Company began the questioning. It was obvious, Masterson had been holding forth about his First Sergeant and

125

the others were there to get his measure. "So what do you think of NET training, First Sergeant?"

"It is good as far as it goes. The NET does what it can in the time available. The Army presumes the unit will conduct training on the tank, run exacting Tank Crew Gunnery Skills Testing (TCGST), have critiqued crew practice, work the Unit Conduct of Fire Trainer (UCOFT) and do firing at local ranges near home station. NET training is the first exposure to the M1 - the end of the beginning, not the end of training. Anyone that believes NET is the only training a Soldier needs on the M1 has not thought the problem through."

"How well is your troop trained on the M1, First Sergeant?" Staff Sergeant McCready asked.

"Where are you from, Mac, Oklahoma?" Martin asked, smiling.

McCready replied, "Does it show that much?"

"What are you re-loading now, shotgun shells? You are a re-loader, aren't you?" Martin asked, still smiling.

McCready smiled back, saying, "I just finished some twelve gauge sevens for skeet this morning. Does that show too?"

"I'm not psychic, Mac, you have a primer stuck on your car keys lying there on your tray, you have a Winchester belt buckle and you have gun powder residue on your left palm. Also, I can smell the nitro on your fatigues. I like skeet and trap and just about all recreational shooting sports. It takes one to know one and all of you are probably certified NRA gun nuts like me," he said smiling broadly.

The entire table laughed as one except for Masterson who suddenly realized his First Sergeant was winning over his fellow Master Gunners without even trying.

"Guys, I have no idea how well or how poorly my troop is trained on the M1 tank. I know Sergeant Masterson is the Master Gunner. He has been on the whole series of tanks 11th ACR has had for the past six years, the M551 Sheridan, the M60A1, the M60A3 and now the M1. When he needs my help I hope he will ask for it. My biggest near term challenge is the Border. If Smokin' Joe thinks I screwed that up, it won't matter what I know, or think about gunnery, I'm gone. I do hope I can join your group somewhere down the road in time just to talk about tank gunnery and solutions to problems. I'll always buy the first beer for a table full of gun nuts. Guys, I gotta' go, formation calls me," Martin said as he stood up and stretched.

The Master Gunners all noted that the First Sergeant said nothing to Staff Sergeant Masterson about the formation. It was clear the Master Gunner only reported to the Commander and was trusted to be engaged in the work of the Lord at the breakfast. Either way, the stories Masterson was telling about his First Sergeant being in his shit as a micro manager did not appear to hold water with his fellow Master Gunners.

Just prior to the formation, Vic Jackson spoke to the First Sergeant, "The wife says to tell you good job on the formation time and that is good to know some people in the Army know what is important."

"Vic, that Debbie is one in a million. If you ever want to trade her in, let me know and I will pay new car price," laughed Martin.

"When are we going to do the border thing, First Sergeant?" Vic asked. Then he added, "My platoon is ready to do equipment inspection and barracks inspection today. The troops saw you cleaning your gear and working on your wall locker in your office and they fixed theirs before they went out last night."

"Yeah Vic, but is everybody else ready - ask the other platoon daddies. I would like to do the skull session for the Border on Thursday. I need to take a Sergeant Major Academy Test on Friday afternoon at the Education Center while the troop is on training holiday. Friday is off the table. I need the process to be relaxed and deliberate with everybody's head in the game. Let's go to formation."

After the report and an inspection of ID Tags and ID Cards, Martin called the troop to gather at his position for a short talk as was his habit. "I hope you all got re-acquainted with your wives, girlfriends, Class B dependents or the whores at the House Chantal. A lot of you are thinking I am damn nuts and way too hard on you. You may be thinking life is too hard here in the Blackhorse. A lot of you are wondering why we lifers go at this so hard. There were three guys who were laying stones at a church. A passerby asked them while on break what they were doing there. One of them, a guy who looked a lot like Aschliman here, said 'I am making $22 dollars an hour and getting ready for deer season'. The second, who resembled old Sergeant First Class Jackson said, 'I am glad to be drawing a good check and supporting my family'. The third said, 'I am building a church. It will be part of the community where folks will get married, baptize their kids, and bury the old folks. What we do here will live on for many years after we are gone'. Most of us are like one of those three guys. Which one are you?"

"Many of you are just young people. You do not really know who you are or what you want out of life. As for me, I know what I am doing here. I am not just here to make the sorry Soldiers miserable. I am here building an Armor Force. The Soldiers, of all ranks we build here, will serve throughout the Army and some will go back to civilian life. All of you will all be a reflection of your time here in the Blackhorse Cavalry. You need to find a reason for your being that is beyond yourself. If you are just drawing your pay and building your college fund you will be miserable, not just here, but anywhere you go. If you just live for yourself, you will have an empty life. The Christian's Jesus said it best, 'He who would find himself, must first lose himself'. We are making progress. Platoon Sergeants stand fast for a minute. Fall In."

Having the Platoon Sergeants attention, Marin asked, "Guys, can we do the Border skull session on Thursday afternoon, 1300, concluding at 1600 or do we wait until Monday?"

"I can't do it First Sergeant. It will take me up until the last minute on Thursday to get done with recovery and maybe after duty hours," Staff Sergeant Hankinson, Mortar Platoon, stated. All of the other NCOs nodded and thus voted for Monday.

"Do all of the newbies have a copy of the Border study guide - for the third time -I know - I sound like a broken record," he concluded. Again, they all nodded and smiled their assent. "Okay, no excuses for your dancing bears. If they blow the test-we know who their re-medial trainers will be, you jack-offs! While we are doing the planning, they will be tested. I'm turning them over to you as everyone is in a different phase of recovery. I am taking the Border Test over lunch. I am going to study it while you work recovery."

Later in his office, Martin was studying his version of the Border Study Guide as he was planning to take the test before lunch that very day. It was a good test. Authored by the Regimental Border officer and approved by the Regimental Commanding Officer, it was not negotiable and beyond either his ability or responsibility to influence. He was just a TURD (Trooper Under Rapid Development) trying to pass it and become qualified like everyone else. Out in the hallway, the sounds of recovery were heard. BJ was bitching about his truck, the Training NCO was working the bulletin board, and the unit arms PFC was inspecting, accepting and rejecting weapons.

Martin suddenly remembered his new light system for the door and shut it to block out the noise. During the FTX, among their many tasks, he had the rear detachment install a system of two lights above his door, one red and one green. The rules were simple, the red light precluded entry or even knocking if either the message or the messenger did not outrank the First Sergeant. The green light could be bypassed if the immediate attention of the First Sergeant was required. Martin turned on the green light and resumed his study of the qualification handout. He had arranged to take the test between 1130 & 1230 hours with Masterson as his proctor. He was using the last 15 minutes of his time to cram the data on the composition of the Forward Security Element then in vogue for Eastern Bloc forces. He had elected to take the test in the training room. He intended to ride the Horse today and not let the Horse ride him.

After the test, Martin was organizing his Sergeant Major Academy study material. Captain Dawson appeared in his office and congratulated him on passing the Border Test with such a high score. "I am glad you took the test so seriously, First Sergeant. That is just the spirit we need. The Squadron Commander just talked to me about your Sergeant Major Academy Course. I told him we had set aside the time for you to study and that you were taking off early today to prepare for your test on Friday afternoon. He is happy we are taking it seriously. He told me the Sergeant Major School Commandant had written him a letter stating that more than 50% fail the course. Is it that hard? Why do so many people fail the course?"

"Captain Dawson, I appreciate your interest and supervision as well as Colonel Covington's. The attrition rate is at least 50% in the Non-Resident Course. The first examination of any of the sections is multiple guess. If you score less than 80%, the re-test consists of essay questions. Everything is graded, punctuation, spelling, grammar and writing technique. I do not intend to fail any of the multiple guess tests. It is all manageable with the slack you have given me. People fail the course for the same reasons they fail college, they are too lazy or too stupid to do the work or they cannot budget their time," Martin concluded.

"Come in my office and shut the door," Dawson ordered. "Sit down, have a cigar. These are called Al Capones. They're Brazilian and just like the ones Al Capone had imported from Havana. Martin accepted a cigar and they both lit up. Dawson opened a small window and turned on a floor fan to manage the volume of blue cigar smoke.

"They are good seegars, Captain," Martin opined.

"Top, just how are you going to manage the Border to get a turnaround for the Troop?"

Martin thought, "The Captain just left Masterson so the seeds of doubt have been sown. Broad strokes are best for now and if they don't do it, we will get down in the weeds."

"Captain Dawson, it will be the same basic technique we used for the alert. I have the critical actions written down. We will work through them and assign the best people for those tasks and train the rest of the folks. Do you want to see the details now?" Martin asked.

"I guess what I want to know is why you want to use that technique, you have said the troop already knows what to do?" Dawson asked innocently.

"The key to success in a maneuver Army unit is to train the troops so that they do the right things at the right time no matter who is, or isn't, watching them. They have to know the right things to do and know how to do them. John Wooden, the UCLA basketball coach said it best, 'Practice does not make perfect, perfect practice makes perfect'. Meaning, if you are performing an action and you are doing it wrong, it does not get any better through repetition of errors. It either stays the same or gets worse. The only method we have that fits the resources available for the Border is on the job training. The frame of reference, or the standard, is the Handicap Black Message Drill. Using OJT, we train to that standard. We need the trainers to be part of the solution. Soldiers love to show what they know. This troop will begin to win when they think they deserve to win or when they feel worthy. They will not be worthy until they, as a body, believe they are."

"As a former Ole Miss Varsity football player, think about what your coach did to make you feel worthy; two a day practices, a thick play book, and gasser runs. My technique may look like a group grope or some Dale Carnegie feel good shit, or even a damn Amway meeting, but it is none of those. It is simply a way to share information between the leadership who are mostly new, with the folks in the troop who are the most successful. The end state will be when you can assign duties using platoon integrity instead of by drawing on the elite members of the troop to do the work. I want no part of a unit where 80% of the Soldiers who are unqualified, watch the 20% who are experts do the work."

Captain Dawson was incredulous at the pure gall of his First Sergeant and the disbelief showed on his face. Martin was not fazed by his troop commander's facial expression. He knew it well. It was the Southern, good ole' boy sheepish look reserved for carnival barkers, revival preachers and slick Carpet Bagging Yankees.

"You know why I really love the south, Captain?" Martin asked.

"No, why, Top?" Dawson replied.

"Because you Southerners are polite to your elders. You guys keep smiling right up to the point of killing people whom you think are full of shit and who are insulting your intelligence while putting their hand in your pocket. I am not stealing anything. Nor am I going to make anyone look foolish. I am going to work through the problem with the centers of influence in the troop and get them on our side. No one is going to discuss the high priced management theories I am putting into play. We will just employ the techniques. It will be fine."

"Okay, Top, you got me on board. Let's do it this afternoon. Oh shit, I gave you off this afternoon to do that Sergeant Major Academy shit - all right, Monday at 1400 then," Dawson said smiling.

Martin studied the Sergeant Major Academy test in his room until past midnight. After a good breakfast at the snack bar, he reported to the Education Center to take the test. He was surprised to see the proctor was Dr. Wisner, the PhD in charge of the Education Center. The administrative part of the test was no nonsense. He was provided a clean desk, the test, five # 3 pencils and that was it. Dr. Wisner reviewed the administrative data Martin entered on the test form, compared it to his Army Identification Card and told him, "Once I sit down in the examiners room behind the window, I will start the stop watch. You will have two hours to complete the examination. You may use neither notes nor any other reference source. If you do not understand a question, raise your hand and I will explain the wording of the question. I cannot help you with the understanding of the material. Do you have any questions?" Martin shook his head no. Wisner then said, "You may begin," and clicked the stop watch as he walked away.

Wow, that was all business and professional. The Academy would be proud.

While not easy, the test was confined to the material of the section he had studied and finished the 100 question test in 40 minutes. He knew he had passed it easily and did not pause to worry about getting a perfect score as anything above passing was overkill in his situation.

The Sunday with Dawson was a good time. Martin and Dawson watched movies that included "The Professionals" ,"Valdez is Coming", and "Dirty Harry" with John Wayne thrown in. The Lieutenants were astounded that both of their leaders knew the dialogue of several of the movies. They also noted that while both leaders drank their booze straight, scotch for the Captain and Jack Daniels for the First Sergeant, neither got even slightly drunk. The food was great and appreciated by all of the bachelors. The young officers all had places to go after dark on Sunday night. They made their manners to Mrs. Dawson and went off in search of female companionship or to their girlfriends. First Sergeant Martin helped with kitchen police duty and when the kitchen was clean, rode back to the kaserne with the Executive Officer.

Before going to bed, Martin sketched out what he wanted to be the border manning document he would use on Monday afternoon. He both expected and wanted corrections from his audience.

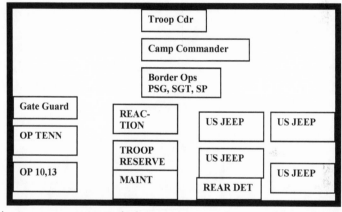

Martin was not concerned about errors as they would spark the discussion. At some point, he would fade into being a facilitator of the meeting and support the Troop Commander as the decision maker. He had been with the troop for nearly a month and knew they were just as good, if not better, than any of the other 11th Cavalry troops in the Regiment. Napoleon was right about some things, there were no bad regiments, just bad Colonels.

On Monday, the entire troop was buzzing. The weekend had restored the spirit of the soldiers and they were ready and willing for PT. They were not disappointed as they got several hundred repetitions of conditioning drills and a slow three mile run to sweat the weekend out. Walking back from formation after the run, Martin waved Ramos toward himself, asking, "Hey hombre', what's the buzz?"

"Shit, Top, you should know. Everybody ees studying their border test since you passed yours. The troop is ready for today's meeting magic. They are ready to wipe out the stain from that stupid ass Lieutenant that crossed the Border, got his picture taken doing it and got relieved. Stupid sucker! They want to win and they can smell it. All of my people will pass the border test and they are all licensed on the M113. Keep the pressure on the leaders, the soldiers can follow if they are led. Hey, Top?"

"Yes, El Jefe?" Martin replied.

"Remember what we talked about on our trip to the border about React being a toy, First Sergeant?"

"I got it, Ramos," Martin replied.

Next Martin diagramed the potential path any Handicap Black message dropped by higher headquarters at Camp Lee would travel in a successful response. Realizing the great experts would think his analysis was overkill; he smiled, and did it anyway. The stick on red arrow would be used to establish incoming information and the green would be outgoing orders and directions.

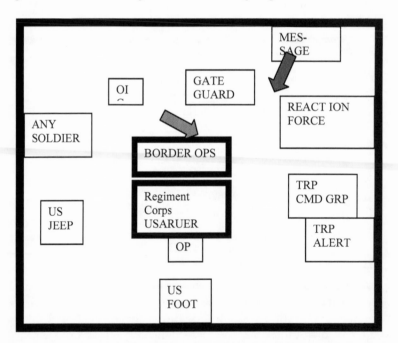

Martin then listed the skills and knowledge for each duty position in his private notebook so as to establish the standards for training. He did not pretend to know them all. He knew the troops would fill in the blanks. Martin knew he was swimming upstream by requiring all of the soldiers to take the border leader's test and did not care.

He wanted PFCs & SP4's to know what their officers and NCOs knew. He knew from experience, the more they knew the more they would begin to infer what was expected of them.

His standard answer to those who preferred dumb privates, "And just who do you think is going to call for fire and for the MEDEVAC to save your ass if not PV2 Schmuckatelli? Smart officers train their enlisted guys to take their place during times of relative peace. Hell, B-17 pilots trained their waist gunners to fly home and to land four engine bombers. My buddy, Herb Lenhart, landed his B-17 wheels up with a dead copilot, a pilot who had no lower face and a dead bombardier. He and eight guys from the crew of that B-17 are alive today because of one Captain's vision. It's a self-fulfilling prophecy either for good or evil. We are going to strive for smart, tough, competent enlisted guys who know their leader's jobs and support them by being top performers. Any leader that prefers his soldiers to be dumb is not worth a damn."

The troop did not particularly like his rule that everyone had to have a military driver's license, but they were working hard to achieve it. The rule was simple. "Soldiers who are not licensed drivers of the specific vehicles as directed by their platoon sergeant, will not have a pass after Thanksgiving Day weekend. This is an Armored Cavalry Unit. If you can learn to drive and be licensed, you are an asset. If not, you are a liability and will be chaptered. Inevitably, it is the unlicensed driver thrown into a tough spot that produces accidents."

Martin had previously told the Platoon Sergeants which of their troopers were to attend the meeting in the Troop Commander's office. They were a bit surprised when he told them he wanted the best: Gate Guard; radio operator; REACT crewmen; Outpost Operators; mounted patrol drivers; and finally, BJ McMasters to be at the meeting. Each platoon was told to bring one or two NCOs that knew the border inside and out. He knew Staff Sergeant Masterson would be present as he was the Training NCO as well as the Master Gunner. All Lieutenants were to be present regardless of their experience level. The office was filled.

When the First Sergeant set up two easels, there was a slight groan from the bowels of the group. Martin laughed saying, "You jokers are Pavlovian with the groan instead of slobber. The alert ones are easel trained. None of the dumb ones, God Bless 'em, are here. Pavlov, Brother Maldanado, is a Russian behavioral scientist who taught dogs to respond to a bell by using food as a reward. He found that the dogs would slobber when they heard the bell whether food was present or not."

"Shit, Top, Koreans slobber when they see a fat dog. Is that the same thing?" Maldanado said smiling.

"The very same thing, a conditioned response, Sergeant Maldanado," the First Sergeant replied with a smile. "And that men, is why we are gathered together here today. We want a conditioned response from our Soldiers based on training in response to stimulus. Instead of dogs in a maze in search of food we will have soldiers in search of excellence. It is 1308 hours. We will be

133

done here by 1700 hours, at the latest. The objective of the meeting is to develop a plan of action for the border that lets us conduct on the job training for the critical job elements required by the border tour. The standard is the Regimental Border SOP. The overriding objective is to successfully pass each and every evaluation dropped on us by higher headquarters as well as properly respond to real world situations. There has been some talk of that I do not know enough about the Border to lead this discussion. There is some basis for that point of view. However, those that hold that view ain't in charge. I know what I do not know. I also know everything we have to know to run the Border correctly is either written in some Standard Operating Procedure (SOP) or is in the brains of the soldiers in this room."

"The Handicap Black Message is the vehicle for testing border units. The message is very simple in format, sorta' like marriage vows, profoundly simple to say, but complicated to execute."

HANDICAP BLACK MESSAGE

DTG: 032015DEC84

ISSUING UNIT: HQS 11TH ACR, SGM ROGERS

RECEIVING UNIT: G /2/11 ACR

SITUATION: Armored vehicles have been reported vic XXXXXX.

Flipping back the cover sheet on easel #1, Martin let the leaders look at the border manning layout. "What did I miss guys?" he asked pleasantly.

"Looks like it is all there, First Sergeant," Masterson opined.

"Okay, here is the layout for a Handicap Black message," Martin stated as he unveiled easel #2. "The Red arrow represents the message from higher and the green one is our response to it as the troop formulates the orders to respond to the situation," Martin stated.

"That is where you are wrong, First Sergeant. The REACT Track should get the message and move out smartly to the grid given by higher. There is a thirty minute time limit in a Handicap Black." Masterson stated emphatically.

Rather than answer directly, Martin pointed to the Executive Officer, First Lieutenant Brown, asking, "You have input there, Executive Officer?"

"Yes, First Sergeant, I do. The critical point is the reporting process to get the word to Border Ops so that they can notify the Camp OIC, Squadron, and Regiment. The Camp OIC is first among equals in the process. There is nothing to prevent the Reaction Team from being at the gate ready to roll and performing pre-combat checks while awaiting word from the OIC. If the OIC is not immediately available, the Ops Sergeant can dispatch the Reaction Team. The Reaction Team cannot become self-employed and move out on their initiative. I have seen a React take off out the gate with the message and no reporting got done within the time limit. Fast can be the enemy of good with a Handicap Black. Border Ops is the key Command and Control element."

"Those are all good points. Captain Dawson will resolve all Command and Control Issues before we are through here today," Martin stated.

Deftly taking the cue from his First Sergeant, Captain Dawson stated, "React moves out the gate on the final order of Border Ops unless Ops is screwing up badly, then React reports Moving, Phase Lines and Set or Contact overlooking the objective. Men I want to work the maze of what happens when an evaluator or umpire, whatever you want to call them, drops a Handicap Black at a border camp. As the message hits a particular duty position I want to treat that position by figuring out the best Soldier or Soldiers to perform that duty regardless of present assignment. I want to then have each Platoon select the three guys who are to learn the job from the best man. We will not keep the best men on duty waiting on higher headquarters to deliver a message. We will train up and switch off."

For the next two hours, Martin worked each of the Border duty positions using this formula. He also had Masterson list the most common errors that the vastly experienced men assembled in the room had seen and in some cases, themselves committed on the Border, for each duty position. At the end of the period, each phase of the Handicap Black Message's passage through the troop for reporting or execution had resulted in the 'by name' selection of the best performers. The top troops were then matched to selected soldiers from each platoon to be trained for the critical slots. The best performers that were present had input on the selection of the Soldiers nominated by each Platoon for OJT. Many command and control issues were resolved. Each officer who would be acting as an OIC during the border tour gained a clearer understanding of what was expected of them once they were border qualified.

Captain Dawson summed up the meeting at 1630 by saying, "You all are beginning to see why I was so happy to see this guy be our First Sergeant. He is a light year ahead of the rest of the First Sergeants in this outfit. He was the best instructor at Knox but it is a pleasant surprise to see him do such a great job as First Sergeant. That is often not the case. A lot of those guys are great bull shitters on the platform but they cannot hang in the day to day hard work of the Army. The devil is in the details. His method got the information on paper and showed us how to teach the new guys in one swoop."

135

"The Handicap Black Message exists only to prove or disprove we know what we are doing. It is the training of the individual soldier that will get the job done. I am very, very happy about the large number of soldiers passing the Border test and the very high numbers of people passing the driver's test. We will still be very selective about granting people a POV license to drive in Germany. They will not get one just because they passed their military test. That is not to say they can't get one, but everyone in Specialist Fourth Class Schedlapp's chain of command will have to swear a blood oath to me he is responsible enough to have a POV if he is not either married or in the rank of Sergeant. There will be no beer until we successfully pass our first Handicap Black. After that, I will take recommendations on the Spur Candidates for Border Qualification beer privileges from their Spur Brother Mentors. I am the Reitmeister (Riding Master or Master of the Hunt and in charge of Spur Qualification) and since the First Sergeant does not drink beer, I have restricted his Pepsi until he passes the foot patrol."

"Damn Captain, not the damn Pepsi, shit!" Martin said with mock anger. The entire group roared with laughter as it was obvious the two men liked and respected each other and knew who was in charge of what. They also knew 25 kilometers in the snow was long patrol no matter old you were. Most leaders knew Staff Sergeant Masterson had a hand in selecting the terrain for the patrol. By now, Masterson was the only man present who thought the First Sergeant would fail to finish the foot patrol.

The veterans knew the Border always had a few surprises for the unwary. They were all very happy to see the depth of analysis and the level of detail that was applied to make the troop successful. The lack of slogans and buzz-words and the insistence on good, hard training by the best performing soldiers put the effort on solid ground. They all appreciated the closing comment by the First Sergeant, "Any damn fool can learn from his own mistakes. It is a smart man that learns from the mistakes of others."

First Lieutenant Robertson was the best all around athlete, most cultured and most analytical of the junior officers in G Troop. He knew he was going to move to Regiment as the Border Officer at the close of REFORGER. Completely fluent in German and French, he was looking forward to the assignment to Regimental Headquarters, being promoted to Captain and the increased responsibility. He watched everything the First Sergeant did with particular regard to the Border. He knew the formalization of the age old training process of OJT was the only option available to the troop given the frantic pace of the outfit. He admired the manner First Sergeant had of getting his followers to buy into the program.

At the end of the process, no one remembered whose ideas were what, only the end state. It was classic leadership, get assigned a shitty job, get good ideas from the guys who had to perform, fix a course of action and make everyone think it was their own idea. He was not yet ready to employ the technique on a large group but he surely admired the results.

The Spur Program, similar to the Expert Infantryman's Badge, was tied into the Border tour and was another level of performance for the Officers and NCOs. He was glad he had his Spurs and was very happy to see the true goal of the First Sergeant was to assign responsibility for the Border tasks of Border Ops, Reaction Force and the 24X7X365 OP Tennessee by unit integrity when possible.

The methodology would put a Platoon Leader in charge of the entire operation with his own people in each critical node. Robertson understood responsibility assigned by Platoon, squad, and crew produced the best results, conserved resources and developed teamwork through shared experience. From West Point onward, he had been taught to use teamwork at every level because soldiers fight for the man on their left and their right rather than slogans or high level concepts. For the first time, he was certain the platoon would not only succeed, but would perform at a very high level. It was Army doctrine implemented by a master motivator.

Thanksgiving at the Dawson home was a madhouse. Everyone had a task. The Lieutenants who had led sheltered lives were lost in the kitchen and at the stove. Mrs. Dawson would not let the First Sergeant help them past doing the mashed potatoes. Her supervision of the Lieutenants was sparse to nonexistent as she was drinking white wine, kibitzing on her husband's conversations and talking on the phone to her friends and her landlord. The meal got served and was edible. The deserts were from the German Backeri and were wonderful. After several John Wayne movies, the Junior Officers thanked their host and hostess and departed. First Sergeant Martin stayed for cleanup and for leftovers. Dawson took the First Sergeant back to his off post quarters. The Captain had not yet seen the apartment since Martin had just moved in since returning from the FTX.

Martin led the way to his basement room. It was utilitarian in the extreme. It had a single bed, with nightstand complete with table lamp, a sink with an individual water heater, a combination dresser and wardrobe. It also had a desk and chair suitable for studying. The small refrigerator from housing also held a small lamp. Martin's Sergeant Major Course was neatly filed on top of the desk facing the wall. The commode was outside the room in an open area of the basement. It was the size of an upscale chicken coop on a sharecropper farm but very clean, quiet, and adequate for a hard ass First Sergeant. Martin was living off the difference between his housing allowance and his rent. "Damn, Top, this is small. A room in the barracks would be bigger than this. You don't even have a TV."

"Sir, I lived in the barracks as an NCO and I don't miss the TV, I read. The place is small. Upton lives upstairs and he has a nice place with a one bedroom apartment with kitchenette. He is hustling some school teacher

137

from Heidelberg. You know he is an up and comer. It is close and the exercise of walking back and forth is good for me. The old gal that runs the place has six soldiers renting from her and is making money faster than the German mint can print it. She is a little long in the tooth for me but if I get desperate she might have to do in a pinch. Upton would razz me forever about screwing her. The place suits me for now. I am not here enough to worry about it. My life is at the troop. I just sleep and study here. Now don't go worrying about me Captain. I live in my mind not where I am physically located. The walls do not close in and I have no issues about living here."

Dawson continued to shake his head saying, "Well it's okay with me if it is okay with you but this is too much like a jail cell for me. I could not do it, Top. I need more space."

The two parted company but on the way out Dawson stopped in the doorway saying, "I am sending the wife and boy home until after REFORGER. We are going to be too busy and I want her to have some time at home with her folks for the holidays. There are very specific things I want to get done before REFORGER. It will be a winter exercise and it is the coldest time of the year. It will take place 80-100 miles north of Fulda where it is even colder than here. Christmas and New Years do not mean that much to me anyhow and what the hell, you'll be here. I know you are not going home after just getting here, are you?"

"No, Sir, Christmas is not a happy time for me as there is so much bullshit tied to it by the wife, perfect tree, perfect gifts, nothing ever meets the standard, take everything back and exchange it, exchange half of it again, plan a perfect New Years, be disappointed, go to ten parties and be around her damn doper friends. It's no fun for me to be with her anytime but the Holidays are special torture. I'll stay here," Martin said with a smile.

Arriving at the troop the morning of the move to the Border, Martin found the barracks bustling with everyone getting ready to move out. Most of the gear had been loaded on the vehicles on Friday and over the weekend. The personal gear, munchies, books and hobby stuff were the last items packed. Seeing all of the stuff the troops were taking, Martin was still amazed at the contrast between the eras of soldiers, his and theirs. Except for his Pepsi stash, two cartons of Marlboro Reds and some Sergeant Major Academy study material, he was traveling lighter than anyone in the unit. He saw Sergeant Robert Hankinson, Mortar Platoon Sergeant extraordinaire gnawing on Sergeant Bertennelli's ear. When Robbie looked his way, he merely smiled and waved as if to say, keep on doing what you're doing Robbie, it's your platoon. Martin then proceeded to his office to get his maps, Web Gear, weapons, mask, and the ten other things he had to have to go outside properly dressed in the German winter. He felt great and was looking forward to the challenges of the month ahead. He was not prepared for Sergeant Hankinson showing up in the door with a troubled look on his face. Hankinson always paddled his own canoe and like all true Infantrymen, did not ask for help until it was almost too late.

"What's up, Robbie? Is Bertie yanking your chain this morning?"

"First Sergeant, Bertinnelli is up and down. He blows hot and cold. He walked by deficiencies and I chewed his ass. He gets tired of correcting soldiers and I jacked him up. He does not understand leadership and wants the troops to love him," Roberts concluded.

"I know how he feels, Robbie, we all want to be appreciated. He is just a young NCO. Keep the heat on his ass. Tell him and show him it ain't personal, its professional. Make sure he knows it is the Army standard we are enforcing not one we made up on the spur of the moment. Also tell him to make sure the Private knows who gets screwed when the standard is not met. The Private has to know and feel he is letting himself down as this is still, US of Army. We are all in this shit together. All for one and one for all. Once he understands and believes that, he will be twice as effective. Okay, Robbie, all for one and one for all, US Army, keep it simple for the kids," Martin said with a smile. Hankinson gave him his lopsided grin and went back to getting his platoon ready to move.

Just as the Mortar Platoon Sergeant left, the level of noise from the three floors of barracks above increased by at least a 1,000% percent. It was 0515 and every stereo in the barracks was on full blast. The windows of the WWII Old German Army barracks were shaking and the floors were vibrating. It seemed to Martin the whole outfit had gone stark raving nuts. As he started up the stairs to the Charge of Quarters desk, he was intercepted by Sergeant Fairchild, the NCO in charge for the night. Fairchild had a note written on an 8X11 lined tablet as no conversation was possible.

As Martin read the note, he smiled with relief once he realized the troop had not lost its collective mind. Only one man was to blame for the cacophony of rock, country, classical and punk rock screaming coming from sixty sets of speakers. He re-read the note to be sure he had burned it into his memory, "CAPTAIN DAWSON TOLD THEM TO MAX OUT THEIR SPEAKERS 0515-0520 AND SCREW ANYBODY WHO DIDN'T LIKE IT."

Glancing at his watch, Martin saw it was 0518 and the mad Minute had two minutes to run.

His immediate analysis - the music volume was classic leadership at the company level. All young folk want to turn up their stereo to the max at some point. Soldiers live under the strictures of military discipline and the close quarters of communal barracks life. The Troop Commander was exercising his discretion, or lack of it, to the obvious delight of the soldiers. Most stuffy Generals would have called it the wrong thing to do. But if the troop all turned up their stereos at the same time and turned them down at the same time, it was a win for leadership. Dawson had great savoir faire' with the soldiers and lest anyone forget it, he was in charge and no one else.

Captain Dawson saw his First Sergeant come up the stairs to the CQ desk as he arrived from the third floor. He was grinning like a small boy who had stolen the biggest watermelon from the old curmudgeon who grew the big ones down Mississippi way.

"First Sergeant, wasn't that great? They got to max out their stereos," he shouted, straining to be heard.

Martin answered him in a loud voice precisely at 0520, when the noise died as if the power had been cut, "Great move, the troops loved it, it pissed off the rest of the Squadron and nobody else will do it. We need to do it every time we move out."

"You really don't think it was wrong or too much, First Sergeant?" Dawson asked.

Martin turned very serious and faced Dawson and when he spoke did not fully realize at least 15 soldiers and NCO's could hear his answer, not that it would have mattered. "Captain Dawson, you will be the one writing the letters to these kids' folks when they get killed and wounded. You are in charge of them and responsible for what happens to them for good or evil. We are here to support you."

The two of them went downstairs to make their final preparations for the month long trip to the Border.

Later, Captain Dawson met Martin where the road to the Motor Pool ended at the Chapel. The Troop was lined up and ready to move. Dawson made his commo check with all of the leaders and all responded crisply and in sequence. He then told Martin, "Fall back to the rear, Top. Tell me when you have cleared the critical intersections and choke points. Execute any recovery. See you at Camp Lee." Martin saluted and Dawson began the Troop movement to the Border.

The movement was without a reportable incident. Martin knew there was no movement of a military convoy in Germany that did not give the leadership at least one thrill. There were always close calls or accidents that did not happen by just inches. The Cav was a head hunting outfit. In this case all of the close calls of German passing M1s and cutting in and out of the convoy were only that, close calls. The troop arrived at the turn off to Camp Lee intact. The contingent of 1st Platoon Scouts scheduled to replace "E" Troop at Observation Post (OP) Tennessee continued to move north east up Highway B-19 up to and through the town of Mellrichstadt to their destination for next seven days, the OP overlooking the storied Meinigen Gap. The remainder of the troop turned left towards the town of Wollbach and into the compound named Camp Lee.

G Troop had some luck for a change. Of the four OPs, only OP Tennessee was active. This good fortune enabled each of the duty positions, identified as critical tasks by the Wise Men of G Troop, to be trained at the same time. Within 24 hours, the "Stars" were to be released back to their platoons and the newly certified experts would be working the critical jobs. The exception was the Border Operations Center (BOC) Radio Operator and NCOIC. Captain Dawson closely observed the performance of the candidates there and decided to hold the experts over another 24 hours.

First Sergeant Martin spent this time visiting each of the OPs to verify their cleanliness, generator fuel state and becoming familiar with the border. Beyond holding formation and supervising the barracks, his time was spent preparing for his own Border Qualification. After twelve hours in the BOC, Captain Dawson declared him qualified at the strong requests of the soldiers and their Platoon Sergeants. No one was prepared for the intensity the First Sergeant brought to every task. Many, however, noted that this was the longest period the Troop had ever been to the border without a visit from higher headquarters.

Speculation was rife and rumors abounded - the smart money was riding on the Regimental Commanding Officer's regard for the First Sergeant. All of the rumors were about to thrown in the dumpster as the dreaded moment arrived in the person of the Regimental S3 Operations Sergeant Major, Martin's great friend and former Drill Sergeant buddy, Sergeant Major Arthur C. Rankin or ACR. When ACR arrived at the camp gate, he produced his ID Card and was granted entrance for himself and his Chevy Blazer known to the Army as a Cargo Utility Carrier Vehicle or CUC-V.

The senior NCOs were in a group at the steps of the Troop Headquarters talking with First Sergeant Martin when ACR got out of his vehicle. He looked at the group without any sign of recognition, though he knew several of them well, and went directly into the BOC. The NCOs turned as one man to the First Sergeant with Mercado saying, "The Handicap Black. He ignored us to make sure Regiment knows he ain't playing favorites. There is no way he would have ignored you, Top, maybe me and Vic, but not you."

"You're right Maldanado. That is exactly how he would play it, straight down the middle. He is on the Army's side right now. If we do it right, we are back to being one of the boys, if not, we are still on the outside looking in," Martin replied.

At that very moment the siren sounded on blast for Reaction Squad. The track parked in front of the BOC started immediately and belched black diesel smoke from the V8 Chevy engine winding up. Hatches flew open and the TC, Sergeant Brazil, the Portuguese Cajun, assumed his position. The scout crewman manned each of their positions as riflemen and M60 machine gunners with one scout dismounting as a ground guide to the gate. The gate was being opened by the gate guard, no longer a new guy or FNG; he was now part of the solution. The two minute execution by the Reaction Squad was not a record but as Martin would say later, "It may not have been a record but it was a damn good average." All noted the gamesmanship of the gate guard as he closed the gate behind the Reaction Squad track while pretending not to

141

notice the Regimental S3 NCOIC trying hard to get his vehicle going and out the gate to follow. After a minimal delay, ACR was through the gate and hot on the trail of the Reaction Squad as it sped off on a notional mission to verify the size and composition of the Russian horde crossing the border.

"Well, Top, what do you think? The React crew is not an all star team. It is their first time under outside evaluation. Sergeant Brazil is a new Sergeant and Staff Sergeant Coffee will be arriving later tonight," Sergeant First Class Mercado asked and commented.

"I am not worried one bit about Brazil. He has big cast iron nuts. He will represent us as well as anyone we have. He is a Buck Sergeant. He is well trained, he had some good practice missions with the star Reaction Team guys and he has trained his guys. Plus, they respect him. Hell guys, most of the Army will be led by Buck Sergeants two days into the fight with the Russians. They had better be good. ACR will give us a fair shake on the evaluation but he will not fudge it to let us skate by. If we blow it that is what he will write. If he drives back in here before the track comes back and walks up to me smiling, we passed, or we hosed it so bad it seems funny to him."

"Remember, he and I saved each other's career about three times a week as Drill Sergeants in the Knox summertime. We have no secrets and no regrets about what we did or how we did it. It will take a little time. He is going to let Brazil deploy the squad and verify each of them knows his job, role, and mission. That is why Smokin' Joe sent ACR out here to screw with first me, and then G Troop. Joe wants his quarter's worth and he knows ACR will get it for him. Just be happy Smokin' Joe and the RS3 did not make the trip, the whole damn troop would be rolling out. Guys, let's remember, the Regimental Commanding Officer wants us to succeed by achieving the standard. He gets no pleasure out of relieving First Sergeants. Let's move this little group to the BOC, React may call for reinforcement."

"You want we should alert our platoons, Top?" Maldanado asked.

"Good thought! No. Don't do that. We have an hour to move once React defines the problem. If we react early, we will look like a bunch of eager beavers. Never let those bastards at Regiment see you sweat," Martin replied. "Also guys, we all need to remember who Commands this troop. We may run it, but it is Brother Dawson who commands it, he calls alerts and moves the troop, not us," Martin concluded.

First Lieutenant Robertson, the most knowledgeable of the Platoon Leaders was on his second tour as the Border Ops officer for the Troop. After a correction by Captain Dawson to only call out React once for training to verify their readiness and thereafter to meet either a demand by higher headquarters or for a real world emergency, Robertson ensured that the other Platoon Leaders knew the new rule had teeth. As the First Sergeant had hoped when he asked Captain Dawson to correct the star Lieutenant, the React team performed admirably once they knew future call outs were all real. No one wanted to be a trained seal act for the amusement of the Operations Officer. Robertson explained what had happened with obvious pride in his platoon.

"Brazil smoked it. He dismounted the track and took up an over watch position with the field phone at the last bit of cover before the small valley where that farm road intersects B-19. Regiment had guys from the RS3 looking for them playing OPFOR. The OPFOR never saw our guys. Brazil called for fire on them over the exercise net the Sergeant Major established and adjusted it when ACR spotted the fall of shot."

"This is the most involved React exercise I have seen in two years. It goes way beyond the norm. It was a damn good exercise. ACR put in the separate radio net for call for fire and made it work. React is on the way back. The OPFOR has its own truck. We met all of the time hacks up to Regiment and it is all logged," Robertson related with a broad grin. The NCOs shook hands and acted like they had just won a close ball game.

"Top, you are not very happy. We won one," Vic Jackson said loudly.

"Yeah, Vic, but there are twenty more hurdles to leap," Martin said. "It is a good sign. We need to keep the winning habit," Martin added, lightening the moment.

"Lieutenant Robertson, would you write up the Handicap Black episode from beginning to end in the form of a vignette, one page if you can and two if you must. Get the Gator to bless it and add any notes he wants and get it out to the other Platoon Leaders and the Executive Officer. Start it with a timeline. For a lesson to be learned, it has to change the way we do things for the better," Martin stated.

"Already working on it, First Sergeant. It is part of my new Border Officer notebook. Our training plan and ACR's alternative secure radio network will be in there as well," Robertson concluded with a broad smile.

"You're learning, Ell Tee, you're learning," Maldanado said.

"Yeah, he is. When the Gator moves your Platoon Leader to the vacant scout platoon and you to the Tank Platoon Leader slot and makes Willie Williams your Platoon Sergeant, there will be a lot of learning in your outfit," the First Sergeant said with a smile.

"Hey, Top, I do not want that to happen. I'm just getting Chastain on the straight and narrow, cut me a break," Mercado stated with the barest hint of pleading.

"Just teasing you man! I do not know what the Gator will do anymore than you do with officer assignments," Martin said laughing. He then added, "It is about time for the Ranger grads to hit the field, after New Years and thus after REFORGER. One of them will get the scout platoon. For a lot of reasons, Lieutenant Chastain will probably stay where he is."

"Top, why is it that the Rangers go to the scout platoons?" Maldanado asked.

Martin decided a little NCOPD was in order, "You are about to become a Master Sergeant and you other jokers, with the exception of Robbie who will be happy to make E-7 as a Mortar guy, will be one after this tour. The TO&E calls for Ranger Qualified Armor Officers as Scout Platoon Leaders in the Heavy Regiments. The Regiments are the Corps' covering forces. The scouts lead the regiment. Ranger school is an elimination process where the weak are culled out. It is an indicator of potential. Scouts go forward to gain contact with the enemy and report. How that contact is made often determines how long they live. Smart scouts do not fight tanks; they snoop and scoot, not stay and shoot. That is what EDATS do, stay and shoot."

"What is an EDAT, Top?" Staff Sergeant Hankinson asked.

"It is an Electronic Dumb Ass Tanker," Vic Jackson volunteered. "Since we got the M1 we have graduated from being Dumb Ass Tankers.

"On that happy note, it is time to play poker," Maldanado announced.

"Hey, you playing tonight, First Sergeant?" Vic Jackson asked.

"Going to the OP tonight. I think my staying in the PSG room is bothering you guys. Is it? Tell me the truth!" Martin demanded.

Vic Jackson was the First Sergeant's oldest friend in the Troop and he answered for the group, "We have a room set aside for you and have had since we got here. We like you and like you staying with us but you know you are a work-a-holic. If you were to move, it would be okay with us, we would not be insulted."

"Okay, Vic, I'll be happy to move. I understand and no offense taken. I'll bet my gear gets moved while I am at the OP, a sign will be posted on the door and a key will be on the night stand - not that anyone planned on me moving or anything." Gales of laughter from all of the NCOs went on for five minutes.

Captain Dawson walked up and all of the senior NCOs came to attention and saluted. He returned their salute saying, "Just what I like to see, happy NCOs. Who are you guys chaptering to make you feel so good?" More laughter from the group got the young Captain laughing as well.

"The boys have graduated me to my own room, Captain Dawson. My late hours are interfering with their beauty sleep and they want me to have enough privacy to jack off in peace. They are always thinking of my well being," Martin concluded with a smile.

"Good job today guys. It is not a big deal to pass a Handicap Black Message Exercise but it is a big deal when you have a long history of failing them. We should pass them all from now on using the system WE developed," as Dawson said the word we, he pointed at the First Sergeant. "I hope you Platoon Sergeants are taking notes at the leadership clinic that is going on before your very eyes. Even if you never make First Sergeant, civilians would pay big bucks to learn his techniques. Pay attention. I am. Where are you off to, First Sergeant?" he asked.

"I am going up to OP Tennessee, Sir, to finish off my hours for Border Qualification. I lack the foot patrol and the leadership of one jeep patrol to complete it. You waived the REACT portion for me. I will finish the foot patrol in the morning and do the mounted patrol the next morning after a good night's sleep," Martin said.

"I told the Executive Officer to PCI the foot patrol and be the Instructor for you and the two Lieutenants. All three of you will get hosed at the same time. It is a long patrol so that will give everyone a shot at it. I know you will make every step of it. I will meet the patrol at OP Bratwurst and bring your jeep and driver with me, how does that suit you, First Sergeant?" Dawson asked.

"Please do not do me any favors, Captain. I would prefer to ride in the back of the truck with the other swine at the end of the patrol, wet feet and all. I am going to teach them how to cheat and change into dry boots for the ride back anyhow. The shared suffering is important, Sir," Martin stated without hesitation.

"Goddamn, Top, you are a glutton for punishment. No other First Sergeant in this Regiment or the 2 ACR ever qualified for the Border like you. I do not want you to get pneumonia," Dawson said with genuine feeling.

"In future years when I wear my Spurs, Captain, I will know I earned them the hard way. When I am bringing smoke on a squadron or regiment of NCOs to win their Spurs, I can truly say I earned mine without short cuts. I could not look our troopers in the eye if I took shortcuts. That is important to me and I hope you support me, Sir," Martin concluded.

"I damn sure do, First Sergeant. I think you are nuts, but I understand your reasons. I just hope you live through it, that's all," Dawson said slapping him on the back.

It amazed Martin that no one realized that what he had done as a Drill Sergeant was far tougher physically than anything the present situation offered. After running 50 miles a week for ten years he was in far better condition than any of them save the young Buck Sergeants and the Ranger school grads. What was the big deal?

After an early breakfast, the foot patrol formed up for inspection by the Executive Officer, First Lieutenant Robertson, the Camp OIC. Like many West Point varsity athletes who were Airborne Rangers, Robertson was all business. Martin had to admit, the hopping up and down standing in place to sort out noisemakers was a part of foot patrol he had forgotten from his Long Range Reconnaissance Patrol days. He did not share the fact that he had once served in a LRRP platoon as an M-60 Machine Gunner with his present comrades. Life was a lot harder while taking turns carrying the water can for the scout dog. Once these mechanized Soldiers learned the mantra of the Special Ops, "You don't have to like it, you just have to do it," they would be better off.

After the inspection, the patrol of eight Soldiers, two Second Lieutenants, one Staff Sergeant and one First Sergeant set off in the Winter Wonderland of German countryside. BJ was the supply driver and he drove the patrol very carefully to their jumping off point. BJ came to the front of the truck to join the leaders. In addition to his duties as a troop carrier, BJ's truck served as the emergency re-supply point for small arms ammunition, grenades and Light Anti-Tank weapons or LAW Rockets. It was also the emergency medical evacuation vehicle for the patrol. It was obvious BJ was enjoying the potential of the First Sergeant to fall on his face. If it happened, he wanted to be there to see it. Three rendezvous points along the patrol route were established, a final check of equipment made and the patrol started off under the leadership of Second Lieutenant Chastain.

The patrol moved in single file and was from the beginning, breaking trail through eight inches of new snowfall on the footpath. It was a beautiful scene with the mountains, the snow on the trees and the frozen creeks and ponds shining on the land below. The view was marred by the scar across the land-scape that was the fortified East German Border. Given the hills and valleys, the border scar was often out of sight as the patrol wended its way along the prescribed pathway. Despite his high level of conditioning, Martin knew after the first leg of five miles that it was going to be a long morning. Two of the privates were dragging, the medic was whining and one of the Lieutenants was starting to blow loudly from the exertion. It was all very predictable. Foot patrols were Infantry meat and potatoes and not a fit task for mechanized troops. They were just too soft of foot and heart to make it without a struggle.

These jokers will appreciate their Infantry brethren a lot more after today, Martin thought.

At several points along the way, the East German activity was duly observed and reported. The patrol stayed masked by the terrain whenever possible and avoided the skylines. Hearing the reports go up as US Foot Patrol was a novel experience for the three new guys. At the first point of leadership changeover, the five mile point, both Second Lieutenants wanted the First Sergeant to take the next leg of the patrol. Martin was very blunt, "I will take the last leg, Gentlemen. These folks are going to be dragging ass big time on the last leg. One of you will be in the rear kicking ass and I will be up front picking the best route to conserve our energy. I will take the last five miles. It is not their fault. We do not do enough foot marching to prepare the troops for a foot patrol. There ain't but one way to get in shape for foot marching, and that is by foot marching."

After a short discussion about where the patrol actually was located, the two Second Lieutenants satisfied the Staff Sergeant instructor's doubts and the patrol moved on. The Staff Sergeant 'Ranger Walker' Williams was not surprised the First Sergeant knew the patrol's location every minute they were marching. No matter what, it would be his ass if anything untoward happened. USAREUR was very unforgiving in assigning blame and quick to demand a "head" to lop off when something went wrong.

Martin noted the supply truck was always were it was supposed to be. He could not help but admire BJ's ability to stay close enough to assist on the tough terrain. He obviously knew the border farm roads like the back of his hand.

He smiled thinking about BJ's morbid interest about his health. It wasn't personal. Entertainment was in short supply on the border and watching a First Sergeant step on his own crank was as good as it got for a PFC.

At the last leadership changeover point, the First Sergeant was starting to feel the pain of the march. Walking is not running, he reminded himself as he smiled, knowing there was no way in hell he was going to fall out of the patrol. He gathered the patrol before resuming the march and personally inspected each member of the patrol intending to put anyone in extremis on the supply truck. The last leg of the patrol was the hardest and did not support evacuation by the supply truck.

The upside was the patrol was to end at a small kiosk nicknamed OP Bratwurst by the soldiers. The kiosk had hot German sausage, or Bratwurst, French fries, brochen, a delicious hot roll with a hard outer crust and soft center, coffee, tea, hot wine and soda pop on sale for German currency. It was a popular spot for the German populace who walked in the mountains for exercise and recreation. After the inspection, Martin felt all of the soldiers could make it to the end provided they wanted to finish the march.

The last miles were a trial. Martin ended up with the M-60, and the aid bag and each Lieutenant had an M-16 with Chastain carrying the radio. As they arrived at OP Bratwurst, Martin was not surprised to see Staff Sergeant Masterson there. He was surprised to see money changing hands between him, Ramos, and Vic Jackson. Masterson left without a word, driving away in his new BMW. Ramos and Jackson greeted the patrol warmly and razzed the First Sergeant for not wearing his field jacket even though both knew he was not cold until he stopped walking.

Martin assembled the patrol and inspected the rank as the weapons, radio, and aid bag were returned to the soldiers responsible for those items. He then told one and all to fall out, get a snack, and prepare to move to the truck for transport to Camp Lee. Then and only then, did he move toward the Kiosk for his snack, falling in at the end of the line.

Vic Jackson had beaten him to the draw, having a steaming bratwurst, brochen, French Fries and a cold Pepsi waiting for him at one of the stand up tables. The two NCOs entertained their First Sergeant as he wolfed down the food.

"Sheet, First Sergeant, Masterson sheet his pants when you came up the path carrying the '60 and the Aid Bag. You guys was late and he was sure they

147

were carrying you in on a stretcher. I knew his "for sheet privates" from Headquarters platoon would be dragging ass and you would be leading the last leg. That foot patrol is some hard sheet for a damn tanker, no, First Sergeant?"

"It is some hard shit for a First Sergeant tanker, yes, hombre," said Martin. "Thanks for the bratwurst, Vic."

"Don't thank me, First Sergeant, thank Masterson. He bet me and Ramos a hundred marks each you would not make the march. We had to come up and look at OP 10 anyhow and he had to go back to BK to do some Master Gunner shit so we all came up to see the patrol arrive. So he bought the bratwurst and much more."

"Poetic justice eh', Vic?" Martin asked.

"Do you want you ride back with us in the warm jeep, First Sergeant?" Vic asked.

"No, Vic. I'll ride the truck back with cold feet and the wind howling through the canvas with the rest of new guys. I want to squeeze everything out of the experience."

Vic and Ramos looked at each other and laughed out loud as they had both known what the answer would be. "See you back at Camp Lee, First Sergeant, enjoy your truck ride. You know the Lieutenants are going to ride up front with the heater," Vic said with a broad grin.

"That is as it should be, Sergeant Jackson," Martin said as he moved toward the truck.

Both Platoon Sergeants were quiet as they saw the patrol gather up their trash and gear, moving to the truck without order or command when First Sergeant moved. The foot patrol might have made them brothers but there was no doubt who was Big Brother.

Both NCOs had seen Martin take over failed and failing units before and the basic approach never changed, "Follow Me, Do as I do." It was also now becoming their way. It wasn't easy, but it never failed to work. It was as Martin said, "I want the NCO Creed in living color every day. Don't just memorize the words like some damn parrot, Live it!" Well, he was living it.

The training program had worked. The entire unit was now being deployed and employed using platoon and squad integrity except for selected training events such as this foot patrol and the upcoming mounted patrols. No one could remember when the troop had clicked together so well on the Border. The rivalry between platoons in the troop was intense but friendly and the competition between squads and crews within each platoon was developing. Publicly, the platoon sergeants encouraged rivalry, but off duty they remained good friends. As good friends, several of the bolder ones were hatching a plot to encourage their beloved First Sergeant to ease up and live a little bit. Not all of them were convinced, but Vic Jackson had the lead and he was sure he could pull it off.

148

In the nightly poker game, Vic outlined his tactics to tame the First Sergeant, "Look guys, the First Sergeant has not met any women since he has been over here. If he has, it did not do any good as he is as grouchy as an old bear with a thorn in his paw. We need to give him a Christmas Present, a damn Christmas Present from The House Chantal. Maybe some hot babe will settle him down a bit and at least give us a one or two day break. When he played poker with us and took all of our money, he put enough of it back when he left to pay for him and Staff Sergeant Jones to go to The House Chantal with enough left for dinner and a beer. We ain't out nothing."

Robbie Hankinson had to speak up or bust, "Vic, just why the hell did he take all of our money and then put it all in the pot and walk away?"

Ramos answered for the group, "Remember what he said Robbie," 'Joo guys are gambling, I am merely playing cards. Seniors that gamble with Juniors and take their money are not leaders, they are stripe wearers. Joo asked me to play. I played. I enjoyed it. Thanks.' He don't theenk it is right to take our money Robbie. And, he don't give a sheet what joo or anybody else theenks is right."

"Yeah, but he ain't normal. He does not have that kind of money to walk away from hundreds of dollars like that. Nobody does that," Hankinson said mystified.

"Yeah, but nobody else walks the foot patrol and smokes the Handicap Black first time out of the box either," Ramos said as he shuffled the cards.

"Money don't mean shit to a guy like him. Rank don't mean shit. He is here to do what he said, build the Armor Force. That is what makes him so damn dangerous to our esteemed leaders," Maldanado opined.

"Dangerous, what the hell makes you say that, Rich?" Vic asked.

"I am simple. I want to make Master Sergeant, retire, finish college and live my life in peace with my kids and grandkids, if I have any down the road. I will do what I have to do to do it. My plans don't include staying here one day past getting a transfer to Vilseck teaching for the rest of my tour. Bosses can live with that. They understand guys like me. They are just like me; they just have bigger goals, like the War College and fat stock portfolios. Two Cards please, compadre," Maldanado said nodding to the dealer.

"Si, patron," Ramos replied.

"Hey watch the Spanish lingo you guys, you know I hable," Vic said. "Now finish the story Rich," Vic stated as the game came to a pause.

"Our guy has not scared the big guys yet. But he will. And when he does, they are going to jerk a knot in his ass and use us as the rope. When they come after him, if the First Sergeant makes us pay the price for his ambition, everybody will know it was a personal thing - greed and he is phony. If he does not punish or blame us, he will really scare the greedy ones. Call and raise you five bucks," Maldanado said without taking the cigarette from his lips and squinting through the smoke.

149

"Goddamn, tell me the rest of it," Hankinson demanded.

"He is not like the rest of us Robbie. He is motivated from the inside out. He cares what the leaders think about the unit and he is content if the unit does good things. He does not care what happens to him one way or the other. The shit that scares you and me, don't touch him. Once the big guys figure out he is not a threat to them personally, they will quit screwing with him and use him up to cover their asses. If you can talk him into a whore for Christmas with what is really his own money Vic, I am for it. I had three hundred bucks in that pot when he gave it back and was reaching for my car title, now can we play some poker here," Maldanado said with a wolfish grin. The stage was set for the little drama and the assembled group all knew they would enjoy it however it turned out.

As he went off to sleep that night, the First Sergeant shivered as he thought about the mounted patrol the next morning in an open jeep. It was so stupid to take perfectly good canvas off a vehicle, bundle up like an Eskimo and spend a patrol shivering like a Beagle shitting Bowie knives. With any luck, his would be one of the last patrols in the open jeeps as the Regiment was about to issue new Mercedes Sport Utility Vehicles to replace them. Lying in his sleeping bag fighting sleep, Martin tried to compartmentalize the present and the future.

He came to the realization getting out in front of the calendar was a big deal to him but not necessarily to the troop. They were inured to the reaction mode. Jaded with regard to the future, the veterans had been jumping through their asses for so long it had become a way of life. Any concept of long range planning that involved both the long and short range calendars would have to be in small doses. They knew the leadership would not be too critical. After all, they were the ones packing ten pounds of doo-doo in a four pound bag. Hell, here he was dreaming of planning and the troops were only thinking about their last woman and scheming where they were going to get their next one.

Vic Jackson woke up laughing and his fit of joy woke up the rest of the Platoon Sergeant quartet. "I figured it out," he said laughing. He was in a great mood. He had won big at poker, his crew in the Border Ops Center had delivered his thermos with black coffee and he had solved his immediate problem off getting the First Sergeant off his ass for a day or two. A naturally generous man, Vic poured each of the coffee drinkers a Styrofoam cup of steaming hot and strong coffee. After waiting for his fellows to make the trip down the hall to the latrine and light their first smoke of the day, he laid out his plan.

As the Sergeants reassembled for their morning coffee and strategy session for the day, Vic Jackson related the plan. "First we get the Old Man to send the First Sergeant to the rear to study for his next test. Haskins takes him back in his hot rod BMW - Martin cannot resist riding in that thing, he

150

loves fast cars. I will prep the First Sergeant on how it is his duty to accept the Christmas present of the gal at the House Chantal. Besides he needs to go to his apartment and change into civilian clothes so they can go out to dinner later."

"Hey, Vic, why not use the one down the hill at the big intersection?"asked Staff Sergeant Hankinson.

"Shit no, Robbie! They got that transvestite there and there is no telling how the Maddog would react to IT!" Waiting for the laughter to die down, Vic Jackson continued his description, "The House Chantal is on a neighborhood street, is very quiet and they got the best women in town. Jeffery can bring back a full report on how he does with the gal."

As the First Sergeant blithely went about setting up another day of learning and qualifying, he was unaware of the forces conspiring to add some humanity to his stern visage. Immediately after a hearty breakfast of several thousand calories, Martin conducted morning formation. To his surprise, he noticed the Troop Commander and the Platoon Leaders at the rear of the formation. After receiving the report, he left the Troop at the position of attention and faced about in anticipation of the Commander assuming charge of the unit. As Dawson came to the front of the formation to accept the exchange of salutes, he told the First Sergeant to report to him at the Border Operations Center after the formation. Martin was a bit surprised and as he went to the rear of the formation he mused at Dawson's evil smile. The boy was up to something but he did not know what.

"At Ease, gather round," Dawson commanded. The Troop broke ranks and gathered around their Captain in the cold pre-dawn light on the scrubbed concrete of the Border Camp Street. "The beer hall will serve beer tonight." While he waited for the loud cheers to subside he wore an ear to ear smile. "We can do this because our Border Qualification, Drivers licensing, maintenance and last but not least, our successful Handicap Black effort are turning the troop around and you men deserve a break. I am declaring the First Sergeant Border Qualified and he can now have a Pepsi." Again waiting for the laughter to subside, he was obviously taking great pleasure in being the Good Cop for a change. "Don't let it go to your heads. We still have a long way to go to successfully complete this Border Tour. We need to stay safe and be smart. We are getting the new Mercedes Jeeps and turning in the Border Jeeps. We kept the old jeeps long enough, First Sergeant, so that no one would accuse you of being a wussy and qualifying in the Mercedes." The troops predictably roared with laughter though they immediately turned to see how the First Sergeant was taking the joke.

"Sir, when the Chaplain goes AWOL, I want to re-enlist!"Martin answered.

Dawson continued, "The plan is still on for the single guys to man the Border while the married guys go home for Christmas. We will all be back for

151

New Years as Echo Troop will relieve us. The First Sergeant and I will attend each New Year's party to which we are invited. Keep your gear together for REFORGER as it will be cold as a well digger's ass and a long 20 days."

"FALL IN." Dawson charged. "Platoon Leaders, Take Charge of your Platoons."

"C'mon, First Sergeant. Let's take a jeep ride, you drive and fire up the heater. I need to stop in the HQs and sign some stuff you got ready for me last night. Do you ever sleep First Sergeant? You do Border Qualification and supervision all day and do paperwork at night. Do you know we do not have a single case of pending action in favor of a soldier? Getting all of the administrative items up to date has really raised morale. You do not know how much these soldiers think of you. They may respect me but they idolize and love you." Martin just looked at Captain. Dawson and wondered what the Commanding Officer was selling.

No matter, once we get into his jeep he will make his pitch for what it is he wants me to do. He is transparent as hell but pure in heart for the most part.

"I'll go get the jeep ready, Captain," Martin said with a snappy salute. Dawson's only reply was a salute and a smile. He knew the entire Troop had observed the exchange of salutes and made the connection that saluting was truly a greeting between soldiers and a salute rendered was a salute returned. Dawson was very gratified and happy to see salutes were both automatic and heartfelt within the troop. There was no need for constant correction. The First Sergeant saluted the Second Lieutenants, the Executive Officer and Dawson as a reflex and sunk serious teeth into anyone who did not. His example worked - now the entire unit was saluting and exuding military courtesy. Martin stated the principle simply, "If they won't salute the Second Lieutenants, they won't charge the bunker. To salute is to act like a soldier; to pass morning inspection is to look like a soldier and to become Border and Spur Qualified is being a professional soldier."

As Dawson arrived at the vehicle, he had Martin go out the back gate and show him the 2 mile run course for the semi-annual Army Physical Fitness Test. The test was given quarterly in the Regiment as part of the Commanders directive to maintain 90% currency for all on PT, Personal Weapons Qualification, Gas Chamber, Border Qualification, and Drivers Licensing. G Troop spent an inordinate amount of time on the Border, on maneuvers in addition to traveling to all events with its parent squadron. Martin knew from the simple math the troop was being screwed by the Squadron S3 NCO and the Command Sergeant Major. He also suspected Dawson loved the Border and the field so much he did not complain but merely accepted the orders without comment. However, the Regimental Commanding Officer wanted training and certification carried out in spite of the obstacles presented by the whirlwind schedule of the Cavalry. Conversion of the gravel pit behind the Border Camp to a rifle and pistol range, use of the guest shower as an NBC Room as a Gas Chamber, aggressive driver's testing and getting the Education Center for college work and Military Police for Driver's Testing as well as getting the Dentists for dental exams and field care to come to the Border as guests of the troop had all been very successful.

Captain Dawson admired the fact that his First Sergeant solved problems in a way that made sense and met the Regimental Commander's Intent. A little thing such as running the two miles down hill appealed to Dawson's wicked sense of humor and served to gain some small measure of revenge on the system. Dawson did not like PT. He was blessed with great strength, coordination and size, he was able to use his reserves of strength and pass the test without regular exercise. All the running the First Sergeant did as part of his daily regimen was past his understanding.

"So, First Sergeant, I understand everything we are doing to meet the Regimental Commanding Officer's goals. What I really wanted to talk to you about was the Christmas present the troops have lined up for you. You are bringing smoke on everybody in the troop, even me."

As Martin started to speak in protest, Dawson cut him off saying, "Just listen for now and do not argue until I am done! You are bringing so much smoke on everyone; it is becoming a pain in the ass. You need some diversion back in BK. You have an exam coming up for the Sergeant's Major Academy. I want you to go back to BK with Jeffery Haskins in his BMW, go out to eat, and hit the House Chantal. You are all lined up with one of the gals there financed by that big poker pot you pushed back. I want you back on the Border in 72 hours the evening of 22 Dec for duty that evening. Bring your jeep back up as I am sending Staunton back down also. Do this for me."

"Go back, get drunk and get laid. Come back ready to finish up the Border tour and get ready for REFORGER. You and I will spend Christmas here at the Border and New Year's Eve back in BK. You are doing a great job. It is even more than I had hoped you would do."

"There are three things at a minimum that you do not realize, so now listen. These troops love you and they respect you because of the hard ass attitude you showed on your own qualification - particularly when you made an error. Most them have never seen a First Sergeant say, 'I don't know, show me how to do that, what do you think'. I tell them to take a good look 'cause they probably won't see one again."

"They do not love me. They respect and fear me, that's it. They know now they can win at everything they study, train and prepare to do. They are now employed in squads and by platoon. The chain of command is working up, down and side to side. Do you have a clue how rare that is? What you need to do is learn to relax. Learn when to let them be and enjoy this new confidence and competence. Questions, First Sergeant?"

Martin replied, "Captain, I asked you to tell me when I was pushing them too hard. I guess I am guilty. Sometimes I just do not know when to let up

153

and go on to the next item on the list. The people are the most important part of what we do. Thanks for reminding me of that. I guess I can rationalize the hooker as it is after all, my money. If not now, I would have to go buy a woman at some point before REFORGER. Right now, a hooker is the cheapest way to go for me - the alternative of seduction takes too long, is too public and too expensive all the way around. As you know, the young wives are also a big No-Go for me."

"Yeah, First Sergeant, I bet it was hard to turn down Mrs. Hornpipe when she all but stripped in your office," Dawson said laughing.

"Not really, Sir. The fact that I turned her down traveled to the back of the motor pool before she left the building. Troops have a right to expect their chain of command to support their efforts to build a family. Sergeant Jason Hornpipe has a problem with her and I am not going to make it any worse," Martin said with a smile. Then he added, "She is a knockout."

"I'll give you a full report on the House Chantal, Sir. I'll treat it as a Vet Inspection of a meat market," Martin concluded.

"That's the spirit, First Sergeant. Jeff is waiting for you just outside the gate and he has your fag bag and gym bag in the car. The Platoon Sergeants packed for you," Dawson said laughing. As his First Sergeant turned to him with a frown, Dawson was suddenly taken aback as he had not expected this transition from Puritan to rake to be this easy and wondered when it would go off the tracks.

Martin just smiled broadly and said, "Boy, this conspiracy goes deep. Now we have the senior NCOs cooperating with the officers. What's next, mind reading replacing radio calls while you maneuver the troop?"

"As a matter of fact, Top, that is the next phase we are going to work after you get human again. Now, be off with you," Dawson said with a salute he held until Martin returned it.

The ride back to the Kaserne in the souped up BMW was all Martin thought it would be. Staff Sergeant Jeffery (Jeff) Haskins was reluctant to drive the car flat out as the First Sergeant was in his forties, straight laced and very proper. Looking over at the First Sergeant, Jeff said, "The car is really a lot faster than I am driving it. I would like to run hard for a few miles to see if the new fuel pump is working like I hoped it would be."

"Shit, Jeff, if you can drive it, I can ride it. These roll bars should do the trick as the curves won't let go you much over 120 mph. Turn her loose," Martin said surprising the hot rod NCO.

Haskins then gave the First Sergeant a real treat as the competition BMW with special fuel mix leaped ahead and hugged the curves. Jeff had been driving this road and ones like it, for most of his twelve years in Germany. He and his German in-laws had re-built the BMW piece by piece and he really enjoyed road racing it. The only emotion he produced in his First Sergeant was joy. He noted the First Sergeant never grabbed for a hand hold on the

154

roll bars but calmly watching the tachometer go up and down as he ran through the racing capable gear box. As Haskins slowed down to pass through several small towns, he looked over and asked, "Well, Top, what do you think?"

"It is a fine car. Fast, well built and made for Germany. Tad bit of under steer but I guess you want it that way so you can keep up with it, huh?"

Haskins was surprised at the evaluation. "So you know about under steer, First Sergeant?"

"Hell, there is no tellin' what I can learn hanging out with you Jeff!" Martin said laughing.

1700 hours
19 Dec 1984

Right on time, Staff Sergeant Haskins arrived at Martin's rooming house in a quieted BMW having closed the exhaust port cutouts. The two NCOs proceeded to a Yugoslavian place named Zagrebs favored by the Troop leadership. They enjoyed a four course dinner that began with Onion Soup, followed by a fresh salad. The entrée consisted of Jager Schnitzel and a delicious Crème' Brulee' followed for desert. Following after a German custom, they took a short walk though the Kurheim District of Bad Kissingen, marveling at the plush hotels and rest cure establishments. Of course, all of the streets and sidewalks were as spotless as Disney World on its best day.

The German populace and the visiting Germans there for a rest cure at the various Kurheim with their attendant spas and hotels were also out for their stroll, some dinner, and dancing. By now, Martin knew many of the happy "couples" were a pair of Kurheimers. Kurheimers were two Germans who paired off during their state paid vacation to enjoy a short and often blissful sexual liaison during a week away from their respective spouses. During the time they were getting the various cures of hot soaks in the mineral water mud packs, facials and other blandishments, they were also getting their sexual urges met.

The Gasthauses and nightclubs were packed with the Kurheim crowd. They would stay that way until nearly 10 pm when each establishment booking the cure had a form of bed check. Teutonic efficiency required all those being cured to be present and in their room, if not in bed, in order for their stay to be fully paid by the state. It was very funny to the two NCOs that all of these middle aged and older Germans would be reduced to a teenage existence akin to boarding school for five days. Some of them probably went home with their butts dragging and their tongues hanging out after their week of exertions. On that cheerful note, the two happy NCOs arrived at the car and set off for the House Chantal.

155

Martin, a veteran of two previous tours in Germany, was very familiar with the state licensed and sanctioned system in place to manage and control prostitution. The very practical Germans realized man had a lustful nature. Since the dawn of time, prostitutes had been available, willing and able to satisfy man's baser nature. The response of the Federal Republic of Germany was to control the prostitution traffic by restricting it to brothels where sex workers were strictly regulated and the hygiene of their surroundings subjected to constant monitoring.

Street walkers did not exist in the smaller communities. During earlier times, the US Army conducted Courtesy Patrols of NCOs operating jointly with the German Polizei. These three man teams visited the bars and whorehouses to maintain a command presence among the off duty Soldiers and Martin had often been detailed for this duty. Though the requirement no longer existed, along with kitchen police and interior guard, he knew he had learned a great deal while pulling the duty though he did not enjoy it at the time. He was glad he had enjoyed good amateur standing but did not mind "paying for it" in his present situation.

He was pleasantly surprised when he was paired with a very petite and attractive twenty something French girl. Although he had daughters her age, he managed to ignore the gulf of age. Somehow he knew this was another form of testing but one he was certain to enjoy. So far, his sexual appetite had always been as great, or greater than, that of his partners and tonight was to be no exception.

After an initial shower together, the experience moved through every desired position and was a very pleasant change from the furtive and seedy version often found with a prostitute near the Army bases in America, USA. It seemed both Gisele and her "Speise", the German term for First Sergeant, meaning the "Blade," enjoyed their time together. Martin considered it service after the sale and enjoyed it for the moment. She was very convincing that she was thoroughly satisfied by her "Speise" and welcomed him to come back anytime. Jeff's paramour was also cooing and very complimentary. She told them both it was nice to have two obviously married men who knew how to treat a woman.

Yeah, right, thought Martin, must be a slow night.

None the less, the girl was convincing as she hung on around his neck when he got up to leave and proceeded to walk them to the door, closing it gently behind them.

"Damn, Jeffery, what the hell was that all about?" Martin asked.

"My gal in there was great. My little German gal is quite pregnant and we have been shut off for a month so I needed that shot of leg. You might as well have been in jail, First Sergeant. All the women you have seen have been married or at a distance for nearly three months. Shit, those two bitches were lucky to get off so easy. Yours was crazy about you and the fact you spoke some French to her. Her Father is a French officer and she is a run away. Probably a heroin user, did you see any tracks on her, First Sergeant?" Johnson replied.

"The light was too dim. Besides, heroin tracks were the last thing I was looking for tonight. I thought we had a very good time as a man and a woman tonight. If she did not have a good time, she should get an Academy Award. Acting or coming, it had the same effect on me. I loved every minute of it. I am ready to go home and get some sleep, Jeff. What do you to say to me buying us one more drink at that Greek Gasthaus where Tatu lives over by my apartment?" Martin asked.

"Sounds great, Top, I know it well. Tatu will probably be there, he sure as hell ain't at the Border much," Jones opined.

"Jeff, how did he get the nick name Tatu after the Fantasy Island character? Is it just because he is short and fat? He is actually in pretty good shape and can run well," Martin said.

"That's about it, First Sergeant. It doesn't take much in the Cav to get a nickname that sticks like glue. You are living proof of that, First Sergeant. You were Mad Dog Martin in about ten seconds of our first duty day," Haskins said smiling.

"It has a certain ring to it doesn't it, Jeff. I hate to be thought of as a man who cannot keep his temper in check," Martin said quietly.

0500 hours
22 Dec 1984

The mail bags lay on the couch in First Sergeant Martin's office. A collection of parts for tanks, Personnel carriers and trucks was neatly boxed and labeled by the parts clerk. Personnel actions were packaged in individual folders ready for review and signature. A re-supply of personal items for the First Sergeant was ready to go as he did not intend to return until the troop completed the border tour. As his driver arrived, he and the training room crew quickly packed all of the items up the concrete stairs to his jeep idling at the curb in front of the barracks. First Sergeant Martin gathered up three packages, two of which were gift wrapped in the finest German wrapping paper available. With all of the olive drab gear of war surrounding them, they looked totally out of place in the utilitarian atmosphere.

"Damn, First Sergeant, you did not have to go to all that trouble to wrap my presents," his driver Staunton said. "You know you gave me the four best presents of all; separate rations; time off to see my girl; transfer back to being a mechanic; and promotion to Spec Four."

"I did not wrap your present Tommy. Here it is." With that, Martin handed Staunton a Buck Knife complete with brown leather belt sheath. "Open it and read the inscription on the blade."

157

As he did so, much to his surprise Staunton's eyes began to water, forcing him to wipe them so he could read the words on the knife – "HQ7 G, 2/11 ACR '84-85, Cavalry Trooper". He was glad he did not sob but began to smile as the tears coursed down his cheeks. Staunton looked to Martin like a cherub. Staunton's pink cheeks, downy blond facial hair, curly blond hair visible under his fatigue hat and a perfect smile of white teeth completed the picture. The young driver could not know his countenance and joyful youth aroused an instinct in old Soldiers that could best be described as "in *loco parentis.*"

"Turn off the tears, Turd. You're going to rust the damn thing and be careful! I had Kamerad hone it. It is as sharp as an old SS trooper could make it," Martin said gruffly.

"Do I have time to put it on my belt, Top?" Staunton asked.

"Hell, yes! Make it snappy, we should have left ten minutes ago," Martin replied.

As Staunton joined Martin in the jeep, he reached into the wooden console box and handed the First Sergeant a cigar case holding six "Al Capone" Brazilian Cigars. "You topped me, First Sergeant. These ceegars ain't much. I know the Buck Knife is also a going away present and is a replacement for the one I lost on the field problem."

"You're welcome kid. Thanks for my present Tommy. The cigars and the case are a nice present, very genteel for an old sweat like me," Martin said.

"Now get me to the Border in time for breakfast and formation. Go the back way and keep it under seventy," Martin said knowing full well the jeep had a top speed of sixty on a good day with a tail wind.

"Be careful what you wish for, First Sergeant. We put a new engine in this thing while you were off. This is the fastest jeep in the Regiment right now. We can beat Captain Dawson and his Buck Sergeant to the Border anytime they want to take us on," Staunton stated proudly.

"Remember, Tom, the Captain can have the bumper numbers changed and any jeep can be Six," the First Sergeant opined.

"Nah, no way, Top, that won't ever happen. Not after putting that stereo and the hard Plexiglas windows, not to mention the overhead lights and stuff, in it. Those two will never get rid of that ride. It is just too comfortable. Say, First Sergeant, is it true you made a test bench for track heaters and that every one of ours in the troop is working for REFORGER?" Staunton asked plaintively.

"I did not build them. I made a diagram based on one we had in one of my old units. Staff Sergeant MacClincock did the rest, but yes, all of the track vehicle heaters work and yes, the test bench makes it easy to isolate the faults," Martin stated with some pride. "I like to keep the troops warm and the equipment working. Tracks with heaters stay in top shape. The fire control and sights work better. Troops that have a warm place to clean up, sleep and work as well as have access to hot food and hot beverages and are properly dressed, can operate through the effects of cold weather."

"Morale is high when troops know you give a shit about them. They give you a 200% return on any investment you make on their behalf. The experience of the Finns in WW II fighting against the Russians is a close parallel to the one we have here in USAREUR. I am just using their example and some technical knowledge to do what they did. They eventually lost to the Russian hordes but they killed a butt load of them first and made them look bad," Martin said with a smile.

1000 hours
22 Dec 1984
Border Supply Annex

"Hey, First Sergeant, got a minute?" BJ asked with a smile and no trace of a stutter.

"For you BJ, I always have a minute," Martin replied.

"Did you have a good time on pass?" the Texan asked with a big smile.

"BJ, it was fine. I had a great time at the Haus Chantal. I got little Giselle and she taught me to speak French in a brand new way," Martin said with a smile.

"Sheeit, First Sergeant. I know about how much language instruction went on that night. Haskins done told everybody the bitch is in love with you and you are leavin' us to be a pimp," BJ said knowing no one else could hear.

"A pimp I could never be, BJ. Pimps hate women. I love them. You know, BJ, I'll bet the Headquarters Platoon could rent the Haus Chantal for the whole night of New Year's Eve and have a night of a lifetime. Who knows, the pimp may go for it. I'll bet New Year's is a slow night in a state run whorehouse," Martin the agitator stated.

When the light went on in BJ's eyes, Martin laughed silently, knowing he had taken the bait and that the hook was firmly set. "Would you and the Captain come to visit our party, First Sergeant?" BJ asked with slight belligerence.

"Why hell yes, why wouldn't we? We would not partake of the fruit of the flesh with the girls, but we could come by and have a drink. You set it up and invite the Gator, we will be there," Martin replied with a wolfish grin.

1700 hours
22 Dec 1984
Check Point 121

First Sergeant Martin and his driver had been sitting quietly in the wooded area near Check Point 121. They were waiting a radio call to meet with the Platoon Leaders at a nearby Gasthaus. A VW civilian van pulled up in the

159

cleared area in front of them. The driver did not see them. As Martin put his binoculars up to read the license plate in the fading light of the German winter, he saw the plates flip. It was clear the vehicle was equipped with a mechanism controlled from the inside enabling the driver to change plates without leaving his driver's seat. Unless the guy was one of ours, that might not be a good thing. "Tommy, did you see that shit?" Martin asked.

"I did, First Sergeant, that guy is dirty," Staunton replied, putting the vehicle into gear.

"Don't move Tommy, he does not know we are here," Martin said quickly, knowing his driver's youth and quick reaction time. "Let's see what he does next. Have a smoke," handing a pack of Marlboro Reds to the driver.

"I'll fish out the NVG's (Night Vision Goggles PVS-5)," Martin said reaching into the back seat of the jeep. The crew of the First Sergeant's jeep had prepared for nightfall earlier by inserting new batteries and bringing the device up to power in the dark of a winter afternoon.

As the NVGs came up to power, the First Sergeant did not strap them on but held them up to his eyes as if they were binoculars. What he saw next really mystified him. "Tommy, that joker is unrolling a piece of target cloth over the license plates at the front and rear of the vehicle. That guy is an old soldier in someone's Army," Martin stated firmly.

"How do you know that, First Sergeant?" his driver asked.

Without removing the NVGs Martin stated, "It takes one to know one. He moves with purpose, he is erect and has bearing and presence. He is a retired or serving officer, at least a Lieutenant Colonel. I sure hope he is not ours. He has some sort of NOD (Night Observation Device). It looks huge like one of our old Sniper Scopes. Leave the lights off but put it in gear. If he is what I think he is, he is going to do a 360 degree check. When he does he will probably bolt. Puff on that smoke Tommie. He ought to see that if that is a NOD or and if it is a telephoto lens. I want him to Rabbit," Martin said with a smile.

"Why?" Staunton asked.

"It is the silly season Tommy. People all over the world do dumb shit at Christmas. That is why we are here, to prevent dumb shit. I am sure he is not an American so the Border Resident Office will have to handle him."

"BORDER OPS, SEVEN, SPOT REPORT, OVER."

"Seven, BORDER OPS, SEND IT, OVER."

"SEVEN, Roger: One Civilian; Operating VW Van with German License Plates being changed mechanically and draped over with target cloth; Vehicle is directly in front of Checkpoint 121; Continuing to observe. BREAK, call the BRO, talk to the Russian and get his advice, OVER."

"SEVEN, BORDER OPS, ROGER, OVER."

"Seven, Out."

"Top, he's moving out."

"Get on his tail Tommy. I want to see where he goes, at least until we hear from the BRO."

The jeep could match the van's speed initially but it soon became clear the driver of the mysterious vehicle was very highly skilled and the van highly tuned.

"Back off Tommy. It is not worth an accident! That guy is either nuts or an Intelligence Operator, or both. Let him go. We have his plate number or at least one of them. Let's go to the Gast Haus to eat. You okay for money?" Martin asked.

"Top, I could have caught him in the next town," Staunton said, his blood still pumping from the chase.

"It is not about you and me Tommy. It became a safety issue and we have no legal standing to chase him or arrest him," Martin said just in time to hear the radio.

"SEVEN, THIS IS BRO, OVER."

"BRO, SEVEN, OVER."

"SEVEN, THIS IS BRO, CALL ME LIMA LIMA AT MY PRIVATE NUMBER. SUGGEST YOU NOT FOLLOW THE VEHICLE OR TAKE ANY ACTION UNTIL WE TALK, OVER."

"BRO, SEVEN, ROGER, WILL CALL YOU LIMA LIMA IN 10, OVER."

"THIS IS BRO, OUT."

"Pull over at that pay phone Tommy. Oh shit, just go onto the Gast Haus. There is a pay phone there. Tell the Lieutenants I'll be in there with them in a minute and tell them why we were late," Martin ordered.

As the First Sergeant joined the group he had a bit of a hang dog look but lit up with a smile on seeing the young officers. "Gentlemen, good evening one and all. Have you ordered yet?" he asked as he sat down in the fourth chair and regarded the three officers.

"No, First Sergeant, but we ordered you a Coke," Lieutenant Chastain reported.

As the drinks arrived, Martin waited until the waitress had departed before briefing the group on what had just transpired. "The guy at the Border was a Soviet Officer who defected. He managed to get across legally while on a mission under proper authority. His wife and teenage daughter were caught up in the Soviet Counter Intell Net. They were supposed to cross at Eusenhausen. Their fail safe plan was for him to take them out across the road at Checkpoint 121. When they did not show up at the West German Crossing point east of Mellrichstadt he went there. When he looked across the Border, the bad guys put the headlights on his wife and daughter. They were bound and blind folded. They guy never got over it and tonight is the anniversary of their loss. The guy is goofy but is still apparently worth something to Intell pukes so they let him run loose. It is a sad tale and I am glad Tommy and I did not

161

make it worse by chasing the guy until he wrecked. We need to make him part of the assumption brief."

"Gentlemen, you have been up on the Border now for more than 14 days. I know you must have questions. Don't be bashful, ask anything you want. I'll do my best to answer without preaching," Martin said with a smile.

"I notice you never drink alcohol, First Sergeant. We can have a beer with our meal but you never drink. Are you a teetotaler?" Lieutenant X asked shyly.

"Long ago as a young NCO, I was in a bind on Battalion Staff Duty. I called the Command Sergeant Major at home and he was too drunk to help me out. I figured out what to do and it came out all right. I made up my mind then and there that no subordinate would ever see me drunk or have to put up with me being unable to give coherent orders over the phone," Martin calmly replied. "I am also cursed with a staff brain and reputation as a trainer. I will get few chances to be a First Sergeant or a Command Sergeant Major. I mean to enjoy every minute of the time I have. I do drink and I enjoy a good time. Enough about me, you guys tell me about yourselves and how you got here," Martin stated with good feeling.

As they waited for their food, each of the young officers shared with the First Sergeant a brief biographical sketch about their lives up to that point. It was a litany of schools, sports, home towns, parents accomplishments, hopes and dreams along with girls left behind and future marriage plans. The First Sergeant listened to each recitation with rap attention often asking a pointed question and invariably making a pointed reference to the geography of each officer's home area. He gave the impression of having traveled the entire nation and of knowing it very well. Though well traveled, he had made a point of a short map study of the US Road Atlas near their homes of record. He was then able to weave the points of interest in their areas into the conversations with each Lieutenant.

Lieutenant Chastain again asked in his shy way, "First Sergeant, why are you more interested in us than the CO? It is obvious you did your homework for our dinner tonight and you make us all feel at home."

As he homed in for the tough part of the question, his table mate, Lieutenant Martin - an Aggie and tough rodeo cowboy - interrupted him by saying, "First Sergeant, Jack is just naturally curious about everything and he over analyzes everything, even yella' snow."

"Lieutenant Martin, you are going to do well in this Army. You sense when leadership is called for and you provide it. But, Lieutenant Chastain has a legitimate question and he deserves an answer to the question he has yet to ask - if the Commanding Officer is our officer leader, why is the First Sergeant being our mentor and doing the things the Commanding Officer has not done?" Martin stated without a smile.

162

Continuing, the First Sergeant said, "The Commanding Officer knows how he wants to lead. He is aloof like Zeus up on Mount Olympus. He is going to tell you what you need to know and what you need to do. He will not speak often, but when he does, it will be important. There are some things he wants you to figure out on your own. I do not analyze or speculate why the Gator does what he does. The Squadron Commander is his mentor, not me. I am here to be a technical consultant and a sounding board for you. The Executive Officer is your gold standard for PT, dress, deportment, timeliness and professionalism. Most of you are in better condition than I am right now. You look great in your uniforms and you have the basic Army stuff down pat. But you have not seen anything yet. A good example is worth ten volumes on leadership."

"My motivation is simple. You are my Lieutenants. You reflect the troop. If we cannot take wonderful men like you and make you into good platoon leaders then we are not worth a shit. No one with a brain expects you all to be in the running to be the Chief of Staff of the Army. Down here our goals are short ranged. We want you to become Executive Officers, staff officers, and Troop Commanders. We expect you to learn how to maneuver, use supporting fires, report accurately, kill the enemy, conserve all of your resources – especially time and if necessary, die bravely."

0700 hours
24 Dec 1984

Hilda Kurstenberg was a full time kitchen worker at Camp Lee. She had worked for the US Army for 15 years at the small kitchen. Some of the men who had been Squadron Commanders were now Generals and many others were field grade officers. To Hilda they were just her boys, forever young in her eyes. She treated them all the same, like surrogate brothers, subconsciously replacing the two older siblings taken from her during WW II. Hilda was a social lion-hunter during the Christmas Season. It was her task to invite a delegation of the unit serving at the Border to her village Christmas Party. Officially, the party was a function of the Regimental Civil Affairs Office. As a practical matter, it was Hilda's pet project for the year.

Hilda was a big boned, very strong, and hearty Hessian farmer's wife. Her family had over three hundred sheep and worked the land from daylight to past dark - on a good day. Her day started with breakfast for her husband and two sons before the soldiers of Camp Lee were awake. Once her men folk were fed and her coffee with her husband was finished, she made her way to work at the kitchen of the Border Camp. In the early years, the leftover food from the kitchen and the largesse of the Mess Sergeants enabled her family to eat well. She continued to be amazed at the capacity of the Americans to waste food and money. The times were good for her family but she still took everything home the Americans gave her.

She smiled at the memory of her Papa. He always said the forest told the state of the economy. When times were good the forests were full of dead wood and stray branches. In bad times, every stick was scavenged and carried away for someone to burn. At the moment, the forests were full of dead wood. It would be a good Christmas at the Kurstenbergs.

"Good morning, First Sergeant," Hilda said in heavily accented English.

Replying in German Martin said, "Good Morning, gentle lady and how is Hilda this fine day? Do we still have all of the sheep - no wolves last night?"

"First Sergeant, all of the wolves are gone - you know that," Hilda answered in English smiling at the thought of wolves. "Are you coming to the Christmas Party tonight?"

"What Christmas Party, Hilda?" Martin asked innocently.

Poston, in mess line near the First Sergeant immediately spoke up, "First Sergeant, the Commanding Officer wants to tell you about the Christmas Party tonight. He just got the requirement from Regiment."

"What is with those guys? This stuff can't be all new. Why is everything we do with the German Community planned so badly?" Martin said, instantly regretting the outburst when the pain registered on Hilda's face. "Of course we will be there Hilda. Thank you for inviting us. We are the Camp Lee family and we will visit the German side of the house and be glad we have such great friends," Martin said gently with a smile.

Hilda knew she was being charmed and that the gruff First Sergeant meant her no harm or ill will. "We will talk after you eat, First Sergeant," she said with a relieved smile.

These soldiers from G Troop were her favorites. Many were fluent in German and were married to, or dating German women and the horny ones were doing both. Most learned their German from their women. It amused her to hear First Sergeant Martin speak German with a Berliner's accent. She decided the source of his ability to speak German was from the university and not the bed room. He and Lieutenant Robertson were the only soldiers she knew who read the German newspapers and underlined the articles. The intensity of this new First Sergeant was unsettling to her. Though friendly and personable, he was clearly different. Hilda was a child of war. What she had seen, lost, and regained could not be explained to those who had not been there. Above all, she wanted to maintain the status quo. After her past, the present suited her just fine.

Captain Dawson laughed as the First Sergeant joined him for breakfast. He was finished with his meal and having coffee with a big slice of cake. "So, First Sergeant, Poston says you don't like getting the plan from the KPs," he said smiling.

"When I get pissed off about Regiment, I try to remember we are all just pissants at Troop level. It is not ours to reason why but to march and die," Martin said with a smile.

Dawson schooled his First Sergeant, "A lot of the stuff the S-5 does are annual events. The old bat that does the S5 stuff at Regiment has served the last five Regimental Commanding Officers. We get the word late. The Christmas in the town always goes well because of Hilda. G Troop is often here at Christmas. Hilda likes G Troop. We will take three jeeps and a Scout Track to the Christmas party. The NCOs and Officers will all wear a pistol under our fatigue shirts in shoulder holsters. Drivers will only have one beer to be sociable. No one gets even slightly drunk. We will be back here by 2300 and 2200, if we can get away. We do the gift exchange in the Beer hall before we go. The message about potential terrorist activity is applicable to us in a general way but we are all armed and behind the fence most of the time. However, we will be armed in the civilian world, we just won't advertise it. What do you think, Top?" Dawson concluded.

"Sounds like an undercover cop's dream to me, Captain," Martin replied in between bites. "Is the party for us or are we being invited to a party the Germans are having whether we were here or not?"

"We are Hilda's guests at the party," Dawson replied. "We need to be on our best behavior."

"She is a formidable woman, Captain," Martin said with a smile.

"She is scared shitless of you, Top. You probably remind her of the SS," First Lieutenant Brown said teasing the First Sergeant.

"What's the plan for the day, First Sergeant?" Dawson asked.

"I want to visit all of the OPs and make certain we have them ready for turnover to Eagle Troop. Joe James and I are getting along fine and I want to keep it that way. The best way we NCOs can keep you officers out of our business is to do the job right the first time and on time." This statement was greeted by a lot of laughter among the officers. None of them could imagine being anywhere near NCO business with this First Sergeant and on time with him was one day early.

"Oh, I think we are okay on that score, First Sergeant. You know my biggest worry, First Sergeant?" Dawson asked.

"No, Sir, but I would like to hear it," Martin said.

"You and the NCOs will do so much that we will get fat and lazy from watching y'all work and get sloppy on details," he said without a smile.

"I never worry about that, Captain Dawson. We do too much maneuver training for that to happen. We have clear cut officer and NCO authority lines here at the Border. Everybody knows their left and right limits," Martin opined. "Is there anything specific you want me to do, Captain?" he asked.

"Captain McKenzie and I are going to meet at OP 13 at 1400. That OP always suffers from a lack of care. It is the furthest away and gets the least use and attention. I see you had it serviced first. I want you to meet us there at 1400. You got a problem with that?" Dawson asked.

"No, Sir, I'll see you there," Martin replied.

"Everyone remember, the married guys are going home at 1100 today by POV. It is only 18 people so we should be fine without them until the day after Christmas. Officers need to be ready to step in and help if there are problems during the night and on Christmas Day. No need for tank start during the night as it is not going to get below 10 above zero tonight. But it is going to snow some more. Just slow everyone down and don't take any risks we don't have to take on the roads. Let's go get it done people," Dawson said, effectively adjourning the impromptu meeting.

At 1330, Martin and Staunton had Observation Post number 13 open and prepared for inspection. Staff Sergeant Ramos was responsible for the task of bringing the OP to a high standard of maintenance and police. He had done a very, very thorough job. Martin sat in his jeep re-reading William Manchester's "American Caesar", the MacArthur Biography. Staunton was as usual, asleep. Martin knew the two Captains were good friends and would probably be late - at least five minutes late. They were good officers - never early, very thorough and very proficient. Though both were Ranger qualified, Dawson was fond of saying he had "gotten over it" once out of Ranger School and by inference implying his good friend Ted McKenzie was still more of a child of Benning than of Knox.

McKenzie simply loved the outdoor life and the challenge of being a Ranger. *Who but a Ranger would take a heavy rucksack and do solitary foot patrol on the Border. McKenzie could care less about mattress covers being clean. Martin knew this but no one wanted to come up short if Regiment inspected on no notice. Martin admired the E Troop Commander's wife from afar and marveled at the dedication of the young Captain who spent so much time away from her voluntarily. You're a better man than me, Gunga Din, he thought as the two Commanders arrived at the OP.*

"Tommy, wake up. You got the radios. The officers are here," Martin said.

"Okay, First Sergeant, I got it," Staunton said.

"Yeah, well, get out and stretch Tommy or you'll be back to sleep before we make it inside," Martin said as he got out and shut his door.

Martin saluted the two officers and shook McKenzie's outstretched hand. As McKenzie shook his hand he also gripped Martin's elbow, obviously very glad to see him. McKenzie was one lean, tough, physically fit officer. His ruddy complexion with wind burned cheeks, and bright blue eyes burning with that West Point manner of bearing and his superior fitness marked him as a fine officer.

"The other OPs look great," McKenzie exclaimed. "It is going to be a good border handover. You do not know how good it is to have you working so close with my First Sergeant and you guys having the same trust level as the officers," McKenzie stated.

166

Martin smiled and said, "Trust flows from performance, Captain McKenzie. Promises don't mean a thing if we don't meet the standard. You're looking fit to fight, Captain M. Still keeping up with your PT, that's a good thing," Martin said.

"Did you get to run much up here?" McKenzie asked.

"Not as much as I would have liked and certainly not as much as the Armor School, "Martin said.

"Yeah, we just about shit when we saw you coming by the O Club on the last leg of your noon time run. You were in shorts, no shirt, no socks, ratty running shoes, a piece of an old tee shirt for a head band and pouring sweat - scheduled to teach us a class in fifteen minutes in Class A uniform. That was a lesson in time management for a bunch of young Captains," McKenzie laughed at the memory.

"Yeah, I remember you asking me in class if that was me and asking me how I did it. It was simple - shower at the gym, air dry on slow walk to the classroom area, change into Greens, hit the Coke machine and teach the class. But there is no sweat flying off me today Captain M, just snowflakes," Martin concluded, opening the bottom door to the OP and stepping aside for the officers.

Buying the latex paint for the OPs had been a good investment, Martin thought. They looked better than some quarters with no holes, putty in the cracks and freshly painted. The fresh paint smell always sold the rental or the house. It was no exception for these officers.

"Damn, you painted them. That is a tough standard, First Sergeant," McKenzie exclaimed.

"Not really, Sir. I'm leaving the excess paint with your First Sergeant for touch up. If all we have to do is buy a gallon per tour, it will be money well spent," Martin replied. "I have never seen the OPs look any better. I hope we can turn them over to Fox Troop looking like this. It would be great," McKenzie said.

"Damn, it is good to see you here as one of our First Sergeants. We just could not believe it when we got you in 2d Squadron. What are we going to do for gunnery? Do you have a plan for the Squadron?" McKenzie asked.

"I have no plans for Tank Gunnery other than to provide the bullets and the beans to the troop. Captain Dawson has not told me anything about gunnery. Smokin' Joe gave me ninety days to turn the troop around or be fired. I figured I'd better work his list before I worked my own," Martin said with a smile.

"First Sergeant, there is no way you are going to get fired and you know it. There is no hole you cannot work your way out of, you will be just fine," McKenzie stated as he and Dawson walked to their waiting jeeps.

As Martin saluted, Captain McKenzie ignored his salute and shook his hand again. "Glad you are here and great job on these OPs. Come over and see me when we both get back," McKenzie said.

As McKenzie drove away, Dawson smiled and said, "I noticed he did not invite you over to his house for dinner with him and the frau."

"It ain't that kind of friendship, Sir. I wouldn't go if he did. I could not stand to be that close to his beautiful wife without saying or doing something I would always regret. She flips my trigger bad and I feel like the stupid wolf in the cartoon when little miss comes out to perform in the nightclub. The wolf is crazy about her with his eyes bugged out, tongue hanging out, slobber everywhere, steam coming out of his ears. No, I will keep my distance from her. Distance is my only defense from temptation," Martin said without a trace of a smile.

"Don't get all involved in anything out here, First Sergeant. Remember we are going to Heustreu tonight. SP will be at 1900," Dawson said.

"The OPs will pass any battle handover we have. I suspect E Troop is going to send Sergeant First Class Kowalski. Joe James does not realize I know he uses him as a Field First Sergeant. He is smart, tough, and coordinates well on nearly everything. I am going to go back and take a nap," Martin said, shocking Dawson.

1900 hours
24 Dec 1984

Martin looked up at the sky in the relative darkness near the gate of Camp Lee. The night was clear and full of stars. The sky was a European one with many differences from that over South Florida, but beautiful in its own right. It was a cold night but he did not feel it. He was dressed in the latest "snivel gear", a lightweight underwear from LL Bean. When he first arrived in the troop he set off a flurry of activity when he had gathered the Troop around him and proceeded to show them what he would be wearing. All of the troops applauded his policy of "If your snivel gear does not show at the neck of your BDUs no one will say a word. If I am wearing it, you can wear it. Civilian gear is always a light year ahead of the Army. Buy lightweight, dress to avoid sweating and accept it is better to be a little cold in winter. You can wear mountaineer boots, just keep them highly shined. You can wear sneakers inside your overshoes, particularly for the vehicle crewman. Keep your combat vehicles clean to include the sub-floor. Do not give an order you do not expect to be obeyed and do not ask your soldiers to suffer with issue long johns while you wear space age stuff." His campaign to set the example was working.

The Guildhall in the town of Heustreu was packed. The spaciousness of it surprised the G Troop contingent. The Germans had rebuilt the interiors of the buildings to fit the largest of gatherings. The floors were pine on a par with the finest basketball court. There was a large stage with an emcee. On the opposite end there was a large counter fronting a huge and completely equipped kitchen. The far end of the counter comprised the keg corner where free beer and wine were being dispensed. It was now clear to Martin why Captain Dawson had carefully selected the troopers to attend the community gathering. Of course, given the terrorist threat, it didn't hurt that they were among the best pistol shots in the Troop and NRA card carrying members.

Hilda was obviously awaiting their arrival. She immediately made her way toward them with her niece, Irmagarde, close behind. Little Irma, so named because of her ample size, had the rosy cheeks, blond hair, and large features of the German country girl. Irma loved the soldiers like brothers and at a distance. She may have been working in the kitchen but she was a "good girl" and intended to stay that way until she was married. Her stock farmer boyfriend, Hans Gruber, cast a baleful eye from the family table at the soldiers, all of whom were at least six feet tall and over two hundred pounds except for Lieutenant Robertson. Hans quickly appraised the competition and looked down at his beer.

Again Martin noted the selection criteria of his Captain and thought, 'Yeah you brought the Storm Troopers and they all know it'. What the hell, it was good to have an edge and Dawson would always seek to hold the edge.

Hilda led the troops over to her family table. Dawson wisely sent the most fluent German speakers forward to make the manners for the group. As Martin shook the hands of the hardy farmers he did not feel out of place. He might well have been at Preble Tavern seven miles west of his hometown of Decatur, Indiana. These were simple, strong, honest and hard working farmers and workmen. Working the land from 'kin see to cain't see', taking what it gave them and putting back what they must to make it work.

"Hilda, please tell these good folks how nice it is to be among hard working farmers who know how to have a good time and tell them I hope they had a good harvest and that they have a good spring," Martin said. All eyes immediately turned to Hilda as she translated.

Hilda added the thought Martin had but did not say, "The First Sergeant says his people, too, are farmers and that being here tonight is good for him as he can be with you while he thinks of them." The group smiled and registered their approval by again shaking the First Sergeants hand.

"Damn, Top, are you going to run for Mayor?" Dawson asked smiling.

"The competitor searches for differences in a foreign country while the sophisticated man finds similarity, Captain. These folks could be in my home town just as easy as not or at the Lutheran Church Fellowship Hall or the Catholic Knights of Columbus if you wanted to keep the beer," Martin said as he gave a peppermint candy to one of the kids at the table.

"If you kiss a baby and make a political speech you will be all set, First Sergeant," Dawson said with a broad smile.

After the final gift exchange and the requisite number of beers consumed in toasts at the table, their hosts insisted the Americans give their rendition of some Christmas Carols. One of the hulking soldiers, Sergeant Durston, Captain Dawson's tank gunner, went to the stage and sat down at the piano while Lieutenant Robertson did a quick rehearsal of the well lubricated choral group of soldiers. Much to his surprise, Martin really enjoyed singing a medley of Yuletide Carols beginning with Little Town of Bethlehem and ending with Silent Night. It was obvious the young soldiers were into the moment. They were far from home on the night before Christmas and missing what they would have had at home. Martin was just as glad to be with them. He was with his soldiers on the East-West German Border, he was home. Granted their inhibitions were few but it sounded good and the natives of Heustreu loved every song. Lieutenant Robertson then closed the American part of the show with Amazing Grace on the bagpipes. After the soldiers left the stage, many of the Germans in attendance thanked them and began to leave for their homes. A final good bye to Hilda and Little Irma and the G Troop departed.

As they went outside, it was truly a White Christmas as it was snowing heavily. The white lights of the military vehicles reflected off the snow and the slight crust of melted snow reflected a million points of light as the vehicles turned the corner to leave the parking lot. A bevy of what seemed to be a million stars were visible against a foreground of the distant hills and it was a very poignant and beautiful scene for all who saw it. To get his driver's take on it all, Martin asked, "Tommy, didn't Little Irma look nice?"

"Shit, Top, she still looked like she could play linebacker for the Husky Whores in the Canadian Women's League. There ain't enough beer in the world to make her look good," Tommy answered with the utter certainty of one who was a bon vivant and connoisseur of petite women.

"Glad you put it all in perspective Tommy. Home, James," Martin laughingly said.

CHAPTER 8 – REFORGER

"Publicity is like poison, it doesn't hurt you unless you swallow it." Joe Paterno, Coach Penn State

1400 hours
30 Dec 1984

G Troop was closed in the Motor Pool at Bad Kissingen, Germany, at the end of a successful Border Tour. The unit performed in an outstanding manner and achieved all of the goals of the Squadron and Regimental leadership. Moreover, the unit met the standards of the Regimental Command Sergeant Major by keeping the Border Camp Barracks to a very high standard of cleanliness during a surprise inspection. The Border change of responsibility between the two Cavalry Troops went smoothly. The ease of the transition was a positive sign and the troop gained a large measure of peer acceptance. All of the NCOs in combat positions except three and all of the officers were Border Qualified. The three were to be re-tested on a patrol before setting out on the REFORGER trek, time permitting. Vic Jackson was jawing with First Sergeant Martin about the successful border tour with some help from Rich Maldanado.

"First Sergeant, would you at least say we have turned the corner?" Vic asked.

"To paraphrase Churchill, 'It is the beginning of the beginning' and his classic about Dunkirk - 'Wars are not won by evacuation'. Cav Troops don't get any medals for doing their job," Martin said.

"Damn, Top, aren't you ever satisfied?" Maldanado asked.

"Ask me when I PCS Rich, then I may have an answer. Am I happy with our progress, yes. Do we have a long way to go, yes. Will we continue to succeed? Yes, if we continue to learn, grow, and work to maintain the standard," Martin said with a smile.

"What do you guys see as the biggest challenges during REFORGER?" Martin asked.

"Shit, Top, I ain't thought about that yet," Maldanado said, "Have you?"

Vic Jackson laughed and said, "You know, Rich, my loader asked First Sergeant's driver what the First Sergeant talked about in the jeep. Staunton said, 'He doesn't talk much - he thinks a lot.' Like right now, he has twenty things he wants to get fixed before REFORGER. He is doing a course correction by asking us what we think - to make sure he is going down the right azimuth, right, First Sergeant?" Vic concluded.

"More like 120 things, Vic," Martin said.

"What are some, First Sergeant?" Maldanado queried.

"Oh no, compadre', you first," Martin countered.

"Fuel pumps. Gotta' find a way to get the next generation of fuel pumps installed. We got no control over them - they just fail - it is a bad design. Without an engine the tank is out of action, the crew is out of the fight and gets left behind - no food, no heater, no supervision," Maldanado said.

Vic volunteered, "Smart maneuver. Those assholes in the headquarters see roads through the woods on a map and never think about the high centers and getting tracks thrown to the inside. They want to run the whole damn Regiment down one little road."

"MILES," said Martin as the two Platoon Sergeants looked at him. "At some point we will be MILESed up. The leading element of the Blackhorse is going to have to go force on force with someone. There is a lot to learn about MILES and the care and feeding of it. Troops have to want to keep it bore sighted. If you do everything right and screw up the MILES play you might as well stay home. The stateside guys know MILES better than we do - we need to get smarter."

"I can get us our own green keys if you want, First Sergeant," Maldanado said.

"Men, green key and God Gun gamesmanship is out. It makes for dead soldiers in real war. We won't do it. Tell the boys it is an automatic UCMJ offense to screw with their MILES and to bring the dead back to life. Only the umpires can do that. Cheating with MILES is for the Opposing Forces. I know you guys think it is okay to do anything to win - it isn't."

"We have all taught people to drive both in the Army and as civilians. The same logic that governs drivers' training instructors governs the way we have to see MILES. If you cheat and re-key newbies who screw up the fundamentals of maneuver nobody learns. In the case of drivers' training, the instructor knows the rookies he trains will be sharing the road with him and his family. He has a vested interest in the drivers' ability to obey the rules and operate the vehicle safely, his own ass. In the case of MILES, Lieutenant Schmuck-atelli must learn if you can be seen you can be hit and if you can be hit you can be killed. Second place in a gunfight gets a tombstone not a ribbon. The training we must do removes ignorance of MILES as one of the causes of unit defeat in force on force."

The dumb look on Hankinson's face told Martin this sermon was not getting to his brain housing group. Staff Sergeant Ramos had joined the group and helped out his First Sergeant, "Robbie, when your guys take a test at the Ed Center and one of them fails it, do you believe him when he say his pencil damn broke?"

"Hell, no," said Robbie. "He can get a new pencil from the test proctor or get off his ass and sharpen the one he had."

"First Sergeant say that when the Ell Tee get the Platoon lit up or the Ga-tor gets the troop lit up he don't want it to be over no pencil or 'cause the lazy jack did not sharpen it, comprendo amigo?" Ramos asked in his doting parent voice.

"Are you worried about cold injuries, First Sergeant?" Staff Sergeant Hankinson asked.

"Concerned is a better word, Robbie. I plan on the maintenance heater test board keeping the heaters working, getting the Soldiers to a Gast Haus for a hot meal every 48-72 hours, finding a schwimmbad once a week and feeding two hot meals per day. We will have at least one thermos per crew and hot drinks most of the day. Our TA-50 is in good shape and these guys all have four or five pairs of boots except the newbies. We will get water from farmhouses. If we can keep them warm, clean and hydrated - our troop leading procedures should carry us through without serious injuries."

"We need to concentrate on doing our little corner of the Army as well as we know how. I plan on just loading the G Troop Wagon and let the big guys worry about the mule going blind. REFORGER is a geo-political exercise. The leaders will learn a great deal. Generals at Division level and higher have no other means of training their staffs except the CPX. Every soldier needs training at every level. There are many who knock REFORGER because of its notional method of assessing casualties. They miss the point. The big guys don't even get an OER. They either fit into the plans of the Lieutenant Generals and above or they take their asses to the front porch. Again, let the officers worry about the damn mule going blind, load the wagon," Martin said.

"Hey, are you going to the Swartz' New Year's Party, First Sergeant?" Jackson asked.

"Vic, Captain Dawson says we are going to every party we're asked to attend. I plan on being sober at the end of the night and sleeping in on New Year's day," Martin said laughing. "Enough of this solving world issues and watching the dancing bears we call soldiers. You jokers will be home drinking a beer and I will still be here doing damn paper work. Does formation at 1700 work for y'all? Don't give me that look, if you are ready earlier than that, let me know. I'll be in my cage, and we will march back as a troop," Martin said as he went on his way through the track park.

On the way to his office Martin walked by the Troop maintenance shop. Passing by the Headquarters maintenance bay he watched as the HHT team hooked up a ground hop kit (a series of wires, cables and hoses so named for the ability of the maintenance crew to provide an engine removed for servicing the means to run while sitting on wooden blocks on the ground, outside of its parent vehicle) for one of its recovery vehicles.

"What's up, Chief?" Martin asked Staff Sergeant Harry Neeley, late of the Miami, Florida police department and Blackhorse veteran of Vietnam. Now Neeley was Motor Sergeant of Headquarters and Headquarters Troop.

"You know the deal, Top. Every engine I change oil and filters for its service gets ground hopped and tested before it goes back into the vehicle. If the

173

bitch won't start or leaks fluid, it will be sitting on blocks over the drain, not out in the field." Neeley was an extremely self confident NCO who fended off all comers, Officers, NCOs and Privates with a mixture of bluster, experience, humor and sarcasm depending on the audience and their rank, or lack of it. He did not suffer fools gladly. Though he referred to himself in the third person in pidgin Japanese as Watashi or just plain Watash, Martin valued his counsel.

"That is one big long-ass fuel line, Chief, and that slave cable is huge. Did you make it?" Martin asked.

Neeley gave Martin his 'Are you really that stupid look' before replying.

"First Sergeant, it ain't Rocket Science, you take a fuel line add length to it and fabricate a fitting. You have been on the M-577. The slave cable is from its generator kit," Neeley said with a slight huff as if Martin should know everything about tracks. "You have led a sheltered life as a line dog or you're just getting old and forgetful."

"Hey, Chief, I'll take the hit on the slave cable. I was in 8th ID with a lower parts priority than the Chinese National Guard when I did my S3 gig. We never had a generator slave cable until I was the Executive Officer of HHC of 4/69 Armor," Martin said smiling.

"You got a problem, don't you, First Sergeant?" Neeley said with real concern.

"I got lots of them. What I'm huntin' is solutions," Martin said.

"Like what, First Sergeant?" Neeley said with great interest.

"The M1 main fuel pump MTBF." Seeing the startled look," Martin spelled out the M1 acronym of Mean Time Between Failure.

"Damn Jedi Knight shit, that damn piece of shit-can't help you there, First Sergeant. No answers here for that one. The demand history is screwed up for parts and the design fix is down the road. But I'll tell ya' something, First Sergeant, it will be someone like you that figures out the fix and when you do, tell me what it is."

Suddenly seeing a soldier backing up an M-113 personnel carrier without a ground guide for safety, Neeley reacted by yelling and giving hand signals. "Hey, stupid, stop that damn thing. Shut it off," Neeley said making the hand signals to both stop by clasping both hands together and by slashing his hand across his throat. "That's right, I am talking to you PFC Gross, you country shit."

"But, Sergeant Neeley, I am a Specialist."

"No, asshole, you are about to make PFC. You don't need a ground guide. You think you are back home in damn Iooway on your Daddy's 300 acres with nobody around but your ugly virgin sisters. You keep on not using a ground guide and backing up until you hear a statement of charges and you will be a damn PFC, you hear me boy?!" Neeley concluded his voice dripping with sarcasm and feigned rage.

"Would you be my ground guide, Sergeant Neeley?" Gross asked plaintively.

"Hell no! Me and First Sergeant Martin are solving serious shit here. Sergeant Andros, get your ass out there and straighten out your child, Gross. Be an NCO for Christ sakes not just a damn mechanic stripe wearer. Gross, what are you mumblin' about boy?"

"My sisters ain't ugly, Sergeant Neeley, and they ain't virgins neither," Specialist Gross stated.

"I guess not, Gross, you and your brothers probably seen to that huh? After all, if they ain't good enough for their family who would want to marry them?" Neely concluded with disgust.

"Now where was we, Top?" Neeley said shifting gears to be as humble as he could be which was somewhere between a Brahma bull in a rage and an Economics PhD with tenure.

"We were on ground hop kits. So, it is possible for the maintenance shop, any shop, to modify a fuel line to make it as short or long as needed provided they fabricate the fittings correctly and protect the line from idiots and other moving parts. And you guys have a butt load of extra cables for generators you could hand receipt me for REFORGER, correct?"

"Yeah, we can do that just between us though, ten cables, no officers. Your Commander gives me a big pain in my ass and don't send that wussy Wintergreen over here neither. He is too clean at the end of the day to be a real Motor Sergeant. Send MacClincock, him I can deal with. He is clean first thing in the morning, after that he is like Pigpen in Charlie Brown, my kind of NCO. And fer' Christsakes don't tell nobody!!"

"Your secret is safe with me, Chief. I'll send Mac over after the holidays. I know you have your day planned and this ain't no emergency," Martin said.

"Hey, First Sergeant, about the ground hop kit, if I was you, I would get reinforced line with that heavy mesh if it was going to get drug around a lot," Neeley said thoughtfully.

"Now, Chief, why would you think that?" Martin asked smiling.

"Shit, Top, you ain't no maintenance freak. You're an operator. You do enough maintenance to run the shit out of your equipment but you respect your mechanics and services for vehicles. I used to be a cop, remember. You can't shit old Watashi. You're up to something, what is it?" Neeley asked wanting to be in the joke.

"I don't know yet. Guys like you solve similar problems every day. Maybe your day to day work will bleed over and give me the answers. Besides, I am always better off after I talk with you, Chief. Happy New Year."

"Happy New Year to you, First Sergeant!"

The G Troop maintenance shop was a beehive of activity. All of troop maintenance was caught up by virtue of being at the Border Camp. It was one of those rare times when the mechanics could work on their own equipment and straighten up their personal gear and tools.

However, two of the bays were empty and had been washed and cleaned down to the bare concrete. That was a first with fifty years of grit gone and the back and side walls had been painted a brilliant white while the Troop was at the Border. Staff Sergeant MacClincock greeted Staff Sergeant at the 'Woods Brothers'. Hell, we're thinking about tiling the floor in black and white checkerboard ala' Victory Lane. Do you like it, First Sergeant?"

"I am impressed. Paint is the cheapest and fastest lighting improvement you can make. It looks great and is functional. Mac, I'm worried about fuel pumps in the M1. There has to be a way to jury rig them to enable the engine to run full bore if we get an epidemic of broken fuel pumps during the RE-FORGER. Think about solving the problem over the Holidays. Get the crew together and present them with the problem - they will have the answer," Martin directed.

"You mean a modern day version of the bocage cutter, First Sergeant?" Staff Sergeant Mac said with a boyish smile.

"That's it exactly, Mac, the bocage cutter of the modern era," Martin said. "Can't promise to promote the guy who comes up with it but I can damn sure give him some time off, an ARCOM, and some promotion points."

"Now, First Sergeant, you are acting like the problem is already solved," Staff Sergeant Mac said with a worried frown.

"For me it is Mac. I just put the howling monkey on your back and his name is Fuel Pump. Oh shit, he just pissed on your clean fatigues!" Martin said grabbing at Macs shoulder. Mac, always a bit goosy, jumped at the First Sergeant's rough touch.

Knowing better but compelled to look, Staff Sergeant Mac glanced at his shoulder, "Okay, I got it, First Sergeant. Daggett probably already has the answer but he is keeping it to himself because he hasn't been asked. You know how those damn hillbillies are," provoking both NCOs to laugh as MacClincock was from Livingston, Texas and was as country as corn bread. Daggett was from the metropolis of Bucksnort, Tennessee and his two passions were Volunteer football and tank engines.

"Has the boy met any women lately, Mac?" Martin asked.

"I will make sure he gets the time to get some but the boy is shy. I guess he was just raised right and all that Bible thumpin' ain't wore off yet," Mac promised.

"I've been talking to Neeley in HHT. He has some extra long cables used by the M577 guys to site their generators away from the TOC. After New Year's go see him and get ten of them. One for each platoon, including Mortars, and put one on the 577, M-88, the maintenance PC and the Cherry Picker. He also has some steel wrapped hydraulic lines we could use for ground hop kits," Martin concluded.

176

"Top, we got more hydraulic line with reinforced steel mesh in our repair stocks than we will ever use. They are all installed under cover in the tank sub-floor. There is no call for them - hell, they never go bad or wear out," Mac stated firmly.

As the First Sergeant left the maintenance bay, Staff Sergeant MacClincock watched him stop and speak to every mechanic, look at what he was doing, and give him some word of encouragement or praise. The man was into it. It was a good thing. For years no one thought about the guys turning the wrenches in maintenance. Now, he treated everyone like a Cavalry Trooper no matter their MOS.

After the First Sergeant spoke to Daggett, the young PFC looked toward his mentor Staff Sergeant Mac and walked over to him. "I think I know how to do what the First Sergeant wants. He told me to get a tank and experiment with it and to use HQ-66. Is that going to be okay with Captain Dawson?" Daggett asked.

"Yeah, but we ain't doing none of that wild shit until we get your 113 tightened up, all your shit stowed and we have a good time on New Year's Eve. The First Sergeant talked to me and put the monkey on my back to solve the fuel pump issue and I'm putting it on you. Think about it over the next few days and we will work on it together with the whole crew. That is unless you think you got it," Staff Sergeant Mac said expectantly.

"I've got a way to fix it but I don't know if it is okay with you," Daggett said shyly as he looked down at the floor.

Staff Sergeant MacClincock realized that Daggett was embarrassed to be smarter than him, the First Sergeant, and the whole Army Material Command. His modesty needed some encouragement. What a great kid he was!

"Well how about you tell me and I tell them, Daggett? If it works out good, it was your idea and if it is wrong, I take the blame. How does that sound?"

Boy, you are starting to sound like the First Sergeant. The Gator will have me shot if I screw up his tank. Oh well, what the hell!

"Okay, Staff Sergeant Mac. We make the ground hop kit fuel line longer and hook it up to the smoke generator. The smoke generator is just a fuel pump that blows diesel fuel into the exhaust and the 650 degree centigrade heat makes the smoke. We run the replacement line over the back deck of the tank to the outlet of the main fuel distribution pump. We can use reinforced line. The tread heads will have to remember the fuel line is exposed and not get it tangled up in tree branches and stuff hanging off the bustle rack. We can rig it in less than ten minutes. The smoke generator has the most dependable fuel pump on the tank. The fix should last until we can get back here and fix it right with the new main fuel pump if those dumb ass tankers don't pull it loose," Daggett concluded.

"Are you sure you can make it work? It ought to work, huh, Daggett? Can you hook it up now and demonstrate it to the First Sergeant & CO?" Staff Sergeant Mac asked calmly and quietly.

"Yes, and Yes, to answer your questions, Staff Sergeant Mac," Daggett answered. "Is this important?" Daggett asked.

"Daggett, there ain't no casual conversations with our First Sergeant. Everything he does has a reason behind it. Most of the time when he wants something, the deadline was yesterday. Anytime we can be early, it is a good thing. Go measure the distance and make a fuel line that fits with two to three inches of total slack. I'm going up to the Troop. Tell Sergeant Wintergreen where I went if he gets here before I get back," Staff Sergeant Mac said as he departed the maintenance bay.

Enroute, he saw Martin at the communications trailer talking to Sergeant Shirley the Communications NCO. He joined them and listened to their talk as he waited his turn to talk to the First Sergeant. "So Brother Shirley, you can tune the forward gain on my jeep radio antennae to extend the range of my radios, maybe double it. Is there a bad side to doing that?" Martin asked.

"The bad side is if you talk for too long you burn out the radio. Minimizing air time is the key to getting a long life span with an overpowered radio. Just use the proword "Break" after 9 seconds or so and you can use it that way forever," Sergeant Shirley concluded.

"Okay, tune mine up after the New Year. I'll be careful," Martin assured him.

"What's up, Mac?" Martin asked turning to the Shop Foreman.

"Got with the guys and told them to bypass the main fuel distribution pump with a field expedient repair. When do you want to see it?" Staff Sergeant Mack asked.

"First; great work on finding the answer so fast. Your outfit is cooking. Shared information in cooperative effort solves problems. Second; you are probably fabricating the parts right now. You have not had time to try the solution. Do a pilot. Make sure it works, war game it to find the next fix if the primary one breaks. Establish a cost factor. If the cost is zero or out of money we spend anyhow – fine - don't count troop labor time or on parts. Be ready to show it to the Gator after New Year's. Go get drunk, get some good food and some women and forget about this Army shit for a little while. Good job on covering for Daggett - top cover is important. I am proud of all of you maintenance TURDS. It is great to have guys like you in charge, thanks Mac. Happy New Year!"

"Happy New Year, First Sergeant!"

As he peeled off his gear and put it in his locker, Martin noticed the envelopes stuck to the Gator's inner office door and figured them to be New Year's Party Invitations.

Thankfully, Staff Sergeant McKnight had kept the paperwork flowing to the Border plus the First Sergeants frequent day trips to the Kaserne kept the back log to a minimum. However, the troops were back and anything they had been postponing until their return now made its appearance. Martin had finished the mail and had it all in readiness for the Commander to approve or disapprove the actions. The DA Form 6 detailing Soldiers for duty had been completed at the Border to enable them to make plans. Martin believed in utter and total fairness in apportioning duty. Due to the former First Sergeant playing favorites, it had been necessary to teach both the Soldiers and some of the NCOs how duty was supposed to be assigned. His answer to his critics who wanted to keep the process secret was to teach the troops how to make out and maintain the duty roster by the regulation. When the NCOs that were obsessed with authority protested, his answer was simple, "If a duty roster will not stand inspection it is a lie. If a leader will lie about how a soldier gets selected for duty he ain't much and everybody knows it. Cheating on the duty roster is the same as stealing their money because in this outfit time off is more precious than money. These jokers are training and at the border so much they have lots of money."

As Martin finished the last piece of paper in the "IN" box, Staff Sergeant McKnight walked into his office. Martin asked, "Sergeant McKnight, where is the rest of the stuff? Surely we are not caught up," Martin said with disbelief.

"We are caught up, First Sergeant. Captain Dawson emptied your "IN" box and signed or corrected everything. He is at Squadron and said for you to wait here until he got back. He also said there is a copy of Armor magazine on his desk. He wants you to read the Commander's Hatch article to see if it is one that you wrote," McKnight said with a grin showing his full over bite as it did when really pleased with himself.

"Thanks for all of your hard work, Mack. Don't mind my frown. We have the Border done and the troop on the mend but there ain't enough green tape to make this airplane fly well enough to pass an IG," Martin said ruefully as he opened the Armor Magazine. He had not written this Commander's Hatch but authorship in the Army was suspect and not for those with an ego deficit. Every horse holder between the one originally tasked to do the work and the Fort Knox Commanding General, wanted a piece of the credit for a favorable action.

There was no big line up of experts to help with the re-write of Tank Gunnery, the Bore Sight Policy, or Close Combat Heavy Manuals. Their technical expertise faded in front of the Commanding General like the exotic charms of a Louisville stripper the young GI took home to meet his 100 gallon Baptist Mama. Mamas and Commanding Generals are irritatingly practical when someone is trying to con them and screw their Sonny Boy. "Mack, I did not write this one. I'm not sure I could recognize it if I did," Martin said ruefully.

1600 hours
31 Dec 1984

Captain Dawson entered the Troop area and found his First Sergeant reading the Regimental SOP. "You must be desperate for reading material, First Sergeant. They are not going to pay any attention to that shit on RE-FORGER. Are you ready to go eat?"

"I am, Sir. I'm hungry as hell and ready for a great schnitzel at Zagrebs," Martin said with gusto, closing the duty tome.

During a great dinner, Dawson mapped out their travel plans to visit three New Year's Eve celebrations followed by a visit to the Haus Chantal where the Headquarters Platoon had rented the entire whorehouse for the evening. "Those guys will probably have the best time of anyone in the troop for New Year's," Dawson said laughing out loud.

Vicki Swartz loved a good party. She was older than Sergeant Swartz by ten years as she was 35 and he was 25. Vicki had a very good job in Wurzburg working for 3 ID in Resource Management and took the train to work most days. She threw a great party and her platoon sergeant's wife supported her and helped her for the big events. By virtue of her twin girls from a previous marriage, the Swartz family had three bedroom quarters as the girls were off to college in the states. Martin got to meet six of the 19 wives in the troop at Vicki's party. It was a subdued affair and he and Dawson got the idea they were a wet blanket on the party. What Dawson did not know, nor did anyone suspect, was that his First Sergeant, Mrs. Swartz and Mrs. Debbie Jackson had conspired to develop a "safe" house system. It was the first step to provide immediate protection for battered wives while the creaky system got engaged. Martin transplanted the doctrine for Prisoners of War to battered wives - secure them, safeguard them, speed them to the "rear" to prevent the inevitable re-engagement by husbands, and get them into a system not of confinement but of care. Vicki and Debbie quietly established both safe houses and an emergency notification network to provide transportation for battered spouses and their children. So far there had been no need for the network but it was in place and was well maintained by the two dynamic women. It remained secure because no one in authority knew it existed. As he watched his First Sergeant interact with the two women Dawson was happy the wives were so engaged. He knew the First Sergeant would brief him eventually. The dearth of housing in Bad Kissingen meant the Regiment assigned single Soldiers there while married men went to Fulda. Staying twenty minutes longer than they planned, they moved on to the Cumberland's.

The Cumberlands had recently transferred to the community commander's operation from H Company where Sergeant First Class Cumberland was in charge of the bridge tank section. The three bridge tanks were of the

M60A1 vintage and mounted a self-contained aluminum bridge designed to span 60 plus feet and was carried on an Armored Vehicle Launched Bridge or AVLB. He was now acting as the Post Engineer NCOIC. The party was bubbling with talk, smartly dressed men and vivacious women, both black and white. There were some German civilian employees present and Martin enjoyed talking with them and polishing his German skills. Both he and Dawson had a small helping of spare ribs, baked beans and potato salad. Martin did not have enough liquor in him to do well in the impromptu limbo contest but he truly enjoyed watching a slim girl from Jamaica in tight jeans show the mainlanders how it was done.

After one more party, Dawson said, "It is time to go to the House Chantal, First Sergeant."

"Are you sure that is a good idea, Captain?" Martin asked.

"Why, hell, yes. They are in the troop. Prostitution is legal in Germany. We are not going to partake of the fruit - at least I'm not. Are you, Top?" Dawson questioned.

"No, Sir, I am not. I just wanted to be sure you had thought it through and were ready to answer the questions from higher if they come up, that's all," Martin said.

Sometimes it was hard to tell when the Gator was feeling his scotch or just scratching his death wish itch or both. What the hell it was only one NCOER!

The pimp at the Haus Chantal welcomed Dawson and Martin profusely. The Headquarters Section had turned a bad night into a profit for his enterprise. There was a very nice buffet of fruit, cold cuts, chips and dips as well as any number of chafing dishes with hot German delicacies. It was the best catering of anywhere the two had visited. Every soldier had a female. Giesele had to come over to see her First Sergeant and offer him her charms since all was paid for. BJ, acting as the unofficial host was of course willing to share her or any of the others if either the First Sergeant or the Captain wanted. It was by any measure, except that of Judeo Christian morality, a nice party. It had great food, attractive women, and great music. The surprise was a recent transfer from Regimental Headquarters, formerly Sergeant Beamish, now Specialist Beamish, as yet unassigned in G Troop. BJ, ever quick to share both the wealth and the cost of the party, quickly made Beamish aware of the deal and reduced the cost by 20% with the Beamish contribution.

Sergeant Durston, Dawson's driver on Headquarters 66, was obviously drunk and in love with Gisele. Durston was hairy as an ape and nearly as strong as one. Martin was a bit taken aback at seeing him so head over heels in love with a whore and hoped he would sober up. He needed to figure out it was all about the money for her.

BJ sealed the deal as Durston and Gisele left the kitchen, "The boy is in love, First Sergeant. I don't know what you and the Captain are gonna' do about it but he is gone. It is like that Th-Th-Th thunderbolt in the God Father - he ain't got no sense."

"We ain't going to do nothin' about it, BJ. Everybody has to grow up sometime. He ain't the first man to lose his head over a whore and he won't be the last," Martin said laughing.

The Captain and the First Sergeant said their goodbyes and made their way out of the party with light hearts, laughing all the way to the BMW that was now covered in snow. Dragging out the word shit in the southern dialect style of the Cavalry Dawson opined, "Sheeet, TOP, those guys had the best time of anybody in the troop tonight."

1000 hours
01 Jan 1985

As he made his way to his office, Martin noticed his headquarters element moving about the kaserne with long faces. Arriving at the Charge of Quarters Desk he asked Sergeant Layton if anything unusual had occurred in the troop during the night. "No, First Sergeant, it was a quiet night in our Troop. The Headquarters Platoon guys all got the crabs last night from the new guy, Beamish, and they had to get the medics to clear them up before coming back into the barracks. They did not contaminate the barracks and only Beamish had to destroy his linen and mattress cover." Layton concluded his summary.

"No good deed ever goes unpunished does it, Layton?" Martin said with a smile.

As Martin started down the steps to his office, he could hear music coming from Captain Dawson's office stereo. The "Boss" Bruce Springsteen was playing near top volume. Dawson was busily arranging his work for his RE-FORGER map book and obviously enjoying the tunes. "Hey, First Sergeant," Dawson exclaimed turning down Bruce, "We had a quiet and uneventful night for G Troop."

"Not exactly, Sir. Do you remember that old tune with the words to the tune of an old spiritual,
Put on that old Blue Ointment,
Give the Crabs a Disappointment,
Put It on Every Hour of the Day,
Oh it Burns and It Itches,
But it Kills Those Sons-A-Bitches
In the Good Old Fashion way."

"It seems Specialist Beamish brought the gift of crab lice from Fulda to the Haus Chantal and thus to the Headquarters Platoon Party. The lads had an infestation of the crabs. They got the medics to treat them and all are on the mend," Martin said with a smile.

182

Up to the point of telling Captain Dawson about the latest misadventure of the lads, Martin had never seen a truly broad smile or an expression of complete mirth by the Troop Commander. Dawson proceeded to rock with laughter and had to sit down to catch his breath and wipe the tears from his eyes. "Oh Lord, Lord that is funny. They all got the crabs. The crabs did not infect the barracks and they have got the cure now. So they are okay, is that right, Top?" Dawson asked as he held back more laughter only by the greatest will power.

"Yes, Sir, they are all on the mend," Martin replied.

"Well, well, well," Dawson said as he busied himself with preparing a huge Brazilian cigar for smoking-an Al Capone. "That's good," he finally said regaining his self control.

1800 hours
01 Jan 1985

As the Commander and First Sergeant completed work on their map books, the platoon leaders and platoon sergeants began to drift into the Troop. Pizzas, hamburgers, and cold beer as well as some nice wine appeared. Soldiers were in and out of the Captain's & First Sergeant's offices as they compared the example map books with their products. The sound of a saw cutting ¼ &⅜ plywood to serve as covers for some of the books carried through the closed door at the end of the hall. Suddenly, a command of "ATTENTION" sounded from the hallway and stairwell. "Who the hell could that be?" Dawson asked the First Sergeant.

At that moment, the Regimental Commander, Smokin' Joe Bannister said, "Carry On Men." Martin was at the door of his office and greeted him with a salute, "Welcome, Sir. We are working our REFORGER prep, having a beer and some pizza with informal OPD & NCOPD as only the Cav can do. Would you like a beer and some pizza while we show you what we're doing?"

"That sounds great, First Sergeant," he replied. A cold bottle of Michelob and a hot slice of pizza on a paper plate arrived and were placed on Captain Dawson's coffee table. Dawson's map book was being used next door so Martin retrieved his and dragged Lieutenant Chastain and his book into see the Regimental Commanding Officer.

"Captain Dawson gave us the example, Sir. We have taken the 1:50,000 scale maps of the entire REFORGER area and put them into map books. This is mine and this is Lieutenant Chastain's - a work in progress."

"Lieutenant Chastain will give you his idea on why we made the books. Lieutenant, go ahead."

"Yes, Sir, Lieutenant Chastain, Fourth Platoon, Blue. The map book organizes us for maneuver and for combat. It allows us to use overlays and keeps us focused. It has also served as a means for OPD and to acquaint us with the terrain we will be on during REFORGER."

"Good summary Lieutenant, thanks, appreciate it," Smokin' Joe said dismissing the lad in a very nice way.

"Nice kid, Martin. Is he the one you are going to move to the Scout Platoon when we move Robertson, David?" the Regimental Commanding Officer asked.

"Yes, Sir, that's the one," Dawson replied.

"Martin doing you right, David? Not too crazy, not too hard on the lads, not driving the Squadron Commander nuts just yet, I see." the Regimental Commanding Officer teased. Martin remained silent but smiled. "You are doing a good job, Ron Martin, but I knew you would when I got DA to move you to the Regiment. Now do me a favor and let me talk to your Troop Commander. See to it we are not interrupted," the Regimental Commanding Officer concluded.

"Yes, Sir," Martin said and closed the door behind him as he went to the other offices and told the happy crew to hold it down to a low roar. The young officers and NCOs who were old enough to know better, could not know how happy their spontaneous effort made him. It was one thing to talk about élan' and esprit de corps and yet another thing to see it appear out of nowhere, in full flower.

1530 hours
02 Jan 1985

Command Sergeant Major McCall was holding a meeting. His tiny office was just large enough for a wall locker, his desk, two settees, and two folding chairs. This arrangement sufficed for the six First Sergeants and the Operations Sergeant to assemble for his meetings where he "ran" the Squadron. The walls were covered with signed photos from General Officers and various Command Sergeant Major serving at star level positions. The center piece was the photo of his study group from the Sergeants Major Academy.

So far, none of the information imparted by the Command Sergeant Major in the meeting was new to the First Sergeants. Their Commanders had attended the same staff meeting as the Command Sergeant Major. Each had already given the exact same information to their First Sergeant. Much to their surprise a new item was announced. The Command Sergeant Major had called for a formation of the Squadron's NCOs to assemble in the Installation movie theater at 0830 the following morning. The subject was "Financial Planning." When queried by Fox Troop's First Sergeant Swan, who was only the second "leg" Ranger Martin had ever met, as to who would teach the class, Command Sergeant Major McCall answered, "What do you mean, First Sergeant Swan? I am going to teach the class. I have a great financial plan. I am set for life and I want to share my secrets with the NCOs. Too many of them waste their money on bullshit when they would be wise to prepare for their future. I will have an old friend of mine who will help me teach the class. It will be over by 1100 hours. Are there any other questions about the class? Martin I know you have a question-ask it-go on, ask it."

"Sergeant Major, we are all up to our ears getting ready for REFORGER. The timing of the class will not sit well with the Commanders," Martin said.

"You know I would expect something like that from the G Troop Commander. He needs to understand that I am the direct representative of the Squadron Commander and as such I determine the education needs of the Noncommissioned Officer Corps, not him. REFORGER preparation can wait three hours on NCO Education. You will be there with all of your NCOs and be on time. Someone else can give the Troop PT, like maybe your Troop Commander could take your place for a change," Command Sergeant Major McCall concluded with a huff. "If there is nothing else, rejoin your units. Martin you stay." McCall saluted the group and they saluted him in return, all but First Sergeant Martin and Swan.

As the door closed, Command Sergeant Major McCall told Martin, "You need to salute me IAW AR 600-20, the Enlisted Aspects of Command. Why do you not do that?"

"Sergeant Major, if we were outside and reports were rendered or directives given that required a salute between NCOs, I would gladly salute. Nothing requires me to salute you or any other NCO indoors except reporting for pay or for a board. I do not salute you as a reflex nor do I intend to start," Martin replied pleasantly.

"You need to figure out that the NCO chain gets supported first and then the officer chain. You need to do what I tell you to do as a first priority and then if there is time, do what your commander tells you to do," Command Sergeant Major McCall opined.

"That is classic Sergeant Major. You get to tell me what to do, set my priorities, use my unit resources and basically run my unit without taking any responsibility for the outcome. That sets me up in direct conflict with my Commander. I always get done what you tell us to do, I find the time. But I do not stop everything in my unit to do a police call or cut grass or trim hedges," Martin replied.

"Yeah and another thing, how is that after I hold a meeting all of the First Sergeants end up in your office. You take them back there and draw pitchers on the blackboard. Are you interfering with my authority? You better not be doin' that," McCall said with emotion quaking his voice.

"Sergeant Major, the meeting in my office is always informal. I have known all of the First Sergeants except Howitzer Battery for years. What we do is figure out how we are going to get your guidance done at the least cost in the fastest time without bothering you with details. It is an innocent thing and your authority is intact," Martin said without a smile.

"My authority better stay intact, First Sergeant, I got my eye on you. You're doing great work but remember who runs the NCO Corps, us, not the officers," the Command Sergeant Major concluded with a frown while waving a dismissal to Martin, he turned to his telephone and began dialing.

When Martin walked back into his office in the Troop, all of his fellow First Sergeants were present and Captain Dawson was at work in his office with the door open. The First Sergeants were talking in low voices when Martin joined them. "I cancelled evening formation and sent the troop home, First Sergeant," Dawson said.

"Well, Sir, that is damn sure your privilege, you being the MMFIC around here. Shut the door there First Sergeant Swan as we have some counseling to do here. I'm guessing that none of you have to go to your unit right away," Martin said while observing their heads nodding in assent. He then reached down in his right hand bottom drawer and came up with a bottle of Jack Daniels bourbon and a bottle of Chevis Regal Scotch. He got some paper cups and retrieved two Pepsi Colas from his refrigerator. He poured a double shot of bourbon into a cup for himself and opened a Pepsi and sat down behind his desk. Dawson arrived and poured a small measure of scotch and moved his chair to the connecting doorway between their offices. Each First Sergeant save one who had a long drive ahead of him all poured a generous shot of Martin's booze. Martin waited until all had had a taste and proceeded to summarize the talk by Command Sergeant Major McCall. Dawson listened but said nothing in front of the other First Sergeants.

First Sergeant Swan said thoughtfully, "That dumb ass has no clue we are all running on autopilot, helping each other, most of the time without being asked and always when asked. If you led, or are leading, anything, it is an NCO support group for him. If we waited on him and that goofy Ops Sergeant to plan our work we would be screwed."

"He is a damn Earth Peeg. He sees bogey mans behind every bush," opined First Sergeant Rosario of Howitzer Battery.

"Guys, nothing has changed because of our talk. I still support him 100% and I will until the end unless, and until, he presents me with the classic Command Sergeant Major choice, him or my Troop Commander. He already knows what I will do. Absolute power corrupts absolutely and we will butt heads. I will support Captain Dawson and pay his price," Martin said.

"Bullshit, Top. He has no options to hurt you," Dawson said with conviction.

"Thank you, William Westmoreland. He will go guerilla and the big ass-chewing will come from someone outside the Squadron. Between them they will pound on my ass to make the round peg go in the square hole," Martin said ruefully.

First Sergeant Swan rubbed his chin and asked, "And you will do what?"

"I will fix the issues they find with the troop, take full responsibility for short comings and continue to support the NCO chain when it does not conflict with my Troop Commander's guidance. I will not do two wrongs to make a right. Somewhere there is a Command Sergeant Major or Commander above him that will see he is putting us between a rock and a hard spot. G Troop should be known by its deeds by then. The big guys will know me and the troop well enough to judge me by what we do and for our potential, not what we say. That will have to be enough."

0830 hours
03 Jan 1985
Post Theater
Bad Kissingen, FRG

The theater was filled to half capacity by some 340 NCOs from all of the units except E Troop which was currently on Border duty. The First Sergeant had brought all of his troops not engaged on the Ops and patrol to the class. Martin had stepped outside into the bright sunshine of the German morning in the 25 degree temperature to have a smoke. The NCOs of the Squadron were talking quietly among themselves with some but not a lot of cross talk between units. They were behaving themselves and three of the First Sergeants left well enough alone. The other three were using the time to impart information to their units.

As the time dragged on, First Sergeant Martin knew something had gone wrong. He also knew he would not wait past 0900 before gathering his troops and going about the business of getting ready for REFORGER. He called one of his NCOs to the door that he knew had driven to the theater. He had done so in order to keep an appointment for his wife in Frankfurt with a specialist at the hospital.

"Sergeant Barcinas, do a recon for me. Go up to the Squadron Headquarters and locate the Command Sergeant Major. Tell him we are here and we are ready. Try to figure out where he is if he is not there. Spend no more than 10 minutes turning over the rocks up there, come back, report and go get your frau for her appointment."

"Roger, First Sergeant. Thank you!" he said as he moved quickly to his car.

Damn, the relief in his eyes when released to go to his wife's appointment was sickening. They have been waiting for a month. Did he really think Vic & I were not going to let him go to support his wife in favor of this stupid shit, whatever it is? 'Why three hours for the trip First Sergeant?' would be the inevitable question. 'Common sense, that's why,' would be the answer.

As Barcinas returned, he was not smiling, "First Sergeant, his car is not there, no one has seen him and no one, not even the Executive Officer knows where he is. All the Headquarters NCOs are working like hell and my buddy Pabon says the Executive Officer told them not to go to the training. It is a deal from a buddy of his who sells life insurance and the Executive Officer told them to blow it off. Okay, First Sergeant?" Barcinas said concluding his report.

"Good report, Sergeant Barcinas. Go take the wife and good luck with the Doctor. Take her out for lunch and to the Main PX. See you on Thursday," Martin said shaking his hand and patting his shoulder fondly.

"Thanks, Top, she'll like that," the Sergeant said with a big smile.

Vic Jackson joined the group just as Barcinas drove away. Martin shared his instructions to Barcinas with Sergeant First Class Jackson. When Martin finished Vic stated, "That's good First Sergeant. I was just making sure Barcinas did not get roped into some shit that would screw him up with 97th General. He likes you because you can pronounce the names of the Philippine Islands. I figure we are going to split at 0900 if these shit-heads don't show up, am I right?

"I will wait just a little past nine, Vic. I hate to disrespect the man but I cannot wait all day," Martin said. *As he made this comment, he did know full well that any course of action short of sitting there until the Command Sergeant Major decided to show up would be wrong.*

At 0920 Martin stepped to the door of the theater and commanded, "G Troop, FALL OUT and FALL IN ON ME OUTSIDE."

As he walked away from the door, Martin heard Sergeant First Class Thorne, the Motor Sergeant from E Troop say in a loud voice, "Wow, at least one First Sergeant in this outfit has some damn balls."

As Martin looked back into the theater, the NCOs let go a burst of noise and just as quickly quieted down as their First Sergeants stood up to maintain order. Arriving at the formation of his NCOs Martin explained the situation, "Men, I normally do all I can to support the Sergeant Major. We waited too long as it is. We are going to the Troop formation area where I will release you. Anyone whose car is here, fall out and move it if you so desire. Everyone else is going with me marching as a unit. Step out and sound off like you have a pair."

As he gave the commands to move the platoon sized element Martin reveled in the professional manner as they marched. They were not Drill Sergeant Candidates but they were a damn fine looking group of men and he would go with them to gates of hell if it came to that.

As events unfolded, the Command Sergeant Major and his insurance friend did not make it to the theater. No explanation was ever given. The remainder of the unit waited until 1130 hours and departed for lunch and thence to their duties. However, all of those who waited were deemed to be "team players" and G Troop was assigned the role of the "rebel."

It fell to the Squadron Commander to explain to the raging Command Sergeant Major that First Sergeant Martin's rationale of 'A full Professor gets fifteen minutes so a Command Sergeant Major with a GED getting fifty minutes has no complaint' made perfect sense to the Officer Corps. No punishment would be forthcoming for the First Sergeant.

The Squadron Commander did make it a point however to make certain Captain Dawson knew of his displeasure over the visit to the Haus Chantal and Dawson's treatment of the sordid event as a sanctioned party by virtue of his visit. The outbreak of crab lice in the Headquarters Platoon was the last straw as the Medical Warrant Officer called the Squadron Commander himself to report it. Lieutenant Colonel Covington did not know what to think of the Regimental Commanding Officer's visit to G Troop on New Year's Day. If he had known the Regimental Commanding Officer was going to visit the Troop after he and his wife departed from their visit to his quarters he would have accompanied him. He would have had a cow with horns if he had known why the Regimental Commanding Officer had made his surprise visit to G Troop.

The extensive map study by G Troop engendered by the construction of the map books had unintended consequences for future events. The assembly process actually took weeks rather than days given the frenetic pace of unit life. As the ebb and flow of the REFORGER exercise became apparent, a pivotal event began to stand out to the members of G Troop. The bridge over the river at Alsfeld would be crossed twice by V Corps, once in retreat and once in the attack. The generation of the exercise scenario reflected not only what the Intelligence types predicted would happen when the Soviet horde attacked, but what Commanders hoped would happen as NATO forces got fully organized - final victory. Given the Cavalry maxims of 'If you ain't cheatin' you ain't tryin'' and 'Fortune favors the brave', it was inevitable that someone in the 11th ACR would figure out how to stack the deck.

While at the Border, First Sergeant Martin and the NCOs came to realize that if a detachment could be secreted in or around Alsfeld, during the withdrawal phase the bridge across the Leine river could be taken by stealth. History provided many precedents for such an undertaking. The Wehrmacht experience in the Blitzkrieg of taking bridges in Belgium lit the path for the Cavalry soldiers two decades plus later. A small, bold, heavily armed force armed with an abundance of MG-34s, a high rate of fire weapon used by the German Army, was secreted in the vicinity of the bridges during the time of relative peace. Led by German soldiers posing as Belgium Policemen, the unit and local collaborators had waited until the war began to execute their mission to take and hold the critical bridge. The initial assault unit was too small for a sustained fight and depended on early relief by glider and airborne

189

forces to survive. Casualties among the assault force were very high as the initial taking of the bridge was far easier than holding it. The relief force made it to the bridge but missed their time table by nearly forty hours.

Airborne forces were obviously not available to G Troop so the timing of the assault and good communication between assault force and the Troop was critical. There were a lot of details to be worked out but none were too hard for a Cavalry Troop to solve. The process of problem solving and buying in by stakeholders to contribute to solutions was by now institutionalized in G Troop. The 1st Platoon, Scouts, was selected to be the Detachment left behind as the assault force. The fluent German speakers of the troop had been directed to go to relaxed grooming standards while at the border so that beards and length of hair would fit in with the local population. The denim work clothes of the maintenance crews for the roads, bridges and public works of the municipality were available locally and were purchased by the Troopers. A reconnaissance of the bridge and its environs was conducted and excellent photos were taken. The city fathers were contacted and preliminary arrangements were made to house the platoon and their vehicles in a large barn administered by the road maintenance element of the German County. The Cavalry troopers acting as emissaries were generous in their promises of diesel fuel as it was the only real bartering element that interested their hosts. Their mission directive from Captain Dawson was simple, "Do what you have to do but get Red shelter in that town close to the bridge." Every part of the Troop contributed as the Commo Sergeant made an expedient antenna to be used inside the barn and got a set aside frequency from Regiment for the platoon to use for daily reporting at specified times. He also assisted in developing a simple operational report to encode data from the platoon.

Martin summarized the view in the Troop of the impact on the platoon, "The fat guys will get fatter, the Don Juans will manage to get laid, one guy will want to get married and at least one soldier who was never seen to leave the hide position will catch the clap. They will not get caught and their mission will be very successful. Any screw ups will occur on the side of the attacking force. We can meet and solve all of the issues of the hide platoon - they are sterile and can act independently. By that time they will be masters of their environment. But this whole deal is a side show and a throw away by the big guys. It will be on Captain Dawson to get to the bridge on time to prevent the assault force getting killed to the last man and the bridge being blown. It will be high adventure. Sometimes these things take on a life of their own and this could turn out to be a big deal for the Corps. We just gotta' be sure we don't screw up our end of the deal."

Smokin' Joe the Regimental Commanding Officer, was in on the plan from its inception. With the Troop Commander's approval, First Sergeant Martin called him from the Border on the secure phone. He got his tacit approval of the bare bones version of the plan. There was no sense doing a recon or coordination without briefing him. REFORGER was a political animal with military legs and implications worldwide. Only a fool with a career death wish would try a grand stand play to impact the end state of REFORGER. While his troops may have thought he was a wild man, Martin took risks but rarely gambled. He just looked like a gambler to those who had not done their homework. After that New Year's Day conversation, Smokin' Joe had deniability and any errors could be charged to the exuberance of G Troop. Everyone knew Dawson and Martin were crazy as March Hares and needed a tight rein. His visit on New Year's day was confirmation the plan was on and he had the task to brief Corps and Dawson was to brief Lieutenant Colonel Covington. Planning and coordination went at full speed ahead and the hundreds of details required to start and maintain a three week exercise with sustained temperatures below zero, rolled onward.

1530 hours
02 Jan 1985

The hands of the clock were racing toward the departure day for the exercise. The summons to the Command Sergeant Major's office for a meeting, while not surprising, had some degree of foreboding. Whatever it was, it would probably not be helpful. As the First Sergeants assembled, the talk was all about REFORGER and the state of preparation for each unit. As Command Sergeant Major McCall entered his office all of the First Sergeants stood up. The Command Sergeant Major was immaculately dressed in a new set of highly starched Battle Dress with spit shined jump boots and an ultra short haircut. "Carry on men. Be seated. I'm going to stay standing up for a minute. Now all of you can see my uniform. This is how I want all of our soldiers to look next week for Command Sergeant Major Ligon's visit. He will be with us the 3rd and 4th of January. He will tour the border, look at barracks and whatever else he wants to see. Nothing will be locked. Everything will be open for him to see just as it would be for an IG. He is a great old soldier who was brought back out of retirement to active duty by the Corps Commander, Lieutenant General Wetzel. He has the total and complete confidence of the Corps Commander and a blank check to look at any and everything that impacts the Corps and its mission. Just like an IG, no door locked and all containers open. We start off down at the Post Theater at 0800 Monday morning with all of the NCOs in attendance for an address by Command Sergeant Major Ligon. All of your Commanders know about the visit and are in full support. He is not hard to please but his standard is the Army standard without deviation-regulations rule."

We will finish up with a social with wives and all First Sergeants and Platoon Sergeants for a modified dining in civilian business attire – that's coat and tie for those who have not been to the Sergeant's Major Academy. I need to know who all will be there from each unit not later than the end of his talk at the theater. The menu will be chicken, t-bone steaks, or Jagerschnitzel. I need to know how many of each when you give me the head count. The social event is mandatory for soldiers in the duty positions of platoon and First Sergeant. It would be very nice if as many wives and girl friends can be there as possible. The guest speaker will be Corps Command Sergeant Major Ligon. I'm real excited about having him here to visit us. He is a great speaker and will help us in a lot of ways. What are your questions?"

"Martin, do you have a question?"

"No, Sergeant Major, I do not have any questions. I have read his inspection reports from the inspections he has made of the Corps and USAREUR facilities in the V Corps area. A friend of mine told me of his visit to Armed Forces Network studios to chew the Sergeant doing the 6 o'clock news for his sorry looking Class A uniform. It took the Deputy Commanding General of USAREUR to referee that dust up over the phone. It should be interesting. I can find enough deficiencies in my Troop to keep me busy fixing them until I rotate."

"First Sergeant, don't cop an attitude when he is not even here yet," McCall said indignantly.

"Let me restate that, Sergeant Major. I am looking forward to learning about my deficiencies so that I might begin to correct them," Martin said with a contrite look.

"See how much better life is when you have a positive attitude!" McCall said with a wolfish grin. "Okay, let's get to it," McCall said in a gleeful manner.

0730 hours
03 Jan 1985
G Troop Administrative Offices

"First Sergeant, I need to speak to you a minute," Dawson called from his office.

"Yes, Sir, what is it?" Martin asked mindful of the time and the impending class from the Corps Command Sergeant Major.

"I need to speak to all of the NCOs at 0750 in the Troop Formation area. You got a problem with that, First Sergeant? You look like you do," Dawson said without a trace of a smile.

"Yes, Sir, I do have a problem with that. We need to be seated in the theater to hear from the Corps Sergeant Major at 0800 and I need to move the NCOs there now. 0750 will be too late and we will insult the man if we show up late," Martin said.

"Command Sergeants Major are the most worthless things in the Army. They serve no purpose. I do not work for any Command Sergeant Major,

First Sergeant, and you don't either. You work for me and those troopers work for me and nobody goes anywhere in this outfit unless I send them or approve of them going. You and everybody else need to understand that. Any questions, First Sergeant?"

"No, Sir, no questions," Martin answered.

You may be immune from getting your ass chewed by the Corps Command Sergeant Major Captain but my ass is grass and that joker is the lawnmower. I know what the UCMJ says but then so does the Corps Commander. Old Jim Ligon is his ace boon coon and you my friend are merely a very junior officer. It is going to be a long 48 hours if Ligon takes it personal and chalks it up to my inefficiency.

The formation was held at 0750. Captain Dawson talked about RE-FORGER, cold injuries, scheme of maneuver, logistics and the fact that the First Sergeant would be in charge of moving the troop. He also emphasized the point that the movement of the wheels must correspond to meeting the train with the track vehicles at a precise time.

Well Captain you have now talked long enough to prove you do not work for Command Sergeant Major Ligon and it is time for me to take my lumps. I hope Ligon understands I think his message is important enough to show up late to hear what we can of it. I will never tell Command Sergeant Major McCall or Command Sergeant Major Ligon why we are late, but then Dawson knows that without me telling him. They can kill me but they can't eat me, it's against the law.

There was no way to slip into the theater and First Sergeant Martin did not even try. He opened the door and sat his NCOs down in the vacant rows reserved for the now late G Troop. The Corps Command Sergeant Major was just getting warmed up but he stopped his remarks until they were all seated. Then he resumed his narrative. As his audience soon would learn, the words may change slightly, but the basic speech was always the same. The NCO was the man who ran the unit. It was he who enforced standards and provided the day to day continuity. It was he who provided the motivation, training and esprit de corps, not the officers. It was the NCO who when traveling had the supreme duty to patrol the airport while waiting for a flight and correct the appearance of every Soldier in his grade of rank or below. Any uniform discrepancy, regardless of how minor was to be pointed out and corrected at once; anywhere and everywhere it may be found. To walk by a deficiency and leave it uncorrected was the mark of a weakling and contributed directly to the downfall of the Army.

Each item on the Corps Command Sergeant Major's list of failures and faults of the NCO Corps was illustrated by a vignette from his past either as a follower or a leader. Each was fully illustrative with the names of all involved with a description of their present position in life or where they had been buried with honors. It was a magnificent performance of a man selected for a mission by a Lieutenant General and turned loose to do it. Command Sergeant Major Ligon was from a different era in time. He knew it and his audience learned it. What they did not know, but were about to find out was the depth of detail he was prepared to inspect and the depth of his knowledge from 20 years of turning over anthills in barracks, arms rooms and motor pools from Fort Riley to Camp Casey Korea and everywhere in between. Leaders would learn the Command Sergeant Major went out and stayed out. Accompanied by his trusty driver, a hill country lad who faithfully nodded and gave affirmation to every boast and claim made by his Command Sergeant Major, he traveled V Corps. Their van was a repository for their weapons and basic load of ammunition as well as administrative supplies, field gear, sleeping bags and other sundries required for a week of traveling. Together with his faithful driver, he roamed the German landscape in an unending quest to lift his Corps and thus his beloved Army, out of the doldrums of imperfection and slovenliness.

Not only did he not expect to find perfection, he knew he would not. He did not expect to be loved or even liked. It was clear he preferred to be feared over any other result as if it were his due. Always staying off post in German hotels, he was never a burden requiring any support from the commands he visited. He was never late, always in perfect uniform with immaculate appearance, totally and completely correct in speech and deportment and was altogether the biggest son-of-a-bitch anyone in the command had ever met. Martin loved him because he sensed even though Ligon would bust his ass over the next two days that it was not personal, it was professional. He knew he would survive the experience and improve from it but that he damn sure would not like it. He was right on all counts.

After the Pattonesque performance in the theater was completed, the First Sergeants joined Command Sergeant Major McCall in his office to get their assignments for the inspection. Command Sergeant Major Ligon would walk through a 100% layout of field gear on each bunk, inspect wall lockers, inspect arms rooms, supply rooms, evaluate bulletin boards, check weight control, UCMJ, training, building maintenance-a mini-Inspector General's Inspection by a one man team. Of course, G Troop got the whole five course dinner being the gluttons for punishment that they were.

Command Sergeant Major McCall rarely had a good shot at chewing Martin's ass but the offense of being late to the theater was just too good to pass up. As McCall worked up to a full rage complete with flying spit, any eloquence was lost in Army speak, "DAMN IT! Why did you come late? If you saw you were gonna' be late you should not have come at all. Huh? Why? Why? Tell me why!"

First Sergeant Martin calmly replied, "I thought what he had to say was important and it was better to get some of the message than none of it."

"Damn you, that does not tell me why you were late in the first place," McCall added.

"No, I guess not," Martin replied.

"You're not going to tell me, are you?" snarled McCall.

"None of us like to hear excuses, Sergeant Major McCall, and since I have never given you one I would not want to start now," Martin replied. Martin did not know his neighbor and buddy Joe James was pointing up in a manner McCall could see as he looked about the small office in some measure of triumph. He was pleased to have finally put his resident intellectual and smart ass First Sergeant in his damn place and missed the signal that told him the answer. Joe did not know it was a rhetorical question and merely a means to chew ass for McCall. McCall knew full well why Martin had been late but he was unable to chew Dawson's ass so Martin's had to serve.

What neither of the two antagonists, Dawson and McCall, could know was that Martin had already written rule number one for his future life as a Command Sergeant Major over the past hour as a First Sergeant. Never ask a First Sergeant to choose between his Commander and the Command Sergeant Major. (His impish devil alter ego added *"There are always work-arounds and there ain't no E-10."*)

The visit to G Troop by the Corps Command Sergeant Major started badly and got rapidly worse. The Charge of Quarters failed to call "At Ease" when the Inspecting party arrived. The young NCO's justification that Captain Dawson was present did not sit well with the two Sergeants Major as they chose not to support the Army regulation at that moment.

The Corps Command Sergeant Major accompanied Martin to his office and listened patiently to the initial briefing of the command philosophy and the general direction of the troop. It was clear to Command Sergeant Major Ligon that the First Sergeant was extremely intelligent, respectful, and in the learning mode. It was also clear he was not sufficiently focused on NCO business and was more interested in training than administration. The bulletin board was not to standard, weight control was not being done correctly and the troop Commander was not focused to the Corps Command Sergeant Major standard. After a short interview with Captain Dawson, it became clear to Command Sergeant Major Ligon there was hope for Martin to learn the lessons of the day, but not his Captain. The two sizable egos of the Troop Commander and the Corps Command Sergeant Major had met, bounced off of each other and the short discussion left the two players neither impressed, nor edified.

"If I were king for a day, Captain, you would comply or be relieved. The enlisted Corps has more than enough issues to keep me busy. I will let the officers worry about the officers," Ligon stated in passing as he terminated the session by rising and saluting the Troop Commander.

He immediately led Martin to the Arms Room where the fault line started as a crack and built to the inevitable chasm before the day was complete. "Tell me what the First Sergeant has told you to do about these weapons, son," Ligon said to the specialist on duty as his eye roamed about the Arms Room.

"Sergeant Major, the First Sergeant got me a strong light for inspection, sent me to school in Vilseck to the Armorer's Course, got us new solvent, had me get a work order to get all of the barrels gauged, told me to order head space and timing gauges for all of our fifty calibers and walked me through an inspection of every weapon."

"Is that so? Well, show me how he taught you to inspect an M-16 and tell me what you are looking for as you tear it down!" Ligon stated. To his credit, the young specialist did a creditable job with the M-16 sharing with the Corps Command Sergeant Major all of the tricks and techniques to find the quirks of the weapon. The M-16 rifle is recoil operated and gas assisted. Gasses from the passage of the round are expelled into a gas tube located at the top of the barrel. The tube is staked in place by a pin. The inspector tests the correct installation of the gas tube by grasping and pulling it to the rear to ensure it is staked in place and ready to perform its function of assisting the bolt to travel to the rear enabling the weapon to fire in either the semi or automatic modes of operation. As he demonstrated this technique the young soldier saw a question in his Corps Command Sergeant Major's eyes so he began to school him in the cycle of function of the weapon, much to Ligon's delight and surprise.

The maxim of performance stated by the latrine philosopher Joe Shit the Ragman was about to be proven in spades. "One 'aw shit' wipes out a lot of 'attaboys'."

"So if you know the M-16 so well, why are these M-60 machineguns so dirty? These are your bread and butter, First Sergeant, and they look like shit." Clearly, Ligon had forgotten more about an M-60 than anyone else present had ever known and he proceeded to demonstrate his superiority in every aspect as he ticked off the deficiencies of spare barrels, safety wire on the gas plug, rusty spare barrels and finally the piece de resistance, improper ammunition storage. Reaching under the wall locker containing the M-60 spare barrels, Ligon triumphantly held aloft a rusted and dirty belt of blank ammunition for the M-60 machinegun from a training mission of long ago. Inside Martin was smiling.

How many times Command Sergeant Major have you found incriminating evidence under something in an Arms Room and what Armor guy gave a big rat's ass about an M-60 anyway. That is his point stupid - you are supposed to care about it all - and you have not been doing a First Sergeant's job as good as it could be done.

The supply room was next and was in fairly good shape save the moustache of Staff Sergeant Thomas, the temporary assistant accepted by Captain Dawson and working under his direct supervision. "Who do you work for, Staff Sergeant?" Ligon asked.

"Captain Dawson, Command Sergeant Major," Thomas replied.

"Who inspects your appearance, the First Sergeant?" Ligon asked.

"No, Sergeant Major, I don't go to formation much. Captain Dawson has me working the files and individual clothing records, I don't work for the First Sergeant," Staff Sergeant Thomas reported with an ingratiating smile.

Oh thanks, Tom, you damn idiot, that sure tells him a lot about everything, Martin thought with a sardonic smile.

"Sergeant, your moustache is not in accordance with the regulation, shave it off, come back here and dump your field duffle bag for inspection," Ligon concluded. He then switched gears and calmly talked with the supply sergeant letting the Staff Sergeant Webster lead him through the supply process. Once he was satisfied the Soldiers were getting everything they required, not getting screwed and Webster was representing them as well as the Troop Commander, Ligon then tore his ass up just so he would not feel left out. Falling back on stoves, canvas, and immersion heaters for the soon to be Headquarters mess equipment, the Corps Command Sergeant Major had a field day. The fact that the equipment was prepared for turn in, was not to be issued and was destined for the scrap heap was not allowed to intrude on the moment. It was dirty, it was rusty and most of all, it was present-turn in status be dammed. Get it cleaned up-now-with a roar.

After a turn through the barracks with its ratty furniture that the soldiers had salvaged from married folks sales, gifts as they were transferred, and German junking expeditions conducted along the curbs of Bad Kissingen, the joy of error found and redemption of the fallen begun, was continued. Dirt, slime and filth were everywhere. Nothing and no one was exempt. When the level of detail got down to "Pubic Hairs on Bath Soap" the double standard demands of the maniacal officers and the NCO Academy standards of the Command Sergeant Major approached Catch 22 levels in Martin's mind. Catch 22 being the title of a WW II era novel based on a regulation that said, 'An air crew guy was sane if he claimed he was too scared to fly and therefore fit for duty and required to fly combat missions'.

It was a very long day for the First Sergeant and his Cavalry troop as a whole host of deficiencies were pointed out to him and presented as entirely his fault and thus his to overcome, immediately. The fact that G Troop had but 12 days in garrison over the past 73 was not part of anyone's analysis but his.

"First Sergeant, your troop is screwed up. Your administration is not good. You are too interested in training and in doing officer business. Why in the hell are you the Drug and Alcohol Control Officer and why the hell are you analyzing and designing training? You need to take charge and get that Captain straight or you will both be relieved for inefficiency. Do NCO things and let the officers do their thing. Read the NCO creed and follow it, it is that simple. If I were you, I would get the NCOs together away from here, but on

Post, and I will talk to them after you do. Tell me where it is and when to come," the Corps Command Sergeant Major concluded.

"We will use the Squadron classroom above the Mess Hall, Sergeant Major. We will be prepared for you at 1500 hours," Martin replied evenly.

"I'll be there. Don't let your Captain make you late again, First Sergeant," he replied.

Martin kept his reply short and noncommittal, "We will be there."

1430 hours
03 Jan 1985
2/11 ACR Classroom

The NCOs of G Troop were looking pretty hang dog as Martin arrived and went to the front of the classroom. "Command Sergeant Major Ligon will be here shortly to address us as a Troop. Before he does, I need to clear the air and make sure we are all on the same page. I told you when I got here that you were good men and I had confidence in you. Nothing has changed. We are just the bad news from a different set of snap shots and a new set of eyes. Command Sergeant Major Ligon is here as a direct representative of the Corps Commander. He was retired for Christ sakes. Lieutenant General Wetzel got him put back on active duty to be his Command Sergeant Major."

"What a compliment to Command Sergeant Major Ligon and what a hunting license to give an old fire breathing NCO. He is doing exactly what needs doing to and for V Corps and doing it well. He is ruthlessly pointing out deficiencies and shortcomings in readiness, discipline, training and maintenance. He is far gentler than any enemy would be. They kill you for the same mistakes he is merely chewing our asses about. That is the background and we were all there for the inspection and we know what happened, he handed us our asses. That is done and we need to review our notes, develop a plan of action and move out on it starting now."

"As to the future and my pending relief as First Sergeant of G Troop. That is not going to happen because you good NCOs will not let that happen. I will not get fired for not being ready today but I could get fired for not doing anything about it. I know what the Corps Command Sergeant Major wants and I know how to get there with the minimum pain to the GI and use of resources. I will teach you how to do it and we will be fine. At least no one showed abject terror when he jumped in their shit. Hell, units have had soldiers shit their pants when he chewed their asses. Remember what I said at the beginning of this adventure, Command Sergeant Major Ligon does not take personal revenge on NCOs. That is the mark of a bully. He just wants a very high standard and he has the means to demand and get it. He has helped us far more than he has hurt us if you can get past the ego part - get over it -

it was not personal. You have led sheltered lives here in the Cavalry. If you have never had your asses chewed like that then you are probably overdue."

"Questions?" Spying a raised hand, Martin stated, "Yes, Sergeant Hollyfield!"

"First Sergeant, why did the Gator shit on us like that and make us late to morning speech? He had to know we would get hammered after disrespecting the big guy by being late. I know why you did not rat out the Gator to Ligon but damn, Top, what was he thinking?"

"Command Sergeant Major Ligon is too professional to carry out a personal grudge for any reason. The Gator is the Gator and it is not my job to develop him. The officers have to take care of the officers except in the case of Second Lieutenants and they belong to us all until we get them grown enough to chew our asses," Martin answered to much laughter.

Little did the NCOs of G Troop know the Corps Command Sergeant Major was early while waiting for the Squadron Command Sergeant Major on the stairwell and had heard every word spoken in the classroom.

"Vic, did the Squadron S-1 get the reservations for tonight and their food orders? And is anyone not going?" Martin asked.

"Everyone is going, First Sergeant, and the reservations are in. We are the only ones at 100% by the way. The suckasses that made out like bandits today are blowing it off," Vic Jackson added with a smile.

"Remember why we are going, to honor our Corps Command Sergeant Major's visit and have some fellowship with the NCOs of the Squadron. Command Sergeant Major Ligon knows the deal and is here for more than some isolated ass chewing. He is building units," Martin concluded.

Suddenly, "AT EASE," was given by Command Sergeant Major McCall. Command Sergeant Major Ligon entered the room at a fast pace deciding early to leave his head gear on and to scrowl rather than merely scowl. As Martin started to vacate the podium and the front of the assembled group, the guest of honor pointed to him to stay in place. Ligon then turned to the assembled NCOs. He began without preamble saying, "Your Cavalry troop is below standard. I can tell you know what to do but you have not been doing it. It does not matter how long you have been off doing what. The shit that is wrong with your outfit should never be wrong with it in the first damn place - not for a minute. I am inspecting all over the Corps. I can relieve anyone I outrank, anytime I choose. The Corps Commander backs me up. The First Sergeant of the outfit is the kingpin that holds it together. He is one that makes it go. He sets the standard and maintains it. If the unit is wrong it is his fault. If he can't get it right he gets fired, made into a Master Sergeant or reduced to E-7 and gets another assignment away from leading troops. That is the way it is. It has always been that way and by God, I hope it always will be that way. If you want to keep officers out of your NCO business, you have to do NCO business. Whatever the officer needs you should be able to hand it to him at the time he thinks of it not after he tells you three times. How good or how smart could any of you be if a Captain, or a Lieutenant Colonel for that matter, is out thinking you on how to take care of soldiers. I ain't talking about long hair and free beer. I am talking about kicking ass and taking names - making men do the right thing because it needs doing - all of the time. Never apologize or sugar coat an order - don't worry about how you give it or if you swear and cuss some asshole that needs it. Get in their shit and stay there because I am going to be in your ass until you do and so will your First Sergeant. Questions – no - then I will see the First Sergeant and all Platoon Sergeants tonight for dinner. CARRY ON." On that happy note, Hurricane Ligon departed the classroom. The NCOs who had yet to experience meeting him up close and personal during the day's activities were pale as ghosts and were a little worse for wear having done so.

"Now that we are all suitably inspired, get out your notebooks and I am going to tell you how we're going to skin this cat and meet the Army Standard according to Saint Ligon. Barracks displays. Keep two sets of stuff. One super clean set on display. White towels will be placed in foot locker trays with all new stuff. I need each platoon to appoint one guy in the barracks to be their example. I will get him straight and the others will mimic him to the letter. Every room must be clean and straight when the men walk out of them at all times. Wall lockers must look like mine at all times minus the extra ammunition of course." Hoots of laughter ensued.

"Supply, get rid of the damn excess, legally. Everyone, clean your weapons using the new solvent I am getting from Corps. Very simply, we are going to be ready for inspection 24x7x365 until he comes back and or Regiment hits us for the IG. By then, the routine will be a habit. Do not waste a second blaming the messenger or his boss, the Corps Commander. Men, if he had not done it, I would have had to do it. I know what I have to do to get my shit straight in the Orderly Room."

"Now troop care for the next 30 days. For the shortimers - get them old but serviceable field gear, have them turn in the good shit and clear the Central Issue Facility (CIF) this week. Get their hand receipts clear and transferred, their efficiency reports in and awards done. I want all of the administrative trash done for them before the officers leave for the Recon. We are screwing them bad enough by either taking them or letting them go with us to REFORGER. I do not want to hear REFORGER used as an excuse to screw these good men. The five jail birds will be doing KP throughout the exercise and will be transferred to Headquarters Troop via Tactical Order. The real challenge of the exercise will be keeping our Soldiers warm, dry, well fed, and well hydrated. The lower grades will get a lot of sleep and we NCOs will all have to watch out for each other - me included - to keep from turning into zombies over no sleep. Lots of stripes and Gold Braid do not make anyone immune to lack of sleep."

"Do not stress out about the Corps Command Sergeant Major. It is another lesson and we will apply what we have learned in our own good time. Keep everything clean and neat until we get back - then we will re-create the 7th Army NCO Academy here in our troop. When he comes back it will be clear we have learned our lessons well and we will meet the standard even if it is at 0300 on Sunday morning. From this point forward, Platoon Sergeants will run a DA Form 6 and detail Soldiers to support Charge of Quarters from each platoon. I want unit integrity in place."

"When the great Ligon comes back to inspect, he is going to inspect the CQ Runners wall locker and the CQs, if they live in the barracks, as well as their TA-50. He will also have the CQ open the Arms Room and the Supply Room to inspect them. If all is okay, he will move on to the next unit. If it is not, there will be a total recall and you will do the whole thing again with a new First Sergeant accompanying him. I know, you jokers think I am a psychic - not true. There are at least two hundred companies in this Corps and even Ligon, empowered as he is can only detect and correct so much in the time he has available. The second look is to verify his first visit worked. He will be in and out in less than an hour on the second look. He will be happy as a clam. Okay, go get ready to be social, the three B's are: Be on time; Be humble; and Be gone at the first opportunity. The fourth B is to Be nice, remember, the shit is not personal, it is professional. Questions about anything?"

"First Sergeant, do you want the stay behinds to shave and get a haircut?" Staff Sergeant Jeffery Haskins asked.

"No, Jeff. I want Sergeant Major Ligon to see you guys tonight. That way he will know for sure what we are up to and give our own Sergeant Major a chance to shine to explain the concept of the maneuver," Martin replied inciting raucous laughter among the NCOs along with cries of 'Sheee it'.

"Now, now, men. Give our Sergeant Major every opportunity to lead," Martin said without a trace of a smile. See you tonight and the first drinks, even doubles are on me," Martin said to big cheers.

"Just remember, First Sergeant, I'm easy but I ain't cheap," said Vic Jackson.

1815 hours
03 Jan 1985
NCO Club Annex

Command Sergeant Major McCall's wife had done him proud in the set up for the dinner in Command Sergeant Major Ligon's honor. All of the NCOs from G Troop were present with wives and or girl friends in neat suits or sport coats with nice slacks, ties and all civilian clothes. They could have easily passed for members of the Junior Chamber of Commerce in any small southern town. Staff Sergeant Haskins and Sergeant Bailey of the Mortar platoon and Sergeant Jones from Maintenance were the only ones to exhibit what the military hierarchy refers to as relaxed grooming standards. They were the NCO nucleus of the detachment built around 1st Platoon Scouts that would hide for nearly a week and take a vital bridge during REFORGER. Their appearance drew Command Sergeant Major Ligon's attention to them like a buzzard to road kill on Interstate 15. He put out what troops called the shit hook as he pointed his right index finger toward Martin and crooked it to call him to him. His quizzical look was so out of character, Martin nearly laughed out loud but discretion won out as he made his way to him.

"Why are those NCOs not shaved and why do they need a hair cut?" Command Sergeant Major Ligon asked calmly.

"They are members of 1st Platoon. We are leaving them behind to take a bridge just before we get to the town. They will hold it until the Troop can get there. They also have German workmen's clothes and they will make certain the explosive charges on the bridge for training purposes will not function. They are all fluent German speakers and we are sheltering them in the barn the German county uses for vehicle maintenance. The scheme of maneuver is approved to Regiment and theoretically, the Regimental Commanding Officer has briefed the Corps Commander," Martin concluded.

Martin could see his last statement had hit a nerve in the Corps Command Sergeant Major. "First Sergeant, you will have them all shave and get haircuts in the morning. You will provide me with a written summary of what is to happen in that town. You will make sure they do not act as spies and be out of uniform unless you get specific permission from your Squadron Commander, and then no more than two of them and no Officers. Before the night is over, get me a map of the area and have the ranking NCO of the detachment to be left behind brief me and answer my questions," the Sergeant Major concluded. Martin expected no less of the Sergeant Major to demand the Soldiers conform to Army standard regardless of who said otherwise but he had made his point. The lads may not have passed his barracks inspection but they damn sure went up about ten notches on his innovation tree.

McCall ran true to form saying, "This is the first I heard about this, Command Sergeant Major. Get those guys shaved, Martin, now."

"Yes, Sergeant Major McCall. I will make sure you get briefed after your talk, Sergeant Major Ligon," Martin said as he departed.

The dinner proceeded apace with appropriate introductions and speeches. The food was the best Martin had ever had from the NCO Club. It pays to be married to the head waitress and assistant manager if you are the Squadron Command Sergeant Major. It was not lost on Ligon that Martin bought him a beer and bought the first round for all of his NCOs. Ligon was amused to see some of the NCOs get triple shots of expensive Scotch on their First Sergeant's dime. He also noted their obvious good humor and camaraderie. They were obviously a tight group and got along very well.

About half of the talk was a rehash of the theater with some sanitation due to the presence of the ladies. Command Sergeant Major Ligon used just enough profanity to prove he could do so with impunity and to make his points. The women were bored to tears and the guys faked their attention until it was over. While everything he had to say was true, they had heard him all day in one format or another. The troops were in Ligon over load.

After dinner, Jeff Haskins gave the Corps Command Sergeant Major a masterful tactical briefing to include a summary of how the fight was to be synchronized at each level of command and control using the 5 paragraph operations order format. He walked through each phase of REFORGER and paid particular attention to troop health and welfare at every turn. "Where are you going to be assigned when you leave Germany, Staff Sergeant Haskins?" Ligon asked.

"Drill Sergeant, 1st Brigade Fort Knox, KY, Sergeant Major," Haskins answered.

"Who thought this up, your Squadron Commander?" Ligon asked with a faraway look in his eye.

"Shit, no, Sergeant Major," he replied with a sheepish grin looking at his First Sergeant with an admiring glance.

"We all had our part in it, Sergeant Major. The NCOs thought it up, the officers refined it and it became a G Troop initiative with no one either seeking or getting credit. We just want to have a good REFORGER and do our part. We agree with President Reagan, Sergeant Major, when he stated that you can get a lot done if you don't care who gets the credit," Martin quickly replied.

"You know what bothers me don't you, Martin?" Ligon asked.

"Yes, Sergeant Major, friendly fire and getting to them before the forces of Orange kill them all. We think we have it figured out but luck will have a play as it always does," Martin replied.

"And after today, you think your Troop is lucky, Martin?" the grizzled old Command Sergeant Major asked with a thin smile.

"Hell, yes, Sergeant Major. It is a far better thing to have you point out our deficiencies and shortcomings than to have to learn them from the Russians," he replied with a smile.

"Goddamn, I want to buy you a damn drink. We need to talk. You guys have a good plan. Damn glad to see NCOs thinking ahead and being smart. Make it work and prevent cold injuries. Good Job," effectively dismissing them. The Corps Command Sergeant Major was secretly pleased that the three of them looked to their First Sergeant to receive their nod of dismissal before they took their leave of his august presence.

Over their drinks at an empty table, any hilarity was gone and both NCOs were stone cold sober. "Now listen to me, you let those officers do their job. The reason I know you so well is you are me and I am you from long ago.

You are going to completely take over that damn troop and run it. But, you have to let the officers have their piece of the pie or they won't be worth a damn. You are not an officer. Don't try to act like one. You will be the one who gets used up and thrown away like a used rubber. Officers can get just as lazy as privates and some of these Cavalry officers think more of a vehicle than they do a soldier. I heard every word you said in that classroom. You will be okay as long as you follow through. I have been talking to you or a part of this outfit all day. What is your basic thought?" the Corps Command Sergeant Major asked.

"Sergeant Major, until someone comes up with a tank or an APC that is robotic, men will be operating them. I intend to make each soldier as good as I know how so that when they leave here they will be a positive example to the rest of the Armor Force or a good citizen," Martin said quietly.

"I'll see you on the high ground, Martin. I need to rejoin McCall," he said as he moved away. The troopers were glad to get an early end to the night's festivities. The track vehicles were loading on the train at 0500 the following morning to be joined by the combat trains of the troop led by the First Sergeant at a distant railhead 40 hours later. The train was traveling as space available on the German Rail System but the tread heads would be safe and warm in their sleeping cars until they reached their unloading destination, just a short distance from their first positions. The Troop Commander and the Officers were already enroute to the exercise area for a leaders' reconnaissance and MAPEX. It was already snowing hard with near blizzard conditions predicted for the road march 160 plus miles north of Bad Kissingen.

0700 hours
05 Jan 1985
Track Vehicle Park

As the troopers gathered around, First Sergeant Martin waited for them to get settled. "AT EASE. We are moving down the autobahn through Fulda and north to the railhead that is marked on all of your maps. The rest stops are marked on your strip maps as well. We will camp at the rail head if the train is delayed and will immediately begin operations if it is on time. Maintain your interval. This weather will have Rick the Rad beside himself so give the crazy bastards plenty of room. Staff Sergeant Mack, and trail party, we will police up each and every 2/11 vehicle we find alongside the road that we can push, pull, jump start or drag to the rail head. Everyone, report any strays you see. We will take them all forward and or see to it they have enough food and water to survive until their unit can come after them if it is a blown engine or transmission beyond our ability to fix. If they have reported their position and can wait it out, we will leave them and move forward. Maintain your secure radios and good job on everyone being up in the green. The Golden Rule

204

applies here folks, Do unto others...... Mount up and let's get moving, we're burning daylight."

As he moved the unit forward Martin was glad they had used their exercises and the border to refine their road marching techniques, radio procedures, and sub-unit discipline. It was all training and they were getting better and better. He was shocked to see the first stray at the second intersection after leaving the Kaserne.

"Black 5, Gator 7, break column and determine the fix for the fueler."

"Gator 7, Black 5 Roger."

"7, OUT."

"Damn, Top, you can still see the barracks from here, what the hell?" his incredulous driver asked.

"Don't know Tommy, just hope we can fix it and get it moving," Martin replied.

"Seven, Five."

"Seven, OVER."

"Roger, he is a new guy and was Lima, Lima, Mike, Foxtrot. He is traveling right in front of me and we will take him with us, OVER."

"Seven, Tango Yankee, OUT."

"First Sergeant, what is Lima Lima Mike Foxtrot?" the driver asked with a smile. "Is it LLMF?"

"Yeah, Tommy, it is. But remember, the guy just got here and there will be any number of folks lost before this rodeo is over and we cannot take chances at 10 to 20 degrees below zero," Martin said.

But he wondered, 'How many strays will we find on the way and how much time must I spend recovering them? Better figure out the size of the elephant.'

"Black 8, Gator 7, OVER."

Sergeant First Class Wintergreen was probably surprised to get a call from his First Sergeant.

"Gator 7, this is Black 8, OVER."

"Black 8, move out ahead of us and survey the route for road kill from other units. Make an assessment. Do not go beyond the Fulda exit until we have cleared Wildflecken. Get them ready to move if they can, call me with a SITREP from each exit, acknowledge."

"Gator 7, Black WILCO, OUT."

By the end of the march, the Gators had recovered 18 vehicles and were forced to leave three that could not be jury rigged for the march.

The railhead was a solid sheet of ice covered by snow when the Gator Troop Combat Trains arrived at the railhead. The temperature was 12 below zero and the wind was out of the North at 18 knots and it was snowing. The track vehicles had been on the rails for nearly two days and would likely be hard to start. They would need the First Sergeant's trick bag for sure. E Troop's vehicles were being jump started from trucks pulled alongside the flat cars. Their engines were not responding. The ones that were started could not move on the icy concrete slab of the rail head. Major Bragg was having a full grown 'Texas Longhorn' as he could not get past the NCO incompetence he was seeing.

"Tell me you are going to get G Troop off their train and gone from here ASAP, First Sergeant. Also, tell me you are going to able to move the entire troop to the designated assembly area to meet Captain Dawson later tonight without any issues - can you do that?" he asked as his eyes narrowed to mere slits.

"We will be moving off the rail head in less than 25 minutes, Major Bragg, with no issues we cannot handle," Martin replied.

"And just how are the Gators going to manage that when no one else can seem to get it done, First Sergeant?" the massive Executive Officer asked so pleasantly that it bordered on sarcasm.

"We're going to cheat, Sir, cheat our asses off," Martin replied. As he said the words the recovery vehicle known as the Cherry Picker, the most ungainly looking and hardest-to-start vehicle in the diesel inventory, coughed and started with scarcely more trouble than if it had been parked inside. As if on cue, every single G Troop vehicle on the train began its starting sequence and the rail yard was filled with blue smoke and the sound of diesel engines starting and being revved up.

"Damn it, First Sergeant, get the rest of these damn vehicles going right now or at least tell these people how to do it," the Executive Officer fulminated.

"Yes, Sir, I can tell 'em but whether they want to do it or not is then up to them," Martin said. The words were wasted. The 6'6" Executive Officer had put out the shit hook and was motioning his "boys" the motor sergeants to come to him. They were a hard and nasty bunch of know it all hard-asses. They came to Major Bragg as much out of curiosity as of discipline.

"You are going to need this, Major Bragg," Martin said over his shoulder as he faced about. He then drew a can of ether starting fluid out of his interior coverall pocket and handed it to the Major unseen by the assembling Motor Sergeants and Maintenance geeks. Major Bragg smiled the smile of the inside joke as he slid the ether into his tanker jacket. As the Major faced about, First Sergeant Martin made his move back to his vehicle to solve his next issue, getting these hogs off the skating rink otherwise known as a railhead. The attached engineers had completed off loading their equipment from one of their five ton dump trucks and were using a back hoe to load gravel from a construction firm adjacent to the rail head as well as some sand. Staff Sergeant Webster emerged from the dispatch shack of the gravel yard smiling so Martin knew the trade had been a good one. One hundred gallons of diesel fuel for enough gravel and sand to give traction to the entire rail yard. Each unit had an engineer attachment but as Martin correctly surmised,

Major Bragg was about to take the best ones under Squadron control until he could vacate the rail head.

"Now, Sir, don't start loving those Engineer TURDS too much. Everyone has 'em, not just me. These boys are gonna' have to start thinkin' and actin' on their own. You and me ain't gonna' be right next to 'em during RE-FORGER. There ain't no book of at least half of this shit. I need to take those guys with me to meet the Gator and he will shit if they ain't there," Martin said in his best country boy accent.

"Oh, shit, you're right, First Sergeant. Sand down the exit and take them with you. You done enough already."

Of course, smart ass Neeley said, "Shit, Sir, if we could cheat like that damn Martin we would of brought ether too but the book says you can never use that shit on these engines. It is an old sorry trick to make us look bad."

Bragg replied with a sly grin, "I told him right now you damn guys and I do not need any help looking bad. We are doing a real good job on our own. He saved your butts and did not even laugh about it. Now me, I would have had to laugh. You keep on, First Sergeant, adapt and overcome," saluting as he finished speaking. He could see G Troop was nearly formed outside the rail head.

"Eaglehorse, Sir," Martin said as he saluted and moved to his unit. Major Bragg noted Martin did not gather the unit but merely got into his vehicle and executed a commo check on the troop net by pointing his hand mike at each Platoon Sergeant, clicking his press to talk switch once and receiving two clicks back from each station. Once he knew each element was on his radio net he went to the side of column and gave the hand signal for 'I am ready, are you ready?'

The Germans must have been amused to see the Americans using a signal that bore a strong resemblance to the Nazi salute from WW II, right arm extended first to the rear at a forty five degree angle and then to the front as each vehicle reported ready. Martin had often been the tail-end-Charlie of the column and had been left sitting at the start point more than once. New guys were never ready and he was no exception as a young Staff Sergeant - he was just as hosed as any other new guy. He never forgot and built the silent reporting structure into all of their movements.

He knew Vic and others joked that he was 'Patton Junior' in his fastidious dress in the correct uniform of the day for the well dressed Armor Leader. He knew he was right and did not care what they or anyone else thought. He also knew his soldiers did miss the fact that theirs was the only NCO led troop at the rail head. All of the other units had at least one officer present.

Martin also had Jeff Haskins as the lead track vehicle behind his jeep. Jeff could smooth talk the Germans out of almost anything. The AA was sixty kilometers away and they would be arriving well after nightfall and at least an hour before the Gator could get there with the officers. They had busy autobahns to exit onto and off of as well as country roads to reach their distant and bleak AA in the forest.

As they arrived near the entrance to the road leading to the AA after a hair raising trip on the Autobahn, Martin called Jeff Haskins, "Red, Gator 7, proceed ahead, check it out and set us up."

"Seven, Red, Roger, OVER."

"All elements, this is Seven, slow down to five, say again, slow to five." Soon his fears were confirmed.

"Seven, Red, this is a large tree nursery. I have found a better spot about 500 meters ahead with some maneuvering area and the Gator will like it better than the trees. We will be gone long before daylight, OVER."

"Roger, Red, break, all elements, Seven, move in and occupy using troop SOP, take your instructions from Red on the ground, submit Log reports, acknowledge in turn, White Roger, Blue Roger, Green Roger, Gold Roger, Black Roger."

Martin then found a high hill with a very old church three kilometers from the new position and moved there to report. He did not want the officers going to where they expected to find the troop and see an empty field. Winning and solid information build confidence, losing and iffy guesses destroy it.

"Gator 6, Seven, OVER."

"Seven this is Six, OVER."

"Six, Seven SITREP Follows, Arrived AA Pony, 1930 hours, all organic vehicles and attachments are present. The Troop is Green and local security is set. The AA is 500 meters North of the Old AA Pony. The first AA was a tree nursery, hemmed in by trees and only had a one lane trail. The new one is far better. OVER."

"Seven, this is Six. If you moved the AA you had a good reason. Meet me at the road intersection leading into the AA from the priority road. My ETA is Two Zero mikes, OVER."

"Six, Seven, WILCO, OVER."

"Six, OUT."

While not wild about moving the troop without the officers, Martin did a credible job of it but was very pleased to know he would not be second guessed, at least publicly. He was also happy the fuel tankers they picked up on the march north were able to top off all of the vehicles in the troop.

Everyone had more than enough food and water so he should get some sleep tonight based on how much planning the recon would force. Since time immemorial, Headquarters units have made big circles on maps with bigger arrows for planned advances the terrain would not support. And for the same period of time, Company and Battalion level commanders figured out how to get the missions done in spite of the guidance they got from the big circle boys with their coffee cups.

0700 hours
08 Jan 1985

"Gator Seven, Gold Seven, OVER."

"Gold, Seven."

"Gator Seven, Gold Seven meet me at reference point 2.4 on map sheet 37. I've got something hot that needs to get higher ASAP, OVER."

"Gold, Gator Seven, See you there in One Five Mikes, OVER."

"Go Tommy, get this heap moving down that primary road right there. Go down by the church and up over the far hill. That is where we will meet Sergeant Jackson," Martin ordered.

"What's he got, First Sergeant?" his driver asked.

"Don't know Tommy, but whatever it is, it is important. Old Vic does not get excited easily," Martin opined smiling.

As G-44 stopped, Martin was mounting at the front slope to see Vic in his Tank Commander's hatch. Martin never had Tank or Track Commanders dismount if he could avoid it. He told the troops it was a bad habit for a man with only a quarter inch of homogeneous cloth to separate his fighters from their equipment based on phony ass protocol of rank.

"Look what I got, First Sergeant. A damn map of the entire side of the battlefield down to company level. Peavy stole it from them as we were helping them recover their tank. It is their ELLTEE's map that blew off his tank and they were trying to catch up to them to give it to him. They broke a main fuel pump and will be stuck here for a spell. What you gonna' do with it, Top?" Vic said with a big smile.

"Did you guys make an overlay for the Gator?" Martin asked.

"Of course, its right here. He sent McWilliams to get it for him. Just talked to him on the platoon net and told him I was calling you," Jackson said proudly.

"Way to go, Peavy, you damn crook," Martin told the gunner who looked up at him with a shy smile as he was departing the tank with the purloined map.

Damn Peavy, shake your hand and pick your pocket while he is inviting you to church next Sunday for revival. Love that guy.

"Eagle Horse Six or Three, Gator Seven, Flash Traffic, OVER."

"Gator Seven, this is six, send your message."

"Six, this is Gator Seven, need to do this face to face. Suggest the TOC, OVER."

"Negative, Seven, the TOC is jumping. I will come to you, send grid."

Once the grid was sent, Martin settled down to wait and watched the remainder of the troop go forward. In less than five minutes, Lieutenant Colonel Covington's CUCV slid to a stop beside him. Martin took the Squadron Commander the "enemy" map with a full set of combat overlays showing the

209

positions and designations of nearly every heavy unit of the Brigade and the Division boundaries opposite the Squadron and thus the Regiment.

"Holy Shit," said the SCO.

"We believe it is genuine, Sir. Specialist Peavy stole from a Platoon Sergeant's tank. It belonged to their Platoon Leader who let it blow away. They probably won't realize what happened to it for a couple of hours," Martin said with great glee.

"Is this guy with the dead tank a friend of Sergeant Jackson, First Sergeant?" the Squadron Commander asked.

"The operative word is probably 'was', Sir."

"Oh well, all's fair in love and war and everyone knows you can't trust a Cav Trooper now can you, First Sergeant?" Covington asked with a broad grin.

Martin took his cue and saluted saying, "Eagle Horse, Sir." The Squadron Commander was already on the radio to the Regimental Commanding Officer and they were plotting their next series of moves based on the great level of detail about "enemy" intentions from the map. Something neither man knew at the time the exchange took place was for the first time during the exercise G Troop and 2d Squadron made the headline edition of the USAREUR event summary. During the nightly critique and discussion of each day's events, unusual or fortuitous events were part of the proceedings. Seldom, if ever, were any units below Brigade level part of the summary. The Gators were about to become regulars.

The map enabled the Squadron and the Regiment to counter the tactics and movements of their opposite numbers in the opposing force. The incident made the summary as a Lessons Learned for security, Commanders being at the Center of Gravity, and the immediate application of battlefield intelligence.

No amount of praise could make the cold go away. The exercise sapped the strength and vitality of men and machines. It took all of the considerable talents of the unit leaders to keep the soldiers' heads in the game instead of merely surviving until the end of the exercise. During the enforced break in the action brought on by the judicious use of the information on the map, a pause in the exercise was called at 1400 hours the day it was found. The 11th ACR and V Corps reaction to the Intelligence bonanza made it necessary to reset forces and unsnarl those that had come in close contact. Captain Dawson and First Sergeant Martin took the opportunity to get their Troop to a nice local guest house in a wooded area close to their temporary AA.

Martin was unable to get there in time as he was setting up for the nightly replenishment of food, fuel, spare parts, and receiving replacements. That did not stop the Soldiers from establishing a guard force and going to the Gast Haus for a meal and a beer. The Troop knew the rules, no hard liquor, no carry out, one beer or one glass of wine. They had never let the leadership down and no one expected them to now.

1800 hours
08 Jan 1985
G Troop AA

Martin was very happy to see the big smiles on the faces of the troops. All of them had clean shaves and fairly clean hands and most had a clean uniform or their coveralls. The crews fell to the task of receiving fuel and moved the logistics package through in record time. Nearly all of them ate but wanted their portions reduced due to the great fare they got earlier at the Gast Haus.

Jeff Haskins motioned to the First Sergeant to join him at the front of the Supply Truck. "I wanted to tell you what happened at the Gast Haus. Specialist Grant was in line to pay his bill. We got a new guy I am not sure you have even met, First Sergeant, Sergeant Bull. Bull ordered a shot of Jaeger Meister Liquor as he was paying his bill. As he was about to toss it down, Grant knocked it out of his hand and it broke on the floor. Grant told him, 'Look, Sergeant, you just got here. The Captain and the First Sergeant trust us to have a beer or one glass of wine with our dinner, no hard liquor. Now you were told that. You are not going to screw it up for the rest of us by violating their trust. I'll pay for the shot glass and buy you a drink later'. He paid for the shot glass. I could have kissed the little shit. Didn't know he had the balls but by God he does. Bull took it like a man and I think he will be all right. He is just not used to that much self-discipline."

"Thanks, Jeff, that is great news. It is working, isn't it? Was the food good?" Martin asked.

"It was great, First Sergeant," Haskins said beaming.

"Now I have to find a break in the action and a schwimmbad," Martin said laughing.

"Just try to find it before we go to that barn, First Sergeant. We go in there like this the smell of our asses alone will lead them to us." Haskins said laughing.

"I'll do what I can. Where is your Wild Man Platoon Leader?" Martin asked.

"He is over there with a full plate of mess hall steak with all the trimmings. He ate at the Gast Haus but he be a Ranger and he never leaves food if it is within range. Hell, he ain't a Captain yet and he is still growing," Haskins said admiring the lad's appetite.

"Don't talk, just eat," Martin said to First Lieutenant Robertson. "I am going to take a swag at where we are going to be tomorrow at 1500 hours," smiling as the boy never missed a stroke. "We need to find and coordinate our German schwimmbad before the guys go into the hide. We will get another one after they come out before we go back to BK if there is time."

The omnivore First Lieutenant Robertson had decided to come up for air from his meal and he spoke, "You know, First Sergeant, the best place to go is right under the OPFOR's nose during the nightly pause, especially if we get another early one. If we start at 1500 we can rotate the whole troop and still do re-supply on schedule," Robertson said, as he forked yet another big piece of steak into his mouth.

"I really admire your coyote metabolism Ell Tee. You make Captain and go on staff you better keep up your PT or you'll be a butter ball," Martin said with a smile.

"You keep feeding us like this and sending us to the Gast Haus and we will all be fat. You let me know when to start looking and I will find a schwimmbad, First Sergeant, don't you worry about that," Robertson said with finality.

"What are you two up to now?" Captain Dawson asked.

"We are war gaming the schwimmbad trip for the Troop, Sir. I figure we have to do it soon before they go into the hide and tomorrow afternoon looks good. We can split the troop into Red and Gold and White and Blue for security and maintain unit integrity. I will get by without going in and keep an eye on the process," Martin said.

"Bull shit, Top, I'll go first and as soon as I am out, you go and take the Executive Officer with you. He is stinking like a damn goat," Dawson ordered.

Thus the stage was set for another headline for the nightly meeting of the stars though none of the G Troop players knew it at the time.

1300 hours
09 Jan 1985

"Red, this is Seven, what is your status, OVER."

"Seven, this is Red, have completed recon of the schwimmbad and have effected coordination for the troop to use it. It is closed today but the ladies agreed to let us use it. We need to make sure we tip them well, very well. It's just on the outside edge of the FEBA between us and the OPFOR, break, we should be able to infiltrate and use it without being seen, OVER."

"Red, Seven, what kind of an outfit is it, OVER."

"Seven, Red. It is a DS support outfit with some DISCOM units. They have built outdoor fires, they sleep during the day on guard post, they are not shaving or cleaning up. They are generally pretty sorry, OVER."

"Red, are they MILESed, Up, OVER."

"Seven, affirmative. I don't know why they have MILES, they are too sorry to need it, OVER."

"Guidons, Guidons, Guidons, this is Six, OVER, stand by for orders. Red has found the schwimmbad with the least risk. We will execute split ops with Red and Gold in first and White and Blue in trail. Black and Green will split even. I want everyone not in the schwimmbad to be ready to fight, double check all MILES, re-boresight if you are in doubt, check all wires and make sure we have a full load. The idea is to sneak in and sneak out but if we have to fight, fight we will. I go in with the first group and SEVEN and FIVE will stay with the second. We will wait for the pause to be announced over the net and go in at that time. Do not fall in love with the shower, but get in and get out. Acknowledge."

About thirty minutes into the first rotation, Tommy Staunton, First Sergeant's driver extraordinaire, returned to the jeep clean and shiny as a new penny. "Damn, First Sergeant. I know we are together all of the time and I have seen you do some shit Man but this, this is the shit, First Sergeant. They have a wave machine in there, Top. I had a shower, a swim, a shave, a sauna and they sold me this schnitzel sandwich. I thought you were full of shit back in BK when you told us to bring our swim suits and cut offs and then inspected to make sure we had them. But First Sergeant, I believe in miracles now. You should go on in."

"Hush Tommy, you are so loud I can't hear the radio and someone is calling. I'm glad you had a good time."

"Seven, this is Blue. We are about to lock up with some Bradleys at 1,500 meters. Can we engage, OVER?"

"Blue, Seven, engage. Green, need you to provide support. Is your Fire Support Evaluator present, OVER?"

"Seven, Green, Affirmative, he is back from his shower and ready to go to work."

"Seven, Roger, Stand By."

By this time, the critique at Headquarters was nearly over. The OPFOR net was going crazy and the umpires were getting busy. The OPFOR representative was remonstrating about the Cavalry fighting during the pause. The USAREUR Deputy Commanding General reminded everyone war was like a boxing match and the players had to defend themselves at all times.

"Redleg, this is Seven, status, OVER."

"Roger, Seven, I am in my tank and plotting targets now. Have good Commo with the Battery and Corps. We have lots of idle tubes available during the pause ex so there is a lot of firepower available."

A wave of laughter swept over the senior officers at the conference.

"Guidons, Guidons, Guidons, remain in your hide positions until we get Redleg working on the OPFOR. Engage at long range if you have a shot. Blue, block the roads by killing the lead elements and the last one out of the gate. White, use your TOWs from the ridgeline and kill any of the leakers who take the long way out the back of town.

"Redleg, status, OVER."

"Seven, Redleg, we have a good registration and expect a Corps Six in about three minutes. It was smart to keep us all in the hide. It will take the umpires a little while to sort out the rubble from the first mission. I can shoot them all day from here. They are in our range and we are outside of theirs, OVER."

One of the Generals asked, "Is this Kelly's Heroes or REFORGER? It sounds to me like G Troop on a shower run at a schwimmbad in No-Mans' Land. What unit is trying to fight them there?" he asked.

An efficient Major checked the exercise map and reported, "That is the 1 ID DISCOM, Sir. They have been executing the Bradley issue for the big fight tomorrow. They are going to use the Bradleys to fight the Cavalry Regiment."

"Listen, the Cav Troop is getting ready for something," the GO said.

"Seven, this is Six, SITREP, OVER. Six, Seven, Blue is engaging Bradleys from an issue point in town at 2,000 meters. White is engaging the middle portion of the Bradley column with TOW from his hide position. Both elements are working battle hand over with Red and Gold. Redleg is coordinating a Corps Six on the middle of the column. Redleg probably has come to a check fire while we are doing our handover, break, REDLEG speak to Six."

"SIX, REDLEG, Seven is correct, we have a Corps Six of DPICM at check fire. About thirty Brads are bottled up and ready to die, orders, OVER."

"Redleg, Six, shoot it, OVER."

"This is REDLEG, Shot, OVER."

"Seven, Six, go get your shower and take Five with you."

"Six, Seven, WILCO."

"Guidons this is Six, report casualties this net, continue to engage. Black standby for recovery."

The Exercise Director gave a hearty laugh saying, "Just another day in paradise for G Troop, gentlemen. Their morale is fine. As soon as they get clear, turn off the fight, restore all elements to full capability across the board and get ready for tomorrow's fight. We will see how well BLUFOR does against the team of Bradleys and M-1's on the North German plain. John, find out what MOS the guy holds who is calling for fire with the Gators from the M-1 tank. I want to know that story."

Major John Parks, Field Artillery and Senior Aide to the Lieutenant General directing the exercise already knew the answer. His best friend, West Point room mate and fellow Artilleryman was the Blackhorse Regiment's Artillery Officer. The answer was one that would help provide lessons learned to everyone. "Sir, we already have the background on that if you want it now," the Major stated.

"John, you continue to amaze me. Please continue," the Lieutenant General said.

"Sir, Gentlemen, my best friend and fellow Redleg is the Blackhorse FSO. The Gators have taken full advantage of the Blackhorse method of combined arms. The Gator FSO is assigned a tank. He goes through the TCGST and a gunnery cycle to qualify in it. He is a fully qualified tanker. He operates out of the tank and serves both the Troop Commander and as an extension of the Regimental FSO. All of them have trained together in Fire Coordination Exercises with the tracks and have worked through the various FDCs to include V Corps Artillery. The Gators put him in the tank in the manner of WW II FSOs and ALOs to protect him and to give him a fast vehicle that can keep up with the combat forces. The Gators appear to have fully adopted the program and the FSO as one of their own. He lives with them, does PT, trains, goes to the Border and socializes with them. He is still rated by the Howitzer Battery Commander but for all intents and purposes he is a member of G Troop. This particular officer is Border qualified and has his Spurs."

Major Parks carefully watched his boss for signs of displeasure as he gave his summary. There were none.

"Are you surprised, John, at what happened just now?" the Exercise Director asked.

"No, Sir. The Gators are obviously well trained, idealistic and tend to take advantage of every situation. We should not hold it against them that they do not fight fair and use every combat multiplier we give them. Frankly, Sir, I am surprised they have not called for TAC Air."

In the pregnant silence that followed Major Parks analysis, the Fire Support Net came alive with a call from the mini-battle being waged at the schwimmbad. "Battle Axe," (Permanent Call Sign of the Regimental Air Liaison Officer a USAF Major). "This is Gator, Redleg. Do we have TAC Air available, OVER?"

"There you go John. There is no need to send that guy to CGSC after he commands. He could go teach there now." The whole room erupted in laughter as it was now clear the former Artilleryman, now a Lieutenant General far removed from the mud, the blood and the beer, was very pleased at this demonstration of the health and vitality of his branch.

"Red Leg, this is Six, negative on the TAC Air. I do not want our little blip to become a mushroom cloud at higher. We are going to slink away and get set for the morning fight. No TAC Air, acknowledge."

"Gator Six, Red Leg, Roger, OVER."

"Six, OUT."

"Well, that completes the picture. They may be bandits at heart but by God they are our Bandits and they have discretion. Let's talk cold weather injuries now that the Gators have provided us with a little levity and are slinking away," the Lieutenant General said with a smile.

215

"Six, Seven, back on station and prepared to move. The ladies were happy. The cleanup detail helped but the tips helped more. The lads were very generous. Those women have not seen that many German Duetsche marks lately. Everyone is accounted for and we are ready to move, OVER."

"Guidons, Guidons, Guidons, stand by to move. Road march will be by troop SOP. I will be in 66," (G-66 the commanders M1 tank). "Red, infiltrate to your position. White, take the lead. I will initiate movement of the main body. Seven, drop to trail, report clearance of the AA and all check points to Five, Six, OUT."

0600 hours
10 Jan 1985
Gator Assembly Area

"First Sergeant, how are we making it with these extra vehicles and people?" Captain Dawson asked.

"Just fine, Sir. We just do the math, order the extra fuel and use an extra chow truck to serve from. We are keeping everything integrated. It is good to have First Lieutenant Eggbert to command the tanks. He is a good officer and runs his logistics straight as a string. He is a pure tread head though and trying hard to get into the Cavalry flow. We are fluctuating between 93 and 106 vehicles based on attachments. The ten fuel trucks are a bit much to set up and convoy. I expect the Corps will start using 5,000 gallon tankers soon using big Refuel on the Move (ROM) stations as the distances stretch out from their base ops point. We have 15 ground hop fuel lines left out of our original 30 of those made back at BK. All of these tanks are running but we are using up the kits at a rate of two per day. We do need some water. Tommy and I are going to find a farm house and fill water cans today using jeep trailers. It will take two trips, that's about it from me, Captain," Martin concluded.

"Top, find some high ground and talk to Red in the barn. No other radio in the troop can raise them this far away. I want to know their status and to let them know we have not forgotten them. Tell them we will be there day after tomorrow. Tell him I will talk to him once we get close. I need you to get some eyes on that creek outside of Alsfeld to make sure the material we brought for the hasty crossing will work. You will have to do it at night. I do not want Red coming out of that barn for the next 48 hours unless it is on fire, you tell him that. Tell him this is the Fourth Quarter of the football game. How are you going to do your recon of the creek?" Dawson asked finally.

"WILCO, Sir. Why? You originally reserved all of the communications with Red to yourself and told me to stay clear, now it is just the opposite," Martin asked with a smile.

216

"You have not done as much of this as I have, particularly over the last six years. Soon, the umpires will start killing off the leadership of Colonels, Lieutenant Colonels and even Majors. They will move people up to fill their slots. I know I will be moving up to Squadron either as the S3 or as the Squadron Commander. The Executive Officer will move up to my slot or First Lieutenant Eggbert will. It will come at the worst possible time of the operation and there is no way to plan for it except how we have done it, train a little each day to teach people your job. It won't last long - just several hours. There are too many complications with the civilians, the weather and the tactical plan to let it go on longer than that. We will not look stupid when it comes. I want you to manage Red and to be ahead of the game. As you said earlier, Red is sterile and controls his environment in the barn and during the capture of the bridge. It is getting our units to him so that they are not all killed and the bridge retaken that is the hard part or at least the unknown part. Think it all through and do what you have to do to get it done. If you have to spend any money doing it, let me know and the S4 will reimburse you. Your old buddy is now the real S4 as a brand new Captain. Regiment snapped up Captain Domalewski as soon as your butt-breath buddy Upton got promoted," Dawson said with great derision.

"What is it with you and Upton, Sir?" Martin asked.

"He is a damn Yankee smart-ass carpet bagging asshole," Dawson said, spitting immediately as if to get the taste of the word Yankee out of his mouth.

Martin began laughing loud and long. He had needed to laugh about something for days and now the laughter-associated tears rolled out of his eyes. His cigarette smoke choked him and he gagged while laughing and waving his arms.

"God Damn, Top, don't have a heart attack on me!" Dawson exclaimed.

Martin waved his hand to calm his Captain. "You are a funny guy, Captain. You remind me of a Cavalry Colonel during the Spanish American War who had the honor and the privilege of being a Cavalry Commander in the forces of Robert E. Lee resisting the forces of Northern Aggression. While holding the rank of Brevet Major General, G. Joseph "Fighting Joe" Wheeler's forces decisively routed the Spanish forces opposing them. He was proud and excited as he reported, 'Suh, we have the damn Yankees on the run.' You neither forgive nor forget do you, Sir?" Martin questioned.

"Hell, no, First Sergeant. We Rebels may lose our asses but we do not surrender our souls. The south will rise again," Dawson said without a trace of a smile.

"Well, Captain, if the war gamers elevate you to Regimental Command please try not to refer to the OPFOR as 'Yankees' when giving your reports," Martin said laughing as he saluted.

First Sergeant Martin and his driver found a German farm house and with a buxom and lonely widow about his age in sole charge of the scene. Her husband had died the previous summer. She was 15 years her departed husband's junior and was Martin's age. After coffee, which he detested drinking, she was more than happy to give them all of the water they wanted from her springhouse well. Martin dropped his trailer and had the maintenance driver begin to fill the cans with instructions to drop the cans off with the supply truck and return to fill the remainder. He would return and get him and all would rejoin the troop.

1000 hours
10 Jan 1985
Near Corps Engagement Area Yorktown

After consulting his map, Martin made his way to the highest hill be could find on his side of the Forward Edge of the Battle Area. The position was almost in enemy territory but he was confident he could remain unseen. The hill was dominated by an old church with an old but well kept cemetery. It was clear the church was not abandoned but was not in use except for special occasions. There were large formations of boulders forward of the church on the military crest of the hill that almost resembled the Druid Stones but lacked faces.

"Park here Tommy. I'm going to walk up over the hill and look down into the valley, then we will call 1st Platoon."

What a hardy bunch of true believers it must have taken to build this church on this lonely hill top. It was made of stone and there damn sure wasn't any drywall with fake rock on its front-no brick veneer for these guys. I wonder home many Soldiers have used these rocks for a latrine like I am. Looks like some activity down there. What the hell is that. Stupid, use your binos. Oh shit, that is at least a Battalion Task Force refueling in the open.

All of his radio calls to the Squadron and Regiment went unanswered. Not bashful, he switched to the V Corps frequency and was very surprised he did not get an answer from them either.

"How come no one is answering, First Sergeant," Staunton asked.

"Not sure Tommy. The FM should be blasting them out of their TOC swivel chairs. Maybe they all jumped locations and are moving all at once and the Tactical Ops Guys are ignoring anyone below the grade of Lieutenant Colonel.

"Any Victory element, this is R4N 87, OVER."

"Gator Seven, this is Red."

"Red, Gator Seven, I have you loud and clear, OVER."

"Seven Red, SITREP follows: All elements in the Green. Charges neutralized on the bridge. The town is jammed with traffic through the passage points. We are set here and prepared to execute on command, OVER."

"Red, Seven, The Gator wants you to know you are on his mind and he has not forgotten you. We have been successful and have 97 vehicles in the troop with attachments. We will be seeing you the day after tomorrow. Gator sends, this is the fourth quarter of the game. Stay hidden, don't get stupid, and wait for his call to break out. Use the artillery and hit 'em where they least expect it and hit 'em hard, how copy, OVER."

"Seven, Red, WILCO, OUT."

"Gator Seven, This is Victory Six, OVER."

"Victory Six, Gator Seven, Spot Report, OVER."

"Seven, Victory Six, send it, OVER."

"Enemy Tank Battalion Plus, Refueling in the open from 5,000 gallon tankers in retail mode, Corps Engagement Area Yorktown, OD paint scheme fresh from Depot, 1008 local, Scattered light clouds to 10,000 feet with winds approximately 10 knots north east, Continuing to observe, OVER."

"Gator Seven, where are you?"

"Victory 6, I am on the high hill just north of Yorktown. I have you in sight. Your aircraft just made a pedal turn below us over the river. I am 3 clicks from you at about 187 degrees waving the towel, OVER."

"Gator Seven, I have you in sight. I need you to move to the north side of the river. It is about to start raining aluminum and I do not want you to become a casualty. You have unfinished business in less than 48 hours do you not, OVER."

"Victory Six, Gator Seven, Roger, returning to the Squadron Net, OVER."

"Gator Seven, Victory Six, good job First Sergeant, Victory Six, OUT."

Later Martin would tell the TOC Crew of the Gators around the stove that it had truly rained fighter planes. "I did not know we had that many fighters playing in the exercise. They were lined up taking turns. That Task Force scattered to the winds, driving over hoses, running into each other and tankers, damn fuel flying everywhere - it was a huge goat rope. It will take the rest of the day to get them back together and unscrewed. If that was the attack force we expected, they are going to have to do a major reset. Old Sam Wetzel sure hosed them today. He may be a three banger but he was a field rat today. The boy found the center of gravity and pounded the hell out of them. You know he had to enjoy that shit. Red is fine and is set to execute. They are using their head and are glad you had me call," Martin concluded.

"How did Red sound, Top?" Dawson asked.

"He sounded like a man who had aged about five years in five days. There is nothing that grows a leader faster than detached service that makes him take charge and live by his wits. That is why the Cav grows strong leaders and

219

why Ranger School and service are great character builders - there is no one to ask what to do - you have to adapt, overcome obstacles and achieve mission success," Martin concluded.

"Now we have to do our part. JJ, do you have my car bodies and are they environmentally neutral?" Martin asked the Motor Sergeant.

"Shit, First Sergeant, those were fine looking cars. Some of them are cleaner than ones our own soldiers are trying to drive," First Lieutenant Brown said in answer for his Motor Sergeant.

"That's right, First Sergeant. They are in good shape. Do you think they will hold up well enough to get a platoon of tanks across that creek?" JJ Wintergreen asked.

"JJ, we are going to cross that creek and go up that bank to the road below the town. We are coming from a direction no one expects us from because they think it is impassable to tanks without bringing up bridging. The AVLB is a distraction. As the defenders focus on the AVLB upstream, we will cross the creek and the bottom land two kilometers downstream. The idea is to be on them and at the bridge before they know it. The M-1 moves at 44 feet per second at top speed but 20 per second will do it just fine if we are shooting as we go to defend Red on the bridge. Besides, tactics are not our problem. We get the stuff to the officers to lead it into battle and die bravely – right, Executive Officer?" Martin said, laughing.

"Yes, First Sergeant," the Executive Officer screamed while doing a West Point brace against the canvas wall of the M-577.

"Why would you know or care how fast the tank moves in a second, First Sergeant?" Sergeant Shirley asked as he was tightening the last of the mounting screws on a radio in the Command Track.

"When you are writing the tank gunnery scoring table it is useful to know how far an M-1 tank travels per second for each ten miles per hour of speed. Crews are measured against what they can do in seconds. Ranges, particularly ones with targets that come up when prompted by the firing tank running over a sensor on the road, are only effective if the speed of the range matches the speed of the tank. You see, Spur Brother Shirley; we have a butt load more capability in the M1 tank than we have ranges to fully exercise its capabilities. So when one designs the scenarios to test the crews this side of Fort Irwin and the Mojave Desert or Dona Ana at Fort Bliss, you have to plot it with some precision. Make sense?" Martin asked.

"I guess so, First Sergeant. Is that what you did, write the manuals and design ranges before you got here?" Shirley asked.

"Yeah, I did but don't tell me to go back there because it is more important than being a First Sergeant. The Army will have me back on staff before you know it Sergeant Shirley, so if it is okay with you I am going to enjoy this First Sergeant gig for as long as I can," Martin said as he left the Command track to go meet the logistics train being brought forward by the Supply Sergeant, the Great Webster.

As the tent flap shut behind him, Sergeant Shirley looked at his idol First Lieutenant Brown, a Mechanical Engineering Grad of West Point for confirmation. "That's right, Shirley, speed is speed be it miles per hour or feet per second. The First Sergeant needed the data at some point to match seconds available and he calculated it. Then when some dumb ass tried to jam up a range design somewhere in a briefing cramming five pounds of exercise into a two pound bag of land, the First Sergeant stuck it up his ass. First Sergeant just made sure he had hard data as opposed to theory. When we were at the Armor School he told us as we gained rank and made big decisions on future systems to remember experts with half ass data theorized, hypothesized and got ready to apologize to save their companies or their jobs. It was our job to save soldiers from half assed equipment and half-baked tactics and doctrine. We learned a lot from him and the NCOs at Knox, a lot more than just about tanks," the Executive Officer said, stretching like a big cat and yawning. The pace of REFORGER and the cold was wearing out the Airborne Ranger, Two Sport Varsity Letterman and they still had days to go. "I'm going to get some sleep guys. Call me when chow gets here or if something happens, okay?" he smiled at the "Yes, Sir" Chorus, curled up on a cot wrapped in his parka and was asleep in less than 1 minute.

0600 hours
14 Jan 1985

The air had a real snap in it and almost took one's breath away it was so cold. Today was the day of the break out for the Red platoon and the hasty attack to take the bridge for G Troop. The weather was cooperating as it had been more than 11 degrees F below zero thus freezing the ground deep enough to prevent serious maneuver damage to the fields. The troop had had a very early breakfast, all of the vehicles were full of fuel and the attachments were still in wonder over their meal at the German restaurant last evening.

The soldiers were clean, warm, and full of food. Their morale was high and the end of this long and cold exercise was in sight. This was the hard part of the exercise for the First Sergeant and the Captain. Just when everything was solved, the coordination was nearly automatic, the orders process was second nature, and the damn thing would end. Martin realized only true lifers wanted exercises without end and war on the horizon. They would have the border to keep them sharp and the leadership would have to insist on following the principles of leadership, the SALUTE format and the great maintenance standards there and at home station.

"Top, I want you to make certain the hasty crossing of that canal goes perfectly. You know what to do. What problems to you see?" Dawson asked.

221

"My big problem is going to be to get them to the LD. The road to get there is downhill and slick as a cat's ass. It has a 90° turn at the bottom with a walled off barnyard right against the road. We have sand and gravel on the engineer dump trucks but letting a dump truck lead the attack ain't exactly doctrine, Captain," Martin said with a wry smile.

"First Sergeant, from what I can see we will be the only thing moving on the road. Nobody but us has gravel in their dump trucks, not even the Germans. They are all holed up by the snow and the ice. You just need to get us around the corner and then shoot up to the ford. We will do the rest. I want you to take my Track to do the ford. I don't want the umpires to kill you off. They were going to kill you off the other day but they could not find you. Where in the hell were you?" Dawson asked.

"I was right where I told you I was while you were acting as the Squadron Commander, Sir. I was just a thousand meters off. I saw them hunting for me. I was using my map and my radio to run the fight. Then the Executive Officer came up on the net and I was relieved in time. Him they were not going to kill. The Regimental Commanding Officer wanted to watch him sweat a little before giving him Killer Troop. He did well," Martin opined.

"Hell, you did well. You maneuvered the troop better than most officers in the Squadron could have done. No one did well against the Bradleys with M-113 scout tracks and the Hammerheads, forget about them damn things. At least we turned on their MILES with the tanks and the LAWs. No one expected the UMCP (Unit Maintenance Control Point) to fight like they did. Our mechanics held them up long enough for the tanks to kill them. We were the only unit to kill them. They just drove through everyone else," Dawson said proudly. "It was great to tell that full bull umpire grading me as Squadron Commander that I knew somehow G Troop would contain the Bradley force and they did," Dawson said with glee.

"Yeah, and right after that the same guy brought Lieutenant Colonel Covington back to life and sent you back to the troop, is that what happened, Sir?" Martin asked.

"Not just that, First Sergeant. Yesterday we became the focal point of today. Everybody and their damn brother is going to be up in helicopters watching us attack Alsfeld. The bigs are having a real early chow call to takeoff before first light to see us conduct the attack. As of right now, no one is to call Red but me - no one. I do not want any conflicting guidance or impressions going to him. If it gets screwed up, either he or I will be at fault. As you said earlier, First Sergeant, this attack has taken on a life of its own. It is not just a story, it is the story. It is at the end of the exercise and has just enough drama and troop initiative to strike a chord with the GOs. They will be on this like stink on shit and critical of everything we do or don't do, First Sergeant," Dawson concluded for the benefit of the assembled orders group.

222

"As you know, Sir, that is why we blindfold officers who are facing a firing squad. If we did not, with their last breath, they would be correcting the firing posture of the troops. 'You there, 3d man 2d rank, curl your wrist under the weapon',", Martin said laughing.

This statement led to more steady hold factor coaching from the peanut gallery and Dawson listened to it all with a wry smile before holding up his hand to silence it. "We have to be there for Red. If we do not get there they will kill them all and the trick play will not be worth anything. MILES or not, I want this to work, dammit. We will make it work. Does everyone understand?" Dawson asked with a very serious look on his face. "Yes, Sir," came the chorus from the orders group.

Martin made his way to the AA for Vic Jackson's platoon. "Good morning, Gold," he said waving to Vic Jackson's tank crew.

Damn, Vic's driver looks like he has a turd in his pocket. The tank was backed into a deep snowdrift and was not running - not a good sign with his departure time for the attack less than ten minutes away.

"What's wrong, Vic?" Martin asked as he climbed up on the tank.

"Damn fuel pump, First Sergeant. I ain't had one thing go wrong with this tank until now. The Gator is going to shit," Jackson said with obvious disgust.

"Vic, call Black 9 and tell him to get Daggett up here. The maintenance team is hidden just behind you in those trees. Tell him your main fuel pump is out and you need a ground hop line installed," Martin said emphatically.

After he had made the radio call, Vic turned to Martin saying, "Shit, by the time those guys get here, my platoon will be long gone, First Sergeant."

"Oh ye of little faith. Here they come with their little red wagon," Martin said with a smile. No one could have misunderstood the situation, not the First Sergeant and not the Platoon Sergeant and certainly not the four helo loads of VIPs watching the platoon and tableau unfold. The M88 recovery vehicle bounded out of the woods behind the platoon knocking over small trees as it bull rushed forward. The driver, Sergeant Edwards, his black face shining and marked with an ear to ear grin of beautiful white teeth drove the M88 right up against the back of G-44, Vic Jackson's tank. PFC Daggett moved like a monkey out of the maintenance vehicle onto the back deck of the disabled tank with a fuel line and two wrenches. He smiled at his First Sergeant when he saw the turret turned and the engine compartment open to allow him to work. Sergeant Edwards promptly moved the M88 back to the wood line to conceal it once Daggett was at work. Martin waved to Sergeant First Class Jackson and returned to his vehicle and stood alongside it drinking a Pepsi and smoking.

The helicopters were holding their position as if they had all day to sight see and they probably did he thought. Old Daggett was nearly done with rigging the fuel line from the smoke generator to the main fuel pump outlet.

223

As Brigadier General Simone looked at the scene on the tank and listened on the Troop Command Radio Net he marveled at the ingenuity of the American Soldier. He was very familiar with the fuel pump design failure and knew the mechanic had to be using the smoke generator fuel pump as a field fix. It was clear the unit had reinforced the line or was using hydraulic line which came with its own mesh. He was smiling behind his binos and when he looked inside the other a/c it was clear nearly all of the Generals were watching the scene intently. But everyone could tell what happened when the young mechanic closed the access doors to the engine and told the tank commander to move out on his mission. The young mechanic waddled to the rear of the tank and did a back flip into the snow. He began doing snow angels as the tank drove away. Martin drove over and Daggett accepted a Pepsi from him and jumped up on the hood of the jeep for transport back to the maintenance area. Nearly every one of the GOs smiled and many laughed out loud to see the snow angels and the exchange between the First Sergeant and the Private. They knew the unit was organized, had great morale and that the chain of command was taking care of soldiers. No one was huddled by a fire bitching about the cold in that outfit.

Shortly, the audience in the helos got another surprise. The movement to the LD was being led by dump trucks spreading sand. Other dump trucks were interspersed in the column. An M-88 waited at the bottom of a hill with a sharp curve at its base. The unit First Sergeant was cutting through the traffic to reach a line of HEMMTs hidden behind a factory warehouse on the outskirts of the town. The First Sergeant led the HEMMTs forward to a point beside a small canal that was opposite a boat ramp. Engineers attached to the troop met the HEMMTs and began to off load their cargo of car bodies from the salvage yard into the creek to form a hasty crossing point for one platoon of tanks. Martin was upset as it appeared he brought too many car bodies. As the bodies were crushed by the 60 ton monsters, new ones were added from the trucks. It seemed to the Generals watching from the helos the tanks were across the canal in seconds but it seemed like an hour to Martin. The five tanks were all up on the road way and hauling ass for Alsfeld. They were covered by the brow of a hill and could not be seen from the town. The other 24 tanks were proceeding over the low ground adjacent to the river. Only four remained in the open part of the maneuver ground and vulnerable to TOWs fired by the defenders of the town.

The third to the last tank in the attack column suddenly disappeared from Martin's view and then reappeared in binoculars. All of the heavy movement had dislocated the sewer or the storm drain system of the area. Huge culverts, some six foot in diameter were churned out the ground like carrots from Grandpa's garden. The Fox Troop tank got traction and kept moving without looking back. Martin did not hesitate to pick up his radio, "Elements held up by the sewer system turn around and go to the alternate crossing site. Do it now." He was gratified to see them turning around and hauling the mail to the alternate site. As he turned to look, the Engineers immediately began to repair and strengthen the expedient site without an order or command. He decided to see if the Gator wanted the tanks to follow the herd or to go around to the back door of the town but he could not get on the net.

The Gator was lashing the ponies, "Dammit Blue and White, do not screw around with that stupid shit. Get to the bridge or it will be too late for Red, move it, move it!"

At this point, Red was heard from, "Six this is Red. We are okay here. There is complete pandemonium. We have a two star trying to separate two one bangers intent on beating the shit out of each other. A bunch of these shit heads surrendered to us. The artillery is really working well and so far, we have zero casualties either from MILES or assessed. You can come ahead as fast as you can get here as there is nothing between you and the bridges; we waved the enemy across as if we were in their unit."

"Seven, Red. I would not send anyone around the back. The Gators have totally screwed the game for the Exercise Director and we will go to reset in a few minutes, OVER."

"Seven, this is Six, send them around the back and tell them to shoot up the DISCOM. Maintain 200 meters distance. They are not to run over anyone or hurt anybody, OVER."

"Guidons, Guidons, Guidons, this is Six. Continue mission, do not stop shooting or moving unless I tell you to stop. Leave the officiating to the umpires, we are here to fight. Red keep the artillery simulators coming, Kill everything and everyone with MILES. We are still a couple of clicks away, Six, OUT."

By the time HQ-66 crossed the bridge and relieved the 1ST platoon, the inevitable reset of forces was in motion from the highest level. The capture of the bridge fully intact, the encirclement of the town and the trapping of forces to the west of the Leine river by TF Dawson was a coup of the first order.

Before the Generals could work their magic, the Cavalry did what it did best, moved swiftly under control. Though suffering from real attrition due to M1 tank fuel pump failure, nearly 29 of 43 tanks had been equipped with the G Troop jury rig fuel lines. These vehicles under G Troop control were fully operational and created the impression of a much larger force than they actually were. The practice of keeping the Troop trains well forward also contributed to the deception. Commanders who saw the support vehicles to include the Engineer Company believed themselves to be overrun by the Regiment rather than a heavily reinforced Company.

The flight of the forces opposite V Corps became head long. The Corps brought 8,000 gallon tank trucks far forward to maintain the fuel flow of the diesel fuel guzzling M1s. G Troop's head thief, Staff Sergeant Webster, took the opportunity to refill all of the logistic vehicles and fuel tanker trucks accompanying him from the captured retail size tankers during a lull.

At a very clear and cold nightfall, the troop found itself with 43 attached tanks, all of its organic rolling stock, an Engineer Company, an NBC Decon Platoon, the USAF ALO unit from the Regiment and ten fuel trucks, and some 135 vehicles total. The Gator picked a high hill as usual but in this instance it appeared to be more of a mesa due its flat top. When he saw the final aggregate number of vehicles in the assembly area, it dawned on Martin how successful G Troop had been. He knew the Army reinforces success and lets failure die on the vine.

He also knew he had been providing support to one troop fulltime and another part time as they had "lost" their First Sergeants. He had also provided support when the normal system failed to work. However, the Squadron supply system had functioned very well. The Gators had only missed one meal of hot rations and certainly never went hungry. Granted, they had Chicken ala' King for breakfast twice but there were no complaints. Martin had learned a valuable lesson with the Chicken ala' Commode. He was not going to go pick it up as it was not a traditional breakfast and he thought the troop would rather eat an MRE.

Captain Dawson was blunt, "First Sergeant, go get the food. It may be Chicken ala' King but it is a hot meal. The cooks busted their asses to do what they could and we will take what they have. Take my track so I know you will get through the snow and up that damn hill where the Squadron trains are sitting." Martin did not want to take the track, but in for a penny, in for a pound.

The Mess Section was very proud of their Chicken ala King and somewhat put out as Martin was the only one to show up to get it. The Mess Daddy lavished his attention on G Troop in return for their loyalty. Martin was glad he took the track. He got cases of canned fruit, fresh fruit and so many MREs he was forced to tie them down on top of the track. It was a true gypsy wagon for the trip back. The troops were glad to get the food, did not complain, and loved the one gallon cans of fruit and treasured the fresh fruit. It was Christmas all over again.

The Headquarters Crew in the Squadron Combat Trains also got a lesson when they asked First Sergeant Martin, "How in the hell can you work for that crazy son-of-a-bitch Dawson?" None of them would ever forget his answer, "He may an SOB, but he is our SOB, right or wrong. Besides we're used to him and we like him like that. It ain't never boring in G Troop."

1200 hours
17 Jan 1985

Captain Dawson was returning from an orders group at the Squadron TOC. When he was certain he was in range of the troop he called his Executive Officer, First Lieutenant and soon to be Captain Brown.

"Five, this is Six, OVER."

"Six, Five, OVER."

"Assemble the orders group at your location. Tell them to drive their vehicles. I will be there in one five mikes, Six, OUT."

"Oh shit, he is pissed. We either did something real bad or the exercise is over and we are going home," the Executive Officer said to the TOC Crew.

"Damn, Sir, why would anyone be pissed to go home?" Pvt Burkes asked.

Reaching up with his big paw that could hold a basketball and make a football almost disappear inside it, the Executive Officer ruffled Burkes bald skull saying, "You are too innocent, Burkes. Don't you know Captain Dawson and First Sergeant Martin love this shit. They live for it. They do not need food, booze, women, or sleep. Those things are for weaklings like you and me. They are lifers. They live for challenges and opportunities to excel. Shit, they can sleep when they are dead. Isn't that what you think? By the way Burkes, you are the truly new guy here. What do you think of our intrepid leaders?" the coffee latté colored Lieutenant said with a smile.

"Sir, my daddy was an old soldier and he told me not to volunteer an opinion but since you asked I will tell you what I think. I think you, the Captain, the First Sergeant, and the NCOs in this outfit are some of the craziest sons-a-bitches on earth. But I am damn glad I am on your side. There are a helluva' lot of Russians but they are gonna' need everyone of them to beat this bunch of lunatics," Burkes said as he braced himself for what he thought would happen next.

"I agree with you Burkes, but I do consider myself to be a reasonable man when compared to the Commanding Officer and the First Sergeant," First Lieutenant Brown said with a contrite look on the most innocent baby face in his bag of tricks. "All right, clean up this pig sty and get the stove going. Start stowing all of this gear and get ready to move to the Border. Pack the track for the Border from here. We will just take it out if we go to a wash rack before we get on the train, so put it in here neat. Get the supply truck up here for the excess junk. We will use the maintenance trailer for chow runs. Chop, Chop, people, move it. Just can the noise when the Gator gets here," First Lieutenant Brown who was about to become Captain Brown said with a smile.

Miss this shit as a Commander, not hardly, but it was a great learning experience and I am surely ready for K Troop. Will miss the First Sergeant and Vic and the other strac

NCOs and the Gator to some degree, but Bad Kissingen the town was like an impacted wisdom tooth, starting out in life as worthless and getting worse.

Among the staccato flow of orders coming from the Troop Commander in support of recovery from the exercise was one for Martin to go find a wash rack for the troop that was enroute to their train loading site. Martin thought it odd that he was going to coordinate something that Squadron was better staffed to do but he did not question the efficiency of the order. He just wrote down the parameters of the task and decided on the German Army base to approach for use of their facilities. Paderborn was the closest, was part of their school system and probably had everything they needed to get the job done. He was surprised to learn he was to work the issue immediately and to keep Captain Dawson informed.

It was a simple task and he made contact with the First Sergeant of the Bundesfehr who had the rear detachment of school troop support. It was their down cycle as they would not receive their new set of draftees until spring and only had technical courses going now. He was very amused when the NCOs he asked if they were the First Sergeant responded by saying, "Oh, no, I cannot drink enough beer to be a First Sergeant," or "Oh, no, my parents are both married, and I cannot be a First Sergeant!" and a final closer of "I am a faithful husband; I cannot screw all of the wives when the men go to the field."

When meeting the actual First Sergeant in front of these NCOs Martin had his words carefully translated by Jeff Haskins, "Jeff, please tell the First Sergeant his men have been extolling his virtues. Tell him I am very glad to meet a man who can out drink, out fight, and out screw everyone in his outfit. He is a true Speise and I salute him."

The German First Sergeant swelled up like a toad, his stomach in and his chest out as if he was on parade, answering in perfect English, "First Sergeant Martin, my men never lie, except when they are awake!! Tell me what I can do for you today." At that point the two First Sergeants from different Armies became fast friends and co-conspirators.

First Sergeant Haertel was more than happy to accept some extra MREs, coffee, eggs, butter, bread and cold cuts from his American guests. In return they got everything they wanted, which they would have received anyway, they just got it cheerfully with some NCO assistance to help them operate the wash rack and control traffic.

As Martin was reporting the results of the recon to Captain Dawson, he was surprised to see Major Bragg pull up to his vehicle.

"Six, seven. Standby. Eaglehorse Five is here and I will get right back to you, OVER."

"Seven, Six, standing by, OUT."

"What in the hell are you doing, First Sergeant?" Bragg asked, obviously pissed off.

"I am coordinating for a wash rack, Sir, as directed by Captain Dawson," Martin said after assuming the position of attention for what was sure to follow.

"The Squadron Commander did not tell Troop Commanders to make their own arrangements. We were all in the same meeting, First Sergeant. He told them to prepare to wash vehicles on command from the squadron. Now we get to look like idiots in front of the Germans with two of us coordinating for the same thing and the same time period, don't we?"

"I don't see why, Sir. Here are the keys to the wash rack, handing them to the Major. An NCO is getting his POV and will meet us there to show us the traffic pattern. One of the NCOs from the detail company in their Red Cycle will be at the wash rack the entire time the Squadron is going to use it. You have the key, you are present, I will introduce you to the NCO and we are back on track. You tell us when to come to the wash rack and we will show up," Martin concluded.

"Your commander is going to get his head chopped off being out in front of the Colonel and the staff some day. It ain't your fault. You are doing what you were told by lawful order. Let's go see the luger head at the wash rack, and then you can go back to your troop. At least you picked the right German Army Post to come to for a wash rack. We will probably rail load right here on Post all except for G Troop. You load about 40 clicks away since you guys are not dragging anything," Major Bragg concluded.

Martin simply saluted and moved to his jeep to get mounted and moving. Enroute to the wash rack, he completed his report to his Captain without embellishment, merely saying Major Bragg had arrived and coordination was now complete for what was now a squadron effort. He did not know the Executive Officer had switched his radio and was listening to his report to his Captain. His driver, Staunton did not miss it however.

Staunton waited until his First Sergeant was off the radio before saying, "Hey, First Sergeant, every time you keyed our net, the Major's aux light lit up. He was monitoring you talking to the Gator."

"Tom, all Majors are sneaky, some are just sneakier than others. Bragg is a good shit and his heart is in the right place. The Gator rubs him the wrong way and sometimes, so do I. I am not worried what he hears or does not hear on our net. I have no intention of talking bad about a superior, particularly on the radio. We accept orders as given if they are not illegal or immoral, and execute them with our subordinates as if they were our own. Ain't nothing worse than having a wussy in charge that says, "Gee guys, if it was up to me, we wouldn't do this shit, but it is old so and so who is making us suffer."

"First Sergeant, that is what the old First Sergeant said all of the time," Staunton said with some embarrassment.

"Tommy, you are going on your third month with me. Do you see and understand the difference between leadership styles?" Martin asked with a smile.

"Yes, First Sergeant, I've got it. Can I go back to maintenance when we get back? I am sure my knee is okay and Sergeant Wintergreen needs the help," Staunton asked unexpectedly.

"Sure, Tommy, you can go back to being an honest man and turning wrenches when we get back. I will get the Scouts to give me a driver, Martin said.

"They already got a guy picked out, First Sergeant."

" Oh really! And who might it be that you and the Platoon sergeants have figured out to be the next First Sergeant Driver?" Martin asked in the mildest tone he could muster.

"It is Specialist Fourth Class Young, the big Mormon guy. He has four kids, his wife is pregnant and he is a straight arrow but he ain't no lifer, First Sergeant," Staunton said rapidly trying to get it all said.

"Oh, you mean Home Boy, the defensive end who cannot be blocked and who can run down a half back in the open field? The big red faced guy who does not smile much and drives the Lieutenant's track, is that the one?" Martin said.

"Yeah, Top, that is him," Staunton answered without looking at the First Sergeant, afraid something was going to go wrong and screw him out of going back to maintenance and then to PLDC. Staunton had become a lifer when no one was looking, he just did not know it.

"You know Tommy, if I didn't know better, I would think you are making plans to succeed in this man's Army. Hush, don't interrupt! I never stand in a man's way when he tries to better himself or when he wants a harder way to go like Airborne, Ranger, OCS or even West Point for that matter. I do not need to know the reasons you want to perform in your MOS nor do I want to know them. It is enough you want to be a hard ass and do what the Army hired you to do, be a wheel mechanic. It also means Sergeant Wintergreen is doing a good job. We will fix it on our return once you and Home Boy recover your vehicles, we will do the deal, okay?" Martin said laughing.

"What's so funny, Top?" Staunton asked.

"Tell me the rest of the story, Tommy," Martin said smiling.

"Staff Sergeant Jeff will let Home Boy come when we get back so he can do the recovery on the jeep and I can go straight to maintenance, if that is okay, First Sergeant?" Staunton asked expectantly.

"Are there any other decisions and initiatives you have fully coordinated in the Troop, Tommy, that I should be aware of? Maybe you should write me a list. I guess it is my own fault. You have watched and learned to tie up the loose ends and be able to do what, Tommy?" Martin said rhetorically

"Answer the question before it is asked, First Sergeant," his driver replied.

230

"Right, good job Tommy. Can you get us back to where we left the Troop, Tommy? I need a nap," Martin said.

"Go to sleep, First Sergeant, I will keep our bargain up on my end," Staunton said smiling at the memory of it from their first days together.

Look Tommy, I need you to remember the way back from places so I can get some rest. Your job is to follow my direction and get us to the meeting or whatever, pull some after ops, clean the windshield and go to sleep. You should be the most rested guy in the Troop. Shit, this damn guy needed a day driver and a night driver. It was hard to believe he was in his mid-forties.

0550 hours
29 Jan 1985
G Troop PT Formation

First Sergeant Martin was talking to the Platoon Sergeants at the front of the formation. "I want the troops to have their baseball caps in their right pocket. We will wear the pile cap to the Squadron formation. It is the Regimental uniform of the day. I realize the Regimental Command Sergeant Major will have a cow. But I want us all to have the pile cap on for working in the track park after the formation and I want to make a point to the REMPFs from Regiment. When the Regimental Command Sergeant Major is through having his cow and after I complain a little, we will switch hats. When the ceremony is over, we will switch back and go back to the track park after we retrieve our winter coveralls from in front of the maintenance bays. The directive is Prepare to Rotate Head Gear, and the command of execution is Rotate. Have Festus guard the gear, Sergeant Wintergreen. He is a magnet for the Regimental Command Sergeant Major and I want to keep him out of the line of fire. There is something about his white red-neck face that sets off the black preacher in the Regimental Command Sergeant Major and I don't want to hear it today. We won several plaques for REFORGER, reenlistment, and there will be some impact awards. PT today will be the daily dozen without contact with the snow and the run will be by individuals for two miles eight laps around the quadrangle, starting there and ending on the other side of the hedge. The minimum time is 18 minutes. Anyone that beats me gets a three day pass from the Border. Anyone but an officer that is. Any questions?"

"First Sergeant, I have a question."

"What is your question, Lieutenant Robertson?" Martin asked.

"Why are the officers excluded from the pass? You always do that to us," he said with a false whimper. "I'll be glad to race the Gator for two miles for a three day pass," he said quietly.

"When I start rating you, Ell Tee, I can start giving you a pass, and stop sniveling, it is unbecoming of an officer and you a graduate of Hudson High, the most august four year institution of the US Army," at which point all of the officers in the troop said in loud voices, "Hell, it is the only one in the Army, First Sergeant."

"All right me lads, everyone can have a pass what beats me on the run but the officers, the officers I say, have to wait until the July fourth weekend," Martin said in a fake Irish accent imitating First Sergeant Quincannon from John Wayne movie fame. Though the Troop had heard the same exchange before, it drew a hearty laugh as the platoon sergeants made their way back to their platoons for Reveille.

1000 hours
29 Jan 1985

True to form, the Regimental Command Sergeant Major did have a cow when he saw G Troop dressed in the prescribed Regimental uniform of pile cap, field jacket, neck scarf and black gloves.

After some fencing, First Sergeant Martin gave his commands and the scarves were pushed below the necklines and the winter caps exchanged for the summer. The Regimental Command Sergeant Major was not amused and of course saw no conflict between what his staff had put out in writing and his personal wishes. *The pile cap just did not look good and it was only an hour long ceremony. Their ears could take that much cold. Today might be a good day for a surprise inspection of G Troop. They had done a great job on REFORGER. Ought to see if they have learned their lesson from the Corps Command Sergeant Major before he re-inspects them.*

The Regimental Command Sergeant Major looked at his watch and realized he had a few minutes before the scheduled arrival of the reviewing party. He took the time to walk over to the rear of the G Troop to speak to First Sergeant Martin. "First Sergeant, I want to walk through your barracks after the formation. Have that assistant supply sergeant layout his gear on an empty bunk and let me see PFC Festerman's wall locker, TA-50 and living area. By the way, where is Festerman, First Sergeant?" the Regimental Command Sergeant Major asked pleasantly.

"Command Sergeant Major, he is on guard duty at the motor pool. I will have him standing by in the barracks with the others, the Arms room and Supply rooms will also be open," Martin said without a trace of a smile.

He was hoping the Regimental Command Sergeant Major thought he was worried but what the hell, maybe he was just trying to help and get them ready for Hurricane Ligon's return. I deserve it for messing with him. Few leaders realized just how smart and capable 'Festus' Festerman really was. He was jewel of a turret mechanic and was always learning. His deep voice and polite small town boy reticence coupled with a long chin did not do his brain or his values justice. He was typical of what the Army did for a man with its sometimes Darwinian method of sorting out the weak and inefficient through tough standards

232

and arduous service. Festus would be all right. He wasn't a Morales guy but he would do fine, Martin thought.

After the formation, Captain Dawson had the First Sergeant move the troop to the only theater they had access to, the second floor hall way of the barracks. He gave them a great talk as he reviewed what they had accomplished and he told them how much he appreciated everyone's efforts. As he was talking Martin's mind wandered to several evenings before as they were having a beer in Dawson's office. Dawson had sent for PFC Daggett and told the Charge of Quarters to have him report to the Troop Commander. Dagget knocked loudly and reported, obviously very nervous and apprehensive about being summoned to see his Captain, a remote and august figure. Martin had not been told why Daggett had been summoned and he was quietly curious.

"Daggett, what would you think if I told you the Regimental Commander was going to give you an Army Commendation Medal on Monday Morning?" Dawson asked softly.

If Martin lived to be a 100 he would always remember Daggett's nonverbal response. The boy did a 360 degree pirouette on his right foot, exactly as the character CW Moss did as he was being recruited for the Barrow gang by Bonnie and Clyde. Neither Dawson nor Martin laughed when Daggett did the spin. Dawson then asked, "And what if I told you the Regimental Commanding Officer was going to promote you to Spec Four at the same time for your great work on REFORGER in keeping all of our tanks and all of those other tanks running with the ground hop fuel lines." The boy did not answer because he just was too happy to talk so he did another 360 degree spin. That tore if for First Sergeant Martin. He had to laugh a little but this was the Troop Commander's show and he meant to ride it out.

"Are you happy Daggett, you can't tell anyone until after the ceremony. It has to be our secret until then, okay? You got anything you want to say?" Dawson asked gently.

"Thank you, Sir, and thank you, First Sergeant. I know you done this for me but I really don't deserve it and I really don't want to get out in front of all those people and have them looking at me," Daggett said looking down at the floor.

Dawson then said the magic word, "First Sergeant, explain it to Specialist Daggett will you?"

"Specialist Daggett, nobody is giving you anything. You are being recognized for your contribution to an effort far bigger than any individual. You have to remember you were being watched by more than 20 general officers as you fixed G-44. As far as they are concerned, you are the Army. You are the Army they want to lead and believe they are leading. Your initiative to come up with the fuel line and find a way to hook it up was great. Your tremendous enthusiasm for your job is catching. There were soldiers with cold injuries and others were just plain sniveling all over Europe while you were

233

outside working on a tank. What did you do, you executed a perfect back flip off a tank and cut snow angels out of joy. Generals often decide things from snap shots, pictures of things in their minds eye. You made their day and probably motivated them. Later when they found out you were the inventor and fabricator of the fix that kept so many of the Squadron's tanks going, they insisted you be recognized. Medals are not just for the hero or the guy that earned them. They are also for the guys in the ranks to show them that they can win one as well. So get this straight my friend, no one is giving you anything. You earned it many times over and you will stand there, accept the praise, the ARCOM and the Promotion so don't give me no more shit about what it is you ain't gonna' do, okay! You, my young friend, are now a Standard Bearer whether you like it or not."

"Okay, First Sergeant, I understand, but I can't tell nobody?" the Army's newest Specialist asked.

"Do you want to call your Mom, Daggett? You can use the Bundespost phone in my office and dial direct. Talk as long as you want," Martin said.

"Salute the Troop Commander, Trooper," he said as Daggett was ready to walk away and call his Mom. The kid was on cloud nine.

Martin realized that the reason Dawson knew all about Daggett was because of a quirk of fate. It could have been him turning wrenches. Dawson knew how lucky he was to have had a stable home with a father who was an Army Armored Cavalry veteran and a solid mother who provided a good home. He had the sophistication that came from being a varsity football player at a Division One School, an Army Officer as well as an Airborne Ranger and a Deputy Sheriff. Yet he and Daggett were linked. He knew Daggett because he was once Daggett. That was the egalitarian beauty of the Army. Dawson truly enjoyed telling the soldier of the good things to come and knew he had to prepare him for the ceremony. Martin had learned yet another lesson in human nature.

1800 hours
29 Jan 1985
Troop Commander's Office

"So how did the Inspections by the great Regimental Command Sergeant Major go today, First Sergeant?" Dawson asked, though his spies had already brought him up to date.

Martin answered with a broad smile, "They went very well, Sir. All of the field gear was spotless. Festus had a picture perfect wall locker and display with all new and unused stuff. The Regimental Command Sergeant Major looked everyone over very carefully for haircut, shave and moustache trim. There were no deficiencies. The sample wall lockers, leadership example of the Spec Fours and the constant cleanup are part of the troop now. I doubt Ligon will return, but if he does, we will be prepared. No one is ever ready for that guy."

CHAPTER 9 - GATOR GRAN PRIX

"Beware the man who only owns one weapon. He probably knows how to use it."
Anonymous.

1830 hours
1 Feb 1985

Sergeant Monte Markham was a sharp operator and was a far wealthier man than his peers in the low paying rank of Sergeant E-5 in H Company, the tank Company of 2/11 ACR. Monte was, as befitted the nature of a man who lived by his wits, a student of human nature. He knew that he was not the sharpest knife in the drawer but then he felt with his experience, modest goals, and the shortcomings of his fellow man, he didn't have to be to be a success. Monte believed in the Las Vegas Casino owners' private credo of, "If God would not have wanted them shorn, he would not have made them sheep." Monte had a sizeable bank roll gained from playing percentage poker at the Veterans of Foreign War Post in nearby Schweinfurt, Germany. Less than thirty kilometers away from Bad Kissingen, the VFW provided a continuing source of income for the sharp NCO from poker games and money lending. Monte had heard about the new First Sergeant of G Troop, his ability to play cards and about his unusual attitude about taking money from subordinates. He saw the First Sergeant come into the NCO Club at BK in civilian clothes and decided it was time they had a talk.

"Hey, First Sergeant Martin, how are you doin'? Let's have a drink, I'm buyin'," Monte said with a smile. Martin looked at the short, compact Sergeant and made a quick decision to see what was really on his mind. It had been some time since he had talked to a hustler and his brain needed the exercise. His CID informant alarm was going off in his head but he silenced it until he had heard the pitch.

"Sure, Sergeant Markham, I've got a minute, give me a Jack Daniels straight up with a Coke chaser. I'll hit the latrine and meet you at the table over there," Martin said politely.

When Martin joined him, Markham appeared to be lost in thought. He smiled and looked Martin in the eye as an equal even though he was outranked and always would be. He had a flattop, a beard heavy with five o'clock shadow, was wearing Levis and lizard skin cowboy boots, and sporting a rodeo winner's belt buckle. It was up to the First Sergeant how equal they would be, but Martin decided to let it play out to see what the man had on his mind. "What's on your mind, Monte, besides marked cards, big poker money, loan sharking, hot women, old whiskey, and your DEROS?" Martin said with one well enunciated phrase.

Monte was impressed, "Damn First Sergeant, that sounds like my epitaph! All but that part about DEROS. Hell, Kamerad (GI slang for a German male) will rotate to CONUS before I do. I ain't never leaving here. I wanted to see if you wanted to play poker down at the VFW in Schweinfurt tonight. The game starts out with quarter half, two raises, Jacks or Better five card draw followed by a round of Seven Card, strictly according to Hoyle, no stupid shit."

"Sounds good, Monte, but I've got some questions. How are you doing in the game, Monte? Are you winning, making any real money or is it just guys having some fun playing poker? Any black guys who stay over here? Any black guys period? Do I need a piece?" Martin asked in a most calm and matter of fact manner.

"It is a mixed crowd, some are good card players but most ain't worth shit. There ain't no niggers there, no where. If there was, I wouldn't go there. It is as white as a Klan meeting. You won't need no piece though if you carried one with all this terrorist shit, no one would care. There ain't violence over no card game, that is amateur hour shit that don't happen there," Sergeant Markham stated.

"My last question, are black people excluded from the VFW post?" Martin asked. Monte finally figured out Martin did not share his racial views. He was astonished the tough First Sergeant was color blind.

"No First Sergeant, the VFW Post don't discriminate. They have black members but like the country song says, Red Necks, White Tee Shirts and Pabst Blue Ribbon beer. They let German women come in as guests and there are some great lookers our age that show up there on Friday and Saturday nights. So what do you say?" Markham asked.

"Sounds like fun. When do you want to go?" Martin replied to the great surprise of the hustler.

"How about 2000 hrs? We'll be back by 0200 or 0300 at the latest. If I get lucky, I'll get you a ride back. Here's the phone number for your CQ in they need you for some First Sergeant shit. Somebody will come find you. They are all old Army guys, retired over here. They know the deal with First Sergeants - all dedicated and all that," Monte said with a mocking smile.

"I am going to go into the dining room and have some chow. I'll meet you back out here unless you want to join me, Monte," Martin offered.

Martin had not missed the fish eyed look that Monte had given the waitress from the dining room as she picked up a drink order from the bar. If he would have had a hole available, the Hustler would have crawled in it and drug it in after him.

"Is she a friend of yours Monte?" Martin teased.

"Shit no, First Sergeant, not no more. In fact, if you want her, you can have her," Monte replied.

"That's mighty generous of you, Monte, giving me a real live human being like that out of the goodness of your heart," Martin said with more than a little sarcasm.

"We went out a couple of times. She's a damn clinger. I want her to leave me be. I got hotter stuff in Schweinfurt and I ain't got time for her, that's all I meant. Besides, she wasn't looking at me, she was eyeballing you. You would be doing me a favor with her. You better go eat if we're going," Monte said draining his beer and moving to the bar.

Fraulein Marlene Zander was interested in the handsome First Sergeant but she was all business as she took his order. They chatted briefly about the States and her erstwhile home there, California. He had a simple dinner of a large hamburger, French fries, and a Cola. On receiving it, he inhaled the burger and fries. By the time she had returned to check on him, he was smoking a cigarette.

"Did you like the food, First Sergeant?" she asked.

"It was good and I enjoyed it all. I was very hungry but I will probably eat again later. Do they let you eat here, Marty?" he asked after reading her name tag.

"They do but I always eat with my Mother before I come to work. I eat three meals each day with her to be certain she eats properly. I also help fix meals for my Poppa. They are both retired and in their eighties," she said with a smile.

"I am going to Schweinfurt with the Shark to play some cards and to have a look around. Do you work Saturday night, Marty?" Martin asked.

"Yes I do and I get off about nine," Marty replied.

"Well, if you're not busy, maybe you can show me the town. I'm new here. We have been gone a lot so I don't know my way around very well yet," Martin said, turning on the charm.

"I would like that, First Sergeant. Until tomorrow then. I'll get your change," she said holding her tray down at her side rather than against her upper body in a defensive posture. It was clear to Martin she was doing the hunting and he was the hunted. Oh well, he thought.

"No change, Marty, you keep it," he said as he stood to leave.

"Okay, Monte, all set to travel if you are," Martin said as he arrived next to Markham's barstool.

"Hell yes, we can go right now, Top," Monte said draining his beer and picking up his smokes. Martin followed him out to the parking lot. Monte had a top of the line BMW sedan. It looked like an officer's car except for the NRA sticker on the driver's side rear window. The vehicle was spotless, inside and out. Martin was surprised as Monte looked neat but not fastidious. Monte saw the look and volunteered, "This is my good car. I never wash the Opel. I only drive it to work. My neighbor kid loves cars and he keeps the Beemer up for me, real cheap, $25 marks a week. I never touch it. I bring it home dirty, park it, and it's clean the next time I see it. I give him a bonus if it gets too dirty. You know me, First Sergeant, I wouldn't screw over a kid," Monte said with a self-righteous sniff.

As Monte was starting the Beamer, he looked at Martin with a wolfish grin and asked, "So, First Sergeant, if the VFW did discriminate against black people, would you go there?"

"No. Look Monte, I don't want to sleep with black women, marry one, or invite them to marry any of my children, but I don't hold their color against them as a group. I deal with each soldier as an individual. If crime is present, then it is the UCMJ, fairly and justly applied to all. As a First Sergeant I support Army policy, period," Martin said without a trace of a smile.

Monte is far too stupid to understand that the guys who will help you when you are really down in the Army are usually other than white so why tell him. He is comfortable in his hate blanket.

"Hey, I got it, First Sergeant. Hey, we will be going right by the turnoff to the BGS Post. I hear the Gator is trying to link up with them for a partnership unit. Hell, those guys got started as a rehabilitation outfit for the Hitler Youth after the war. You think I hate black people, those guys made lamp shades by skinning Jews and Gypsies, alive. Good luck on singing kumbaiya with those BGS hard asses," Monte said laughing.

Monte's news is dated. The Gator had established Partnership with a Bundesgrenz-schutz (BGS) Kompanie. It was an Aryan outpost and probably did originate with the Hitler Youth in some fashion but he has seen no bias on their range training together. I am going to let that pass and not say a word.

The local VFW post was what Martin expected, a bar with a grill, card rooms, and a club area with booths and tables. It was complete with stage and dance floor downstairs with a meeting area and offices upstairs. It reminded him of the Moose Lodge in his home town. The bar area was purely German, a direct transplant out the Gast Haus genre' of Germany. It was spotlessly clean with a faint smell of Lysol.

Monte was greeted as the Prodigal, returned for the feast. At the insistence of the poker crowd, Monte and Martin sat down with them for a large deep fat fried pork tenderloin sandwich which no one referred to as a schnitzel, and a large order of fries. Monte smiled as a large decorative beer stein, obviously his personal drinking vessel, materialized from "his" bar.

As they ate, various patrons, young, old, male and female came by and handed Monte money. He never counted it, he just stacked it in the order he received it alternating each new stack as it came to him. He had a kind look, smile, or word for everyone. There was an order to the procession as well as a purpose. Monte the Shark was not just socializing, he was holding court with his subjects. He must at least be a benevolent loan shark, Martin thought.

"So, you need to borrow any money, Top?" Monte asked as he wiped the ketchup and the mayo off of his chin and mouth.

"If I do and if I think I can afford the Vig, I'll let you know Monte," Martin replied evenly as he referred to the Mafia custom of not only collecting the principal owed but also the 'Vigorish," known as usury in polite society. Vig was an amount based two factors, what the borrower could pay and how scared he was of the lender.

"Hey, there ain't no vig for you. It's even money, unless it is out of the poker pot and at the table, then its twenty percent. I hate gambling against money I already won, you know," Monte said with his patented wolfish grin.

Commonly known as never give a sucker an even break, Martin thought. He was glad he came to see this guy in action. If the players in the game were hard edged bastards who had retired here to be financial or sexual chicken hawks, swooping down on newbie soldiers, it would be a pleasure to take some of their money.

2045 hours
1 Feb 1985

As the game got under way, Martin bought $40 worth of quarters and stacked them in front of him. He was glad to see they used money rather than chips. There was no danger of being raided. The VFW had private club status and the Polizei could not have cared less. Being the new guy Martin provided a modicum of background information to his fellow players, expatriates to a man, about the state of Fort Knox, REFORGER, the 11th ACR leadership climate and his relative degree of contentment. He was not surprised to meet men there with whom he had served and who knew the same people that he did.

There was much laughter as they discussed one of their mutual friends, a true Army character Martin knew on his first tour to Germany in 4/69 Armor. They loved his account as the game progressed. "The great Sergeant First Class Burner C. Martin was at that time about 6'5" and 275. He and I and another guy you may you know, Robert L. Doolittle, a distant relative of Jimmy of Tokyo Raider Fame, had courtesy patrol at Grafenwohr on payday at the 48 State Enlisted Club. Margaret the infamous Jamaican part time dancer and full time whore, with the 20 inch belly scar was the headliner. The 48 Stater had cooled off somewhat but anyone could still get a Buck knife buried in their gut for little or nuthin'. Burner Lee was about to be our platoon daddy but we did not know that. We were quite happy when he waved us over to his table and poured us each a glass of beer out of one of two pitchers on his table."

"It was the full pitcher. Burner Lee was eating two full sized baked trout dinners and drinking straight out of the other pitcher. His napkin was a small table cloth secured inside the collar of his fatigue shirt. RL and I were damn glad to see Man Mountain Martin in that Bloody Bucket. Back then, as you all remember, if you wouldn't fight, you would not be on Courtesy Patrol at

Graf. RL and I had each drank one sip of beer when two privates started to argue over Margaret. As we started to get up to fix the problem, Burner Lee motioned us to stay seated. He stood up and yelled in a voice that froze the room, 'Hey you two!' The intrepid fighters looked over our way to see what idiot was buying into their fight. When they saw Burner with a trout in his right hand and a pitcher of beer in his left they wisely came to AT EASE. Burner Lee took a big drink out of the pitcher before he spoke again and it left his moustache full of foam highlighting his beady eyes. 'I'm trying to have my supper and drink a beer. If you two idiots keep up your shit I am gonna' have to quit eating and go on Courtesy Patrol. If you assholes disturb my dinner again I am gonna 'stomp you through the floor. That dancer is only here to get you worked up, not to do anything with you two shit heads. Now sit down and shut up or get out. That goes for the rest of you. Have a good time but keep it clean'," Martin finished his tale to gales of laughter.

The rest of the table all seemed to have another story about the famous Burner Lee and then started on 3 AD stories about Elvis, as Martin had hoped would be the case. Burner Lee was an Old Soldier with five tours in 'Nam. He had been a Private with Elvis Presley with both of them becoming NCOs together in the 33d Armor of 3 Armored Division. Burner Lee had always liked Elvis and spoke well of him as a man and as a soldier. Martin's answer surprised the group when an old Sergeant First Class asked him what was the most important thing he had learned from Burner Lee. "Listen to your Commander and execute his last lawful order in the spirit it was given," Martin replied almost with a tear in his eye.

Thanks, Burner Lee, for who you were and what you did for me and all of those other guys. What a Trooper you were.

As the walk down memory lane continued, Martin quietly listened to the war stories as he nodded and smiled. He was winning steadily. The stakes were increased at the request of the losers who were trying to get even. The guys who were playing to buy a stereo or a new pair of shoes for their baby, lost their stake. They borrowed it back from Monte and hoped it would pay their bills until mid-Month payday. Inevitably, the plungers just had to see who had the most luck and wanted to keep playing until they were head to head with Martin and Monte, who had nearly all of the money. The percentage players who were there for enjoyment packed it in early. Their poker strategy was based on logic and was low key. They were playing cards, the drugstore cowboys were gambling.

When his turn to deal came up, Martin passed it to his left saying, "I'm a lousy dealer, and I give myself bad cards." During the evening, he won steadily. It was no surprise when the last three players insisted on a $50 ante with $50 dollar bets per card for five card showdown. All of the cards dealt face up. He won every hand but the last one, losing $300. The big losers had long since given up and went home. Martin and Monte adjourned to the bar for an

American Truck Stop breakfast where Monte's German Frau, the flavor of the month, was cooking them Bratwurst sausage, Gravy, Fried Potatoes and Over Easy Eggs.

A grizzled old Sergeant First Class (Ret) asked Martin while he played a quarter slot machine why he was not drunk. "I made up my mind as a young Staff Sergeant that if I ever got to be a First Sergeant, the CQ who called me for help would never have to listen to a drunk. I sipped Jack all night and enjoyed it. This breakfast topped off a fine evening with good companions. I'm going to call a taxi and go back to BK. I'm sure Monte has other plans, huh Monte!"

"I appreciate you takin' a cab home 'cause you can damn sure afford it, huh, First Sergeant?" Monte said with a wry smile.

The Old Sergeant First Class turned to Monte and said, "You brought him, Monte, and we were glad you did. If you are what they are making First Sergeants these days, Martin, the Army is in damn good shape. It was nice to meet cha'," and he and the percentage players departed. By that time, a clean white Mercedes taxi driven by an off duty policeman, was waiting.

0330 hours
02 Feb 1985

After a fast but uneventful ride driven by an off duty cop moonlighting as a taxi driver, Martin arrived to his small apartment. He checked with the CQ by phone and got an update.

Boy, these guys have a system. The whole place has off duty cops on the street day and night, with radios in perfect cover as cab drivers. Criminals are caught before they get a good start.

Command Sergeant Major Ligon had picked that night to re-inspect G Troop at 2000 hours. He and the Regimental Command Sergeant Major conducted a surprise re-inspection of the Troop. As predicted, the Charge of Quarters and his runner were the troop sample since both lived in the barracks. The Arms Room and Supply Room, as well as appearance of the barracks passed with flying colors. Ligon was ecstatic to see the bottom of all of the boots under the bunks were clean and polished. The Corps Command Sergeant Major went out of his way to forbid the CQ to call his First Sergeant. His words to the CQ were, "If First Sergeant Martin needs to be called after I take a look, I'll call him, not you, got it youngster. He needs some time away from the job and the VFW is a good place to get it," as he put his big paw up beside the young Sergeant's cheek and patted it rather roughly. The Regimental Command Sergeant Major confirmed the Regimental IG re-inspection was still on for April.

It had been a helluva' day. Won some money. Met a cute German gal. Passed the Corps Command Sergeant Major re-inspection and got home one piece. Doubt I'll be in-

vited back to the VFW and glad of it. Monte is glad to get rid of Marlene. She probably has her own agenda as do we all.

As it turned out, Marlene, or Marty, was a delightful companion. She was very neat, well groomed and in good condition from walking. She followed a strict regimen of physical exercise. She was into Yoga and was very supple. Marty was a gourmet cook, an artist and had her own condo under development in Bad Bocklet, a small community north of Bad Kissingen. Her dancing was far better than Martin's who was a mediocre but enthusiastic dancer to rock and roll, swing, a Texas two step or a waltz. She made him look good on the dance floor but then she could follow a gorilla.

Marty was quite a surprise as a lover. In addition to her other fine qualities she turned out to be a 'screamer'. She managed to wake up everyone in the Austrian Frau's apartment house. It was a performance that evoked memories of the lady gym teacher in the cult classic "Porky's." The young officers of the Squadron were still laughing a week later. Upton in particular enjoyed repeating Martin's pithy explanation, "What can I say, Sir, Cupcake is a screamer. I am in trouble and will have to move." None of them knew "Cupcake's" identity and Martin did not elaborate.

05 Feb 1985
Local Training Area

It was time for the Troop to again go to the Border for a month. It was hard for Martin to see why it could possibly be G Troop's turn in the barrel again. Five units with one month of total relief should mean two border tours per year per unit with one having three trips. 5X2+1=11, any idiot could count that well. If Squadron was not deliberately screwing them, the Gator must be volunteering to go. However you cut it, four trips per year was too many for one Cavalry Troop.

The Border tour was both boon and bane. Boon because the Troop, Company and Battery Commanders got to run an operation far enough from home station to be autonomous. The Platoon Leaders acted as Officers in Charge of the Border Camp and were responsible to the Commander to respond to all sorts of challenges. The NCOs ran Observation Posts, conducted convoys, arranged re-supply, led dismounted and mounted patrols, called in spot reports to a number of headquarters and managed a myriad of details. It was an experience rarely encountered by NCOs of their grade elsewhere in the Army and was a priceless training opportunity.

All leaders were on the spot every day of the border tour. There was nowhere to hide. The cycle of mission receipt, planning, reconnaissance, back briefing of unit leaders, orders briefs to soldiers, mission execution, recovery of men and equipment and After Action Review occurred without let up for a month. The maneuver rights area, an area set aside by treaty of ten kilometers wide, along the Border let the troop commander set two platoons at a time against each other in mock combats. The pace could, and did, crush those few leaders and soldiers who did not, or could not, learn to manage their time and focus on the mission. Service in the Border Cavalry taught combined arms employment and decentralized operations with a vengeance. It was a great leadership learning laboratory for officers and NCOs. It was no secret why many of the officers who served in the Border Cavalry advanced to positions of great responsibility in the Army. It was a leadership forge in between wars. It was Darwinian development, only the strong thrived. The weak merely survived or were eaten by the system.

It was a bane due to the lack of time to execute the tasks of a garrison Army deemed necessary by Army policy. Physical Training suffered as many units failed to do PT at the Border and almost none ever did it at the training areas of Graf and Wildflecken. Specialized training requiring facilities such as the Gas Chamber, Rifle Ranges, Mini-Tank Ranges and the Unit Conduct of Fire Trainers for the M1, and soon to be M3, were out of reach at the Border for most units. The dual workload was very hard to manage.

Martin approached the puzzle as he nearly always did, by assembling data. He knew detailed plans were viewed with great suspicion, particularly by the Cavalry and Airborne communities. This prejudice, as with most bias, was deeply rooted in personal experience in both Army Tribes. Most detailed plans never held up past the Line of Departure for the Cavalry and landing on the Drop Zone for the Airborne. The phrase "No plan survives contact intact," was the mantra of both tribes populating 11th ACR. Planners were looked upon with scorn and improvisers were exalted.

Martin created a fold out chart covering the major events for the next two years of planning. The simple chart filled out in pencil showing holidays, gunnery, M3 fielding, border tours and exercises told the story. He could not exclusively train the troop at home station. He would have to bring the resources to the Border as it was the only place the unit was physically static for longer than two weeks. The rest of its life was spent in motion.

He did not need his chart board to figure out the head Gator's next move and it was not long in coming, "First Sergeant, I want you to be in overall charge of local tank gunnery training while I split my time between here and the Border. The Troop minus will run the Border and the tank platoons will focus all of their efforts on tank gunnery. Masterson has a schedule worked up and I have approved it. I need you to make sure my guidance is carried out. Be a hard ass and be tough on these guys."

"You know I would prefer not to do that, Captain Dawson. The Cavalry way of tank gunnery train up is not Crawl, Walk, Run, it is more like Run, Trip, Fall. I will do as you ask but you only get what you are willing to pay for," Martin stated firmly.

"What do you mean by Run, Trip, Fall, First Sergeant?" Dawson asked in an accusing manner.

"Captain, I believe you and the tankers believe the M1 will do it all. It will do a lot of the work if properly prepared with trained crews. I will look at the training layout and make recommendations," Martin said hopefully.

"No need, First Sergeant, you will carry out my orders. The schedule is set and only I can change, modify, or cancel any part of it. Your job is to execute what I have set up, period," Dawson stated with finality.

As he expected, Martin lasted about four days as the tank gunnery straw boss. His insistence on a strict Tank Crew Gunnery Skills test and other building block issues was over ridden by Dawson as unnecessary Armor School bullshit. Matters came to a head on the Tank Crew Practice Course over the set up of the course by the Squadron and the conduct of the course by the G Troop Tankers.

"First Sergeant, are we glad to see you. We can't see the targets to engage them. The Squadron Commander will not listen to Staff Sergeant Phillips and will not alter his personal design of the course to fit the terrain. It is too stupid for words," a new NCO, Sergeant First Class Collie, stated strongly.

"Put me in the gunner's seat of your tank, Collie, and let me see the course," Martin said simply.

After occupying three carefully prepared defensive positions Martin agreed. The targets were not visible from the firing tank position due to the failure of the Squadron Commander to verify the target locations through the Gunner's Auxiliary Telescope. This instrument was slaved to the cannon and worked independently from the sophisticated systems of the tank. For safety, the main gun barrel of the tank had to clear the berm or embrasure of the defensive position and be able to see the target and the telescope located right next to the gun made certain it did. The primary fire control of the M1 allowed the crew to see, range to and prepare all systems to engage the target with a 98% probability of hit while remaining virtually hidden. This ability was a feature that sold the tank to anyone who wanted to live to fight another day. Staff Sergeant Phillips, an NCO who had worked for Martin at Fort Knox as an instructor, had placed the target array. He knew better but either could not convince the Squadron Commander or did not try to convince him of the un-workability of the arrangement.

When apprised of the situation, Lieutenant Colonel Covington immediately defended the target placement saying, "First Sergeant, my very best Troop Commander proofed the course from the gunner's seat of his tank and I was his TC. And now, you are telling me he is wrong?"

"Sir, I checked them all myself. They are wrong. I can have them fixed in less than an hour," Martin stated calmly.

"You know why this happened and you are not telling me. Tell me, First Sergeant, don't sugar coat it," Covington said.

"Very well, Sir, if you insist. Captain Filterbind is a suck ass. He baby sits your kids and walks your dog. He told you what you wanted to hear when you wanted to hear it. He talks the talk but he don't walk the walk, Sir," and as he finished Martin came to the rigid position of ATTENTION for the inevitable dressing down.

Surprisingly it did not come, the Squadron Commander merely said, "Fix the targets, First Sergeant, and thank you."

When Martin told Sergeant First Class Collie to put one of his tanks in every battle position and fix the targets with his troops in concert with the Master Gunner from Fox Troop NCOIC, Collie was incredulous. "How did you get him to change his mind? Must be a First Sergeant thing, I guess," he stated.

Collie the inveterate wise guy with all of the answers, Martin thought before he answered.

"Collie, give the man some credit where it is due. He is out here and working hard to make it right, not back in his office drinking coffee. He was an S3 in combat as a Junior Captain with Freddie Franks. We will support him. The Fox Troop NCO & I were at Knox together, he will cooperate," Martin said simply.

Collie immediately saw the light. The Squadron Commander had overridden the Master Gunner and put the targets where he wanted them. No one had the balls to tell him he was wrong. Collie did note Martin never said a negative word about the Squadron Commander or his target locations; he just got permission and moved them.

Later in the evening a severe thunderstorm swept into the area with both driving rain and lightning impacting the ground in the distance with huge claps of thunder. As Martin watched the training, Sergeant First Class Collie and Sergeant First Class Vic Jackson came to his jeep. Both were wet through. "First Sergeant, we need to cancel training due to the lightning. We have live ammo on these tanks and we should not be out here in this thunder storm," Collie stated.

"Bull shit, Collie, those tanks are on rubber tracks and you are safer in one of them than in your car or at home. Two; it doesn't rain in the Army, it rains on the Army. If it ain't rainin', it ain't training. I can see it now in 1999, Command Sergeant Major Collie is briefing the press, 'Well folks we were beatin' hell out of the Russians at the Meinigen Gap and then, it started raining with thunder and lightning.' Keep training guys. If this was light infantry, we would hunker down until it passed. We aren't canceling mounted tank gunnery training due to lighting."

At this critical juncture, Captain Dawson arrived and went to his tank to make his night run. In short order, the tank platoon sergeants convinced him to send the First Sergeant to the Border and to take his rightful place as the Panzer leader. The old guy was too nuts they said and offered examples.

245

Dawson was quietly amused to hear their stories of the Gator Gran Prix. During day light hours, after each tank had engaged the gunnery course twice, boredom set in with the troops. The First Sergeant had organized drag races among the nine tanks to determine the top eliminator and the fastest tank. He then had them race their tanks around the proficiency course as if it were a Grand Prix circuit until platoons produced winners and a troop champion emerged to be duly crowned. The puritans were terribly upset that one of the winning tanks had an armored skirt pin break forcing them to temporarily remove the piece of armored plate from a tank. He was not surprised to learn Martin beat them all on elapsed time around the course on the initial demonstration. The fact he was willing to take turns at high speed on one track removed many of their inhibitions as did his talk to them later, which was reported word for word to Dawson.

"These M1s are instruments of war. Their purpose is to defeat the enemies of the United States. In war, you will do things with these tanks no one ever thought you could do. You will have to take them to the limit to survive. Stretch your limits now to the maximum. If you break it, we will fix it. Now get out there on that course and let me see what you can do. I would hate to tell anyone my 46 year old grandpa First Sergeant beat me one on one in an M1 tank race because I had no balls."

Concurrently, he had the crews not on the course practice assembly, disassembly, and function check of tank weapons blindfolded. Of course he did it first and let them time him. He beat all of them but two NCOs. He also devised a drivers' training course progressively narrowing the lanes to smaller and smaller lanes forcing drivers to learn to judge distance from the driver's seat. He also taught them all how to override the fuel filter system in a combat situation.

Talking at once, the three NCOs said, "Sir, you shoulda' seen 'em. He made 'em run it three times. Skirts were flying, they had rub marks, one crew had to jump a track back on, they were bangin' into each other, I thought we was gonna' get somebody killed. First Sergeant just kept cheering them on. He is nuts, Sir. We are lucky we did not lose weapons parts and have injuries when they tried to earn a three day passes by beating him on weapons assembly blindfolded."

Dawson was laughing inside. Good for you, First Sergeant. The Gator Grand Prix was just what they needed. The drag race was a nice touch particularly since G-66, his tank had won Top Eliminator. The First Sergeant told him "Whenever possible, never let them know they are training, just playing." Staff Sergeant Willie Green was the Road Course winner, which was a surprise. There might be more to Green than he first thought. He also knew the First Sergeant turned their training into games to make their reactions to contact instinctive. It was Genghis Khan's hunting party all over again. Ole Genghis gave the best of the best the privilege of fighting the tigers with the short sword once the encircling drive to herd them was over. The blindfolded assembly of weapons was a great idea, taking the

246

TCGST one step further - train for war by achieving the impossible in peace. The key was being able to lead them and beat them at every turn using guile. He then goaded them until they could beat him with youth and strength, praising them as they did so. It was vintage leadership by personal example. They had learned to do seemingly impossible tasks under the toughest conditions. But, he was going to send the First Sergeant to the Border and take charge of Tank Gunnery, tonight. He made too much out of the technical aspects of the M1 and had the tankers in an uproar. He was a zealot and there was not enough time and energy to teach them all he thought they should know. Besides, it was really a simple thing. The damn tank did everything for you.

"All right men, I hear you. Pack it in for tonight, line up and get ready to go back to the barracks."

Once they were gone from him to line up their vehicles, he keyed his jeep radio, "Gator 7, Gator Six, OVER."

"Six, Seven, OVER."

"Roger, Seven, meet me at the start of the course door to door, OVER."

"Six, Seven, WILCO, OVER."

"Six, OUT."

As they traveled, Dawson's driver asked him, "What are you going to tell the First Sergeant, Sir?"

Dawson smiled saying, "Change of mission, starting now. The First Sergeant takes all of this gunnery shit way too serious. He wants to train everyone up to his level but it ain't necessary. The damn tank does everything for you. Masterson and I hit everything in record time at the gunnery for NET. He just does not get it, the troops are trained well enough and they will never learn all he knows about the tank."

His driver persisted. He was headed to OCS. This was a clinic in leadership to him, "How is the First Sergeant going take getting pulled off a mission you just gave him for doing exactly what you told him to do?"

Dawson laughed and replied, "You better hope you get a Platoon Sergeant and a First Sergeant like him. He does what he is told and does not bitch unless it involves safety. He gives his opinion before the decision is made but once it is, he spends all of his energy on the task and none on complaining. You just have to remember as an officer you are the one responsible for the final outcome. The Army puts officers in charge. It is when you make your unit do the impossible that you are in command. Watch and learn Grasshopper."

The Commander dropped his fancy plexiglass window as his First Sergeant merely opened his door for the meeting, disregarding the light rain and saluting.

"Yes, Sir, you have orders?" Martin asked as the rain took that exact moment to slack off to zero.

"First Sergeant, you have got this off to a good start. The races were great. The guys loved it. The Squadron Commander told me you fixed the course and that he appreciated all you did for him. I need you to go back to the Border and take charge up there. I've got this now."

Martin looked past his Troop Commander and saw the tanks forming up in column and knew the deal. Saluting his commander, he asked, "Is there anything else, Sir?"

Dawson replied, "No, First Sergeant, nothing else. I know you would prefer to run the tank gunnery training. There is no need for both of us to be here. That leaves the Border without adult supervision."

"Sir, I am enroute to the Border," closing his door as his jeep pulled away.

His new driver was Specialist 4 Keith Harrington, a 19D from a CO-HORT unit, who had volunteered to remain in Europe when the majority of his unit's soldiers' time expired on their enlistment. Keith asked the First Sergeant, "Top, did we just get fired?"

"No, Keith, we just got a change of mission. The tankers neither like my training methods nor my philosophy about the M1 tank. They think the tank is automatic. It is no longer my job to train them on Tank Gunnery. I was willing to do it. I am an expert on the tank. I want them to do well for all of the right reasons and a few of the wrong ones," Martin replied.

Keith was a very perceptive man and the best driver Martin had ever had. He was also very curious. Given his other fine qualities, Martin often indulged his driver's thirst for knowledge using it to clarify his own thinking. "Which is which, First Sergeant?" Keith asked.

"The tank qualification course represents preparation for individual tank combat. The course teaches and tests tank killing skills. Each engagement trains and assesses the crew's ability to fight their tank. The wrong reasons are my big ego and what I think is a big reputation as a Tank Expert. I want the troop to do well to validate me as well as them. That is not going to happen. Dawson will let them off the hook. Their egos are too big to learn right now. The M1 tank computer compensates for errors and refines accuracy by eliminating the physical factors of what is known to the eggheads as the error budget. Old tankers like me used 'steam gunnery' with all sorts of training fixes we might, or might not, remember in a crisis. The M1 resolves most of the questions in nano seconds."

"What is a nano second, First Sergeant?" Keith asked.

"One millionth of a stopwatch second, Keith," Martin said.

"Shit, First Sergeant, you tankers hurt my poor Infantry head. How do these guys remember all of this shit?" he asked.

"It is not necessary they know what I know, Keith. I had to know it all to answer student questions and write the manuals and procedures. The knowledge is in the tank systems. The hard part is to train the guys to put the data into the system correctly and update it. The easy way is to use an aircraft checklist. These guys are too proud to do anything like an aviator does it.

They want to remember it all or use the goofy Technical Manual written by maintenance guys."

"I am too far gone today to tell you about the error budget and you would not sleep a wink tonight if I did. I'll show you on the tank at Wildflecken and let you shoot one. Practical work is always best."

Maybe, down the road something good will come out of this gunnery. If they get their asses handed to them maybe they will listen to a course like the one Sergeant First Class Jimmy Pierce did in Korea many years before.

"So what are you going to do, First Sergeant?" Keith asked.

"I am going to go to the Border and do the best I can to perform the mission Captain Dawson gave me," Martin said. "Cheer up Keith! You are going to be around the scouts and not see a tanker for the next month or so - that should make you happy," Martin said laughing.

"It sure will, First Sergeant. Are we going to do anything wild up on the Border?"

"I hope not, Keith. I want to get our training up to date on the NBC Chamber, rifle range, driver's training, dental exams, the PT test and work on the fine points of the IG inspection we have coming up in less than 70 days. That should be enough to keep us busy," Martin laughed ruefully.

The Regimental plan for maintaining unit readiness was a good one. Company level commanders were responsible to maintain a 90% level of individual training readiness in five critical areas: The Army Physical Training Test a semi-annual requirement, NBC Mask confidence and Individual weapons qualifications, annual requirements, and Driver's Training & Licensing. Medical and Dental qualification rounded out the list. Each Troop, Battery and Tank Company Commander participated in quarterly training briefings with the Regimental and Squadron Commanders.

This forum gave the Regimental Commanding Officer an opportunity to interact with his Captains, enabling him to give guidance, assess unit effectiveness and to determine what resources they lacked to accomplish the mission. G Troop was routinely ranked number 12 of the Regiments 12 ground cavalry troops in training readiness. Martin knew the Regimental plan was reasonable for most units but hard for G Troop as it was never in garrison long enough to do the tasks. It was the quarterly gate that made it hard. No one up until now had made it happen in G Troop. It was time for Mohammed to go to the mountain as the mountain was damn sure not moving.

Gathering the NCOs, Martin led them through an analysis of the training resource problems associated with training and testing on the five areas while deployed to the Border and subsequently to quarterly tank gunnery and maneuver training at the end of the border tour. Of course, for G Troop, it would then return for another Border tour immediately after the trip to Wildflecken for gunnery with the scouts assuming the Border duty while the tankers finished their training.

It was easier than anyone thought it would be. The stakeholder philosophy was by now firmly a part of G Troop life. The First Sergeant used it to layout the objectives, gain information on local conditions and secure the support of the stakeholders, the NCOs and Junior Officers of the unit. The resources and answers were right in front of their noses. No one up to now had ever asked them the right questions.

The shower room in the guest barracks was certified as the NBC Chamber as it had a ventilator, tiled walls, and was easily de-contaminated. The rock quarry at the rear of the Border Camp provided a convenient .45 caliber pistol range, submachine gun range and a zero range for the M-16s. Tunnel C targets allowed full rifle qualification to occur at 25 meters. By adding dirt, the unit was able to test fire machine guns in the quarry as well. Several of the officers brought in twelve gauge shot guns and together with Martin, bought clay trap targets and several cases of twelve gauge number seven shot from the Hanau Rod and Gun Club.

The officers and the First Sergeant thus began to teach wing shooting to those soldiers who had never led a target. They learned how and had a lot of fun doing it.

The driver's training officer agreed to travel to the border to administer the test once he was assured of a high passing rate. The troop had borrowed his training aids for training on the two weekends prior to his arrival and 98% of those tested qualified. The PT test was problematic but Martin set up the two mile run on a downhill slope in the country side behind the camp.

It was also very easy to get the Regimental dentist out to the Border Camp with his entire field kit to include a canvas chair. An enterprising Scotsman, the Regimental Dentist, Major Fitzpatrick, got several of his colleagues from the big dental clinic in the sky at Frankfort to come to the Border to help him with exams. They all got a border tour and were taken for a flight in either the front seat of an AH-1 Cobra or on a UH-1 Red Catcher flight right along the fence. As a result, G Troop was at 100% dental readiness for the first time ever. The First Sergeant was the first one through the dental gate with three root canals and two fillings.

The Troop now met every gate on the Regimental Commanding Officer's chart for the quarterly training update briefing, honestly without penciling in any qualification scores. One of the officers asked Martin why he bothered being honest when it seemed Regiment's methods were often questionable. He never forgot the answer, "The Regimental Commanding Officer is not in the troop. I am not responsible to develop his character. I am responsible for yours. We do not lie about readiness. That is a criminal act. We do our best and report it like we see it, period."

What no one knew was that the Regimental Command Sergeant Major had a mole in G Troop. The mole was PFC Jeans, a Bible Thumping member of the Church of Christ from way down in Bivens, LA. He was in the Bible Study group led by the Regimental Command Sergeant Major in Fulda.

First Sergeant Martin had defended Jeans from all comers when he was being harassed for his faith and his dedication saying to the Platoon Sergeants, "Jesus already told Jeans he would be reviled and spat upon for his faith by heathens and to love them that hate you. What I ask is that you be publicly neutral. Keep your opinions to yourself. Let the troops that look up to you make up their own minds about their faith. I know it is strange to hear that from me. Get over it. It is a civil rights issue. I am a Christian who strays from the path of righteousness from time to time."

The last statement caused the assembled NCOs to burst out laughing but they got the message and the harassment of the Christian stopped. It was also how he knew Jeans was the Regimental Command Sergeant Major's rat. The Regimental Command Sergeant Major made a point of telling Martin he appreciated him defending the Christian. The cock hounds were certainly not talking to the Regimental Command Sergeant Major at the camp meeting. If there had to be a rat with a direct line to the Regimental Command Sergeant Major, a Christian rat was good. At least he would tell him the truth.

As Martin and Keith made their way to the Observation Posts with coffee and soup, they began to be overcome by CS gas fumes. Martin had kept the capsules used on a burner in the makeshift gas chamber in his briefcase. One or more of the capsules had broken. He and Keith along with the Commo Sergeant had to stop, evacuate the jeep, and perform a hasty decontamination exercise on the road against the Border fence. Naturally, they had an audience of the East German OP and the American crew in OP Tennessee. The US crew had the benefit of night vision devices. Anything slightly different in their area got their instant attention. The sight of the First Sergeant and crew pouring water on their eyes and washing on the road was hilarious. The event entertained the troop for days as the OP crew regaled their friends with detailed accounts of the event.

For a month or so thereafter, Martin took perverse pleasure in the gasps of rear echelon personnel as they received documents carried in the briefcase. The Squadron Command Sergeant Major got so sick of the powdered tear gas fumes from the infamous briefcase; he requisitioned a new leather one, issued it to Martin as a replacement and had the old one burned.

As he roamed the Border checking on the many tasks, the patrols, the barracks, and just sightseeing, Martin reviewed what should be happening in preparation for the first gunnery cycle of the M1 tank in the 11th ACR.

Tank gunnery training is done in phases. Home station training begins with the administration of the Tank Crew Gunnery Skills Test (TCGST). Each crewman demonstrates the ability to safely prepare the tank weapons to fire, operate them using correct commands and procedures, correct malfunctions of the various weapons and apply safety precautions during range firing. The TCGST was the initial test for the Tank Master Gunner Course and routinely caused between 25 & 50% of the candidates of the tanker 'finishing' school to be dismissed and sent home in disgrace. The message sent to the 'field' by this action was to support the fidelity of the TCGST. The interpretation of the "field" was the members of Master Gunner Faculty were all pricks anyhow and would fail the highest percentage they could to maintain their exclusive club. The fidelity of the TCGST varied widely between units. Although Martin was not a Master Gunner, he fully supported straight arrow TCGSTs. In his previous unit, failures were re-trained and re-tested until they passed. After riding several hundred tanks from V Corps while grading their crews as a Staff Sergeant Assistant Instructor and helping investigate a number of accidents, he knew from bitter experience lackadaisical TCGSTs led to accidents and poor results.

The second part of home station training was the Tank Crew Proficiency Course. This was generally a circular road with targets arranged in the manner of the qualification range. Crews would engage the course followed by a control jeep manned by unit officers or NCOs. The control officer briefed the tank crew before each engagement using a tactical scenario for either a stationary defensive engagement or a moving engagement. The governing metric for success or failure was time measured on a sliding scale of points measured against time graduated in seconds with the fastest time being awarded 100 points and slower times receiving fewer points less as the scale slid toward zero. Errors made by the crew were assessed against each engagement. This system assumed the enemy tanker to be just as motivated to stay alive as his US counterpart. Second place in a gunfight sucks. The fastest tank round's time of flight is nearly a mile per second, ergo, most engagements occurred at ranges less than a mile and never successfully more than three miles. (The range was a factor of the M68 gun and the ammo. It would change dramatically when the 120mm came on line). Seconds counted in war. The appearance of a target started all engagements. The control officer operated a remote radio set which sent a signal to a target erecting mechanism to present the correct target setup for each engagement. The control officer and his assistant also timed the responses of the crew via a radio net from each tank. The tank crew's time for score began when their vehicle was first exposed to enemy fire. Exposure was universally accepted as beginning when the target was first visible to the control officer when the tank on the course was moving. For defensive engagements, the time began to count when the tank pulled forward into a firing position from a hidden position exposing it to enemy direct fire. Control officers started their stop watches when they saw brake lights on the firing tank. Thus the critical elements of detecting the target, exposure to enemy fire and being the first to shoot were all evaluated. The entire procedure was also captured on audio tape to keep everyone honest at the de-briefing. Crews engaged targets after a short briefing from the control officer. Smart units used the same words and procedures crews would hear on the final phase of testing, Tank Table VIII, throughout the training. Martin was considered cruel as he used very small targets of one quarter scale on the beginning courses and never one larger than the smallest NATO target. It was the size of a BMP, a Russian Personnel Carrier turret, or just about the size of a big bean bag chair. When the crews arrived at Tank Table VII they shot against half scale targets. He knew what the troops did not. Acquiring the target was the critical skill, not shooting at it. You had to see it before you could shoot at it and the human predator is geared to movement. Crewmen trained to what they thought of as an

252

impossible standard with a small bullseye. When they got to the final exam and saw a target the size of a garage door they shot it down instantly earning maximum points. Over training was going out of fashion in the US Army. But he knew his method was win-win once he could get it past the whining leaders.

The third part of home station training was the maintenance preparation of tanks and automatic weapons. Martin was again at odds with his commander and the majority of the tankers. Most leaders wanted to hold off on tank repairs and machineguns until they went to gunnery. He was dead set against such a strategy. Gunnery training is marksmanship training not maintenance. Only an idiot started his family out on a cross country automobile trip with four bad tires hoping to find some new ones on special as he traveled. It also belied the legend that the Cavalry was the tip of the spear and meant to blunt the Russian thrust. If your automatic weapons did not fire first time, every time, you were a failure as a soldier and your leaders were negligent criminals for tolerating your low standards.

The intermediate phase of gunnery prior was accomplished for the Cavalry by firing at Wildflecken at shorter and narrower ranges that would be found at the annual qualification range at Grafenwohr. Each Squadron of the Regiment was allotted time on the ranges and each rotation was managed by the Squadron S-3's.

A task often neglected was the range training and certification of unit leaders to run ranges as safety officers and officers in charge. At the First Sergeant's insistence, all of the NCOs and officers would be required to become range qualified at Wildflecken. Martin knew from long experience that the best way to run a safe training exercise was to qualify all leaders as range safety officers. It was his way of eliminating ignorance and excuses in the whole unit in one fell swoop. It also enabled the Commander to maintain unit integrity by assigning platoons to run ranges and train together. Training on tank ranges was stressful for leaders but it did not hold a candle to war. If you can't run a tank range in a time of relative peace you probably can't lead a tank outfit.

The Wildflecken Training Area was run by 7th Army, Training Command, on behalf of its parent, 7th Army, the Combat element of US Army Europe. Wildflecken was a compact training area consisting of ranges sited in an area ten to twelve miles in circumference firing specific weapons into a large common impact area and dated from the time of the WW II Nazi Wehrmacht. It was noted for hills, fog, rain and generally nasty climate. The Germans had a saying that roughly translated to: "Six months of the year it snows at Wildflecken and the rest of the year it is winter." A monastery was located adjacent to the Post atop a small mountain called the Kruezburg. It was known for its strong dark beer, tasty bread, Friars in traditional Monk garb, a menagerie of peacocks, huge mastiff dogs the size of ponies and other animals found there. The monastery began life in 1731 and was the only one in Germany that still made its own products as the others were co-opted by breweries.

The Wildflecken Training Area could host all of the combined arms of the Cavalry though the TOW missile. All direct fire weapons were generally restricted to training ammunition with inert warheads. Artillery and Mortars fired Smoke and High Explosive rounds. Many a promising Army career was ended or impacted by rounds going out of the impact area at Wildflecken. It was a place of survival as much as of training. The common saying of "There ain't no flicken like a Wildflecken" was more truth than jest. The small impact area required strict observance of horizontal firing limits and moving vehicle lanes to ensure projectiles stayed within the impact area. The population density adjacent to the ranges also mandated the shooters adhere to regulations written to make the neighbors happy. The training area was a short road march of fifteen to twenty miles depending on the route from the 1 & 2/11 Border Areas. This close proximity added great flexibility to the Cavalry's ability to train and man the border concurrently.

Martin was lost in thought as he and Keith waited for the fueler to show up at OP 13. Wildflecken was a new place for Martin to get used to as his last unit trained at Baumholder as part of 8th Infantry Division. Wildflecken had a lot of potential even with its many shortcomings. He was determined to learn all he could about the training and land available for future operations. It was his lot in life to get drafted into the S3 shop of every unit he had served with and the potential for that happening in this outfit was high. These poor bastards caught up in the cache' and mystique of "The Regiment" did not know what they did not know about the M1 tank. For once he was unable to do anything about the train wreck but watch it happen and it made him want to puke.

The final phase of gunnery was performed once each year at the Mecca of European based troops at Grafenwohr. A large training area that pre-dated the Nazis of WW II.

Ranges there were run by the Regiment. Scoring was by the NCOs and officers from sister units. No slack was asked and none given. It was a 14 day training cycle and the weak would be quickly devoured. If those ranges were run correctly, 1/11 ACR Commanded by Lieutenant Colonel John Abrams, Son of Tank, would probably out qualify the whole Army. The pity was Abrams would be glad to share his techniques with his peers but they would never use them. As the Squadron Commander he often went to Graf for the land conferences and stashed float tanks there, flying crews to meet short notice range opportunities via 4/11 helicopters. It was too much work for his peers.

0630 hours
28 Feb 1985

"Are we ready for Wildflecken, First Sergeant?" his driver asked.

"Keith, watching these guys on an M1 reminds me of a pig looking at a Rolex," Martin said ruefully. "Don't repeat that, please," he added. "We are ready for everything but the learning process. We will do all of the surface stuff correctly and to standard. Hopefully we will hit targets and I will look like an old woman, worrying about shit that will not come true. But we still have a Border tour to do before Wildflecken and the IG."

"Gator Seven, Blackhorse 39A, Your Net, OVER."

"Blackhorse 39 A, this is Gator 7, OVER."

"Gator 7, this is 39A, meet me at OP Tennessee, OVER."

"39A Gator 7, WILCO, OVER. 39A, OUT."

"Who was that, First Sergeant?" his driver asked.

"That was the great Regimental Border Officer, late of G Troop 2ˢᵗ Platoon Scouts, Captain Robertson, West Pointer, Bag Piper, Varsity Wrestler, Swordsman, Airborne, Ranger, Pathfinder and all around stud duck," Martin replied as Keith made his way toward OP Tennessee.

"What do you think he wants, First Sergeant?" Keith asked.

"Whatever it is, Keith, it will be interesting. We'll see what is on his mind shortly," Martin said smiling.

"Isn't he the guy that helped you hold the LSD dealer out the third floor window until he told where his stash was?" Keith asked with big eyes.

"Keith, that is just a rumor. The dopers told that lie to discredit Captain Robertson and me. Besides we found the dope and they were never prosecuted for having it. No harm, no foul. Those guys cried like rats eating onions when that shit was flushed down the commode," said Martin laughing loudly. As they approached OP, Martin noticed Captain Robertson standing outside his vehicle.

"Keith, he is going to want to drive this vehicle. Get a soda and go shoot the shit with the guys in the OP or in the scout track until we get back," Martin's tone was soft but it was a command. Keith realized he was not going to get to hear this conversation. He reached into the cooler and retrieved a cold Pepsi as the vehicle came to a halt. He got out, retrieved his rifle, stuck the Pepsi in his pocket and saluted the Captain as he opened the door for him.

"Thank you, Keith, we will be back in about 20 minutes. I am licensed for the vehicle but just leave the trip ticket alone," he said returning a second salute from Keith, smiling at his immediate agreement.

Captain Robertson got into the vehicle saying, "Nice kid, best driver I have seen you have, how did that happen? Did you turn into a Waco when I left?" he asked laughing. Martin smiled at the reference to a WW II movie which portrayed a paranoid Infantry Captain AKA Waco after the city of his birth, Waco, Texas, who took his two best soldiers, fellow Texans, to watch his back. They of course had the best and latest weapons while his line platoons had to scrounge to remain equipped and lived like dogs in the mud while the chosen lived in a house with 'Waco'.

"Not hardly, Captain Robertson. Are you adjusting to life at the puzzle palace?"

"I am but they are keeping me hopping. With all of the shit they want done yesterday I wonder how their last bitch Border Officer survived before I got there," he said as he drove the jeep up to a deer stand overlooking the border trace. "Get your binos, First Sergeant, and we'll go up in that deer stand. Bring your map, please," Robertson requested.

Once there Martin told him, "This is where the Great Jesus brought me on my first day on the border, the Saturday before the Stallion Stakes at Schweinfurt."

255

"It is a good spot. They can't see your jeep where it is parked. If we are quick, they probably will miss seeing us get into the stand. Let's move it, Top," Robertson said leading the way up to the elevated enclosure.

Once there he explained the purpose of his trip. "My task is to get a piece of the East German communications fence and determine if we can tap their hard line. The only way I can see to do it is to go over there at night with NVGs, clip a buried piece and cover up the spot. What do you think, Top?" he asked.

"I think you need some nutty Cav guys to go with you. Guys that don't much care what happens to them as long they get some adrenaline flow. God knows we have enough of them around," Martin said with a rueful laugh.

"Yeah, I got all that, but how do we get across their fence and back without a lot of noise and barking by the dogs?" he asked his old First Sergeant.

"You use our key. It just so happens we have a set of keys to the lock on the gate right in front of you. You get a rake, unlock the lock, go through the gate, re-lock it, rake out your footprints in the sand and patrol around the dogs, up to the fence, snip, snip and sneak out the way you came in," Martin said cheerfully.

"How the hell did you get a key, First Sergeant?" Robertson asked.

"We took the hasp loose and put our own lock on it during the night. We then got Ricky the Rad Locksmith to make us one at Schweinfurt Engineers Housing Department for a can of coffee. That night we switched it back. Just thought it might be nice to have unobstructed entry into East Germany. Just another good idea that bubbled up from the rank and file of the enlisted swine," Martin said laughing heartily.

"As you know Captain, the East Germans use the ropes outside the tower window to tell everyone how "short" they are. They are draftees and the shorter the rope displayed out of the tower, the less time they have to go in the Army. When they get close to the end of their term of service, the rank and file get really sorry. They play cards, sleep and screw off. We just waited until the tower across from the gate had two short ropes and pulled the switch one foggy morning at 0200," Martin continued calmly.

"What the hell if you had been caught and they fired on you?" Robertson asked.

"My old Warrant Officer on the Missile Site in Florida swore his Pappy told him, 'Son, they's only two kinds of people in the world, they's the guilty and then they's the caught'."

After letting that sink in Martin said, "And that is what you and your band of merry men are going to be, Captain Robertson, guilty only if you are caught."

"You need to take some thugs with you who are used to sneaking around screwing married women and being cat burglars. You had enough of them in 1st Platoon to do ten bag jobs like this one. Take Washington, Jesus, Johnson, and Smitley. Washington is black, former Marine, fearless, and bad to the bone. Jesus is smarter than all of you put together and he can control Washington. Johnson is a fluent German speaker and has a future in the Army as a Scout. He needs to know how to do shit like this. Smitley is a new guy, small but strong. He is a work out freak who was a gymnast in college before he dropped out. He is also a very good martial arts guy. Plus, dogs love Smitley, don't know why but they just do," Martin concluded his advice.

"You left out the one guy I came to get, First Sergeant," Robertson said.

"Who might that be, Captain?"

"You, First Sergeant."

"Shit, Sir, are you sure? I'm getting a little long in the tooth for Airborne Ranger life of danger patrolling adventures."

"I'm sure. We'll have all the speed we'll need. What I need is a steady slack man at the rear of the diamond to cover our trail and ease my mind. If you're back there, I can handle anything that happens upfront. What do you say, Top?"

"You know I'm going. I don't want anyone to think I'm a candy ass," Martin said.

"No one would ever think that, First Sergeant," the Captain said with disbelief.

"I'll put Keith, my driver, on for a spare man. He is very good, ultra quiet, great condition, quietly tough. We also need to get some urine from the vet from female dogs in heat. The East German dogs will whine and want to screw us but they probably won't bark and try to bite. Besides, they will all be in their houses at 0200 anyhow."

Robertson stared at his former First Sergeant slack jawed in astonishment, finally asking. "Where in the hell did you come up with that?"

"Long ago I was a young Buck Sergeant. I got put in charge of the MPs at a missile site. The dogs there were the old attack variety, bite everything and everyone. Their handler had to choke them off intruders. Mean sons-a-bitches. Any man who could not get in on a dog in his kennel could not win their respect. I noticed none of these mean ass dogs bothered the Vets. The Vet told me his secret, female in heat urine spray. Someday, Captain, I'll teach you how to hide a tank using ordinary office supplies, but not today, the limit is one trade secret per day for all officers below the grade of Brigadier General."

"Can you get everything we need by tonight, First Sergeant?" Robertson asked.

"Probably, but it will be hard to get the squad together, get them checked, rehearsed and rested in the time we have available. Let's ask Jesus if they can hang, he is in the OP. They all belong to him. There is some extra fencing behind the motor pool we can bury and you can test it for sound and hardness. Shit, most them chase women until that time of night anyhow so a patrol should not be a challenge. We will give them the next half-day off. Does the Gator know you are here poaching, Captain Robertson?" Martin asked.

"I am surprised you waited to ask that question, First Sergeant," Robertson said with a smile.

"First Sergeant advice is free, Captain. People and resources are not. No one is authorized to commit resources, especially people, of a unit, except for the Commanding Officer. That goes double for Captain David W. Dawson's Cavalry Troop. He is signed for it all, he weighs the 5 W's and assesses risk, not me."

"I talked to him, First Sergeant, and he sent me to you. The Gator is the one who told me to make you ask 'the question'. He also said you, personally, could not go across the border. I will take Keith. You run the support on this side. I just wanted to see if you really had the nuts to go over with us," Robertson said in a very detached manner.

"You might make an officer yet, Captain Robertson. You have the killer instinct and the sense of mission it takes. Let me go get it all together, particularly if you want the estrus spray," Martin said.

"You aren't too disappointed about not going over are you, First Sergeant?" Robertson asked as they walked to the jeep.

"At some point in every senior enlisted man's life he realizes he is not twenty five and his greatest contributions will be from teaching and supporting the younger NCOs and Junior Officers, not leading the charge. I am never unhappy when the young guys out perform me when I challenge and train them. That is the way of life, the coach coaches, the players play. I am very, very happy with me. I am content to teach, coach, and mentor the guys coming on. One more thing, I can get you a silenced 9 mm with a catch bag. Just don't ask where it came from and don't lose it. Do you want it?" Martin asked.

"Yes please, First Sergeant. I will take good care of it, wherever it comes from," Robertson said with a sly smile.

After a busy day of assembling people, gear, a rehearsal, and a hearty meal, the squad rested at a patrol base in the forest near the gate they were to pass through to cross the border. At 0200 the young lions had to be awakened by Captain Robertson and First Sergeant Martin as all of them were sleeping soundly. The two leaders smiled. They had the right men, no fear, no misgivings, no conscience.

Except for Washington slipping a large nail in the hasp at the bottom of the guard tower and effectively penning the East Germans inside, the patrol went off without a hitch. Forewarned by his First Sergeant who was watching Washington like a hawk, Staff Sergeant Gilberto Jesus Ramos made Washington remove the nail on the way out. No Eastie woke up or saw anything. There was a bonus as Smitley found a piece of discarded communications cable in a drainage ditch. That would give the spooks something to sniff. Martin learned to appreciate the agony of command that officers feel as he watched the patrol disappear into the fog bank covering the Border and sweated it out until they were back. He was proud to see them slink back without a sound and for the East German side to remain unaware that they were ever there. He was damn relieved to see them return.

Back at the patrol base that was made up of tank tarpaulins for a tent, they all talked at once until Captain Robertson began the AAR. The First Sergeant had beer, soda, and bologna and cheese sandwiches available once the weapons were on safe and wiped down. The sandwiches were sliced by Army Cooks and were slabs of meat and cheese. The soldiers wolfed them down as if they were finger food at the O'Club. The snack and the beer surprised them as did BJ from Supply showing up to take back the 5,000 rounds of ball, 4 to 1 tracer, and linked 7.62 mm that the First Sergeant had signed for. "Damn, First Sergeant, you really did have extra ammo to cover us," Robertson exclaimed.

"You are my guys, Captain. No one would have cared how many rounds I had to fire to get you back, they just want you back. Smokin' Joe is a Jesuit. The ends justify the means. Don't think this request was a Regimental brain fart, this was an order someone up high can deny if you got caught. You guys done good. Sleep until you wake up and I'll see you in the afternoon. Keith, you have had enough fun for one day, finish your beer and I will drive us back to the Border Camp. I need to wake up there about 0700." He left to a chorus of "Good Night, First Sergeant," with the unfired silenced pistol inside his field jacket, smiling and happy. He was not at all surprised to see Captain Robertson unroll his sleeping bag under the tarp with his old Platoon.

Martin loved those guys and was glad to see it all turned out so well - it could have been double ugly. He also wondered how often the East Germans were crossing over to just have a beer, probably every other day. The soldiers and politicians of post WW II never stopped to realize the impact of the East/ West line demarcation on the German people. Hell, people on both sides of the fence had relatives just across an artificial barrier. What an emotional gulf it must be. He knew the answer of the WW II soldiers of his hometown, "They started it and we finished it. The German people deserve everything they get after the war. Go see a concentration camp and tell me again what I owe those assholes."

1330 hours
14 Mar 1985
Wildflecken 7th Army Training Area

Captain David W. Dawson was not a happy man. The machinegun range had turned into one snarl after another. It wasn't that bad but it was not good. There was no flow to the training. He wanted the range, one of the first training events at Wildflecken, to get a better start. Nothing he had tried worked to move it along. He then smiled as he saw his First Sergeant arrive with the Motor Sergeant and the Supply Sergeant to brief them on the machinegun course. The range had three lanes large enough to accommodate tanks. There were four moving truck targets total. One set was made up of two targets that moved simultaneously, two of which had one, four stationary truck targets and eight sets of pop up troop targets. It was a valuable training site.

Martin was determined the Headquarters Platoon with its eight .50 M2 Heavy Barrel Browning Machineguns would learn to fully employ them. He personally inspected each weapon, had the barrels checked, ordered new ones to replace those judged worn out. This was the second time since his arrival they would be fired. The first was at Home Station at the local rifle range where the Headquarters Platoon engaged targets with the iron sights on the heavy weapons firing them single shot. They had to call each shot. They then reviewed the result comparing where they said it would strike to where it actually hit after inspecting the target at 1,000 inches or 83 feet. All Headquarters Platoon soldiers learned the weapons inside and out on that day. They thoroughly enjoyed it as none of them turned a wrench on a vehicle the entire day.

Today was the pay off as the First Sergeant was going to run them down a tank range with live ammunition and a variety of targets. Sergeant First Class JJ Wintergreen was to lead the maintenance section in two elements and Staff Sergeant Webster was going lead the two supply vehicles and one M113. The range was old hat to the tankers and scouts but was high adventure to the maintenance types. They were pumped. No one had ever taken the time to teach them, inspect and correct weapons faults and then let them engage the same targets the trigger pullers used.

Martin knew the technical guys had tremendous combat potential. They were inventive, calculating and were motivated to show up their combat MOS brethren. What no one knew was that Martin was going to teach them to fight stationary tanks from the Unit Maintenance Collection Point. He knew everything behind the first infantry squad was considered to be a REMPF by the grunts in the OPFOR and he had a surprise for them, fighting mechanics.

"Okay guys, that is the layout of the range, the training thrust of it and the potential engagements. Go back and get your guys some chow, relax and get ready to go down the course dry and then live. Tell everyone to use the sights initially and lean into the gun. Make sure everyone knows to put the first burst low. It is okay for the first burst to hit dirt in front of the target. You can adjust short machinegun fire. The sound of the ricochets scares the shit out the guys you're shooting at. Rounds fired over the target are tough to sense and give the enemy a false sense of security. Any questions?" Martin asked.

"No questions, First Sergeant, I think we got it," Sergeant First Class Wintergreen said with more confidence than he actually felt.

There was a lot of shit going on at this range at the same time. Tanks moving, targets moving, range fires, Captain Dawson yelling at the tankers. Shit, the tankers get paid to do this all of the time. If they are firkin' it up will I be okay?

"Remember men, either Lieutenant Fontane or I will be your OIC in the tower and we will guide you through the deal. You will do fine," Martin said with a smile.

"This is great, First Sergeant. My guys will really enjoy this," First Lieutenant (P) Fontane said with a happy smile. He had been a line dog for two years and six months. He knew the lot in life of the mechanic and meant every word.

Martin never forgot Junior Officers were supposed to be excited about training and idealistic. They had yet to be stationed at the Pentagon and learn how to be cynical.

At this point, Captain Dawson pulled up in his Jeep on the small hill where the HQs orders group had convened for the range briefing. He began to speak while the vehicle rocked to a stop in a low and measured tone that implied rage, "Goddammit, First Sergeant, the range is screwed up. There is no sense of urgency, targets are not being engaged correctly, the AAR process sucks and I want it fixed, right damn now if you please."

"Sir, as I recall, you told me to keep my hands off gunnery. What is it you want me to do?" Martin asked.

"These are your NCOs. They are screwing up this range. Go fix it, First Sergeant," Dawson ordered.

"Yes, Sir," Martin said as he saluted and departed for the tower.

"Damn, Sir, you did tell him to stay away. I was there," Sergeant Poston offered.

"Yeah, but watch what happens to this range now. It is about to come alive," Dawson said grinning ear to ear, not the least bit angry. It was clear he had merely wound up the First Sergeant to watch the fur fly.

Arriving at the tower, it was clear to the First Sergeant that Staff Sergeant Masterson thought he had all day to run nine tanks, eight scout tracks and two mortar tracks through the course. To his credit he was not getting a lot of help from the Platoon Sergeants. Martin's first task was to change the name of OIC of Record for the Range from Dawson's to his. He then rapidly took charge of every phase of the operation using the radio to professionally but firmly crack the whip on the unit.

He did not raise his voice but modulated it one octave lower than normal. His confidence and competence carried the moment easily. In less than 30 minutes, the range was running wide open and safely engaging targets. In two and one half hours every combat vehicle had engaged the course three times and the requirement was fulfilled. No one in the troop had ever seen such a performance except Sergeant First Class Vic Jackson. He had cheated. Once he saw Dawson talking to the First Sergeant and pointing, he knew what was

261

going to happen. He got his platoon organized and they were available to meet the high speed technique of the First Sergeant and finish the range with high scores in record time.

"Sergeant Jackson, how did you know what the First Sergeant was going to do?" Second Lieutenant Chastain asked.

"We been together before, ELL TEE," Jackson drawled, pouring them each a cup of coffee from his thermos. "He was my First Sergeant at Fort Knox. He managed to get H Co, 2/6 Cav, a school support outfit, a full gunnery cycle using scrounged ammo and excess capacity on Armor School Ranges. Nobody, and I mean nobody, had ever done that before. But most people are not willing to set up and run a TCGST at 0300 either. He is not unsafe, but he is quick. He calls it using the unforgiving moment. If three tanks will fit on a range, he will run them on it. He is very confident, knows his safety diagrams and exactly what this tank will do in any given situation. He is not taking chances. It just looks that way sometimes because the people watching do not know their shit. He then backs up the vehicles on the range with the next set letting the NCOIC run the firing portion. Next he is going to put those HQs dancing bears out there with the M88 and Deuce and a Halfs with ring mounts. That is a challenge."

"Why is he doing that, Sergeant Jackson? They are just mechanics," Chastain asked innocently.

"Sir, don't ever let the First Sergeant hear you use that word "just" to describe anybody in the Army. You need to listen up when he says shit like, 'Everyman in this unit is a Cavalry Trooper no matter what his MOS'. That is not bullshit, he means every word of it. Before you know it, you will be an Executive Officer and you will wish to hell your First Sergeant felt that way. There are no second class citizens with our First Sergeant. Everybody is in the shit together up to our necks."

"But do you think they will hit anything, Sergeant Vic?" Chastain asked.

"Martin trained them on those weapons himself. He checked 'em out and he is giving them a dry run. I will bet you they set the targets on fire on the second run. That .50 on a Chrysler mount is not a pop gun. It is a bitch to get used to and fire correctly. You'd better get on up to the tower ELL TEE, it is your turn to be the Safety Officer. I'll make sure your tank is ready for the night run. Think about what I said about the First Sergeant's bee in his helmet - everybody is a Cavalryman in this outfit."

"I will, Sergeant Jackson, and thanks," Chastain said as he hurried to the tower.

As the Headquarters Platoon finished their last dry run with the supply contingent with an M113 added to fill lane three, the Maintenance Section was at the start points of the three lane range. The M88 recovery vehicle predictably had spare parts stowed in their boxes lashed to its rear. Duffle bags and gear were stowed according to load plan but it looked like what it was, a maintenance vehicle stuffed with everything driven by working mechanics. The maintenance M113 looked slightly better but had tow cables still crossed across its front and secured with muddy straps as if it had just returned from a recovery mission. The maintenance truck still sported a broken window from REFORGER and was towing the trailer carrying the lubrication spare supplies behind it.

In short, the Maintenance Section looked like a bunch of mechanics with their work faces on taking time out to play. The sight of which pleased the Commanding General of USAEUR and Seventh Army immensely. He was about to see a unit training event, not a dog and pony show. It reinforced his practice of showing up unannounced whenever possible, as he did now.

He was a sparely built man, wiry and tough with all of the badges of the hard side of the officer corps. He wore his four stars easily and put soldiers at ease without familiarity. A veteran of both Korea and Vietnam, he had fought as a tanker, an Infantryman and as an advisor to the Vietnamese. This was probably his last command and he was enjoying it to the fullest.

As he made his way to the control tower on foot with his entourage trailing him and his helo landing nearby, he stopped at the de-briefing tent to listen. He heard a very professional Staff Sergeant walking a crew through their engagements. The NCO guided them as they talked through what they had seen, had done both right and wrong and what their fixes would be for the next time. It was a very good snapshot. He looked at the chart and then at a tank bumper number. This was G Troop. He remembered them from RE-FORGER and the great time he had watching the attack into Alsfeld and the schwimmbad caper. He also recalled the troop was the size of a battalion when REFORGER was over.

Arriving at the base of the control tower, his day was truly made. The vehicles getting ready to fire were the M-88, a maintenance M-113 and the maintenance truck. In the on deck position were the Supply truck, the parts truck and another M-113. Having spent some of his life in mechanized units as a Company commander and a Battalion Motor Officer as well as an Executive Officer of a Tank Battalion, he was very surprised. He hoped they were for real, as the troops said.

As he entered the tower, "ATTENTION" was called. He quickly he gave "Carry On." He walked to the front of the tower and accepted a pair of M19 binoculars from the Second Lieutenant. "Sir, we have run the Troop through the machinegun tables twice. This is the Maintenance Section of the Headquarters Platoon. They have had a dry run to verify procedures and are about to engage the course."

"So Lieutenant, you are telling me those HQs guys are about to engage targets from their Chrysler mounts as wing men supporting each other commanded by radio from the M113 by their Motor Daddy, is that right?"

"Yes, General, that is correct."

"Well, turn 'em loose son. I want to see this."

Reading from a script, Lieutenant Chastain intoned "Black 7, this Charlie Six, you have reports of truck mounted infantry moving across and away from your direct front. Continue your movement forward to provide support to the troop, OVER."

"Charlie 92, Black 7, WILCO, OVER."

"Charlie 92, OUT."

The fire commands and crew duties were on another radio net and were being recorded. The group gathered in the tower could hear the Motor Sergeant talking to his driver and everyone heard the maintenance track observer call out the pair of moving trucks, "Goddam, Sergeant JJ, trucks." The Commanding General joined in the laughter but he also cheered loudly when the NCO opened fire with the first rounds low on line with the target in the dirt and with the next burst hitting in its very center. As the target continued to his right, he directed the M-88 to take it under fire. The M-88 handed it off to the maintenance truck. The two right elements set the moving truck target on fire with long, accurate bursts of .50 Armor Piercing Incendiary Tracer (API-T) rounds.

As the section moved down the course, their firing techniques improved as they became very comfortable with fire distribution. The observers in the tower could hear their confidence grow on the radio net and see the results as they fired the heaviest machine gun in the inventory. Setting the targets on fire said it all.

The Commanding General was doing Cheetah Flips of joy. When he began to ask how it was that the Maintenance Crew was being combat trained, Second Lieutenant Chastain said it all, "General, we are all Cavalry Troopers here. At some point they will have to fight. Those caliber .50s are too much combat power to waste." At that everyone in the tower came to attention anticipating the Commanding General's departure. They were mistaken. He waited to see the supply section engage the course. Staff Sergeant Webster, the First Sergeant's Junior Ranger did not disappoint. He engaged every target from his supply truck ring mount and did a superb job. Every engagement report was crisp and sharp. He gave a section fire command and all three vehicles engaged the one set of troop targets whose location permitted the tactic.

The deafening crescendo of three heavy weapons plus the M-60 machineguns from the track closed in on and wreathed the row of fifteen infantry targets in smoke dirt and dust the second they came up. Everyone in the tower roared with laughter as the driver of the M113 fired his M-16 on automatic when the targets came back up. "Guys, do they know I am here?" the Commanding General asked.

"No, Sir, they don't," Captain Dawson replied.

"I want to meet that driver of the M113. They are going to be de-briefed at the tent, aren't they?" he asked.

"Yes, Sir, they are," Dawson replied.

"Walk with me, Captain Dawson, and tell me about the driver," the Commanding General ordered.

"Sir, you have seen him before. He is the kid who fixed the tank outside of Alsfeld, did the back flip into the snow and did the snow angels. He got his ARCOM and his promotion as you directed. He's as country as a cornfield and is the salt of the earth," Dawson stated.

The Commanding General turned to his aide and told him, "Get out some of those impact ARCOMs, that country boy is going to get another one from me and so is the Motor Sergeant and the Supply Sergeant."

"How did you arrive at doing this for the Headquarters guys, Captain Dawson?" the Commanding General asked disarmingly.

"Sir, my First Sergeant is new to Cavalry. He has been a straight tanker before now. Between us we decided to maneuver the Headquarters Platoon as close to the troop as we could get it, at all times. It really paid off during RE-FORGER and is continuing to be a good thing. He trained them up on the caliber .50 and the M-60s teaching them to move by bounds and report correctly. This is his baby and his doing, I just encouraged him. I told him early I wanted the whole troop to be cavalry. The trigger pullers are lost without support and they are in the minority in the Army," Dawson concluded.

As was his way, the Commanding General insisted they wait behind the tent wall next to the entrance until after the debriefing. They then surprised the maintenance guys and the Commanding General gave an impact ARCOM to Sergeant First Class Wintergreen. At Dawson's suggestion, Sergeant First Class Wintergreen waited for the arrival of the Supply contingent and attended the Commanding General as he decorated both Staff Sergeant Webster and Specialist Daggett. Dawson was quite pleased to see Daggett had a very good appearance and that he did not repeat his 360 degree spin of joy for the Commanding General.

"Tell me about the line you put on the tank at Alsfeld," the Commanding General asked conversationally. Daggett looked at Captain Dawson in utter terror.

He did not know Alsfeld. What in tarnation was an Alsfeld?

"Daggett, the Commanding General is asking you about the fuel line replacement you made up that kept the tanks running. Alsfeld is where we were in Germany at the time you did the snow angel," Dawson stated, glad to see the relief on Daggett's face as he thought he was about to pass out cold.

"Yes, Sir. The First Sergeant and us was sure we was going to need lots of fuel lines for REFORGER. The central pump that comes with the tank was giving us trouble. So between us all we had the idea to take the fuel line from the ground hop kit, make it longer with reinforced hydraulic line and hook it

265

to the smoke generator. The central fuel pump is the worst pump and the smoke generator is the best one. I designed it and made forty spares. We used thirty seven with all of the attachments. Some of them are still using the fix. They are running fine, Sir," Daggett said to his new best friend wearing four stars.

"Do you have one you could spare for me, Daggett?" the Commanding General asked politely.

Daggett brought a big smile to the Commanding General when he looked at Dawson first to get his nod before he answered, "Yes, Sir, I'll run over to my track and get it."

Once Daggett had departed to get the line, the Commanding General looked at Dawson and said, "That look was priceless, Captain Dawson. I may command 7th Army but there is no doubt in Daggett's mind you are his Troop commander. That is iron discipline, pure and simple."

"Walk with me to my helicopter. What are your problems, what do you need or want?" the Commanding General asked.

"Sir, I do not need a single thing. You have given us everything we need except PT gear and we are getting along fine without that. We are an ALO 1 unit, we don't want for anything," Dawson said.

"Tell your First Sergeant good job. Good work, Captain Dawson."

The arrival of the maintenance M-113 with Daggett gave him another smile. Daggett handed the fuel line to Sergeant Poston, Dawson's driver. He saluted the Commanding General as he caught his eye, reversed the track and spun it with a neutral steer maneuver to clear the take off pattern. After receiving Dawson's salute the Commanding General moved into and boarded the helo, handing the fuel line to his enlisted aide. He did notice every soldier on the range, even the target detail downrange, saluted when his bird took off.

Turning to his aide he asked, "John, did you see any indicators they were going to fire that course at night?"

His aide, a Special Forces Officer of the Airborne Infantry Tribe, smiled and said, "Sir, they are planning on firing it at night in three vehicle elements, stationary by the support guys. The wing man senses as the muzzle blast of the firing vehicle washes out the shooter's night vision goggles. They also have a plan to use a thermal sight from an M60A3 if they can scrounge one in a jeep up on the Border but that is pretty hard to do at their level."

The Commanding General turned sharply and stared at the aide, "John, where did you get that information?"

"Sir, Staff Sergeant MacClincock is the Shop foreman. He is from my hometown, Livingston, Texas."

The Commanding General gave his aide the 'tell me more' hand signal. "Sir, his Daddy has a garage there with a towing service. The whole family works it. They can fix about anything. There were eight of them. Staff Sergeant Mac came in the Army and stayed over here with his German wife. His Daddy eats breakfast in the Whistle Stop Café across from the courthouse every morning with my Daddy. We used to fish with them when I was a kid. They are very inventive. His Daddy once made a Chris Craft copy. Mr. Mac put a 327 Chevy in it with six two barrel carburetors. It could pull eight skiers on Lake Livingston. Sir, if a MacClincock tells you he can do something, he probably can." The last comment drew a smile from the Commanding General and he appeared to be lost in thought.

Just last week, a group of deep thinkers from the Army scientific community had briefed him on the potential of M60A3 thermal sights for the new family of HUMMV's. A thermal sight package was part of their program. A company sized element of the Army, one of his Cavalry troops, was thinking about doing the same thing. God love soldiers, they were always thinking ahead. They could probably field one in Border Cav in a 113 before it could get out of committee in the bowels of the Army. Those guys had made his day. He was not looking forward to the social event scheduled for that evening and would rather have stayed home and read a WEB Griffin novel but that was part of the price and he had to pay it.

0630 hours
18 Mar 1985
Mess Area Range 23
Wildflecken Training Area Germany

"First Sergeant, the BGS is coming to visit us today. I want you to teach the Commander, the First Sergeant and the Motor Sergeant how to crew the M1 tank and take them down a Tank Table VII run and a simulated Tank Table VIII run. You can use G-66. Make sure they leave with a VHS of both runs NLT 1500 hours. You know those guys, if it ain't done by 1630 they were inefficient," Dawson concluded.

"Damn, Sir. Why did it take so long for us to figure out they were coming to visit?" Martin asked.

"Their schedule opened up and now was the best time for them, First Sergeant. They were mighty good to us and it is our turn to reciprocate. They will be here about 1000 hours. I will get my day run done and have the tank in perfect shape for them. All you should have to do is check it for safety, if we are hitting everything, and we will be. Is there anything you need, First Sergeant?" Dawson said with quiet confidence.

"I need Haskins about 0900 to poop him up on the tank. I can't be teaching the interpreter at the same time I am teaching them. It would make him look bad. He has been here so long some of the German character traits have rubbed off on him," Martin said.

"Yeah, but your German is good enough to do the job," Dawson replied.

"Not for the technical stuff it isn't, Sir. Besides, Jeff is a comfort to them. Having him there makes sure they know we respect them sorta' like a Hallmark greeting card," the First Sergeant said with a smile.

"Jeff, come and join us when you are done with your breakfast. We'll be in Six." Dawson said. As Haskins waved his acknowledgement of the order, Dawson explained to Poston, "Stay here and get the stuff for the softball team straight with the guys. Same deal as with football, 200 PT score exempts the team from daily PT. We will only be about ten minutes or so with Haskins," Dawson said with a smile as Poston had his mouth crammed full of French toast and could only nod and smile. "The boy loves to eat, don't he?" Dawson said to Martin as they walked to the Commander's jeep.

"They will break him of that shit in OCS," Martin said.

The mental picture of Poston in Candidate Brass, with knife and fork cutting his food into tiny pieces almost convulsed Martin. He laughed so hard tears came to his eyes. Then he thought of the special training he had given the Warrant Officer Candidates in his basic training platoon on the weekends many years ago, damn almost ten years had flashed by since then. Did they owe Poston a train up of some sort for OCS?

"What's so funny, Top? I could use a laugh right about now," Dawson said.

"I was just wondering if we should run a little school for Poston before he goes to OCS to prep him for the ordeal," Martin said thoughtfully.

"Hell no, if he makes it, he makes it on his own. He is a tough kid and very adaptable. He has butchered and brought out elk and big horn sheep on pack mules in the Rockies. Those OCS TAC Officers won't faze him," Dawson opined. "When Jeff gets here, tell us both how you are going to train up the BGS, that way you will only have to tell it once," Dawson ordered.

After a few minutes of Dawson preparing the first of his three Al Capone Brazilian cigars of the day, Staff Sergeant Haskins made his appearance at Dawson's center of gravity, his Jeep, saying, "Gentlemen, how can I be of service today?"

Dawson looked up and said, "You want an Al Caponee?" smiling as he mimicked the German pronunciation.

"No, thank you, Sir, I'll smoke my own."

"Jeffery, we are hosting the BGS First Sergeant, Company Commander, and their Motor Sergeant today. I am their primary instructor using G-66. You will help me answer technical questions. The mission is to introduce them to the M1 tank. The Commander means for them to safely engage Tank Table Seven and a simulated Tank Table Eight. We will do this by doing a walk around of the tank, driver's training for each one, a short Tank Crew Proficiency Course, a dry run with laser only down the range and then four wet runs. We will do the night courses using thermal sights and closed hatches. I will walk you through the tank first so you will be familiar with it. You are my back up. As you know, the First Sergeant's Bavarian German

268

confuses me at times. I'll be the loader and will keep the turret action safe. You man the radio with Captain Dawson here in G-66. I run the show but as always, the Captain is the C2 for the troop," Martin concluded.

"First Sergeant, the technical aspects of the M1 are over my head. I don't see how a short familiarization is going to help my technical explanation. I don't want to screw this up," Haskins stated modestly.

Smiling, Martin reassured his modest young Staff Sergeant, "Jeffery, these guys have all served in the Bundesfehr on the M-48 tank. They already know how to tank. What they need to learn are the bells and whistles. Once they see the gun tube jump and the sights align after the laser feeds in the range, they will know what to do. They are the Bundesgrenzschutz, some of toughest and smartest policemen in the world. Except for the Motor Sergeant they have killed men and slept like babies. Combat Stress to them is running out of beer during a soccer match. You just keep me straight, I will worry about them. You worry about me."

"Okay, First Sergeant, since you put it that way. How did you know about them and their tank experience?" Haskins asked conversationally.

"They have told me their life stories over time, at least the short version. I just listened and remembered," Martin said.

Yeah, they were good. They had been together as First Sergeant and Company Commander in the same outfit for 22 years. They communicated more in a glance than he and Dawson did in a twenty page memo. The BGS handled riots and terrorism for Germany. They had requisitioned horses locally and broken up a riot in Munich without breaking a head or firing a shot. The First Sergeant climbed up on the roof of the Schweinfurt American Express on the US military Kaserne with his custom built 9 mm with a silencer and killed a terrorist. He was a 6 foot 6 inch US Army Chapter case who was dumb enough to take a 5 foot 2 inch hostage, a choice that still amused the BGS. The Captain had seen to all of his demands to include a limo. The First Sergeant shot him in the forehead as he turned and threatened the crowd. The Captain had personally apprehended an international terrorist on a Bad Kissingen street using classic judo moves from his days as an Olympian and perfected in the dojo in Frankfurt, in civilian clothes. They could both fire ten of ten shots with a machinegun into a 3x5 card at 50 feet. They were polite, cultured and erudite. They feared no man. They knew who and what they were and made no pretense of being anything else. They were treasures to their friends and terrible enemies to outlaws and assholes. Martin liked and learned from them. He was better in every way for having known them. Their association with the troop was another home run for Captain Dawson as they were not a popular choice for a partnership unit in some quarters. As if Dawson gave a shit what a higher headquarters thought. As he said, "If they did not want me to pick them, they should not have had them on the list. Screw higher. They are with us now and we are sticking by them, all the way." It helped the V Corps Commander agreed with him.

0900 hours

Martin led Staff Sergeant Haskins through a general briefing on the M1 tank. He talked through the exterior, the driver's compartment and moved on to the turret. Martin did a brief check of the tank systems using his Instructors Checklist from the Armor School. As he did so he maintained a running patter of how the parts of the M1 interacted. He was careful to use terms and techniques that related to high powered rifle shooting. This played to Staff Sergeant Haskins' extensive small arms experience and sniper training. By the time they were finished, Staff Sergeant Haskins was much more comfortable and knew he would not look foolish to their sharp eyed German guests. He too highly respected the BGS and supported the principle of partnership units.

1015 hours
18 Mar 1985
Range 23 Wildflecken Training Area

"Guten Morgen Minen Freunden!" Martin greeted his German guests. They smiled at his Berliner pronunciation much as an American Southerner would smile at the accent of foreigner speaking with a New York accent. It marked him as one who had learned their language in college as opposed to a pillow dictionary from a German consort. It endeared him to them. They patiently corrected his speech in the manner of Germans everywhere. They were glad to see Staff Sergeant Haskins as his German was of the local dialect and flowed smoothly. It was music to their ears.

Captain Wertz and First Sergeant Rogos were the best of friends on duty but off duty, they for the most part went their separate ways unless they were needed by the other. Their wives were friendly but the officer-enlisted social gulf was ever present. Their off duty interests diverged as First Sergeant Herbert Rogos remained the vigorous physical specimen of his soccer or foosballer youth, running and walking in Volksmarches and officiating and coaching youth soccer. Captain Wertz's off duty pursuits were more cerebral and he had put on a great deal of weight in his later years. They were both looking forward to today and learning about the M1 tank. They knew First Sergeant Martin was an expert. They were sure he would remain positive and remember they were old tankers. They would not be disappointed.

"Gentlemen, the M1 remains just a tank similar in many ways to the M48 of your youth. Think of it as an upgrade that removes the need for the crew to adjust to conditions that impact on accuracy," Martin began. He then proceeded to give them an introduction to the tank explaining the outside nomenclature of the tank in English depending on Staff Sergeant Haskins to translate. He always spoke directly to the three men, not to Haskins. He was

270

well aware of Captain Wertz's ability to speak fluent English as well as French and Russian. His very manner was positive. He was certain his students would learn rapidly and master the M1 in short order.

For each piece of the M1 that eliminated a part of what he termed to their great amusement, 'steam gunnery', from their days on the M48, they were able to relate their experience and understand the M1. As they progressed to the crew stations, Captain Wertz assumed the Tank Commander position while the First Sergeant became the gunner and the Motor Sergeant observed. As Martin had predicted, they were apt pupils and quickly absorbed the technical nuances of the M1. As each took their turn driving the tank it was clear they were true policemen. They were willing to drive the tank wide open but only in the correct conditions. The hardest part of the driving experience came as they had to extricate Captain Wertz' huge bulk from the driver's hatch. He was clearly embarrassed his bulk presented a problem but they got past it with a laugh.

After a dry run, they loaded weapons and engaged the course. Martin loaded the main gun, serviced the coaxial machinegun and coached them while acting as a sort of super safety officer from inside the tank. Everyone in the troop not actively engaged watched them on their course run. They did not miss a single target. They improved their time and technique on each engagement. By the end of the modified Tank Table VII they had adopted abbreviated fire commands in the manner of advanced and expert crews. Martin smiled as he heard "LOS" instead of "FIRE" as well as other modifications in German.

After their "Qualification Run" they were de-briefed using a video tape complete with an audio track of their run down range. They were also presented with certificates in Army picture frames that commemorated their qualification and their assimilation as members of G Troop with Certificates of Achievement. They also received a copy of their qualification video. It was a very successful day of partnership and friendship. They were able to make their departure time and return to their Kaserne outside of Schweinfurt. Staff Sergeant Masterson obeyed but did not understand First Sergeant's order to dub an extra copy of their video of the BGS run for Captain Dawson's partnership file.

As the BGS departed, Staff Sergeant Haskins asked the First Sergeant, "How did you know how well it would go in such detail, First Sergeant?"

"I didn't know Jeffery. I just adopted a positive outlook. Most of our thought process is self-fulfilling. If we think something is going to be bad, it usually is. There was too much good going for this effort for it to turn out badly. I will tell you this. I am glad those guys are on our side. If they can learn the M1 fast enough to go to abbreviated fire commands and fire Distinguished on Tank Table VIII with two hours instruction, we do not want to fight them again if we can avoid it. They will be damn hard to kill if they can find enough folks like those three. Never believe those guys who say the German military mind set cannot adapt to a changing environment - they are full of shit. They are chameleons who grasp technical details in a flash. Granted, these guys are at the top of the food chain for Germans but they are so good it is scary," Martin concluded to a silent and thoughtful group of Gators.

The BGS contingent showed their video tape to their chain of command. The BGS Commandant showed his opposite number the German Army Chief of Staff the video of "his men" qualifying an M1 tank. The head of the BGS knew the German Army had yet to even sniff an M1. The protests of the Army guy echoed through the US Army Europe Chain of Command but came to an abrupt halt at V Corps Headquarters. The Regimental Commanding Officer had beaten everyone to the draw by sending a report and a copy of the tape to both Corps and USAREUR. Forearmed, the Corps Commander told all comers to back off. G Troop had done exactly what he wanted them to do, establish a firm partnership with the BGS. Other Armor units should follow their example with their German Army Armor counterparts. The USAREUR Commander agreed and he secretly hoped his US crews would shoot as well as the BGS.

G Troop was up to its neck in Border Tour and tactical training for the platoons. It was time for Pony Fights and for Stallion Stakes. In the former, Scout platoons went at each other force on force in the Border rights maneuver area. The tank platoons also conducted Pony fights and all elements served as Opposition forces against the other elements of the Squadron who came to the Border to train. Again, Captain Dawson had the troop in the field for an extended period of time. The training was invaluable in that Platoons got to fight against units led by their Captains. Most of the time, G Troop Platoons held their own and did very well. The banditos of Staff Sergeant Ramos platoon defeated all comers in every phase of operations. Ramos' force soon taught the maxim of "be prepared to defend yourself at all times" in the combat zone. They struck without warning and in unconventional ways, defeating and demoralizing those who thought themselves to be superior tacticians. If the exercise started at 0001, it was best to be on guard from 2330 forward and if in command, to not let one's jeep trail one's tank thus giving away a prospective next move.

It was during this Border Tour the great Sergeant First Class Collie got his first lesson in true First Sergeant leadership. Collie had heard through the grapevine the Scouts and the fill in guys, the mechanics, clerks and truck drivers who were taking the tankers places on the Border while they trained for tank gunnery under the aegis of Captain Dawson in the rear, were going to conduct a horse patrol. Collie was a rodeo rider, bronc buster and a horseman of some reputation back in his native Texas. He wanted to go on the Horse Patrol and did not care a damn what it would cost him to do it. Collie was convinced not only were the tankers the chosen ones of the Army, there were First Sergeant Martin's favorites and he would do anything for them and by inference, Sergeant First Class Collie.

As was his wont, Collie just went at his task head on as he knew the First Sergeant would be in his office.

"Say, First Sergeant, good morning," Collie greeted.

"Good morning, Collie. What can I do for you this morning?" First Sergeant Martin asked pleasantly as Collie was one of the very best NCOs he had ever known.

"Well, First Sergeant, I want to take a couple of my guys who are great riders on the Border Horse Patrol. How is that working out? Do you have it all set up?" Collie asked innocently.

Collie knew full well all of the details of the Horse patrol. He knew the Scouts had gone to Martin to ask him as the Troop Commander's eyes and ears at the Border if they could conduct a Horse Patrol and would he help them set it up. Much to their surprise, Martin agreed but added the caveats and provisions of a true hard-ass First Sergeant. There would be no publicity from the German newspapers or the Regiment; every man had to be a rider with experience; all money had to be paid down front; the ride would be twenty kilometers or less with a halfway switchover for riders; all attention and care possible would be given to the mounts; it must be a real patrol with secure radios, weapons, live ammunition, back up ammunition; water points for the horses must be on the map and known to have water; reports would be submitted to Regiment and to Corps as US Horse Patrol just as they would have been sent as US Jeep or US Foot; communications would be established with the German wrangler and the location of the nearest veterinarian capable of treating a horse would be known. First Sergeant Martin bought an Inland Marine Insurance Policy that covered the horse and liability from a German Insurance Agent who shopped the re-insurance to Lloyds of London.

The guy did not miss a trick, Collie mused to himself. Martin got all of his requested conditions fulfilled with the exception of one and the ride was on. The one condition not fulfilled was the request for period uniforms to be drawn from the Cavalry Museum. It was not honored as there was not enough time to notify the Russians, the Brits and the French to get their approval for a uniform change.

Martin responded to Sergeant First Class Collie saying, "Collie, I would love to honor your request but I cannot and I will not. You and I both know the tankers 'hooraahed' the hell out of the scouts and the support guys about getting over and not having to go to the Border. You guys also teased them terribly about taking care of their wives and girlfriends during the time off you were going to have from your training back here in the rear. This deal is all set up, paid for and organized. You guys wanted to be special and you are.

You are training for tank gunnery and riding a $3 million dollar steed so enjoy it," Martin said with a wry smile.

Collie tried for another ten minutes to sway his First Sergeant with every argument in his arsenal but it was to no avail. However, being the good sport that he was, Collie finally said, "Damn, Top, I thought I could convince you to take care of your tankers in this instance but I see I was wrong. Have a nice ride," he commented as he put out his hand for a vigorous handshake with his First Sergeant.

Sometime later while in his jeep, Martin followed the horse patrol led by his new Second Lieutenant. The thought crossed his mind that he would gladly hand over to Collie or anyone else the whole damn Border Horse Patrol exercise for a quarter. None of the senior officers he had briefed and extended an invitation to had shown up to observe despite the fact that all of them had sworn they would be present. As usual, that meant his ass was ODF or 'Out Der Flappin'. Horses could make the smartest of men look very stupid when they decided to act like horses and do dumb shit. The Lieutenant was a great rider and a college rodeo guy who could really handle a horse. Malcolm Rodney, or Rod the Wad as he was known to the troops, had the look of a comer, and was thought to be a future four star hiding in a Second Lieutenant's body. He had it all, looks, charm, intellect, private money, true interest and concern for soldiers and just enough modesty to avoid being considered a jerk.

About a mile before the turn around point, Second Lieutenant Rodney called a halt to the patrol and waved the First Sergeant forward. As Martin's jeep arrived, he got out and spoke to the Patrol Leader, "What's up, Ell Tee?"

The answer surprised Martin, "Top, my ass is killing me. This little mare is a fine horse but I have not ridden in 'forty for-evers' and I am not going to be able to walk if stay on her much longer. Can you ride her for me?" Rodney asked.

Martin began to smell a rat in the young officer's pleas when the great Staff Sergeant Webster and two other photography nuts showed up at the position with their cameras and lenses hanging on them like Associated Press guys in combat. As Martin got acquainted with the horse, he adjusted the stirrups, tightened the cinch and mounted. The plot thickened as he was then urged to wear the Lieutenant's Cavalry Stetson as Martin did not yet own one.

Immediately on donning the Stetson, the cameras started to whir from both the patrol and from the self-styled historians led by Webster. Martin's mount was startled by the cameras and reacted in a typical 'startled' horse fashion. As Martin coaxed the mare to back up in order to put some distance between them and the cameras, his mount suddenly went into her Trigger imitation by rearing onto her back legs and pawing the air with her front hooves. Martin was a far better rider than any of his soldiers knew. He simply patted her neck, brought his weight forward, and turned her head to the left with proper neck reining technique. He then gave the hand signal for 'move out and follow me' to the patrol and started out at the trot. The patrol followed in high spirits as their First Sergeant once again demonstrated that he was always one step ahead of the game.

The truth however was somewhere in between. Martin was always responsible for the Horse Patrol. He knew the squadron commander had only agreed to Captain Dawson's training arrangement because he knew the First Sergeant was backing up the Executive Officer at the Border. He was now in the exact position he did not want to be in, leading the Horse Patrol. *Once more, he found himself thinking, "All I sought was peace and beauty and all I found was toil and duty". Well shit, I'm here in the Blackhorse Regiment, mounted on a Blackhorse, leading wonderful young guys on the live East/West German Border with all of us armed to the teeth. I'll be damned if I am not going to enjoy myself for an hour or so.*

As he slowed the Patrol to a walk, Martin raised his binoculars and glassed the half way point. He could see the outline of the supply truck and knew it was on time and at the exact spot spelled out in the Operations Order for the changeover of riders. By splitting the ride, the tyro cavalrymen spared their butts and split the cost of the rental of the horses into manageable parts. He smiled and said to the trusty Specialist Daggett, "Well, Daggett, that Lieutenant is not going to flim-flam me into doing the whole damn ride."

"First Sergeant, what are all those guys in Russian uniforms doing over there?" Daggett said pointing toward East Germany. "Damn, First Sergeant, that looks like a weapon they are carrying!" Daggett added.

"Men, fall in line formation here with your mounts," Martin said indicating the edge of the farm road. As they lined up with their horses, Martin turned to face them.

"The Russians are setting up a Television Camera. The other guys are using personal cameras with the one guy using a telephoto lens. The TV camera looks like a weapon because of Russian Technology and because they build their shit tough to withstand field service. Unlike our Army, they know Soldiers can ruin a ball bearing with a q-tip without supervision. We are in no danger from those guys. We drew their Public Affairs Officer since we did not allow ours to even know we were doing this Horse Patrol. This is big shit for them and they are apparently going to make the most of it. Daggett, do they look like they are about set up?" Martin asked.

"Yes First Sergeant, they are shooting tape with that big-assed camera. The little fart is doing commentary," Daggett said.

As Martin and the Patrol arrived at the changeover point, an MI-26 Hind helicopter appeared on the scene. Everybody on the helo had a camera and was engaged in taking pictures of the Horse Patrol. The door gunner from the Hind was holding up a sign that said, "Wait, Film". He was obviously changing rolls and did not want the action to stop or for the patrol to leave before he got a shot. As the Hind taxied across the fence to stop just within East

German Airspace, Martin figured it out. The bastards wanted to play. There was no brass present, not theirs, not ours, just Soldiers. However, Martin was wary. He was not going to get into any form of informal truce with these assholes nor was he going to encourage his soldiers to recreate some Civil War Reb and Yank frontline coffee and cigar exchange. He looked down from his black horse and told the troops, "Stay here. I'm going to go give these guys what they want and we are going to leave. Get your gear adjusted, get mounted and do a commo check with Border Ops and my jeep. Whatever happens, stay here," Martin said as he took out his pistol and unloaded it slipping the round he had chambered into his pocket and the magazine into his ammunition pouch.

Knowing his weapon now to be clear, Martin rode his black mare a short distance away from the assembled group toward the Hind. Almost on cue, the Hind gunner swiveled the turret toward Martin. As the gun moved, Martin backed up the mare and she did her Trigger imitation to the accompaniment of twenty or so 35 mm cameras on auto advance on both sides of the Border and in the Hind. He then put his trusty steed into a full gallop belly down across the wheat field directly at the Hind while pointing his pistol at the helo. He was followed by Daggett with the guidon, an act that was shortly to truly surprise Martin.

The Russians and East Germans loved the scene and applauded wildly, shouting their approval with the word 'Bravo' as if it was a curtain call at the local opera house. Martin continued his charge up to the edge of the West German border sliding his mount to a stop in a cloud of dust with a defiant look at his foes in the Hind. He holstered his pistol in the shoulder holster, snapped the retainer and only then did he notice Daggett behind him with the guidon. Looking at the hovering Hind backing up across the East German Border he asked, "Daggett, what the hell are you doing here?"

"Why, First Sergeant, all Yankee Cavalry has to have is a guidon to make the charge behind the Commander, don't they?" Daggett asked.

"So, Daggett, you were giving me what I needed not what I asked for, is that it?" Martin asked.

"Well, First Sergeant, you do it all the time for us, I just had to it for you!" Daggett said.

"Thanks, Daggett. You did not know it but those guys were not about to shoot us with that Hind. You are going to amount to something in this Army, Daggett. Let's get back to the Patrol," Martin said, turning his mount to see the patrol formed and ready to ride.

As he waved his jeep forward, he leaned down and told Lieutenant Rodney, "I will take it back to checkpoint 132, then you got it. Here, take your Stetson before I start sweating into it. You guys have had your fun now or have you?" Martin asked.

"Damn, First Sergeant, I have never had so much fun wearing fatigues this side of Ranger School," Lieutenant Rodney answered with a big smile.

Martin was very saddle sore and weary at the end of his short ride. He had ridden for many miles as a youngster but had not ridden for many years. He was damn glad to change places with the young officer and to get all of the animals and troopers safely back to the border camp. Without being told, all of the riders turned to and cared for the horses. The German wrangler did not want them washed at the camp wash rack but was gratified to see them rubbed down and to find them in such good condition. It had been one of Martin's longest days in the Army and although he never used the word stress, he knew it had been a very stressful experience but one he would not trade for anything. Just seeing the scouts and mechanics ride horses on the Border was worth all of the angst.

The preparations for the Inspector General Re-Inspection continued apace during the period. The unit also prepared for annual tank gunnery, set up a 7 day trip to Spain and began to use the newly operational Conduct of Fire Trainer for the M1. There were few idle hands anywhere in the Squadron.

CHAPTER 10 - HARD REALITY

A dream is a state of mind with hope as its primary method and depends on luck to succeed. A plan is a series of assumptions buttressed by facts requiring 90% perspiration and 10% inspiration to carry it out. Army Lore-Timeless

0530 hours
08 Apr 1985
G Troop. 2/11 ACR
Bad Kissingen, West Germany

Staff Sergeant Haskins planned an early start inspecting his scouts' wall lockers and field gear CTA-50 901 and thus arrived at the troop an hour before PT was to start. Seeing the light on in the First Sergeant's office, he decided to give the troops a few minutes more and visit with the First Sergeant. He had a lot on his mind.

He knocked on the doorframe of the First Sergeant's office. The First Sergeant was working on his wall locker. He was the only First Sergeant with an office wall locker subject to inspection in the Regiment. Haskins smiled as the subtle nature of the instruction in leadership that he and the rest of the soldiers got by seeing an E-8 prepare a wall locker for inspection. Simply, when First Sergeant Martin was working on his wall locker the troops knew they were next and if they had any questions about the display or the standard to be attained, they could look at his locker for their answers. When he was done, the troops knew they were next. He was just finishing replacing his collar brass on his uniform. He had polished it using a modified tent pole as he had for 17 years. The method was almost ancient. It reminded Haskins of a pre-flint or match stick era woodsman or a Boy Scout, starting a fire with a spindle stick and dry shavings.

"Come in, Jeffery. Stewing over Drill Sergeant Duty are we this fine morning?" the First Sergeant said with a smile.

"You are psychic, First Sergeant. I am worried about more than that," Haskins confessed.

"Of course you are, Jeffery. You have been living in a protected environment here in Germany. You have a little petite German girl for a wife that adores you and a handsome son. You speak the language, have lots of German friends your age, are an accomplished leader and a great scout, have a nice hot rod BMW, your wife has her beauty shop, a great income, your In-laws love you and life is good."

"Then some asshole in DA you have never met, does the old round peg in the round hole routine and voila', you are a Drill Sergeant Candidate. You are being forced to go to a school you do not want to attend and qualify for a job you have avoided. One in which you must either succeed or be chaptered out

278

in disgrace. You are wondering why the hell don't they just leave you alone. You want to stay a Staff Sergeant and retire over here and never go back if they will let you. How am I doing, Jeffery?" Martin said pausing for a response.

"You got it pretty well pegged out, First Sergeant. Did you miss anything?" Haskins said balefully.

Martin lit a cigarette and with his Pepsi took a seat on the settee opposite Haskins rather than behind his desk. "I guess I did forget to mention the esteemed Haskins family now being forced to accept a beautifully coifed, dressed, and well mannered European in the latest fashion. You think that the belching and farting that goes on near Crab Orchard, West By God Virginia will drive her nuts and she will miss home so bad she will make you miserable," Martin said smiling as Haskin's head drooped lower and lower as he talked.

"There are several things you need to realize, Jeffery. One, you will get more out of being a Drill Sergeant (DS) than you ever thought possible. Two, it is a two year tour of duty, not three. Three, Lufthansa and other airlines run both ways across the Atlantic. Four, anyone who does not love your wife is stupid. Your Momma and your Daddy are going to love her like one of your sisters. I will bet that black haired boy looks just like your Daddy. You have never failed any school you ever went to. You never will. DS is almost civilized now-there is no live in requirement, the course is by modules and there are only two PT tests, one at the start and one at the end. You will be a better technically qualified DS than I was in my day and you will be a success."

"DS verifies your potential for Sergeant First Class. It is just you and those Joes. What they become, or fail to become, is on you. There is no one to turn to for help, most of the time. Success as a DS gives you immense self-confidence. You learn more about people, basic soldiering and yourself than you can imagine. It is one of the hardest and most rewarding jobs. When you do it right, you lose yourself in the purity of the work. Ambition, future promotion, peer approval and all of that petty shit fades away in the intensity of the task."

"Look around, Jeffery. How many former Drill Sergeants are there in the Squadron? What are their ranks and what type of leaders are they? There are 1,000 men here, nearly 350 of them NCOs. Five are former Drill Sergeants. They are all Sergeant First Class or First Sergeants. DS duty makes the impossible look easy in a unit. It is a discriminator for the promotion boards all the way to Sergeant Major. If it was not tough duty it would not mean a damn thing. You'll do fine. Remember 98% of what man worries about never damn happens," Martin said smiling.

"Thanks, Top," Haskins said with a rueful smile.

"You know once you get there, you may be the only one in the family that wants a quick return to Germany. Your wife may be able to find a way to do

279

hair in Radcliff or on Knox and not want to come back to Germany except to visit. Do not get corrupted by the long cycle of One Station Training if you get stuck in 1ST Brigade. Try your best to get to the 4th Brigade for pure basic training. I'll give you some names to help you along at Mother Knox. They are always glad to help a hard ass. It is easy to get back to a Cavalry Regiment in Germany - volunteer. No one in their right mind wants to be here. Now move out, I've got shit to do," Martin said.

1030 hours
22 Apr 1985
G Troop Formation Area
Bad Kissingen, West Germany

The Regimental IG Team had finished their in depth look at G Troop. They had combed every nook and cranny of the buildings, records, wall lockers and the Soldiers for two days. The team sampled the Annual Physical Training Test, NBC Training, Rifle and Pistol Marksmanship, all vehicles and all weapons. While the results were not perfect, they were good and it appeared the troop would pass on this second go around. Martin got considerably more than the original allotted 90 days to fix the unit. The performance of the unit at the Border, on REFORGER and at off season gunnery was very positive. The last hurdle was underway, the Regimental Commander's In Ranks Inspection. Until the Regimental Commanding Officer stopped to inspect PFC Roosevelt Washington, a great looking figure of a man with a chest full of ribbons, it was mostly positive.

The Regimental Command Sergeant Major did not like PFC Washington, Washington was trouble. He did not like trouble makers, especially black trouble makers. The Regimental Command Sergeant Major was despised by half of the young black soldiers as a "Super Nigger" and the other half because he was a "Bible Thumper." Right this moment, the "Preacher" had Washington right where he wanted him, in front of the Regimental Commanding Officer. He also had First Sergeant Martin where he wanted him, center stage. He did not miss his chance to try to get rid of a troublemaker.

"First Sergeant Martin, why is this man still in the Army and still in my Regiment?" the Regimental Command Sergeant Major asked as his boss was inspecting Washington's gleaming M-16 rifle. The piece was perfect in every respect. The Regimental Commanding Officer had rarely seen weapons as clean as what he was seeing in G Troop this morning. First Sergeant Martin did not hurry his answer. He waited for the Regimental Commanding Officer, who Martin knew was happy, to look up at him. The Regimental Commanding Officer did so with a shy smile.

When he had his eye and thus his attention Martin answered the question. "Command Sergeant Major, I will discharge Washington when the Regimen-

280

tal Commanding Officer stops sending me across the Border to steal stuff from the East Germans. He is going to compete on the Boselager Team Competition as one of the best scouts in Europe. If we are going to use Washington to do our bidding, all of us, then I will keep him. Washington received Jesus as his Lord and Savior as a young man and has strayed from his Christian upbringing. He has begun Bible Study with PVT Jeans and is on the path to righteousness. I have hope for him, Sergeant Major," Martin replied with a straight face.

The Regimental Command Sergeant Major looked to his Christian rat, PVT Jeans to see him nod thus confirming the First Sergeant's assertion. The Regimental Commanding Officer saw the rat's head bob and nearly laughed out loud but managed to hold the serious demeanor he had assumed for the inspection. There was no bigger drunk or more serious cock hound in the Regiment than Smokin' Joe the RCO. He loved it when an ornery First Sergeant got over on his Regimental Command Sergeant Major.

"Fine looking weapon, soldier. Good luck at Boselager," Smokin' Joe was smiling broadly as the weapon was snatched out of his hand on the exchange by the super soldier and former Marine, Washington. The wild look in Washington's eye took the now almost elderly Regimental Commanding Officer back to 'Nam and he was a young Troop Commander again with all of his hair and his youth. Washington looked just like one of the jailbirds Smokin' Joe had on his track in 'Nam as a young Captain and Major.

As he looked at Washington he could again clearly see the three soldiers from his crew across the time and distance back to Vietnam. Those bastards were so damn mean it was a toss up between them and the VC as to who would kill the Officers of the Blackhorse Cavalry. Old PSG Higgison once briefed them they would sweep through what was briefed as a NVA R & R center and kill the officers. PFC Smith, a jailbird, now dead, killed outside of Swan Loc by an RPG and a dead ringer for Washington asked, "Theirs or ours?" Higgison gave him the classic answer from the Dirty Dozen movie, "We'll start with theirs, Smith," and added, "They be the ones shooting back at your dumb dusty asses." God, that Higgison was a MAN and no damn Bible Thumper!

It was obvious to the Regimental Commanding Officer that these troops he was looking at with his eagles shining from his epaulets were well schooled. In every respect save combat experience, they were finer raw material than the soldiers of his G Troop he had commanded in Vietnam long ago. They were crisp and sharp executing the exchange of weapons with an officer or answering questions. To a man, they were well turned out and self assured. They would mature and conduct themselves well in war. There was no point in belaboring the Inspection. The Regimental Commanding Officer asked kindly, "Any more questions, Sergeant Major?"

281

The Inspecting party then moved through the rest of the unit without halting except in several cases where the Regimental Commanding Officer stopped to talk to a favorite officer or senior NCO with whom he had served. Say what you will about the man's personal life, he never forgot a friend or forgave an enemy. Martin was surprised he was ending the inspection.

"Gather round, men," the Regimental Commanding Officer directed. "When I sent First Sergeant Martin here and filled up this troop with good officers and NCOs I expected it to rebound. It has met my expectations and more. You have all done well. You are only as good as your last failure in the Army. We all know that one 'aw shit' wipes out all of the 'attaboys'. You now have a good reputation. That is a bigger burden than a failing unit carries. You are now expected to do well because you have proven what you can do when led and motivated. Captain Dawson, take charge of your unit and give them the rest of the day off. Give them a four day weekend when it fits your schedule."

"FALL IN," Dawson commanded. He then waited until the Squadron Commander, Regimental Commanding Officer and Regimental Command Sergeant Major had moved away and directed, "First Sergeant, POST." As they exchanged salutes, he told him, "Secure the weapons and all of the gear and turn them loose. Tell them we will look at the four day weekend and to stand by. It is my option when we take it. He surprised me with that. He was impressed."

As he waited for his commander to move out of the area of formation, Martin noticed the junior officers remained. That was not always a bad thing and he let it slide. He did not want to turn them into super platoon guides and become responsible for their total development. That was a job for the Troop Commander.

"STAND AT, EASE."

"Men, the Commander is going to work the schedule for the four day weekend. Good job men. I know you did a good job because I am still here."

"TROOP, ATTENTION. PLATOON SERGEANTS TAKE CHARGE OF YOUR PLATOONS."

He was glad to see the armorer come to get his .45. He cleared the pistol and handed it to the young PFC with the slide locked to the rear saying, "Thanks Allison. Good job in the Arms Room. Follow up on those .50 barrels. You're still the fast draw king of G Troop."

PFC Allison smiled. He was the only man in the Troop that could out-draw the First Sergeant with a shoulder holster on dry fire. However, he could not outshoot him on the pistol range, yet. Like his Dad, the First Sergeant was coaching them, but to fight not play baseball. The challenges, contests, official and unofficial games with the weapons made them better. The weak hand shooting and one-handed reloading was only taught in G Troop. The fun of the games and the contests trained them in the best possible way. He and several other troopers were scheming to best the First Sergeant on the AK-47 on the Grafenwohr trip. So far he waxed their butts at 500 yards with the Russian rifle and he was murderous at shorter ranges. Allison had not been in favor of Martin's policy of sending one soldier from each Platoon to the Armorer's Course. He now knew he had been wrong. It was a big help. They acted as his assistants and he became the head weapons guru. The improvement in maintenance and cleanliness was like night and day.

"First Sergeant, you have a phone call from some woman from the Comptroller's office. She said she would wait," the CQ runner reported.

"Thanks, Specialist Festerman. Do you have your greens ready for the Soldier of the Quarter Board?" Martin asked.

"Yes, First Sergeant, Sergeant First Class Wintergreen inspected them yesterday," Hagen replied.

"Okay Festus, keep studying," Martin said using his nickname after the character on Gunsmoke.

Answering the phone, "First Sergeant Martin here, how can I help you ma'am?"

A sexy German voice purred back at him over the wire, "I am the Comptroller today but who knows what disguise I will assume later," Marty said mischievously. "Can we go to Coburg tonight sweetheart? My friend Irmegard from Hollywood wants us to have dinner with her and drinks afterwards at her aunt's house. I don't want to drive there by myself with these awful German drivers. I want to go the back roads and you know them all."

"I will go anywhere and do anything you want Marty. I can get away by three and we should be there by five, have dinner, depart at 7 pm and be home in time to play if you are not too tired from the trip."

Marty laughed a deep throaty life, "I am never too tired for my First Sergeant."

1500 hours
22 April 1985
Bad Kissingen

Marty and Martin drove away in her small German car bound for Coburg via the Border. They drove and talked about their lives up to now and discussed their own future. Irmegard was an extra who spent her time at "cattle calls" waiting to be picked or at home waiting on her agent to call her to work in a movie. While she waited to be called, she sipped Red Wine in her condo. If there was no call by afternoon, she was usually slightly smashed. She had been a very attractive woman. According to Marty, she got some work and even some roles. It was enough money for her to live well in Hollywood. Marty told him during the trip to Coburg she would dominate the conversation and talk about everyone from their former circle in America. Martin was always willing to learn from the folks he met and he looked forward to meeting a Hollywood extra.

Irmegard did not disappoint. She hugged them both and gave kisses with pursed lips at the side of one's head facing away and never touching, pure Hollywood kisses. Her makeup and clothes were perfect. She appeared to be a fifty five year old Valley teenager transported by a time machine to Coburg. Her tight jeans and open midriff top, big hair and extensive jewelry probably wowed the locals she had gone to school with years before.

God save me from any desire to be an old fool trying to look young forever. It is a pitiful sight was Martin's first thought when he saw the aging wanna be.

After a very nice dinner at a corner restaurant, the three of them walked back to Irmegard's aunt's home on one of the main streets of Coburg. The house was a magnificent structure and was hundreds of years old. The wood was dark, the banisters and rails were baroque and summoned up visions of Wuthering Heights. Tante Elsa, Irmegard's eighty year old aunt, was a delightful lady. She had declined their dinner invitation. She remained devoted to her diet of a left over two minute soft boiled egg, cold sausage, thick German bread, butter and strong coffee for her supper. She and her husband had been farmers with the stable below the house in a basement and large fields outside of town. She had made tea for Martin and coffee for Irma, Marty and herself with a sliced Marzipan with a hard icing of chocolate over a fruity yellow cake. Martin was having a great time.

He noticed a large crack in the wall next to the street and asked Tante Elsa what had happened to cause it. She told him, "Soldiers lost control of an artillery piece and it struck the house."

"Marty, help me out here as I explain to Tante Elsa what her rights are." Martin then proceeded to tell Tante Elsa in less than perfect German that 2d ACR could, and would, pay for the damages. They had special funds to do so. If she would agree, he would call the Duty Officer right now and they would send someone to assess damages to pay for the repairs.

Once Marty embellished his remarks, Tante Ilsa patted Martin on the knee and said, "Not today's soldiers, Napoleon's soldiers."

Getting over his embarrassment, a somewhat less than ultra confident First Sergeant learned a valuable lesson about living history. In the German way, they continued to add floors to the original house for succeeding generations as children married and had families. They could only add on in the vertical plane as land was too costly to do anything else. The three ladies all had a good laugh once it was clear Martin's good nature let him laugh with them. Tante Elsa got out the family photo albums and took Martin down memory lane while Elsa and Irma talked about Hollywood and their circle of friends. She had relatives who served in everything from U-Boats to the Hitler Youth, most of whom did not survive WW II or died in the Russian POW camps.

Almost too soon, it was time to call it a night and say good bye. Marty and her First Sergeant made their way back to Bad Kissingen and to her condo in the country. There was no PT scheduled for the next morning and first formation was at 1000 hours. That gave them a restful and quiet night as the only residents of the building and a wonderful German breakfast of bacon, eggs, and rolls.

0800 hours
23 April 1985
Bad Kissingen

Marty dropped Martin off about two blocks from the Kaserne at 0800. He was glad there was no PT. Marty had worn him out. She was truly a handful.

The Troop was still in the afterglow of the IG. Martin was surprised to see Captain Dawson in his office so early.

"Hey, come on in, First Sergeant. Sit down," Dawson directed. "Talked to my wife last night. She is going to come back after Grafenwohr. There is a chance I am going to change command early to give the new guy a chance to do the Bradley Transition. Smokin' Joe is giving me another command at HHD Regiment if I leave early. What do you think, First Sergeant?" Dawson asked.

"I am happy for you. Fulda is nicer than BK. A second command wires you up for Major. You are very fortunate to get one. I am surprised the Regiment is thinking that far ahead to tell you the truth, Sir," Martin said.

"What are you going to do, Top?" Dawson asked.

"I am not wild about remaining here with a new guy. He will be someone who is below the zone and smart as hell from the staff, probably a First Lieutenant. This is my third Company with nearly three years as a First Sergeant, all of it in balls to wall outfits. Maybe something good will happen out of it Captain," Martin said pensively.

"You realize the TO&E is changing with a Staff Sergeant Major position being added to all of the Cavalry Squadrons and Armor Battalions don't you, First Sergeant?" Dawson said quietly, adding, "You are already in the Sergeants Major Academy and on track to graduate in June of 86. Who would be better in the job than you?"

"Did you just sandbag me, Captain Dawson?" Martin asked with a smile.

"Not really, First Sergeant. The Squadron S3 has been understaffed since I have been here. The Command Sergeant Major and the Operations Sergeant could screw up a wet dream with the Border Schedule. With all we have going on, the Squadron Commander is going to need an operator that can plan and execute. It would set you up for the E9 board to have worked as a Sergeant Major before you are eligible. Think about it and talk to the Earth Pig after

285

Tank Gunnery. No need to commit to anything now. This heads up just gives you time to think through your options," Dawson concluded.

Martin thought, *He is right. It is something to think about. No job is harder than that of the Operations Sergeant in any combat arms outfit. The addition of an E9 slot in every Armor Battalion/Cavalry Squadron S3 grade expands the enlisted personnel pyramid for the Armor Force. I hate to give up being a First Sergeant for staff duty again. Better take a fresh look at it after Grafenwohr. The issues will stand out by then.*

1300 hours
18 May 1985
Rod & Gun Club Parking Lot
Grafenwohr Training Kaserne
W. Germany

"Gator 7, this Eaglehorse 5, your push (radio frequency) OVER."

"Why the hell is the Squadron Executive Officer calling me on the radio? My loose ends are tied up tight and the Troop Cdr told me to get lost from the range."

"Eaglehorse 5, this is Gator 7, OVER."

"7, this is 5, what is your fix, OVER."

"5, I'm at the Rod & Gun Club Parking Lot waiting for the Guest of Honor to show up for the Command Sergeant Major luncheon, OVER."

"7, these tanks are not hitting anything even though their bore sight and confirmation went well. The TPT is flying high. I have brass coming. Can you fix it, now, OVER?"

"5, this is 7, Roger, Break, Gold 44, this is Gator 7, SITREP, OVER."

"Uhhhh7, this is Gold 44. I am on range 275 firing Tank Table VI. Rounds are all high and right of target. No one here can fix it. It has 5 and the rest us treed, OVER."

"Roger Gold 44, we are going to zero your victor with HEAT. Follow the same procedure for SABOT once I talk you through it, how copy, OVER.

"7, Gold 44 standing by.

"Roger 44. Is Code Name Collie there?"

"Standing right beside my hatch. He can hear you."

"He needs to go to his tank and sense where your rounds hit. Have him draw the target with chalk on his loaders sponson box top. He will watch you fire three rounds and mark them on his sponson box lid. You will then using the zero procedure, refer your Gunner's Primary Sight to the center of that shot group and fire one more round for confirmation. How copy, OVER?"

"This is Gold 44, Roger and he understands what to do, break, I am still going to overshoot the target, OVER."

"Gold 44, not anymore you won't. Divide the target in thirds. Use a clean target. You will be firing at the lower third quadrant. Put the GPS on the inside of the lower left corner. Use the same aim point for all three rounds - Open the TM to the section on zeroing and follow along as we do it, OVER."

"7, Gold 44, that will be hard to do, we never got the change to the manual, OVER."

"Gold 44, it does not matter, just do what I tell you when I tell you. I'll get you going and be there personally in about 90 minutes. Duplicate what I do with the remainder of the Troop, OVER"

"Gator 7, Gold 44, Roger."

Martin then talked his 4th Platoon Sergeant through the zeroing procedure from memory.

He used Sergeant First Class Collie's tank to observe the hits. As he knew would happen, adjusting the firing tank's point of aim to the lowest portion of the target would get them "on the paper" and provide a point of reference. Up to this point, the crew aimed at the center of the target and missed. In less than ten minutes, First Sergeant Martin had the tank zeroed for High Explosive Anti-Tank or HEAT. Following the same procedures, it was then zeroed for Armor Piercing or SABOT. Sergeant First Class Victor Jackson then began hitting all of his targets dead center. This occurred just as the VIPs were arriving on the range. The Dog & Pony demonstration went off without a hitch. Martin went to his luncheon and got the latest news on Department of the Army promotion boards, failures from the NCO Academy and other information the Command Sergeant Majors could have put in a newsletter and mailed to him. It was just a friggin' power trip. Another lesson in negative leadership to be filed in the Command Sergeant Major notebook. As soon as the meeting concluded, he departed for the range. By the time he arrived, firing was over for the day portion of Table VI and the crews were preparing for night firing.

"Gator 7, Eaglehorse 5, what is your location, OVER."

"Eaglehorse 5, Gator 7, I'm in your parking lot, OVER."

"Roger, come to my location now, OUT." As Martin looked up, he could see the Squadron Executive Officer out the door of the tower, waving him forward.

"Can you tell me, First Sergeant, why no one knew what to do to zero these tanks and you could get it done over the damned radio?" Major Bragg asked accusingly before Martin could even get his jeep door closed.

"Do you want the long answer or the short one, Major Bragg?" he asked.

"I want the short one first then the long one," the Major replied.

"The crews are not trained properly. The long answer is the Army adopted the bore sight policy to preclude zeroing the M1 tank to save costs and because the practice of zeroing has so many pitfalls," Martin told him.

"What in the hell is wrong with zeroing? They are knocking all of the targets down. That is what we're here for ain't it?" Bragg thundered.

"Major Bragg, policy is made at the highest echelons of the Army. Zeroing is time consuming, expensive, and not always possible to verify in war when changes occur. The capability to zero the tank was designed into it before there was a bore sight policy. You like zeroing because it is what you know. You understand it. Electronic soldiers do not understand zeroing. It is real popular now because they are hitting. What neither you nor they understand is a zeroed tank is good only for that date and time while conditions remain the same. When any one of those conditions that were present for zero are not present at the time it fires next, all this good feeling will go down the toilet. The variance for Bore sight in the vertical plane corresponds to the height of a T-62 turret. Bore sight policy is a direct Army response to a predicted demographic that speaks to the long range economic health of the nation. As entitlements continue to rise and the welfare state becomes entrenched, the Army will be forced to cut back by populist politicians. Zero is a logical cut point as bore sight makes it unnecessary. That's the long answer."

"First Sergeant, it is a hell of a note when a First Sergeant in the US Army can even spell demographic and a goddamn dirty shame when he knows what it means. I have two damn Masters Degrees and I begrudge no man an education. It just makes me puke when we officers have infected enlisted men to the degree you just demonstrated. However, I will forgive you personally. That deal of drawing the shit on the sponson box lid was pure Army Kabuki Dancing. You took all of the theater, angst and worry out of the target area with chalk and drawings as well as chopping the radio traffic to zero. Seeing that was worth a lot. Why the hell are you not an officer?" the Executive Officer asked wistfully.

"I did not qualify, Sir. My parents were married," Martin answered softly.

"You dirty SOB. I am serious," Bragg thundered.

"I came in too late at age twenty five, got hurt in a car wreck and just got too old to qualify, Sir," Martin said.

"The rest of the long answer is it all goes back to prepare to fire training. The rounds exist in the inventory to permit zeroing of each round type and the verification of zero daily for each tank but as a point of doctrine, they will not be issued. What little I did was like putting a few band aids on one or two of the holes the 700 ball bearings made when the 682 grams of C4 from the Claymore propelled them into the elephant," Martin concluded.

"What is the final solution, First Sergeant?" Major Bragg asked.

"The tankers need to be thoroughly trained to learn Why as well as How to prepare a tank to fire. If a man knows why things happen he can reach logical conclusions. Right now, if something happens outside of his 'monkey see, monkey do world' of How, he is lost. Logic enables deductive reasoning. At the moment, the tankers are operating with a one quart brain in a one gallon world."

"So tell me, First Sergeant, if you know so damn much why you have not trained your soldiers?" Major Bragg asked with a measure of sarcasm.

"I obey orders, Major Bragg," Martin replied evenly.

"Your Commander told me he took you off the mission the day after he did it. I'm just ragging you. This gunnery does not look good, First Sergeant. What is your next move?" Bragg asked.

"Going to see if the tankers need anything, go see the Scouts to make sure they are okay and then check on the Mortar Platoon. I will do anything I can to help, if I am asked, but I won't be," Martin stated.

Saluting Major Bragg said, "See you later, Gator. I won't be the one keeping you from your appointed rounds." Martin returned the salute and left smiling.

To the Gators' great chagrin, only one tank out of the nine assigned to G Troop qualified without a re-test, the one Martin zeroed over the radio. The set of failures seemed to be all Technical Knockouts. Each and every one could be traced to training, or the lack thereof, and the lack of a standard operating procedure. They were in good company, 38 crews in the squadron failed their first try at Tank Table VIII. All subsequently passed by re-firing the engagements they missed, some of them re-firing the same engagement two more times.

First Sergeant Martin attended each and every de-briefing of every tank crew in G Troop. It was of no consolation to have seen it coming. He never said I told you so. He was positive and upbeat no matter how poorly they did. He shared his past failure with the tankers of the troop. He had failed as a fill in Tank Commander to qualify the tenth engagement of a TT Table VIII run while also serving as a First Sergeant in H Co 2/6 Cavalry. He thought he got screwed by the AI grading him from the tower on his .50 target. Several of the calls could have gone either way, but they did not go in his favor that night. His advice to his soldiers was blunt, "Winners never bitch about the officiating. Losers who bitch never get any better until they correct their errors."

He could not share his disappointment with anyone. The troops already thought him to be nuts. He knew they had adjusted to the re-fire philosophy. He was conditioned to believe only first time qualification counted. Years of service in straight shooting Armor units to whom gunnery was the sum total of their existence made it his standard. The Troop was blasé about gunnery because of the frantic pace of Cavalry life. It was not crawl; walk; run; it was run; trip; fall. It was just another event and a welcome distraction from Border duty. Any serious training effort would have to be incremental and fit into an already full calendar.

1/11 ACR led by Lieutenant Colonel Abrams scored 9 first time qualifiers while 3/11 found 3 crews who passed the first round. The Regiment's score was 15 of 123 tank crews qualified. While abysmal, it was the best in Europe that year for M1s. Martin was not happy. To be judged the least screwed up Kop in a Key Stone Kops car chase was nothing to brag about.

First Sergeant Martin knew the Master Gunners of the Squadron felt the same way. As the debacle unfolded, a plan was forming in his mind for the Squadron for the next year. The syndrome of 'Not Invented Here' got every one of his suggestion he made this year shot down. No one wanted to listen. Something would have to happen to change the mindset of the leaders for the lessons to be learned and a fix applied.

Years of teaching, training, testing and firing of hundreds of tanks plus growing up with the Vietnam veterans and the tough standards of 4/69 and 1/33 Armor had taught him what he needed to know. God knows he had been a big enough doofus in 1973 to learn humility. If he could, he was going to repay the Army for all he had learned from the old dogs. The old tanks and their archaic sighting and computing systems had been hard to learn. However, knowing how and why they worked gave him great insight into how to train for the M1. It was time to payback those old soldiers, the alumnae of the Army who had trained him so patiently and so well, by training the new soldiers on the M1. If it was to happen, it had to incremental and done in small bites. There were too many events feeding the OER and the Officer Ego Monster in the 'Horse to do anything else.

Clearing Post at Grafenwohr Training Area was far simpler in 1985. Back when, if the barracks or tent site was screwed up you simply left it better than you found it and bribed the inspector with a bottle of Jim Beam. Things had changed greatly in ten years. The troops reported to the ranges and slept when they could in the metal buildings that were a combination of a dining hall and barracks buildings with flush toilets and hot and cold running water with showers. They could be hosed down with squeegees available to push out the water. The squadron and the unit trains had barracks or tents on main post.

When the tank crewmen, scouts, mortar men and maintenance men were finished with training and training support, they went directly to the railhead and loaded vehicles onto a waiting train. Bus transportation to home station met them at the railhead and once the German train crew accepted the equipment, they departed for home station. Martin smiled he watched the German who measured the overhang of the track projecting from the side of the flatcar. The troops called him by the same nickname of the 1970's, the Millimeter Freak. Using a metric system ruler, this Bundesbahn official would require drivers to move the tank left and right to meet his exacting eye. As with most nicknames bestowed in irony, "Millimeter Freak" was actually a term of respect. The trains moved at up to 100 mph through tunnels barely wide enough for the tanks to clear their walls. The Millimeter Freak was both in charge and riding on the train. He thus had two reasons to be exacting.

The Headquarters element drove home in their wheeled vehicles led by the First Sergeant or the Executive Officer. The troops looked forward to the trip knowing they would stop at the German McDonalds on the autobahn. The movement to and from distant training areas was a very well orchestrated event with no room for error. As a tanker, Martin liked riding the train home in a sleeper car. Even that small pleasure was becoming a thing of the past. Sleeper cars cost too much. Soldiers had to sit up in day coaches if buses were not available, rarely getting sleeper cars.

1000 hours
06 June 1985
Bad Kissingen, W. Germany

"Sergeant McKnight, where is the First Sergeant?" Captain Dawson demanded of the Training NCO.

"He's in the track park, Sir. You know how he is about topping off the tanks," McKnight answered the CO.

"Go get him or send for him, no, as you were, I'll go up there myself," Dawson replied as he started out the door.

The Troop Commander found his First Sergeant sitting on the right front fender of Sergeant First Class Vic Jackson's tank watching a crewman fill Sergeant First Class Collie's vehicle. Martin came to attention and saluted Captain Dawson in full view of the troopers working there, "Good Morning Captain Dawson. The troop is engaged in Maintenance and topping off fuel tanks, both timeless rituals of the Armor Force," Martin said with a smile.

"Let's take a walk, First Sergeant. You may not be smiling when we get back," Dawson said.

"The staff meeting today had some surprises. The S-3 Sergeant Major slot in the TO & E is approved. The Squadron Commander has been extended for a year to improve tank gunnery and to oversee the Bradley transition. We need to send at least two guys from each troop to be Bradley Master Gunners. All three troop commanders will all rotate before August so the new Troop Commanders can become Bradley qualified during the New Equipment Transition at Grafenwohr. The Corps Commander wants all gunnery improved. He is not happy with M1 gunnery results. Tank ammo will be fenced to force everyone to use the Unit Conduct of Fire Trainer. The UCOFT is to become a big part of train up. Main gun ammo is limited by an Army wide ceiling of 110 rounds per year. We have more Master Sergeants than units to assign them to as First Sergeants. You need to talk to the Earth Pig if you want to move to the S3. I want you to move while I am still in command of the troop. That's all the news that is the news," Dawson concluded.

"Damn, Sir, that must have been some meeting. I will talk to the Command Sergeant Major. Was he present and did he see the 'burning bush' with the rest of you?" Martin asked.

Dawson nodded and added, "He was there. He has hurt his back and he is not really up to speed right now."

"Great, I will get to be three people, Ops Sergeant Major, Master Gunner and fill in Command Sergeant Major," Martin said smiling.

"Yeah and love every minute of it. You know how I feel. What is the good of power if you don't abuse it now and then," Dawson added. As they found themselves at the front gate of the track park, Martin took his leave of Dawson and walked down to the Squadron Headquarters to see the Sergeant Major. Dawson, having nothing better to do at the moment, went back to his vehicle line to check on the topping off of fuel and maintenance.

The Captain had heard the First Sergeant once say he would throw any going away gift costing more than the limit allowed by the Army Regulation into the dumpster. Shit, he would get something he would not throw away. I am going to miss this shit. It would be better all the way around with a second command and a better hospital now that they were going to have another baby, maybe a girl. One of each and that was that. Two more years here and then back to the States for CGSC. The Squadron needed the First Sergeant's brain more than the troop. If the Squadron Commander got extended, he would be all over Top to train up the tankers and the Bradleys. The Regimental Commanding Officer would be gone by then, well on his way to being a Brigadier General and me to being a Major, I hope. I should still be able to get together with the First Sergeant from time to time stationed at Fulda. I'm going to keep in contact with him for as long as I can. He had decided he would find out why the First Sergeant took it so hard about first time No-Gos at tank gunnery. Well, the Earth Pig should be having a Major Heart Attack about now when the First Sergeant tells him he will do the Ops Sergeant Major job.

Dawson was wrong about the mental state of Command Sergeant Major McCall. He was elated by First Sergeant Martin's willingness to take the Ops job. He was actually amazed at the effect the Sergeants Major Course was having on Martin and how well he was doing. He had a very hard time at the Academy as did his entire "life group." He would never have taken it as a non-resident. It was just too hard to grasp all of the material. The testing was harder. There was no one to talk with about it. You learned a lot from your fellow students and they learned from you. Martin never asked McCall's advice or troubled him in the least about the course. He knew he talked with other members of his class by phone and helped several of them as a peer instructor. Even Command Sergeant Major Ligon, the Corps' fire breathing legend, commented on how much help he was to his fellow students. One of the guys he tutored was one of Ligon's best friends, a Brigade Command Sergeant Major. Martin got him back on line and kept him in the course. Everyone was concerned about the 80% failure rate of the non-resident course.

292

What a chance this was to get his best First Sergeant for training, analysis and motivation into the S3!!

Command Sergeant Major McCall's happiness showed through as he had the biggest smile Martin had yet seen on his face, "You mean you would do that? Leave G Troop, let me put Master Sergeant Black in your place, work as the Master Gunner, schedule the Border rotations, devise a train up for the tankers and get the Bradley vehicle train up started in parallel with the tankers."

Martin replied, "Yes, Sergeant Major. I am getting a good deal here as well. I get qualified to be a Sergeant Major before I'm eligible, train the Squadron the right way on the M1 and the M3 crews later in the year when we get the Master Gunners back from Fort Benning. It won't be easy but it will teach me a lot and I will be able to do some good for the outfit. That is what is important."

"It's obvious the Academy has had an impact on you. What changed in your thinking?" Command Sergeant Major McCall said.

"Sergeant Major, it has taught me Sergeants Major primarily work for the good of the entire Army. Command Sergeant Major collar brass is Army brass, not Branch. Command Sergeants Major strive for their units to be as good as they can make them but not at the expense of the greater good, the Army standard. If we serve the Army standard first and honor it, we will have a good unit. That is the long and the short of it Sergeant Major," he said. He thought McCall was going to shed a tear.

"Goddamn right you're right. That is the primary mission. You remember that when they ask you to teach there. They will want you on the faculty. Tell them yes if you ever want to be at a higher level than Battalion. Will you?" McCall asked.

"Probably not, Sergeant Major. I have had enough of schools and teaching. I want to be in tactical units the rest of my time, which will not go much past 20 years, if at all," Martin stated emphatically.

"But you're willing to sacrifice that here - why not there?" McCall asked, sincerely wanting an answer.

"It is not a sacrifice here, it is duty. Schools and the folks who man them very quickly forget how life is in the unit. The Sergeants Major Academy is a Zebra farm there are so damn many stripes there. Hell, Sergeants Major call each other Sergeant Major there if they are outranked by a day. No thanks. It is not for me," Martin stated.

"You will never get a brigade thinking like that," McCall stated.

"'Please don't throw me in the Briar Patch Uncle Remus' said Brer Rabbit," at which point Martin wiggled his Clark Gable sized ears and wrinkled his nose, shocking McCall into laughter.

"So what do you want to accomplish as the S3 Ops Sergeant Major, First Sergeant?" McCall asked.

"Establish a good S3 section, devise a fair Border Rotation, Qualify 41 of 41 of M1s, first run and 38 of 38 M3's, pass all alerts, re-do the Ground Defense Plan, respond to Regiment, do great ceremonies if tasked for Regiment and Corps," Martin told him.

"What are your personal goals?" McCall asked.

"Finish USASMA by March 1986, attend the Resident phase that summer, rotate to Fort Knox, make E9, serve two years and retire," Martin stated bluntly.

"You mean you do not want to be a Command Sergeant Major, Ronald, I don't believe that," McCall said with a big smile.

"If Command Sergeant Major comes I will be happy. If not I can live without it," Martin said calmly.

"Don't worry. It will come. You will get selected as a Command Sergeant Major designee before you pin on Sergeant Major based on your course work at USAMA and your record here. You are getting notes back from instructors praising your research and both the Corps Command Sergeant Major and the 7th Army Command Sergeant Major appreciate your tutoring their slow learners. You have made powerful friends," McCall said.

"I did not ask for their thanks. Every time I see them they each chew my ass about something," Martin replied.

"That is why they like you. You are doing it because it needs doing and USASMA asked you. If they did not like you, they would not harass you. It is their way of making conversation without favoritism. What is the last thing they say to you?" McCall asked.

"They ask me if there is anything I need, Sergeant Major," Martin said.

"See, that's what I mean," McCall said laughing.

"I need you to take a look at my briefing book and re-do it for an update. You will be the alternate to give the enlisted in-briefings and to give my portion of the training briefing to the Regimental Commanding Officer. Redoing the book will get your feet on the ground. My back is bad. I need to get you ready. You are not the ranking First Sergeant. But you are the one who always steps forward and acts. That is what counts. You will lead the others. None of them wants the job. The first requirement of a leader is to want to lead. As a stand in, you will get help from the other Command Sergeants Major in the Regiment and the Corps. We will work well together. Keep me informed. If I am out and you have to do my job, use everything we have to help you execute. Don't take any shit from anyone. I will get you in to see the Squadron Commander."

The Squadron Commander was more than pleased Martin was to be the Ops Sergeant Major. He had a list a mile long of things he wanted done in the S3. He also told him he would personally show him everything the S3 was responsible for in terms of real property. His guidance was clear, "I am going to be extended for Level I Tank & Bradley Gunnery at Grafenwohr. Nothing

294

is going to slow down; this is not an Armor Battalion. I need you to find a way to train up the Tankers first and then the Bradley crews when they complete New Equipment Training. Don't rush it. Think it through and show me the whole thing from concept to end product. Mostly, you will have a free hand as long as I can see and approve of the syllabus. Involve the Troop and Tank Company Commanders. When you get the troop turned over and First Sergeant Black spun up, we will get together. Fast is the enemy of good for training. For goodness sake, keep up on your course work for the Academy. Can you handle being the Ops Sergeant Major, Part time Command Sergeant Major, and M1 Master Gunner concurrently?"

Martin replied with a smile, "Yes, Sir. It won't take long to get a decision out of the three of us."

"Come and see me next week," the Squadron Commander said as he answered his phone ending the interview.

Upcoming for the First Sergeant was the hard part, letting go of being the First Sergeant for the troop. No matter who was to come behind him it would not be the same. Martin realized that he would have to stay out of his way and let him develop his own technique as the First Sergeant.

0930 hours
10 June 1985
G Troop, Bad Kissingen West Germany

First Sergeant Black made his appearance at the Troop. Over the next three days Martin took him around to show him the people, places, property, and things he needed to know to function as a First Sergeant in the Cavalry. He appeared to be very calm and quiet. He gave the distinct impression that he had his own methods of operation and the best thing that Martin could do would be to get gone and let him begin his tour as the First Sergeant. Black lived in Bachelor Enlisted Quarters; his wife was in the States and was not coming to join him. It was very clear he was going to be a desk, safe and duty roster First Sergeant. He had no intention of becoming a primary trainer or logistician. He would do the bare minimum to get by and would make no waves. Black was a moderate to heavy drinker, a one to two pack a day smoker, extremely neat and very conscious of his appearance. It was going to be a case of do as I say, not as I do, tour of duty for him.

First Sergeant Black had come with a set of unit orders making him a First Sergeant and moving him to G Troop. Martin was on the same order and was made a Master Sergeant and assigned to Headquarters Troop as the S3 Sergeant Major with additional duty as the Squadron Master Gunner.

The order was effective 14 June 1985.

Captain Dawson outdid himself with First Sergeant Martin's farewell. The officers and NCOs took him out for the evening to their favorite restaurant,

Zagrebs', in downtown Bad Kissingen. A good time was had by all and although there were many toasts and some hard drinking, there were no incidents either during or after the festivities. At the last formation First Sergeant Martin held, Dawson presented him with three Gator Certificates of Achievement and a Smith & Wesson, Model 29, .44 Magnum pistol. The pistol came in a very nice cherry wood case, was nickel plated and had a four inch barrel. It was a beautiful going away present and it did not get thrown in the dumpster. How much of it Dawson bought and how much the soldiers paid was open to question but Martin did not raise the issue. He was overwhelmed.

CHAPTER 11 - ON THE SHELF

My highest ambition is to be an E7 with a P3 profile assigned to the S2 shop of a Tank Battalion. Staff Sergeant R.J. Miller, DS, C-19-4 circa 1977.

0530 hours
18 June 1985
HHT, 2/11 ACR
Bad Kissingen, West Germany

The initial tour of the S3 domain was interesting for the now Master Sergeant Martin. He did not realize the extent and the range of the S3. Few people did. It was a big operation. There were lots of training devices, ten buildings, nearly 1,600 acres of training land and millions upon millions of dollars of US property. Lieutenant Colonel Covington was a former S3. He had very specific guidance and a long list. It was mostly clean up and disposal. A very good Corporal could have done everything he wanted in a week. After the all day tour, Martin had a single spaced list two pages long of things to do.

The Headquarters Troop First Sergeant was an interesting character. He was a Texan by birth and a Louisiana Red Neck by choice. He was Master Gunner qualified, a former sniper in Project Phoenix and a combat veteran of G Troop in RVN. He knew all about the tour and Martin's project list from the SCO.

"Well, what do you think about your new job?" First Sergeant Waters asked Martin.

"You'll laugh," Martin said.

"I might," he said, already smiling.

"If Baron Von Stueben saw all the shit we have available to train these troops and ain't using, he would slap the taste out of our mouths," Martin opined.

Waters immediately began to laugh, "Boy is that Colonel in for a ride," he continued. "He don't have a clue about you boy, does he?"

"Whatever do you mean, First Sergeant? I am just a simple old soldier trying to do his duty," Martin said with a grin.

"I know it is an adjustment for you not being a First Sergeant. It would be all right with me if you did PT by yourself there, Sergeant Major," Waters said without a trace of a smile.

"Okay First Sergeant, I'll do that," Martin said.

I guess I hit a nerve and pissed off the Headquarters wussies by trying to motivate their weak sisters during PT. The concept of smoke is unheard of in HHT and is not wanted. Since I cannot be depended on to keep my mouth shut for on the spot corrections it is probably best I leave it alone. He is right and I was wrong.

Waving off his next comment, Martin said, "There can only be one First Sergeant at a time in a Cavalry Troop. Good intentions do not always produce good things. You are right and even if you weren't, you are in charge. I need to remember that but then I'm sure you will remind me if I forget."

"I will and I appreciate all of your support. With you here, the S3 guys will realize they are in the Troop and will become my strongest support. That attitude is coming from you and I know it," Waters said with sincerity.

Yeah and as a former Army level champion heavyweight boxer you are a gentleman and I am glad of it, Martin ruminated.

"How much time you got, Don?" Martin asked.

"Why, what's on your mind?"

"I want to run a Master Gunner problem by you if you have about 30 minutes or an hour," Martin replied.

"I'll take the time right now, shoot Luke, you're faded," Waters said intrigued.

Waters was an old time Master Gunner and one of the first NCOs in the Army to go through the course. He was qualified in combat on the M-551 Sheridan, and M-48 and also on M-60 series in Cold War Germany. He had been a Master Gunner for the M60A1 and knew the M60A3 thoroughly. He knew the theory of the M1 but became a First Sergeant before transitioning to it. He was a hands on guy and very, very wise in all phases of tank gunnery, including training, ballistic theory, and range layout and design. He had been a Master Gunner through the Brigade Level in Korea and was highly successful, though low key. Moreover, he was a borderline overweight guy who always passed the PT test and never failed to complete a run though he dropped back, he never dropped out. He was not bashful and would tell anyone who asked his unvarnished opinion. After rendering a strong opinion, were he to be insulted, or physically challenged, he could, and would, whip some ass in the bargain. He would become the de facto leader of the First Sergeants by force of personality now that Martin was on staff. He was the quintessential "good man."

"I mean to reverse the gunnery results next summer with a goal of 41 for 41 tanks and 38 of 38 Bradleys. Using the Master Gunners, I am going to develop a unit school using the Master Gunners Course and Weapons Department Instructor Checkout Program as a baseline for the one week course."

"Crews will take it together with six to ten crews in a one week course. There will be a pre-test and a post test over the same material with no nonsense. We will teach theory in the morning, do hands on in the afternoon, and conduct prep to fire using a checklist read by the driver. Each Master Gunner will have a day of the course he is responsible to develop and execute and the rest of us will be Assistant Instructors. Each crew will check out each tank with unit turret mechanics present on the field day. Each class will take a week. Commanders will be trained first," Martin stated.

Waters had listened closely to Martin and looked wistfully off in the distance as he thought about what he had heard. He smiled and said, "Boy, are you sure you aren't a former VC (Viet Cong guerilla from the Vietnam War)?

You sound like a damn Communist. You want these stiff necked Cavalry Officers to actually admit they do not know every damn thing on the face of the earth and go to a school run by a bunch of Sergeants."

"Worse than that, you want them to go to school with Privates and Sergeants and take tests and show their ignorance. Don't get me wrong, you are right and it is a great thing to do, but you are swimming upstream. You could end up like the damn salmon and dying once you get your eggs spawned or worse yet, getting speared during the trip. Toward the end of your journey, you are going to see everyone desert you. When that happens, come to me."

"You are an idealist. You think everybody loves the Army as much as you do and wants to be the best tanker he can be. It may work, but you had better develop a tough hide," Waters said shaking his head.

"Don, I know I appear to be naïve, but I am not. I know people are motivated by self interest. I also believe when you do something like this, you have to be doing it for the right reasons. I am going to take to the high ground and stay there. I appreciate you hearing me out," Martin said.

"Who all knows about this?" Waters asked.

"Just us two roosters. The Master Gunners and I have developed a straw man. They are with me all of the way. You are my Devil's Advocate. I can trust you to give me your unvarnished opinion. I am going to brief the Squadron Commander in a week or so," Martin replied.

"You know this Sergeant Major gig you're doing is not going to last. They will have a newly minted Sergeant Major here to fill that slot before you know it," Waters said.

"Fortunes of War old buddy. I am here doing it now and that is all I know. When we get a Sergeant Major I will be his strongest supporter. Hell, something will turn up," Martin said with a laugh adding, "This ain't the Air Force where everyone is in the right job. Here we just keep pounding on the square peg until it fits in the round hole. The trick is to make the peg believe all the pounding is for his own good."

1000 hours
25 June 1985
Squadron Hqs

Martin had seen the briefing the Squadron Commander used for the Regimental Commanding Officer. It was on butcher paper hung on an easel with hand drawn cartoons with balloons and bullet comments to make the pertinent points. He was feeding the Squadron Commander his own format. The baseline would be the test. A handout published by General Dynamics and the manuals would be the texts. Each crewman would get their own set of everything Martin had from the Armor School in his trick bag. There would be no secrets. Every book and pamphlet would be opened and explained for its purpose and relevance. In concert with the unit Master Gunners, Martin was going to show him the straw man outline for the course. Day 1 would be a review of all systems inside the turret with emphasis on the items impacting on accuracy and the error budget. Day 2 consisted of vehicle identification and conduct of fire-commands and crew duties. Day 3 was preparation to fire and bore sight with a thorough inspection of each tank by the crew supported by the unit turret mechanic in the morning with practical work in the afternoon. On day 4, automatic weapons were inspected and test fired at the scaled mini-tank ranges. Sub-caliber training devices were installed on each tank and exercises conducted to train manipulation. The morning of Day 5 consisted of a review and a question and answer period with no time limit followed by the Post Test but generally the little school that could, would be complete by noon. The General Dynamic booklets would be made available to all at least a month before their training iteration.

The Squadron Commander appeared to be comfortable with the format and was glad to get a fact sheet with all of the details. Martin also used an overlay to show the highlights of training for the intervening months before Level I Gunnery and to include his absence from gunnery to attend the Resident Phase of the Sergeants Major Academy in June. He hated to miss the big dance but if he did his job correctly, his fledglings were be fully feathered and in flight on their own. He expected Lieutenant Colonel Covington to make some changes but was surprised to see he offered very little guidance and had few questions. Most of the questions came from Major Bragg and Command Sergeant Major McCall.

As expected, Major Bragg had the first question, "So First Sergeant, you expect the guys will read this book on their own time? And you think you can get enough of them printed to do the job?"

"The answers are: Yes, and Yes. Most soldiers by and large like their Troop Commanders and their NCOs. If they set the example and tell them this is a good idea, they will read the book. Soldiers want to succeed. The book will be printed by the Corps Print Shop in Frankfurt. Sergeant Major Ligon told me to use his name and to keep him informed about every stage of the school. I'm going to get 500 copies," Martin answered.

"But if you give them the answers and teach them the doctrine and give them a book that spells it out, they are going to cheat. How will you handle that?" Command Sergeant Major McCall asked.

"They have to pass the post test. The theory behind this method of training is to discard the unnecessary and only teach what is vital. We will tell the student the bottom line upfront. If they cheat and memorize the answers to the 150 questions, it will be great. They will know the information. The key is for them to learn why and how the tank works and get exposed to using an aircraft style checklist read by the driver to get it ready. It is the old Army method Sergeant Major, we're gonna' tell 'em what we're gonna tell 'em, we're gonna' tell 'em and then we are gonna' tell 'em what we told 'em and test 'em." The big difference is we are not hiding the answers and daring them to find them. We are teaching the answers down front. I am taking a page out of Eisenhower's playbook, 'Always tell the American Soldier 'Why' and get him on your side'."

"The second big payoff is getting all of the Master Gunners in the unit energized and used to working together. The third is getting the crews to associate with the other crews from their sister units. That will give us cross talk, information sharing and asset sharing down the road. The unofficial networks in organizations are twice as fast as the official ones," Martin concluded.

"You really know how to do this Martin, don't you?" Bragg asked.

"I should, Sir. I did it for the whole Armor Force to include the Marine Corps and 7,000 total tank crews. Surely we can teach 41." Martin said with a smile.

The Squadron Commander summarized brilliantly, "2d Squadron conducts a unit School tentatively called SABOT Academy with crews from each unit scheduled by the Troop and Tank Company commanders on dates of their choice spread over four months time. The Commanders and I will attend the pilot course and make changes. The school will last five days with pre-test and post test. If one of the crewmen fails, the whole crew repeats the course. It continues until all tank crews are trained. A make up course will be held in the spring at my discretion. An accelerated SABOT Academy for the Bradleys will be held after NET and before Wildflecken for the scouts. The tank Master Gunners will help the scout Master Gunners develop their course."

"Now here is our guidance for Level II gunnery. The Wildflecken train up will be run by the Squadron. All the Troops and Company will have to do is show up and shoot. The final range at Wildflecken will mirror Tank Table VIII engagements. Can you fix it so that crews will be able to practice a given task until they pass it?" the Squadron Commander questioned.

"Yes, Sir."

"Good, I want video and audio for crew de-briefing on the largest TV set we can find. Each crew will get a copy of the VHS tape for their run. The debriefing tent will have coffee and soup, decent chairs, tables and a dry floor with straw if nothing else, and will be heated- using the best canvas we have. I want the largest telephoto lens available for the TV camera from the Graf Training Support Office. I want no doubt, arguments, or even heated discussion about who hit what target when, particularly the far mover. It's the far target from the tower and the baseline. It is uphill. Rounds fired short, but on line will look like target hits. Video does not lie. It documents. I want metal on the targets to give a flash for sensing. Visitors will be cleared through the S3 and through me. No dog and pony shows; visiting fireman will see us as we are, warts and all. Crews are the focus. Be prepared for the Regimental

301

Newspaper to visit SABOT Academy. I want the least possible manpower possible to be expended in support of this gunnery. Cut it to the bone. You are doing a great job Master Sergeant Martin. First class briefing with just the right amount of information for now," he concluded.

Great. A true Commander. He gave me simple guidance. The Master Gunners and I researched the problem and developed the details. He absorbed it all and refined the guidance and expanded it to include a follow on mission. The big guy is not supposed to do it all, just see that it gets done. We have guidance. Now what we have to do is write it, teach the pilot, modify it and teach it to make it come true. The hard part would be getting the Squadron Commander to keep the Troop and Battery Commanders honest. Given their schedule, they would start chipping away at the resources midway and shafting SABOT Academy to "feed the glory bulldog."I wonder if the Squadron Commander has figured out no one in USAREUR has the stroke to delay ten Battalion Commanders from the War College Class date DA has set up. What a goat screw the video will be with generator power. What did Churchill say about the Mulberry Harbors to his staff, "Do not argue the difficulties, they will argue themselves, get moving forward!"Good advice! The difficulties of this enterprise would soon surface.

1000 hours
27 June 1985
Squadron S3 Conference Room/Work Area

A series of phone calls got the Master Gunners assembled for the meeting. Martin knew it could be difficult. The Squadron Commander had personally briefed the Troop and Tank Company Commanders. By doing so, SABOT Academy became his idea not the Master Gunner mafia at work.

"Thanks for coming fellas. The results of the last Level 1 gunnery sucked. No one in this room wants to repeat that experience. Whatever happened is in the past. There were enough errors at every level to go around. It made me puke to watch it. We have good soldiers, good leaders and good equipment. They only lack polish and practice," Martin began.

As he looked at the group of young NCOs he was very optimistic. He knew they could pull the school and training off with ease. Staff Sergeant Masterson with G Troop had finally learned Martin was not his enemy and was highly principled. He was still a cocky SOB but that was okay. Staff Sergeant Jester from H Co was a Command Sergeant Major hiding in a Staff Sergeant's body. There was nothing he could not do. Staff Sergeant McCready of Fox Troop was a card carrying member of the NRA and a certified weapons nut who loved anything that went bang. Staff Sergeant Phillips from E Troop was a former Armor School Instructor with Martin and one of ten men Martin had sent to Master Gunner School as a standby using his authority as the Chief Enlisted Instructor of the Gunnery Division, Weapons Department, Fort Knox. (The Master Gunner faculty believed the TCGST was Kindergarten for tankers. If they could not pass that simple test, they could never master the details of the Master Gunner Course. The success of Master

Gunners in the field was so complete and absolute not even the Commanding General challenged the administration of the course even when the tough NCOs in charge failed 25 of 25 candidates and no one graduated. When up to half of unit candidates failed the TCGST and were sent home before day one of the Master Gunner Course, Martin was not willing to waste the slots when he had outstanding men serving as Instructors under his command available. The Master Gunner Faculty agreed and it was an easy thing to set up."His" guys took the TCGST, passed it and went on an informal order of merit list. When openings occurred, Martin released the candidates for formal entry into the Master Gunner course. However, once in the course, all buddy bets were off and the Knox guys were at just as much risk, if not more, than the guys TDY from units. Of course, they did have the advantage of the support of the entire Gunnery Division and all of its assets).The men sitting at the table were all thoughtful, confident, intelligent, well trained veterans of years of service with the Regiment or with other Armor units. No one could ask for a better group of companions for a tough enterprise.

Martin continued, "There is nothing we have proposed to the Squadron Commander we cannot do. I know you all want to contribute and have a lot to say. I want you to know where this idea of mine came from."

"In Skidgel Hall, Jimmy Hanks is a civilian turret mechanic instructor from the Maintenance Department. He is a veteran of WW II, Korea, and Vietnam. All of you had him for your classes as a Master Gunner. In his office he had a photo of himself and his fellow Platoon Sergeants in Korea in the 72d Armor. I asked him about the picture. He told me it was taken during a unit school he organized to train the unit up during a brief lull in combat in Korea. They had a few days and Jimmy was fresh from teaching AOB at the Armor School. He organized the course to serve as a refresher for old tankers and a crash course for their Infantry Replacements drafted as tankers from 2d Division."

"A few days prior to the picture being taken Jimmy had arrived in the unit on the supply truck after dark. At the time, the Company was under attack by the Chinese Communists. Very few of the company's .50 calibers were working. There were few if any, head space and timing gauges. Jimmy brought his own gauge from the Armor School and proceeded to get all thirty six caliber 50's in the company going during the fight, beginning with his platoon. He then went back to the rear, about 400 yards, and got a dozer to bury the dead Chinese and push the piles away from the front of the tanks to clear their fields of fire. That is a lot of dead Chinamen. After Jimmy's impact on their fortunes, he had the Company's total respect and they were ready to listen. It is hard to get pissed off at someone who probably saved your life. They wanted to live and he had the answers."

"Well, guess what? The Squadron Commander was extended for Level I Gunnery for 1985 and he wants to survive as well. His motivation gives us an opportunity to train our soldiers. I realize we cannot make them into Master Gunners in the time we have but we can teach them what they need to know

303

to begin to learn the M1. I will always remember that sign on the wall at the troop entrance to Skidgel Hall, 'The knowledge you gain here is not yours to keep'. Based on our earlier talks to assemble the straw man, I sold big wolf tickets to the Squadron Commander. He bought them. I told him we could teach a one week course to the tankers and back it up with a Wildflecken Gunnery that would turn M1 gunnery around and get the M3 program off to a good start."

"I know I am not a Master Gunner graduate. I do not pretend to be. I am in the job because there is only one of you per company. No Commander will give any of you up. I am spare parts and on the shelf with the staff. My role will be to coordinate and be responsible as the Squadron Master Gunner and Operations Sergeant Major with Sergeant First Class Scott acting as the Operations Sergeant."

"There are four objectives for this meeting: 1. Divide up the responsibilities for the course content; 2. Critique the Test; 3. Approve the prep-to-fire checklist; 4. Approve the initial outline of the crew schedule - knowing it can be fudged here and there."

"We need to divide up the course and figure out who is going to teach what. You know what you are most comfortable teaching although any of you could teach any subject. Each Instructor will develop his portion of the course and then talk the rest of us of through his portion. We are the murder board. We will make changes based on intellectual honesty. If you cannot defend the content of your class, it will have to change. We will use the pre-test as our guide. We will teach the test, so the test has to meet our needs. It is our baseline. We will fix the test first. Review and critique it."

"My prep to fire checklist from H Co 2/6 Cav is a good one but whoever picks up prep to fire may not like it. The reason I am so hung up on a checklist is obvious. The manual sucks. It was written by maintenance types. It jumps all over the waterfront. The Pye-Watson Bore Sight Device is not part of the manual and neither is the Bore sight Policy. The changes to the preparation to fire procedures for the M1 tank have moved too fast for the Army system to keep up."

"We cannot hope to teach these rookies all we know. We have to use what we know to give them a series of simple systems that will carry them through combat. Try to remember most of them are double screwed, they are new to tanks and the M1 is new to the Army. We all have been on the "Steam Gunnery" tanks as the system evolved. We lived the error budget, they can't spell it and neither can the officers. We are training for war, not Tank Gunnery at Grafenwohr."

"The checklist is logical and arranged to flow as the crew gets the tank ready. The driver reads it as he is the least employed crewman during the event. He is usually the best candidate to replace the gunner in combat. Review the tank crew schedule. Does the schedule I coordinated with your

Commanders still fit? None of it is carved in stone. It is almost all negotiable in some degree. This is not my course. It is our course. The crews listed by the course dates are guides, not something dictated by me or the Squadron Commander. No one wants to tell your Commander when Staff Sergeant Tommy The Tanker is going to take his crew through the course. That is a Commander's Call. Any questions, input, complaints, bitches?"

Staff Sergeant Jester surprisingly was the first to speak, "Damn, First Sergeant, how long have you had this stuff sitting in your trick bag? And why the hell didn't you use it last gunnery in G Troop if it is so great?"

Staff Sergeant Masterson had turned beet red and was about to speak, but Martin waved him off, saying, "In a minute Bob. That is a fair question, Dave, and it deserves an honest answer. The Commander of G Troop chose to train his soldiers differently than I recommended. Not better, not worse, but differently. He was in charge and I supported his right to command without complaint or comment, either then or now. Okay, Bob say your piece."

"We screwed up, Dave. We did not know what First Sergeant Martin had because Dawson was not interested in it. He thought First Sergeant was overboard and wrapped too tight to run gunnery. He only called for him to fix stuff when the train went off the track. I thought he wanted to do my job and be the Master Gunner. We were both wrong. I can see that now," he said after his face had returned to a normal flesh tone.

Martin patted his shoulder saying, "We all support our chain of command in different ways from where we are assigned. My only interest here is to teach and expose these soldiers to a way to train that is so thoroughly professional and completely accurate so that it changes the way they think. As I told G Troop, I may look like a First Sergeant or in this case a Master Sergeant in 2d Squadron, but what I really am is teaching the future leaders of the Armor Force how to be fight and win. At some point many of you are going to be involved in a desperate fight in a far off land on a mission no one can see from here. When that time comes, I want you to have a foundation in training and experience that lets you apply what is learned here to the situation you find yourself in there, and win. Simply put, I want all of our soldiers to have one gallon brains to fix one quart problems."

"As far as SABOT Academy goes, I want to teach tank commanders everything I can to see them prevail in their first four engagements of the next war. After that, they will be blooded and they will know what to do. This little course and some OJT will make them equal to the M1 tank. The tiger is built into the tank. We have to grow some claws on these kittens to make them worthy of it. We need to make sure they strap it on rather than just ride in it. We can learn from last year and concentrate on 1985. 1984 is over."

Staff Sergeant Jester asked, "What are you going to teach?"

Martin replied, "Characteristics and data, the one thing you all hate. I would hope you are going to teach prep to fire."

305

Those are the biggest and broadest smiles I have ever seen on some of these guys. Guess that was a good choice, Martin thought. Let the old guy take the first day with the hardest and most boring shit they are thinking. They need to see the Head Man in Charge (HMFIC) take the hardest task and do it to perfection. While they are struggling with their portion they can all say, boy I am glad Martin is doing that shit and not me.

"Can I?" Jester asked.

"Better ask your peers, Dave. I do not care who has it. You are a good choice for it," Martin replied looking at the other men present. Jester looked over the group as well and saw no objections to his adoption of the difficult task.

"All right, then, I got it," Staff Sergeant Jester said.

As the two hardest nuts to crack were taken, Staff Sergeant Masterson took Armored Fighting Vehicle Identification, Staff Sergeant McCready took machineguns and ammunition, Staff Sergeant Phillips happily accepted Conduct of Fire and Fire Commands. It had all gone far better than Martin had hoped. It was clear the unit's performance on the last gunnery had embarrassed these NCO professionally and upset them personally. Now to get it written, rehearsed and approved. They had months but it would take time to develop the course of instruction given competing demands.

0630 hours
09 Oct 1985
Squadron Hqs
Bad Kissingen, West Germany

As the time passed, Martin found the execution of the three jobs, Master Gunner, Ops Sergeant and Command Sergeant Major was difficult but the chain of command was short and he got a lot done. He took care to accomplish everything the Squadron Commander wanted done first. Oddly enough he had little reporting to do as Lieutenant Colonel Covington showed up at the various sites needing attention either in the middle of the job or at its end. The Ops Sergeant Major task was made much easier once the unit commanders realized he was going to apportion the border duty strictly by the Army Regulation for the Duty Roster. The Fox Troop Cdr demanded to know how it was Martin thought he knew for certain E Troop had the Border over New Years the past year, implying Martin was lying.

He did not like the answer, "You may think me a liar, Captain, but I asked Miss Deidre, the Echo Troop Commander's lovely wife. She told me she did not get to wear the gown she bought for the Gala on New Year's because you sniveled out of the Border at New Year's at the last possible second. Would you like to tell her she is a liar?"

Each task that the troop, company, or battery had to perform that was critical to the mission or the performance of the commander was balanced

with the border and with Sabot Academy. Other tasks were fairly appor-
tioned, known well in advance, and were generally few and far between. The
only taskings received habitually late came from Regiment and these were
handled without a fuss. It was a very productive and good time for the unit.

There was much to learn about being a Command Sergeant Major for
Martin. Much of it was nuance and not book-learned skills or knowledge. It
was a matter of experience and judgment of which he had precious little as a
Command Sergeant Major. Fortunately, he had the great Command Sergeant
Major of 1/11 as a guide. He just tried not to wear him out as the man had
his own unit to run. Earlier, he got a very early call from the Regimental
Command Sergeant Major. The farewell the Regiment was putting together
for him was faltering. He was not a popular man. Getting folks to shell out
money for gifts and to attend a testimonial dinner with a bus ride both ways
was a very tough sell, especially in 2/11 ACR. Already somewhat of a provin-
cial unit, it was composed of mostly single soldiers and unaccompanied geographical bachelors. Of the three installations making up the Regimental
footprint, 2/11 had the fewest family quarters of the three units and by de-
fault became a bachelor outfit.

The NCOs did not like the Regimental Command Sergeant Major and did
not want to support him, period. Martin could not believe the guy was calling
him to drum up support for his own farewell party. After a quick call to his
mentor, he called a First Sergeant Meeting and got one dozen tickets sold. He
would send the money with the distribution and mail run to the Headquarters.

"Now that you have that straight, who is going to present the plaque from
the Squadron and make the speech if the Command Sergeant Major is still
laid up in the hospital?" the Tank Company First Sergeant asked with a big
smile.

"I guess that would be me, First Sergeant, unless of course you are volunteering given your vast experience at public speaker as a Drill Sergeant and
all," Martin said with an evil eye.

First Sergeant Bascomb was known for his deep aversion to speaking in
public and did not do so unless there was absolutely no other choice. He was
a fine First Sergeant and took wonderful care of his outfit in every regard. He
knew Martin liked and respected him and he was very glad all of the First Sergeants in the unit got along so well with any rancor or divisive behavior.

"What I mean is, Ron, how in the hell are you going to stand up there and
tell everyone what a great guy he is. Everybody knows he was ready to throw
you in the dumpster to keep Ligon off his ass. Even Ligon knew that," he
said, confirming Martin's long held belief he and Ligon were old buddies
from Fort Riley.

"Well Carl the lawyers have a saying, 'When your client is innocent, try the
case law. When he is guilty, try society!' I am going to adopt the spirit of that

307

technique. Rather than praise him, I will praise the audience as soldiers and let it wash over onto him. The ones that are listening will get it and the ones that miss it would probably never get it anyway," Martin said.

"Yeah, but do you have it written yet, I mean your speech," he asked with an intensity Martin had never seen.

"Hell no! I don't intend to write anything. They only want five minutes or so and I can pull that out on my way to the podium. Hell, Top, every First Sergeant in the Army but you and maybe two others, has a five minute speech on any subject concerning the Army in his hip pocket," Martin said teasing him.

"The joint is going to be packed with dignitaries from Corps, USARUER, the Fulda Community, 8th ID with the women all dressed up and us in dress blues. The Corps Commander and Ligon are going to be there. My wife and I are going especially to meet the Ligons and stay over in Fulda," Bascomb said almost beside himself. "I ain't shitting you Ron, this is a big deal."

"Look, you tell your wife, the Ligons, and old Sam Wetzel the Corps Commander, if they want to see how it is done just watch my tracer. You might learn something as well because I sure as hell am not worried about it, but thanks for your concern, bud," Martin said sincerely.

0900 hours
18 Oct 1985
Restaurante Orangerie
Fulda, West Germany

Martin was the one who learned a lot. All of the Command Sergeant Major gathered at Fulda in the Orangerie, a very beautiful and well appointed combination restaurant and musical hall with a disappearing stage as well as a fantastic bar. The Colors he had brought from Bad Kissingen were on a short staff modified to fit in the Squadron Commander's office and had a large stain across the center of their field. Beside the other Colors so perfectly maintained by the other unit Command Sergeants Major, Martin's looked like a pigmy on an NBA team. Martin felt like an idiot and knew he was over his head for social events, particularly of this type.

The 1/11 Command Sergeant Major immediately snapped up his colors and loaned him a nine foot 6 inch staff on which to display Martin's. They got an iron from the staff and watched approvingly as Martin pressed the colors and each streamer. The collective effort made the Colors look a great deal better but it was obvious they were stained and not as well cared for as the other Squadrons, which were immaculate.

As his mentor, the Command Sergeant Major, told him, "Look, we all know you are a one legged man in an ass kicking contest right now. You did not pay any attention to the colors. Keep the staff and fix them when you get them back to BK. Just have it fixed for the next time. Don't you say nothing about thank you. Before you are through you will have helped so many new First Sergeants, Color Sergeants, and Sergeants Major no one could count them all. We are all just glad to see you here and fully participating in every task. You don't duck or back up from nothing. You may not be wearing Command Sergeant Major rank but by God you act responsible and that is enough for us. Did you write a speech?"

"No, Command Sergeant Major. I figure I can do five minutes off the cuff and the last thing I want to do in front of that crowd is reach inside my National Guard Blues and pull out 3x5 cards,'" Martin said quietly.

"Good. That confirms everything I thought about you. I wish to hell I could have got you up here with me as a First Sergeant but it was not to be. You will do fine tonight now that we have your colors fixed," he said and with that he moved on to continue to rehearse the event as if it were the Presidents Inaugural - yet another lesson. He took nothing for granted and made sure everyone with a moving or speaking part in the event knew what to do. They rehearsed it three times and then once more with the Regimental Command Sergeant Major, the Regimental Commanding Officer, and the Corps Ops Sergeant Major, Command Sergeant Major Ligon's representative.

The most important learning experience of the event was yet to come for Martin. From the posting of the Colors to the Invocation everything went perfectly. The plan was for each Command Sergeant Major to make a short speech and present the Regimental Command Sergeant Major who sitting adjacent to the speakers dais with his gift and to exit stage left. After the meal, the presenters lined up in numerical order. None of the Command Sergeants Major were even remotely nervous and they noted Martin was very loose as well. Several of them knew he was a bit of a character and they were looking forward to his talk more than their own. It was clear to Martin that although none of the Squadron Command Sergeant Major had a reason to either like, or respect, the Regimental Command Sergeant Major, not one of them gave anything but a full and total effort to the event. He then realized that this was not about the Regimental Command Sergeant Major. It was about their love of the Army. They intended to put the best face possible on the NCO Corps. It was pride, élan and Esprit de Corps and they had them all in spades.

Using an old public speaking trick, Martin gripped the sides of the dais and looked out over the audience making eye contact with the Squadron Commanders, the Regimental Commanding Officer, and the Corps Commander and guests. His quiet presence silenced the slight murmur of the crowd and focused their attention on the speaker, which was his intent. "Recently I was at Grafenwohr out near Hofenoh Church. The ruins of a small town can be found there as they are in many places in Germany. As you see them you cannot help but wonder who the people were, what were their dreams, their aspirations and how did they meet their end. There are also

309

many monuments in this country to soldiers, presidents and saints. What then are the monuments to the soldiers, the soldiers of the Blackhorse and of V Corps that are here tonight going to be. It is not likely that the ruins of a town with be unearthed to show any of us have ever passed this way. Very few of us will ever have a statue commissioned or a building named for us. No, that will not be our legacy."

He looked about the room and knew he had them listening now. It was not a trick, it was the truth and those that could believe would, and the rest were just along for the ride.

"Our enduring legacy is soldiers. Soldiers we have trained, taught and had an impact on for the better. Soldiers, who will man and lead the Army through the years ahead. The impact you have on them will last the rest of their lives and beyond. Yes, beyond. It will be passed on to their soldiers. Don't be worried about the lack of manmade monuments. No, we won't have statues for the most part. What we have will endure long after the statue is rusted away and its purpose forgotten. We will live on the hearts and minds of the soldiers we touch every day. Just like we will not forget, as the Regimental Command Sergeant Major goes on to bigger and better things. Command Sergeant Major if you would please."

Martin was a bit surprised by the strength of the ovation he got at the end. The other guys must have been a bit pedestrian because he sure had the crowd warmed up. He had grown close to the 3/11 Command Sergeant Major who was a real character. He had once won two Bronze and a Silver Star in one day in Vietnam. As he came to the dais, he grasped Martin's hand holding him fast saying, "You son of a bitch. I'm never following you again."

The next learning event for Martin came in the social time after the presentations. The wives of the senior leaders were the most moved and most vocal about what he said. They were also very cognizant of the distinction between the guest of honor and the body politic. He would need to be very careful and circumspect if he ever became a Command Sergeant Major particularly at rat screws like these. He still did not like to come to them and never would. But at least he was better able to understand how to put on a good one and how to avoid catastrophe through rehearsal. He was glad to find his driver and make his way back to Bad Kissingen.

29 Oct 1985

As the temperatures grew colder and the time for the pilot course drew nearer, even the Master Gunners started to get uptight over the content of their classes. As each class was presented, the Murder Board's ability to assist rather than merely correct or "sharp shoot" the instructor improved greatly. It had become clear to each of the instructors they not only faced the possibility of teaching any of the blocks, they had to know the information to guide the practical work. Martin had known his biggest challenge would be to establish collegiality among these ultra competitive NCOs. The murder board and the learning process had done it for him.

Walking down the hall of the Squadron Headquarters, Martin walked softly by the Executive Officer's door. He was busily assembling a book and Martin hoped to ease on by to the S-1 Personnel Sergeant and escape the attention of the Executive Officer for the moment. It did not work. "First Sergeant, come in here and see me," Major Bragg thundered.

"Yes, Sir, what can I do for you?" Martin said.

"You can give me a cigarette and talk to me," Bragg said with a smile. Martin shook out a Marlboro Red and produced his trusty Zippo lighter as he knew Bragg rarely if ever smoked and had no lighter.

"How is the course development coming?" Bragg asked.

"We have the instruction and handouts done and checked. I am going to give it to the Old Man tonight when he gets in from Regiment. If he approves it, I will get it printed in enough copies to get us through the pilot and go final after that. The big stuff he has no say about is already printed up and ready for issue, "Martin concluded.

"Go get the packet. I want to see it," Bragg ordered.

When Martin returned with the packet, Bragg motioned for another cigarette and began to leaf through the material.

He looked up and said, "Get us some hamburgers. Miss Virginia is at a nursing seminar tonight and the girl is at the German Babysitter. I'll pay for supper, you fly to get it. Oh, and say hello to old whats-her-name while you are there, no hurry on my burger!" Bragg said with a shit eating grin.

Well, there goes that cover. The junior officers must be talking to him if he knows about Marty. He just had to let me know he knew I was engaged in some form of conduct that is questionable though proving it would be very hard to do and prosecuting me even harder, even if they chose to do so, which was very unlikely. If the Army prosecuted everyone with a foreign girlfriend while on an unaccompanied overseas tour they would stay busy.

Martin walked over to the NCO/All Ranks Club and got two large cheeseburgers with fries to go along with a box of Twinkies from the PX with a quart of milk. Field rats ate junk food while they had a chance and if the great Bragg was smoking, there was no chance he could resist the Twinkies. Martin got the whole box of ten. He had a nice but short visit with his German paramour and arranged to meet her after she was off work later that evening.

On his return, he found Major Bragg deep into the Preparation to Fire checklist and pamphlet. The meal did not stop, or even slow Bragg's review down. He did not appreciate the Twinkies and the milk. He knew he would help Martin eat them all if he had a chance. By the end of the burger, the fries, and three Twinkies and a pint of milk, the large Major was ready for another cigarette.

"Can I trouble you for another Marlboro, First Sergeant?" he said laughing as Martin pointed to his Master Sergeant rank insignia. "You will always be a

First Sergeant to me, not no damn Master Sergeant. Now Black, he is a master Sergeant, not a First Sergeant even though he has G Troop. He will never get an ass chewing until the troops go hungry or someone gets hurt or the IG or Chaplain figure him out. Your buddy, the Earth Pig Command Sergeant Major loves him because he has all of that stupid admin shit lined out and perfect. Enough of that shit, he ain't here to defend hisself. Let's talk about you. All of this tells me how you are going to do it but it does not tell me why. Tell me the real why, First Sergeant, and no bull shit!" Bragg concluded, blowing a perfect smoke ring toward the high ceiling.

"When we were in the checkout for Instructors for the M1, I was learning to drain the chip collector from the hydraulic reservoir. It is the device that traps pieces of metal to prevent the hoses and valves from getting clogged. One of my buddies, a fellow Sergeant First Class, came to the rear of the tank and told me our Master Sergeant Chief Instructor Brookman wanted me on the phone. Brookman called to tell me I was selected below the zone for Master Sergeant and that he was locking me into a Master Sergeant slot as mission essential if that was agreeable with me. I told him that was fine. He wanted to shoot the shit with me about making E-8 and all of the stuff he had lined up for me. He then told me I was the last man to be notified and asked me if I had any questions. I said no. He was a little put out I wanted to go learn a maintenance task rather than talk to him. As I was walking back to the tank to finish draining the chip collector, one of my buddies asked me where I was going. He was astounded I was going to drain a chip collector and probably get soaked by hydraulic fluid. As he was one of the first guys to be promoted from the new list, he was telling them to stuff this Sergeant First Class shit up their ass. He was done learning about the M1 or any other damn tank."

"I told him this, 'I need to know where the chip collector is and how to drain and inspect it. As a First Sergeant, I may be the only one in the company to know where it is and how to drain it. The M1 is brand new to the Army. I want to know everything I can learn about it so I can teach and help my soldiers as a First Sergeant and as a Command Sergeant Major. We will all be learning about it for years to come'."

"Our discussion drew a crowd, most of whom thought I was nuts and should stand on my dignity as a soon to be E8 standing to one side with my arms folded like them to watch the task rather than learn it. I closed the scene by telling one and all that I had managed to make the E8 list in eleven years doing it the hard way and I was not going to change now, no matter what they thought. I got that damn hydraulic fluid all over me giving them some great entertainment."

"When I got here, I was the only man in the Squadron who had ever drained a chip collector and was able to coach the G Troop turret mechanic to drain it. The devil is in the details. There is always a chip collector in the deal. I owe it to the new kid in the fourth rank to know the answers. Smart

312

leaders never stop learning. Are you going to eat all of those damn Twinkies or can I have another one, Sir?"

0915 hours
31 Oct 1985
V Corps Hqs
Frankfurt, West Germany

Command Sergeant Major Ligon looked out a rear window and saw Master Sergeant Martin coming across the back parking lot of V Corps Headquarters in the old IG Farben building. Ligon was an old soldier not just in age but in outlook and habit. He could tell one of his men at any angle, day or night, once he knew them by their walk and carriage. His fearsome countenance softened and he smiled.

That son-of-a-bitch is damn up to something. He is walking like a man about to damn steal something. What the hell is it? Whatever it is, interrogating his ass will be more fun than anything else I've got to do today.

"Mary Ann," Ligon said, addressing the Command Secretary.

"Yes, Command Sergeant Major Ligon, what is it?"

"Call the MP checkpoint at post three. Tell them First Sergeant Martin is to be told to report to me after he clears through them."

Mary Ann Leighton was accustomed to brusque requests from the crusty Command Sergeant Major and limited her reply to, "Yes, Sergeant Major," and made the call immediately.

At Post Three, Sergeant Mattingly answered the phone in a perfect military manner, "Post Three, Sergeant Mattingly speaking, may I help you?"

Ms Leighton replied, "This is Miss Leighton, Command Group, please tell First Sergeant Martin to report to Command Sergeant Major Ligon immediately when he arrives at Post Three."

Sergeant Mattingly knew full well who Miss Leighton was and where she worked. She was a very attractive, middle aged, single woman of mystery who was very good at her job and who did not flaunt her status as the Commanding General's Secretary.

"Yes, Ma'am, he is approaching now. I will tell him," he replied, tactfully waiting on her to hand up her phone first. One did not hang up on one of the Commanding General's crew except at some peril. Sergeant Mattingly was handpicked to be on an interior guard post at Corps Headquarters and he was very good at his job, particularly the unspoken nuances that went with it.

As the Master Sergeant passed his ID card for screening, Mattingly instinctively did the MP scan. Six foot tall, about 200 pounds, Master Sergeant, not a First Sergeant, immaculate appearance, all sewn on rank, close hair cut, fresh shave, direct gaze, bold combative aura, in command of himself and all he surveyed. Mattingly hesitated as he checked the ID card against the roster

313

for entrance to the building, then found Martin's name listed under the block for 11ᵗʰ ACR.

"Has Sergeant Major Ligon busted me already, Sergeant Mattingly?" Martin asked politely.

"You are supposed to report to him as soon as you pass through this post, Master Sergeant," Mattingly replied.

"You gave me the message Sergeant. He has his schedule and I have mine. I'll report to him in the next ten minutes. Will that fulfill your obligation to the Command Group?" Martin said disarmingly.

"That will be good, First Sergeant," Mattingly relied, coming to attention in spite of himself. He was amused to see Specialist Jones, his partner quivering at attention beside him.

"Who was that guy?" Jones asked his Sergeant.

"Nobody you would want to 'jack' with Jonesy, that's for sure," Mattingly replied. "Anybody that makes Ligon wait has big balls, a death wish, or both."

Martin made his first stop at the Corps print shop. It was not busy. In the authorizing official block, he carefully printed Command Sergeant Major Ligon's name for each work order. Handing the German National, a Mr. Krautz, the work orders and the master copies Martin blithely waited while he checked every block and reviewed the print requests for the substantial order. Ligon's name worked magic. The German could not have been nicer and he promised all of the work much faster than Martin could have hoped it would get done. Martin told him he would be sure Command Sergeant Major Ligon knew what great work the print shop was doing on his request and thanked him. The thanks were genuine and Martin hoped Ligon would not even find out about the requests until he had the material in hand.

Realizing he was pressing his time limit given to the MP Sergeant, he quickly strode to the elevator and timed the jump to make it. The elevators in the Abrams Building were small, two to three person cars that moved in perpetual motion requiring some degree of agility and coordination to get on and off the conveyance. There were conventional elevators for freight, the disabled and large parties, but the denizens of the building and regular visitors disdained them.

Miss Leighton found herself standing when Master Sergeant Martin arrived at her desk. Once she realized he was just a Master Sergeant, she recovered and sat down. *This guy had presence and what a deep resonant voice, what had he said, she wondered, flustered and blushing.*

"Yes Ma'am, Master Sergeant Martin to see Command Sergeant Major Ligon as ordered," Martin repeated in a soft voice.

"Get your ass in here and report Martin. Stop trying to make time with Miss Leighton," Command Sergeant Major Ligon bawled from his office.

314

Martin went to the door of the Corps Command Sergeant Major's office and went through the procedure of reporting as if he were a trainee. Ligon returned his salute and told him to sit down.

"What the hell are you here to loot, pillage, and steal from the Headquarters today?" Ligon asked.

"Sergeant Major, I came up here to use your name to steal some printing services and some machinegun ammunition for weapons test fire as well as some GS/DS weapons support for Bad Kissingen. Your object lesson in my Arms Room opened my eyes and I realized we need to get ready and stay ready with our bread and butter, automatic weapons. We have a range to test fire them and your Corps level guys rarely get to test fire what they fix. If we get them to BK for a couple of days, we can get all of our bad automatic weapons fixed, they can shoot them to test the ones they work on and everybody gets some great Sergeants Time instead of bullshit."

"No shit. You are going to test fire every automatic weapon you have and get the broken shit fixed. By God, I want to be there to see that shit. You son-of-a-bitch. You wouldn't pull my chain would you about that ass chewing you got?" Ligon concluded.

"Sergeant Major, ass chewings are like bubble gum, they don't last long and they don't cost much provided the chewee listens the first time. You are trying to shake up and straighten up a whole damn Corps of 75,000 soldiers. The Corps Cdr did not bring you back on active duty to sell damn AMWAY. You were doing what you had to do to get my attention and you got it," Martin stated.

"Tell me about these print requests you used my name to get done. I don't give a shit you used my name and I did not let on to that damn Luger Head Krause. What's it all about?" Ligon demanded, switching to his Dutch Uncle tone of voice.

"This is it in a nutshell, Sergeant Major Ligon," Martin replied as he handed him a master copy of the publications for the course from his Army briefcase. "It is probably the last time any of these soldiers will see old time Army standards applied to teach modern weapons before they get to the Master Gunner course if they ever get selected. The reason they did so shitty on tank gunnery in V Corps is they all had one quart brains trying to solve one gallon problems. This course teaches everything they have to know to be successful and provides them a reference library to guide them as they learn. They are getting all of the secrets. It is Hogan in the 1980's." (Hogan being the semi-mythical Platoon Sergeant hero of Command Sergeant Major Ligon's fables and war stories he used habitually as practical examples in his speeches for the soldiers of the Corps.) At the mention of Hogan, Ligon gave Martin a hard look and then smiled a wolfish grin.

Ligon motioned him to a chair, lit a cigarette, threw him a clean ashtray and began to methodically study the notebook. Martin lit a cigarette and sat smoking quietly as the Corps Command Sergeant Major perused the material as if he had all day to do so. "What did you get on your PT Test last time," Ligon asked.

"290, Command Sergeant Major," Martin replied.

"Why not 300, First Sergeant?" Ligon said coldly.

"I had them score me at the eighteen year old level Command Sergeant Major. I had a bad day with pushups," Martin replied somewhat indignantly.

"This is some damn fine training. It is too bad you cannot stand the unit down to do it. It ain't the EIB is it? Anybody that cannot learn how to shoot that tank or the Bradley after this course needs a Chapter 13. Damn good job Martin. I know you are going to tell me a lot of other people helped you get it done but I know who done it. Make sure I get the dates for that test fire when you get it set up. You use my name to get shit done at Corps and I will back you up, just be smart about it. Now go back and get to work and leave Mary Ann alone," Ligon said with a wolfish grin Martin saw for the second time since he had known the man.

I'll be a SOB, the man has a sense of humor. Glad I passed his surprise inspection and got on the good foot with him. I would be long gone counting sheets and blankets somewhere otherwise. The experience taught me not to take it personal and to respond in the Army manner with discipline, order, and common sense, without anger. That was a long day he spent with me in good old G Troop and one I made certain would not be repeated. Mary Ann was safe from me, too close to the throne.

"Good–bye, Ma'am, thanks for your help," Martin said as he departed the office. He did not need to look over his shoulder as he knew the Corps Command Sergeant Major was in tune to his every move regarding the lady.

His next stop was the Corps G3 office where one of his fellow students in the Sergeants Major Course, Correspondence Study, was newly assigned. Sergeant Major Newbourne was a walking wonder. He was about the most efficient NCO Martin had ever known. He had it all going on and his troops invariably loved him everywhere he went even though he was an exacting leader.

"I heard Ligon yelling at you. Is everything okay?" Newbourne asked with a somewhat worried look.

"Yeah, I was using his name to get some back door stuff printed in a hurry and the print shop guy ratted me out for signing his name to the request. Ligon is an old soldier. He waited to see if I needed an ass chewing for lack of integrity until he verified what I was doing, God Bless him for that. Somehow I got on the good side of the guy and I am glad of it," Martin said with a wry smile.

"Hell yes, you did. It was that damn REFORGER that did it, not the maneuver crap, the Swim Bad. You getting them all clean with hot showers once or twice a week and no cold injuries. That and very few Companies pass his midnight raid after their initial ass chewing, very few. You had him pegged right. The only way to get out from under his thumb is to soldier your way out by executing what he wants you to do. He still thinks you over think the mission rather than act like an NCO but knows your heart is in the right place. Now what are you going to try to screw me out of today. I know this is not a social call or a casual conversation, First Sergeant," Newbrourne concluded with a smile.

"You remember that deal we talked about with the DS/GS guys and the machineguns?" Martin asked. When Newbourne nodded, Martin added, "Now I have the ammo and the range is certified for it, let's talk some dates with the leaders of those outfits."

"No need, you give me the dates and they will have teams there. Talked to both of them at the Corps Commander's NCO cook out at his quarters. He got in on it and now, everybody is hot on it. You were exactly right and they laughed like hell about your analogy of tuning up a jeep and never getting to see if it started and how it ran. I helped you out by telling Victory Six it was because of Ligon inspecting your arms room the deal was happening," Newbourne said, laughing.

"Victory has a thousand fathers," Martin's thoughts were racing, Kursk-Best tanks and tankers but no machine guns-Russians ate their lunch-Have to be ready to go wide open from a standing start-no more steady build up ala' WW II-maneuver warfare, decentralized ops-no more attrition-shut up take the help, credit does not matter, this won't last once the new wears off - Dear Mrs. Smith, there just was no time to get your son's machineguns working on his tank. We had 75% of the tanks in good shape-too bad his wasn't one of them.

"I appreciate everything you are doing up here for us. You have been there and know how it is. It is hard to push a log chain, you have to pull it. I gotta' go, there are a lot of loose ends to this Sabot academy thing and the pilot is next week," he said taking his leave from his old friend.

"Promise me one thing?" Newbourne asked.

"Sure, Top, what is it?" Martin said smiling.

"Give them a No Bullshit Crew Skills Test. Remember that nightmare at Graf in '75!" the new Sergeant Major concluded.

"How could I forget, Top, it will be a good TCGST," Martin said.

In 1975, Martin was a Staff Sergeant working for the then Master Sergeant Newbourne at Grafenwohr grading tank gunnery for an Armored Division. As they were packing to go home, the graders were told they had one more unit to grade. Newbourne selected eight "graders" to remain another week, live in officer quarters and work their butts off. Martin was one of the men selected. A unit scheduled to transition to the M60A2 was forced to conduct a graded tank gunnery in their old M60A1's to satisfy Unit Readiness Reporting Standards. They had fallen through the crack on the calendar, an error compounded by switch of tank priority and dithering by their leaders. Circumstances and tired unit leaders made it a slapdash affair. They were just going through the motions. Somehow, the leadership missed the point. Tanks are objects. They do not demonstrate proficiency,

317

people do. The accident rate was sky high. The Grafenwohr Commander relieved a safety officer from the unit for cowardice, and put Martin in his place without relief for 24 hours. Unit NCOs were busted and sent home. The unit field grades had been out of tanks for years and were not proficient. Main guns went crashing out of battery and in general, every problem that lack of maintenance and training could produce, happened. Not one of the accident victims had taken Tank Crew Gunnery Skills Test. Shoulda, woulda, coulda was little comfort for a guy picking his nose with his wrist when his fingers were left in the breech of a cannon. The graders were all hand selected from the 8th Infantry Division, Third Armored Division and the 11 ACR. Instinctively, they tried to lead the crews through the challenge. The leaders of the tested unit dug in their heels and fought them at every turn and in time, became stupid and proud of it. It was classic. A crew of the best tankers in Europe was grading the worst unit and applying the highest possible standard. The unit came apart at the seams once they figured out they had to pass, no matter how much it hurt or how long it took. There was no slack. Some crews fired Tank Table Eight Targets five times before the passed with a minimum score of 70%. The experience was a painful, negative leadership lesson no one that lived it ever forgot.

0900 hours
03 Nov 1985
Squadron Classroom
Bad Kissingen, W. Germany

"Good Morning Men!" Martin stated firmly.

"Good Morning Sergeant!" the pilot class of the Sabot Academy answered with as much hardiness as a Girl Scout Meeting. He decided to let it pass and be positive. Most of them had never seen him in the instructor mode so that would be shock enough for one day.

"Why are we here today? This is the pilot course for SABOT Academy, a short one week course that is going to answer your questions about the M1 tank and take away many of the mysteries that surround it. We the teachers do not have all of the answers. We are learning the M1 vehicle as you are. Our perspective is a bit different because we have seen all of the others that have come before it."

"We designed this course to be taught in one week. It is to teach you what you absolutely have to know with no frills or extras. To that end, it begins with a pre-test. This will serve as an inventory of the knowledge you have on hand. It is not an intelligence test that tells how smart you are. Everyone here is more than smart enough to learn the systems of the tank. It gives you a baseline to begin learning about the vehicle and separates what you do know from what you don't know. The test you take today is the same test you take to graduate on Friday. The test is yours to keep once it is graded and the score recorded. Do not write on or in the test booklet, just blacken the answer keys."

"The reason that the pre-test and the post –test are the same is simple. The course teaches you the technical aspects of what we believe you must know to win with the M1. This course is about combat skills and winning a no-notice war with the Soviet bloc. Tank Gunnery at Grafenwohr will be easy once you complete this course and the Wildflecken train up. Graf will hold no mysteries for you by the time you will arrive there in June. Once you begin to take the test, continue with it until you are finished. You have until 1130 to complete it. This is an inventory not a contest. You do not need permission for a break during the test except from your Tank Commander or NCO. Begin to work and do your own work."

As each student finished the pre-test, one of the Master Gunners graded it using an answer key and the student went outside to take a break or downstairs to get a coke or cup of coffee. The bratwurst lady from the railhead was to arrive at 1015 with her little truck and stop by the classroom before going up to the Motor Pool. Her visit was a part of the school house strategy for the course. Martin wanted everyone to have a chance to sample her wares and socialize during the break.

The Bratwurst Lady was a survivor. A child of WW II, she had over the years assembled a nice VW with the amenities she needed to sell snacks to soldiers at the railhead. Her male relatives worked on the railroad with the Bundesbahn so departures and arrivals were no mystery. Martin personally loved the bratwurst, the pomme frites, and the hard rolls or brochen she served along with the hot German mustard and the semi-cold Pepsis. He was probably breaking a few PX rules by having her here but so be it. The troops loved her.

As he watched her work the crowd of officer leaders and their handpicked command crewmen he thought about her early life. In his mind's eye he could see her in the Hitler Youth in a white blouse with nubile teenage breasts and hard nipples marching in formation with the rest of the girls from Hesse. Most Germans would tell you the Holocaust was a figment of Jewish imagination. Martin had seen the concentration camps and knew soldiers from WW II that had tried and failed to save the denizens of the hell holes. He had toured one of the camps near Grafenwohr and felt he knew from more than one source, it had happened. It was a lot easier to believe General Eisenhower than it was a camp guard. He also knew the German psychic was as Churchill characterized, "The German, either groveling at your feet or clawing at your throat." He was not going to lay all of these sins at the Bratwurst Lady's feet but he retained a healthy skepticism.

As the last test was scored, Martin began the critique of the test. He had not intended to discuss every question, just the ones: everyone missed; instructor pet peeves; misunderstandings; rationale for asking. The critique went very well. It was clear the soldiers had read over the handout material in advance and some of them had studied it in great detail. The Troop commanders who tended to pontificate were on their best behavior with their efficiency report rater present and sitting in the first row. Fortified by his coffee and

319

bratwurst, the Squadron Commander was almost eager to begin the course. He could smell the success in the air. This was a winner if he had ever seen one. He thought Martin gave the deep thinkers a little too much information in the critique but decided to let that percolate a bit and not interfere. The NCOs were doing great so far and the soldiers were far more interested than he had ever hoped they would be.

"Okay, let's talk about the characteristics and data of the M1 tank. We are going to talk about the theory and then adjourn to the tank for hands on to find all of the systems and make certain we have all of the parts and they all work. That is why we are being joined in the afternoon by the turret mechanics."

"You are very fortunate. You are mounted on a tank that can hit an enemy and kill him before he can shoot you. Add the thermal sight to the equation and neither night nor fog nor smoke will allow him to hide. Even if Ivan gets the first shot, he is probably not going to kill you because of the Chobham armor."

"This tank was designed by a team of geniuses, built by guys with Doctorates, checked by guys with masters degrees, is maintained by guys with AA Degrees to be fought by High School grads who love video games. The key to accuracy is preparation to fire using every system on the tank to its full capability and when one of them is not working, knowing the work around. On its worst day, in Emergency Mode firing battle sight, this is still the best tank in the world."

"This tank is designed to eliminate the reasons for missing targets. The geniuses call reasons we miss, the error budget. If you are shooting the M1 and missing, the first place you must look is within its parameters. The factors are divided into two categories, the automatic inputs and the manual inputs. The automatic inputs are those caused by the environment surrounding the tank- Cross wind, cant, tracking rate and range. The manual inputs are bore sight, Muzzle Reference System, air temperature, ammo temperature, barometric pressure and gun tube wear. If you are missing the target, these are the first places to look for the error. If they are all correct, the fault lies with the equipment and can be isolated. Remember, this tank will not let you fire unless the firing solution puts the round within one quarter of a mil to achieve a target hit. This is called a firing inhibit and will be explained in detail during the practical work. It has happened to me. As an Instructor at Knox, I set up the conditions to make it happen so I could see it. Most of you will never experience a firing inhibit failure to fire in peacetime."

The characteristics and data class went on with Martin doing his best with humor, varied voice inflection and other histrionic tricks to keep the class interested and awake. Mercifully, it was complete in one hour and they were on their way to a late lunch.

When they returned from lunch, the students were very surprised to be handed a large trash bag. Part of the exercise was to clean all of the tank sub-floors of all trash, debris and foreign objects. This was done concurrently with the instruction in each of the tanks. As the door to the sub-floor was opened, the turret was traversed so that the cant sensor, hydraulic lines and other components under the tank floor could be pointed out to them and inspected. They were shown the various modes of operation of each of the sights and instruments inside the turret. The turret mechanics from each unit were also peering down into the turrets and checking the tanks out for broken, worn or missing components. For some of them, it was their first look at the sub-floor of their Commanding Officer's tank. Many of the crews were very embarrassed at the collection of filth, Coke cans, leaves, training munitions, tools, and other items were found in the sub-floors. The import was clear to the leaders, if this was in the sub-floor of their command tank, what the hell did the rest of them look like. The smart ones also now fully understood why each crew brought their own tank to the training. It was not to be mass training but rather training of the mass. To their surprise, Master Sergeant Martin never uttered a word as the sub-floors were cleaned and the trash taken out.

As the afternoon wore down, in the training bay of the S3 exercise building, Martin called "AT EASE." When he had everyone's attention he spoke, "Today you found out the location and importance of the turret fire control, inputs and service items. You can see there is no room in the sub-floor for litter, trash and anything that does not belong there. Be a-holes, insist your troops keep their sub-floors clear. Categorize your misses by system, know why you missed and know how to hit with the second round. Train your troops to the point they can put their hand on a component in the dark, tell you its nomenclature, its purpose, what it does and the work around for it if it breaks. Tomorrow's instruction covers, machineguns, ammunition and vehicle identification. Your release time is up to your Master Gunners. In case you are wondering, I was not happy to see all of that shit come up from beneath the sub-floor. Now you know better. You know what is down there and how important it is to keep our dumb asses alive. It is past time for me to be angry about it. It is your turn to be a standard bearer. It was a good first day."

The next day four of the .50 caliber machineguns were dead lined and unable to be fired. Two barrels were shot out and unusable for accurate fire. They appeared to be of WW II vintage. Two of the coax machine guns had covers with the feeding mechanism incorrectly installed and would not have worked correctly. Tempers flared immediately and Martin jumped in with both feet.

"Shut up, all of you. Deficiencies are everybody's fault when found and no one's when fixed. Here are two new barrels from HHT's excess stock for the caliber .50's. Observe how the gauge fits the forcing cone where the head of the projectile would fit. That is what gets shot out and ruins the efficiency of the weapon though the pitting and rust spots don't help anything. Get me a ball peen and a punch and I will fix the feed trays in the coaxial machine guns and teach all of you 'how' in the process. The feed pawl of this caliber .50 is upside down. We will punch it out and flip it as well. No one is dead. No one is even hurt. Save your anger for the enemy. Cooperate! Help each other! It is us against the Russian hordes! We can survive if we are combat brothers and we kill them by the bushel."

Wednesday was dedicated to preparation to fire with a short class in the morning and the movement of the tanks to the local training area for the afternoon hands on work. The work was truly progressive as one block built upon the other. It was not necessary to go into detail about the components because they all knew where they were and what they did. Machine guns had been checked in great detail. Martin skipped the classroom portion going instead to the field to set up the targets and place vehicles for long range thermal viewing. He claimed the long communications cords he had built by the G Troop Commo shop. The class was very surprised to see each tank was being issued a long cord connecting at the driver's Combat Vehicle Crewman's commo station enabling the tank commander to speak to and hear the crew as he worked the Pye-Watson Bore sight device at the end of the gun tube. Previously, it was a convoluted affair with a lot of shouting, walking back and forth, and relaying commands by the driver. All of which were poor substitutes for the command and control now made possible by the cords. It was yet another swift stroke of the sword on a Gordian Knot of stupidity by the Master Gunners of the unit.

A key element of the course was the requirement for each and every crewman to operate the Pye-Watson bore sight device and demonstrate the ability to determine the bore sight adjustments needed. Staff Sergeant Jester made certain each crewman demonstrated he knew what to do to bore sight the tank. It was clear the checklist was a hit, and the cord solved the biggest issue of bore sight, communication. The sight of friendly vehicles in the thermal sight with thermal targets for comparison to prevent fratricide made the best of sense. The sight of a Bradley borrowed from Corps beside the thermal target was very scary to the soldiers. It was difficult for some of the soldiers to learn to fine tune the thermal sight but they now understood after seeing the potential for fratricide why just a blob would not do. Everyone realized however, in a maneuver involving a mass of vehicles it was command and control that would reduce fratricide.

The conduct of fire course caused the greatest controversy of the week. Staff Sergeant Mixon taught the standard fire commands. He also taught abbreviated fire commands. The Squadron Commander came alive and forbade the use of abbreviated fire commands. He wanted to hear it all and thought

322

the short version was potentially too dangerous. It was the most animated he had been during the course.

"The tankers are not ready for 'TANK, FIRE'. I only want to hear: "Gunner, Sabot, Tank, Up, Identified, Fire. I will allow LASING and RE-LASING." He was very receptive to the techniques shown in the defensive position. The ability of the M1 to remain in the hide position exposing only the gunner's primary sight and tank commander's cupola, setting up the entire engagement before pulling forward, firing with zero seconds exposure appealed to his sense of gamesmanship. It was a brutal expression of the tank's design.

Martin scared them all until they thought his comment through when he said, "Men, we're not looking for a fair fight. The M1 lets you set up for the shot and take it with one second or less exposure. The Regiment has 164 tanks with 50 rounds each or 8,200 rounds to kill 3,000 plus enemy vehicles."

When one of the young Captains protested the degree of preparation that appeared to be dedicated to defeating a range, Master Sergeant Martin defended the approach. "Captain, we did not design the Tank Table VIII engagements. TRADOC did that based on Israeli/Arab war experiences. What you see is armored warfare in the flesh and a policy of train as you expect to fight."

"But you wrote the shit at Knox, I know you did," the young Captain Kestner insisted.

"True, I wrote, tested it and qualified it. But I did not determine what the engagements were to be. The Commanding General of TRADOC & Commanding General of Knox did that. What I wrote fit their guidance. We do not have the time for discovery learning or inference, Captain Kestner. We have to be direct," Martin stated. "You call it teaching the test, I call it training as we fight. No matter what you call it, the crew still has to do everything right to get the tank ready and hit the target. They are on their own when the engagement starts," he said with a smile. "Also Captain K, I know I am getting there when good men like you think I am cheating. Were I you, I would train my outfit using ¼ scale targets for acquisition and half scale targets for firing up to Tank Table VIII. When the crews get to the scoring round the targets will look as big as houses. The hardest part of tank warfare is target acquisition by the crews. The element that sees first, decides first and shoots first will survive." Martin stated to the audience of commanding officers.

All too soon it was Friday morning. A pre-test review was held and the Squadron Commander gave his guidance on what was to be changed for the course. The post test was uneventful as everyone did very well and aced the test. The class provided some minor feedback that was useful.

Captain Kestner approached the instructors as they huddled after the students had departed, "I was about to ask you why you let the tests go out with the class with all those notes on them from the critique. Then I figured it out, finally, you could care less if the following classes all memorize the answers. It does not matter how they learn the material if they learn it and can demonstrate it. They can get it from osmosis for all you care, right Master Sergeant Martin?"

"You have a real future in the Army Captain Kestner. You have a great time awaiting you in Fox Troop after your period of servitude to the S3 is complete. The course is the wave of the future with a figment of past woven in it. Having a pre-study component as well as providing study material two to three grades above the responsibility level of the soldier, is old school. Determining the essentials for combat survival and teaching that, and only that, is not new. It fits the Squadron Commander's guidance. I only have to make him happy, not you and not these NCOs or even myself - just him. He is happy as hell and we are not changing anything."

After the second iteration of the school everything was executed like clockwork. The instructors knew what to do and did it. Some support evaporated but by and large everything got taught and taught correctly. On a Friday night in early December, Martin was buttonholed by a drunk at the NCO Club.

"I guess you know they are laughing at you, Martin. They memorized the test and they ain't studying shit but they ain't gonna' flunk. Guess they showed you huh?"

Martin's reply hit home, "Yes they showed me all right. Did it ever occur to you if they were memorizing the material they were also learning it?"

What a damn idiot and what an amazing grasp of the obvious. As he made his way to the annex for a reception and dinner party for Command Sergeant Major Ligon, Martin reflected on the school and what it had accomplished. He thought about what yet needed to be done and the long road ahead for the Bradley New Equipment Training and integration into the Army and the Border Cavalry. He was glad he had sent the best Scout NCOs with the most mechanical aptitude in the unit to the Initial Master Gunner Course. What a struggle that had been.

The great commander of F Troop had insisted on confronting Martin when he was the acting Squadron Command Sergeant Major, Ops Sergeant Major and Master Gunner in the weekly staff meeting about his selection of Staff Sergeant Gilberto Jesus Ramos as a candidate. He complained Ramos could not speak English well enough to be a Master Gunner or an NCO for that matter.

As the Squadron Commander turned to him for a reply to the scathing assault on his selection and his character, Martin gave a reasoned reply. "Ramos is the best man for the job as he has already struggled through a great many challenges in the Army. He can do many things. I would like to see a show of hands of the highly educated, erudite, and extremely competent men in this room who have my complete respect to illustrate why he was selected. I will list the reasons that made up the rationale. If you would just hold up your hand if you can do the following: Fly an OH-58; Defeat every scout and tank platoon one on one during Pony Fights OPFOR portion with minor losses; Pass the Scout Platoon Test at Graf

324

and end it with all vehicles running; Qualify every man in a scout platoon as an Expert with every weapon; Qualify an entire platoon on the Border; Patiently coach and teach the platoons from other units who you defeated so they win their next force on force engagement; Score 300 points on the PT test at the 18 year old standard; Rebuild a VW engine from the ground up and install it on one Sunday afternoon; Rewire the fuse box at OP 10 when the Post Engineers gave up on fixing it; Never quit smiling. Ramos is going to the course. Your guy is going to the next one. The selections of the first guys have to hurt. If there is no pain for their Commanders, we sent the wrong guy. I would not be surprised to see the Infantry Center move heaven and earth to keep Ramos there as an Instructor."

To answer the murmur that swept the room, the Squadron Commander waved Martin to explain his last comment as other than a knife twist into the gut of the Fox Troop Commander. "The Infantry is being tasked to do a new thing with a new vehicle. Most grunt two stars, their staffers and leaders believe vehicles on the Infantry battlefield suck up resources and draw fire. They avoid them like the plague in war and in peace. No one has to tell a senior grunt what he doesn't know. When they find folks with great aptitude who speak four languages-Korean, Spanish, German and Portuguese, like Old Jesus, they hang onto them. Infantry leaders are people oriented. Armor leaders are vehicle centric. As a 19D with an EIB, Ramos has one foot in each world. He will be a star at Benning," Martin concluded. He guessed that he didn't make a lot of friends that day.

The last two iterations of the Sabot Academy were very hard to execute. The Squadron was spread all over Germany in a variety of missions, the most difficult one being umpires for a downsized REFORGER run by VIII Corps. It took all of the leadership, the staffs and the support crews for the unit. When they were forward the calls for support, equipment, vehicles and replacements was a constant drain on the rear detachment. They went out three weeks early, ran the exercise for two weeks and chased the parts and pieces of the equipment and settled maneuver damage for two weeks. It was two months all but lost. For the first time, Martin had to call on First Sergeant Don Waters to help him set up the field portions of the course. When he went to see him, as usual, he got more than he bargained for. Sometimes he was sure Waters saved the heavy shit in his bottom right hand drawer just to hit him upside the head with it.

"Do you know this Sergeant Major Burton coming in here?" Waters asked Martin.

"Is it Nicholas K. Burton, 19Zulu, white guy, half-Cherokee, an Okie, multiple Blackhorse tours in Vietnam, Silver Star, Bronze Stars, Purple Heart, etc," Martin replied.

"Yeah, that's him. He was Patton Jr.'s lead dog tanker when I was a PFC. He was nuts in 'Nam," Waters replied.

"I know him. He was my Drill Sergeant in AIT in 1969. He is one of my personal heroes and there is nothing I wouldn't do for that man. If he is coming here we are indeed fortunate. He is a winner of the first magnitude. Let me be his sponsor," Martin said, surprising Waters.

"He arrives in Frankfurt Rheine Main at 0830 12 Dec. He's all yours. Since he is taking your place it is a good thing you are his sponsor. I told you it would happen. I would never have left G Troop if I was you," Waters said crowing the last part in his teasing way.

"I got it, Top, don't worry about a thing," Martin said.

"I ain't worried. If you want something done, give it to a busy man. What's one more thing on your plate?" Waters said laughing uproariously at his own joke and the situation. Waters knew full well Martin was a one legged man in an ass kicking contest and that the man loved it. True operators loved chaos because they were in charge while the non-operators were scared shit-less they would get blamed for something.

"Now what can I do to help you get this last two evolutions of your little school finished? Just tell me the five W's and spare me the motivation bull-shit. I can do that little bit of punk ass shit in my sleep, Big Sarge," Waters said with a sneer.

Martin replied, "Here it comes military genius: What: M-113, M3 Bradley, M577, NATO 59 with lifting device, ten e-type infantry targets unheated, ten heated polyurethane, one bore sight panel; Where: LTA in accordance with this diagram; When: Wednesdays by 1200; Why: Preparation to Fire Targets-Bore sight & anti-Fratricide training."

"So that's why you have the NATO 59 and the Bradley side by side with a 100 meter split, damn that is smart. You know sure as hell some dumb ass tanker is going to bust a Bradley with a TPT round at some point along the way if you do not do that. You really surprise me Martin. You are a lot more practical than I gave you credit for. That one thing is probably as good as the rest of it put together," Waters said grandly.

Waters, you are so full of shit. You have watched this whole thing like a hawk on a fence post looking at a rabbit nest. You puttered around as HHT First Sergeant and coasted along doing your thing. But, by God you said you would help me when my ass was in crack and they had all deserted me and you are, bless you, you old fart. But he is right. Fratricide will come when they are all very tired with no good sleep for days on an advanced exercise in the night with scouts forward. Have to somehow get these thermals tuned up and get the damn goldfish out of them. These kids think they look great when they really look like shit. Degraded conditions cause fratricide. Tired people and tired equipment engaging esoteric training scenarios equal dead or injured soldiers in training as screwed up orders and graphics do in war.

"Don, could you put your ear to the ground and see if there is anyone working thermal sights diagnosis and repair at the depot or Army level in USAREUR? Your buddy at USAREUR, would he be any help to find out? I know there is a contractor over here somewhere," Martin asked.

"Goddamn, Sergeant Major, I help you do one thing and you give me an S3 tasker any good Master Gunner should already be doin'. Well, I guess I can check it out for you since your Master Gunner element of your personality is so screwed up," Waters said with a sly smile.

"Yeah, you had no trouble remembering who was the Acting Command Sergeant Major when it was time to present the Regimental Command Sergeant Major his award and make a speech about how great he was as a leader, unless you wanted that job," Martin said giving Waters as good as he got.

"Oh no, I'll leave all of that schmooze stuff in your hands. I was in my room on quarters that night, too sick to attend. I was as close to that Bible Thumping Hypocrite SOB that night as I ever wanted to be," Waters said with a deep long laugh.

"I want all of the M1 thermal sights checked and repaired before we go to Wildflecken," Martin replied.

"You don't want much do you? You are unreasonable!" Waters replied scoffing at the thought.

"Reasonable men never get anything done. They let other reasonable men talk them out of it. Assholes get stuff done because they won't take NO for an answer," Martin replied with a smile Waters knew he did not mean. When it came to the mission and his troops no one was a bigger asshole than Martin.

"Yeah, you and Rommel, the best form of troop welfare is good, hard training, right Martin?" Waters said with a big grin.

"You have me in some fast company but I do agree with him on that one," Martin said.

True to his word Waters came through and helped Martin through the last two iterations of the Sabot Academy when the entire chain of command lost interest. As they watched last class of SABOT Academy do the practical work for the preparation to fire class, Waters spoke very quietly to Martin, "I see why you worked so hard to get it done. It is great for these troops. With the NET training, a failed gunnery, the new Unit Conduct of Fire Trainer and a Wildflecken Gunnery to practice on, they ought to smoke Level I gunnery at Graf. The aircraft checklist alone is worth 20 qualified tanks and is invaluable in combat. Someday, the average tanker may be able to get the M1 ready to fire without a detailed checklist but it is still a good thing to have. You focused on the weak link in the chain, getting the tank ready and diagnosing faults. The written list; the long cord for the TC; having each crewman learn how to do the bore sight; and the detailed test, are all surefire methods to institutionalize the process," Waters opined in a quiet voice.

"Why, Don, you just used a three syllable word. I think I'm going to have your subscription to the Army Times canceled for high brow thinking," Martin said, moving instantly to his right. His quick move thwarted the larger man's grab for him and they eyed each other laughing as Martin stayed out of Waters' reach.

The big man knew he could not catch him but before he could fake him out for another try, they were joined by Major Bragg, the Squadron Executive Officer. "Well, this is it, First Sergeant Martin, the last roundup, call in the dogs and piss on the fire, Sabot Academy for M1's is over. I see the First Sergeant Mafia led by Don Waters here saved the day for you. Are you a convert, First Sergeant Waters, or do you think he is Mad as a Hatter like the rest of the Regiment?" Major Bragg asked with a big smile.

"Hey, Sir, just 'cause I helped him don't mean he's not nuts. He is a dangerous man. He is an idealist. I did not do it to see him succeed. I just did it to make those Troop Commanders that screwed him look stupid. Oh no, he is crazy! That is for sure," and they all had a good laugh, Martin most of all.

"Seriously Martin, can you tell me something?" Waters asked.

"Sure, Top, what is the question?" Martin replied.

"You know that Sergeant First Class of yours that threatened suicide, Fogararty. Well the shrink said he was a paranoid schizophrenic. Can you tell me what that means in terms I can understand?" Waters asked sincerely.

Martin looked at Major Bragg before answering as he knew the Major's wife was a Psychiatric Nurse with her Master's Degree. She was also a runner. He had it all with her, whip smart, good job, in top shape, good mother, attractive and hot.

The look provoked Bragg to say, "You know I would like to hear your answer to that, First Sergeant. Soon you will be a Command Sergeant Major and you need to translate shit like that for guys like me and Waters - I sure as shit don't know the answer."

"Gentlemen, paranoids build castles in the air and schizophrenics move into them," Martin replied.

"Why did you put an NCO on him to keep him from following up during the night?" Waters asked.

"The shrinks say if the unit can keep them alive until morning, the outlook for a complete recovery is good. Besides if they commit suicide successfully, prevention is no longer an option is it, First Sergeant? And the other reason is there is no way his mental state is not connected to his service in Vietnam. He was on a flame thrower PC in the Blackhorse. The shit he saw is more than enough to give any rational person nightmares. He got crazy in the service of his country. To me he is walking wounded because of his head just as sure as he is from that shrapnel he still has in his knee. Just because they don't give purple hearts for mental injury doesn't mean it didn't happen. He will be okay with the therapy and happy drugs. He won't ever be a First Sergeant. He retires next year when he rotates. The S3 has plenty to keep him busy until then. He is a good man. We will continue to watch over him and help him," Martin replied.

"I'm surprised. I thought you would want to chapter him out," Waters said looking off to his left preventing either Major Bragg or Martin from seeing his expression.

"The Army Regulation forbids the Chapter of a soldier over 18.5 years service by administrative discharge. He has survived for 19 years. No one is putting him out now. I am not a Vietnam Veteran but I damn well know Fogarty is walking wounded from that war. There ain't nobody putting him out of the damn Army except over my dead body, First Sergeant."

"Hey, hey, take it easy, big Sarge. I'm just checkin', that's all," Waters said smiling.

"You love to pull my chain. At least I am consistent on people screwing over wounded veterans and glorifying Jane Fonda," Martin replied. "As to the question you have not asked, yes, I am damn glad Sabot Academy is about over. The last couple of iterations without full support were too hard."

"Did you see the writing on the guard tower wall, Sergeant Major?" Waters asked laughing.

"Yeah, I saw it. The question is, do you agree with it?" Martin said with a rueful smile.

"What was it?" Major Bragg asked always glad to hear one on his favorite NCO.

"Master Sergeant Martin, a Legend in His Own Mind," Waters said and both he and the Major laughed heartily while looking at Martin expectantly to see his reply. He did not disappoint them.

"Now I know how Moses felt when his brother Aaron made that damn golden calf. Here I am trying to lead you people up from the pit of ignorance and you want me to develop an ego deficit and become humble. I am sure the Private that wrote that could have easily thought up and taught Sabot Academy in between Jet Pilot School and Brain Surgery if he did not have so much guard duty. Shit, the Privates are entitled to make fun of me and every other guy who talks like a used tank salesman. No Private can understand someone who is serious all of the time and trying to save the world. But then I know something that Private don't. The Army puts you in charge of a unit but you don't command it until you make the jack-offs in it do something they either don't want to do or think they can't do and it works like a charm." Martin said with a broad smile.

"It is time to plan Wildflecken but I want to be sure Sergeant Major Burton is in on that effort. We are going to be bending the rules like pretzels to meet the Squadron Commander's guidance. When those rules involve live ammunition, you have to be honest with yourself and meet the spirit as well as the intent of the laws and regulations," Martin stated.

"Do you ever get tired of the shit, man? It never stops, one operation right after another," Waters asked.

"Never, when that starts to bother me, I will retire. The real challenge for me is remembering that Generals seem to forget. Units do not stay trained. People are the main ingredient - not a tank or a PC. Unit turnover is about 20% per year. What we know from experience, the new guy has never seen. We do not have time for them to learn from their own mistakes. Any fool can do that. How we integrate the new guys and teach them determines everything. As long as our demands make sense and we avoid a double standard we will have a good unit. Drill Sergeant Duty drums that into your head. The guys standing in front of you in new fatigues in the afternoon are not the guys you trained for eight weeks and shipped out that very morning - they are newbies and they do not know shit," Martin said with a broad smile.

"I'm glad you weren't my Drill Sergeant," Waters said.

"Me, too. Your first demerit was probably horseshit on your saddle blanket with Custer," Martin said dodging away from the lumbering giant.

CHAPTER 12 - PERFECT PRACTICE

"Practice does not make perfect, perfect practice makes perfect" John Wooden, UC-LA Basketball Coach.

0900 hours
10 Dec 1985

"Sergeant Major Martin, you had a call from some Warrant Officer at USAREUR Headquarters from the G4. Here is the information. He wants you to call him as you as you come in to the office. He said it was very important. He has called twice since 0730. Who did you piss off up there now, Bud?" Sergeant First Class Scott Jackson said. Jackson had known Martin well when they were both at Fort Knox as Instructors, Jackson in Maintenance Department and Martin in the Weapons Department. Before that the two had been Drill Sergeants in the same Battalion as Staff Sergeants. When there was no one else present no formality existed between the two old friends but Sergeant First Class Jackson was never familiar when they were not alone.

"Beats the shit out of me, Scottie. I have been talking to some folks up there about trying to get some old Service HEP* issued to us but not anyone of high rank," Martin said looking at the note.

High Explosive Plastic is an ammunition type of 105 mm that was intended to be used to destroy bunkers, buildings and material and as a last resort, armored vehicles. It was often unstable and had been withdrawn from the Armor Force when the leadership elected to only store and issue two types of ammunition, SABOT and HEAT for tanks.

"Yeah, right. Somebody ratted you out and this guy is probably her boss. There is a woman in this somewhere, I'll bet," Sergeant First Class Jackson said with a wry smile.

"My source is a cute little Spec Four and I did promise her a night out in Heidelberg and a space on the next Ski Trip from G Troop. I found out from a grunt friend of mine that they have a lot of extra service HEP at the ammo dump at Miseau. The OIC is dying to issue it to someone. It is a total of 5,000 rounds in four different lots. I laid on the transport from the 561st Polish outfit to get it moved to our ASP (Ammunition Supply Point) for tank gunnery. I got special permission to fire it at Wildflecken. Shit, I had to give up a thousand rounds of it to get Smokin' Joe to let me do it," Martin said with a rueful smile.

"Does Lieutenant Colonel Covington know about this shit?" Scottie asked his buddy.

He replied, "What do you think Scottie? I kept him and Smokin' Joe out of it officially in case the deal went sour, but no, I did not tell him I was doing it. Better he not know. He still has a bright future in the Army," Martin said looking at the note as if he could determine its import by re-reading it. Smiling at his own stupidity, he said, "Guess I had better call the Chief to see what is on his mind."

"USAREUR Ammo Chief McKutcheon speaking, Sir," was the answer at the other end of the line.

"Morning, Chief, Master Sergeant Martin here returning your call. What can I do for you?" Martin asked.

"Are you First Sergeant or Master Sergeant Ronald E. Martin, late of G Troop, service number 304-46-9918?" the voice at the other end of the wire asked.

"Yep, that's me, Chief," Martin said, about to lawyer up and not say anything more. He did not like the turn of the conversation. The Chief knew everything about him and he knew nothing about the Chief, never a good sign.

"You know, First Sergeant, you almost had it made. Specialist Timothy was all set to issue you that 5,000 rounds of service HEP. Except for one thing, I am the sole authority for the issue of ammunition by order of the USAREUR Commander, General Otis. As a former Instructor at the Armor School I am sure you are aware that DA has put a cap on the number of training rounds issued annually for tank practice at 110 rounds to make people use the UCOFT. You do know about the cap don't you, First Sergeant?" Chief McKutcheon asked.

"You know, I heard something about that Chief. But Chief, you and I both know that old HEP is just going to sit there in that old ammo dump and rot away if no one shoots it," Martin replied.

"For your information Martin, General Otis told me at 0600 staff call today he knew there were people like you in USAREUR and he wanted to know who they were and where they were assigned. He said he remembered you from REFORGER and to tell you nice try, but no cigar. Tell me something, how the hell did you plan to move it? That is a bunch of dangerous cargo for a Cav outfit to moving around Germany using unit transport," the Chief asked conversationally.

"Now Chief, you would not want me to tell all of my secrets would you?" Martin asked.

"When I became a Warrant, I was an Sergeant First Class on the E-8 list with twenty years service and I am a Chief Warrant Officer 4 over thirty now, serving at the direction and pleasure of the President. It is the Commanding General's question, not mine. I already know how you were going to do it; he just wants to see if you will lie about it. I told him you would not lie once your ass got caught trying to steal the rounds," he answered laughing in the background.

"I was going to use the Polish Truck Battalion to move it for me Chief. We go back a ways with those guys," Martin replied.

"Damn, Martin, those guys are a USAREUR asset tasked out to V Corps. You have some balls partner. You were stealing Otis' ammo and using his trucks and workforce to move it for you to home station. He will 'shit a brick' when he hears the whole story. Who else down there knows about this Martin?" he asked pointedly.

"Chief, this was NCO business. None of my officers knew a thing about it. The way you tell it we were coming over the fence in the night stealing the shit. Other than the cap, which specifically applies to training ammunition, not service ammunition, I did not do one thing that was illegal, or outside the Army or USAEUR Regulations. Chief, you know the CAV, if you ain't cheatin' you ain't tryin' and if you get caught, you ain't tryin' hard enough. This is an administrative matter that got stopped by a Commanding General USARUER directive. It ain't no double naught, naught spy deal that Jethro Bodine has exposed to Uncle Jed," Martin said.

"Okay, First Sergeant Martin, it was legal. But you still ain't getting the ammo. You need to brief your chain of command up through V Corps and you had damn sure better tell Ligon yourself. He is an old buddy of mine and you do not want him to find this shit out from the USARUER Command Sergeant Major," and with that being said, Chief Warrant Officer 4 McCutcheon with over 30 years service, hung up his end of the phone.

"Goddamn, what was all of that shit?" Scottie asked.

"That was the head ammo puke for USAREUR being the big man, Scottie. He is a damn paper pusher whom I am sure they love. He makes them look good. He has probably removed more than one thorn from the paw of the Otis Lion. I had scored the rounds but the system won out. I guess I better tell Smokin' Joe the jig is up but I'd better tell Ligon first," Martin said.

"Damn, you're going to call Ligon direct?" Sergeant First Class Randolph asked.

"Oh, hell, yes, of all the people I have to confess to, he will take it the best. He thinks less of Warrant Officers than he does Arabs and he thinks less than nothing of them," Martin said with a smile.

Martin was right, Ligon was the easiest call. "Screw that son of a bitch Warrant Officer. You are right. That shit will be sitting in that ammo dump when Kamerad rotates. Don't worry about it. I've got it. Were any officers involved?" Ligon concluded.

"No, Command Sergeant Major, no officers were involved it was just me and the US Army Sergeant First Class who is the liaison to the Poles. He never knew the details but then there was nothing illegal about it as far as they were concerned," Martin replied.

"I know some of your officers were involved. You are protecting them, that's good. This shit will all blow over. Is there anything you need down there? If there is, you call me," Ligon said just as he hung up the phone.

When he called the Regimental Commanding Officer he was too busy to talk so Martin left him a short message, "Yes, we have no HEP today. Uncle

Otis says nice try, no cigar. Ligon knows," The secretary was curious but Martin assured her Smokin' Joe would figure it all out very quickly.

The new S3 Major Jared Klenk came into the back office to say hello. "Well, I'm all in processed. How are we doing on the MOI for Wildflecken?"

"We are not doing so hot, Major Klenk," Martin replied, then added, "I have the boiler plate on the word processor but the details have yet to be worked out. The guidance the Squadron Commander gave has to be worked against the ability of Wildflecken to support us with the space, targetry and land we want. Plus, the Squadron Commander wants to review the entire round count for the year for the tanks and order the 25 mm for the Bradley to get the account started once NET is complete. I am sure that will be a three man effort and we will be helping him figure all of that out. The cap on 105mm is weighing on the senior leaders of the Regiment. The Squadron Commander is going to count the shit himself. No staff summaries on this one. A Lieutenant General has told him he sucks on tank gunnery and he is giving him one more shot to get it right. He wants data he can trust, his own. Can't say as I blame him. It will only take a morning for the three of us to thrash it out. The Squadron Commander is working on his third BZ promotion, the big one, Bird Colonel. He is doing more right than wrong, that's for sure."

With that, Major Klenk closed the door saying, "How far do you really trust the Squadron Commander? Is he a true blue guy or does he say one thing and do another? It is hard for me to figure him out."

"Before I take that one on, tell me something, O' Great S3," Martin paused.

"Of course, esteemed elder Sergeant Major, ask away," Klenk said in the way of soldiers who trust each other.

"How in the hell did you get through Ranger School with your bum foot?" Martin asked.

"It must be that Drill Sergeant thing. You don't miss much. They liked the way I ate. I went to Ranger School in between my Junior and Senior year of college. I was a varsity football player with the foot. They loved it 'cause I played Safety. I did everything everyone else did in Ranger School. I never quit, never bitched and cooperated when I was not leading, plus I cheated by stealing a truck and they loved that. Most of all they liked the way I ate. I ate everything on my tray and was out the mess hall door before the instructors had salt and pepper on their food." Major Klenk said.

"All of that plus you have a lovely wife. That gets you the brass ring Major. Lieutenant Colonel Covington is a complex man in a simple business. He believes the troops are as smart as he is. As such, they should be content to finish a solid second as second is only one step from winning. Now you and I view second as the first loser, he does not. He plays the percentages. He wants to win the most ground at the least cost in treasure, sweat and blood.

He believes running more than two miles for PT is a waste of time and energy. He does not understand to over train physically is money in the bank. Men who play the percentages bother guys like us because we are idealists who want to give it all for every task. You and I will never understand him. The best we can do is co-exist and accept him for what he is. He is in charge and what he wants, rules, regardless of what we think or believe. The Commander wins all ties and all arguments. The good part is he has more humanity than most and is not a micro-manger about everything. He gives a lot of leeway to subordinates, is a good tactician, a true friend to his fellow Commanders, a devoted husband and father and a true patrician," Martin concluded.

"So you like him then, right?" Klenk said.

"I respect him. He is not my beau ideal of a Cavalry Officer but he is in charge and I honor the system that put him there. He could have hung my ass out to dry more than once as a First Sergeant and he chose not to do so. So respect will have to do for now," Martin said with a smile.

"How about me?" Klenk asked.

"You! You are a butt head with more brains than common sense who is here to get qualified as a Major and move on as fast as you can get gone from this crazy outfit. You! I like you because you overcome obstacles and achieve success in life. You are a cowboy from Wyoming out where men are men, a defensive football player, a math whiz, an Airborne Ranger and a BZ Major. I also respect you because you ask the right questions and you listen to the answers. Plus you are writing my last efficiency report as an E-8 that goes to the E-9 board and I need a good one," Martin said laughing.

"You a-hole. I am going to say, 'This NCO has hit rock bottom and continues to dig' or maybe, 'Soldiers follow this man out of curiosity to see what he will screw up next'. You will be lucky to get to retire as an E8 when I get done writing that report. What is all that sauce about my wife?" Klenk said with a big fake smile.

"Sir, your wife is way too good for you. She is a lot of woman who loves her man. You both married late and kids are not in the picture. She reminds me of the one that got away in my life and I regard you as a lucky man to have her. Plus she is a far better cook than my old heart throb. Never worry, you are the one for her and she is country enough to kill any man who gets stupid with her. Anyone who would mess with a woman who can skin an elk deserves all they are going to get," Martin said with pride.

"Who was the one who got away, Top?" Klenk asked playfully.

"She was Miss Trudy, a thing of beauty. She was 5'4"with 48 inch double E's, an 18 waist and 36 inch hips. In a black sheath dress and heels with long red hair, I watched her cause five car wrecks in the noon time traffic in Indianapolis just walking to lunch. She was a great dancer, played the piano, sang

335

like an angel, was a CPA and loved me more than anything," Martin said wistfully.

"What happened?" Klenk asked.

"I was a draftee. I was bound for Vietnam and got snatched out of line for the plane at Oakland. She was used to good living and I guess I just could not believe it was the real deal," Martin said with finality.

Just then, the Squadron Commander began banging on the door saying, "Okay, open up and face the music."

As Major Klenk opened the door, Lieutenant Colonel Covington said, "Change of plans, bring the ammo charts and training calendar to my office, now. I need to see it all this morning. The Regimental Commanding Officer has called a late afternoon meeting. I want to determine the allocation for each training event for the 105 mm and 25 mm we have now before I go into the lion's den tonight."

As the three of them entered his office with the Squadron Commander leading and Martin and Klenk following carrying the traps they would need, Lieutenant Colonel Covington told his secretary, Mrs. Carolyn Baumgartner, "I want you to take all of my calls while these two are in here Carolyn. I'll talk to the ones that outrank me, my wife, and emergencies. Everybody else has to wait but the Executive Officer, he can just come on in, okay? Thanks!" and with that he shut the door. It was obvious he was about to enjoy himself as he lapsed into being an S3 again, if only for an hour or two. He saw Martin smiling and asked, "What's funny, First Sergeant?"

"It's nice to hang out with people who enjoy their work, Sir," Martin said with a smile. "Before we get started, Sir, I suggest we develop some assumptions that frame the effort and keep us on track to accomplish the mission. You may need some butcher paper for a hip pocket briefing to take up there in your briefcase. You may not need it but 1/11 is at the flagpole and 3/11 will have coordinated with them. I don't want you ODF."

"By ODF, I surmise that means Out Der Flapping. Thank you, Sergeant Major. You're going to be a big success when you get promoted. Just a minute guys." Lieutenant Colonel Covington then proceeded to hit speed dial on his classified phone and very quickly had set up a conference call with the other two Squadron Commanders on speaker phone. It was not necessary for him to tell his two subordinates to be quiet.

"Guys, are you doing a dog and pony for the ammo allocation for the meeting tonight? I am a bit concerned about it and I am doing a little bean counting here today. I did not want to show up with a big hairy brief on ammo and have the Regimental Commanding Officer ask you for yours," the Squadron Commander concluded.

Both of his fellow Commanders agreed counting the ammo was a smart thing to do but briefing it without being asked was dumb. They then all agreed to have a set of charts in reserve but not to bring it up unless asked.

336

They also agreed to have another call at 1200 to resolve ammo issues among them. As he hung up, Lieutenant Colonel Covington was very pleased an issue he had raised was settled so well with his peers. His fellow Squadron Commanders were not total back stabbers but it was clear to Martin and Klenk, Lieutenant Colonel Covington was a most faithful peer. Neither of those other two guys would have ever made that telephone call. Of the two, Martin knew Lieutenant Colonel John N. Abrams was in a league of his own. The other two commanders would have been happy to just to have his brain farts. He had been Martin's S3 as a Captain and was usually at the finish line waiting on the maddened crowd to decide which way to run.

Martin mused about reading the Creighton Abrams Sr. file years before. It had been a PhD course for Martin to read his Captain Abrams Dad's old MOIs and orders from his days as a Battalion and Division Commander. The adage that brevity is the soul of clarity was personified by the writings of Creighton Abrams Sr.

His present Commander broke that reverie with bantering. "Let's see your assumptions Sergeant Major. After all, you have had ten whole minutes to develop them. I am expecting them to be prescient and topical."

Martin went to the chart and listed the assumptions:

- HETs to and from Wildflecken-Save Tank Wear and Tear
- PH- 98%-SABOT, HEAT & Prep to Fire
- PK-100%-Plywood targets-no one should have to fire twice
- Follow on Level II is in Oct 86-No legacy issues w/New SCO
- No cap on Machinegun Ammo-Fire extra 1,000 rounds per tank-Swap barrels
- No cap on Training Device Ammo
  -Use 1/64 size targets
  -Train acquisition even if it causes failure on early tables
  -If it moves it dies
- Mini-Tank Range is squadron Asset-Assign by Troop & Company
- U-COFT is running 24x7-either CSM/S3/SXO/SCO see each crew perform x 2
- Tables VI & VII & Modified VIII day night can be fired in one 24 hour period
  -Eliminates 2xdays of verification firing =6 rounds
  -No target larger than a NATO # 59 (BMP Turret) until TT VIII
  -Range 23 can handle all three tables w/creativity
  -Emphasis -Lay, Dump, Laze and Blaze
- No ammo point-pre-loading tanks eliminates need
  -Support Plt, Inspection, Tank Guards remain (Headquarters overwatch)
- De-Briefing at Wildflecken includes VHS Tape-each crew
- Flash Cards –Key Points each engagement

- Table IX not fired –Plug in Mad Minute if Rounds available

Based on these assumptions, the three Cavalrymen began the task of allocating the ammunition to each task. Lieutenant Colonel Covington was giving guidance; Klenk, ever the graduate level expert in Math, was working his trusty calculator and Martin was taking notes. The notes encompassed the changes required for the written order, the quantities of ammunition and a running total of what ammunition remained.

"What the hell are you doing, Master Sergeant Martin?" Klenk asked with alarm.

"I'm writing down the ammo and tracking it, Major Klenk," he replied.

"But how? You don't have a calculator. No one can do calculations in their head that fast. I have been watching you. The Squadron Commander speaks and you write down the numbers before the answers come up on the calculator, and you are always right," Klenk exclaimed.

"Major Klenk, the multipliers remain the same for the tanks, there are forty one of them. If the task is day/night, I use the total rounds he wants fired for one tank's iteration and multiply it by 41 and then double it for Level I. I have been doing calculations like this for years in my old units and at the Armor School. It is just second nature. Why don't I just wait for you and your calculator to catch up?" Martin asked pleasantly.

"Watch this Major! Martin, tell the Major how to calculate the arrival of air support when you know the distance from their orbit point to your fight. Go on, tell him," Covington said with a broad smile.

"Sir, UH-1, 1.5 miles per minute; Ch-47 & Cobra gun ships, 2 miles a minute; fully loaded jets, 9 miles a minute," Martin said without looking up from his chart while continuing to add ammunition totals.

"Major, don't worry about how senior enlisted men know, just employ them to do the work of the Lord," Covington said.

In less than two hours the allocation and verification process was completed. The finer points of the administration of the off season gunnery were hammered out and final guidance given. The points that were not solved would wait for the arrival of the new S3 Sergeant Major and the scheduled trip to Wildflecken Range Operations and G3. The S3 would then make the modifications needed to resolve differences to meet the Squadron Commander's guidance given the multiple tasks the Squadron was facing. Lieutenant Colonel Covington surprised them both by assigning each of the Squadron leaders a unit for monitoring during home station training. He took F Troop and assigned Martin the Tank Company, Major Bragg G Troop, and Major Klenk E Troop. Each would retain their squadron duties but would visit training, with emphasis on the UCOFT during the ramp up phase at home station. The group would meet on command and report as needed between meetings. Each would be the Champion of their assigned unit and a mentor for them.

0800 hours
12 Dec 1985
Rhine Main AFB, Germany

Martin did not envy his former Drill Sergeant, Sergeant Major Burton, Nicholas K. AKA "Nick." He was walking into a hornet's nest. But, if they had it all done in concept and made the trip to Wildflecken they could work out the details. It was not rocket science, just details, where the Devil lived and lifted weights on steroids. Pre-positioning of assets, combining security, strict ammo accountability, training to the toughest possible standard early in the process, recording results on TV video, teaching fundamentals and employing everything the crews had learned in SABOT Academy were all steps making up the total effort. Nick would understand. His task was not to do it but to see that it was done. Be good to see him again. Wonder if he remembers me. He has no idea of the impact he had on me and many others. I know now he was just doing his job. He did it very well. He used every leadership principle in the book and a couple besides. Wish I knew more people at Wildflecken but never had the time. I hope he does. It will help us all if he can make an impact right away. The key to Wildflecken was to develop the youngsters into pros. Pros practice so that they never get it wrong. Amateurs just practice until they get it right. Each crew had to turn that corner. It was going to be painful. It will be sweet if we can get at least half of them to learn to strap the tank on like a pistol instead of it being a ride.

The Squadron Van used to transport family members and usually the exclusive property of the Squadron Commander was the vehicle of choice to pick up the new S3 Sergeant Major Earl K. Burton. Martin had decided to use the Command Sergeant Major's driver as he was extremely familiar with the van, the route to Frankfurt and with Rhein Main Air Force Base. He was also probably going to be Sergeant Major Burton's driver should he decide to take on Command Sergeant Major McCall's duties during the latter's frequent periods of absence for medical treatment and hospitalization.

Sergeant Hardaway was leery of Master Sergeant Martin. The young NCO kept his distance and was cautious around him. From his hospital bed in Wursburg, Command Sergeant Major McCall told him to support Martin every way. He had done so but he was happy Sergeant Major Burton was here. Sergeant Hardaway did not want his Command Sergeant Major supplanted by Master Sergeant Martin or anyone else but a Sergeant Major. He certainly had not wanted to leave Bad Kissingen at 0600 but Master Sergeant Martin was very strict on all matters of safety and it was a foggy morning. He could not figure Master Sergeant Martin out or classify him easily. He was very tough but fair, using Hardaway only for those duties directly connected with the office of the Command Sergeant Major. He always took him along when he visited Command Sergeant Major McCall in the hospital. He treated

339

him very well, particularly on overnight trips. He used the S3 guys for S3 business. Hardaway knew them well. They had a large fund of tales and anecdotes about Master Sergeant Martin whom they idolized. They were a cohesive and happy group of soldiers. Hardaway decided he would see what he could learn about Sergeant Major Burton from Martin.

"Master Sergeant Martin, Command Sergeant Major says you know Sergeant Major Burton from before, that right?" Hardaway asked.

Martin looked up from the Sergeant Major Academy text he was studying and regarded Sergeant Hardaway with a baleful eye. "Yeah, I know him. He was my Drill Sergeant in 1969. Another Drill Sergeant was determined to put my ass out of the Army any way he could to make the Commanding Officer happy. Burton bucked the Commanding Officer and kept me in the Army. Good thing. I was at rock bottom and had no place else to go. Burton taught me a lot about taking care of soldiers, tank gunnery, ranges and armor life in general. He was a great Drill Sergeant and I owe him a lot. I intend to pay him back over the next year, in full, whether he remembers me or not. I never forgot him and I never will."

"Now, as for you, Hardaway, you are Sergeant Major McCall's pick for a driver and you are his guy. I have respected that and used you strictly for duties in support of his office. You need to figure out what you are going to do next. You are a scout, a 19D, in an unauthorized position, at least for now. You need to seriously consider going to a tough scout platoon and learning how to be an effective Squad or Section Leader. For all you know, the next Command Sergeant Major may drive himself and not want a driver, let alone an enlisted aide. In any event, you need to decide what you want for your future. You have done all I asked of you, but it was not much. I owed you counseling. You just got it. You have had a good little gig hanging out with Sergeant Major McCall but your clock is ticking, bud. In this Army people are either moving up or moving out. If you are not moving toward Staff Sergeant you are walking backwards. Right now, you are at dead stop in this job of yours. Questions, Sergeant Hardaway?" Martin concluded as the young Sergeant shook his head east/west.

"Good, I'm going to go inside and find our new S3 Sergeant Major," Martin said.

"Do you want the sign, Master Sergeant?" Hardaway asked referring to the sign he had made.

"Hardaway, you must be two people. One person could not possibly be that dumb. He was my Drill Sergeant for two months and I served with him for six months after AIT. I could pick him out of the crowd at a night game in Yankee Stadium if the lights went out!" Martin said walking away from McCall's dog robber, smiling and leaving him in shock.

Rhein Main AFB was not O'Hare International. The flights were few and far between. The incoming charter flights were turned around quickly and became the outgoing flight as soon as the aircraft was cleaned and serviced. Martin walked to the gate where the passengers would be getting off the Delta Airlines DoD charter, thinking as always.

Whoever the genius was that figured out a way for the government to finance the airline aircraft purchases under CRAF (Civilian Reserve Air Fleet) and thus get first call on their assets in time of war, was a smart guy. Do the math, the personnel costs for troop carrier pilots balanced out the finance charges. Hell, a lot of the pilots were in the USAF Reserve anyway. Too bad the "coastal artillery" guns were all facing the wrong way, against yesterday's enemy, shades of Singapore. DoD was all set to fight yesterday's enemy with tomorrow's weapons. At least they had half of the equation right - new weapons - the new enemy was the x-factor. I'm sure I'll know him, I wonder if he will know me past the name tag and the welcome letter.

As befitting his grade, Sergeant Major Burton was one of the first passengers off the plane behind the pregnant women and the families with small children. He did not have a carry on except for his briefcase. Martin greeted him, "Welcome back to Germany, Sergeant Major. We are glad you are here. We have a van to take you to BK after we pick up your luggage."

Sergeant Major Burton looked Martin over with a big smile. "Boy did you make rank fast. How long did it take you to make E8, Martin?"

"I got lucky, Sergeant Major, fourteen years. About average I guess for a tanker. Nothing special. It must have been that great AIT you gave us in 1969," Martin said with a smile.

"Yeah, shit. It was a hell of a lot more than that. Tell me about yourself and what you have been doing," Burton asked.

Martin could see Burton had changed very little physically in the past seventeen years. He was still a tall, slender, immaculately turned out soldier with just a hint of Indian bloodline. He still sported the same jug ears, big smile, beautiful teeth and the hint of terrible menace lurking behind the kind eyes. A strong handshake and elegant manners but country at heart. No one could fake the Oklahoma cowboy way, you either was one or not.

Martin gave him a thumbnail sketch of his career since AIT and said he wanted to wait until they were in the van to fill him in on the unit and the current events there.

Burton was shocked by Martin's obvious weight lifter physique. He had been so damn skinny in AIT and afterward. He was obviously strong as an ox now and an outdoor guy with great self confidence and assurance. When he moved, people got out of the way in the terminal with some of them flattening against the wall. No wonder his buddy said the older Command Sergeants Majors called him Sir Ronald.

Martin asked Burton about his girls and how they were doing. Burton reported the oldest was married with two small children and a good husband. The youngest was still at home with them, about to start college and would be with them in Germany for at least a time. Both girls were toddlers in 1969 and Nick had to care for them as his wife was deathly ill with ovarian cancer. The great hospitals in Louisville took very good care of her and she had recovered completely. Nick's wife was as he recalled, a very fine looking, dark German gal with elegant clothes, looks and manners from a good family in Bavaria.

"I always wanted to have a chance to tell you how much it meant to me to have you for a Drill Sergeant after Plowhaven rode my ass until my tongue was in the dirt. It was such a relief to be treated fairly. I have always appreciated your role in that part of my life. I know you were just doing your job, but the fact is, the way you did it saved my ass. The result was when I got to be an HFMIC, I tried to treat everyone the way you treated me and let them step on their own crank. Then I hammered them, but not before. I saw Sergeant First Class Plowhaven after I made Master Sergeant at the Armor School," Martin said.

"What did the boy have to say about that, Martin?" Burton asked.

"He told me he had more fun losing his stripes than I did earning mine and I suspect he meant it. He also told me I was foolish for running at noon in the heat and was sure to kill myself. I promised him I would be careful and told him not to worry, he would be retired by the time I came back as a Command Sergeant Major to Fort Knox," Martin said laughing.

As the bags came onto the carousel, Martin noticed a young Specialist come up to Sergeant Major Burton. Burton motioned to Martin to get his bags and he went off to the side with the soldier. He was obviously counseling him, probably finishing a conversation begun on the plane. Martin smiled as some things never changed. Sergeant Major Burton was still making a big impact on the Army, one soldier at a time. It was no trouble for Martin to get the duffle bag onto his shoulder and set up the suitcase for travel on its wheels while Burton finished talking to the youngster. As Burton joined him he tried to take the duffle bag but Martin would not let him, giving him the suitcase instead saying, "Oh no, I missed PT this morning so I'll carry the duffle bag, Sergeant Major. I need the exercise. I'm getting fat on staff, 'cause I never miss a meal."

Once the bags were stowed in the van and introductions made to Sergeant Hardaway, Sergeant Major Burton took the seat in the center rear of the van and Martin turned sideways in the front seat so they could talk.

"I thought we would stop and get a bratwurst and a brochen at this little kiosk on the way, if that is okay, Sergeant Major?" Martin asked.

"That's fine, Martin," Burton agreed.

During the ride, Martin briefed his former DS on every facet of the unit beginning with the mission through its organization and equipment, personalities of the leadership, current status and future training. He spent some time on SABOT Academy and demonstrated more parental pride in it than he had intended. Sergeant Major Burton was very impressed and somewhat in shock to see the "training monster" he had created from long ago. He was also very grateful Martin had held back on publishing the Wildflecken Memorandum of

Instruction until they could make a trip there to meet all of the people Burton knew would help them. Burton knew everyone there and "owned the joint" in city street terms. Once he had heard the conditions the Squadron Commander had demanded, he knew it would be an interesting trip to the training area, to say the least.

"The guy that really runs the training side of Wildflecken is a German civilian named Richard Rheinhardt who runs the G3. He will do anything and everything it takes to make training a success. I know him very well. He is a genius, always thinking and scheming to make training better and more realistic. He does not get a lot of help from USAREUR. If we can find a way to help him the return will be like the Bible, 10 times 10. Just having him on our side is enough. Waiting for me gives me some ownership and responsibility for the process - it is just what I need to get off to a good start. I want to meet the Command Sergeant Major right away even if we have to go to the hospital to do it. There is some of that stuff I want you to continue to do especially if it will make the First Sergeants more comfortable. How do you feel about that?" Burton concluded.

"I only did the bare minimum as the Command Sergeant Major. A lot of the soldiers think I have the big head as it is but it ain't so. I would prefer working the training hard and letting you do the ceremonial stuff. There is hardly any to do. The Regiment is too busy for formal balls, dances and formations and so is the Squadron. I think the great Sergeant Major McCall will be back soon and knowing you are here in the flesh will probably do him a lot of good. You will give him someone to talk to and he can bounce ideas off you," Martin said with some enthusiasm.

"You seem awfully positive about him. He must be a good man," Burton said with an obvious question in his voice.

"He is a good man. He's a grunt in a Cavalry world. He does things like a grunt and he thinks like one. That is not all bad. He takes care of soldiers and demands everyone else take of them as well. He wants the simple things done first before the panache. He has done very well to make Command Sergeant Major and has given a lot of himself to get there. He is our Command Sergeant Major. I have, and will continue to accentuate the positive and eliminate the negative as far as he is concerned. His nickname among the senior NCOs is "Earth Pig" but I have never used the term and I never will. He has been good to me although he and the former Ops guy screwed G Troop and lied about it. I fixed the Border schedule once as a First Sergeant and they screwed me. When he was stove up with his back the Squadron Commander piled it all on me. I did it my way. The Squadron Commander backed me up instead of agreeing with the last Troop Commander that kissed his ass. It is as fair now as it will ever be. Besides Top, we have an S3 Major, a Major Klenk. I'm sure he has some very definite ideas of how he intends to employ you. I am your sponsor and you are here now. Your quarters are ready and I am signed for them. My influence will end when you sign in and the system takes over. I am yours to command. We will have a great time until I have to go to the Academy in June of next year."

"I feel we will have a great Level II gunnery at Wildflecken and we will put into practice all I taught those jokers in SABOT Academy. These officers do not really get it. No one has seen tanks and tankers shoot the way these guys are going to shoot at Wildflecken. I am going to place spare targets on the ground behind the target berms to enable us do quick replacement throughout the days and nights. These guys are going to shoot out the center of the targets to the point they will not get a laser return." Seeing the question in Burton's eyes, Martin explained further. "The laser beam will go through the holes and won't be reflected as it would with a new or repaired surface. I know I sound like a used tank salesman but I know that tank inside and out. In the hands of trained tankers it is the most deadly instrument of war to hit a battlefield since the German Tiger with its 88 in WW II. If the damn Russians had a clue how good it was they would give up right now, join OPEC and own New Jersey in six months. I'm excited," Martin finally said.

"No shit, you are excited. Do you know why I love you as much as you like me - for real?" Burton asked seriously.

"No, Sergeant Major, but I would like to know," Martin replied.

"The day we went to the range at Knox and I was the field first I was wearing my fatigue cap from Vietnam and my Jungle Fatigues with a double Blackhorse patch set. I had spit shined Cochrans and was looking good. Then the first round out of a fifty cal went off and I dived under the water trailer and got dust and dirt all over me. You and the combat veterans were the only ones not laughing at me. You guys knew the deal. I was still in Nam in my mind. I was out of my tank, in the open and a machinegun was firing. It was instinct but the laughing really pissed me off. I was a little short on temper and understanding during that time and just plain mean when it came to killing folks. I knew then and there you were going places in the Army. In tough times, events move in slow motion for you for the most part, don't they? I mean if you can get just an inkling of what is coming. Nobody can do shit when a round from a tank is fired into a mess hall except duck and cover. It is instant analysis and calm under pressure. Sometimes I think guys like us are more afraid of screwing up than of getting killed, don't you?" Burton asked.

"I feel that way. You have put me in a category I have not earned, Sergeant Major, but I am glad to hear you feel that way. I just hope I can live up to it," Martin said with some humility.

Martin continued, "You are going to hear people tell you that I am giving away the farm to get crews qualified at tank gunnery. I just wanted to take the time to tell you there are two camps in the unit. I will give both sides of the story."

"There are people in the Army and our unit who believe while discovery learning and failure are painful, they are good medicine for our soldiers. That school of thought believes we should give the troops the facilities to train on and let them find out and work the details on their own. Teaching details is cheating the test and should not be done. If you make it too easy, everyone will qualify and the test loses both validity and prestige if everyone passes it the first time."

"I disagree with them completely. Two reasons, the first is obvious, no one knows when we are going to go to war; the second is less obvious but just as true, there is no virtue in having units where half of the soldiers are ignorant. We do not tolerate a culture of 'haves" and "have nots" for supplies and equipment, we should not do so for knowledge and skill. I do not believe in telling people the range to a target or backlighting targets for them with IR searchlights or in giving points not earned."

"What I do believe is our superiors think Table VIII is the test of critical skills our tankers need to be ready for war. The tactics required to defeat the course are simple when compared to war with an active enemy also trying desperately to win and to stay alive. I believe in training with the use of flash cards with key indicators spelled out for the crews as teaching points. I am working on the draft set of flash cards now. I have them when you want to review them."

"My technique says the test represents war. Teach them everything they can absorb now. Give them written notes to help them remember. Write out the steps to prepare and bore sight the tanks so that they can execute it perfectly with a crew checklist read by the driver. Bring in technical experts who work above depot level to inspect sights and machineguns before gunnery. Again, be ready for war now. Use the smallest possible targets through Table VII to teach target acquisition so that when the full size targets come up on the final test so they will see them move. Video review with audio for take home after Level II gunnery for each crew-that is the Squadron Commander's pet rock-I agree with him. I probably sound like a broken record to you. This is a lot of info to get in a short period of time. It may be more than you want to hear Sergeant Major," Martin said.

"Let me see the flash cards, Martin," Sergeant Major Burton said.

As Martin opened his briefcase Sergeant Major Burton saw it contained more than flash cards. There was a Model 29, four inch barrel .44 magnum pistol with two speed loader clips of spare ammunition in the brief case. "Damn, Martin, what is that damn cannon doing in there?" Burton asked.

"We never go anywhere unarmed, Sergeant Major Burton. It was too much trouble to go to the Arms Room so I just brought this one from home. This was my gift from G Troop when I left there. It is very accurate out to 100 meters as long as you hold high past thirty meters. The drop is about 18 inches at 100 meters," Martin said as unloaded the pistol and passed it to Sergeant Major Burton with the cylinder open and empty.

Sergeant Major Burton closed the cylinder and hefted it for balance and trigger pull, smiling at the hair trigger for single action, "Don't take much, does it?" as he handed it back. Once Martin had the pistol back, he reloaded it and passed Sergeant Major Burton the flash cards.

Sergeant Major Burton may not have realized it but Master Sergeant Martin was going to school on the way he conducted himself. Burton carefully looked at each card, smiling at some of the comments on the cards. Martin gave him the space to review them without uttering a single word. Instead he lit a cigarette while the Sergeant Major was reading and watched the road unwind ahead.

"Master Sergeant Martin, I didn't know you smoked," Sergeant Hardaway said.

"I do, Sergeant Hardaway, just not very often, about ten a day when I'm not trying to stay awake in the field for days at a time," Martin said smiling.

"Martin, I would not change a thing on any of these cards. They are very good in all respects. They are not slick like a training aid or a GTA. I don't think we want them to be, do you?" Burton asked.

"I agree with you, Sergeant Major. They need to stay homespun. We will keep copies available as replacements," Martin said.

"Shit, it would be a damn fool that would lose this set of notes. These kids will have these notes for years until they are yellowed and faded. From what you have told me and from what I see, if we have a good Wildflecken, we should have a great gunnery. I do not have a lot of thinking to do or planning either. What I have to do is make the people part of it work, starting with Richard at Post G3 Wildflecken. You have everything else covered like a blanket. It sounds like SABOT Academy was great. Can you get me all of the materials you taught from so I can review it before my wife arrives? It will keep me off the street," Burton said with a smile.

"Yes, Sergeant Major, I can do that. Basically, the fact remains there is no body of work to support the M1 tank. It does not exist yet because there is no one with any practical experience on the tank. What we did was to use the school to infuse the crews with knowledge. Putting them through it together had some rough edges, particularly for the Captains. Wildflecken will put the icing on the cake. The problem is all of the field exercises, training, umpire duty for REFORGER, and reinforcement of USAREUR units will take us to zero manpower. There will be little, or no, ability to train up except for the UCOFT and it too is an entirely new thing for everyone. The solution is perfect practice for each crew. They will have to repeat the engagements they screw up until they cannot make a mistake if they wanted to on them. It will be a lot easier than it appears to be now. We just have to set the conditions that will enable them to have a perfect practice session," Martin said.

346

"Sometimes it is good to make a mistake in training. Mistakes promote learning when they are pointed out and the crews and soldiers understand what they did and how to fix it. Perfect rehearsals nearly always result in lousy operations because no one learns anything. It almost makes me cry to see everything we have for these kids. I wake up sometimes at night and think about how many of guys who got killed in 'Nam that would be alive today with someone like you to run a SABOT Academy and a gunnery program like we have going on here. Hell, the MILES alone would have saved 10,000 lives but then a little smart leadership from LBJ would have been great. He never figured out the VC were not American politicians whose arms he could twist and who responded to gradual pressure. Those jack-offs just needed killing and that is the only thing that impressed the North Vietnamese. His dumb ass strategy and our rotten allies made it damn hard to come out ahead. But, what can you do but go soldier where they send you and do the best you can, right?" Sergeant Major Burton concluded with a million dollar smile.

After a short pit stop at the Bratwurst stand, the three travelers remounted their trusty VW steed and continued on to their Kaserne. It was amazing to Martin that Nick knew people that the lady who owned the bratwurst stand knew in the German State Police. They had a nice chat about mutual friends. It would be an education to serve with Nick for Martin and everyone else in the unit as well in all probability.

The reception for Sergeant Major Burton in the unit could not have been better. Martin's prediction was on target. Major Klenk grabbed onto Nick like glue and took over his unit orientation - as well he should have. Martin resolved to pick him up when it was time to go to his quarters and told him so. Burton's reply was unexpected, "You don't have to do that Martin, just give me the keys to the quarters. My brother-in-law is bringing me one of his cars to my quarters tonight and will take the train home. My USAREUR driver's license is still good from my 1st AD tour and I have my International Driver's License from England so I am good to go for transportation. My Ford pickup will be here soon and the wife will drive his car back to him in Munich. You got to understand I am as much at home here as in the states. We are back and forth to Germany all of the time. You got stuff to do, go to it, I'm okay, okay?"

0900 hours
18 Dec 1986
Headquarters 7th Army Training Command
Wildflecken, West Germany

"Richard Reinhardt, meet Ronald Martin. I have been anxious to get you two wild men together just to watch the sparks fly. Have you had a chance to

347

read the summary of what we want to do when we come to your house, Richard?" Sergeant Major Burton asked.

Martin and Richard shook hands and exchanged greetings. Richard Reinhardt was a tall well set up German with the appropriate size beer belly but with an appearance befitting a German working in US Civil Service at the GS-13 level. His countenance was that of a man with a very active mind totally dedicated to his mission of providing training facilities and devices to the US Army and the German Army, the Bundesfehr. As Martin was to learn, Richard was a veteran of the US Army with four years service as an instrument repairman. When asked to describe his latest projects by Sergeant Major Burton, the Americans were totally astonished by his response in idiomatic English spoken without any trace of an accent.

"I have read the summary. It is not doable at the moment but it may be if we can get some help and some damn big dump trucks."

"We are proud of our silencer for the 20 mm cannon on the Marder. The sound of firing does not project off Post, at all. It won't be a stretch to do it for the Bradley when it comes. We are ready for the new SABOT round for the 120 mm, the one that dies at 2,200 meters. It will open up a lot of land for impact area that is closed for now. We have these hot targets. I took two plastic targets and glued them together back to back. We then cut a hole in the bottom of them and put a hair dryer in the hole. We put an electrical inhibit switch on the target lifter to heat them in the down position. When they come up, presto, they are hot and the gunner sees a 3D set of hot targets in his thermal sight. The small holes from the machineguns do not cause much heat loss and besides, not many tankers even hit them. They are still being treated like area targets. This is the concept for Range 23. I am having a lot of trouble getting enough dump trucks to move the dirt I need to construct the second moving target and the far targets to enable 1,500 meter plus ranges for the M1 to shoot at on the move. I need some help. The Colonel is all over my ass but he has no assets to give me and you don't either except for your engineer company. We can configure Range 23 to let you shoot the early tank tables to save moving the tanks from range to range. We can let you park, here, just off to the south of the bleacher area of Range 23, in between interactions during the months of March and April. But, if I can't move the dirt, it won't matter. You will have to move from range to range and you will not be able to meet your timelines for the other tasks the Squadron must do. Finally, your plan to load all of your ammo on board the tanks and cut your guard force to just the Headquarters guys requires you to use Range 23 exclusively for all of your operations."

"Martin, get in touch with your buddy with the Polish Labor Battalion, what's his name, oh shit, you know who I mean," Burton said as he tried to remember the point of contact.

"I'll call him now, Richard, if you will let me use your phone," Martin said politely.

"My house is your house, Martin. Just don't haul any of it off and sell it on the black market," Rheinhardt said smiling broadly.

As he dialed, Martin said, "His name is Richter of all things guys and he is nearly always by the phone. It's ringing. Hey, Richter, Martin here. Do you still need some work for your twenty ton dumps? Yeah, rations, quarters, fuel and full support. The mission is Wildflecken, is support of your parent USA-RUR Seventh Army Training Command so you get full credit. Let me put Richard Rheinhardt on. He is the honcho here. He is a an old US Army vet and a German citizen GS-13 so no bullshit is needed, just tell him what you need for support for the drivers and he will provide it. I will square it with the Corps G3 Sergeant Major while you two talk, here's Richard."

"Richard, this Sergeant First Class Richter who is looking for a GS job over here by the way. He is the coordinating officer for the Polish Transport and Labor Outfit attached to V Corps. His word is good," Martin concluded the introductions and handed the phone to his namesake and now an obviously relieved German civilian.

Martin immediately went to Richard's work table and used the other phone there to dial up the Corps G3 Sergeant Major and coordinate the contact. "Yo, Sergeant Major Newbourne, I just put Sergeant First Class Richter in direct coordination with Richard at Wildflecken for an asker not a tasker, to provide twenty ton dumps to move some dirt for a couple of weeks. Wanted to give you a heads up."

"Always out there hustling like Crap Game in Kelly's Heroes ain't you, Martin?" Newbourne said with a smile."What's the short version for my boss?"

"Richard at Wildflecken has a great plan to re-make Range 23 into a viable Tank Table VIII for V Corps. The twenty ton dump trucks of the Polish unit will enable him to complete the project in time to train V Corps prior to next gunnery in support of the Corps Commanders directive to Armored Unit Commanders. How does that sound bite grab you, bud?" Martin asked.

"Damn, are you looking for a job, Ron? We could put you straight into PAO. Seriously, is that what is going to happen?" Newbourne asked.

"It is that simple, Sergeant Major" Martin stated.

"Okay, Martin, thanks."

"It's all set guys. The Corps G3 is on board," Martin said as he hung up the phone.

"You get thirty 20 ton dumps to move the dirt on Range 23 when you and Sergeant First Class Richter figure out the time frame you want to do it. You owe them quarters, rations, laundry, fuel and individual health care at the clinic. Sergeant Major Burton and I are out of the picture, it is between you guys to coordinate," Martin said with a smile. He had really grown to like Richard in the short time they had spent together so far and knew how important getting the ability to move the dirt was for him. Richard had done what so many hard chargers do, he had planned a big event, got it approved and then resourced it on a wing and a prayer. That might work in resource rich USAREUR but it could get you fired at most other places. The three of them then adjourned to Range 23 to nail down how they would skin the cat for the Squadron event.

Richard was nearly over the shock of his good fortune by the time they arrived at the range. In less than thirty minutes, everything Martin and Burton needed to do to meet the needs of the unit was approved. Richard was the approving authority for ammunition storage, range layout, HET downloading, environmental cleanup, target selection and range sequencing. Once everyone understood the unit would be responsible for the set up and teardown of the stationary targets for Tank Table VI, all barriers to their strategy were gone. The German workers were responsible for the set up and tear down of the ranges. It was outside their purview to allow units to fire all four exercises in one location and beyond their ability to support it with workers. Richard knew the unit would simply use fixed targets at fixed locations down range with pre-sited butts. The unit would simply erect the targets he would build for them and repair or replace them on the spot for the units that followed. Unlike the soldiers of the modern era, Burton and Martin were used to building their own targets and emplacing them at positions directed by range control. While the new system of McDonald's Drive Through was great, there are times when the old ways are best, provided you knew what to do and how to do it. Between the two of them, they both knew every trick in the book to range set up from the days when it was ugly. As they went down range to ride the moving tank target to check the track, the two of them looked at each other and roared with laughter.

Richard had to know, "What is so funny guys? This is a great mover."

Martin answered him, "It is not your mover we are laughing about, Richard. It is a great piece of machinery particularly since you built it all here in house, congratulations. We are laughing about the last time we did this in 1969. We were sitting on the front of the mover carriage with our feet hanging over and the full size tank target erected behind us. It was a great day at Fort Knox, the morning sun was out, we were early, all of the tanks were operational and the trainees were going to be thirty minutes late. Sergeant Major Burton was a Staff Sergeant and the NCOIC of the Range and I was an Acting Sergeant Private First Class in hog heaven. Sergeant Major Burton looked at me and said, 'I hope that stupid ass Sergeant Parkinson does not take a shot at the mover'. He was going to do some crew drill with his trainees. No sooner were the words out of his mouth than the damn target vibrated and a 90 mm hole appeared in the dead center of a virgin target. The vibration was followed by the sound of the shot. We were glad for the cover of the protective barrier and got on the radio to the OIC to tell him to cease fire. Technically we were not in any danger as the track and rail car we were riding was far below the top of the safety berm. But, it was hairy to be down there with a tank firing on a range not yet opened for firing."

"You tankers think that was funny? Armor guys sure have a strange sense of humor," Richard said.

"Hey, Richard, if it doesn't kill you, it makes you stronger," Burton said with a smile.

"Richard, stop the mover," Burton said abruptly as the device reached the last fifty meters of its permissible engagement area."You are going to need to put in a lot of gravel here Richard. The tankers will shoot short on the mover and the rounds will go under the tracks from here to the barber pole marking the firing limit. The upward angle of the target increases the range of the target. Slow shooting crews will shoot short line and swear they hit the target. The fast shooters will never notice. The slow guys will have to adjust their point of aim like our flash card tells them Martin or they will miss this mover. Tell the engineer calculating the grade of the track to add more dirt to the barrier or your tracks will be shot to hell in no time."

Richard stoked his beard and agreed it could happen but it was clear he was still stuck on the incident at Fort Knox from 1969 while the two old lifer dogs had merely laughed and moved on to the business of the day.

The three of them decided to eat lunch at the monastery atop the mountain named the Kreuzberg outside of the Wildflecken training area. It was a short distance by civilian roadway from the range where they had passed the morning but a light year in terms of tradition and values. For most, the strong beer served by the monks was the attraction but the two senior NCOs would not be drinking. Richard would have to hold up the honor of the group and have a beer with his lunch. Beer was, after all, mother's milk to a German at lunchtime. Whatever was on the menu would be fine for the three of them as there was hardly ever a bad meal in Germany.

Richard knew all about the Kreuzburg and gave them a mini-travelogue on the way up the mountain. The monastery church construction began in 1681 and continued until 1692. It had been home to the monastery since 1681 when construction began on the church. The brewing of the dark beer began about fifty years later in 1731. For Martin, raised among the Amish, the contrast of the cloistered Monks with their Friar Tuck bowl haircuts, flowing brown robes and sandals even in winter was understandable. It was more of a way of life than a religion. Hard bitten soldiers tend to be cynical when confronted by religious iconoclasts. When one group of idealistic folk encounters another, their first search is often for common ground, provided they have some degree of erudition. Their second objective then becomes a search for hypocrisy. The monks may have dressed funny but they had phones, electricity, fax machines as well as portable radios and a Rolex or two. Intermingled with the peacocks and very large mastiffs walking about, the scene could have come straight out of the Middle Ages.

The interior of the restaurant could be best described as rustic. The tables and chairs were of finished wood and were devoid of amenities such as table cloths. The fare was very good, tasty and hot. It was not expensive for the area and the three had a hearty lunch with the boys in uniform having cola and Richard drinking a large Kreuzberg dark beer with his lunch. Martin never ceased to marvel at the huge piece of pork roast he got with French fries for a very low price. He could not eat it all and suffered through the inevitable questions from the waitress about the quality of the food and his health as he left some food on his plate. In a previous tour to Germany, Martin had begun to order the children's plate as the great fare along with the generous portions would make an old soldier fat in no time.

"So my friend, this is your first time here?" Richard asked.

"No, Richard, but it is my first time here in fatigue uniform. Every other time I have ever been here we were restricted to Post and I could not sample the wares of any of the attractions nearby," Martin stated without hesitation.

"You mean you obeyed that and never left post as a young Soldier, even for Graf and Baumholder?" Richard asked, incredulous.

"Listen Richard, I don't know what kind of REMF outfit you were in but in those hard ass outfits I was part in, you either obeyed your Battalion and Brigade Commanders' orders to stay on post or you got hammered. A lot of senior NCOs, some of them with five combat tours, either got terminated or their careers were halted in grade for off post misconduct at a training center. We were cleaning up the Army from the bottom up and not taking any prisoners. There was no place for a double standard though it did happen. One Article 15 as an NCO and it was all over for future promotion, and it still is. Some of the alcoholics made it through for twenty years but most did not. They flamed out," Martin concluded remembering the wild men from those times.

The Wild Man, Captain Ford, AKA Pecos Bill, sent me and Robert L. Doolittle to Weiden in his M-113 to drag some senior NCOs out of a bar and get them back to Range 42 on Grafenwohr. I did not have the heart to tell him I did not know where Weiden was. I broke into my combat supply of maps to be able to navigate to it and return. Doolittle was pissed he had to go along and was determined to at least get a beer out of the deal. He was trying hard to stay on the straight and narrow. Having his Platoon Sergeant go get drunk and leave him home on Range 42 pissed him off beyond reason. He damn well knew the way but since the Commanding Officer had put me in charge and he out ranked me, he said screw it and refused to help in any way. I made it, dodging MPs, avoiding highways, and hiding the PC in the woods. We got the dozen NCOs from three Companies of the Battalion out of the Gasthaus. I got Doolittle two beers to go and made it back to Range 42 before daylight for a couple hours of sleep. What a nightmare! The Commanding Officer would have left me out there hanging! Me, the junior of juniors, the Battalion Commander's dud of the week and the dumbest cherry NCO in the outfit. Shit, I was probably the only NCO who did not know where Weiden was. I surely did not know it was a hotbed of Communists. Once word got around my little foray had beat the MPs to the scene by less than 20 minutes, my stock went up some. When the Battalion commander wanted to replace me with a smart ass Captain, the NCOs told him they would all bolo deliberately if he did. I skinned that year with 20 points to spare. The slick Captain failed. But, the Big Guy got 51 first round qualifiers out of 54, followed by 52 of 54 the next year, the best record in the Army. It made him a bird Colonel and if it didn't, the road march of his tank battalion 240 miles from Mainz to Graf without dropping a track vehicle, surely did. It sure scared the shit out of the Russians. We had so many Soviet Military Mission Liaison vehicles in our convoy we should have given them unit bumper numbers.

After dropping Richard at the G3/DPTMS, Sergeant Major Burton said, "The wife will be here for Christmas. What are you doing for Christmas?"

"I have not told you about my German friend. She has invited me to spend Christmas with her family out in the country near the Border Camp. She lives in an apartment upstairs over her folks' place. I will stay one floor below her in her brother's old room. No hanky-panky or guitar playin' will happen around her Momma. Her brother and his family live on the first floor. I got them all some small presents, a large goose, some steaks, booze and nice snacks that are hard for them to find. Hell, they would rather have a large can of Planters mixed nuts than a fifty dollar bill. Throw in some American ice cream and you are king for a day. They are very well off, have very nice kids and are all very well educated and cultured people," Martin said.

"You are keeping that mighty quiet. No one I have met knows about her," Burton said with a smile.

"Scottie knows but he is close mouthed, as you know. Other than that, the Squadron Commander suspects something as he has seen us in a social setting but only as friends. I just keep my life away from here as private as possible. She is very attractive and nothing to be ashamed of but regardless of a faithless wife at home, to the Army I am a married man and need to act like it," Martin said with a rueful smile.

"Is it anything serious, Martin?" Burton asked.

"Not for me it isn't. I have never promised her anything nor has she asked me to commit to anything. She is a couple of years older than I am and I will not fit my life into her long range plan for life in the states. She wants to live in California, a definite no go for me. I hate the climate and cannot stand the "me" people. She has a good job with some very, very rich folks as their household coordinator and I can be the combination security man, butler, major domo etc, no thanks. The first time that billionaire cussed me out he would need to see a Doctor to get my foot out of his ass. I would pick shit with the chickens before I would be a servant to him or anyone else," Martin said dismissively.

"What's the pay?" Sergeant Major Burton asked curiously.

"It doesn't matter what it is as far as I am concerned but for your information it is $75,000 per year each with living quarters provided on the place in Palm Springs and free chow while they are in town. With my retirement pay and her investment income we would draw about $230,000 a year with limited expense. Shit, those people fire their help like we change socks on a foot march and with about as much emotion, no thanks," Martin said with finality.

"But I am going to spend some time in the LTA and get a good course layout figured for the Tank Crew Proficiency Course and figure a way to set up a Mini-Platoon gunnery table there," he added.

"That is probably an okay thing to do but you need to get away from the Army and let your brain go to idle for a while. All of the effort you put in as a First Sergeant, this SABOT Academy and Wildflecken is a lot to ask of any man. Take it easy for a week or two and re-charge your batteries. Having told you to take it easy, I was going over that material you gave me. I noticed the first engagement is different from the rest. What is that about? I saw the sight is displaced. It was not center of the target," Burton questioned.

"The M1 tank is as good in the degraded mode as any tank in the world is with all systems working. The first engagement tests the crew's ability to fight in the degraded mode using the telescope or Gunners Auxiliary Sight. The gunner sets up for it by closing the ballistic doors on the Gunners Primary Sight or GPS leaving just the telescope. The tower can both hear the lever move to shut the doors and see the dog ears of the sight. Cheaters will not prosper and will get zero points."

"The reason the sight picture is on the target for the mover is the SABOT round is moving at a mile per second and at that range the aim off is slight. The manual is wrong. If the gunner follows it he will miss. I've fired it from the GAS with the sight picture on the flash card and hit it every time. The information came from the mistakes of others, mostly mine and the NCOs of the Armor School. Any fool can learn from his own mistakes. I want our troops to learn from mine, like you taught me way back when," Martin concluded.

TASK 1A-DEFENSE
ENGAGEMENT: 1 STATIONARY TANK (T72) & 1 MOVING TANK (T-72) AT
               900-1300M, USING GAS BATTLESIGHT
SCRIPT: FIRING TANK, THIS IS CHARLIE- 92, YOU HAVE COMPUTER
               AND LRF FAILURE. CLOSE YOUR BALLISTIC DOORS,
               BATTLE CARRY SABOT (RECEIVES READY REPORT –FIRING TANK)

               FIRING TANK, THIS IS CHARLIE- 92, SUSPECTED ENEMY ARMOR
               VICINITY OF TRP _____ & TRP _____

(TOWER ORDERS TARGET OPERATOR TO BRING UP TARGETS, VERFIIES THEY ARE FULLY
PRESENTED AND TIMES THE TARGET EXPOSURE)

UPON COMPLETION: FIRING TANK, THIS IS CHARLIE -92, OPEN YOUR BALLISTIC DOORS
AND MOVE TO THE COURSE ROAD

354

PREPARATION

TC	GNR	LDR
INDEX 1,200 M BATTLE SIGHT	CLOSE BALLISTIC DOORS	LOAD SABOT
	INDEX SABOT REITICLE, GPS	
	USE 1,200 METER SABOT AIM POINT	
	AMMO SELECT TO SABOT	
	FIRE CONTROL TO EMER-GENCY	

FIRE COMMANDS

TC

TC		
TWO TANKS, STATIONARY TANK FIRST	IDENTIFIED, DRIVER STOP	UP
DVR MOVE OUT, GNR TAKE OVER FIRE	ON THE WAY, FIRES	UP
TARGET, MOVING TANK FIRE	IDENTIFIED MOVING TANK ON THE WAY, CONT TO TRACK	UP
TARGET, DRIVER BACK UP,		
CEASE FIRE		

NOTES

1. FIRE THE STATIONARY TANK FIRST. YOU GET A TWENTY POINT CREW CUT IF YOU SHOOT THE MOVER FIRST.
2. ACQUIRE THE TARGETS FROM THE TURRET DOWN POSITION USING THE CWS.
3. PLACE THE GAS RETICLE EXACTLY AS SHOWN ABOVE
4. GET FIRST ROUND HITS TO QUALIFY
5. TRACK, FIRE, TRACK ON THE MOVER. TRACK UNTIL THE TARGET FALLS, YOU HEAR CEASE FIRE, YOU ARE OUT OF AMMO, OR THE LOADER GETS HEAT EXHAUSTION

TIME: TO SCORE 100 POINTS: STA TANK= 6 SECONDS; MOV TANK =10 SECONDS

2000 hours
23 Dec 1985
Cold Water Flat
Above Greek Gasthaus

Marty and Martin were finishing packing his bag for the four night stay at her parents' home. He had all of the presents for her family in two large cloth bags and her present in a small jewelry box. It was a very nice Bulova watch he had purchased from his brother at a bargain basement price. His brother, an ornery man with a wicked sense of humor, was tickled his little brother had a German friend as he loathed his sister-in-law and wanted to see him leave her at any price. The watch was worth several thousand dollars but it had only cost him two hundred dollars. Paul had made it work by simply dipping it in trichloroethylene; a fluid Ron had introduced him to after using it in missile electrical cable maintenance. Besides, he would never charge his "little" brother retail price on anything. She was a woman who had everything. It was hard to buy a present for her. Seeing the box in his bag, she could not wait so he gave it to her. Seeing the watch led her to cry all of her makeup off and she had to redo it before they went out. This was not his first meeting of the family but it was the first time he had stayed in their home overnight.

Marty spent a great deal of time reviewing all of the do's and don'ts of the household with him. It was amazing the power the old German parents had over their wild child when she was under their roof and how little they had when she was off and running free in her fifties. She loved to talk and he loved to listen to her. She was a wonderful woman. He cared for her and wanted her to be happy, particularly this Christmas as she would be returning to the States before next Christmas and be living in Palm Springs far from any snow, pine trees and her German family. He was fortunate in that he could sleep anywhere. The Germans loved big comforters and sleeping cold as he did as well. He was looking forward to the trip.

The two of them arrived at the parents' home and slipped in quietly. Muttie however had the ears of a mouse and called her daughter to her bedroom. They giggled over the watch and she gave Marty one last admonition about each of them sleeping in their own beds as they were without the benefit of clergy to bless their union. Marty tucked in her wild man for a nap and went to be by herself. Martin slept with one eye open in strange places. He was mildly amused to see Muttie creep out to make certain he and Marty were sleeping alone before padding off. Soon, Marty appeared in Martin's room and coaxed Martin out of bed and back to the car to drive even though there had been a huge snowstorm blowing all day long. They did not drive far, only into the forest down a farm and logging road with a gravel base. Marty attacked him and woke every animal for ten kilometers with her lusty screams as they made love in the car. She was a very enthusiastic lover and unlike any other he had ever known. They had been gone for three hours and it was time to return to the house and the bosom of the family unit. All of them had been amazed that the modern American First Sergeant had so much to talk about with the aged Unteroffizzer of the Wehrmacht, her father. He was a veteran of both WWI & WW II. He had served on the Western front in communications in WW I and on both the Eastern and Western Fronts in WW II. He told Martin a number of amusing and wonderful stories as well as a couple of hair raising tales from WW II.

Between the wars he and his brother had taken their families to the occupied lands of Poland and were farmers. They bought some German Army horses for draft animals and used them on their adjoining large farms in Poland. The German Army was on maneuvers. They were fertilizing their field with a manure spreader pulled by their German horses. From a distant meadow came the sound of the bugle. Their horses ears perked up and the team took off toward the bugles. The two horses could not be stopped, slowed or controlled. They ran into the middle of the parade ground occupied by a German Cavalry force. The units were aligned for an inspection by the Division Commander. Their team fell in on the far left flank of the Division in perfect order with the other horses. Both Oscar and his brother were former soldiers. As the General came to their position in front of their steaming manure spreader, their proud steeds seemed to drop years of toil and labor as they stood straight, proud and quivering in excitement from the band and the presence of so many other horses. The Pavlovian reflex took over and both brothers popped to attention and executed eyes right. The Commanding General honored them with a salute of his riding crop and he gave the old cavalry mounts a rub between the ears, saying to them, "So it is farming you have turned to lads. Look at these splendid horses and you will know how I regard you both. You are four proud veterans and we are glad you could join us today." His children could not understand that Oscar and Richard connected even though their experiences were worlds apart. They understood each other in ways their families could not fathom as none of them knew anything about being a soldier.

01 Jan 1986

All too soon for Marty's family it was time for the holiday to end. While it had been enjoyable, Martin could not wait to leave. It was time to leave the dominating mother behind. She had brought her family through the aftermath of WW II in fine fashion with brilliant planning, tough love and true grit. He admired her for that but a little of her went a long way. He knew she had at least one ulterior motive and felt others would surface in due time. She could not know she would come up with an empty sack if she thought he was the Senior NCO she could use to scam the system for her and Marty down the road.

Marty insisted on taking Martin to the LTA to do his recon and layout of the Tank Crew Proficiency Course. She was a devotee of Edgar Cayce and had a new book by him to read. She parked on a hill while he walked the course road and figured the angles for target placement. Suddenly, she saw a new Mercedes sedan driving across the training area. This was not unusual as many of the local Germans used the road to cut across between two German highways. What was unusual was as her man tried to step aside to let the Mercedes driver past, he kept moving the car to give the impression he was going to run over Martin.

Suddenly, the Mercedes stopped and began backing up as fast as it would go in reverse. As she started her little Opel, she saw the reason for the fast exit by the wacky German. Her Master Sergeant Martin was pointing his .44 Magnum at the driver with a two hand grip in a combat stance. There was not a doubt in her mind the driver was about to meet his maker had he persisted in his attempt to bully what he thought was a helpless and lonely pedestrian. It was very amusing to her as she held no love for German men and their driving habits. She knew Martin would simply resume his mission and finish his drawings. Once he was cold, wet and miserable, he preferred to stay that way until his task was complete. Getting warm just made it harder to resume the task.

1000 hours
02 Jan 1986
HQs 2/11 ACR
Staff Meeting

Martin was beset on all sides by everyone except the G Troop and Howitzer Battery Commanders. The Squadron Commander was theoretically neutral and listening to the body of evidence pile up against an initiative promoted by the erstwhile Sergeant Major Martin, now relegated to Master Gunner. Chief Warrant Officer 4 Fitzhugh, the Motor Warrant produced facts and figures showing the cost of diesel fuel, parts and time. The E and F Troop Commanders were joined by the H Company Commander as they thoroughly debunked the rationale and usefulness of the initiative. Martin was secretly amused as he knew the arrival of Sergeant Major Burton and emergence of Command Sergeant Major McCall from the hospital had prompted this officer revolt. They were allied against his policy of each unit having an organized detail to start track vehicles once after 2200 hours during the cold German winter.

Lieutenant Colonel Covington made his decision, "Tank starting detail is only to be done as a Troop, Company and Battery initiative. It is no longer a Squadron initiative. Any comments, Master Sergeant Martin?"

"Sir, I did not know the degree of angst this detail caused in the unit. I see these august and erudite officers allied firmly against the policy. You are surely correct in making it a unit responsibility. I was incorrect in thinking it was something a Sergeant Major should address."

"I'll leave the subject with this thought. There are three kinds of leaders, the kind that makes things happen, the kind that watches things happen and the last type who wonders what happened. One fine morning after a long cold snap, we are sure to get alerted by V Corps to move to the Border. When that morning comes, everybody here will know which one of the three types he is and he won't need me to tell him," he said with a smile.

After the meeting, Sergeant Major Burton pulled Martin into his office and shut the door. "What the hell was that all about Martin?"

"I got a lesson in playing nice from the people I had been jamming up when I had unlimited power conferred on me from three different jobs. I guess I pissed off the biggest part of the outfit. Plus, nothing is more unpopular than tank starting detail. Hell, most of the time it does not do a damn bit of good if it is not linked to specific temperatures. It was tailor made to stick up my ass, and they did it. Not to worry, Boss, about our section. Our recall rosters are straight, our equipment stays warm and combat ready in the simulation building. There are six outlets in there that allow six tanks or other combat vehicles to plug into a 28 volt power supply. On alert, we fire up our vehicles and drive out the back gate to our initial alert position on a high hill that lets us talk to the Border, Regiment and every place in between. The twist I authorized for the three S3 Soldiers who live along the route we travel is for some of them to stay home. They stand out in front of their house and we will stop and pick them up having drawn their weapons for them. We then hand receipt the weapons to them as well as night vision devices and other sensitive items for their use. Two of them meet us on top of the hill as they live just past it and can hump it there in ten minutes. They act as the quartering party for the TOC. The rest of us drive and command the vehicles from here to there. Time will tell if they made the right call but I can tell you they did not. That is one morning that will be a nightmare for the lazy folks," Martin concluded with finality.

"We will still have to help them get going, won't we?" Burton asked.

"We will if you tell us to help them but the truth is, we will be long gone before they even start to show up. We are called first, and we are small and highly organized. Our barracks rats will have the doors opened in the Simulation Center and everything fired up by the time you and I get here. I will stop by the Arms Room and verify the sensitive items got drawn and get my .45.

Sergeant Major, do you want to walk through the drill to dipstick it?" Martin asked.

"No, but I had better get my gear ready to go. It is not ready now and I see your point," Burton said with a sly smile.

0400 hours
26 Jan 1986
Bad Kissingen, Germany

Martin could hear a bell ringing from a long way off and he was deep in sleep in his apartment. Marty woke him saying, "Sweet heart, your phone is ringing. I would have answered it but it might be the Barracuda." At the thought of his wife calling from America, Martin came painfully awake. She was the last human he wanted to talk with on this day.

"First Sergeant Martin, here," he said automatically as he answered.

"So you been reassigned, Top," Scottie said at the other end.

"Screw you, Scottie, we both know it is Master Sergeant, what's up?"

"Lariat Advance, Top," Scottie said as he was the Squadron Staff Duty for evening, adding, "You are the first call so you'd better boogie, you ain't get-ting' no younger, home boy."

Martin said "Thanks" to a dead phone. Scottie was already on to the next victim. Flipping open his troop notebook, Martin called everyone on his list himself. It was so much faster and it gave all of them extra minutes to get into the Kaserne. Marty was getting dressed as he made his calls. The S3 was high-ly trained and motivated to execute alerts and few words past the magic code of 'Lariat Advance' were necessary. By the time he had finished his calls and began to dress, Marty had her small coffee pot going and was dressed but without her makeup.

"I'm taking you. It must be twenty below zero outside and I don't want you walking in this cold," she said.

"Marty, I'll be riding in it at 20 miles an hour in a few minutes," he said, adding, "You worry too much, woman, but I thank you for it."

"You can freeze like as an example to the troops. For right now, I will take you and drop you off near the gate where no one will see us. I will go start the car now. I go home after you go in so lock the door with the dead bolt honey," she said presenting her lips for a kiss which he promptly gave her.

As he dressed it was clear she wanted to be a wife and could adjust to be-ing married to a soldier. They would have to see what developed.

"Here you are, when will you be back?" Marty asked as she pulled up on the side of the wall surrounding the Kaserne.

"It will probably be tonight sometime. These things usually do not last too long at my level. Will you be at home or in the Condo?" he asked.

"I'll be in the condo if you will promise to come there. I will have to build a wood fire and I do not want to leave it once I get it roaring," Marty said with a sweet smile.

"I'll be there tonight about six or so," Martin said kissing her good bye and hurrying off to the controlled chaos of the alert.

A quick stop at the Headquarters Arms Room confirmed the system was working as Martin only had his pistol to draw. Sergeant Major Burton had not yet drawn his weapon and no commander was yet present. Martin would not leave without Sergeant Major Burton. He was confident after their discussion and walk through of the process that he would show up at the Simulation Center shortly.

The winter storm had been even more severe than he thought. When he checked the incline leading from the Simulation Center to the Motor Pool it was a sheet of ice beneath the snow. He went back to the building and began pitching sand bags into the back of the M577 Command Post vehicle that would be leading the march.

If the sand did not work, the only alternative was to drop the fence and go across country. That should make the S3 real popular with the S2 Physical Security pukes.

The sand worked and all six vehicles cleared the step. All they needed now was for Sergeant Major Burton to show up.

It was good to see the heaters come on in all of the vehicles. It would be a bad enough day to go to the field at -15 below zero but it would be very hard to do it in the ice box interior of the large slab sided personnel carriers. Last but not least, the two trucks of the section with the large tents, stoves, chairs and troop tent for the staff fell in with the small convoy. Martin was surprised to see the S3 arrive in his vehicle at the back gate and Sergeant Major Burton dismount and quickly walk toward them.

"You were right. G Troop and How Battery are just now getting ready to move. One or two privates of the starting detail started all of their vehicles. Are we ready?" Burton asked with a smile.

"Affirmative, Sergeant Major, we are ready to move on your command once you get mounted," Martin replied. It was 0455, less than one hour after the first phone call had been received by the S3.

"Let's boogie. Lead us out Master Sergeant Martin in the TAC 113. I'll take the 577," Burton directed.

As he went forward to his vehicle, Martin saw Specialist Fourth Class Stroud opening the hatch cover over the engine. Stroud reached in and handed Martin a C Ration can of Ham and Eggs that was warm with engine heat and shouted words to the effect his Pepsi was inside but had not been opened. What a crew, Breakfast at Tiffany's.

In short order, the Squadron Tactical Operations Center was established in the field. Only the track extension or tent, from the main personnel carrier was extended with a stove. The Fire Support and the S2 vehicles backed up to the openings of the tent and sealed off the entrances to keep it warm inside. On board snow shovels cleared the macadam street that was now the floor of the tent and was covered by duck boards in front of the maps and by dry straw in the meeting area. The chairs were set up and the lights were working. Long range antennas were erected and all radio nets were functioning within ten minutes after the small caravan stopped in the morning darkness. Burton was very glad to see the efficient group deliver on their early promises. He then told them all as they gathered in the track extension tent, "You guys all told me how this would go. It went exactly as you said it would. As they say it Texas, 'It ain't bragging if you can do it'. You did it! Good job! Let's get those reports in and transmitted to Regiment."

As Martin went to his M-113 Stroud spoke to him, "Did you eat yet, First Sergeant?"

"Not yet, Stroud, but I will," Martin answered with a smile.

"Now, First Sergeant, you know what the Major said to me. I have to see you eat something. He knows you won't eat or sleep unless we stay on your ass. Who knows when you will have a chance to eat today," he said insistently.

Martin decided Stroud was right and he sat down in the troop compartment of the track and finished opening his C Ration can and wolfed down the still warm ham and eggs washing it down with his ice cold Pepsi. The ever efficient chow hound Stroud had coffee in a silver spouted urn and was about to finish making bacon and eggs in an electric skillet powered by the generator.

"Mike Golf, Eaglehorse 6 A, OVER. Mike Golf, Eaglehorse 6 A, OVER."

Stroud asked, "Top, why is the Squadron Commander's driver calling you? Shouldn't he be calling the Sergeant Major if he wants you to do something?"

"Tell you what Stroud, I'll answer the call while you decide how best to educate the Squadron Commander on following the Chain of Command," Martin said squeezing the burly soldier's arm as he squeezed by him in the narrow track.

"Eaglehorse 6 A, Master Gunner, OVER."

"Master Gunner, this is 6A. Six needs you at the Mike Papa now. He needs all of the slave cables from the G3 and all of the vehicles from the TOC that are running except HQ-3. He also wants your secret stock of ether. BREAK. He needs what you have on the tracks and what you have stored in the rear. Where is it back here, OVER."

"6A, Master Gunner. Go to the Simulation Center. See the NCO there. He will provide you with everything the Commander needs to start the dead vehicles, OVER." Martin noted Stroud was almost finished with the eggs to go with the pound of bacon he had cooked. He pointed to Martin indicating he should make them each a bacon and egg sandwich to go while he finished the hot breakfast for the rest of the crew that wanted it. No one had to call them. They could smell it and they all came to get their sandwich, with Burton leading the charge.

God bless you Stroud. What a morale builder that skillet was at -15 below. Troop coddler he may be called but Martin knew he got the max out of these guys and the skillet was part of the deal.

In no time Stroud had the skillet clean and packed away and was in the driver's hatch ready to roll.

"Eaglehorse 9, Master Gunner, did you monitor last from 6A, OVER."

Burton answered Martin very professionally, "Master Gunner, Eaglehorse 9, roger. Move out and execute, OUT."

"Is he mad at you, First Sergeant?" Stroud asked.

"No, Stroud, he is being short so he can stay professional. He is too pissed to say more," Martin laughed as Stroud turned in his driver's hatch and gave the universal shaft salute with his forearm. All of the soldiers knew about the revolt over tank starting detail but none of them ever suspected the S3 crew would have to return to the motor pool to fix it.

Sergeant First Class Fogarty was the long standing rear detachment NCO for the Squadron S3. He did not go to the field for any reason short of total war. He ran the simulation center and was signed for a myriad of training devices. The list was so long and varied, only he knew where all of the 'bodies' were buried. He was also an expert on the operation and recovery of track vehicles under all conditions. He was about to become invaluable in the motor pool.

It seems the great Chief Warrant Officer 4 Fitzhugh, the warrant officer in technical charge of the squadron's vehicles, having led the effort to sabotage the tank starting detail, had a must do appointment in Frankfurt at 97th General Hospital that morning and would not be present. The main NCO power they had in Squadron Maintenance, Master Sergeant Ramirez, was on a well deserved leave. It was now clear why Martin was recalled from the field. Between the three of them from the S3 they would help the unit maintenance guys get the unit out the gate and rolling to the Border.

Sergeant First Class Forgarty met Martin at the back gate with two cases of ether based starting fluid and ground guided them to the tank company. With the long "jumper" cables Martin had scrounged for the past REFORGER, the tanks of H Co rapidly came to life. Stroud worked on F Troop across the aisle from the tank company with another cable and the generator. The long cables let the track stay centrally located until four vehicles from each unit were running. Between them, Stroud and Martin started a tank every two minutes. These four tanks then began to jump start the others in their unit. Others were heated by backing an M1 up to the engine compartment and letting the 650 degree centigrade exhaust of the tank warm up the dead vehicles. In a little over an hour after the rescue crew arrival, some two hours into the alert time, all of the vehicles that could be started using operator level skill were running.

Stroud was back in his driver's hatch warming up and preparing to return to the field headquarters location. He could see their work in the motor pool was nearing an end as it was becoming vacant and while he was tough, there was no sense freezing you ass off if it was not necessary. He began waving for Martin to come back to the track. He did so putting on his Combat Vehicle Crewman or CVC to listen to the radio. Major Klenk was directing the S4 to task organize the support platoon for fuel and other services to the remainder of the squadron. V Corps had decided to deploy the unit forward for Border Condition One, later amending the order to place them near Camp Lee in a position around a gravel quarry.

As Martin gave Stroud the 'What the Hell? look, Stroud keyed his helmet to intercom and said, "The stupid 'jacks' from Fox and the Tank Company ran out of fuel and strung their shit from here to Bad Neustadt - just like you told them they would. The S3 is not about to let the Old Man Task the S3 to pick up that dog turd."

"Hell, Stroud, you are just pissed because of when I busted G Troop's ass on cold weather starting last winter and these guys got over!" Martin said ruefully.

"Bull shit, Top. I am going to be a Sergeant one day and as you always said, if they won't salute the Second Lieutenants they won't charge the bunker. It is a lot of little things that make soldiers and units great when they do 'em and sorry as shit when they don't."

"Today, those suckers are sorry. And again as you used to say, our buddies in units on our flanks are depending on us. And then finally, there is the all time saying that went, 'Men, I know it sounds corny but the Chairman of the Joint Chiefs really believes all of his vehicles, ships and planes at rest are topped off because he knows we follow orders and we in our little troop ain't going to disappoint him'. Well, First Sergeant Martin, somebody ought to tell the Chairman not to make those two sorry Captains into Majors where they can screw up entire Battalions as Executive Officers," Stroud said as seriously as a Specialist Fourth Class could speak.

"Okay, Stroud, I got it. Let's go back to the TOC. Stand by a minute, Eaglehorse Niner, Master Gunner, OVER."

"Master Gunner, Eaglehorse Niner B, Niner can monitor, OVER."

"Roger, does Niner have any other missions back here? If not we're about to return to your location on the farm trails since the traffic is now on the streets, OVER."

"Master Gunner, Niner sends, Return to this location, OUT."

0730 hours
13 March 1986
2/11 Conference Room
Weekly Staff Call

The Squadron Commander came out of his office and headed for the conference room in a wonderful mood. He had just learned he would be going to the War College and would change command in June as previously scheduled. He had of course, immediately called his dear wife and helpmate of these many years. She was overjoyed because both of the twins were ready for their Sophomore year of high school and their oldest daughter would have finished her first year of college at Heidelberg. He was more than ready to now joust with the minor problems of the day as befitting a man who had just learned his next promotion was a sure thing, had ten more years service waiting if he so desired, and most important to him, a happy wife.

As the Adjutant called attention as he entered the conference room, his ebullience transferred to the group. After all, when he was happy, they were happy. "Good News, Sir?" asked his faithful subordinate commander of Fox Troop.

"As a matter of fact, Rex, it is good news, but I'll cover that later. Let's get the meeting started, we have a full plate today," he said happily. His happiness evaporated rapidly as the first unit of 41 tanks began to roll out the front gate of the Kaserne. The sound of the engines and of the track on the cobblestones made conversation nearly impossible in the conference room. The continuous roar told him, and anyone else of any experience, this was not a detachment movement but was all of the tanks under his command.

"Can someone here tell me why all of my tanks are moving?" he said with a hint of Frank Burns on MASH.

"That would be me, Sir," Master Sergeant Martin said, "I'm the one you need to ask about that. It is one of the events of Sergeant's time. We have a guy in town from Frankfurt who is going to inspect and repair all of our tank thermal sights today and any overflow on Friday. You approved that three weeks ago for Sergeant's Time and Regiment has been notified. As Command Sergeant Major I set the agenda for Sergeant's Time, as Ops Sergeant Major I did the schedule and briefed it to you and as Master Gunner I got the guy to come down here and put him in the Soiftel Hotel next to the LTA. We also used parts from G Troop and built a thermal test bench at Squadron Maintenance to assist in troubleshooting and repair. The whole instrument repair section from Corps is also here for Sergeant's time and they are in the LTA in bivouac."

If looks could have killed, Martin would have been dead. No one in the room had ever seen the Squadron Commander's killer face until now. He stood up and over the roar of the last element of tanks said, "Sergeant Major, in my office, now." Martin's foes were delighted and his friends were in shock. This was bad. Everybody in the room knew what was happening but the head man. Clearly, it was Martin's job to have made sure he knew. Friend or foe, all were glad it was his ass in the Squadron Commander office and not theirs.

As the Squadron Commander reached his office he stood aside and motioned Martin inside and slammed the door so hard that two pictures came off the wall and shattered the glass in both. Martin, no fool, assumed the position of attention in front of the Squadron Commander's desk. Lieutenant Colonel Covington looked up and saw Martin at attention.

"Sit down in that chair. Dammit! I have wanted to do this since we got the damn tanks and I could never get it done. You come in and do it off hand, like a two foot putt for Christsakes! Dammit! Say something, dammit!" as he spat out the words.

"Sir, I told you three weeks ago what was happening but you were busy on other things.

"I came in again to tell you about the funding expenditure for his TDY and permission to put him in the Soiftel but the Squadron Executive Officer told me to proceed and assured me you knew all about it. When you signed the training schedule I hoped that would do it. I am not sure what else I could have done that I did not do," Martin said with genuine regret.

"Do you realize that all of the tanks he deadlines will impact on the USR? Today is Thursday and we only have until Friday at midnight to clear the books? No, that would not enter into it for you, would it," he said sadly.

"No, Sir, it would not. Your philosophy has been you did not want your subordinates to even think about consequences but to report faults and get them repaired. The USR did not cross my mind. However, I believe he will be able to fix all of the faults and there will be not big jump in the deadline rate. Sir, this guy was present at the creation of the sight. He went through all of the permutations as it was being invented. The process was part of his master's thesis. He is also working on his Doctoral dissertation on Thermal Dynamics in the Cryogenic Spectrum. It is sort of like having an astronaut change a spark plug in a lawnmower. They guy does theoretical calculus in his head to relax when he is stressed. As for who got it done, Sir, that does not matter. If it is good it is because of you and your example. If it is bad it is because some son of a bitch did not do what you told him to do and you can hammer his ass. You will be the only Squadron Commander in the Regiment whose tanks thermal sights will get done before Tank Gunnery," Martin concluded, trying to be as positive as he knew how to be.

For a long moment, Lieutenant Colonel Covington stared at the diesel smoke cloud of the last of the tanks leaving the Kaserne enroute to the training area. He turned away from his window with a painful smile and said, "It is good the sights are getting checked. You will monitor the situation and report

366

to me every two hours. You will find me wherever I am and render all reports in person and get an acknowledgment from me. You will use every legal and proper means to limit the number of tanks to be dead lined for thermal sights. Your mission today is thermal sights. Work it through until it is done or until the troops get too tired to be effective. We will visit the test site when the command and staff is over. Questions?"

"No questions, Sir," Martin said, glad to be getting off so cheap.

Returning to the meeting, the Squadron Commander decided to drop all of the bombs at one time and proceed to tell one and all about the new Commander, the Change of Command and the thermal site flap and its resolution. He also confirmed the change of command dates and the New Equipment Training dates for the M3 Bradley or the Cavalry Fighting Vehicle. He then did a summary review of the upcoming Wildflecken training. He then asked for input and adjourned the meeting establishing a record for the fastest command and staff meeting in living memory. After asking the Commanders, Executive Officer and S3 to remain, the Squadron Commander politely, but pointedly, dismissed Martin and Burton. Both of them decided on breakfast at the snack bar before they went to the LTA to check on the thermal sight rodeo as Burton called it.

As they ate, Burton asked, "What was the big deal about the thermal sight rodeo? It is a great idea. Are they that messed up?"

"The big deal is that the Squadron Commander did not think of it or direct it. He was thinking about doing something like the rodeo. He just never moved it from his mind to action. I told him about three times but it never registered. He knew he was wrong and more or less apologized. The soldiers do not realize that while the sight will show you a deer in the dark, they need to be able to count its antler points. You have to know what to look for in the sight to know if it is screwed up. Today, we are going to show them pictures and use the bad sights as examples. Right now, they do not know bad when they see it. They think tuning the sight until they see a blob is okay. A lot of times the turret mechanic can clear it with nitrogen. As to how many are bad, I would guess 75%. Whatever it is, it will be a lot uglier than the officers want to see written down. Someday I hope the officer corps will want unit OR rates to go up on an alert instead of down. Honest maintenance evaluations can be subjectively upgraded but lies will always just be lies. Vehicle road kill on the way to the border does not lie."

Both Burton and Martin got an education from Chaim Bevelheim, AKA CB, thermal sight guru from General Dynamics. "As Master Sergeant Martin probably told you, these lines represent the failure of the sight to correctly process the information from the IR spectrum. It is a component failure and easily repaired. Martin calls the lines Goldfish because at times they appear to move across the viewing area and to some people, appear to be swimming."

"So, CB, how many bad ones so far?" Martin asked.

"So far, 20 of 21 I have checked. All tanks but one are dead lined for thermal sight. Either a DS support guy or I can fix all of them I have found so far," CB replied.

"What did you tell that guy last week, Martin, about mechanical faults, something about the Russians?" Burton asked.

"I tell them their one true critic who will not lie to them about how bad they prepare, fight or maneuver is a Mongoloid looking guy under 5'8" in a T-72. Save your anger for the enemy, I am on your side," Martin said.

"That makes sense. My girl is coming down today. Am I still okay with the room even though I may get them all fixed today?" CB asked.

"You let us worry about paying for the room CB. You go out and have a nice meal tonight with your girl friend. What doesn't get fixed tonight gets fixed in the morning or evacuated to Frankfurt for parts," Burton said giving Martin some needed top cover.

"It sounds like the bottom line is going to be no more than 3 or 4 thermals out of 41. How is the test bench working?" Martin asked.

"The test bench is saving our butts by getting the Depot guys into the effort. I'm glad you listened to me and had it ready today. It saves so much time. Your Chief Warrant Officer 4 gave me a hard time right at first but I won him over. He is on board now," CB said even as he inspected yet another sight as the clacking of the compressor rattled in the background.

"Look at this sight, Sergeant Major Burton. It has what the troops call goldfish. We will purge it and that should fix at least part of the problem," CB continued to teach as he worked the maintenance issues.

As usual, the hand wringers felt compelled to run to the Squadron Commander after their visit to the site to tell him all of their tanks were now dead lined as a result of yet another hare brained scheme by the iconoclastic Master Sergeant Martin. Their Blackhorse Icarus, Martin, was taking them all down in flames with him. Summoned back to the Headquarters via radio, Burton and Moran reported to an obviously distraught Lieutenant Colonel Covington.

Sergeant Major Burton did most of the talking and Martin was grateful for his help. "Sir, one of your troop commanders is pissing on your leg telling you it is raining. His sights are so full of water and out of calibration they would never hit anything in periods of limited visibility. He and everybody else should be damn glad *you* and Master Sergeant Martin organized this event to straighten out their maintenance issues in one swoop. While we are at it, Martin is a big part of your outfit and working to make it a success. From what I can see, there are a few folks here who let personality rule their brain and who would rather carry tales than fix problems. I wish you would tell them to either get on board or shut up," Sergeant Major Burton said in summary.

The Squadron Commander remembered full well his earlier guidance and did not appear to have heard a word Sergeant Major Burton had said as he glared at his Master Gunner, "Well?"

"Sir, the expert has inspected twenty one thermal sights. Twenty were dead lined. Fifteen are now fully operational. Five are being repaired. One is being evacuated to Frankfurt for direct exchange. I estimate three tanks will be dead lined for thermal sight deficiencies at the end of the day with one of those on a vehicle with other issues for a net loss of two pacing items on the USR," Martin reported.

The Squadron Commander merely looked at his watch and said, "It is now 1130 hours? When is your next report, Master Sergeant?"

"Sir, the next report is due at 1330 hours," Martin replied.

Through the day, the numbers got worse as the repair process slowed as tanks returned to the motor pool with their sights still broken. CB was a genius but a one man band by design. Though the support crew was a big help, they could only replace parts, not make intricate adjustments to interior components - only CB could do that. However, the entire process was an eye opening experience for everyone, including CB. He saw for the first time how his idea of having the Direct Support unit working with a unit test bench while he inspected sights and taught crews, turret mechanics and unit leaders, was a winning combination, albeit a slow one in relative terms. The squadron was truly committed to "teaching men to fish" rather than handing them a fish for their next meal. CB smiled as he recalled this homily Martin had used. CB knew now he was in the company of at least two ruthless SOBs, Burton and Martin, who took bad news as a means to an end rather than an end unto itself. They projected the calm and unruffled demeanor of men who had been there before and were confident of the outcome. He liked them and he really enjoyed being around the Cavalry troopers. They were sponges for learning and did not have to be told anything twice. They now knew how to tune their sights and knew a bad one when they saw it. They now had another arrow in their quiver, knew the 'why' and the cure for bad thermal sights.

1830 hours
13 Mar 1986
Squadron Maintenance Shop
Bad Kissingen, West Germany

CB turned from his labors to see Master Sergeant Martin standing beside him in his Class A Uniform with a white shirt and a bow tie. "Damn, First Sergeant, you did not have to get all dressed up for me."

Answering the budding genius with a smile, Martin said, "Don't worry CB, I didn't. I am about to report the final status to the Squadron Commander. He is going to a piano recital down town I have also been invited to attend,

369

though he does not know that. He told me to find him every two hours and report and so I shall. What are the final damages from today's thermal sight bar fight?"

"We inspected 41 systems and 38 were faulty. We corrected, repaired or replaced components or complete systems in 35. We ran out of parts and three will have to wait until Friday morning to be fixed. I am going to go have a great meal, a beer and get re-acquainted with my girl friend. I will see you here in the morning about ten o'clock. We will finish the last of the sights before noon," CB said, ending the report.

"That's great, CB, thanks for all you did today, the diagnosis, repair and especially the teaching of the young crewmen. It was invaluable and will have a long lasting effect on the squadron and the Army. Have a nice evening. See you in the morning," Martin said shaking his hand.

1900 hours
13 Mar 1986
Bad Kissingen Mayor's Reception

The Bad Kissingen Mayor had a great many social events, occasions and while some were political, this one was truly a community event. His own daughter had performed in the musical revue early in her career before he had been elected and he and his wife thoroughly enjoyed the evenings with the youngsters. There was something magical about young people with musical talent who studied and practiced to produce for their recital. He enjoyed this evening as much, or more, than any event in the whole year. It was why he insisted on sponsoring the reception to open the evening with a buffet, canapés and light wine and champagne. The music hall itself was worth the price of admission. Rebuilt after the war, the acoustics were so perfect it often served as a recording studio. He was especially glad to see the US Army present, many of whom had children who had been part of the music festival over the years and one who was performing this evening.

When the Bundesgrenzschutz contingent arrived the Mayor was surprised to see an American Master Sergeant with them. They acted as if he were part of their unit and introduced him as if he were. The Mayor was a snob and he did not recall any connection that would have included an NCO in tonight's activities. He then saw the real reason the Sergeant was present. He was there to meet the daughter of one of the patrons of the Musical Societies. Long unmarried and late of America, living a life of God knows what in Hollywood, Marlene Zander had arrived. She and the party of the BGS exchanged Hollywood kisses while her greeting for the American Army Sergeant was notable for its restraint. He went off to get her a flute of Champagne though drinking and eating nothing himself. He appeared to be waiting for something

370

or someone. Well, never mind, he had other guests and those two would have to sort out whatever game they were playing.

Ah, there it was. Lieutenant Colonel Covington and his wife were here. What a beautiful couple. These American Army officers certainly knew how to marry well. He was very handsome in his Army Dress Mess uniform and she was very, very elegant in her black cocktail dress with pearls. Attentive, her husband made certain she had a glass of wine, while he had a whiskey highball that appeared to be an Old Fashion. Both of them spoke fluent German and were conversing with the elite of Bad Kissingen when the NCO approached Lieutenant Colonel Covington. He was undoubtedly one of his subordinates.

"Good evening, Sir," Martin said pleasantly. "I have a final report for you if you want to receive it."

"Oh, I do indeed, Master Sergeant Martin. You look very nice in your greens. I am a little surprised not to see you in Blues as it is after six," he said in a slightly stuffy manner.

Martin smiled and said, "I don't own a set of blues, Sir. If I make the E-9 list I will buy a set, otherwise I have no use for them. 35 of 41 thermals were bad. 32 of the 35 are now fully functional. The final three will be fixed by noon tomorrow."

Lieutenant Colonel Covington smiled a thoughtful smile and said, "Now tell me how you came to attend this event."

"Sir, it is the proverbial two birds with one stone. Your order for me to report was specific with regard to your location. This invitation was of long standing from my good friend Oberst, (Major) Wertz, formerly commander of 2d Company for 22 years of the BGS. His daughter is having her recital tonight and is playing a Chopin Sonata. It is one of my favorite pieces. Knowing that, he and his wife invited me to attend. I accepted some time ago," Martin said.

Almost immediately, Lieutenant Colonel Covington's attention was taken away by the Mayor who came to say hello.

"It is quite chilly tonight, Sergeant Martin. If you need a ride, you can ride back to the Kaserne with us," Mrs. Covington offered sweetly.

"Thank you, ma'am. I have a ride home to my humble abode after the concert. I won't be joining the BGS officers and their wives at their reception afterwards at their Kaserne. I have other plans," Martin said politely. He did not know Mrs. Covington well and never would but he had no desire to be rude or unkind to any family member regardless of their husband's rank.

"All up and coming NCOs with a great future, particularly married ones, know how to conduct themselves without their wives when they are overseas alone. Wouldn't you agree?" she asked sweetly without a hint of hidden meaning.

"Yes ma'am, I would certainly agree and again, I thank you for your kind offer," Martin said.

"So, Martin, where were we?" Lieutenant Colonel Covington asked as the Mayor had moved on to a constituent to schmooze.

"Sergeant Martin was just leaving to rejoin his friends. He has his own transportation and it was nice to see him here, wasn't it dear?" she said in a most pleasant way.

"Yes dear, it was. See you in the morning, Martin," the Squadron Commander said without another thought about the NCO or his report. He was determined to have a good time out with his wife tonight and was glad the report was positive.

When the lights went down for the series of recitals, Martin was sitting with Marty. When Ms Hildagarde Wertz finished her recital, Martin and Marty slipped out when the lights went down for the next number and no one saw them leave but the observant Mayor. They immediately left for her condo in Bad Bocklet for what both knew would be a far better time than the recital with all of the stuffy folk convincing each other how great they were, and they were right.

1400 hours
20 Mar 1986
S3 Office
Bad Kissingen, West Germany

As he returned to his office, Martin checked on the TV camera and 2,000 mm lens he had set up earlier. He had a short course from the experts at the Grafenwohr audio visual section when he drew and signed for it but was not yet comfortable with the equipment. He wanted only the very best presentation for the tankers of the outfit and was also determined to establish a rigorous standard of excellence for the Bradley gunnery to follow. One of his former NCOs from G Troop was now the Bradley Squadron Master Gunner and most of the other Soldiers were present. When he had returned from the course at Fort Benning, he came with two Sergeants First Class. The Command Sergeant Major of the Infantry School had as Martin predicted, selected Staff Sergeant Gilberto Jesus Martinez to teach the course. He sent two Sergeants First Class to take Martinez's place and Staff Sergeant Tim Duncan was out of a slot and a job. All had been involved in a long and arduous support of the numerous exercises at the USAREUR, Corps and Regimental level. They were about to depart for a rare four day week end but were there to get the word on their assignments for the upcoming Level II gunnery at Wildflecken. Martin looked at the view on the TV set and was immediately angry.

372

Look you stupid ass, control yourself. These are very good men. They have never even remotely disobeyed your instructions. They probably have not moved anything. Take it easy and feel your way. You can let the wolf out later. Probably good that Tim Duncan's wife was here to civilize the process although she was a hell raiser in her own right. He finally trusted himself to speak. Realizing it was his own fear of failure at the new business of video and audio critique driving his apprehension.

"Guys, who moved the damn camera? I asked everyone not to touch the shit," Martin said mildly looking at Staff Sergeant Duncan for an answer.

"First Sergeant, no one moved anything. We have just been in here talking about Wildflecken and Bradley NET. Honest, no one moved anything. Hell, you told us not to and who in here is going to blow YOU off?" he said with a sincere smile.

Janet was sitting behind everyone else and everyone was looking at him. She slowly shook her head no telling him nonverbally that no one had moved the camera. Martin realized Tim would never lie to him no matter what. There had to be another explanation. He went to the window and looked outside. The day long fog had finally cleared. He went back to the camera and checked it. The traversing mechanism was still locked so it had not been moved either left or right in traverse or up or down in elevation.

"Men, help me out here. That is a live picture. There is no tape running. That is not a picture from downtown. What the hell is going on here? Tim you guys drive by downtown every day when you go home. What am I missing, it has to be simple," Martin asked.

It was then the troops looked at the monitor and the camera in a new light. Staff Sergeant Jimenez laughed saying, "You have not been downtown in quite a while, First Sergeant. They have moved in that heavy crane just last week. It is set up for repairs to the top story of that big hotel just beyond down town."

"My ass, Jorge, that hotel is miles and miles from here. Get my map board and do your scout trick and tell me how far that crane is from here. I'm going to look for something I know in the meantime," he said as he began to move the camera.

"There is the tower of the gingerbread house. Aha! It is in the foreground by a long ways. That crane is not visible to the naked eye and neither is the ginger bread house. That damn lens can see for miles, I am an ass and sorry I thought you all moved it. The power of the thing was beyond my knowledge. I feel like Jethro Bodine trying to cipher or granny mistaking a Kangaroo for a rabbit."

"I know how to write a script and give shooting directions but actually setting up and running a camera with a telephoto lens is new to me. Tim, you and I and Stroud are going to get smart on this set up starting now. Get Sergeant First Class Fogarty on the phone and ask him to come down here would you, Jorge?" Martin directed.

373

For an hour and a half, they played with the camera and the lens trying to establish how they were going to accomplish their mission to video each tank's qualification run, use video tape to debrief crews and provide each of the 41 crews a tape of their performance to take home before they left the range.

The S3 crew had been working hard and Martin did not know what Sergeant Major Burton had told them as he was working other issues during the hectic period. Mindful of that, he called a halt to the experimentation with the camera, videotaping and recording devices so that everyone could attend the safety formation by the HHT Commander, Cone Head Bates. The sobriquet had been coined by soldiers while Captain Bates was the S2 of the Squadron while awaiting command of Headquarters and Headquarters Troop. Convinced of the power of pyramids, Captain Charles Hanson Bates had fashioned one and suspended it over his desk. The pyramid morphed into a Cone in troop lore and thus he was, and would remain, Cone Head Bates in the unit until he died or rotated.

Sergeant Major Burton came in as the troops were leaving for formation and said, "Come on here Master Sergeant Martin, you don't want to miss the Safety Briefing."

"You go ahead, Sergeant Major. I am not welcome at HHT formations. First Sergeant Waters made it quite plain. I just stay away. It is easier that way. There are no hard feelings, I understand his position and I respect it," Martin said without rancor.

"You gotta' be shitting me. You support the hell out of everything they do and they do not want you there. What the hell, OVER?" Burton asked.

"Air Force gloves (Hands in one's pockets while in uniform), trash, PT drop outs, sniveling, usual HHT bullshit. He does not want me doing on the spot corrections in his formation, so I do not go because I cannot watch it and be silent. When I am the Command Sergeant Major I will go but right now that is you. I'll be here when you get back, Sergeant Major," Martin said cheerfully.

"What about the Commander? What does he say?" Burton asked.

"Shit, he is even happier that Waters not to see me. He thought he was an expert on the word processor. He wiped out the entire four hundred page GDP we had just completed updating with one or two stupid key strokes. I chewed his ass for it and he went to the Squadron Commander and wanted to bring me up on official charges. I guess him wiping it out did not hold a candle to me having two copies of it in our classified safe. The kicker was when he asked me when I decided to break regulations and keep my own copy of the GDP."

"Wait a minute! Do you mean he lost the entire Ground Defense Plan?" Burton asked, clearly angry.

"Yep, the whole damn thing," Martin replied.

"So what did you tell the Squadron Commander when you decided to go rogue?" Burton asked.

"That was what tore it I guess. I told the secretary to make copies of it the minute he insisted on typing his own annex," Martin said.

"The Squadron Commander took his part for a short time and asked me how it was Mrs. Beeler thought she could correct Captain Bates, another sore spot for him. I then explained to him how I took her up to the GDP on three very cold winter days when nothing was shaking in the Squadron. She is a school teacher with a Masters Degree and working on her PhD. I taught her to read a map after she had completed the map course by correspondence from Fort Benning, you know the one with the Leavenworth, Kansas map. At the end of one day she was navigating and telling Stroud where to go. She learned where each of the points of interest cited in the staff annexes of the GDP. Brother Bates put the POW cage where the Squadron Commander directed we put the Unit Maintenance Collection point. When she pointed this out to him, he went ape shit and told her she could not read a map and insisted he would do his own typing. It went downhill from there," Martin said.

"So what he was really mad about was this tall, gorgeous blond haired, blue eyed Army wife knew how to read a map and knew the ground at the GDP better than he did because you, her leader, had taken her on a two day recon."

"It was really three days, Sergeant Major," Martin added.

"Have you screwed her yet?" Burton asked with a leer.

"No, Sergeant Major, I have not. She is a married woman. I got her promoted and paid at a higher step because she went the extra mile to learn her job. She did her job and several others very well. It had nothing to do with her looks or an after duty hours thing. My approach to duty makes enough people mad. I cannot add misconduct to the list and do not intend to in the future. Marty is about all of the risk I am ready to accept," Martin said.

"I felt that was what you would say and I am glad of it," Burton said as he then went out the door.

1000 hours
28 Mar 1986
Range 23
Wildflecken Training Area

The Squadron Commander was obviously trying to drive the Range Crew crazy. Just when they had one thing fixed he found two more that were broken. It was set up day and the complicated equipment was not cooperating with the Korean War Era generators available. The TV sets in the de-briefing area required constant and regular voltage or they would turn off and on dis-

375

rupting the process. Martin felt like a ping pong ball as he bounced around the range behind the Squadron Commander fixing things, some real and some were just "I am smarter than you stuff." Unless he could get a handle on it, it was going to be a long 15 days on this high, windy and wet hill. The BGS NCOs had it right when they said in German, "Six monat in Wildflecken ist winter, und den six monat of schnee or Six months a year there it is winter and the rest of the time it snows." Soldier humor was of no comfort at the moment.

Burton asked, "What can I do to help? You obviously need to be training soldiers not chasing electrical connections. It is all important but you cannot do it all. We need some division of labor and we need it now."

"I thought this would happen. I told Sergeant First Class Fogarty to come up and be prepared to stay after his appointment with the Shrink yesterday. I expected him before now and do not know where he is or what happened to him. When he shows, we will put him in charge of the tent, generators, TVs and VCRs. Could you call Richard and get him to loan us a commercial generator out of their emergency equipment back up pool for the post? He knows we will bring it back if he needs it. That will solve my most pressing issues, that and Sergeant Fogarty," Martin said.

"I will go get the generator from Richard. I will find Fogarty and bring him back. What do you want on your hamburger from Burger King?" Burton asked with a big smile.

"Everything, Sergeant Major, everything. It will be as cold as a brick bat when you get it here but I will eat it anyhow," Martin said with feeling. It had been a spell since he had anything to eat.

He was very glad they had one day to set up and rehearse the de-briefing sequence and the target scenarios with the Range Operator. Richard had given the range operator very strict instructions to fully cooperate with the unit and to go the extra mile. After all, they were the saviors of the Wildflecken G3 with the big dump trucks. However, the operator was still a German and orders were orders to him and if it was new, then it must be bad and was probably illegal.

1000 hours
28 Mar 1986
Range 23
Wildflecken, West Germany

Master Sergeant Martin had just finished briefing the Eagle Troop Tankers on the modified Tank Table VII they were to fire on Range 23. They had done well firing their verification rounds and Table VI at stationary targets. He noticed the Troop Commander was extremely agitated. He seemed particularly upset as Martin went down the list of range handouts that were to have been distributed the week before by each unit Master Gunner. The reason for his angst was not clear as the troops had been issued everything and were eager to begin shooting. Martin had known the Captain previously.

"What is bothering you, Captain, anything I can do or fix?" Martin said pleasantly.

"Everything is bothering me. Do you really expect that these guys can go execute these engagements like you wrote them up on the cheat sheets? Can you do it? I'll bet you can't! I think it is all just big talk on your part, Master Sergeant Martin. I would like to see you do it and prove it to me it can be done. After all you are the expert tanker here, are you not?" he said emotionally spent.

I'll be damned. The famous hunter and former Infantryman, Airborne, Ranger is scared. He is going to fail and he knows it. I guess when he talked his boss into clearing the way for his branch transfer that this shit looked pretty simple after sitting next to a General Officer who had been doing it all of his professional life. Now he got a good look at it here today after having chased women and drank scotch instead of studying these past months. He blew off a special make up of SABOT Academy a month ago as beneath his dignity. Now he is like a defense attorney with a guilty client, he wants to try society for the crime. It couldn't be him that is screwed up; it has to be the course right? Of course it's the course, it just has to be.

Martin dropped all regard for rank and respect even though he knew everyone there was being pin drop silent and could hear every word. "Pick an engagement Captain and I will demonstrate it to you using your tank while you sit here and watch. You can hear the fire commands on the Safety Vehicle's Radio."

"Oh, hell, no. I want to see you do the whole thing," he responded.

"Can't do it, won't do it. The rounds are all counted and set," Martin said with finality.

"You'll do it if I order you to do it dammit."

"You forget yourself, Captain. I do not work for you and I do not report to you. You are empowered to correct my deportment, bearing or conduct when we are both at the position of attention. Beyond that you have no authority to order me to do anything on this range. Quite the contrary, I'm charged to direct you through the field grades. I am only going to do the demonstration for your soldiers not for you. You have cast doubt and aspersion on a noble effort. Someone needs to set it straight. The best man to do that is me. So please select the engagement you find most disagreeable to your sensibilities."

"The BMP with troops, Mr. Expert. Let's see that one."

"Okay 66 crew, let's get mounted and I'll give you a preview of the course."

The soldiers eagerly bounded up on the tank. They had been through SA-BOT academy earlier with the former Commander and knew Master Sergeant

Martin well. He had been their neighbor in G Troop and had orchestrated the exchange of responsibilities between the two units at the Border. He had also fed them for three days during REFORGER when their First Sergeant got separated from the Troop. They trusted him and secretly looked forward to seeing him show up their prick Captain.

Despite time being of the essence for the Troop, Martin rehearsed the fire commands and crew duties with the crew of E-66 so they would be used to the cadence and the sound of his voice. He would not be hurried at this point. He called the tower and shifted the Safety Officer duty to one of the Captains present and briefly explained the demonstration. He then reviewed everything for the crew. He talked them through how they would set up for the engagement explaining he would fire first and why. He emphasized the loader would continue coaching him on the caliber fifty machine gun until the target was destroyed. After one rehearsal in the defensive position, Martin reported to the tower and reported he was ready for his engagement.

It was clear to Martin the crew of E-66 was superbly trained before he ever got on their tank but that was no surprise to him. The unit Master Gunner took good care of the Commander's crew and busted their asses every chance he got with tough love. Everything they did was sharp and the tank was immaculate on the inside even though it was a loaner. The tower began the engagement with the standard briefing of "Suspected Enemy Activity vicinity of TRP 314, OUT.

The target representing the Russian made troop carrier, the BMP came up and at the same time a set of troops appeared to the far right of the BMP target. The objective was for a tank crew to be forced to engage troops firing an RPG at the same time they were within the lethal range of the Infantry carrying BMP. The engagement went off like clockwork following a crisp fire command from Martin of, "Gunner, Heat, BMP, Fire and Adjust, Caliber Fifty, Driver move out." Followed by the Gunner directing the crew with Identified, Driver Stop, the Loader clearly said Up, the Gunner sounded off with On the Way, followed by target Cease Fire. It was clear Martin was firing the Tank Commander's Machinegun before the tank was stopped. His targets went down just as the main gun fired and before the brake lights came on for the tank. His first rounds were short and he rapidly adjusted the gun to bring them all down. It could not have been executed any better. Zero seconds had elapsed and both targets were destroyed. Burton was amazed to see the Commander hang his head while his troops whooped and applauded the performance.

There was no joy apparent on the radio from the firing tank as Martin shifted the responsibilities for Safety Officer back to himself via the officers in the tower, moved back to the baseline and left without speaking to anyone but the Master Gunner of the Troop, the Gunner on E-66.

The Troop commander spoke up to say, "What, he left without gloating?"

378

The Master Gunner replied, "Sir, it all happened out there, didn't nothing happen back here. It's our turn now to go out there where it happens. He didn't do the demo for you, he did it for the soldiers to give them confidence. They know he is past his prime as a Tank Commander. Seeing him train up for the engagement was an eye opener. He knows he needs to rehearse."

It was indeed their turn and they did a magnificent job. The first four tanks were Platoon Sergeants and Platoon Leaders. They all fired perfect scores for day firing of seven hundred points each except for a crew cut of twenty points on one Platoon Sergeant. No crew used more than one round per main gun target. The last four crews consisted of the junior members of the Troop and the troop commander. Each of them dropped one engagement and the troop commander had to be brought to a cease fire for firing outside the range markers on the very engagement he had insisted Martin demonstrate. It was an easy mistake to make and in fact, Martin had done the same thing when testing the engagements at Knox before the manual was printed. The M1 traversing ring for the commander's machine gun was tricky for a novice, particularly when the tank was moving and then stopped suddenly. But, that was what practice was for, so that the men could not do it wrong.

As the last tank fired for the evening, Burton showed up with what was becoming a tradition, a cold Whopper and a watery coke and said, "Just think, ten more days and you will be gagging on a hot hamburger 'cause you ain't used to it."

"Any more cheery thoughts, old friend?" Martin said with a mouthful of cold burger.

"Yeah. This shit is tough but going well. You were right. I have never seen tanks shoot like this, anywhere, at any time. That shit of shooting through the fog with you in the safety tank is damn scary man. We fired the whole Table VI without ever seeing the range markers with the naked eye. Jesus Christ and General Thomas Jackson that scares the living shit out of me to think how far we have come. Now I don't mind killing folks that need killing and most of the time the jack-offs they sic us on need killin'. But these tanks are downright sinful in how they let you go about it. You've been right about everything so far. The targets do not last. The middle of them are shot up in no time. The chicken wire does not work. There is not enough of a spark from the rounds for the tanks to sense a hit. The flashcards really help the crews. Their confidence is sky high. The guys that have to re-do an engagement take it well. They take it even better out on the course road. The whole thing seems more like college baseball practice than tank gunnery but I sure cannot argue with the results. Godamm, Godamm, these jokers can shoot their asses off. This tank is bad, bad man," Burton said.

"Are you having a flash back, Nick?" Martin asked.

379

"You damn Skippy I am. Watching this shit today put me back in "Nam in the middle of a hellacious firefight in damn Cambodia. You know we invaded that place on a FRAGO over the radio. I was screwing off and my troops got off the tank and looted this store. They brought back a lawn chair for me. Nothing to do but I plop my sorry ass in it going down the road wearing my CVC drinking a Cambodian beer we had liberated. It never fails, start screwing off and all hell breaks loose. We ran into this NVA Regiment of Infantry that wanted to fight. We had been screwing off and it took us a minute to get into it but once we did, we killed nearly every one of those assholes. That is how these guys looked to me today, like my Echo Troop of back then once we got our shit wound up and threw away the lawn chairs and the beer. These guys were all business here, all day long. They are bad to the bone and a light year ahead of where we were in Cambodia. We were just more vicious but they'll catch up on that. Once they have a few casualties, they will be more than mean enough. Besides which, they will be sober," he said hitting Martin on his shoulder to break the moment.

1200 hours
30 Mar 1986
Range 23
Wildflecken, West Germany

The great Fox Troop was on the range and doing great. They had four maximum scores already and the remainder of the troop was very solid. It was evident they had been listening and paying attention. They were fully ready to fight. The Squadron Commander called for Martin on the phone to tell him to report to the debriefing tent. He was hardly prepared for what he found.

One of the very best NCOs he knew was at severe odds with the Tank company Master Gunner. The argument centered on the crew's shot at the moving tank. Martin had seen it happen. It was definitely a miss that went under the target. The Platoon Sergeant was a very good man. He was a former Drill Sergeant, about 6'2," a solidly built handsome Texan with as yet unlined face and blond hair and blue eyes. A stone Texas Redneck if there ever was one. He was also a ranch kid who had gotten enough of that life early and did not care if he ever saw a cow or a horse again. He was a soldier to the bone and though the list was not out yet, was a sure bet to make Master Sergeant.

At the moment, he was being an ignorant Platoon Sergeant, choosing to ignore the video evidence of the event and making an ass of himself. Martin motioned to him to come outside of the tent so he could talk with him. Sergeant First Class Delbert Murray shook his head and indicated he wanted to stay there. Martin reached up and pointed to his Master Sergeant rank and was vigorous in waving him to come outside.

380

Murray came outside but he was not fond of the idea. Martin came straight to the point, "You are not acting much like a First Sergeant. I know you ain't one yet but you will be one as soon as the list comes out and you are on it, and you know you will be on it. The Squadron Commander cannot wait to put you into a Cavalry Troop as a First Sergeant. He thinks you are ruled by reason and not emotion. Right now you are wrong as two left feet. You are emotionally involved and pissed off because you believe you hit the mover. You did not, you missed. You were screwed before you started. The mover is going uphill and away from you and is changing direction in two planes vertically and horizontally. You wanted your gunner to establish a smooth tracking rate, and then fire, didn't you?"

"Yes I did. How did you know that? Oh yeah, you can hear us up there, can't you?" he said with a shy smile.

"All of the guys that shot battle sight or shot fast, hit it. All the guys that tracked it for its length, like you did, shot short. It is a quirk of the Wildflecken Range 23 set up. Richard had to run it that way in order to get a double mover set up installed. It is the only way it would fit into the range footprint. It is 90% gamesmanship and 10% luck. Everyone that shot it short, as you did, missed. They have all creamed it dead center the second time."

"I don't want to shoot it over. I hit it," Murray said stubbornly.

"I hate to be the one to break the news to you, Tex, but Joe Shelby is not waiting for you down in Mexico and the South is already risen so it ain't rising again. The slaves are free and they are stayin' freed. For the here and now, if you choose not to fire that engagement over again, then someone else will be in command of that tank and of your Platoon. They will fire it cheerfully with your crew. Staff Sergeants do not make Master Sergeant. Use your head and take the practice for what it is worth - it is practice and Level II - not the Canadian Army Trophy shoot."

"Okay, I'm going but I still think I would have hit if it had been a real tank," he said in a parting shot.

Lieutenant Colonel Covington asked Martin on his return to the tower what he had told him. The young Captains were all ears. "I explained how the range was built and why the layout of the mover made it tough to hit the far mover for slow shooters. I then told him the convincing phrase that usually works, Staff Sergeants don't make Master Sergeant."

Using the new Captains in the S3 as a jury during a firing lull, Martin polled them. "What do you think about the training on Range 23, men?"

Captain James L. Corleone (AKA Vito) was a New Jersey pure bred Italian. He had gone to Princeton as a freshman and finished his undergraduate college work at West Point. His father was a WW II veteran who served overseas continuously from North Africa to the Elbe ending the war as a directly commissioned Captain of Armor. His dad had raised him to be a rational and independent thinker as befitting the son of a CPA turned business man. His

381

mother was a High School Principal and a former mathematics teacher. He was to be in the S3 for a year and take over Eagle Troop. He took his time answering and surprised everyone in the tower with his detailed response.

"The Squadron's analysis of the situation was nearly perfect. The pre-staging of the tanks and the elimination of all requirements for the troop to support itself with details was very smart. The ability to shoot all three tables on one range using troop labor for target detail only, is the key to success given the time available. The ability of the leadership to order re-fire engagements using ammo left over due to the extreme accuracy of the tank and proficiency of the crews are critical elements of the success. The immediate feedback and application of knowledge is great. The critiques are very well and professionally done. Making the soldiers discuss what they saw is the new way of teaching and is how the Armor School is doing it. The take home VHS tape is the smartest thing I have seen to date in the Army. What a training tool! They all tape skin flicks and can always find a VHS to show them, why not a tape of their range firing. From what I have seen so far, the Squadron is operating about two levels of proficiency above the rest of the Army in tank gunnery and maintenance. The firing during periods of fog and reduced visibility while appearing risky by putting the Safety Officer in a tank, it is not. It is a great time saver but most importantly, it teaches everyone in a most graphic way what the tank can do."

Captain Jared Winslow from the Arizona desert country just looked at everyone and Captain Coreleone before he spoke. "I agree with Vito. Master Sergeant Martin summed it up when he said those immortal words to a tank commander who was nervous before his run to calm and motivate him, 'Stevie Wonder could qualify this tank with your crew. Get your ass out there and show us how good you are and stop this stupid sniveling'." The entire tower broke out laughing to include the Major from V Corps who was visiting training.

All of them looked to Martin to see his reaction to the two Captains analysis of the Level II Gunnery. "You two gentlemen are really fitting in well. In the S3, we are a lot like the studio in Hollywood where the actors ran the show. A head of a rival studio once said, 'Oh great, the inmates are in charge of the asylum'."

Captain Winslow waited for the buzz to die and asked Martin a question, "When you started SABOT Academy did you know it would turn out like this?"

"Yes," Martin replied, not intending to say more.

"Oh come on, we want more than a 'Yes'," Winslow said, adding, "You're among friends."

"I am cursed to some degree, Captain Winslow. When I think up a course of action, I have learned to see the whole thing with the probable end state as the clearest part of the vision. It is the first thing in my mind rather than the last. I then work it backwards for planning with the unit calendar providing the gates. It is then just a simple matter to fit the resources to the time available and smoothing out the bumps in the road to get there. It had to be done and we had everything one could want to get it done. I had some great leaders and teachers and the rest of my time in the Army is just payback for what I have already been given," Martin said with some emotion.

"So you are now going to get ready for Grafenwohr and Level I?" Captain Corleone asked.

Martin thought for a moment before answering in this way, "No, I'm not going to be here for Graf nor will I be here for the Change of Command. I depart on 6 June for leave and TDY to the Sergeants Major Academy and will return after Level I and all of you are back in BK. We will also have a new Regimental Commanding Officer by then. The Regimental staff is already being re-loaded to meet the new Regimental Commanding Officer's desires as evidenced by the Squadron Executive Officer going to be the S1. I'm sure the new crowd will publish a very detailed MOI that leaves the new Squadron commander very little wiggle room. I know where you are going with the question. Know this! After this little rat race here at Wildflecken, my time here has passed. I am no longer needed at the Squadron S3. My purpose has been fulfilled with this gunnery and past helping set up the Bradley SABOT Academy. I am a lame duck."

"That sucks. You won't be here to see the results at Graf!" Winslow said.

"It was never about Graf, or Level I, or even beating the scores of the other Squadrons or even the rest of the Army, Captain Winslow. It was about the Squadron killing at least a thousand Russian armored vehicles in the Meinigen Gap in the role of the Corps Covering Force and giving the V Corps Commander some time to organize his forces. Level I gunnery is just one more measurement for Commanders to use until a war comes along again to sort out the flakes from the players."

CHAPTER 13 – TRANSITION TWO STEP

"Remember, when yo fights wit yo wife when you is in the Army, you is guilty 'til prov-en innocent or you go broke." SP4 Bennett, AKA -Cousin, Generator Man and Philosopher, Circa 1972

The Headquarters was empty of all but the Squadron Staff Duty crew consisting of an Sergeant First Class, a Driver and the Duty Officer. Even the Executive Officer, AKA the Iron Major, had gone home for the night. The only remaining souls working on the entire floor, which also included the ad-ministrative offices for the Headquarters Troop, were First Sergeant Waters of the HHT First Sergeant and Master Sergeant Martin, the temporary Tank Master Gunner stand-in. Waters was sorting the mail and establishing priori-ties for the next day's activities in his troop office and Martin was finishing a recorded presentation for the Sergeants Major Academy on the double enve-lopment of Nancy, a WWII battle.

It was his last course assignment before attending the 2-week course at Fort Bliss, TX and formal graduation from the Non-Resident Course of the Sergeants Major Academy. The effort spanned two years and had begun while he was assigned as Chief Instructor of the Gun Division at Knox. It contin-ued through assignments as, First Sergeant of two units, Ops Sergeant Major, Command Sergeant Major & Master Gunner. Martin was in the Secretary's medium sized office, sitting at her desk listening to the playback of the brief-ing he had just recorded and prepared for mailing to the Academy. He used two sets of paper slides as if he had two projectors. It was a complicated presentation but he knew the Major grading it at Fort Bliss would be able to follow it easily.

He could hear the loud and raucous guffaws of the HHT First Sergeant echoing down the hallway. It was clear the great First Sergeant Waters was coming down the hallway to visit someone in the Command and Staff section of the building and Martin knew it was not the Staff Duty crew.

"Hey, Martin, where is you, Man?" Waters called in imitation of Jamaican patois. Martin opened the door to the office and put his finger to his lips to shut him up and wave him forward. This was his last hurdle and he was de-termined to get it done no matter what the interruption.

First Sergeant Waters, never one to waste a learning opportunity, peered over his shoulder as he turned the pages of the briefing, matching the words on the recorder to the slides. As it ended, Martin took the tape from the play-er and placed into a padded envelope and sealed it. "Okay, First Sergeant Wa-ters, what is so damned funny it caused you to walk down here to find me?"

Waters was not quite ready to spring his surprise. He was still savoring the potential for humor he had seen in the Academy assignment Martin had ob-viously put so much effort into completing. "What in the hell does a Sergeant

Major give a big rat's ass about tactics at the Army level? Shit, a Sergeant Major isn't supposed to be able to spell envelopment and he sure to hell isn't supposed to know who Varo was."

Martin had long ceased to be surprised by the depth of Waters' knowledge. He may have looked and acted like a Klingon, but was far from it. He had just stated the obvious with a taste of irony about the esoteric nature of the assignment. He had also proven beyond a doubt he was conversant with tactics at the Army level no doubt arrived at through self study and interests. Waters knew Varo was an idiot and a political General qualified only by social and political position to lead a Roman Army. The phrase 'to be a Varo' for the tacticians of the world implied that it took an idiot on the defensive side to allow an attacker to successfully pull off a double envelopment. A competent commander with interior lines could, and most often did, make any attacking commander who elected to split his forces pay dearly for his decision.

"No need to hold back there, First Sergeant. Tell me how you really feel about the Sergeants Major Academy," Martin said with a big smile.

Waters became very serious and then adopted a shy smile. He was a country Texas man and he took great care not to insult anyone who was sincerely trying to serve their country. "I was not selected for the Academy. I was lucky to get to be a First Sergeant and lucky to survive three tours in Vietnam. The Academy is not for me. I'm going home to my sweet little wife in Louisiana, getting a job at Range Control at Fort Polk and living the good life, fishing and huntin'. This First Sergeant job is it for me. I would not do what you have done for two years for any money, rank or position in the world."

"Not even for Sergeant Major of the Army?" Martin asked sarcastically.

"Shit, not even for Sergeant Major of The Earth. It ain't me brother. Do you remember the day the Squadron Commander gave you your PT Test for record? I do. The whole damn squadron and half of the 2/41 Artillery were looking out of the barracks windows onto the street cheering, booing and insulting the shit out of you while you ran your two miles around the quadrangle while he timed you. You ran it in twelve minutes and change, bowed to the four compass points and did fifty pushups to cool down. You are what they want, an Arabian Stud, you can run all day and First Sergeant all night. I am a Clydesdale Gelding with a bad heart. I can walk part of the day and sleep most of the night. I don't fit the mold. I'm going home while the getting is good. The good news is I will be there to greet you at Fort Polk. Here is your Welcome Letter and your packet," he said with a great guffaw that echoed through the high ceilings and off the concrete tile floors of the old German barracks.

"I am not going to Fort Polk. Armor Branch told me I was going back to Knox. We own a house in Radcliff. Our plan is to return there and retire to Florida. No way in hell I'm going to Polk. This welcome packet is an error," Martin stated with great conviction.

385

His ardor only stoked the fire for his buddy Waters. "Bullshit my friend. Your ass is going to Fort Polk. A place you think you hate. Your life is about to change when you become Sergeant Major Martin, First Sergeant. You are about to lose control of your destiny. Shit, a Speck Four gets more consideration than a Sergeant Major or a General. DA moves you Sergeant Major types around like you ain't human. You'd better call Armor Branch and talk to Miss Peggy. The zip code for DeRidder, LA is 70634. That is where all the Bible thumpers stay but they buy their beer in Leesville," this last statement ended in another burst of braying from Waters.

Martin got a sick feeling in the pit of his stomach as he thought of the possibilities of being assigned to Fort Polk. Shit, in a soldier's mind, there is no better place than the one he just left and no worse one than the one he was going to report to next. All of it was relative. He would call branch and straighten this whole thing out with Miss Peggy. It had not been more than a month ago he had called to check. Then, his next assignment was as a First Sergeant in a Basic Training Battalion on Fort Knox, Kentucky.

In his small cold water flat, Martin had dialed Armor Branch direct on his Bundespost telephone and he was on "hold". The West German post office also owned the telephone service along with the rail service. Martin's phone was metered. The meter was on the face of the telephone. The cost of calls was expressed in terms of pfennings, the German version of pennies. The cost of each call could be monitored by the caller by observing a meter on the phone. Since Miss Peggy had put Martin on hold, his pfenning meter was going ape shit as it spun upward into bankruptcy altitude. The cost no longer mattered to him. He intended to hold the connection as long as it took to find out where he was headed. Miss Peggy finally came back on the line.

"First Sergeant Martin, I am sorry it took so long to get back to you," Miss Peggy said.

"That's okay, Miss Peggy, I appreciate all you do for us," Martin said honestly.

Miss Peggy was probably a lifelong resident of DC, black, rode a bus to work, had two kids, was divorced, a Baptist, a Democrat and had never been outside of DC unless it was a bus trip during high school. She was a vanishing breed as he was. He could not have explained the pfenning meter on his phone to her if he tried.

"Your file is no longer in the Armor Branch. It is signed out to the Sergeants Major Branch. You will have to call them to find out about any future assignments! Okay? Sorry I took so long," Miss Peggy said, only understanding the file was longer hers to worry about without realizing the impact to her caller.

Not hearing an answer and aware overseas connections were sometimes fragile; Miss Peggy wanted to verify the connection, "First Sergeant Martin, are you there?"

Thankful her question had broken his reverie, he answered her, "Yes, Miss Peggy I am here. Thank you for your help, I have their number over there at Sergeant Major Branch. Good bye."

I won't be calling them anytime soon until the list comes out. Time to shut up and go serve at Polk or anywhere else. Made the list in 17 years. Must be a cutoff point in the Sergeant Major course where it is safe to promote folks. But, they have you by the stacking swivel so it really does not matter. To hell with the pfenning meter, it will be a pleasure to pay the bill in a good cause, peace of mind!!

Martin would not miss the run, trip, fall execution cycle of the Cavalry instead of the crawl, walk, run cycle of the Infantry Division. The Squadron Commander now wanted the S3 to move to and occupy a position near the border to conduct a briefing for over 100 NATO General and Senior Officers and Officials. The briefing would be in a large tent known as a General Purpose Medium. The tent would have bleachers in it as well as a sand table built and set up to reflect the terrain on the Meinigen Gap. The activity on the sand table would be mirrored by a demonstration team from the Cavalry Troop assigned to the Border. It was to be augmented by the tank company and the howitzer battery in the movement in the valley below hill 746 maneuvering their M1 tanks, M-113 personnel carriers and M-109 howitzers. As these troops in their vehicles moved on the actual ground, observed by the VIPs, the Squadron Commander described the actions of the US Commander countering the tactics of the Russian Commander. The red dots of two lasers manipulated by well rehearsed privates moved in response to the narrative keeping the audience focused.

The laser dots were emitted by the M-55 training devices originally designed to fit in the coaxial machinegun ports of tanks to give a focal point for indoor manipulation exercises for gunnery training. The Squadron Commander would be akin to Cecil B. DeMille, directing a small piece of an imaginary epic battle complete with real moving parts, artillery simulation, tank gun firing and MILES force on force battles in the valley below.

The battle of the Meinegen Gap had achieved the mythical status of a real battle through repetition. Past history helped as it was a traditional invasion route used by Armies attacking both east and west in Germany for many years. It was now the darling adopted step child with blond hair and blue eyes come to be the star of the annual school play. Now clothed in modern garb and hopefully alluring, attractive and youthfully exciting, the Gap story was to the men in charge of weapons procurement and budget what a busty waitress was to old men with prostate trouble. Selected facets of the story provided inspiration for those who needed it. For that reason and the desire to meet the needs of each constituency in the military-industrial complex, each and every commander in the chain above Company level changed their minds ten times before the final curtain went up. Lieutenant Colonel Covington's task was to change the narration to fit the last change by the highest ranking "coach". It was his next to last "ARTEP" as a Squadron Commander and he damn well meant to pass it.

The final form for the map representation was not a sand table. It had morphed into a huge map board measuring 50 x 75 feet. Richard, of the Wildflicken G3/DPTMS, made certain it was sturdy enough for the Squadron Commander to walk on it wearing a wireless microphone and carrying a pointer six feet long. Detailed rehearsals enabled soldiers concealed in deer hunter stands to project the laser beams from the clumsy training devices onto the map board below. Clearly, the Squadron Commander had more than enough sophistication to make rapid changes to his narrative and moreover, the patience to coach the soldiers with the lasers. Richard also provided a bleacher set up of a most clever design that allowed seating for 200. It was an engineering marvel that folded up into flat packages easily transported on a five ton truck.

The set up, rehearsal, ammunition supply and troop control as well as the reception and care for the VIPs was an absolute nightmare for Sergeant Major Burton and his S3 section. Nothing worked right from the beginning for the unit. Nearly everything had to be replaced or altered that was issued by the government. The bright spots of the entire process for the S3 crew were the fabrication of maps and bleachers from Richard and the state of training of the soldiers and their leaders. The rehearsal was an abortion. The laser pointers failed, as did the communications gear. Communication problems between the demonstration troops and the hill top conductor, the G Troop Commander, Captain David Dawson, were common. He and his old First Sergeant had a short moment to chat and to coordinate, "Top, do you have some shit stashed somewhere? We are out of Hoffman Devices for the tank company. Some asshole hooked up his device wrong and shot his one whole load during prep to fire checks. That will run them short," Dawson asked Martin.

His former First Sergeant then surprised his old Commander by asking, "What is the complete bill for all of the pyrotechnic shortages? I know there has to be more than just Hoffman devices that got screwed up. I also would hope that you are not letting these assholes scam me to build up their secret storage. I have enough of everything to do it at least two more times but I would not want that to get around. I did screw with the Squadron Commander a little bit. He does not realize all of this shit never got forecasted in advance. The numb nuts he had in the S3 never bothered to plan ahead. I did an emergency supply request a month ago when I caught the first glimmer of this event, but it has yet to be filled."

"The shit you see here is from the big exercises we have been umpiring this winter. Lieutenant Colonel Covington did not know I had an S3 stash, he just knew G Troopers have a bad habit of hiding shit away for a rainy day under less than legal conditions. In G Troop the word illegal means a large, white headed sick raptor," he said as they both laughed like the small boys they really were.

"God it must be so hard to be morally straight and need to come to a set of pirates like us to keep the Regimental Commanding Officer's teeth out of your ass. Oh the Shame of It All Seamus. It is a terrible thing for a nice English Lad like him havin' to deal with heathen devils like us and maybe losing his mortal soul, just terrible," Martin said doing his imitation of an Irish accent he knew Dawson would recognize from a John Wayne movie.

"Damn, First Sergeant, I never heard you do that one before. You sounded just like Barry Fitzgerald in the 'The Quiet Man'. Where on earth did you ever learn to do an Irish accent like that?" Dawson asked.

"The abilities to act and to shoot pool are both merely the evidence of a misspent youth, not any great gifts from God, my Captain. It is all just pure sin. Why, do you realize the Puritan faith has the ability to stay in a state of contrition because someone, somewhere on earth, is always having a good time?" Martin said with an impish smile.

"What in the hell has wound you up?" Dawson said, starting to get worried as his old First Sergeant was acting so far out of character he thought he may have been drunk.

"I called DA to check with Armor Branch about my assignment when I got a Welcome Letter from Fort Polk. The branch file girl told me my file was signed out to the Sergeant Major Branch and they would have to be the ones to answer all my questions from now on out," Martin said with a broad smile.

Dawson was truly and completely surprised and happy for his old First Sergeant. It was as if one of his uncles got promoted. "Damn, First Sergeant, that is good news for you and for the Army. I guess I am now going to have to say I have met one Sergeant Major who was worth a shit instead of saying all of y'all are worthless," he said bluntly.

"You can hold off thinking bad thoughts and calling me a scum bag for a year or two as it will take that long to get promoted," Martin said with a smile. He was sure Dawson knew it did not make a shit to him what he thought about the rank of E-9. Dawson was entitled to his opinion and Martin was entitled to ignore it.

"Stroud, break out the emergency pyro and take Captain Dawson shopping please. If he needs help delivering it, you take it down to the EDATS in the valley over there by that church house. It is too late for anything but execution now - no sniveling - by anyone. Jackson, what is the definition of sniveling?" Martin asked though all present knew the question was formed in a Pavlovian like format and called for a rote response.

Sergeant Jackson came to attention and shouted, "First Sergeant, the definition of sniveling is to sob without tears."

"Good Man! Sir, Stroud will square you away. I am going to do some maintenance on your commo gear before the big show," Martin said.

"First Sergeant, what is an EDAT," Stroud asked. "I know what a DAT is, but what is an EDAT?"

"Stroud, you are supposed to be a hip scout. An EDAT is an Electronic Dumb Ass Tanker. The new acronym reflects the fact the Army has spent another $3 million dollars per tank to provide a thousand new excuses why they can't hit shit," Martin said playing to the scout prejudices strongly held by Stroud and all 19D's who held themselves superior to the rest of the Army. "Hell, Stroud, soon you will be an EDAS, when you get your Bradley," Martin added.

"Not me, First Sergeant. That big sonofabitch is gonna' draw more fire than a gas can at an arsonists' convention. I'm changing my MOS to draftsman," Stroud shot back.

"Is Jackson worth a shit?" Dawson asked smiling at Stroud's quick come back to his old First Sergeant.

The Old First Sergeant had always liked a quick witted soldier. He never came down on them when they gave him back as good as he put out. Not many NCOs could do that. They did not have the self-confidence. Good natured banter among soldiers was not for Commanders. Better he kept his distance and said only what was necessary to get the mission done. Familiarity breeds contempt. OCS was open.

"He ain't bad, ain't bad at all. He has a bit of a payday soldier in him but not enough to hurt anything. Wry sense of humor, loves the booze, his body stays hard as Japanese arithmetic, works hard as hell, just a good Cav Trooper, why?" Martin asked, always on guard about his people.

"The Regimental Commanding Officer is looking at him to be his last driver," Dawson said.

"You know my philosophy. Cheerfully give the leaders who they want to support them when they want them and they will keep your unit full of folks. He can have him this afternoon if he wants him. I know you have never agreed with that philosophy of support for others. You like to tell people 'No' just to see if you can buffalo them. One of us, any of us, telling the Regimental Commander 'No' because he wants a specific soldier, is like a baby buggy colliding with a freight train. Some day that stubborn streak of yours is going to cost you a big price if you are not careful," Martin said.

"I'll keep that in mind, First Sergeant, but I will reserve the right to tell any, or all, to jack off even when I know I am going to lose, when they want my men or my equipment," Dawson said with finality.

None of the high ranking folks got their feet wet or muddy thanks to the duck boards, straw, tent floors and gravel walkways. The rolls, coffee and fruit trays were a big hit as many of them had missed breakfast trying to travel to the site.

When the American Officers found out by following their noses there was a soldiers' breakfast of eggs, creamed beef (SOS), biscuits and bacon available, they made a beeline for the mess tent in the nearby woods. Led by the three and four star Generals, no one else in the group had any inhibitions about taking the time to eat breakfast.

They ate as if they had not eaten in years. It was yet another lesson learned for Martin. Most staff pukes were former field rats who really missed being in a TO & E unit. Food, particularly in the field, was a very big part of the Army. It was Sergeant Major Burton who insisted the Border Camp cooks make enough food to feed all 150 expected guests plus all of the soldiers in the demonstration that made it a winner. Burton also made certain the plates were from the commissary and of the China variety, no trays, plates or metal flatware. They were strong, the size of meat platters and could have held a roast. He also insisted on stout plastic silverware. Most of the Allied Officers could have cared less about the American food and stayed with the light continental fare. The Special Operations types among them waded into the breakfast with the Army Rangers. The slight delay caused by the breakfast was used to good effect by the "stage crew" to make last minute adjustments to equipment and re-distribute some of the "ammunition". Who is going to tell the USAREUR Commanding General he cannot visit a field mess hall and have creamed beef on toast AKA, SOS (Shit On a Shingle)?

Sergeant Major Burton and Martin had little or nothing to do once the extravaganza was rolling with the Squadron Commander on center stage. He did a superb job. When it was over, Sergeant Major Burton said to Martin, "This is when you find out how it really went. Pay attention and just give this guy whatever he asks for," as they both watched the One Star approach them.

They saluted as one when the Brigadier General was within three steps of them, saying in unison, "Eagle Horse, Sir."

He smiled and said, "Tell me everything and don't leave anything out. I really need to know about the bleachers and the map boards and how long it will take to make me a set of them."

Martin answered first, "General, the bleachers are yours to command. We can get them to you today, if necessary. The map boards can be made within ten days at Wildflicken or by one of the other G3's you control. The ammunition, pyro and vehicles are also yours to command with just the 5 W's. They can be moving in two hours. This is the listing of ammo and pyro and this listing shows the tentage and parts for the whole operation on one sheet of paper."

"You mean I can have the bleachers, the tent, duckboards, lights everything right now?" he asked.

Burton simply pointed to the name tape over his left breast pocket of his field jacket and said the same thing to the Brigadier General he had said to Martin and his trainees long ago, "General they put the US Army on the left over our hearts. The needs of the Army are more important than the individual name tag on the right. We are all in the same Army. Our equipment is your equipment if you need it. Tell us what you want done. We will make it happen."

"My Ops Sergeant Major, will be here in a minute. We need the equipment on this site to go to Oppenheim. It will be set up above the river there. It needs to go there today for use next week. This was a great event. It is hard to believe it was set up and run by a Battalion size element without additional support except for the show boat stuff like the paper map boards and the bleachers. Be sure and show him how to do the red dots on the map board. You guys did a great job, thanks and thanks for being so helpful. I appreciate it and the Commanding General appreciates it," he said as he saluted and left.

"When the big guys steal your ideas and borrow your shit to cover their asses you know ya' done good!" Burton said turning to shake Martin's hand.

"Can Staff Sergeant Duncan handle the SABOT Academy for the Bradleys?" Sergeant Major Burton asked.

"Tim Duncan has a history of competence with me. He has never failed me. He did fail as a recruiter. He was fired and got an enlisted efficiency report that rated him somewhere below whale shit. After seeing him operate, and watching some other guys in his fix, I decided to rehabilitate the 19D's and 19K's, who were also failed recruiters, by sending them to Master Gunner. It was the only way I had to get them back on track."

"It was as much a decision for the sake of the unit and the Army as it was for them. The Bradley Master Gunner selection was the hardest to make because the initial course was sure to be a near gimmie'. It had to be. It was the first one. The guys that went to it had to be of the finest character, and they were. They kept the best one we sent. The Benning School Command Sergeant Major sent two great guys to take his place."

"The Tank SABOT Academy is more than a blueprint, it is a forged pattern. The 19D's can simply overlay the technical jargon of the Bradley and the processes unique to the vehicle over the tank syllabus. Plus, the Squadron is familiar with the moving parts of a unit school and they have a successful model."

"So short answer, Tim Duncan will produce a very, very successful SABOT Academy for the Bradley. It will turn out better than the tank version or at least as good. The critical difference is the ability of the scouts to acquire targets. If we use smaller targets initially, the flash of the sun off the big ones with the morning dew on them will draw the attention of the scouts. They will be knocking them down in zero seconds. Out of 38 Bradleys, we will have at least 18 perfect scores and maybe more, on their Table VIII," Martin opined.

Staff Sergeant Duncan did not disappoint. He designed a great course of training for the new Cavalry Fighting Vehicle. He had every critical element in its proper place. His range selection at Wildflicken was superb. Although Martin did not agree with the range he picked for Table VI, he did not interfere. The targets were on the side of a hill across a windswept valley. The firing point was on a sheltered mesa. The result was an accuracy nightmare for the crews due to the crosswind and half sized targets Duncan selected. When asked, his response was from a bygone era, "Good training, there is always going to be something wrong. Here it is a crosswind. Tough, we just have to figure it out."

Staff Sergeant Duncan's decision to take the Squadron Commander's Bradley to lead the Squadron through Wildflicken paid big dividends. Duncan's crew was not spectacular but they were very steady and finished in the top ten in scoring. Staff Sergeant Duncan and Lieutenant Colonel Covington's leadership helped all of the crews see what the vehicle could do and that the training worked. The Squadron Commander really enjoyed firing the Bradley and did a great job. Each unit fired better than the one before it. The fact all of the Master Gunners shared information and trained up the next unit proved Staff Sergeant Duncan was a good choice.

The Bradley crews progressed through the ridiculously small targets on the beginning ranges. They became highly adept at acquiring targets. Their marksmanship was honed there on the difficult windswept and miserable range. By the time they encountered targets the actual size of Russian tanks and personnel carriers, average crews were knocking the targets down before they could come up and lock in position. To the uninitiated, it appeared as if the targets were malfunctioning though they were not.

It was as Martin had hoped it would be when modern technology met the US Army Infantry School. Tough, no frills, training conducted early under the worst possible conditions employing artificial handicaps produced crews whose performance exceeded all expectations.

Before he knew it, it was time for Martin to return to the states for the two week Sergeant Major Course and 21 days of leave. He was not looking forward to the constant conflict of a nagging wife in the stark contrast with the sweetness of a German mistress. He felt he had to lose a few pounds to preclude the possibility of the autocrats at the Academy judging his height to be 5'11" instead of 6' even. After two years of work and study and 16 years of service, he wanted to be absolutely certain he was 15 pounds under the maximum weight standard. He had served at Fort Bliss and knew the climate of the high desert in June was far removed from Bad Kissingen, Germany. When he boarded the train to catch his airplane ride to the states it was snowing. He knew that if the Command Sergeant Major Commandant got a wild hair up his ass, they could all end up taking a PT test for the record during the school. He had his one required presentation ready and was as prepared for the experience as possible.

393

1400 hours
10 Jun 1986
Family Home
Naranja, FL

Nothing had changed in his home. He was still the meal ticket and an un-welcome visitor. His wife treated him alternately hot and cold depending on what she needed at the time. The yard work he had been doing plus his daily PT program that included long runs in the South Florida summertime had peeled the extra ten pounds of schnitzel and beer from him in no time. He was tanned, fit and relaxed as one could be living in an unhappy home. As he was dragging a large tree limb to the pile, a lady stopped her car as if to ask directions. He was dressed in just a pair of shorts and old sneakers with no socks, no shirt, hatless, and covered in sweat and tree sap.

He approached her open window and saw an attractive middle aged lady about his own age that was immaculately groomed with very nice jewelry. "Yes ma'am, how can I help you?" he asked.

"Do you live in this house, I'm looking for the man of the house who is a soldier and home on leave named Ronald Martin, is that you, Sir?"

"Yes ma'am, that's me," Martin answered with a smile as she was really very, very good looking and in great condition.

"I am Charles Burden's wife. He is carrying on an affair of long standing with your wife Dinah. He spends a lot of time here and they go off on week-ends together in our motor home. He went out with her before we were mar-ried while she was still married to the Air Force officer. I am sorry to have to tell you this. I am at my wits end and am trying to save my marriage," she said as the tears welled up in her pretty blue eyes.

"Well I am certainly glad to meet you, Ms. Burden. I knew your husband and Dinah were lovers before but I did not know they never broke it off. Why don't you park your car up on the lawn. We'll go inside and have a chat with Dinah. She can bring us up to date about this state of affairs. This is a red letter day for me," Martin added with a huge grin.

"Oh, no, I don't want to do that. I just came by to see if he was here. I need him to sign some papers for our business that we run together. But, I meant to tell you if I saw you. I did not want you to be blind to what has been going on for twenty years duration, through three wives for Charles and two husbands for her," she said, her errand and her courage having come to an end at the same moment in time.

Shit, just what we need an honest person caught up in the messy married lives of three hedonists, Dinah, Charles and me. This should provide a few laughs during the leave pe-riod. I see Bertha from across the street did not miss a thing as he watched the shades flip and the drapes being closed as Mrs. Burden drove away. It was a little embarrassing for the neighbors to know about their business. Of course Dinah's girls, his step daughters, knew

394

everything. Guess I'll go see what lies this development will bring. They should be some whoppers.

Martin was greeted by his wife, with her inevitable questions, guidance and complaints. "Are you done with the tree yet? I have other things for you to do. Nothing much got done as there was never enough money to keep it up correctly. The Army just does not pay you enough for you to live there and me to live here. So when you come home on leave, you have a lot to do and it can't get done with you sitting in the house. You can have some Kool Aid. There's no money for soda or beer. You are losing too much weight and are making me look bad."

When she appeared to pause for breath, he told her, "I just had an interesting visitor. Mrs. Charles Burden stopped by and told me of the long standing affair Charles is having with you. She seems like a nice woman. I wonder where she could ever come up with that idea. How could she say you of all people, the paragon of the virtuous wife, was having an affair? Why it is ridiculous! Don't they have nine kids between them and a thriving business to run?"

Gotta' give the bitch credit, she was a cool customer as she started her lie. He knew exactly what she was going to say before she said it. It was ironic that her own words convicted her more than any video or testimony could have done.

"Charles is an old love and he does stop by here to see me and to rest. He has done some work for me here. She does not love him or understand him and he only comes here to cry on my shoulder. There is nothing between us. That is long over. He had his chance and did not take it. You are the only man in my life. Any of the neighbors or Billie can tell you the same thing," she said avoiding eye contact.

Yeah, right. They are all used to lying for you and are happy to do it. They probably told your husband that when you were seeing me and telling me you were legally separated from him while he was on an unaccompanied tour to Korea and to Thailand.

"I guess the extra money he earned fixing stuff over here came in handy. He never charges me full price to do anything. She never lets him spend any money and keeps all of their money tied up in the business and paying off her debts," she said.

"That is some lame shit you are telling me Dinah. I am living on nothing while you plead poverty and you are paying your lover to hang out. I'll try hard to remember that the next time I need a pair of tennis shoes and the damn check bounces. You need to think about how much money you have to have. Old Charles is going to need a new Sugar Momma or you are going to have to get a job to keep his ass in style because you ain't doing it with my money," Martin said with emotionless finality.

"I did not give him hardly anything. It wasn't like that," she said angrily.

He did not take the bait. "Whatever you gave him was not yours to give. You have several hundred thousand dollars in assets to draw on if you want to give him money. You can give him all of your money if that is what you want to do, but Charles nor anyone else you choose to let cry on your shoulder, gets anymore of mine."

"Just what do you mean to do?" Dinah asked.

"Tell me how much you believe our expenses to be and list them for me on a single sheet of paper. We have income and we have expenses. Your old story of everything you had before marriage was yours, is still yours and everything I had before marriage and now have is also yours, is not true anymore. It was only as true as I let it be to make you happy," he said with the greatest calm. He knew she was about to move into the attack mode as she could not surrender her hard won position with so little struggle.

"So, while you were having your great love affair in Germany, what was I supposed to do? Don't think I am stupid and do not know you were seeing someone over there. You had a lot of money from the housing allowance. You did not need any of our money. You are not going to do anything that would cause us to get a divorce. You want to be successfully married. I know you do," she opined, sure of herself.

"No, of course not," he said appearing to give in to her without a struggle. "I'll go out and finish the work on the tree and get the limbs over to the dump in the station wagon. I need to go to the hardware store to get John a new chain saw blade. The tree sap has ruined his. It was brand new when he let me use it," he informed her.

"How much is that going to cost? He does not care about the chain saw blade. They borrow stuff from other people all of the time. Don't throw money at people. If he does not like the way you bring it back, wait for him to say something. Don't assume you have to bring it back perfect," she barked now that her confidence had returned somewhat.

"Don't worry about it! It is only a few dollars. I will not take it back to him without cleaning it and putting on a new blade. He saved us a ton of money and time by lending it to us. What was the estimate for trimming the tree from the professional - $600 dollars wasn't it? They are our best friends on the block!" he said with finality.

He decided then and there to give her a fixed allowance, separate their money and to begin the total separation of funds and property. He would get a divorce - no matter what the cost or the pain. The contrast between Dinah and Marty was too great. She was just too much of a self-centered, penny pinching, bad tempered witch to live with anymore. Bitching about the chain saw blade and her willingness to screw their oldest friends in the neighborhood over $15 was the last straw. Martin could not believe he had lived with her as long as he had.

He would have to be careful. Her stupid temper knew no bounds and she was capable of total self destruction to get what she thought was her just due. If she could, she would take the last person who pissed her off along with her. He was determined not to be in the blast cone of the hand grenade when she did her own dumb ass in for the final time.

0500 hours
15 Jun 1986
Holiday Inn
El Paso, TX

Martin eased out of their room to go for his morning PT effort of exercises and a five mile run. He and his fellow Non-Resident Course Students of the US Army Sergeants Major Academy had until 1800 hours to report to the school. The course was the culmination of a two year effort to complete a detailed course of study but was only for the slim. There was an inevitable weigh in and if necessary, body fat measurement segment. The faculty would also verify student documents and schedule one formal briefing by each candidate to verify he could walk and chew gum at the same time. He would take Dinah coffee, a breakfast roll and fruit when he returned to the room.

As he did his warm up exercises he noticed a number of men about his age wandering about the hotel, some of whom were dressed in PT clothes and others who were already in their Class A uniforms sipping coffee. Every one of them he saw in dress uniform looked fat and worried. It was hard to believe anyone would put in two years of work and then show up to a school proclaiming that it was the paragon of E-9 fitness and be fat. But, he realized he had a lot to learn about the Army outside of combat arms.

The desert did not disappoint. It had not changed since his time there for an AIT as a Nike-Hercules Missile Launcher Crewman or for his many visits there during three years with an Air Defense Artillery Battalion for exercises. The road next to the Holiday Inn led out into an expanse of desert. The handout the Academy made sure each arrival had covered every detail of the two week school. The first lines reflected the fact the desert environment was one of low humidity and required acclimatization prior to PT. The handout was piously written in the manner of Sergeant Major communications the world over. The stress was on drinking lots of fluids, gradual increase in exercise and to impress upon those there for a two week TDY that they did not have enough time to get used to both the altitude and the summer heat of El Paso. He grabbed a bottle of water from the lobby of the hotel and began his run. Running out for twenty minutes and turning around should give him his six miles in 42 minutes. He would follow it with an hour of the heavy weights in the hotel gym and a swim. His wife should be ready for a full breakfast by then and he would in process, giving them time to tour the Academy, see the sights of El Paso, Las Cruces and maybe Juarez.

The run was a great way to start out in El Paso. Martin had a lot of great memories of the place and had spent a lot of time there over the years. It was a unique Post. The civilians that ran it were 90% Mexican-Americans and many were former soldiers. If it rained, all military traffic stopped as the majority of the residents did not know how to drive in the rain. When it did snow, everybody stayed home. There were no cars whatever on the road to nowhere leading away from the hotel. Martin decided the hotel was the first part of a development trend by the City/County development agency and other businesses and venues were not far behind. He hoped he would not be back to see it grow. El Paso and the famous Dyer Street had grown exponentially since his last visit there 10 years ago. As he looked at his watch, he was approaching the hotel with 38 of his allotted 42 minutes elapsed. Deciding the faculty of the Academy probably had some empirical reason for telling the know it all E-8's and E-9's to chill out, he began to walk to cool down. After drinking another pint of water in addition to the pint he drank on the run, he got a Coke before going to the weight room and sat outside on a bench sweating out the water.

Out of long habit, he reached down into his sock and fished out a Marlboro Red with a lighter and had a cigarette with his Coke. Off balance, he was surprised to feel someone stumble into him on the bench. As he started to raise hell with whoever it was, he saw it was Pete Simmons, a fellow Drill Sergeant from long ago at Fort Knox. He and Simmons were the only two Drill Sergeants who ran during cycle breaks or at any other time when it was not mandatory. Simmons was now a Sergeant Major and in his Class B uniform. Martin immediately stood up and said "Morning, Sergeant Major Simmons. Out perfecting your Dale Carnegie Course skills a little early aren't you?"

"Damn, there for a minute I thought you may have mastered the social graces, Master Sergeant Martin," Simmons said with a big laugh. "I saw your name on the list and told my boss you would be up at 0500 and running at least six miles and pumping iron before the weigh in and in processing. I'm glad to see you heeded the warnings and backed off with the walk at the end. I assume you went to the end of the road and turned around."

"I did," Martin answered his old friend. He added, "I did back off. I figure if it was important enough for you guys to write it down in the welcome packet I should pay attention and do what you advised. It probably came from having to police up old farts from cold climates and guys trying to get back in shape in one day after doing nothing for years before reporting to the Academy. It is too little, too late by then. BOHICA baby," (Bend Over Here It Comes Again) they both said in unison from their Drill Sergeant days being led by 82 AA NCOs.

"So hey, you got your ID Card, we can do you right now. No need to wait. You're all set for the weigh in. Take a towel so you don't sweat on the tables and shit, hell take a couple of them. The damn sweat is jumping off of you as usual man. I wish to hell I could sweat projectiles. Two extra tacos and I'm overweight. You got the metabolism of a flippin' coyote, home boy."

Taking Simmons at his word, Martin did his in-processing right then and there. He did not argue when his height came in at 5'11"as he knew the Academy would always round down no matter what the measurement unless you were 6'1". At 170, he was 20 pounds under the standard and would not be re-weighed over the next two weeks of the school. He finished his in processing and said goodbye to Simmons vowing to catch up with him during the next two weeks. Clutching his new schedule and welcome packet, he got Dinah her coffee and snack and returned to their room all set for the day and to begin class on Monday.

1900 hours
27 Jun 1986
NCO Club Main Dining Room
Sergeant Major Academy Summer Class
Dining Out

The Dining Out was looking more and more like an imitation event being held to check the block. The Resident Course had one, ergo the Non-Resident course had to have one. Of course, there were skits and the normal toasts and formalities. It had been an interesting two weeks but overall it was a pro forma requirement and Martin for one, was glad it was about over. He had enough of the Army School scene. Like the tomcat making love to the female skunk, he might not have all he needed but he had damn sure had all he could stand. Three years as a Drill Sergeant and three on the Armor School faculty and the past two had topped off his Army School tank of knowledge.

His faculty advisor, or FUGM, Sergeant Major Barnhill, had cornered him and two other combat arms types while the wives were in a long discussion about Germany, clothes and kids. The women were having a good hen party while Sergeant Major Barnhill was picking their husband's brains and sizing them up as future instructors at the Academy. If he so recommended, the Commandant could have them assigned immediately with orders sent to their units to pack up their personal property, automobiles and household goods for shipment to Fort Bliss. He had watched them closely throughout their time at the two week course and he wanted both of them as Instructors.

Master Sergeant Washington was the most intelligent NCO that Sergeant Major Barnhill had met in 25 years of service. He seemed to know everything about everything. He was an Intell guy with a thirst for knowledge and a sponge for a brain. He had a photographic memory, was a recruiting picture book soldier, had two Masters Degrees and was a great conversationalist. He was very interested in becoming an Instructor and was fully cognizant of the benefits of doing so. His ambition knew no bounds and he was certain he would be at least a Division Command Sergeant Major by virtue of his time at the Academy. Based on his interview with the Commandant, a very crusty Air Defender with 18 years in grade as a Command Sergeant Major and 35 years service, the next morning, he would join the faculty.

First Sergeant Martin was a walking paradigm of a hard driving NCO. He obviously held up the Army Standard. He was leadership personified. Everyone in a room, officers and all stopped talking when he entered it. He had led his group to do things no other set of students had ever done. They solved problems that were not supposed to be solved. Their solutions actually scared some of the faculty, most of whom were not easily cowed. In one instance, the time for the solution was growing short and the group wanted to give up, quit, and take a break. By force of personality, Martin would not let them quit. He divided them for responsibilities a second time, summarized what they knew, defined what they had yet to find out, and browbeat them with humor, irony and veiled threats. They found the answer in the last 30 seconds. No one had ever solved the problem nor had a group ever continued to fight until the end.

The problem was a leadership test. Martin was in a subordinate role. He had himself appointed Chief of Staff and designated each of his classmates in staff positions befitting their mission in the Army and the Reserve. The problem had various red herrings designed to confuse the unwary. The factors were expressed in a language concocted by the author to make the problem extremely difficult, and it did. None of that mattered, the small class of Non-Resident scholars of a Cavalry Scout, an Infantryman, a West Point Bandsman, a Food Service Cook, a Quartermaster and a Finance guy, figured it all out. Martin deflected all praise and attention to the appointed leader for the event.

In a leadership test involving the detection and correction of uniform violations at the Fort Bliss PX Snackbar, those students whose service with troops was limited, were at a severe disadvantage confronting the salty scouts of 3d ACR just in from the field. Martin saw that one of the field rats had a classmate Sergeant Major backing up. Martin fixed that very quickly and gave some pointed lessons to his fellow students.

Nose to nose with a nasty looking Specialist, Martin confronted him saying, "Just how many years are you willing to do over your nasty appearance? Just shut up, button your shirt, blouse your damn boots, reverse your belt and try to look like a Soldier, and do it now, right now!" all of which was spoken softly and directly to the miscreant in a tone of implied menace by an experienced troop leader. When one of his classmates did not want any help and disdained any assistance, Martin waited until the soldier being corrected had reached out and grabbed the diminutive Sergeant Major while the young E-9 was doing his best trying to get in the Privates face and chew his ass. None of the soldiers took it badly and were glad to get off with a verbal reprimand.

400

The NCOs, some of whom had never made an on the spot correction learned their lessons as well.

Back in the classroom, Sergeant Major Barnhill asked Martin to define the Cavalry standard for an on the spot correction. "Gentlemen, when a Non-commissioned Officer walks by a violation of a standard without correcting it, he has just set a new standard in the mind of any soldier who saw it happen. In combat arms, NCOs learn early that: As you walk, you inspect; when you stop, you teach; when you detect error, you correct it; never stop preparing soldiers for NCOES at their next level."

This was the last part of their formal instruction. The Director of Instruction (DOI) was listening in the back of the classroom though his duty position and place in the hierarchy of the school was not known to the students. Each student was asked to briefly state the impact that the course had on their life and career. The faculty was always interested in this feedback but particularly for the non-resident course.

Martin's response was a classic and the DOI was determined to record it.

"It was a hard two years. The field Army fully supports the non-resident course. I got more than enough time and more attention than I wanted or needed to get it done. The Academy gained a lot of respect from some very smart officers when they saw the course requirements."

"It is a big Army. Trigger pullers are a small part of it and getting smaller. We must all develop support guys and treat them like soldiers. I learned a lot in the two weeks I spent with you guys as the only trigger puller in the group."

"I am here to support the Commander's intent for the unit, not the commander's personal ego or whims. We must give our commanders what they need as well as what they think they want."

"The guys and gals that got thrown out for overweight and cheating deserved to get hammered and I have no sympathy for them. They would be liabilities in combat. Honesty is a given and nobody gets any brownie points for not lying."

"The Air Force guys lie about the Army corps denying air support to the frontline soldier. You cannot allocate assets you do not have. The classic choice for the Air Force leadership is Air Superiority versus Close Support which they are starting to call mud bombing. For them, it is a no brainer, air superiority wins every time."

While at the Dining Out Sergeant Major Barnhill told Master Sergeants Washington and Martin they were being formally invited to be instructors at the course pending an interview with the Commandant Graduation morning. Master Sergeant Washington's eyes teared up and he accepted on the spot.

Martin was happy to see a good man get matched to a job he truly wanted. "Congratulations Enoch, you will be a great instructor. They got themselves a fine man."

401

"You'll be there too Ronald Martin. They are not going to let you get away," Master Sergeant Enoch Washington opined.

"I am not as ambitious as you are, Enoch. I have to think about it over-night and give my answer to the Commandant in the morning. If the answer turns out to be no, I do not want the Sergeant Major Barnhill in the blast ra-dius of the Commandant explosion. Best the Commandant only remember me saying no," Martin said smiling like a man who already knew the answer.

"Damn Ronald, don't you want to be a Brigade and Division Command Sergeant Major? If you say no, you are throwing that away for certain," Ser-geant Major Barnhill told him.

Martin motioned Barnhill in close so he could answer him without being overheard by his life group members, "I do not care if I am ever a Command Sergeant Major above Battalion level. I will be fine if I do not make Com-mand Sergeant Major and retire as a Staff Sergeant Major. I have watched the politics and seen how worthless many Command Sergeants Major become above Battalion. It holds no appeal for me. I have had enough school as a student or an instructor. I just want to be a field rat until I retire."

Sergeant Major Barnhill was aghast at the answer. "But you do everything so well. The whole faculty loved your leadership of this group. They valued your presentations and research ability, particularly when you were isolated up on the border without a big library or resources. You were one of only eight students singled out on academic reports for praise. Your work as a peer in-structor has made the next class. It saved the percentage and maybe the non-resident program for another year."

"Sergeant Major, I did well in the course because I was learning to be a Command Sergeant Major, not burning with ambition. I am too old to be able to count on my body much longer. I have been very lucky so far. It will all turn out okay for me and for the Army. I helped those other guys because my Corps and USAREUR Command Sergeants Major asked me to do it. On-ly an idiot says no to those two guys, especially Ligon," Martin said as the time grew near for skits.

"Is Ligon as big an asshole as I hear he is?" Barnhill asked.

"Ligon is an old, hard core NCO. He loves the Army and the NCO Corps. The shit is not personal for Ligon, it is his job. If you are soldiering hard and trying your very best to do the right thing, you will never have an issue with Command Sergeant Major Ligon. It is the slobs, skaters and jerk offs that hate Ligon. They are terrified of him because he lives on a different mental plane. He takes no shit. He knows in his Command Sergeant Major, Two Star CIB heart that none of us is operating to his or her full potential. He simply thinks the way you look is a direct reflection of your ability to fight and that sorry is sorry, wherever he finds it. So he works his way from first appearances to the rest of you and tells you in no uncertain terms how to get straight. He is a national treasure even though he chews my ass about something every time I see him. It ain't personal, it is just professional correction."

If he had been on the fence on whether or not he would join the faculty of the Sergeants Major Academy, the reaction of the commandant to the skits sealed his fate. Skits at events such as the dining out serve as outlets for frustration for subordinates and let some of the air out of over inflated egos of some leaders. It takes a good leader to take a good joke and a great leader to take a bad joke and turn it on the perpetrators for a gentle lesson.

One group declared the then popular song of "Red Necks, White T-shirts and Blue Ribbon Beer" personified their group. They also made reference to "coyotes" the barracks term for those females habitually attaching themselves to the available members of each class living in the BOQ without wives. These denizens of the Fort Bliss area were often widows or divorcees searching for husbands or companionship or both. The issue had come to a head during one of the resident courses when a "tree hugger" wife had complained to the Post Commanding General that Sergeant Major Academy students were keeping wild pets in the BOQ, coyotes no less. The Commanding General, unaware of the euphemism for the unattached females, told the Commandant he should look into the fact his students were keeping wildlife in the barracks. Coyotes may look like dogs but they were wild animals.

As they say in the tank park, the shit went rapidly downhill from that point. It got a lot worse for the last Resident Course. Just before Martin's Course arrived for the non-resident course, after duly warning the BEQ residents overnight guests were not permitted, the Commandant led a 2 am health and welfare inspection by the faculty NCOs complete with SJA lawyers. Of course, the inspectors found nearly twenty geographical bachelors with "coyotes" in all states of imitation marital bliss in quarters provided for bachelors. The sin of the Non-Resident guys was to poke the sleeping "coyote" issue to spice up the Dining Out. It was a poor choice of Command Sergeant Major Americana to portray as satire. It was too recent and too painful for the Commandant to let slide.

The Commandant chose to attack the problem head on. He went to the dais and took over the program from the Class President. He restated the mission of the Sergeants Major Academy in no uncertain terms and told the group presenting the offending skit to be in his office at 0600 the following morning, with their faculty advisor. There was no way Martin could work in that atmosphere. If the guy could not take a joke, he should not insist on skits and if he was so sensitive, he should have withheld script approval.

It took a minute or two for the ripple of understanding to make it through the room but all of the old soldiers knew what had just transpired. Six irreverent guys who did not know the lay of the land had just screwed the pooch for their instructors and possibly for themselves. When the fat guys were sent home and the dumb guys were caught cheating, even at the end of two years of effort, there was universal understanding of their fate. They deserved what they got, instant dismissal and immediate retirement for those eligible, after an Article 15. No one could overcome an Academic Report citing a lack of intellectual integrity or being found over weight. No one could hope to balance out an Article 15 for blatant misconduct as an E9, nor should they.

These guys that did the skit were dumb but not criminal. A good ass chewing should have sufficed. Martin hoped that is all they would get, but who knows how far the pendulum of officialdom would swing. The old adage that satire offends the most those who cannot afford to laugh at themselves was destined to again be tested.

Martin reported to the Commandant's Office for his interview at 0700. The atmosphere was that of ground zero after a nuclear strike. He had just thrown the three of the six skit guys who showed no repentance, out of the school, reassigned their faculty advisor to an embassy in Africa and raised holy hell with his clerk over his vehicle dispatch. He was truly sorry he was about add pain to what was already a bad day for the Commandant.

The Commander of Fort Bliss had dropped by to say hello and wish them all luck on graduation day. When the Commandant told his clerk to get Martin into his office the clerk told him Martin was in deep conversation with Major General Duplantis. As the Commandant came out of his office, the Commanding General turned to him saying, "This is one the best NCOs I ever saw in Air Defense. I was a young Major and he is one of three NCOs I saw who could make old General Hirsch smile. Remember General Hirsch, Command Sergeant Major Barrett?"

"I do remember him, Sir. He was a fine officer and a great leader. I never made him smile but I never made him mad, either," Command Sergeant Major Barrett said, adding "Won't you come in, Sir, and have a cup of coffee?"

"No, I won't keep you, Gary. You are doing a fine job. I just wanted to congratulate you on turning the Non-Resident Course Failure rate around and getting so many through it. Martin here was one of your surrogate instructors in Europe helping people to achieve their potential, legally. I'm going to leave you to do what you have to do. It is a busy morning for you. I'll see you Sunday at the golf tournament. We're on the same flight with the two city councilmen again. You take care of yourself, Ronald. You were a damn good Staff Sergeant and you'll be a good Command Sergeant Major someday," he said shaking hands all around before departing to the resounding call of ATTENTION by the Commandant.

A stickler for procedure, the Commandant went into his office, closed the door, and sat at his desk awaiting Master Sergeant Martin's formal report.

He was not disappointed. After a very brisk knock, Martin entered and reported perfectly with a sharp salute saying, "Command Sergeant Major, Master Sergeant Martin reports to the Commandant as directed."

As was his right, Command Sergeant Major Barrett left Martin at the position of attention for the interview. "So Martin, are you ready to join us as an Instructor at the Sergeants Major Academy?"

"No, Command Sergeant Major, I am not. I wish to return to my unit and remain with field forces until I retire," Martin stated in a calm voice.

"You realize that you are forfeiting your best chance to ever become a brigade or Division level Command Sergeant Major. You might make it otherwise but what you would learn here and the people you would meet could employ a soldier like you to your fullest potential. Why would you turn such an assignment down?" the Commandant asked politely.

"Command Sergeant Major, I am not a thirty year man. I am in for twenty and some change. I have spent ten years of my career either in a school as a student, an instructor or on the staff. I like life in the unit with the soldiers. That is where I wish to serve out the rest of my career, if possible," Martin stated with politeness.

"That will be all, Master Sergeant," the Commandant said without emotion.

Martin saluted smartly and left the office with his mind racing in relief.

I am glad I did not have to serve here. I know I have sealed my fate but that is okay. It was not for me. I would have been in trouble from day one with those humorless, ambition filled perfectionists. Serving above Battalion without a combat patch would make me puke. Besides, being that close to Juarez and all of those hot females for two years, I would probably get busted to E-7 long before getting promoted to Sergeant Major. It is too bad the Commanding General closed the border for US troops due to the political climate in Juarez for our stay here. I know some of the guys went anyway but that is double stupid. It is dangerous enough when it is on limits. Some of these guys have a death wish. They forget they are not at home with a Commanding Officer who will forgive them. They are at a school and ripe to be hammered by a guy who does not know them from Adam's Cat. He cares only for the support of the Army Standard of behavior, as he should, but he is without humanity. He has no sense of humor and he cannot laugh at himself. I'm glad I did not have to tell the crusty old bastard how I really felt. It was no good backing a guy like the Commandant into a corner in his own "house". No upside. After all was said and done, the old guy was still standing at the top of his assigned shit heap, with over 35 years service, a milestone I will never see.

The trip back home to Florida was done at mental idle for Martin. He was done with wife number two but she did not know it yet. She thought nothing had really changed and believed she was still in charge of all that mattered. She was, except that it was an empty victory as none of it mattered to him anymore. He was only interested in getting through the next few days and getting back to his true home, Germany, and to Marty for the remainder of the summer. Whatever stupid penny pinching, bitchy, cranky moods and screaming fits she pulled out of her bag of tricks would just have to play out as the calendar slowly moved ahead.

405

The trip could not have been made in greater comfort in the four door Buick sedan with every known convenience. It was a great car and he enjoyed traveling in it even though she was there. Her condition required she travel stretched out in the back seat propped up on pillows. Her ego required her to vent her rage at every gasoline stop over a penny per gallon price difference either across the street or a mile behind them. He hoped her love of self would be of great comfort to her in the days ahead when he was no longer there to support her and take care of her needs. He had loved her once but no longer. The combination of her constant and increasingly strident litany of invective and complaint, combined with her faithlessness and egotism had taken its full measure and left him empty of feeling for her. Work was his refuge and his salvation, and he missed it.

The four days enabled him to begin to think his situation through and to analyze his future course of action. He suppressed a loud laugh to just a smile as he recognized he was using the five paragraph field order as a baseline.

Enemy Situation: She had thirty plus years experience under her wampum belt and the scalp of a senior Air Force NCO on her lodge pole. She was a determined and borderline insane opponent without either scruples or apparent emotional weakness when defending. She was unable to work. She hated to fight at night. Their money was commingled. They had property in three states that amounted to nearly $350,000. Their total cash reserves were close to $125,000 while their securities and mutual funds were steady at $100,000. His income provided the bulk of their living expense. They had no installment debt. All assets would be on her side during the fight and unavailable to him. The Army system was fully in her corner until the civil process could begin. He was guilty until proven broke or the divorce was final, whichever came first. It would be a Florida divorce. She would get to fight on her home ground.

Friendly Situation: Last promotion to E9 was certain with assumptions well known and achievable. Credit line available was $10,000 on charge cards with $100,000 available for long term obligations for housing and transportation. No spouse was in waiting nor would there be. Family would be neutral though resources up to $250,000 were available should they be required from millionaire brother for absolute emergency. It was first come, first serve on lawyers and he was determined to get the best before she could retain him. The one he wanted was a great advocate in all respects. Like his father before him, Martin never hired a cheap lawyer or doctor, slept on a bad civilian mattress or wore cheap shoes. One way or the other, quality required some sacrifice.

The analysis continued until he arrived at the end state: Attain and maintain an ability to wake up in peace after retirement. Everything in between would be tactics. He would deal with it as it came up. He normally did not

406

like the philosophy of crossing the line of departure and improvising but at the moment it was all he could do.

CHAPTER 14 – LESSONS GREAT AND SMALL

"Figure out what your boss wants and give it to him." General Bruce Clarke, former USAREUR Commander and outstanding leader in WW II.

0700 hours
11 Jul 1986
Miami, FL

Life in America with Dinah was summed up by the manner of Martin's trip to the airport. As was his custom, he took the city bus to the airport as the girls and their mother were all too busy to take him to the Miami airport. It was just as well as he wanted to hear no more from any of them about anything. He was looking forward to several months of personal peace and relative happiness before reporting to Fort Polk in the fall.

The Sergeant Major branch representative during a private interview told him at Bliss that any request for an extension in Germany would be disapproved. He also hinted Martin's selection as a Command Sergeant Major was forthcoming, probably before he ever pinned on his Sergeant Major rank. The message was very clear: Shut up and don't rock the boat.

As a seasoned international traveler, he went to sleep as soon as the airplane was airborne waking only for meals and the bathroom. Turbulence, crying babies and the in flight movie never woke him. He knew not what awaited him on his return but whatever it was, there was no upside to jet lag and no slack for it in the Cavalry. His return to his second home would prove to be anything but uneventful.

0730 hours
12 Jul 1986
Rheine Main USAF Base
West Germany

"Morning, Top, Welcome Home," Specialist Fourth Class Stroud said by way of greeting as he extended his hand to Martin.

Glad to see a familiar face, Martin shook Stroud's hand saying, "It is good to be back. There's no place I would rather be right now than here, I'll tell you that Stroud."

"How was school and your leave?" Stroud asked.

"The school was a rubber stamp for the most part. They sent some dumb asses home and kicked out some who did not know how to act, told us where we were going next and how our next couple of years looked. I got the yard all cleaned up, ate some great food, worked on my tan and got reacquainted with the wife and kids," Martin said, sparing all of the personal details.

As they waited at the carousel for the baggage, Stroud asked, "Well, ain't you going to ask me how gunnery went."

"I'll play your silly game, Stroud. How did gunnery go?" Martin asked.

"How do you think it went, First Sergeant?" Stroud asked playfully.

"I think we smoked it so bad Regiment and Corps were so shocked that they did not say shit about it one way or the other. They probably thought we were cheating or had target malfunctions, especially for the Bradleys. At least I hope that is what happened. How many bolos did we have? I figure three bolos for the tanks and none for the Bradleys with 10 perfect scores for the tanks and 12 for the Brads," Martin replied.

Stroud looked almost hurt as he replied, "I meant for G Troop, First Sergeant!"

"Damn, Stroud! I have only the best of feelings and hopes for G Troop but it was a squadron effort for me and that is how I think about it. My time in G Troop is past and I just did not think about in terms of the troop. So tell me old Gator, how did our Troop do?" Martin asked with a smile.

"You know, you are acting different somehow, First Sergeant. But unless I miss my guess, you are going to be a lot more interested in G Troop than the Squadron and pretty damn quick," Stroud said with a big shit eating grin as the carousel started to move with the bags.

"I figure all you got is a duffel bag, right, Top?" Stroud said smiling, adding, "You lifers all travel light."

"There's my bag with the red tape on the lock. Let's go get some breakfast at the Air Force Mess Hall. I'm buying, big spender, huh, Stroud?" Martin said laughing.

"Don't forget to get your copy of the Stars & Stripes before we leave the terminal. Wouldn't want to upset your routine," Stroud said teasing his old First Sergeant. Martin's penchant for the newspaper was well known. "Besides, the best news is yet to come. I'll tell you at breakfast, First Sergeant. It is too complicated to get told in pieces."

It's nice to be one step ahead of the Maddog for a change. Those jokers in G Troop are about to get the shock of their young lives when the Squadron Commander meets the Maddog. When he sees what he has sitting on the bench, the Wildman is going to get back in the game. That will be something to see. I'm damn glad to be able to watch it from Headquarters and not in a scout platoon in G Troop. I wonder if I should tell him the entire skinny or just give him a hint - what the hell, in for a penny, in for a pound, Stroud said to himself. He would tell his old First Sergeant all.

As was their custom, both men ate a huge breakfast with everything the Air Force had on the menu. The little skinny Airmen thought they were both nuts as they got bacon, eggs to order, fried potatoes, hamburger gravy, toast, pancakes, biscuits, juice and sodas, and a cinnamon roll with a huge hunk of butter. Though both men looked big, Stroud was the heaviest at 240 pounds against Martin's 200. Both loved to eat, particularly breakfast. Both usually skipped, or had very little lunch, instead using the time to run and work out at the gym or the makeshift troop weight room. Each could bench press his own weight and run as far as necessary at any given moment, with a sprint at the end of the run. Stroud was extremely intelligent, analytical and had street smarts.

He and his father had raced motorcycles on both the outdoor and indoor circuits in Motor Cross with some cross over to flat track racing. Neither racing venue took any prisoners. Softies were soon eliminated. Stroud's father, AKA Birdman, was so called after one of their distant relatives, reported to be the murderer Robert Stroud, serving life at Alcatraz. Both Stroud boys pimped the legend on the circuit. Martin had run a number of Moto Cross races when Stroud's father was in his prime and while he had not won any, he placed high and raced clean. It pleased Stroud to know he was one of a very people to know Martin was twice as crazy as anyone thought he was in the straight laced Army and he loved to tease him.

As they worked their way through the sumptuous breakfast served in an immaculate atmosphere as compared to their 'hole in the wall' dining facility, Stroud did most of the talking and Martin listened and nodded with an occasional question when his mouth wasn't full, which was not often.

"The gunnery went way past everybody's expectations. It is too bad you were not there to see it. You out there at Fort Bliss eating great Mexican food, drinking Cruz Blanca and Corona chasing Mexican women in Juarez, in tandem. That's one behind the 'tother, First Sergeant," Stroud said transposing dialogue from the "Wild Bunch."

"For your information, Stroud, you got it almost all wrong. But you keep thinking I had a great time in Juarez if it will make you feel better about going to Graf," Martin said laughing.

"The only people to bolo a tank were officers. The Squadron Commander was too new to know what to do and said and did some dumb shit on the tank and had to re-fire two engagements. He got re-trained, paid attention and qualified no sweat on the second time through. The other two were hopelessly messed up. The E Troop Commander, you know the one that messed with you at Wildflecken, would not listen to anyone about anything. He did not get it right until late in the game. He was the last man shooting and him with an E-7 gunner, Christ sakes. The platoon leader from F Troop was a safety DQ and never got to re-fire. He was just too big of a snatch to be an Armor Officer. He should have sent his dyke sister from the Illinois gymnastic team in his place. I hear she is more of a man than he is. He cried when the Squadron Executive Officer chewed his ass. You know what you told us about officers taking care of their own and their utter lack of regard for feelings if they even think one of theirs is a coward. Nobody ever saw him again – poof - the little joker was gone," Stroud said with a wave of his hand as he continued the monologue.

410

"There were at least 18 tanks with perfect scores and 15 more in the 900 point range. The scores were off the chart and nobody in the chain of command was expecting to see anything like it. I was in the tower with the S3 when the Commanding General from 1AD came to see his Canadian Army Trophy guys shoot. He and the Three know each other. He said our tankers looked and acted like combat veterans. He said they made the course look like child's play and the rest of the Army look like amateurs with the M1. The Three told him about SABOT Academy and gave him a packet. He told the Three he would be back to see another troop to see if this one was a fluke and by God he came back. He took notes, First Sergeant," Stroud said watching his old First Sergeant closely for some form of feedback.

"I know that General. He is one of the smartest men ever to wear a uniform. He sees past the fluff and spit shined boots into the soul of a unit. That level of praise from him about our guys says it all for me, regardless of scores," Martin said as he attacked the last of his food, the sweet roll while drinking his hot chocolate. "Now the Bradley tale if you please, Jester" he said recalling Stroud's nickname from the Moto Circuit as a youngster.

Being a 19D and a new Bradley crewman, Stroud was going to lay it on thick for his old First Sergeant. As he started to speak, he saw Martin holdup his hand with a closed fist in the universal hand signal for halt and say, "Like Joe Friday, just the facts, save the steely eyed killer bullshit for the fräuleins on REFORGER."

"Okay, First Sergeant, but remember you asked for it. 38 fired and 38 qualified first time. No re-fires. 23 of 38 fired perfect scores day and night. 12 fired 900 or above but less than 1,000 and three fired in the high 800 range for a 971 average score. There were no safety violations reported on the Bradley qualification ranges. There were five missed TOW's fired with three being bad birds. The Squadron Commander is still walking on cloud nine he is so freaking happy. I do have a question, First Sergeant," Stroud concluded.

"My question is why isn't Regiment anymore excited about the result than the ho-hum they showed? Why isn't the USAREUR Commander trying to figure out how we did it to duplicate it throughout his command? Are they crazy not to see how great a thing it was to shoot like that? Nobody shoots like that as a Squadron, nobody."

Martin thought a moment before answering, "Stroud, I really do not know what General Otis' marching orders are but he made four stars without any coaching from you or me."

"This is the Regimental Commander and Staff's first gunnery with these two new systems. Every Squadron Commander was promoted below the zone for Major and Lieutenant Colonel. There ain't nothing wrong with them. The Army has a great deal of patience while units are learning to use new systems. I suspect the entire chain of command is treating 2/11's gunnery as a pleasant anomaly or they saw what a bitch SABOT Academy is to put on and

411

want no part of it. If the leaders see it as a personality driven thing for me and the former Squadron Commander, they will not try to duplicate it. And worst case, and I hope this ain't true, they may not feel any pressure to be combat ready. In their view, the Border Mission may be the Border Myth and they are just riding the wave. What is the rest of the news, Stroud?"

"In the Joe Friday mold, the engine of Major Klenk's CUCV taking you to BK will still be cooling down and you will be the new First Sergeant of G Troop. The Squadron Commander has had a gut full of First Sergeant Black's half ass approach to being an NCO. The troop is missing meals, the log pack cycle is screwed up, the duty roster is unfair, their paper work disappears, so I guess everything he touches turns to shit. What do you call it, First Sergeant, the Reverse Midas Touch? Well he has it. But he is a nice guy who never chews ass or calls people out who are dogging it. He never does PT and has never led it. He does not inspect, detect or correct gear, attitude or behavior. He does not lead the troop on road marches 'cause he gets lost. The Commanding Officer can't do recons or teach the officers. He does not feed it in the field or do any of the thousand and one things the great First Sergeants do. There is no top NCO leadership. We still got some great individuals, but as a troop, they are Lima, Lima, Mike, Foxtrot."

The Commanding Officer is a First Lieutenant (P), A West Point Golden Boy, Rhoades Scholar, ladies man, Airborne Ranger and a well rounded guy with great potential. Big, tall skinny guy, runs like a deer. But, he is learning to command by OJT with only 5 out of 8 cylinders firing. It is like professional baseball, Top, you can't fire the team and the Commanding Officer is like the owner, so you fire the player manager. In this case, First Sergeant Black is not worth a shit and a guy like you is sitting on the bench, a .400 hitter with 60 home runs. Who do you think the Squadron Commander is going to put into the game?" Stroud said with some satisfaction.

"Stroud, if you are all finished with your Obi Wan Kenobi impressions for the day and have enough energy left to herd the CUCV to BK, we best be on our way. Any more advice for me? I still have at least two brain cells unoccupied," Martin said laughing.

"Yeah, you better stop and get some Al Capone seegars, they ain't got none in BK or Fulda for some reason," Stroud advised. He knew full well Martin did not smoke more than one of the long, black, strong Brazilian cigars per day in garrison but used them to stay awake in the field.

"You are good man, Stroud. Stop at the shop down by the zoo. It is close to here. The shop at the Flughafen too damn high or stop at the place in the Nazi puppy farm. They always have them there, and it is on the way," Martin said.

"I hate that place, First Sergeant, the whole damn town. Those people give me the creeps. Just thinking about all of those women having babies by SS

412

guys, one after the other, all through the war," the young soldier said with a shiver.

Martin merely smiled and said, "Okay, Eleanor Roosevelt, just stop in front and keep the motor running. I'll be in and out before you can get infected."

As they departed for the trip back to their Kaserne, the First Sergeant in him took over his thought process. The boys of G Troop will not be happy to see their sweet life come to an end. But, they had to know it would not last. Same rules as before. No bad words about the old guy, be positive, start small, build on little successes, see what the Squadron Commander & Troop Commander want, give it your best shot, step lightly with the new Command Sergeant Major, get a feel for the Ligon monster's current MO, move your shit into the Troop until you can get it straight and enjoy it. There will be all too little time left as a First Sergeant before it is time to step aside and be a staff puke again for who knows how long.

The country had never looked so beautiful to Martin. It was mid-summer and everything was green and lush. The lakes and resorts were packed and at least half of the populace was on vacation. No one appreciates summer like people living in cold climates and the Germans damn sure made the most of what little warm weather they had. He would have no real issue with staying over here forever but was not an expatriate at heart. It would not be the same either as a contractor or a GS employee.

It was good to be back though. Martin immediately went to the troop latrine to shave, shower and change into duty uniform. The water heater had recovered from the drain of troop PT and he damn near scalded himself before remembering he was not in the USA.

He dressed quickly as his intuition told him he needed to get ready for something to happen that very day. Whatever it was, it would not happen in Class A uniform.

1100 hours
10 July 1986
HHT Shower Dressing Area

He had just finished dressing when Sergeant Major Burton tracked him down. "Welcome Home, First Sergeant," he said with a wide grin.

"It is good to see you too, Sergeant Major. Why is everybody I see is trying to hand me a set of First Sergeant chevrons? Is it that obvious?" he asked.

"That's because everybody but you knows the deal. The Squadron Commander wants to see you right now. Give me your towel and shit and I will hang it up outside your wall locker. This guy is full of nervous energy and when he says right now, he really means right now," Burton added.

"Do you know him, Nick?" Martin asked, clearly in the friend mode.

413

"Yeah, I knew him in 'Nam. He was a great officer with combat integrity. He was pure nuts about the fight but used his head and listened to the NCOs. He got the Silver Star and the DSC with damn few Purple Hearts in his Troop. G Troop killed so many gooks with such small losses the other Captains did not talk to the boy. He is an okay guy for a top performer. Come on slick, let's go. I am the acting Command Sergeant Major, so show some respect, okay!" he said chuckling.

Losing no time, Sergeant Major Burton dropped Martin's stuff in the Command Sergeant Major office on the floor and immediately went to the Squadron Commander's office. He knocked on the door facing and when the Squadron Commander looked up, he said without entering, "Sir, Master Sergeant Martin is here and reporting for duty."

"Good, Nick. You got the stripes?" waiting for Sergeant Major Burton's nod, then saying, "Get him in here and let's get moving."

Martin reported to the Squadron Commander in perfect fashion. The Squadron Commander returned his salute and came out from behind his desk to shake his hand, saying, "Lieutenant Colonel Bob Milliard First Sergeant. I am glad to meet you. Adjutant, publish the order." As the young Captain whom Martin had never met, read the order, Sergeant Major Burton handed the Squadron Commander the pins and he and Burton pinned them on Martin's collar, leaving him one pin on for his hat with extras. The three men all congratulated him and shook his hand. The Adjutant was the last to do so and handed him the orders he had published from the local personnel service detachment. The orders appointed him as a First Sergeant and transferred him from Headquarters Troop to G Troop effective today. Following paragraphs made Black a Master Sergeant and transferred him to headquarters in the S3 shop.

Unsure of what to do next, Martin merely stayed at the position of Attention. The Squadron Commander confirmed the wisdom of that decision as he began speaking in a rapid series of staccato sentences, "I feel like I know all about you that I need to know, First Sergeant. I read the after-action on the '85 REFORGER. I got a hurry-up version of SABOT Academy for the M1 and the Bradley and qualified in both of them. Your squadron registered the highest scores in the Army for gunnery. Everybody thinks you're a genius. Everybody but three people, me, you, and Sergeant Major Nick Burton. We *know* who the genius is in this room. You are, First Sergeant Martin."

"I need G Troop unscrewed. Quick, fast, and in a hurry. You are my fireman. I am relieving the present First Sergeant. If you think the Troop Commander needs relieved or he won't listen to you, you tell me and his ass is gone. Now listen carefully, go to G Troop. Tell First Sergeant Black to report to me, now. Clean out his shit while he is down here seeing me. Put it in a box. Send the box down here to Sergeant Major Burton with the CQ runner. Take over the troop at the 1300 formation. Tell me by 1700 today if I need to conduct an Article 32 into anything you find amiss in the troop that smacks of misconduct or misappropriation. Any questions?"

"No, Sir," Martin replied.

"Welcome back. Good job on SABOT Academy, both of them. One 'aw shit' wipes out all of the 'attaboys', First Sergeant! That's all!" the Squadron Commander said coming to attention as Martin saluted and departed.

"A man of few words, isn't he, Sergeant Major?" Martin asked as they arrived in Burton's office. "How does he romance his wife? 'Hi baby I'm home, you look great, let's do it'."

Burton laughed saying, "That is why you are such a happy guy, Martin. You never let them see you sweat and you keep your sense of humor without being disloyal. He is a good guy. You and me ain't got the first worry with him. You'd better get moving and ensure my new Master Sergeant makes it up here to the Three Shop, his last stop in this outfit."

It was the longest short walk Martin had taken in a long time. It was less than 100 yards from the Headquarters to G Troop. He had decided he would carry out the Squadron Commander's order to the letter.

Before he could get to G Troop, he encountered Master Sergeant Ramirez. He and Ramirez did not get along. Ramirez was one of the biggest Mexicans Martin had ever seen. He stood 6' 4" and weighed over 250 pounds. He was strong and hearty in the manner of a man who had performed hard labor on heavy track vehicles for more than 25 years. He had more time in grade than Martin had in the Army. His five years in Vietnam with the Regiment ensured he knew all of the current leaders who like him, wore the Blackhorse sandwich of patches on both shoulders. Ramirez had of course taken his Chief Warrant Officer 4's side against Martin at every issue during SABOT Academy and the thermal sight episode as well as the cold start. Martin was not looking forward to meeting him today of all days. He was about to be totally surprised.

As Ramirez got to Martin he stopped and put out his hand. Surprised, Martin took it and was immediately engulfed in a bear hug by the huge Mexican. He felt his feet leave the ground and realized he had picked up like a child and then gently set back down.

"Damn, Ramirez, I'm glad to see you too, what the hell, OVER?" Martin said smiling.

"Martin, I was a damn fool to listen to my crazy Warrant. He was all wrong. I guess the booze fogged up his brain. You were right. I was wrong and I apologize. I ain't never seen a gunnery like that. My maintenance guys did not have nothing to do, I mean, damn nothing," he said slapping Martin on the back so hard he lost his footing.

"Everything went right. Not one machinegun broke. If something in the turret broke, the PFCs and Spec Fours knew exactly what was wrong when they called it in. When we took the part to them, they had the old one out and

415

waiting on top of the turret. They would not let my guys put the new parts back in, they did it and had my guys check their work. It was like they were combat veterans they way they knew their shit. Shit we had three big barbeques out at the range maintenance area. We cooked a whole pig that accidentally got killed. Used a Hawaiian pit. It was great. I also won five hundred bucks from the other two Master Sergeants in Squadron maintenance from 1st & Third Squadrons on who would qualify the most tanks first run. They would not bet on the Bradleys, no guts, I guess. Anyhow, here's a hundred bucks of the five, since I spent most of your share and all of mine on a party for the section when we got back. I made sure I saved you a hundred. Damn it's good to see you. I know, you gotta' go take G Troop back over. That's a shit sandwich. Let's have a beer. I'm still drinking down at the German place at the end of town by the river with Monica. We own it together now. Hell, we might even get married. See ya'."

As Martin looked down at the hundred dollar bill, he was suddenly the richest man in the world. When your worst enemy becomes a friend and your most severe critic turns into your biggest supporter, it's a good moment. Of all the things that could have happened, the welcome by the fierce Ramirez was at once the most unexpected, most sincere, and most welcome. Ramirez would never know he was a metric to measure success. If SABOT Academy had won him over, it was a success. All of the effort by the Master Gunners to teach it and the tankers and scouts to learn the skills and absorb the material had been worthwhile. Well, that was then, First Sergeant, and this is now and all that hand clapping won't feed the bulldog, onward to G Troop and the Shit sandwich that Ramirez and everyone else but you knew about.

Martin walked into the G Troop First Sergeant's office to find First Sergeant White busily moving papers about on his desk, organizing it. He gave him the message from the Squadron Commander without emotion or inflection in his voice, "Morning, First Sergeant White. The Squadron Commander directs you are to report to him without delay."

First Sergeant White arose, put on his fatigue cap and sauntered out of his former office without a word or a backward glance. He never returned to G Troop again in any capacity. The Squadron Commander's orders and intent were carried out to the letter. All of his personal items barely covered the bottom of an emptied Xerox paper box.

Martin knew before looking what he would find. A DA Form 6 Duty Roster improperly filled out shot through with favoritism and errors; personnel actions undone; correspondence overdue; and counseling for Quarters Allowance undone. These were the items that required leaders to care about and for their soldiers. Decisions were involved. Someone had to look a soldier in the eye and say no. First Sergeant White could not bring himself to say no so he just didn't.

As always when picking up the pieces behind a failed First Sergeant, he would take care of the money items first, followed by career concerns and finally would tackle the duty roster. He would make certain he was not the Drug & Alcohol Control Officer on what looked like his final turn at First Sergeant duty. His first order of business past posting the order on the Troop Bulletin Board that appointed him First Sergeant of the Troop was to find the Commander and make certain he knew he had a new First Sergeant.

Picking up the phone, he switched it to the outside line so that he could call the Charge of Quarters desk upstairs. There were two reasons he was calling himself up. He wanted to hear how the current crop of soldiers answered the phone and he wanted to make certain they knew they were to track the Commander's location. "G Troop, 2/11 ACR, Specialist Aschilman, How may I help you, Sir?" came the answer to his first question. It may have seemed elemental and a useless thing to sample but the Charge of Quarters was the first look that any outsider had of the Troop. There was only one chance to make a first impression.

"Specialist Aschilman, this is First Sergeant Martin. I am down in my office just below you. Where is the G Troop Commander?" Martin said with a pregnant pause. "Aschilman, wake your happy ass up and tell me where the Commanding Officer is or tell me you don't know, one of the two!" Martin said firmly.

Aschilman had heard many stories about the wild man First Sergeant who held forth in G Troop before First Sergeant White but as a new guy, First Sergeant White was the only First Sergeant he had known. He was greatly relieved to see the tall, spare Commander bounding in the door like a gazelle headed down stairs to the admin offices of the troop. "First Sergeant, he is headed your way right now. He just went down the stairs," Aschilman said greatly relieved to have fulfilled his first task for the Maddog.

"Good job, Aschilman. It helps to be lucky doesn't it?" Martin asked with a smile in his voice.

"Yes, First Sergeant," was all he could croak out.

"Relax, Specialist. You are doing a good job. Hang in there and keep those messages coming," Martin said as he hung up the phone. Realizing the Commanding Officer must have made a detour to the Supply Room, he went there.

He found his new Commander working on Individual Clothing Records while the Supply Sergeant and the two clerks watched him work. "Good morning you TURDS, Martin said cheerfully. Noting the young Lieutenant's obvious displeasure at his soldiers being called turds, Martin said, "Sergeant Webster, define the acronym TURD for Lieutenant Douglas."

"Sir, the acronym TURD means Trooper Under Rapid Development and if under UCMJ, Rapid Deterioration," Webster screamed in his imitation of Beast Barracks.

"Webster thought maybe you were lonesome for West Point and Beast Barracks, Sir. You turds take a walk and shut the door," Martin said.

417

"Sir, why pray tell why you are doing their work and letting them watch?" Martin asked pleasantly.

"I was a Supply Officer and my Supply Room got the highest grade in the Regiment, First Sergeant. Perfection in Supply begins with the individual clothing record. If I want it done right, I have to do it myself. It is that simple and that is the way I want it, okay First Sergeant?" he said proudly.

"Sir, let me be responsible for the Supply Room and every other administrative detail in this outfit. I wish you would concentrate on teaching schemes of maneuver, check on driver's training and testing, get the Officers through the Border Test and counsel the Lieutenants on the way they should go. The way this is supposed to work is best illustrated in the words of Moltke the Elder, 'The good Commander is a bit lazy. He never does anything himself. He makes sure the officers, NCOs and soldiers are kept busy and learn through the toil of being a soldier, how to be one. The followers of such men often complain about how little they do and contribute in terms of labor to the goals of the organization. It is after success in battle they understand they have learned their trade well at the hands of a seemingly indolent Commander.'

"If the Supply Records are not right, then Webster, the Supply Officer and all of their minions will work them a few hours each night and on weekends until they are correct. You, with your knowledge and the winning record to prove it, can tell them what you want done and go on to other fields of endeavor. Remember the words of the Centurion to Jesus, when I tell a man to go, he goeth, and when I tell a man to cometh, he comes. Nothing has changed since the time of the Romans and Jesus in 33 A.D. They are still yours to command and they have no choice but to obey. Our goal must be to employ them intelligently and with their manhood intact. We make sure they clearly see the mission and expect them to be willing to go above and beyond the call of mere duty to gain our respect."

Martin noted the young Troop Commander's mouth was hanging open in wonderment at this new vision of NCO leadership. He was not sure if he should resist or join this wild man. "Let me show you what I mean, Lieutenant Douglas. If what I am about to do is not what you want, please take it back over and I will shut up," and with that Martin summoned the Supply Crew in from the hallway.

"I do not care how the Supply Records got screwed up or who did it. What I want is for you guys to make out the records for me, the Commander, the Officers and for your selves. When that is done, bring the ten completed records to the Commander for his inspection and correction. Make certain they conform to all pertinent regulations. When the pilot product meets the Commander's expectations, coordinate with each platoon sergeant. Get one or two smart guys from each platoon and supervise their preparation of the remainder of the clothing records. You have seven days. The Commander and I have got to go do important shit and we ain't time to do your jobs for you. Questions? None. Good execute," Martin said smiling.

He knew Webster would not let it go at that and he did not, asking, "First Sergeant, are we going back to the old way of doing logistics?"

"We are, Sergeant Webster. You are the best Supply Sergeant in the Regiment, bar none. I intend to employ you to the fullest, just like always. Pretend I never left," Martin said with a broad smile.

"We tried, FFFFFFFust Sergeant," BJ said, stuttering with emotion. BJ hated failure particularly in the field.

Martin went to BJ, patted his burly shoulder and shook his hand saying, "BJ, do not hesitate to school the Commander and I on logistics when you think we are screwing up, okay?"

"It may take a few beers but I'll be coming to see you geniuses if I need to counsel you!" BJ said with a leering smile.

First Lieutenant Douglas was aghast at the prospect of having to learn anything from BJ but he kept his counsel, secretly amused at how Martin mixed the words and techniques of Moltke the Elder, Ligon, and Baron Von Stueben techniques in one situation. He and Martin adjourned to his office.

Walking with the CO, Martin was glad to be back in the company of the Texas cowboy even though he was borderline overweight, balding, in need of a shower most of the time and greasy from pulling maintenance on his beloved supply truck which gleamed as if it were new. BJ was a former Sergeant who had fallen on hard times and had only recently been promoted to Specialist Fourth Class for the second time. The wags asked him if that meant he was an E-8 since he had made E-4 twice. They got a stuttered "SSSSSSSSSSScrew you," from BJ for their trouble which of course made it even more hilarious. Without the slightest stutter he closed that discussion by saying, "None of you assholes will even make a pimple on a First Sergeant's ass."

Knowing how Martin dogged them all at times, the head wag asked, "I guess you are not including your buddy Martin in that group, are you, BJ."

His reply was classic, "Especially him and the Fox Troop First Sergeant. They don't have any peers 'cause there ain't nobody else that good. The next time you get your hot chow in three feet of snow and we be the only ones getting a hot bath in the German Spa at twenty below zero outside, tell me how great First Sergeant Black is and how great you guys would be. Talking it is easy, walking it is hard. Those two don't talk, they just do!"

"What I want to do is to find out what it is you want me to do above and beyond what a good First Sergeant does, Lieutenant. You have not had a good First Sergeant up to this point so it is hard for you to know what one looks like although there are great ones in 3d Squadron. I am going to clear just about everything I do or say through you ahead of time. It is your intent that counts, not mine. I advise you and you take it or leave it or modify it. It is no different than being the Regimental Commander or on the Regimental Staff at West Point except, here; lives can be in the balance even in peacetime. There is risk in any outfit that lives with live ammo day in and day out."

"The best way I've found to start is for us to review the day ahead and figure out how we are going to execute it. Who is going to do what and be where with what level of assets. We will then execute. At the end of the day we will meet to see what got done, what jobs remain undone and what got screwed up for lessons learned."

"It is my intention to fill out the scheduling board that got exiled to the NCO room so everyone in the troop knows what is happening when. It really helps the troops figure out when they are going to be able to take leave and to let them brief their wives. So to sum up, we want to form a team with known objectives. We train up and work toward them and meet the expectations of the Squadron Commander."

"I'm going to begin preparing the Troop for alerts and give the scum bags an out they must use by next Wednesday. I doubt we will have any takers but the objective is to get everyone on board as a pure volunteer. The best way to do that is to give the ones on the fence a chance to bail. If they don't take it they have to shut up and perform."

"I'm going to be in their shit in a million little ways until they reform to some degree and realize we are in charge, not them. That whine ass do as you please, do I have to do that First Sergeant, but whyyyyyyyyyyy, is dead! They will not be abused or debased or degraded, but they will become Cavalry soldiers, every last one of them."

"First Sergeant, just tell me when you think I am wrong or you have a better way of doing something and I will listen. The Squadron Commander sent you to me. You are a First Sergeant already qualified to be a Sergeant Major at the top of your game. I appreciate it more than I can ever say."

"I am living in Fulda with a German woman. I'll be commuting. I make the trip very quickly in my Mercedes or my Corvette. If you think I should go straight to the border for some events, then I shall. I intend to live at the Border and just go on pass when the troop is deployed there. I hope my relationship with my German lady friend does not bother you," the Commander said to his First Sergeant, hoping he was not going to rat him out.

"Sir, any man that won't screw, won't fight. I have a very dear German girl friend and a witch wife in the states who is doing her own thing. Your secret is safe with me. I would like to meet her sometime," Martin said pleasantly.

He continued saying, "Sir, we are not going to be able to plan everything we do to the nth degree in advance. But as we can learn to trust each other to do the right things for the right reasons, we will build a great organization. I have no special knowledge about a coming alert. The Squadron Commander may have some inside dope from Corps but he is not talking. My thought is he wants to make his mark with the outfit and getting it off the dime with an alert is the method he's picked. There is no downside to getting out of the gate quickly."

1300 hours
10 Jul 1986
G Troop Formation Area
Bad Kissingen, West Germany

There were some wide eyes in G Troop as First Sergeant came striding out to the formation area to take his position. He was pleasantly surprised to see all but one Platoon report "All Present," with Maintenance the only element reporting with personnel accounted for. After the reporting process was complete, he called everyone to gather around him.

"I just got back from leave and the Sergeants Major Academy this morning. By the order of the Squadron Commander, First Sergeant Black was to report to him and I am now your First Sergeant. I did not ask for the job. It is my duty to do it. I am very happy to be back among the best men in the regiment. I do not want to hear any bad words or gossip about First Sergeant Black. He was here. Now he is not. We will leave it at that except for if you were promised something and it has not happened. Staff Sergeant Mac and I will be here tonight for as long as it takes to get all pending personnel action done, signed and forwarded to Squadron."

"Some of you know what to expect and some do not. Our task is simply to be combat ready to kill as many Russians and East Germans as we can. We are going to kill those Mongoloid Midget suckers in their T-72s by the bushel. They are going to wish they were anywhere but the Meinigen Gap and fighting anyone but the Eagle Horse. It is a damn hard day for the Russians when we will be killing them before they see us. We will be killing them when their best shots bounce off our Chobham Armor. We have the best tank and cav fighting vehicle in the world. They have dog shit. We have professional soldiers, they have conscripts who are barely trained to goose step. Our commanders are very skilled in maneuver and theirs rely on attrition. You see, they think we will run out of tanks and people before they do. If their raggedy ass shit could penetrate our armor or see us at 4,000 meters in all weather, they might have a chance. It won't. They are not packing the right gear. I almost feel sorry for the stupid bastards."

"There are a number of things that have to go my way. No negotiations. There will be German marks at the CQ desk to pay for Taxis - no drunken driving or drunken spree walking. If the assholes from E Troop are tearing up the town as they make their way back to the barracks, get a cab and stay off the street. Remember, off duty cops drive the cabs in the wee hours of the morning. Use your heads when you party. No arrests for drunken behavior will be tolerated. You will not be given an order from a drunk nor are you to obey one. If you are a leader, stay away from troops when you have been drinking. Alerts are different. We will all stumble through them half in the bag now and then."

421

"Take care of each other. You will never get in trouble for helping an out-numbered buddy in a fight nor will you be forgiven for leaving him. If he is being an asshole and won't listen, leave his dumb ass and come on home. New guys, listen to the old party animals when downtown. If they correct you, listen the first time or you will deal with me when you wake up."

"Keep the barracks clean and picked up at all times, period. Time off is no excuse to live like pigs. This is not the British Army nor is it the Air Force. It is the US Army and there is only one kind of discipline, perfect discipline. I know we all make mistakes from time to time. You will get a fair hearing and if at all possible, extra training will take the place of Company punishment, if the Commanding Officer agrees. We ain't having an Article 15 factory."

"Starting immediately we are going to dress in accordance with AR 670-1 at all times. Look down at your boots. If they are not laced left over right, re-lace them, now. If your belt is not fed from the left to the right, fix it now. Men dress from left to right while women dress from right to left. I know some of you were raised by your Mommas so your sexuality is still under de-velopment. Here we all dress like men."

"Whatever it is we are doing, we are going to it right be it PT, drill, march-ing from Point A to Point B or singing cadence. Half ass effort will not feed the bulldog men. The military cemeteries are full of damn good men who died doing their best. Alongside them there are some sorry soldiers who never learned the right way to fight. You will have the chance to learn how to sol-dier correctly and while you are with me you will live up to that standard."

"Speaking of standards, you men have all been in the Army long enough to know right from wrong. You are capable of being standard bearers. In times of old before radios, telephones and signal flags, it was the unit stan-dard, the colors and guidons, that soldiers followed into battle and rallied around when the going got rough. Be worthy of following where the stan-dards of this great unit are going to lead you. Be a standard bearer for the Blackhorse. Serve where you are with pride. If you do that, you and I will get along fine."

"Now for those of you who are just coasting and have no intention of ev-er amounting to a tinker's damn, you have until next Wednesday to come to me and ask for a General Discharge. You don't have to French kiss your pla-toon sergeant or pork the Squadron Commander's poodle, just come and see me. I will send your happy ass home to flip burgers at McDonald's. After Wednesday I will assume everyone here is fully engaged and on the team."

"I have no special knowledge about a higher state of alert for the Squa-dron. I suspect the new Squadron Commander has a plan. When he makes changes, we will execute them immediately. When he tests the squadron we will not sleep in the motor pool or in cars. We will make our preparations and when released, we will go eat a nice meal, have two beers and get some pussy if we can. When recall comes we will do our best from where it finds us in our normal life. It has to be that way. If we stack the deck we will fail when the mission comes out of the blue. True cheaters never prosper."

"Platoon Sergeants, review the alert rosters and then resume maintenance by Platoons. We will all march together from the Motor Pool tonight after standing Retreat there. Questions about anything we have covered?"

"Yes, Specialist Bonham, what is your question?" Martin asked.

"I know for a fact First Sergeant some of the units are going to sleep here until the alert stuff is all resolved. Aren't you worried they will get ahead of us?" Bonham asked.

"Bonham, bring your ass up here." When he arrived Martin hugged his neck and said, "God Bless you, Bonham, you are a competitor. You want to win and you hate being screwed over by assholes violating the spirit and the intent of what the Squadron Commander is trying to do. Listen to me you crazy shit heads. What we are doing is simulating recall under normal circumstances when there is absolutely no warning. It does no one any good if we violate the spirit of what the Squadron Commander wants. Anyone who cheats the alert by sleeping in their vehicles violates the spirit of his orders, is lower than dog shit and stupid. I do not judge those who will cheat. It is up to their rater and senior rater to develop their character but we will not be among them."

"Here is what I predict. The cheaters will go sleep in the motor pool. G Troop will go eat and get ready to go downtown. About 1920, the Squadron Commander will send up the balloon. No vehicle will leave the motor pool for the alert. About 2100, the Squadron Commander will gather the leaders and tell them everything he wants changed. G Troop will fix everything he tells us to fix right then and then we will go to our quarters and go to bed except for some of you single guys who will go to town. Sometime before morning, the balloon will go up again but we still will not move a vehicle. He will inspect to see what was corrected by whom and what was not. Once all corrections have been made, he will wait a few days and move G Troop to Border Condition One prior to our assumption of the Border mission. He will flame those dumb asses sleeping in their vehicles in the motor pool and mess with them until they meet the standard."

Specialist Bonham looked first at the First Sergeant and then out into the troop seeing the heads nodding, he turned back to First Sergeant and asked, "How do you know exactly what is going to happen, First Sergeant?"

"Bonham and men, one last comment and we go back to work. It is easy to predict what men of integrity will do. The Squadron Commander has combat integrity, so do most of you. You just don't know it yet. What does that mean? Simply, you may not want to go into combat and if you are smart you will be afraid, but you know your buddies are there and you will go in spite of your fear. The Squadron Commander is going to do what is right because it is right but also because he wants you, and you and you, to know he is predictable. He will always pick the harder right over the easier wrong. For most of us, a good example is worth ten sermons. I trust him. I know what he will do next. It is no mystery to me and if you watch him and your Troop Commander it will not be a mystery to you either, become like them and like your NCOs. FALL IN."

Martin spent the remainder of the afternoon refining the recall roster, streamlining weapons issue, defining details required for the supply room, inspecting weapons and making sure each and every vehicle had full fuel tanks by topping them off. He was not surprised to find some of them take a hundred gallons or more of DF-2. The support platoon cheerfully brought up the big new fuel trucks, the HEMMTS, to do the work.

He was also not surprised to find the generators for the command post track wouldn't start. He merely said, "Engineer equipment is a big challenge. When I stole Stroud from the Troop for the S3 shop I knew it would suffer. Get the shit running guys, now! If you have to, go get BJ off the supply truck. He is about to wax it if he gets any more time to work on it."

The result was predictable. The practice alert was called after G Troop moved off to their quarters at 1800 hours. G Troop made rapid progress and fixed every fault and changed every procedure the Old Man wanted fixed. The Squadron Commander also predictably went nuts when he found crews sleeping in tanks and vehicles after he had specifically forbidden the practice. He did some smart things. He put the machineguns on the tanks, allowed the on board storage of duffle bags, issued the combat map package, and issued the night vision devices. To the soldiers of the troop it appeared the First Sergeant was living inside the Squadron Commander's head. However, after many of them were present for the changes and the trial efforts of selected tank crews, they bought into the process and were enthused about getting out of the gate quickly. They were very happy to see crews execute pilot projects to see if a technique would work instead of trying everything en masse. It was at this point the Squadron Commander's pleasure at how well his unit was responding led his enthusiasm to put his butt out on the proverbial limb.

"Men, if for any reason, I am late for the 55 minute meeting and we have troops ready to roll, roll them to the ASP, to the alert training area and to the Border if that is part of the exercise from higher," Lieutenant Colonel Millard said with great conviction to the assembled officers and First Sergeants.

Looking up to see Martin rolling his eyes, the crusty Lieutenant Colonel asked, "First Sergeant Martin, you got a problem with that?"

Martin answered him instantly, "No, Sir. I trust you to back up what you say. I just hope you appreciate how fast your changes have the unit moving. The process is streamlined and by that order you are telling us there is no final control measure for the alert. The meeting at 55 minutes is a control measure. If you remove that, until the lead troop gets where it is supposed to go, they are operating under Corps guidance, not yours. But hey, Sir, if you can drive it, we can ride it."

0500 hours
17 Jul 1986
Bad Kissingen, West Germany

It had only taken a week for the predictions to come true. It seemed the Russians had decided to smoke the entire Meinigen Gap on a fine summer night with little or no wind. They began the operation in the middle of the night after Observation Post Tennessee reported a bright flash on the ground in the vicinity of the tank range in the center of the Gap. Russian intentions were not known but smoking the whole gap could hide a Division from the naked eye until it was too late. There had to be a reason the bad guys would blanket an area three miles wide using artificial smoke.

Predictably, Corps called an alert. The Squadron moved like a well oiled machine. G Troop was lined up at the Chapel and ready to head out the gate at H+48 minutes. Martin had called First Lieutenant Douglas in Fulda on his private German line from his apartment Commander and suggested he meet the troop on the Border. Martin called his commander at his girl friend's number in Fulda. He suggested he go straight to the Border from her apartment. In their special code he told him the troop would meet him there and would be in Border Condition One when he arrived.

At H+55 minutes, there was no sign of the Squadron Commander or his staff. Without further orders, Martin rolled the troop to Border Condition One to include the upload of missiles. As he turned the corner in his jeep at H+56, he saw the Squadron Commander with a most incredulous look on his face watching G Troop drive by. "Gold 34, Gator 7, OVER."

"Gator 7, this is Gold 34 your push, OVER."

"Roger 34, pull over at the commissary and brief the Squadron Commander. Recommend he go straight to the Border Camp. Tell him this is real world and no drill. Then catch up. I will slow up as we drop off the Mortars at the ASP. We are going to tail gate the TOWs at their fighting positions."

"Gator 7 this is Gold-34, roger, OUT."

Martin knew the Squadron Commander trusted Vic Jackson and had known him in Vietnam.

Slowing at the ASP entrance for the Mortars to peel off, Martin was glad to see Vic Jackson boiling down the road with his M1 wide open to catch up.

"Gator 7, Gold 34, OVER." Vic called with a grunt when his ribs hit the edge of his hatch as his tank nosed over hard when his driver slammed on the brakes whipping the two antennas.

"Gold 34, 7, send it."

"7, Eagle Horse 6 will meet you and our Six at the Border Camp. He is flying up there in the 58. You are to go directly to the Border Camp once we all split out. He knows we are on auto pilot at the LD. He was surprised you set the dispersal point so far back from the Border. Told him we are very familiar with the farm roads and would not be seen. He knows we are uploaded for war and are at Weapons Tight, no rounds to be chambered without order or a hostile act."

"Gold 34, 7, what is his mental state, OVER?" Martin asked his buddy.

"AHHHH 7, he has his map board and he said he is ready to get it on, OVER."

This last comment caused the G Troop net to erupt with the sound of dogs barking. Martin smiled, the troops thought they were ready to fight and displayed the attitude of all virgin soldiers who have yet to see their first dead man.

The movement to the point of departure where individual platoons moved to the Battle Positions was executed without issues. As the Commander's driver came forward from his position as tail end Charlie for the convoy, Martin signaled him to follow and moved off to the Border Camp on B19, the German State highway.

As he arrived at the Border Camp, Martin saw the Squadron Commander was already there with his map board across the hood of one of the Mercedes Border jeeps. He was alone as the Fox Troop currently manning the border had gone on alert and vacated the camp. As Martin joined him, he looked relieved and happy to see him. The two of them immediately became co-conspirators as they laughed with the Squadron Commander speaking first.

"You were right, Martin, I about shit my pants when you rolled by and then Jones told me it was a full ammo load out for all weapons and a full occupation of the border ordered by V Corps. What the hell is going on? What the hell are the Russians doing, Martin, I need to know and know now?" the Squadron Commander asked almost plaintively.

"Stand by, Sir. We should have eyes on the gap with 4th Platoon. Blue 30, Gator 7, OVER."

"Gator 7, Blue 30, OVER."

"Blue, can you see through the smoke? OVER."

"Gator 7, affirmative. It is an aircraft crash site. I was in the Civil Air Patrol and I have seen them before. There is a debris field and what looks to be some big pieces, turrets, rotor blades and stuff from a HIND, OVER."

"Good news, Blue, stand by that location and keep your thermal on the area. Good job, stay curious. Chow is on the way along with fuel. Get your reports flowing."

"BREAK, GUIDONS, GUIDONS, GUIDONS. All elements confirm WEAPONS TIGHT with all prep to fire checks complete and zero rounds locked and loaded. Five, pass Blue's report to all elements."

426

Martin and the Squadron Commander smiled as the rapid confirmation came in from each platoon. The Squadron TOC requested the same report from Fox Troop for their section of the Border.

The Squadron Commander nodded with approval, thinking that the last thing we needed was a stray bullet whizzing over to the other side sent by a doofus via accidental discharge. Can't shoot it if it ain't chambered.

"We lucked out. We practiced and got fast just in time for V Corps to call a real world alert. We got the Cav troop deployed along the Border backing up Fox before V Corps could get a command element up here," Martin told the Squadron Commander.

At that very moment, an AH-1 Cobra from Thunder Horse came out of the mist to land near the small group. Martin was very glad to see his Troop Commander show up just as the Cobra was landing. He had all of his LBE complete with pistol in new fatigues looking like a million bucks. He reported to First Lieutenant Douglas with the Squadron Commander looking on: "Sir, The Troop is at Border Condition One. We moved IAW with directives, without orders, at H+56 minutes. All elements are uploaded to include TOW Missiles for the Bradleys. All ammo packaging is stored at each fighting position. Weapons are Tight. Re-supply is ongoing by Tailgate by Sergeant Webster. Blue reports we have a HIND Crash in front of his position. That is the only activity in our sector. The Squadron TOC is up and consolidating reports. We are up to date on both nets. How Batt is in DS to the Squadron. Our FSO is in direct contract with the battery and the FS net is operating. I doubt the Russians at the crash site know we are here. There is no TAC Air and Thunder Horse is not playing. There are no issues. We are in the wait and see mode. End of report."

"Good report, First Sergeant, thank you," First Lieutenant Douglas said gratefully.

As the Deputy Corps Commander made his way to them, he was smiling broadly. "Just got off the VHF with Corps Headquarters. The Russians are finally telling us what all the fuss is about, it is a HIND crash. They are exercising their well known paranoia to the maximum. They did not know what to think when their overheads showed the Eagle Horse motor pool lighting up and in two hours, uploaded vehicles on the Border ready to fight. It would not be much of a fight with just the smoke outfits. They have not alerted their other forces in any way. Bob, the Corps is damn proud you were able to do what you did with no notice. The fact you have been in command less than a month speaks volumes about your leadership. Repack the ammo and get the heavy stuff off the border. Sooner would be better than later. I assume you are Weapons Tight and have your tigers on a short leash," he said smiling.

"Yes, Sir, no one is authorized to have a round chambered unless I order it or is facing a hostile act. They all know they are authorized to defend themselves without asking permission," the Squadron Commander stated plainly.

"Damn, Bob. That is the first time I have ever heard a Field Commander over here say soldiers can defend themselves and then report during the Cold War. You are exactly right. Let's go see the troops! What are we going in?" he asked.

"Sir, we will take this Mercedes. I'll drive us. I'm licensed for every vehicle in the squadron as are all my officers," the Squadron Commander stated bluntly.

"So, Bob, all of your officers are licensed to drive all of the vehicles they command?" the General asked.

"All of the ones with a pass, yes, Sir. Until they can get trained and licensed they are restricted to their quarters, the post and the Border. It works wonders. We are approaching 95% of the squadron," he said.

As they departed, his Troop Commander turned to Martin saying, "So, in summary, the Squadron Commander stepped in shit and came out smelling like a rose. That is some good luck isn't it, First Sergeant?" First Lieutenant Douglas opined.

"You could call it luck but in this case luck is what happened when preparation met opportunity. The Squadron Commander busted our asses for the past week to refine our ability to respond to an alert. He gave us an order to move without command when the situation is unknown or unclear using the control measures of the Border SOP. He backed us 100% when we did as he directed, to the point of breaking open the TOWs and uploading the cheese on the Mortars. He is a risk taker but not a gambler. I like that, plus he is lucky, a rare thing," Martin said.

"Once the Deputy leaves, I want the support platoon to come and get the war ammunition from the Bradleys and I want our supply guys to use their deuce and the five ton from the Mortars and turn in their ammo. Tell Red & White to do the best they can on re-packaging the TOWs. Leave the machinegun ammo on board the tanks and we will replace it in the conexes when we get back to the motor pool. Thanks for having Six trail you everywhere. I'm going to go visit the platoon leaders, our TOC, and get up on my tank. Everything worked great. I worried a little about you making all of the calls on the phone tree but it must have worked to perfection," Douglas said.

"It worked great. It took twenty minutes to call 19 people," Martin said.

0600 hours
21 Jul 1986
Camp Lee, Near Wohlbach
West Germany

G Troop was back on the border. First Lieutenant Douglas was talking with his First Sergeant about the subject of spot reports, "My buddies at Regiment tell me no one is getting enough spot reports. The Regimental Commanding Officer thinks we are on our asses and either not patrolling or not reporting. He thinks there are 25 – 50 potential spot reports per day on each Squadron's frontage."

"So what you want done is for the Troop to generate more spot reports but to maintain a high standard - no messages describing an East German Police Dog licking his nuts. The troopers tell me nothing is happening across the way and there is nothing to report. The truth is somewhere in between. If we were to immediately generate 25 spots today and maintain that rate and increase it to 50 and then to a 100, we would meet your intent," Martin said giving feedback to verify the guidance.

"How are you going to make that happen, First Sergeant?" Douglas asked with some skepticism.

"Oh ye of little faith. Were it not so I would have told you. You should study your Bible a little more, Herr Loitnant!" Martin said.

"I really want to know how you are going to do it, First Sergeant," his Commander said.

"Come on, I'll show you," Martin said.

Walking from where they were sitting to the Border Operations Center he and First Lieutenant Douglas went into the office.

"How many quality spots did we send up to Regiment or higher yesterday guys?" Martin asked.

Specialist Aschilman replied, "Eight, First Sergeant. Ten were screened out by the Ops Officer as insignificant. The screened out ones were about the dogs being fed, dogs sleeping, etc."

"Thanks guys. Are you guys coming or going?" Martin asked though he already knew the answer. Shift change was at 0600 for Border Ops.

"We are coming on, First Sergeant," Staff Sergeant Burdette answered, his eyes smiling.

Martin did not disappoint Burdette, "You'd best sharpen your pencils guys. This AO is going to heat up some today. Keep the same high standard but be prepared for a minimum of 25 solid spot reports during the next twenty four hours."

Martin left the Border Ops Center and walked to the administrative office where a small chalk board was affixed to the wall beside the door. The chalk board served to keep the troops up to date on changes to life in the camp. Securing chalk and the eraser from inside the admin office, Martin erased the board and wrote the following on the board:

20 Jul	8 good spot reports
21 Jul	Goal 25 good spot reports
	First Sergeant & Driver=8
	CO & Driver=8
	Net Increase for Ops & Patrols: 1 for total of 9

"Let's go get some breakfast, Sir. I'll brief the lads at the 0700 formation," Martin said grandly.

"If nothing is happening, First Sergeant, how am I going to find 8 spot reports?" his Commander asked querulously.

"Shit, that's easy, Sir, I'll give you 7 of my first ones and still get my 8 by dark. I would hate to know the Regimental Commanding Officer had a mission I could not fulfill. By the time we're done, we will be sending 100 spots to Regiment. They will be like Jeremiah Johnson wanting to see a grizzly bear and we will be like the old trapper. We will run the son of a bitch right through the cabin. They will have more griz' than they can kill or skin."

At the 0700 formation First Lieutenant Douglas watched his First Sergeant motivate the Troop. "Everyone here is a scout. We all see things out on the border in the performance of our duties when we are on patrol and when we are doing other missions. Regiment wants 25 spots a day per Squadron slice of the Border. Many of you think that is too high and unreasonable. That is why the Commanding Officer and I are going to give you a hand today. Let's see what we can do together. Border Ops will track the total."

After the formation Martin's new driver, Keith Richards, came up to tell him he had the gear that Martin had told him to get. Martin took the Commander to his jeep to show him the gear. It consisted of 300 feet of ½ inch nylon rope, a set of tree climbers and a leather safety belt. As he inspected the gear, and talked to Keith, the Commander listened, "The leather belt is dry rotted. You lean back on it and you will take a fall for sure. Take a piece of rope, tape and burn the ends and use it for a safety rig. I climbed an Army pole with Army climbing gear once and it damned near killed me because the belt was rotten and my platoon sergeant was a doofus. You see, Sir, a high hill with tall pine trees will let us see a long ways into East Germany and they will never know it."

He inspected the TA-1 and TA-312 telephone and made sure both worked. Keith had their cooler loaded with Pepsi on ice and some sandwiches. "Sir, are you ready to go?" Martin asked.

"You go ahead, First Sergeant. I'll meet you at OP Tennessee. Wait for me there," he ordered.

Martin and his driver took the long way around to the Observation Post. They were able to make five good spot reports beginning at Check Point 132. The subjects ranged from construction crews on the control road, to a 10 man GAK foot patrol on the outside of the fence. Even seeing a GAK was a rare event.

430

Once the Commander arrived at the OP Martin led the way to a high hill that was almost in the 1ˢᵗ Squadron's sector. Keith put on the climbers and scrambled up the tree like a monkey. "Holy shit, First Sergeant. They are having some sort of family day or something over there. They got one of every kind of vehicle in the East German and Russian Armies. I am going to write out the spot and drop it taped to this rock."

Martin held out the phone so Keith could see it. He got the idea and began reporting to First Lieutenant Douglas over the phone line. It beat screaming, Martin thought. It might be a family day but it was here, they saw and they were reporting it. The sheer volume of what Keith was seeing could have made one report into five but Martin counseled against that and it went in as one spot. Corps wanted a Red Catcher flight launched even though it was explained as a Family Day. There was a Soviet General there and that was a separate spot. Seven spots down, 18 to go.

Throughout the morning, the headquarters patrol easily found 12 more good spot reports making their total 19 before lunch. Of course, there was no way First Lieutenant Douglas was going to stay on the ground. He put on the climbers and went up a large oak. His climb was worth the sweat as he got to report an orders group of a Border Police meeting of senior officers, equivalent to Battalion and Brigade Commanders. That one was worth the Red Catcher. The exercise was in a location that the sensitive equipment on the helo could listen to their talk from a discrete distance.

The guy on duty at Regiment did not know what to think when he began to get spot reports directly from a Troop Commander and a First Sergeant. The Regimental Command Sergeant Major and the S3 Sergeant Major were talking in the S3 when he came in to report this strange occurrence. "Who was it, G Troop, I'll bet!" Sergeant Major Rogers opined. "The Regimental Commanding Officer wants spots so Martin is out working the trace with his young First Lieutenant Douglas, busting the kid's hump and leading the way for the Troop. I'll bet a dollar to a dog turd he has a tracking system on the chalkboard of the Camp Lee admin building. I can hear him now, John Wayne in the flesh 'What the hell! Me and my driver and the Commanding Officer and his driver are doing more than all of you combined. Life is hard but it is harder when you're stupid. Are you going to have it said that a 43 year old Grandpa is better at patrolling than you - I hope not', he'll say," said Rogers laughing loudly.

Hearing the laughter, the new Regimental Commanding Officer walked into the S3 and read the spot reports. He was everything Smokin' Joe was not, West Pointer, Army Cheer leader, BZ promotions from Captain forward, Honor Graduate of every course he ever attended, leader of the highest caliber and a moral family man. He was the only Regimental Commanding Officer to be known to do the road march with the Expert Medical Badge Candidates to the point of blood squishing in his boots from blisters. The Second

Squadron qualified all but three soldiers of their medical platoon building on the year before when they had 22 win the badge.

"Looks like the G Troop leaders listen to their Regimental Commanding Officer and lead the way. Keep me posted about how many spot reports come in from Second Squadron. I particularly want to know if it jumps up dramatically tomorrow or the next day. I know how they are playing the game and I want to see how far they can go. Day after tomorrow, Sergeants Major, I think we all should visit Camp Lee and the Eaglehorse Squadron. They should be up to fifty spots a day by then or I miss my guess," he said smiling at the thought.

1000 hours
23 Jul 1986
Camp Lee near Wohlbach
West Germany

The Regimental Commanding Officer was always happy to visit the Border. He was not at all surprised to see exactly what ACR predicted they would see, a chalkboard that tracked the past numbers, the current numbers and the goal numbers of spot reports from G Troop. The 50 listed for a goal put a big smile on his face. Obviously, First Sergeant thought big and was focused on the Regimental intent. The Regimental Commanding Officer turned to the Lieutenant escorting him and asked, "What is the meaning of the starred reference to dogs, Lieutenant?"

"Sir, the First Sergeant uses the dogs as illustrations of what is not an acceptable focus of a spot report. I believe his favorite phrase is – 'A dog licking his nuts is not something higher wants to hear'," Second Lieutenant Chastain reported.

"Not exactly what you would hear back at good old Norwich is it, Lieutenant?" the Regimental Commanding Officer said.

"No, Sir, but the First Sergeant is rarely misunderstood."

"Is it realistic to expect 50 spot reports per day on a Squadron's frontage?" The Regimental Commanding Officer asked the Lieutenant.

"Sir, the First Sergeant is not a reasonable man. He says reasonable men never get anything done because they can always be talked out of their goals, usually by another reasonable man. Being unreasonable is a virtue in his mind," Second Lieutenant Chastain remarked with some irony.

The visit to the Border confirmed the Regimental Commanding Officer's opinion of 2d Squadron. They listened, formed a plan and acted to support his intent. The camp was completely clean, straight and met all of his expectations. He was particularly happy to learn the Reaction Team was only tested until it met the standard of being out the gate in five minutes. Further testing by young officers to watch their own power in action was not permitted. The only disturbing thing he and his ad hoc team found was the amount of ammunition carried by the foot patrols in G Troop. 270 M-16 rounds in ten magazines per rifleman, 10,000 rounds for the M-60 and four AT-4's was too much ammo for a patrol. The Regiment had failed to put a limit on ammo and that would be fixed.

"Lieutenant Chastain, is the amount of ammo issued to the patrols excessive?" the Regimental Commanding Officer asked.

"The First Sergeant is the guy who told us what to carry. He said he did not want the Commanding Officer to have to write a letter that said, Dear Mrs. Smith, your boy would be alive today if his chain of command would have had enough balls to trust him with enough ammo to win. It is heavy and it is a pain to carry the extra 7.62, plus the spare barrel, but it terrifies the East Germans. They see one of our foot patrols carrying bandoliers of 7.62 and they run for cover. They harass the other troops but not the Gators. The dedicated sniper scares the shit out of them as well, Sir."

"Oh really, what dedicated sniper would that be Lieutenant?" said the Regimental Commanding Officer with great interest.

"Sir, we have an M-14 tricked out with a scope on loan from the SF guys at Bad Tolz. It is government issued with a nice 4x16 scope. Our best shot carries it and he and his spotter wear those sniper suits with the burlap pieces and the cammo net. He and his spotter set up above us terrain permitting and then move by jeep ahead of us. When those two stand up near the fence that really scares the shit out of the East Germans on patrol, hell they scare me appearing out of nowhere and they're on our side, Sir," he said with a rueful smile before continuing. "Staff Sergeant Fowler gave us a class on snipers out at the mini-tank range complex using a demonstrator wearing the suit. He had him stand up about fifty meters out from the bleachers in the tall grass and walk in to the gravel. No one saw him until he stood up, Sir."

"Do you think the First Sergeant is deliberately provoking the East Germans, Lieutenant?" the Regimental Commanding Officer asked.

"No, Sir. He is giving them something to think about without a threat to harm them or a hostile act. The East Germans treat everyone but us like shit. They respect us for how we do our job, not what we say. We don't confront them or talk to them."

1000 hours
Oct 1986
Hofenoh Church
Grafenwohr
Training Area

The quartering party from G Troop moved into the first Assembly Area of a 24 hour Live Fire Exercise. Led by a scout platoon Bradley, each element

433

had specific tasks to execute which included surveying the ground, staking positions and verifying a secondary route into and out of the position.

The exercise had been designed by the Regimental Staff and was modeled on the activity at the latest wrinkle in Army Training, the National Training Center at Fort Irwin, CA. The staff was acting as Observer Controllers with the Chemical Company, selected members of the Engineer Company and the Regimental MP Platoon acted as the Opposition Force under the command of an Infantry Company Commander from the 3d Armored Division with his entire unit in M-113s. Every vehicle and each soldier of G Troop would have MILES after the live fire. The staff was clearly under orders to overload the leadership of the troop with scenarios to tax both the SOPs of each level of the Regiment and the mental resilience of the NCOs and Officers.

"We will be the first unit to undergo this exercise out of 12 troops in the Regiment. We will not be the best rated unit in the Regiment. I know, I see you wincing and can hear the groaning. The Regimental Commanding Officer has spoken. He is new and all of the OCs are about to go command somewhere in the Blackhorse. They will all want to show what bad asses they are to make a good impression. Also the rules will be shaken down by the first unit."

"No one here has ever been through one of these. The idea is to learn, not necessarily to win. The key point for all of us is to follow our own SOPs, not make the same mistake twice, and apply what we have learned to the next set of events they give us. It will be grueling and it is supposed to be hard. It is also of short duration since we know we have to be on the train in 72 hours. It will appear to you that you are not worth a shit, are impossibly stupid, do not know your job and part of a hopelessly screwed up unit. It ain't so Joe. I can write down more things on a sheet of paper in two minutes than you can do in five years let alone 40 hours," Martin said watching the irrepressible PFC Boudreux's hand go up.

"Okay, Boudreux, what is it?" Martin asked.

"I can do your list, First Sergeant, what is it?" he asked smugly.

"For you Boudreux, being a registered Coon Ass or Cajun, your first task is to alter the course of the Mississippi River so that it flows to the east of the LSU campus instead of the west. You have 2 years to do it and you can only use a wheel barrow from supply and the D-Handled shovel off your Bradley."

"Well shit, First Sergeant, couldn't nobody do that!" Boudreux stated indignantly.

"And the lesson in that story is what, Boudreux?" Martin said holding his hand to his theatrically.

"They are gonna' give us more shit to do than we can get done and they want to see if we do the important shit and let the dumb shit slide," Boudreux said sheepishly.

434

"Boudreux, unless you make it as an officer, you ain't leaving this troop until you PCS. You are too smart, too valuable, and too brave to let go. At least you know what you don't know and will admit it. Men, we can correct ignorance. It is a temporary condition cured by learning. Stupid is forever," Martin said before continuing, watching Boudreux swell up with pride.

"Remember the mission the Commander briefed, move to and assume a defensive position to fight and hold until ordered to move. Everything else is just bullshit and of secondary importance. We do all of that other shit as we get to it. Our priorities remain, defend, care for and evacuation of casualties, maintenance of equipment, conservation of resources - to include sleep and chow. Once we make the move to the fighting position all of the coaching and impact scenarios from the OCs stop until the firing is over."

"During the LFX, there will be a lot of distractions. You will see artillery rounds impact as you have never seen them before but on the enemy, not you. You will see A-10's and Cobras firing live TOWs and rockets as well as 40m grenades. The A-10s will also drop bombs. At one point, tanks will fire over the scout platoons and our own mortars will be firing in direct Support."

"Our job is to enter the Assembly Area, receive a Chemical Attack, eva-cuate casualties, report, perform decontamination after requesting assistance and setting up the decon station enroute to the range. The casualties will come back to life once the proper reports are complete and decontamination is performed correctly. Simulated or real casualties will not cause the exercise to halt. It goes on regardless of death or injury unless or until a pause is called by the OCs to conduct a critique."

"The Range will then be the scene of a first ever LFX employing the guns of the howitzer battery in Direct Support, Thunder Horse, AH-1 Cobras fir-ing live TOWs, the Mortars of the troop and A-10s all controlled by First Lieutenant Douglass on six different radios strapped to and inside of G-66."

"All weapons of the troop are to be used with the CFV Bradleys firing in-ert TOWs with the M1 tanks firing over the Bradleys from a higher elevation. The scouts will then make smoke with their on board red phosphorous gre-nade launchers and displace behind the tanks. The targets will appear to ad-vance on the troop in bands to simulate the echelons embodied in Russian attack doctrine. At some point the Troop Commander will order us to dis-place, we will go get a critique and move into the MILES or maneuver part of the drill."

"Keep your head, be proud of who you are and remember the guy with the clip board is king today and dog shit tomorrow when it is his turn to be evaluated. I have held the clipboard. Even when you press it tight against your forehead, you do not get a mind meld like Spock."

"I will make a prediction. We will rank no worse than third. Killer Troop will be first, Fox Troop will be second and we will be third out of the 15 graded elements in the regiment. Third for the first guys through will be as good as first for the rest. Everyone will know how great you are because you will have been first in the fight and you will show more class than the OCs screwing with you. They may be acting like Drill Sergeants on Day One but at the end they will be thinking, 'Damn, I hope the guys in the unit I'm getting are this good!'"

The O/C's got a big surprise as Martin coordinated for Thunder Horse to fly in water blivets to the decontamination site and casualties out to include the dead. Staff Sergeant Ardouin found, laid out and made the coordination for the drive through site. The engineer squad attached for the exercise from the Regimental Engineer Company merely cut a road through a long low spot on a trail just off the main tank trail around the reservation for a slurry pit. The water from the blivets was used to fill the ditch and the simulated bleach and decontamination powder enabled the troop to take advantage of the equipment organic to the squadron. It was an approved solution to the problem of performing a hasty cleaning of contaminated vehicles in the field. No one anticipated the Troop would request and get the helos from 4th Squadron for support. Looking on as the Troop negotiated the makeshift field 'car-wash', the Regimental Commanding Officer, the RS-1 and the Command Sergeant Major all reached the same conclusion at the same time. The Regimental Commanding Officer said, "Damn Sergeants Major Academy got them over that hump. Now Martin will teach that to Fox Troop and it will be an institution. But, this is a learning exercise and that includes us. When you send them away to school and they come back smart, it is dumb to get mad about it. They just use resources better than we gave them credit for when we planned this. Don't stop it, Three, let it go on until complete."

The troop moved onto the live fire complex without halting. The Combat Trains took positions in the woods behind the firing range. Martin went to a hill between the two elements where he knew he would have line of sight for his radios in case the Commander need his help.

The Regimental Commanding Officer was monitoring the G Troop Command net during the live fire exercise. Lieutenant Douglas was doing a great job. He was working the six radios of his make shift radio net superbly. His ubiquitous First Sergeant was on a high hill behind the range giving him a lot of help, too much in the opinion of this Regimental Command Sergeant Major. The Regimental Command Sergeant Major was sure the First Sergeant was running the troop and the First Lieutenant was just a figure head. His O/Cs strongly disputed this fact. The Regimental Commanding Officer believed them over his Regimental Command Sergeant Major only because they had spent the time down in the troop. The Regimental Command Sergeant Major did not like the way G Troop moved with their combat train of support within the Troop formation for protection and immediate support.

The Regimental Commanding Officer loved it. It was brilliant but simple and he knew it was the way of the future. He had heard Martin had been a big part of writing the doctrine of close combat heavy and it showed. He also loved having a First Sergeant just like Martin when he had a troop. But, the type needed watching. His Command Sergeant Major was right, the First Sergeant would slowly take charge and run the whole show if the Commander ceded his authority or was not capable.

Martin was acting as the radio relay to the G Troop TOC track who could not maintain commo from where he was required to be by Regimental order. The location had been selected to put the Troop Commander under as much strain as possible as well as overload the troop reporting procedure. But Martin did not know all of that, the Regimental Commanding Officer mused, he just knew his young First Lieutenant was in deep kimchi and he was helping him out. Trouble was, he was doing it so good, the stress strategy of the exercise was not working.

Watching it all happen, the Regimental Commanding Officer said, "Command Sergeant Major, G Troop is cheatin' with that radio relay. They cheated and massed fires on the far targets and erased the Russian horde. The scout platoon leaders got cross talking after that First Sergeant ass chewing and found ways to shoot their cannon from the flanks with the tanks. There ain't no more targets once they shoot up the near set and they are all BMPs. He is massing the troop and will kill them all. Damn they're good. They do not rattle. They got it together after that little flurry between the platoon leaders."

"Yeah, that's all well and good but the First Sergeant is still acting like he is in command of the troop. I sent the O/Cs to find him and kill him with the God Gun but they cannot find him. I'm going to chew his ass out at the critique for failure to exercise log pack at the very least," Command Sergeant Major Bodrotsky said.

"Yeah I would like to see him figure that one out. We will keep them in the classroom and take up all of the time they think they have to refuel. Then we give them an immediate FRAGO to move. The tanks will run out of fuel before they get to their next objective and the OPFOR can hit them in the flank and from the rear to chew them up," the S4 Major opined.

"Bragg, you aren't saying much about your old unit," the Regimental Commanding Officer said.

"Sir, that First Sergeant is one of the most resourceful men we have. I don't know what he will do but it will be a surprise to us, of that you can be sure. If he even thinks we have resorted to cheating to beat them, and we are, he will show us what cheating looks like," he said smiling.

"By god, I will break his ass!" the Regimental Command Sergeant Major said.

"Why, Command Sergeant Major, you are making this personal? Just because he is an old friend of yours you didn't think he would slack off, did you?" Sergeant Major Rogers said with a mischievous smile.

437

"What happened with the scout platoons? I missed that," the S4 said.

"The stress got to the two platoon leaders and they were snarling at each other about to screw everything up. The troop commander was doing the last of the air support coordination on the radio and the First Sergeant jumped in their shit in a fatherly sort of way, like a Command Sergeant Major would straighten out two Captains when his Squadron Commander was busy. He told them to go to their quick fix, you know, the high band. He really jumped in their shit and told them to spend their time figuring out how to help kill the BMPs and to apologize. We knew they were just going to switch to the other band and we listened as the three of them got their act together and conspired to help the tankers. The guys that wrote the book never thought of that one but it sure worked. Maybe we ought to institutionalize it, it was a hell of a move, a little hairy, but hey it worked like a charm. Martin knows he ain't the troop commander. We will find a way to settle his ass down and make certain Lieutenant Douglas is capable of being in charge or not, before we are through," the Regimental Commanding Officer said, calming the group.

The entire troop was in the classroom but the First Sergeant and his driver were not. The support team from the support platoon was excluded by the O/Cs from the meeting due to lack of space and input. The Regimental Command Sergeant Major was beside himself that Martin was not present at the meeting and was ignoring all radio calls and messages for him to report. As the meeting droned on, it dawned on the troop they were being played against the clock for re-fueling and re-supply. They were about to be screwed without getting kissed or lubed.

"Goddammit, give me a God Gun," Command Sergeant Major Brodtsky yelled. Then he added, "That damn Martin is out there refueling the damn tanks with his driver instead of coming to this damn meeting." The first three God Guns failed to function. By the time the Command Sergeant Major was suitably armed, Martin's jeep was going over the hill and disappearing into the trees. No quitter, the Command Sergeant Major went outside without his helmet no less, God Gun in hand. All he found was the dust of his quarry's mount to fire at.

He turned to see the Regimental Commanding Officer at his elbow smiling, "Command Sergeant Major, do like I do with that guy."

"What's that, Sir, court martial him?" the Command Sergeant Major asked.

"No, Command Sergeant Major, just be glad he is on our side. Come on back inside and let's get them on the road. Oh shit, too late, here they come, they've got the FRAGO," he said as the two of them moved out of the way of the charging herd that was G Troop. Noting their demeanor, he was pleased to see none of them had laughed inside the building but they were damn happy when they were back on their vehicles and he was happy to see some of them give the finger to who ever needed it. Good outfit, lots of spirit.

The answer on how to jerk a knot in the G Troop First Sergeant's ass came to the Regimental Commanding Officer like a gift from heaven. Someone had left the First Sergeant's Communications and Electronics Signal Operating Instructions or CEOI, in the latrine next to Regimental Headquarters. One of his clerks who know of the antipathy between the Regimental Commanding Officer's staff and G Troop over the FTX was very happy to give it to the Regimental Commanding Officer. As of yet, the troop had not reported the item as missing. The loss of the item, with its real world listing of frequencies of everything in the Regiment, was a serious matter and must be reported. The Regimental Commanding Officer smiled as the radio in the S3 came alive with Martin reporting himself in a very matter of fact manner. After the report was concluded and Martin was standing by for confirmation, the Regimental Commanding Officer told the radio operator to direct him to come to Regimental Headquarters, notify them of arrival at the rear of the building and to await the Regimental Commanding Officer at that location.

When Martin arrived, the Regimental Commanding Officer began his informal investigation. He already knew it was the driver who had left the document bound with plywood and with a tough string of parachute cord enabling it to be worn around the neck as a "dummy string." Martin approached him and reported formally, "Sir, First Sergeant Martin reports."

"First Sergeant, who is responsible for this breach of security?" the Regimental Commanding Officer asked.

"Sir, I am responsible for everything regarding security that happens, or fails to happen, in G Troop," Martin replied.

"What punishment do you believe you deserve for this heinous crime, First Sergeant? What should I give you?" the 52d Colonel asked quietly.

"At worst a letter of reprimand, Sir, and at the least a thousand pushups," Martin said.

"First Sergeant, your punishment will be as follows: You will not talk on the radio after midnight. You will sleep. At the conclusion of this exercise, you will deliver and install the souped up AN/VRC-46 radio now in your jeep, the one that makes AFN flutter when you key it up, to the base of the tower on range 82, install it in my jeep, and do a commo check with my Command Sergeant Major. One more time, stay off the radio after midnight." With that the Regimental Commanding Officer handed Martin the CEOI and returned his salute. He waited until he walked back into the building before pumping his fist and saying softly "I got your ass that time, First Sergeant. Oh it is good to be the King. I would do this shit for NOTHING."

Martin got over his shock quickly and was back to himself once in his vehicle.

"What happened, First Sergeant? Damn, I'm sorry," his driver Keith said almost in tears.

"The Regimental Commanding Officer troop led me Keith. We have to sleep tonight without talking on the radio after midnight. We will do frequency change and not talk. The Regiment thinks I am running the troop and letting the Troop Commander get off easy so they want him to sweat tonight without my help. Whatever we do, between midnight and 0600 we do not talk on the radio, just listen while we sleep. Then when this is over we have to DX our radio with the Regimental Commanding Officer's immediately," Martin said.

"He didn't say nothing about refueling the tanks, I guess," Specialist Richards said.

"No, Keith, he kind of likes the no surrender, never quit stuff," Martin said adding, "Shit like the CEOI happens. We are just going to have to be more careful about doing a quick check for our sensitive items when we leave one place for another. We are both so damn tired we couldn't find our asses with both hands."

At precisely 2400 hours Martin and his trusty companion Keith changed frequencies.

At 0002 their radio come alive, "Gator 7, Blackhorse 6, radio check!" Keith nearly stopped his First Sergeant's heart as he reached for the hand mike getting his hand slapped in the process while Martin shook his head violently. Twice more the Regimental Commanding Officer called the G Troop First Sergeant on the radio.

He then sent a final message to clear the call in the correct manner, "This is Blackhorse 6, nothing heard from Gator 7, OUT." And that was the last anyone heard about the lost CEOI.

Through the night, First Lieutenant Douglas did everything he was supposed to do and did it well. Staff Sergeant Webster and his team consolidated reports and re-supplied each of the platoons with all they required except a few tank parts. At 0600, the First Sergeant was again alive and on the radio. He had previously ordered egg McMuffin like sandwiches and fruit for breakfast. He and the supply crew issued the brown bags of food as the tanks rolled by and exchanged coffee thermos jugs with the vehicles from the supply room overstock. The tactics of the Regimental S3 to force them to operate without food or rest were blunted but not thwarted. They were still some tired puppies responding to yet another change of orders.

After assuming a defensive perimeter on a hilltop they were ordered into their Chemical Suits for a complete inspection by their respective O/Cs. The O/C's did not reckon on the utter proficiency and efficiency of Staff Sergeant Raefel Ardouin, AKA Tatoo, so named after the character in Fantasy Island, a TV Show then in re-runs on AFN. Staff Sergeant Ardouin had a slight drawl from New Orleans in his speech and was a fine Chemical NCO. He was also the NCO in charge of Sports Betting Pools, the Assistant Coach of the Football Team, the catcher for the Soft Ball team and the NCOIC in charge of booking excursions for troop trips to ski and to visit places of interest all over Europe. Tattoo was proof positive of the merit the effort by DA made to increase the Chemical Defense Posture of line units. The assignment of a certified Chemical NCO to each line outfit was a winner.

The troops loved Tatoo and if he did not know of something that was happening in the troop, it was of no importance. He was a human bulletin board. However, to stay on his good side, one needed to know his NBC stuff and keep it in top condition. Captain Dawson's influence was again felt, even months after his departure. He knew instinctively that making Staff Sergeant Ardouin into Mr. Everything put him in a position to influence the troop to be good at a facet of the Army that they loathed. The unofficial social director had the troop prepared to the highest level of NBC readiness in all phases, equipment, training, mask confidence, and knowledge of procedures and SOPs.

After running the troop through every NBC trick, the O/C's gave the all clear to all platoons except the 1ST Scout Platoon. The Chemical O/C, an Airborne Ranger, fell them in and marched them to a sealed GP medium that served as a field gas chamber. Four soldiers in four groups entered the chamber. Each set faced a different O/C for inspection and mask confidence exercise. The inspectors took their time inspecting so that any leaks would show. Not a single mask leaked and surprisingly, the groups were released without being forced to unmask inside the chamber. The reward for this proficiency was the privilege of joining the remainder of the troop at the Grafenwohr central testing site of the Physical Training test.

While surprised by this unexpected development, Martin was present at the site and led the Troop through the test scoring, passing each event with ease. He told the troops to pass the test and not to give their maximum effort. They were too tired, under fed, and dehydrated for a maximum effort. It was not for record, it was to see how much vigor they had left in them after the 36 hours of the exercise. Passing would be enough. They still had to go to the wash rack and get on the train or buses or drive their headquarters vehicles man miles home to Bad Kissingen. Martin had made up his mind that no one was driving anywhere without a full nights rest at Grafenwohr no matter where they had to sleep. Everyone passed the PT test easily with three perfect scores of 300 recorded.

The end result for G Troop was uncannily what their First Sergeant had predicted, third highest score in the Regiment. Fox Troop, schooled by G Troop before beginning the event, made appropriate changes, practiced the drills G Troop recommended. They did not adopt the practice of traveling with the trains in the center of the Troop for protection. They were an easy first in the Regiment. No one else was even close. It was G Troop's total dedication to schooling F Troop that impressed the Regimental Commanding Officer the most. The teamwork between the two units was the most gratifying thing he had seen on the trip. He went by to see the train up of Fox Troop. While there he made certain that Martin got to see him use his new radio.

"Tell me how you felt about the information sharing there, Martin," the Regimental Commanding Officer directed.

"Sir, at war we would want our brothers in our flank unit to know all we know when we knew it, without any delay. We have to train as we fight so teaching us all to do this now is smart. The old saying of 'He, who would learn, let him learn to teach is true'. We had the privates join in because they speak the modern language of the other young guys. They have more credibility but it also lets them buy into the process and become stake holders," Martin said seriously.

"Did you get your radio tuned up yet?" the Regimental Commanding Officer asked with a raffish grin.

"Yes, Sir, I did," Martin answered.

"You guys did a good job. It is always hard on the first unit. We will have to see how the scores hold up when Third Squadron is done," the Regimental Commanding Officer said returning their salutes.

1800 hours
29 Oct 1986
G Troop Admin Area

Captain Douglas came out of his office and sat on the small couch next to his First Sergeant's desk.

Martin stopped his work and gave his complete attention to his Commander. "The wives meeting with the Squadron Commander's wife is in the conference room Thursday night. Friday is a teacher's workshop so the kids are out of school. Attendance is spotty at the meetings for the troop because it is so hard to get a good baby sitter for the kids. Is there a way we could have a Halloween Party for the kids of the Troop during the hour or so of the meeting and keep them occupied, maybe with some Halloween events?" the Commander asked.

"Stand by, Sir. We need more brainpower and I need to see if the troops will help us out," Martin said as he turned to dial up the CQ desk.

"Specialist Harvey, this is First Sergeant Martin. Go through the rooms and get me one man from each down in my office. It don't make a shit how any of them are dressed. It ain't no detail and no work is involved. It is for planning a troop Halloween Party for the kids. Yes, right now, dammit! Thanks!" he said as he hung up the phone.

442

He then went to the butcher paper and drew some balloons, writing Trick or Treat = Soldier rooms; House of Horrors= Down Stairs Hall Way; Camp Fire=Troop formation area; Ghost stories=Videos small day room area (mattresses); Treat Costs: Cdr, First Sergeant, Troops. By the time he finished treats, the Commander had gently taken away his magic marker and crossed out all donors except himself. "If you guys do all of the work, I will pay all of the money plus buy everyone who runs a station a beer and every room a six pack or a bottle of wine, your choice. I will buy the hamburgers, hot dogs and marshmallows for the campfire as well as the buns. What is the estimate, First Sergeant, about 15 kids?" Captain Douglas asked.

The First Sergeant thought a moment before answering, "Let's plan on 24 kids and let the guys buy their sacks of candy for their rooms. Their rooms are their houses and they will receive the Army brats as if they were back home in America and they were their little brothers and sisters," he said looking up to the nods of approval from the guys from the two floors upstairs. "Let us take care of everything Captain and I will tell you what you owe when it is all over."

Martin got Sergeant Major Burton's very beautiful daughter, a college freshman, to act as the baby sitter for the small kids in the day room with the videos. On Thursday night he asked Second Lieutenant Chastain to pick her up and bring her to the troop. She arrived in a Witch's Costume looking more like a Princess than a witch with her gorgeous blond hair, blue eyes and her full woman's body doing full justice to the bodice of the dress. The small dayroom with mattresses turned into a jumping ground more than a video viewing room. As usual, the kids discovered a use for it the adults had not contemplated.

The Troops had a great evening of answering the door and guessing the identities of the Batmen, Pirates, Hoboes and Ninja Turtles. They handed out only the best of candy with no generic cheap stuff, it was all Hershey, Mars, Ritter and Tobelerone with nice apples and bananas as well.

The bigger kids loved the apple bobbing barrel while the young ones loved the fishing hole. A piece of canvas covered the roll around events calendar and blocked the end of the hallway from viewing by the kids. Cane fishing poles with clothes pins on fishing line were cast over the wall and then a bite was simulated by the soldier yanking the line once the prize was loaded.

The downstairs hallway was the house of horrors. Martin had to admit, the troops outdid themselves in the basement. Their diabolical natures came through. The Arms Room was the home of the cookie monster, with clanging chains and ghostly music. The training room became Freddie Krueger's bailiwick with a soldier in disguise in jeans and old fishing hat with moulage applied from the mass casualty kit. All of the light bulbs were removed and replaced by chemical lights. Large black plastic contractor bags from the maneuver damage kit were fashioned into hanging vines and traps canalized passersby so that they could be grabbed around their ankle by a hand from the Arms Room. There were several black lights and along with the green, purple and red chemical lights cast eerie shadows among the steam pipes and the hanging plastic bags.

Outside on the formation area paved with cobble stones, a large fire was burning complete with a hidden CO2 extinguisher. Logs were placed around the fire for seating while coat hangers and green sticks of wood were provided for roasting hot dogs and marshmallows, while the hamburgers cooked on a fireplace grill and popcorn popped in old fashioned fire place poppers with long handles. The shadows cast on the trees and the hedge by the fire provided just enough ambiance to scare the kids into a form of good behavior without their mothers present. There was also sweet cider and hot chocolate by the fire as it was getting nippy outside for children after dark.

The mothers could hear the delighted screams of the kids bouncing on the mattresses and they were content. They trusted the First Sergeant and the guys in the barracks. They looked out the Squadron Executive Officer's window with his wife and saw the fire blazing in the formation area with the kids roasting their hot dogs and laughing. Suddenly it occurred to them as if they were one person. Their kids were having a hell of a lot more fun than they were and they should adjourn their meeting and join the kids.

There was nothing for it but they had to see and do everything the kids had done earlier. The soldiers were delightful gentlemen and remained fully dressed for the wives to see their treats. The House of Horrors scared the Squadron Commander's wife so bad she peed her pants. Everyone loved the camp fire. Martin offered to have chairs brought out of the HQs to keep their clothes from getting dirty. Not a single chair was used or wanted. None of the wives wanted any comfort beyond a seat on the log beside their children roasting a hot dog or a marshmallow.

Each of the wives made a special point of thanking Captain Douglas and telling him what a great, once in a lifetime event the party was for them and the kids. He of course demurred and gave the credit to the soldiers and to his First Sergeant. He was very happy the event brought a smile to wives who attended the meeting. There were nine present that included an increase of six in one month. It was something to build on and not bad for a single guy in command without a wife.

Afterward, Captain Douglas was looking at the fire roasting a hot dog sitting by the First Sergeant who was having a cigar and drinking a Pepsi sans alcohol. "What do you think, First Sergeant?" he said.

"I think everybody had a damn good time, Sir. The troops got as much or more out of it than the kids. They act tough, but they miss home and Halloween is still a big deal in the small towns of America. They also miss their little brothers, sisters, nieces and nephews coming by the house with their costumes and shit. So it gave them a touch of home," Martin said.

"I just can't get over the level of detail, First Sergeant. Every station was engineered for safety, the guys on it were screened and briefed, we got Sergeant Major's gorgeous daughter, the damn fire is contained by rocks and you have a CO2 extinguisher that would put out a flaming Huey and it got done in just hours - what the hell? And oh, did I mention there is not the first clue there was ever a party in that barracks?" Captain Douglas said with a degree of wonder.

"I guess you're really gonna' miss it when you get out, aren't you Captain Douglas?" The First Sergeant said staring into the fire.

"How did you know? I haven't been slacking off, have I?" he asked.

"True lifer dogs do not wax nostalgic over a kids Halloween party. You are too good at making money in the stock market to stay in the Army. Plus there is too much stupid shit along with a double standard you cannot and will not accept as a life style," Martin said. He added, "You will finish troop command, go back to CONUS and resign at the end of your five year West Point obligation. You will make a million bucks, get box seats over the home team dugout and rarely get to the ball game after you have more than five employees. You will marry a beautiful, chic, smart, thin, small-breasted wench whose daddy has money. You will buy a house with six bathrooms, have one boy, one girl and live happily ever after," Martin said without smiling.

"And you, First Sergeant?" Captain Douglas asked staring into the fire.

"Ah yes, me. I will divorce my current wife, live alone for years, marry a younger woman, get a nice government job and retire with her in a place far from my home and be very happy and very broke," Martin said with a smile.

"But not Marty?" Captain Douglas said.

"No, not with Marty. In Germany we fit. In the States we would not. I have a hard time hanging with anyone from California. I hate the 'me first' life style. I will not be anyone's servant and that is how she intends to get re-established in California working for some zillionaire. He would cuss me out and I would choke him out and that would be it. No Captain, I'm going to go to Fort Polk, make Sergeant Major and retire in just a little over twenty years. I've done what I wanted to do and it is time to move on. You know we have the Dining Out coming up but if it is okay with you, I would like to hold off on planning that and just enjoy the afterglow of the Halloween Party. I'm going home now, Sir. I'll be in to do PT and some awards stuff and organize some stuff for the movers and hold baggage," Martin said.

"I am taking the Training Holiday. Brigetta and I are going to Belgium and the North Sea this weekend to see friends of ours. We are leaving about 0300. That is why I had the order cut for the Executive Officer to take charge, so it is good you will be here. I'll see you on Monday for PT, First Sergeant," Douglas said standing and saluting Martin who had stood up as well. It was time to go home, another good day with a good ending.

445

0600 hours
30 Oct 1986
First Sergeant Office
G Troop
Bad Kissingen, West Germany

Sergeant First Class Vic Jackson was waiting for his First Sergeant when he walked into his office. "Dammit First Sergeant, I was up half the night with Ryan. I'm just shitin' ya but he was sick as a dog from all of that candy, popcorn, hot dogs and cider. He threw that shit up until I was checking for toe nails. He said, "Oh Dad, we had so much fun." Debbie and I cried like babies over them kids and their great time last night. You know that they had a shitty life before we adopted them and last night was one of their best nights over here, ever. Debbie told me the women packed up and came over here with the kids. The soldiers woke up talking about it this morning. I know you hated to do it but damn we're all glad you came back. We hate to see you leave. Have you thought about extending?"

"Vic, I can't extend. I have to go home and face the music on my divorce from that old gal and E-9 is a lot different as far as assignments go. I am a newbie E-9 and I need to spend my first assignment in an Armor unit S3 shop and then my first assignment as a Command Sergeant Major, if I am selected in an Armor or Cavalry unit. I wish I could stay here but it is not to be," Martin replied with some sadness.

"How is that German gal taking that, First Sergeant?" Vic asked.

"She is a survivor. If we can figure out where we are going to live, we may get hitched but I doubt it. I have a good job offer to come back here with GE down the road and work simulation as a civilian. The money is really great but she never wants to come back to Germany except as a US citizen with a Visa. I will not do the job she has found for me, so there we are, two stubborn mules, neither one of us willing to give in to the other," Martin confided to his good friend.

"I told Debbie you would wait until you made E9 before getting a divorce. That way no matter what happens you have a job until age 55 and a good retirement but you can only do 29 years, not thirty right?" Vic asked, knowing the answer.

"No, I can't and wouldn't if I could. I am 43 now. Men who are not General Officers get awful sorry looking over the age of 45 in the Army unless they are exceptional athletes. It becomes a sinecure rather than a profession and I am not going to lose the respect of soldiers just to have a job. Very few Generals get sorry physically. They are exceptional men who are lifelong athletes and are too proud to go to seed. They are not going to put up with an old worn out Command Sergeant Major," Martin said thoughtfully.

"Who is taking your place in G Troop?" Jackson asked.

"Beats the shit out of me, Vic. What have you heard?" Martin asked back.

"I heard from the Knox grapevine that Murray made the list. Like how many Delbert Murrays are there in the primary zone for 19Z. Besides those damn guys have an inside line on that shit, it will be him and it will be damn quick, you know that Colonel. Probably be right after the dining out, ain't that the last thing he told you he wanted to happen?" Vic asked.

"What was that Vic? What did you say about the Dining Out? I was still stuck on Murray being the First Sergeant. He will do a good job. He is a faithful, loyal guy who likes and takes damn good care of his soldiers. He never quits and he is very thorough. I'll do all I can to help him," Martin said.

"Yeah, well if it is him, Douglas is gonna' have to command this mother for sure 'cause old Delbert ain't gonna' do it for him like some people we know. He ain't a bad guy but he is gonna' be an average First Sergeant, not a barn burner like the Squadron Commander thinks he is," Vic stated with a snort.

"Douglas has grown into the job, Vic. You have to admit he is doing well. He is a fast burner and they never get to be true experts. They move onward and upward too fast to learn everything about command they should. They either become quick studies or they learn how to cover their asses and fight to the last Staff Sergeant. Do you realize Lightning Joe Collins stayed in command of a Regiment for seven years after WW I?" Martin said pulling on his PT clothes.

"Top, there ain't no PT today. It's a training holiday," Vic said laughing.

"Vic, I don't do PT for the Army. I do it for me and I just happen to be in the Army," Martin said smiling. "I know what you are going to say, yeah and you will be doing that shit when you're 70, and I hope I will. And if they ever find me dead on the running track Vic, you tell them I said screw them all but nine, six for pall bearers, two for road guards and one to call cadence and oh yeah, the aluminum issue casket will be just fine."

As he ran up the slight incline to the track park, Martin could hear the sound of a VW van behind him. It was the Staff Duty Driver. "Colonel wants to see you, First Sergeant, he says right now for five minutes and then you can go back to PT," Martin just shook his head slightly and got into the front seat of the van.

Knocking on the Squadron Commander's door Martin could see him arranging his project cards on the beautiful mahogany holder he had made in the Wursberg craft shop before taking command. "Come in, First Sergeant," he said.

"Sir, First Sergeant Martin reports," he said knowing a formal report was rarely out of style.

"Thanks for the great party last night for the kids and then for having the wives see what the kids got to do. It literally scared the pee out of my wife but it was all she could talk about last night, that and the great improvement in G

447

Troop wives participation, thanks for that as well. I read your memo on the Dining Out. My wife and I will be there with bells on. You have done a superlative job as the First Sergeant of G Troop. It has been above and beyond anything I could have hoped to see. I want you to show Sergeant First Class (P) Delbert Murray of Fox Troop the ropes starting 10 Nov. Between then and your PCS work with him about two weeks and then come up here and work for me until you PCS. I am going to assign you up here. You need some slack time. If anybody wants you for something they are going to have to go through me. I know you have worked night and day for two long years with just one leave and you need to power down, questions?" he asked.

"No, Sir, no questions," Martin replied.

"How far are you going this morning, First Sergeant, six miles?" Lieutenant Colonel Millard asked with a smile.

"Yes, Sir, can't let the sweat get dry," Martin said, smiling as he saluted his commander who merely waved at him and resumed shuffling his priority cards.

As he ran, Martin was thinking about events to come, particularly the Dining Out. It wasn't his idea. It was the Squadron Commander's. He probably had one in his outfit along the way as a Lieutenant or a Captain. Martin did not like formal functions for Company sized units. But he understood how hard it was for the Border Cav to have a Squadron Social function of any kind. Somehow he knew the Command Sergeant Major would send regrets and he could count on Sergeant Major Burton as the guest speaker. He wanted to honor his friend and his wife. He was a great soldier. He might never again get a chance to speak to the troop he had served with in war so many years before. The First Sergeant was responsible for the event but he was happy knowing his NCOs would take care of the whole thing. His only desire was for a great band but knew they could not afford the price of a civilian one and he did not have the stroke for an Army one. There was no way he or anyone else could see far enough ahead to schedule an Army Band if they did qualify for it, which in the name of sense they could not. He told the group planning the event he wanted a piano player at the very least and a drummer for the posting of the Colors. Providing a band for company functions rated up there with giving 15 year olds Ferrraris to drive to school. Having a band would drive the ticket cost over the budgets of the troopers. It would be the last Troop event for him. His replacement would be on board and learning the ropes.

1630 hours
06 Nov 1986
G Troop
Bad Kissingen, West Germany

The Commander and the First Sergeant were getting dressed for the Dining Out. The First Sergeant was escorting the guest speaker, Sergeant Major Nicholas Burton and the Squadron commander with their wives to the func-

448

tion. They would use the Squadron van for the event. The guests did not know they would travel the last mile of the journey in an open carriage escorted by one officer and three G Troop NCOs mounted on Black and Roan colored horses wearing sabers and Stetsons.

The two of them discussed the event until Captain Douglas was certain all was in readiness and nothing more could or should be done to ensure its success. It was time to go fetch the guests and that was the First Sergeant's duty tonight. The Captain, as usual, had plans after the event and intended to sky up for his love nest in Fulda as soon as possible.

During the late morning reconnaissance of the Hotel where the Dining Out would be held Martin began to feel the event would come off well. Just seeing how the driveway to the Hotel led through an arch of oaks before reaching a very nice structure of stone with lead glass windows untouched by WW II added to his ease. Hearing the Hotel had remained in the same family for over 200 years was even more good news.

The dining room was very well appointed with large tables for eight, a head table for the Commanders, Sergeant Major Burton and the First Sergeant. The entrees for the evening were either baked chicken or Jaeger Schnitzel. A nice fruity wine was available for toasting. The tablecloths were of good white linen, the table service was good stainless flatware and the glasses were crystal. Candles adorned all of the tables. There was a nice dance floor and a very nice bar with every sort of liquor choice to delight an epicurean palate.

There was also a very nice baby grand piano and a curious mixture of band instruments. It dawned on Martin that these lunatics may have hired a one man band. A one man band would have been too much parody for him to stand on one of his last nights in charge of a unit.

"Guys, tell me the entertainment is not a one man band playing a drum set, honking a Zeppo Marx horn while blowing a harmonica and farting in ¾ time," he said.

"No, First Sergeant, but given the ticket price, all we could float was a trio of a trombone/sax player, a drummer and a guitar player who can also play the piano during dinner. I made sure he can play Chopin," Sergeant First Class Vic Jackson stated.

The staff, led by the owner Frau Hilda Brumfeldt, were German country girls who could have stepped off the pages of any one of a hundred years of Germany history. Their jutting breasts, ample hips, sturdy calves, blond hair and lovely smiles were marvelous. They projected good health and sold the place with their cheerful attitudes.

Frau Hilda led off saying, "Your Sergeant was very clever, Herr Speise. His choices enabled us to make a profit and your company to have a good time. It was vonderful doing business with him."

One look at Sergeant First Class Barnes told Martin he had nailed the old gal at some point along the way. "That is good to hear Frau Hilda. He is a good man in every respect," Martin said with a slight smile. Barnes was one of two Sergeants First Class the School Command Sergeant Major at Fort Benning had sent to replace the great Staff Sergeant Gilbert Ramos.

Every time Martin looked at Barnes he laughed inside at the Officers who bitched about his selection of Ramos for Bradley Master Gunner training because of his apparent lack of English skills. Ramos was so apparently 'screwed up', that Benning had kept him after the course, sent two Airborne, Ranger, Scout guys in his place, had promoted him to Sergeant First Class and made him a Division Chief. Yeah, that was one screwed up greaser all right! Fricking gringo officers, what did they know! Wish to hell old Jesus was going to be here tonight but it was not to be. He would be teaching his last class as they were posting the Colors.

As the carriage stopped at the entrance to the Hotel, Martin dismounted from the footman's step on the rear and opened the door helping the ladies to descend. Their beaming husbands followed. Lieutenant Colonel Milliard took Martin's elbow saying, "This is where Debbie and I spent our honeymoon when I commanded G Troop, 14th Cav as a second command. We love this place. Thank you so much for selecting it for the Dining Out. It has a special place in our hearts."

Martin could see Sergeant Major Burton's look and he nearly laughed out loud but knowing the Squadron Commander would take it wrong, he said instead, "I did not know, Sir. I'm glad you approve. I'm sure we are all going to have a nice time."

As the Troop commander came forward to escort the group inside, Sergeant Major Burton handed Martin his notes for his address saying, "You have more dumb luck than anyone I have ever met, picking their honeymoon spot." Sergeant Major Burton then followed the troop commander into the hotel shaking his head and looking back smiling.

A good time was had by all. Martin got drunker than he wanted. The Squadron Commander spent more money buying everyone a drink than either he or his wife intended. The waitresses got into the act late with some of the single soldiers. Hilda provided some free champagne and it was a lovely evening without a single reportable incident or accident of any kind.

Sergeant Major Burton gave a good speech. A magical evening for love ensued and at least three conceptions happened that could be called accidents with some lovely children as a result.

A great tradition for a fall Dining Out was established for the unit. It was a great way to close things out for Martin after his most rewarding assignment to date. There was just nothing better this side of war for an E-8 to do than serve as the First Sergeant of a forward deployed Cavalry Troop.

Martin and Marty made plans to meet in California in the spring. Both knew that would not happen. They spent two very happy weeks living a ho-

450

neymoon existence in the country condo. They laughed and danced in the small cafes of the town that catered to the working class Germans there for the rest kure'. He really enjoyed her company and could have easily spent the rest of his life with her there were it not for her Teutonic dedication that sent her straight and unswerving to her short term future.

It was amusing to see the couples paired off for their night on the town and to see them all scurry back to their rooms for bed check. The German Nanny state was paying for their rest cure and rest they must, in their own room at the prescribed hour for retirement. After bed check it was anybody's guess where they would end up though most were monogamous with their kure' friend they met during their trip. Martin often mused about their return home and if they would put a different move on their respective spouse that they had learned on their trip. All societies have their quirks and the rest cure taken alone without the spouse was just another unique thing of many for Germany.

Life in Germany was full of lessons and Martin learned yet another on his time away from the unit. Although working directly for the Squadron Commander, he had to contend at least one more time with Command Sergeant Major Attleborourgh. The Command Sergeant Major was an artilleryman who wangled the assignment to Bad Kissingen in order to get him as close to his wife at Amberg as possible. He spent every feasible moment there rather than in BK. He deeply resented anything and anyone that detracted from the ability to visit his wife. He would sort through the DA 4187s and Requests for Personnel Action that he kept in rows on his desk top, make wise observations about the obvious to his six First Sergeants and be gone at 1630 daily. He had sent for Martin with four days remaining on his time on leave to the country.

"Yes, Sergeant Major, what can I do for you?" Martin asked.

"You can do your damn job, First Sergeant. That damn guy, what's his name, Jerrold?" he said trying to prompt Martin to give him Delbert Murray's name having failed to learn it in the three weeks of his assignment as one of his First Sergeants.

Martin was not playing the game today except on his terms, "I don't know anyone named Jerrold, Sergeant Major."

"The hell you don't. He is the guy taking your place as First Sergeant of G Troop," Sergeant Major Attleborourgh said without embarrassment or chagrin. "He is asking me, me, his Command Sergeant Major, First Sergeant questions about how to do shit in the unit. You were supposed to tell him everything and get him straight before you left. You did not do it and he is acting like he don't know shit. I ain't here to answer his questions and teach him to be no First Sergeant. That was your job. You are going to stay here with him until the day your plane leaves. Do you understand me?" he added with the spit flying and wild eyed as a March Hare.

451

"Good evening, First Sergeant Martin. I see you violated my orders and are in fatigue uniform. Could you tell me why you did that?" his Squadron Commander asked quietly.

"I would rather not be the source of that report, Sir," Martin said politely.

"I want to know and I want to know now, First Sergeant," he said.

"The Command Sergeant Major is not happy with First Sergeant Murray's ability to function after our transition and he is particularly upset that he would have the temerity to ask him questions about how to proceed," Martin replied.

"First Sergeant, I command this Squadron. Until I send for you do not return except to sign out before going to Frankfurt one day early to catch your flight. That is all," he said saluting Martin. As Martin departed he saw the door closing to Command Sergeant Major Attleborourgh's office. He would have loved to have been a fly on the wall for that heart to heart.

CHAPTER 15 – LAST GUIDON

"You only get one chance to make a good first impression." Anonymous.

0930 hours
01 Dec 1986
Miami, FL

"Good Morning, Command Sergeant Major, this is First Sergeant Martin calling you from leave in Florida. I have a reporting date of 28 Dec 86 to your Battalion," Martin said on the kitchen phone of the Florida house watching the kids do their morning swim.

"Yes, First Sergeant, you be taking over Headquarters Company on your arrival!" Command Sergeant Major James R. Washington stated.

"Sergeant Major, I was hoping to get a tank company as I have never had a TO&E one with so few people. The last thing I wanted was an HHC," Martin said politely.

"So you tellin' me you refusin' to go to HHC, First Sergeant?" Command Sergeant Major Washington asked testily.

"No, Sergeant Major. I will go where you send me without complaint. It will be my fifth company sized outfit so I am very confident I will be able to do the job. I was merely staring a preference not an objection, Sergeant Major," Martin said honestly.

"All right, all right, I got you now. We lookin' forward to you comin' and to meetin' you, First Sergeant. If you need a little more time or somepin' happens, call me, gotta' go to formation," Command Sergeant Major Washington said hanging up his phone.

His bosom buddy, Sergeant Major Jerome Arbuckle had been listening at the door. Arbuckle had 34 years service with 12 years in grade as a Sergeant Major as he asked, "New First Sergeant givin' you trouble already huh, James?"

"Nope, he figured out real quick he needed to shut up and execute. He the rankinest man and he gwin to Headquattters, and that be all there is to it, uh huh! He be all right. He be an Academy Graduate, and is all set for E-9 when the list comes out in the spring. We won't have him long. He sounds like he has a lot of confidence but we'll just have to see about that. Hey, we need to go hear what the Wild Man got to say this mawnin'. What a guy huh?"

Arbuckle who fought a slight stutter his whole life chimed in, "There ain't no tellin' what the great man has come up with today to sway duh masses and mystify duh leaders but it will be different, you can bet on that."

Both senior men laughed as they made their way to the Brigade formation area. At least once per month, the Cold Steel Brigade held a Brigade Formation at a small amphitheater in the front of the Brigade Chapel. Everyone not

453

required for phone watch, not in confinement, hospital and present for duty was expected to be present. Formal reports were rendered by Battalion Commanders and the formation was conducted in accordance with FM 22-5, the Drill and Ceremonies Manual to the last detail. The Brigade Commander conducting these formations was truly one of the last of a breed. He knew and his men knew it. An OCS Graduate, he had been selected for that course one smoky evening in Central America by the Commander of the 82d Airborne Division known at Fort Bragg by its old soldiers as simply, The Division. The singular reference implying that it was the only one rather than merely the only one of its kind, which it became as a result of budget cuts in later years.

Earlier, the Division Headquarters was under fire by a highly motivated sniper operating just outside the unit's perimeter. Several members of the Division had been killed and wounded by this individual. The present Colonel of the Cold Steel Brigade, then First Sergeant Noble Barrett, was delivering some administrative papers to the Headquarters. The sniper fired his normal three rounds and promptly disappeared. The Division was inhibited by the State Department rules to avoid collateral damage. These admonitions precluded use of the proverbial baseball bats of artillery and recoilless rifles to kill the proverbial pissant.

The Division commander had had enough and he reverted to type as an Infantry Officer. Seeing First Sergeant Barrett in the back of the Division Tactical Operations Center waiting patiently for the meeting to be over in order to transact his business, he made up his mind. Standing up he halted Division Intelligence Officer in mid-excuse as to why the Dominican sniper was still killing and wounding his men.

"Thanks, Jim, I think we have the picture. Gentlemen, we have a problem. This damn sniper is doing what he damn well pleases secure in the knowledge we are limited in how we can reply. Well, we have a very potent weapon we have yet to employ to silence him once and for all, the US Army First Sergeant. This is a lesson in problem solving for all of the aspiring officers out there who want to become Division Commanders, so pay attention. First Sergeant Barrett, come up here."

As Barrett arrived at the front of the crowded and smoky TOC to stand with his Commanding General in front of the assembled leaders of his Division he was neither awed or frightened. He was only awed by God, never by men. Whatever was to come, he could handle it.

"First Sergeant, we have a sniper operating within this area," the Commanding General said drawing a small circle on the map with a grease pencil, and then filling in the words 'eliminate him.'

"What do you have there?" the Commanding General asked.

"Reports, Sir," First Sergeant Barrett replied.

"G1, take these papers from First Sergeant Barrett. Get them where they have to go," the Commanding General ordered.

"Any questions, First Sergeant?" the Commanding General asked.

"No, Sir!" First Sergeant Barrett replied with a stone face.

Barrett knew all about the damn sniper and the goofy rules of engagement. The enemy operated from behind concrete block walls, he fired no more than three rounds, he used firing positions in schools, churches and family homes as he killed and wounded US soldiers. The mission from the Commanding General was to eliminate him. That was simple enough for Barrett, he would kill the bastard. He had no ethical issue with the mission, he was from Arkansas and down there a man was taught from childhood that some people just needed killin'.

He would do so in a way calculated to be efficient and that would discourage similar behavior. Barrett brought up a .50 caliber M2 Heavy Barrel Machine Gun. He personally set the head space and timing of the weapon and configured it for operation. He interviewed the soldiers serving opposite the circle the Commanding General had drawn on the map. The soldiers narrowed the sniper's known choices to three favored locations.

Predictably, the sniper fired one shot and ducked down behind the concrete cinder block wall from one of the locations described by the privates. First Sergeant Noble Barrett fired the M2 heavy barrel at the wall the sniper elected to hide behind some 600 yards distant. The shock action of the .50 caliber ball round produced a huge amount of pieces of concrete spall from the inside of the wall. The pieces of concrete became ballistic projectiles akin to buckshot from a shotgun when they were displaced by the single round of .50 machine gun. The concrete "buckshot" splattered the sniper all over the back wall of the small apartment in what was to be his last firing position. It was the last sniper fire the division received. It had been done within three hours of receiving the Commanding General's mission.

The object lesson was not lost on the Division leadership as the Commanding General succinctly summarized at the next day's tactical update, "There are few new lessons to be learned. There are only new people to relearn the old ones. If you want something done, give the mission to a busy NCO and leave him alone to complete it."

First Sergeant Noble Barrett was named to the next class of Officer Candidate School at Fort Benning, Georgia, where, to no one's surprise, he was the Honor Graduate.

The Division was Darwinian in that it embodied the doctrine of survival of the fittest both in its conscious and subconscious mindsets. Each member of this tribe within the Army was measured first and foremost against the standard of jump status. That is to say the demonstrated physical and mental ability to hurl oneself out the door of a perfectly good airplane at a height selected as best for mission accomplishment. A height selected with a first

455

consideration of future operations balancing risk of ground fire against the probability of main parachute failure rather than individual safety. At 600 feet altitude, a reserve parachute is of no use. The dictum of mission first needs no more emphasis than executing a parachute jump without a reserve.

The next measurement applied against each member of the tribe with leadership aspirations was the ability to pass through a series of schools originally designed to develop soldiers physically and mentally for Infantry operations under the most arduous conditions. As the leaders of this tribe advanced in knowledge and experience, they were awarded badges for wear on their dress uniforms and to be sewn onto their fatigues. Initially, in the eyes of all who then saw the array of badges, the 82d tribe member gained instant credibility. The badge wearer then either improved upon his first impression or lost ground depending on the results of his leadership on the fortunes of the unit he led. It was not a perfect system by any means. Its many trails through the human psyche were, and would remain, a mystery to both civilians and those "leg" soldiers who had not shared in the hardship, danger and privation of this unique Army tribe.

Tribe members who left the familiar surroundings of the insular world of the 82D to serve in the big Army were regarded with a mixture of awe, fear and respect by the soldiers who either could not, or would not, match their accomplishments. The insular nature of the tribe was a source of great strength within its ranks. Its lack of organic assets to sustain itself in the "fight" past 96 hours made it a fire brigade. Rushed to trouble spots around the world from Arkansas to enforce school integration to the Dominican Republic to buttress the chosen government, The Division was an instrument of US foreign policy. An inside joke portrayed the Secretary of Defense as in charge of the 82d but the Secretary of State as in command.

None the less, notable members of the tribe were graduated and promoted to other duties outside the tribe. Others were banished for physical or mental failures also left to take their places in the Big Army as their faults were minor there. It was in the Big Army they learned they were outnumbered 1,500,000 to 15,000. Not awed by numbers, they simply set out to make the Big Army conform to the best standards of The Division in so far as the candy ass nature of the "leg" wieners they were forced to lead could be expected to progress without being airborne.

The more erudite expatriates from the 82 Tribe demonstrated over time the intrinsic value of the tribe by infusing the remainder of the Army with their spirit, courage and dedication to noble causes by daily example. During times of relative peace, those who risk their lives with abandon assume the leadership role of those who do not. Through their qualities of balls and brains these few influenced the behavior of thousands of soldiers of Combat Arms.

At today's formation of the Cold Steel Brigade, the Brigade Commander was to give a short talk on the goals for the Brigade and read from a letter of a former Command Sergeant Major for the unit about courage in war. It was cornball to the extreme for any latent civilians in the crowd but the true soldiers loved it.

Noble Barrett loved his soldiers. When he justified his seemingly harsh methods of Article 15 under the Uniform Code of Military Justice of fines for not wearing the helmet, failure to fasten a helmet chin strap, failure to apply camouflage face paint, building of a sleeping "hooch" with a cover over a jeep in a Division where canvas tops were issued but forbidden to be used, failure to dig in, tampering with MILES, failure to salute, failure to be armed at all times in the field or the loss of equipment, he knew he was saving lives of his beloved men.

He knew he was right because of his service on six tours in the Republic of Vietnam in the toughest units and in the some of the biggest battles ever fought there. A second offense caused the modest fines of $50 & $100 to increase to ½ month's pay for two months and for those with the temerity, or stupidity, to be found wanting a third time, immediate discharge in Chapter 13 for Unsuitability. The rank of the offender was irrelevant. It was the offense that was paramount in his mind. A Major got the same treatment as a PFC.

Colonel Barrett accepted every chance he could get to train at the National Training Center. He had four palm trees, each signifying one NTC rotation, painted on his trusty steed, Cold Steel Six. He was noted for leaping from his OH-58 onto a retreating OPFOR Recon Scout riding a motor cycle to prevent him reporting the location of the Brigade Tactical Operations Center. To say he was zealous in his pursuit of excellence was a classic under-statement. Presumably the OPFOR Scout got over his broken shoulder, an injury that Cold Steel soldiers dismissed as "the fortunes of war."

It was to this environment First Sergeant Martin reported on 7 Jan 87. He was assigned to HHC 3/70 Armor in the Cold Steel Brigade of Colonel Noble Barrett. The 5th Infantry Division was in a cycle of two weeks in the field and two weeks in Garrison. The schedule was killing the unit.

The most telling comparisons between where he had come from and where he found himself soon became starkly clear to Martin. The 5th Mech had a supply priority lower than the Chinese National Guard and it was on Formosa.

These poor bastards, as you were First Sergeant, you poor bastards now, ain't got nothing. They are not even allowed to have canvas on their wheeled vehicles and it is always raining here. Some leader in the Division's past history had decreed canvas cuts down on visibility. Vision to see the threat is life in combat, ergo, canvas is bad, remove the canvas. Someone needed to tell these poor dumb bastards about the care and the cost of NODs (Night Observation Devices) complex radios and electronic systems,M1 thermal sights, and in gen-

457

eral, modern life. It was amazing seeing an entire heavy division exist as a living anachron-
ism circa WWII. The short version could be "stupid and proud of it." But, if the leadership
judged effectiveness by the degree one adapted, he could adapt as well as anyone. No one had
yet told him he had to check his brain at the door and reclaim it in time to go back to the
Blackhorse, which, oh by the way, had some silly shit of its own to live down.

Lieutenant Colonel Salvatore G. Milano was an interesting man. He was a tanker. He was heavily built with the thick neck, body and legs of a lineman, which he had been at Penn State in his youth. In the manner of some big men, he deliberately couched his voice in nearly a whisper so as to ensure his listener focused on the message rather than the messenger. For an old and nearly deaf tanker like his new First Sergeant, this trait made conversation difficult but not impossible.

"First Sergeant, I want you to raise the morale of HHC. I will be behind you all of the way in order to achieve that goal. You are over qualified for your job like a lot of people in the Army. You won't be with us long and it may seem to you the task I have given you is simple, it is not. But it can be done. The HHC is the engine that pulls the Battalion. The TO & E now has all of the maintenance and support assigned to HHC. The teams of specialists that provide the mechanics, medics and transport to the Line Companies are tasked out during operations from the parent HHC. It is difficult to balance the competing demands from the four line companies with the need to train, supply, discipline and control the soldiers of the HHC. Your commander rarely sees his soldiers and when he does, it is often in a negative situation. Find a balance and make it work. Let me know if I can help you in any way. Keep me informed. We will be seeing a lot of each other in the field and in garrison. Please don't stand on ceremony. Tell me what I need to know when I need to know it. What do you think about your assignment?"

Martin thought carefully before answering saying, "Sir, this is a good assignment for me. It is a challenge but I will be a better Sergeant Major for the experience. There are more supporters than trigger pullers and making them part of the unit effort is important. I'm looking forward to it."

Whispering Sal squared himself at his desk and returned Martin's salute saying, "I'm glad you are with us, First Sergeant."

"Glad to be here, Sir," Martin said and departed.

The best description of the Company Commander was "bright eyed and bushy tailed." Martin learned from him that he had personally been selected by Colonel Noble Barrett as the replacement for the previous Commander whom Barrett had relieved in the field. He also learned that the emphasis in the company was on discipline through UCMJ via 117 Article 15 punishments in the past 7 months. Clearly, the long list of soldiers on the "hot check list," failure to pay just debts, traffic tickets and domestic abuse that was rampant was symptomatic of deeper issues. As he reviewed the "smith files," a file on each soldier maintained by the First Sergeant in a quasi legal manner, the

458

training schedule and the past offenses rating punishment, the problems were clear. Martin knew it was not enough to treat the symptoms; he had to cure the disease.

The Commander was an Infantryman. Captain Frederick L. Sims believed implicitly training his troops in basic soldiering as well as rappelling, ambush techniques, rifle marksmanship and Common Skills Task Testing would get him where he wanted to go. He knew next to nothing about a tank or track vehicle. He remained an Airborne Ranger and light fighter untainted by Armor shortcomings. As such, it was clear to him track vehicles only existed to draw fire and were the refuge of cowards. The fact that his mechanics were charged to maintain the vehicles of the Battalion and his other soldiers to sustain it in every way was viewed as an obstacle to his desire to train them all to be Infantrymen. He sincerely believed that if he could get all of his men to pass the EIB, the reminder of the issues in the unit would disappear. He also took to heart the Brigade Commander's admonition that he was not to worry about property and other administrative details but to bring smoke on the recalcitrant, buoy the few good soldiers of the unit and chapter the rest. He further displayed the disturbing tendency to look first to the Brigade Commander for guidance and direction rather than to his rater, the Battalion commander.

Rather than be put off by these facts, Martin arrived at his course of action within 10 minutes of the briefing by the Commander. He would give the Commander what he needed, not what he wanted, but he would make sure he never figured out the difference.

A series of interviews with the rank and file followed by sessions with the team leaders and some management by walking around would flesh out the strategy for the turnaround of the unit. The boys did not know it yet but the maestro from Carnegie Hall was about to become the high school band director.

Martin knew how good they could learn to play the concert of Mars the God of War. It was the age old problem. The NCO cadre was not meeting the needs of the situation. It was being driven by the egos, prejudices, and ambitions of the officers without the NCO buffer of Sergeants between the officers and the soldiers. It began with the outgoing First Sergeant and the Commander as they had convinced themselves the lash was more fitting than leadership. The soldiers of this unit were just as good as any in the Army when properly led, from the front. Chains like the chain of command were meant to be pulled not pushed. It was hard to push a chain but easy enough to pull one. Chains had a tendency to bunch up, kink and get tangled when they were pushed. This one had been pushed for months and it was damn sure kinked.

The central issue was clear to Martin. The simplistic notion of the Division strategy to deploy all maneuver units for two weeks in the field and two weeks in the rear was not sustainable. It failed as it did not take into account the flow of parts for the antique equipment, the vacancies in low density MOSes, the pace of modernization, the pace of NTC rotations and the price in wear and tear on soldiers and their families. It was training for training sake. Martin did not know if the Emperor knew he had no clothes, if he liked being naked, if no one had told him he was butt naked, or that he had been told and had shot the messenger. He suspected it was the last. It did not matter at his level. The Commanding General was not in his outfit. He was in the FORSCOM Commander's squad.

Martin's job as the HHC First Sergeant was so easy in the field it bordered on the ridiculous after the pressures of a Blackhorse Cavalry troop. The Mortar platoon, the staff sections and the remainder of the unit save the Scout Platoon had organic transport to pick up meals and they coordinated their own fuel delivery. The scouts had six tracks and the very best NCOs and First Lieutenants in the battalion to lead them. Once they understood Martin's method of re-supply and bought into his sense of urgency, they began to complain they were eating too well. The platoon had never been fed three times per day under the old First Sergeant, never got fruit and seldom got hot food. The hardest thing he had to face was keeping his wallet and the administrative papers he carried from time to time, dry. With some ingenuity, plastic bags and some waterproof bags from supply, he made it happen. Sleeping in a tent with a heater was new though the tent was an abortion, the stove leaked diesel fumes forcing him to get two tarps and build a tanker tent for him and his driver. No more stoves.

Four days into the field problem, Martin was summoned to the Tank Range to report to the Battalion Commander. It was raining steadily when he arrived at Whispering Sal's jeep. He found him eating an MRE with great relish and being a true Ranger, licking the inside of the packages before discarding them. "First Sergeant, the Secretary of Defense and the Sec Army will be here in the morning to observe Tank Table VIII. We do not have, nor are we projecting the ability to get the Class V from the ASP to this range with the assets available to HHC. Our vehicles cannot pass inspection by the ASP to be certified to haul ammunition. Fix it."

"Yes, Sir," Martin said saluting and returning to his vehicle.

Martin had an ace in the hole no one recognized. He had Specialist Fourth Class BJ McMasters as his driver, under protest, but he had him. BJ acted as Martin's mental foil telling him when he was wrong, when he was right and guiding him about the local policies and idiosyncrasies of the unit and Fort Polk. BJ and the First Sergeant had a very nice water proof lap robe and a pair of vehicle heaters that could have boiled water. They wore their wet suits; web gear and Kevlar helmets and were almost comfortable even in the rain. The way they laughed, joked, and carried on in the rain was of itself cheering to the soldiers in HHC. The E-9s of the unit and of the Brigade thought they

460

were nuts but their cheerful demeanor was not lost on the senior officers. They knew a good example when they saw one and were very pleased.

Handing BJ a large cigar, Martin lit his as the rain slowed to a mist. Watching BJ light up, Martin said, "The support platoon is broke. I want to go to the ASP and look the person in the eye that is failing the trucks. I suspect it is all our fault but I want them to know we are working the issue hard and will get some ammo today and some by 0600."

"What is the story for the ASP, BJ?" Martin asked.

"The gal that runs the ASP is strict but she ain't mean. She is a Texan and from an old Texas family. She says she is too old and too ugly to go to jail and everything at the ASP is going to be done right or not at all. There ain't nothing special about the vehicle inspection at the ASP. They check the same stuff they do in a roadside but they don't go under it with a creeper. They do check the CV boots."

"All lights and safety equipment have to work and be present to include the jack and spare. The signs and placards have to be right. The driver has to be properly licensed for the vehicle. It has to have its pioneer equipment as well as the right canvas and rear strap. The guys in our support platoon are not trained or disciplined enough to do their jobs. Unlike the Cav, they put duds in charge not studs. They just play at war here, Top. They do not know what is important, but hell; you'll soon show 'em, startin' about now," BJ said laughing loudly.

"Let's go see the lady, BJ, quick, fast and in a hurry."

"Headhunter 6, this is Headhunter Seven, OVER."

"Seven, this is Six, OVER."

"Six, Seven, enroute to the ASP and then the motor pool to fix the Class V issue for the demo tomorrow and for future operations, OVER."

"Seven, Six, where did you get that mission, OVER."

"Six, Seven, the mission is from your next higher, OVER."

Long, long pause then, "Seven, this is Six uuuuuuuh Roger, OUT."

Arriving at the ASP, Martin immediately went inside. Everyone there seemed to have a purpose. The atmosphere was calm, orderly and professional. A lady who could only be Mrs. Hockley asked him politely, "Can I help you, First Sergeant? It isn't very often we ever see a First Sergeant out here. I'm Mrs. Hockley and I am in charge of the Fort Polk ASP."

Martin took her hand and gently squeezed it and shook it saying, "I am happy to meet you at last, Mrs. Hockley. You are much nicer and more pleasant than your detractors would have had me believe. You have a very good and professional operation going here. I am Ron Martin and I am the First Sergeant of HHC 3/70 Armor and we are ignorant at the moment with regard to the transport of ammunition." The entire office erupted in laughter and relief at his honesty and tact.

461

Ms. Hockley smiled broadly but she did not laugh saying, "We do not do courtesy inspections First Sergeant. We don't have time and we are not Motor Sergeants. Here is the form we use to guide the inspection of vehicles prior to issuing ammunition for transport."

"Ma'am, I would not ask you to do a courtesy inspection. You are correct. It is our job to present you with a vehicle that meets the standards for transport of ammunition. I intend to do that here in short order. I just wanted to be certain we could get what vehicles I can put together combat loaded to meet my requirements for the Sec Def and I wanted to meet you. I wanted to tell you we are going to learn as a unit to meet the standard of the ASP and to make whatever happened before now just a distant bad memory," Martin said cheerfully.

"We would prefer to out load everything at once onto large enough set of trucks. But we both know if it gets too ugly, the DOL will be or could be, hauling that ammo to the range. You get us good trucks and we will load the ammo you request, even if it takes more than one load out," she said with a smile.

"Ma'am it was nice to meet you. Hopefully, we can get the support platoon to a state of training and discipline that it will not be necessary for us to meet on a professional basis. It has been a pleasure to meet all of you folks and we will see you shortly with some decent vehicles," he said taking his leave from the group of DA civilians, noting there were no soldiers present in the building.

On arrival at the motor pool Martin found the support platoon at what could most charitably be called mill-around-mill. He sent BJ to get the Platoon Sergeant out of his dry truck, a semi-tractor with canvas and he gathered the platoon in a vacant maintenance bay.

"Men, I am not interested in excuses or war stories about the ASP. What interests me is the successful draw of ammunition by your platoon leader and the ammo NCO this afternoon and at 0600 in the morning, if it comes to that. We, meaning the soldiers of the support platoon, will get it right. There are five bays in this building. Line up the trucks in a murder line to pass over the pit in the next bay for inspection of the running gear and leaks. Drivers stay in the vehicle. We will do the light check in that bay. Until your vehicle passes the leak inspection, we will not make any cosmetic repairs to the lights, horn, wipers, etc; once the truck passes the leak test and we confirm we have CV boots in hand, it moves to light repair. We will not repair any tires until after we draw the ammo but will only do a direct exchange. We will also issue spare bulbs, lens covers and repair tape there. The jacks, triangles, and other OVM will be pooled in order to get six trucks through the inspection at the ASP. We will prepare ten trucks to get six through the inspection. When we arrive at the ASP, I want all windows, mirrors and lights to be cleaned and

462

polished. I want them to see you doing it. Now let's get started. BJ and I will inspect all vehicles out in the motor pool where my jeep is sitting now."

"BJ, find out where they are hiding the good shit and get enough of it for ten trucks. See Master Sergeant Shuster and tell him we need his emergency stash. He has more time in grade than I have in the Army; I know he has a stash."

Seeing the soldiers of the support platoon laugh, Martin said, "Hey guys, I'm not shittin' you, Shuster the Rooster, has 32 years' service and 19 in grade and I've got 16 years of service. I wouldn't shit you guys, you're my favorite TURDS. Move it people."

The soldiers of the support platoon wanted very much to be proud of their contribution to the unit. They wanted to belong to an outfit that had its shit together. Their PSG was a ROAD soldier (Retired On Active Duty) and the First Lieutenant was an idiot. He had failed at everything he ever did in the Battalion and had been stashed in the Support Platoon by the former Battalion Executive Officer. He was very upset at having his platoon taken from him by the high handed actions of the First Sergeant and intended to protest to the S4 and the HHC Company Commander as soon as he saw them. He could not believe his eyes as he saw both of them get out of their jeeps and come walking toward First Lieutenant Snell and First Sergeant Martin.

Softly Martin told First Lieutenant Snell, "Just shut up and smile while I brief the Captains, ELL TEE."

"Good afternoon Gentlemen. First Lieutenant Snell has the effort completely organized and well in hand. While I was at the ASP, he got his lads in action back here. I got here in time to find some extra stuff for him. He is now going to walk you both through his plan for remedial action to get these vehicles through the ASP inspection and take the ammo to the tank range. Go ahead Lieutenant, brief the Captains, it's your platoon and your show," Martin said making a grand gesture with his open palm and stepping to one side.

First Lieutenant Snell might have had some faults, but he knew a good deal when he saw one. Recalling Martin's words he used to organize the effort, he began his briefing by saying, "The First Sergeant was a big help. For instance, he pointed out station one, leak and running gear was the main point of failure. When we got the vehicle through there we will then fix the lights and equip it with the OVM and safety items from a pool of the First Sergeant's driver brought to me ...." Martin smiled broadly as he listened to young First Lieutenant repeat his earlier instructions almost word for word. He was a sure bet to be a great briefer at the Pentagon someday.

As he turned to look at a truck, Specialist Fourth Class Yardley said, "That's good shit, First Sergeant, you taking care of him. First Lieutenant Snell needed a break, he sure ain't getting no help out of the PSG. Besides

463

after you put the band aid on this joker of a platoon, we still have to live with the ELL TEE. I learned something too, First Sergeant."

"What did you learn, Yardley?" Martin asked.

"I guess I re-learned it, First Sergeant. I learned it from my Dad first. He was a county AG agent and knew everybody. He always said you should leave a man his dignity when you were helping him out. He said if a man brought dignity of his own to the job he never had to rob the other fellow of his," Yardley said as he went to work on his truck.

"BJ, post," Martin said summoning his driver.

"Yes, First Sergeant, what now?" BJ asked.

"So, BJ, if we do not have the right number and type of mechanics as we convert from the GOARs to five tons and we have these thirty or so left over mechanic tool boxes, why can't we issue them to the drivers of the wheels?" Martin asked.

"In case you have forgotten, First Sergeant, tools are issued by echelon. If the Army wants a man to stop when he gets to a certain item, it does not give him the tool he needs to take it apart, like say the spindle on a jeep. An operator does not have a wrench that fits it, only a wheel vehicle mechanic does, so that screws your plan right there. I see where you're trying to go but I don't think you can get there from here due to echeloned maintenance," BJ said thoughtfully.

"Regulations are for the guidance of the Commanding Officer BJ. Nowhere in any regulation does it say the Commander can fail to accomplish his mission in war and blame the establishment. The definition of sniveling is to sob without tears, BJ. Using tool boxes and their contents to excuse failure is sniveling. What if we assigned a mechanic a set of vehicles and gave him control over the drivers with regard to maintenance. They would then become apprenticed to him. Like all good apprentices, when they have demonstrated the proficiency to perform a task, he gives them the go ahead to do it and he checks it. Before you know it, they can fix everything and it remains under positive control. Driver confidence goes over the moon, the deadline report disappears and the mechanic has a safety valve. Great Idea, BJ, we'll do it!" Martin said enthusiastically.

"BBBBBBBullshit, FFFFFirst Sergeant. Don't you go troop leadin' my ass like that and sticking that idea on me when it is yours and everybody knows it," BJ sad with a rueful smile on his homely countenance.

"Oh really, BJ! Then tell me why you have a mechanics tool box that looks like the number one common junior? I'll tell you why. You have learned to use every tool and fix everything on every wheel we have. The motor sergeant does not want me on his ass so he made sure you had everything you need to keep old Seven on the road, no matter what. I was born at night, BJ, just not last night. Who is bull shittin' who? If a strategy is good enough for the First

Sergeant and the Commanding Officer, it is good enough for the whole Troop? What's funny, BJ?" Martin asked.

"This is not the Cav and this ain't no troop, First Sergeant, it is HHC!" BJ said smiling, knowing how bad the First Sergeant wished he was in G Troop right now.

Finding the Motor Sergeant rummaging through the parts bins trying to find one more u-joint for Whispering Sal's jeep, Martin briefed him on the plan to apprentice the wheeled vehicle drivers. He also directed the supervising mechanic's name be added to the vehicle windshield in the center, between the driver and the vehicle commander. It was to be done for every vehicle.

In answer to why, Martin said, "It is ownership, Sargie. When is the last time you washed a rental car before turning it in at the airport? The answer is, never. Why? It is not yours. You do not give a damn about it. Do the Battalion Commanders jeep windshield first when you get the u-joints in it followed by the Company Commander's and then mine. When they ask why, act as if it were your idea, not mine. They will accept it better." Martin directed.

It was now 1400 and the support platoon had ten trucks ready to go to the ASP. Martin did a PCI of them in the rain. Everything worked and all placards and signs were in place for the hazardous cargo for all ten trucks. At the ASP, one truck's left turn signal failed to function leaving nine eligible trucks. Ms Hockley greeted them with a broad smile and not a single word was said regarding overtime or the employment of her team. The entire Ammunition supply Point outside crew turned to in order to load the ammunition of 3/70 Armor on the trucks and trailers.

The only reaction from Whispering Sal to the arrival of the ammunition at the range was a very thin and very brief smile. The Battalion commander was secretly overjoyed to see the name of the mechanic on his windshield. He gently silenced the S4 who complained about the new addition on his jeep glass and gave him the Responsibility 101 lecture. He added the background on General Creech and the USAF Tactical Air Force Experience. He did not mention Martin directly in the second lecture to the young Captain. Whisperin' Sal and Martin had obviously been reading the same books by Peters.

The next day after the demonstration had concluded and the Sec Def, Sec Army, and the retinue of horse holders from the Division had come and gone, Whispering Sal was surprised to see Martin waiting outside of the TOC next to his parking space as he pulled up. As usual, night was chasing away the sun and it was drizzling. He was pleased to see his Headquarters First Sergeant standing in the rain as if it were a sunny day.

"Yes, First Sergeant, what can I do for you?" the Battalion Commander asked.

"Sir, I have to report an incident with Colonel Barrett and I have a favor to ask," Martin said.

Having given his First Sergeant the signal for tell me more, he settled in to listen, noting Martin did not even look at the Commander's driver, taking for granted he would be a wooden Indian.

"Sir, my driver was adding camo paint to his face as we were driving down the road. I was holding his helmet in my lap and steering the jeep. Colonel Barrett had us pull over and told me to report to him and give account of why my driver had his helmet off. I told him we had stopped to help some Infantry guys in 1/61 and their camo put ours to shame so we had to adjust it. I assured him BJ would have his helmet back on and would keep it on with chin strap fastened. He accepted our explanation and dismissed me," Martin concluded.

"It is good for you to keep me up to date. He will ask me about it tonight at the meeting. It is the little things that count with him. You did right," he said. "Now what is the second thing?"

"Smitley, I need you to take a walk for a minute," Martin said to the Commanding Officer's driver.

PFC Smitley looked at his boss and got the head nod to take the walk. He was thinking, *Damn, it must be bad; they never exclude me from anything.*

"Sir, when we get back I am going to divide the unit into two sections, Green and White. Everyone will have to be cross trained. Everyone in each section will have to meet a series of standards to achieve full combat readiness in admin and training, not have any DUI's, Indebtedness, or UCMJ to remain qualified. Once they qualify, Green will be off on Fridays and White will be off on Mondays. The standard will be applied by section, not to the entire half of HHC. I want to tell them you know nothing about the plot and let them think it is subversion on a grand scale," Martin concluded awaiting guidance.

For the first time, Martin saw a true smile on Whispering Sal's face. "I will agree to the entire program with one caveat, First Sergeant. If I hear of anyone saying on a Friday or a Monday the words, 'Not my job, I can't do that', for whatever reason, keys, training, experience, whatever, the experiment is ended and no one is off except by my order. I want HHC's morale built but not at the expense of readiness in the line companies. Carry On, First Sergeant," he said saluting as he waved Smitley back to his rightful seat.

During the nightly Command and Staff, Lieutenant Colonel Milano kept hearing a discordant radio voice he could not identify in the background. Waving everyone to silence, he asked his Master Gunner, Sergeant First Class Robinson, "Robbie, who is that on the radio? I do not recognize the call sign."

"Sir, that is the HHC base station. First Sergeant Martin set up a power antenna on the phone pole outside the orderly room that is about 80 foot tall. We are using it to coordinate with the rear and to cut down on unnecessary trips. No one comes back to the field unless they call the TOC and the

ALOC to see if we need anything and them what is goin' in to the Rear check with us before they leave. It has helped us a lot, Sir, and we would sure like to see it continue," Robinson said hopefully.

"Oh, Robbie, I have no intention of stopping it. But when I hear my radio net sounding like United Parcel Service, I want to know why. Everywhere I look, I see new initiatives by the HHC leadership. You guys are on fire over there aren't you, Freddie? Is there anything else I should know about you've got going on?" he asked smiling broadly.

"No, Sir, if the First Sergeant talked to you about Green and White, we are up to date," Captain Sims said brightly, feeling for the first time since Colonel Barrett abruptly assigned him to HHC 3/70 that he was part of the outfit. It was good to have a great First Sergeant though it was a little stressful at times.

The references to the teams sparked the Battalion Commander to ask his four line dogs, "Do you know about Green & White?" he asked and was immensely gratified to see each of the shake their heads yes and smile.

Captain Les Brown could not resist, "Oh is that the program you don't know about, Sir?" as they all laughed softly as co-conspirators.

"That's the one. Let's move on to how we are going to execute the Movement to Contact Rehearsal!" he said.

Over the next month, Martin was very happy with how his concept to move the HHC to excellence using the three day weekend as a reward turned out. Every section achieved the goals. The deadline report dropped to two pages from eight, bad debts went away as the time off enabled the soldiers to pay their bills, Article 15's nearly disappeared through use of extra training and some intelligent time management by the platoon sergeants. Training, efficiency, morale and spirit de corps were all high.

The soldiers were still reluctant warriors and not willing to commit heart and soul to the task at hand. Nowhere was this more true than their unwillingness to sound off with the cadence of singing during the formation run during physical training. They were unwilling to fake it if they did not feel it and their intellects made light of those who did.

It was yet another rainy day at glorious Fort Polk. The uniform was full PT with wool bottoms and tops as well as watch caps. Their cadence sounded like a collection of girl scouts with chest colds. They were wet, miserable, and feeling sorry for themselves. Except for the Rangers, they were about to get the shock of their lives in the Army.

The First Sergeant had halted the unit on the company street. He faced them to the left and commanded, "STAND AT, EASE."

"I don't know what is wrong with you people today. You sound so weak I am ashamed to be seen with you. You are not responding to your leaders. If you don't feel it you are ordered to fake it until you do feel it. If you cannot contribute to the overall good of the unit because you love it then I will make

467

sure you all hate me. At least your thoughts will be united. Together, we are going to low crawl through that large mud puddle. Then we are going to run some more until you sound like combat soldiers. If that does not happen, we will low crawl through the puddle and run until you do, maintenance, training, breakfast all be damned. All of you intellectual jokers get this straight. At some point in your Army career, your brain will say 'no I won't'. It is then that your balls have to kick in and say 'yes I can and I will'."

He then called them to attention, faced them forward and low crawled them through the mud. Once on the other side, they resumed the running formation and returned to the street with a muddy and nasty front and clean butts. Their cadence sounded like basic trainees in the 8th week, loud strong and positive. After another mile, Martin turned them into the company street and left them on a high note saying, "Give yourselves a hand! Good Job! Dismissed!!"

He was very shocked to see Colonel Noble Barrett step out of the formation with the Chaplain and the principal members of the Brigade Staff. They were all covered with mud. "Great PT session, First Sergeant, enjoyed it," Colonel Nobles said with his perfect white teeth shining in contrast to the mud.

"Sorry you had to hear the profanity, Chaplain, I did not see you in the formation," Martin said.

Chaplain Major Rabinski, an Airborne Ranger said cheerfully, "Profanity, I didn't hear any profanity, did you S-4?"

Major Barstow, a fellow Ranger, shook his head and said, "No, not a word."

The lesson hit home and did not have to be repeated. The progress on other fronts was not diminished by any hard feelings by anyone.

Days later, the Company marched better and were about to show their stuff at the Brigade Formation in the amphitheater. Arriving after the remainder of the Battalion, Martin was forced to use right and left step march to align the unit. It was very well done.

As he was making the final adjustments to the Company, some wag in Charlie Company sang out in the prefect stillness that always occurred once Colonel Barrett was near, "Well look at the wussies from Headquarters trying to march like soldiers." The entire Brigade laughed as one man and just as quickly stopped as the Brigade Commander looked up with a steely gaze. Martin did not see any of the byplay with the Brigade Commander as he had his back to the reviewing area and aligning his unit. He did hear the wag sound off and he had an answer the entire Brigade heard as well.

"There is a four day pass for the man that knocks that son of a bitch on his ass," Martin said in a stentorian tone heard by the entire Brigade.

"I got it, First Sergeant," Said Specialist Fourth Class Rudolfo, a happy go lucky Portuguese fisherman from Tampa, Florida. He promptly went through the ranks of Charlie Company and knocked out the offender, whom he knew well, with one punch and resumed his position in formation.

"Good Job, Rudolfo, see the training clerk after formation. In Cadence, Company Halt," he said.

"ONE, TWO, First Sergeant," 350 throats screamed as one rattling the chapel windows. Now the whole area was deathly quiet as Captain Sims came forward.

Martin saluted saying, "Sir, all present or accounted for. The sick, lame, lazy, crippled, blind and crazy are all in the rear of the formation as directed."

"Take your Post ,First Sergeant," CTP Sims stated easily.

The Brigade was called to attention. The Commander received the unit from his Adjutant. He then gave them all at ease and as usual began with a little light humor. "I guess it is clear to everyone we have a new First Sergeant in HHC 3/70," he said sure of the mirth to follow and it did. Not another word was ever said about the event.

He then proceeded to read a letter from a former comrade in arms. The letter described a battle in Vietnam. Colonel Barrett put his own spin on the lesson by summarizing, "We offered those North Vietnamese a chance to surrender. They would not. They came to fight and by God we killed over 300 of those bastards in the Hobo Woods that day. They were men that needed killin' and we were the men to do it and so are you. This is a democracy. We don't pick our wars. We just fight 'em. We fight 'em with what we have at the time, the weapons, the ammo, the vehicles and the instruments of war. We can't fight with what we wish we had. We have to fight with what we've got. We don't have the latest and greatest of everything but we have great soldiers who know how to fight and who are willing to close with and destroy our enemies. I am proud to walk among you Cold Steel soldiers."

It was during the struggle to find housing for his soldiers Martin ran afoul of the Post Civilians. One set of them told him he could sign for the top five floors of a building if he did so that day. The proviso was that he must assume responsibility for painting the interior of it using government paint and troop labor. He did so immediately. It solved his problem for housing and all of his troops were allotted the correct amount of square footage under the regulation. It was a short lived feeling of happiness.

The head civilian for housing had already promised the barracks to another unit. He also had contracted for it to be professionally painted. It was clear to him that Martin and his Supply Sergeant had circumvented the DPW chain of command or at least the hierarchy. No one had asked him because he was not in the chain of command for barracks assignment. Thirty years of organizational in fighting, back stabbing and puffery had not been kind to Mr. Harold Provo but he was an accomplished in fighter who neither gave, nor asked for, quarter in turf battles. The dispute ended up in the Commanding Gener-

469

al's office with the chain of command in attendance. The Commanding General was asking all of the questions.

The Commanding General noted the Garrison Commander was effusive in his greeting of the First Sergeant. His look told the GC to tell him the story, as there was always a story, "This is the First Sergeant I told you about, Sir. He is the one who inspects family quarters in Class A uniform. He began the process informally with a progressive supper and the Class A inspection was for those who declined to be sociable. It really helped us a lot and I sure wish everyone would follow his example of taking care of soldiers and their families."

"First Sergeant, how is it you and the Supply Sergeant contrived to sign for a barracks illegally?" the Commanding General asked.

"General, I do not know the source of that report. We were inspecting rooms in the barracks while the communications command was turning their rooms back to DPW. The barracks is in the 3/70 HHC footprint. The civilian gentleman responsible asked me if in return for signing for the remainder of the barracks if I would paint it. I accepted his offer. I did not know there was any requirement to brief the administrative leadership of DPW about such a routine matter. Should we not be permitted to retain the barracks, there will be no place for the 24 soldiers to sleep except in a tent," Martin said calmly.

"Mr. Provo, what say you?" the Commanding General asked.

"I hold here the barracks utilization report from last month. It says noting of the sort, in fact it shows many vacancies throughout HHC 3/70 barracks," Provo said with a voice quaking with emotion.

As the Commanding General looked at him Martin replied, "Sir, the report is inaccurate at the least and a forgery at the worst. The report Mr. Provo is purporting to be one I submitted, is typed. All of our barracks utilization reports are submitted in pen and ink. I was most careful to ensure the total accuracy of that report. I will agree that he was not briefed by his people about the transfer. That is an internal matter for DPW to fix. I can assure you none of your soldiers lied, cheated, stole or dishonored themselves in the process of signing for the barracks."

If Mr. Provo could have stuck the altered report up his butt he would have. His lie was blown up in his florid, whiskey soaked face and he knew it. He had hoped to beat down the First Sergeant and the other soldiers and he had failed. The air went out of him like a toy balloon.

"First Sergeant, keep the barracks. You did nothing wrong. That is all! Provo and Colonel Richards, remain seated," the Commanding General said rising behind his desk to return the salutes of the chain of command.

Colonel Barrett cautioned everyone with hand signals not to speak until they were outside.

"That asshole. He thought he would just bowl us over. Good job, First Sergeant. There is no next time but if there is, go through the Brigade next time, you hear?"

"Roger, Sir," Martin said glad to escape with his whole skin.

0700 hours
06 Mar 1987
3/70 Armor Battalion Classroom

"ATTENTION."

"First Sergeant, do you mind telling me what is going on here today? Everybody is supposed to be off today in the Brigade," Colonel Barrett said with his jaw jutting out. He was clearly pissed.

"Yes, Sir, this is a voluntary class on the written portion of the MOS test for 19E's. Your guidance targeted several MOSes that were plagued by low scores. This effort is how I chose to attack the problem in HHC. There are other soldiers here today from the line units. What I have done is to teach the soldiers how to write test questions. The correct response must be referenced citing the written authority that makes it correct. It is my theory that many young people do not know how to take a test. It's not so much that they do not know the information. They just get confused and do not take tests well. My strategy to fix that is to teach them to write an MOS test for 19E's on their own. I then graded their responses during the week and came up with an MOS test for them of 240 questions rather than 100. We have a test key and will grade the test today and provide each of them with the correct answers that are of course, referenced. They will then use the test for self study and will take it again before the formal MOS test in May. There is no better way to teach a man to take a written test than having him write one."

"We will then rehearse the hands on portion of the testing by grading each other. Again, learning by teaching, much as the TAC officers learn at West Point and the service academies, learn by doing," Martin said finally.

"First Sergeant, did you do this for all of the MOSes in the HHC?" Colonel Barrett asked.

"Yes, Sir, they are here in these notebooks filed by MOS. The Master Trainer in HHC for each MOS has the final version of the written test for his respective area and he manages the training effort. The one for the cooks was the hardest to assemble. It was like pulling hen's teeth."

To no one's surprise, Colonel Noble Barrett sat down in the back of the classroom and leafed through the MOS training booklets. The Armor class continued as the Brigade Commander was engrossed in his study. After nearly 40 minutes of perusing the note books, the Brigade Commander stood up and signaled Martin to meet him outside the classroom in the now empty S3 shop. "If this effort does not drastically improve the scores of the Battalion I will be very surprised. This is fine work and it shows great respect for soldiers and their ability to learn. Good job, First Sergeant, good job. Proud of you guys but no more Saturday work when I have given the Brigade off, period!"

The tankers who went to "Saturday School" got five perfect scores on the written test and improved their scores by an average of twenty four points. The year of their work and improvement was also the year the Army decided to discontinue MOS testing. It was ironic, but at least a lot of soldiers learned how to train and teach at a higher level of competence.

Standardizing the rooms and their layout was a very difficult task. The rooms were oddly shaped and configured for three soldiers. Any leader knows three is the worst possible number of members of a group to attain and maintain cohesion. Two of the number will always conspire against the third or the third is the odd man out. It was the old saw, two is company and three is a crowd. Martin fell back on his lead dog philosophy.

He assigned one person in each section to lead the way for the rooms. Once they had applied the approved solution, everyone else conformed to the demonstrated standard and was inspected for compliance.

By April, it was clear the unit had done a 180 degree turn. Every leadership indicator for excellence was in their favor. The only remaining problem was to work through the enormous amount of missing, broken and poorly accounted for property of the HHC. It was nearing time for Captain Sims' change of command and he was at least $50,000 in the hole for property. Captain Sims insisted he had been saving some money and that no commander escaped a report of survey and the loss of a month's pay. It was in his mind, a badge of honor to have rightly ignored property accountability and concentrated on making his mechanics, clerks and medics into Infantry.

Within four days, Martin and the company had reduced the property deficit to $2,500 dollars. Captain Sims called a halt to the effort and was quite happy with the result. What the young Captain failed to realize was while his NCOs were determined to reduce his burden, they were also cleaning their property accountability house for future operations. The largest part of the reduction of his liability came from the enforcement of policies already in effect to develop the series of hand receipts for property below the Commander so that the user was correctly identified and signed for the items under their daily control.

"Captain Sims, is there anything wrong with Colonel Barrett's eyesight? He is getting along in years and does not wear glasses even to read," Martin asked knowing the young Captain was on social terms with the Brigade Commander.

"No, First Sergeant, he has twenty –ten vision. He can see bullet vapor trails impact E-Type targets at 300 yards. Why do you ask?" Sims queried.

"Today at Battalion Headquarters, he was coming out and greeted me by saying, 'Good Morning, Sergeant Major'. I thought maybe he needed glasses

472

as I was wearing three up three down and a diamond in the middle, not a star," Martin said.

"Goddamn, you made the E9 list. Colonel Barrett knows everybody that is anybody in the Army. One of his buds called him and told him everybody on the list that is assigned to his Brigade. You made it, congratulations. There is nothing wrong with his eyes, trust me, First Sergeant. That is his way of telling you without telling you. He was smiling ear to ear when he said, was he not?!" Sims said laughing and slapping his First Sergeant on the back.

"Sir, that list is not due out for two more months. I do not see how he would possibly know already, but I am willing to take your word for it and be quietly happy. I have been screwed before when a superior told me I was on the E8 list in my first look in the secondary zone. It turned out he was reading the considered list, not the promoted list," Martin said ruefully.

"First Sergeant, Cold Steel Six has more oars in the personnel water than a Roman galley. People all over the Army love him and keep him informed, believe me it is true. You will be moving right after I change command. There is no slot for you here and they put those on the list in E9 slots as soon as the list comes out. Shit, they are looking at the list right now to see where to put you guys that got promoted. This is great, just great. I am so happy for you. You do not seem happy, First Sergeant. This is the last hurdle for you except for Command Sergeant Major. You will be entitled to be called Sergeant Major for the rest of your life, even after retirement. There are less than 2,000 of you out of a million soldiers. That is some elite company. Damn, this is great news," he said, disturbed because his First Sergeant as not nearly as happy about the news as he thought he should be.

"Don't take it wrong Captain Sims, but the journey was always more important to me than the destination. It is anti-climatic for me to finally see it all come true. It is the beginning of the end of my career as a soldier. I am a twenty year man, not a thirty year guy," Martin said pensively.

"First Sergeant, I would not over analyze it. If I were you, I would just be happy I had it and plan on enjoying it. And you tell me to lighten up. You need to lighten up, First Sergeant," his young Captain said laughing.

"Shit, you had better be planning your ceremony for the change of responsibility and the passing of the guidon," Sims said suddenly serious.

"That is one ceremony that will never take place, Captain Sims. I will not take part in it. Change of responsibility ceremonies are hokey horseshit dreamed up by senior enlisted men who have pretensions to be officers. The change of command ceremony is well defined and covered by FM 22-5 and Army Regulation. There is no such animal as a change of responsibility ceremony," Martin said with strong conviction.

"You can't be serious, First Sergeant. Are you being serious?" Captain Sims asked.

473

"I am very serious. A ceremony with two First Sergeants exchanging guidons reminds me of a little girl's tea party in the back yard with the little plastic cups. People that make up ceremonies to fit their egos are doing their jobs for the wrong reasons. If they want to be officers so bad, they should apply for OCS. Most of the time the NCOs that love that ceremony do not fully support their commanders and have their own agendas. The next thing you know we will have another Battalion where the Privates are saluting the Command Sergeant Major like our Infantry Brethren are being taught by Command Sergeant Major Applegate. He believes he rates a salute due to his august rank as a Command Sergeant Major. He is full of shit and wrong as two left feet."

"When you peel the onion back in his outfit there is more rot from the double standard than the IG can cure. No, Captain Sims, it is a dark and slippery slope when senior enlisted men get confused about the rights and responsibilities of NCOs versus those of officers. I'll have no part of that ceremony. It is enough for the new First Sergeant to introduce himself to his unit at his first formation. If he is worth a shit, the troops will know it and if he is not, their built in bull shit detectors will start humming before that goofy ceremony is over."

CHAPTER 16 – BALLS AND BRAINS

The best leaders know the difference between a risk and a gamble. If they be too smart they never take a risk. If they be too brave they don't stop to think. Best you kin do is fig-ure out the smart play and have the balls to carry out your plan. Sam Cyprus- Sergeant 1969 – Veteran of 3 tours to RVN

First Sergeant Martin, now fully eligible for promotion to Sergeant Major once his very junior number came, was being reassigned to the 4/12 Cavalry, the Divisional Cavalry Squadron on Fort Polk. This was not what his Brigade Command Sergeant Major wanted to happen. He had campaigned long and hard for Martin to be the Division Operations Sergeant Major. Martin had first learned of this from his Captain, a favorite of the Brigade Commander.

Colonel Barrett, a very wise and august man had his young officer ask Martin's opinion. He was pleased with the reply the Captain gave him. "The Brigade Command Sergeant Major has a high opinion of my intellect. It takes experience and credibility as well as brains to make a Division Operations Sergeant. I would be way over my head in that job. I need to learn how to be a Sergeant Major in a Battalion. I am not a combat veteran. No Command Sergeant Major or combat unit commander would listen to a damn thing I had to say. It is all about trust at that level."

At the final formation of HHC 3/70 Armor he was to attend, now Master Sergeant Martin, their former First Sergeant, wanted to leave them with some words to live by. Somehow along the way, the put upon, overworked and un-der supported Company had begun to refer to themselves as dogs. They had arrived at a mutual understanding that summed up their feelings of frustration and their desire to rise above it in a single phrase, "You can't Dog a Dog." Martin had seized upon the phrase from the soldier patois and turned it into a mantra for the whole unit. It was typical for that unit to select the object that was already the lowest form of animal life, a stray cur dog, and adopt it as their symbol.

Martin's going away plaque contained the phrase on a small brass plate along with his term of service in the unit. Like the outfit itself, the plaque was rough and tough. Homemade at the craft shop, it sported an outline of a tank, the unit crest and Division emblem of a Red Diamond. Like the unit it came from, it was tough, heavy, made to last and represented deep and abiding val-ues.

Looking at it in the formation, now held by his replacement, Martin was smiling broadly as the troops gathered around. He held it up so all could see. He completed a full turn. He then said, "I guess all of you know, YOU CAINT" -and they finished the phrase with a roar, DOG A DOG." He knew and they knew the six months he had been there had changed them and their unit. They had responded to him far better than either he or the chain of command had dared hoped they would.

"This is not a surprise. I told you when I got here I would be moving on shortly. It has been a good six months. You have taught me a lot and I have taught you a little. I got the best of the deal. I will be a better Sergeant Major for having been here. I am leaving to be the Operations Sergeant Major of the Division Cavalry Squadron. I will serve there as a Master Sergeant until I am promoted way down the road. I am lucky to even be on the list and as long as I don't pork the Commanding General's poodle at the flagpole I will get promoted." The laughter was long and hard and the Brigade Commander and his chaplain in the rear of the formation laughed as hard as anyone.

Martin continued, "You will hear some stories about where I went and why. We have a good Division Command Sergeant Major and a good Commanding General. They know how to develop soldiers. Sergeants Major need to be trained and developed just like everyone else. Book smarts have to be matched with practical work. Serving with units in the field is the only way the two come together. My promotion will be a long time coming but remember this, 'tis a far better thing to be the last man on this year's promotion list than the first one on next year's. I am very happy with my new assignment. Parting is such sweet sorrow."

"Long ago I heard a story. It seems this guy went forward to help his buddy trapped by heavy fire in WW II. His Infantry Company Commander yelled at him to stay put and not go forward, but to wait until they could get supporting fires on the enemy strong point to reduce it. He was badly wounded and dying when the Commander arrived having called in mortars on the Germans, killing them. The buddy our soldier went to rescue was dead in his arms when the Commander arrived. The Commander was very upset and cursed the soldier, 'Goddammit, why did you go forward? Why wouldn't you wait until it was safe?' The soldier replied, 'Captain, I'm dying, don't curse me. I had to go help Jim. When I got here he said to me, 'I knew you would come.' That is how I will remember you Dogs, when your country needs you; you will come, no matter what."

With that and the applause and cheering of his former Company, Martin shook hands with the new First Sergeant, "Fast Eddy" Felton, a highly decorated practical veteran of five tours in Vietnam, the new Commander, Captain Smart, an Airborne Ranger and the most successful armor company commander in the Division. As Fast Eddy put the troops back into formation for dismissal, Martin responded to the Brigade Commander's hand signal to join him in the rear of the formation. As he did, the two of them walked away trailed by the Brigade Chaplain talking softly so no one else could hear the conversation.

"Thanks for the great job as a First Sergeant in HHC 3/70. I appreciate it. It was a very good idea to reinforce the decision by Division to send you to the Cav and to tell the troops that Sergeant Major need training like everybody else. Hell, Brigade Commanders get trained too you know. What was it you told your troops, you can always tell a Brigade Commander but you can't tell him much?"

"Yes, Sir, I probably said that but I only meant it to apply to former First Sergeants," Martin replied with a smile, knowing full well the Brigade Commander was one of the youngest First Sergeants ever to serve this side of WW II.

"Well, that makes it all right. You know how those OCS guys are, like Cavalry Sergeants Major, all balls and no brains," the Brigade Commander responded.

Command Sergeant Major (RET) RICHARD E. MORGAN

Command Sergeant Major (Ret) Richard E. Morgan was born in Decatur, IN in 1943. He entered the US Army as a draftee in March 1969. Command Sergeant Major (Ret) Morgan served in each rank and enlisted leadership position in the Army.

Command Sergeant Major (Ret) Morgan's duty positions include, Tank Crewman, Missile Crewman, Tank Commander, Tank Platoon Sergeant, Drill Sergeant, Senior Drill Sergeant, First Sergeant, Operations Sergeant Major and Command Sergeant Major.

He was instrumental in the development of doctrine, tactics and training for the initial work on Close Combat Heavy Forces and the M1 tank Bore Sight and Calibration Procedures, Field Manuals 17-12 Tank gunnery and 17-12-1 M1 Tank gunnery, and the development of tactics, techniques and procedures for the Armor Force.

Command Sergeant Major (Ret) Morgan's duty assignments include the 5thID (Mech) as a PFC & SPC and again as a First Sergeant and Sergeant Major; A Battery 2/52, Air Defense Artillery, Homestead, FL; 4/69 Armor, Mainz, Germany 8th ID as a Tank commander and HHC Executive Officer; Drill Sergeant, Senior Drill Sergeant and First Sergeant for Basic Training & Infantry in B & C-19-4, Fort Knox, KY; 1/33 Armor, Gelnhausen, Germany 2d AD as a PSG; Instructor and Chief Instructor of Gunnery Division, Armor School Fort Knox, KY; H Co 2/6 Cavalry as First Sergeant; G Troop 2/11 ACR as First Sergeant; 2/11 ACR, Bad Kissingen Germany as Squadron Master Gunner, Acting Operations Sergeant Major and Command Sergeant

Major; HHC 3/70 Armor, First Sergeant; 4/12 Cavalry as Operations Sergeant Major & Command Sergeant Major; 1/11 ACR, Fulda, Germany; Command Sergeant Major 3/70 Armor, Fort Hood, TX.

Command Sergeant Major (Ret) Morgan's awards and decorations include: the Legion of Merit, Meritorious Service Medal, Sixth Oak Leaf Cluster, Army Commendation Medal, Army Achievement Medal, NDSM, Expert, Rifle and Pistol Badges, and the Drill Sergeant Badge. He was a distinguished Honor Graduate of his Advanced NCO Course. Command Sergeant Major (Ret) Morgan graduated from the US Army Sergeants Major Academy Non-Resident Course in 1986.

Command Sergeant Major (Ret) Morgan also served as the Emergency Deployment Readiness (EDRE) Officer, Operations officer and finally as the Deputy G3 of the JRTC & Fort Polk. He retired as a Department of the Army Civilian in 2006.

He and his wife Linda have four children. They are empty nesters and reside near DeRidder, LA.

Command Sergeant Major (Ret) Morgan is a member of the Order of St. George, is a Lifetime Member of the Blackhorse Association, was inducted into the Order of the Spur in 1984. He is a member of both the National Rifle Association and Adams Post 43 of the American Legion.

He is the author of a work of fiction novel entitled "The First Sergeants" and intends to publish several more books beginning in the winter of 2012.

ACR: Acronym for Armored Cavalry Regiment, a largely self contained unit organized for expeditionary service under the direct supervision of a US Army Corps Headquarters. Organized into five battalion sized elements called Squadrons each commanded by a Lieutenant Colonel (the SCO) with a Colonel in command of the Regiment (the Regimental Commanding Officer).Three elements are ground maneuver squadrons each with three troops of cavalry, with one each tank company, howitzer battery and headquarters element responsible to support the logistical needs of the unit. Of the remaining squadrons one is composed of helicopters and one of support equipment and personnel to provide in house logistics. Separate companies of Military Police, Military Intelligence, Combat Engineers and Chemical forces round out the Regiment. In essence, a Regiment is a Division reduced in scale to fit the mission of finding, reporting and fixing an enemy mechanized force well forward in a Corps operating area.

ADA: Air Defense Artillery is the branch of Army service that defends the maneuver force against air attack using man portable missiles such as the STINGER and the 20mm cannon of the Vulcan. Formerly, the branch was armed with 40mm cannon mounted on M-41 tank chassis as well as missiles such as the Nike-Hercules, HAWK, and Patriot systems. The success of the USAF both in the air and in the halls of Congress doomed this branch of the Army.

AFB: Acronym for a United States Air Force Base. When used by the US Air Force it is often preceded by a single letter to designate a specific base, such as HAFB for Homestead Air Force Base, located at Homestead, FL

AFN: This is the acronym for Armed Forces Network made famous by Robin Williams's portrayal of the disc jockey in the movie "Good Morning Vietnam." It was created to bring a small piece of America to the troops abroad. In Europe it consisted on one radio and one Television station. It sucked but it was better than nothing. In tough units, there was not much time for TV watching.

Agent Orange: A defoliant used in the Republic of South Vietnam to denude the jungle through aerial delivery from C-130 aircraft and others configured for the mission. It fell on friend and foe alike. The American troops exposed to Agent Orange came home with a myriad of health issues lurking in their bodies, many of which would not manifest themselves for many years. The establishment and the Veteran's Administration stone walled early information efforts and thousands of Vietnam veterans died without compensation, care or compassion. Eventually the public hue and cry of forced the stone hearted establishment bureaucrats to act to save themselves politically.

AIT: Advanced Individual Training was a period after basic training where soldiers received the training for the entry level of their Military Occupational Specialty.

AK-47: The AK-47 is ubiquitous rifle of the Soviet Bloc, its allies, surrogates and anyone else in the world that can buy one. It is a rugged, rapid firing, accurate weapon capable of aimed automatic fire out to 500 meters. US Border units were issued AK-47's for training purposes and all were required to be able to learn to operate the weapons to become border qualified.

Alert: The alert is the mechanism used by levels of command to recall, issue orders, conduct logistics supply and move units to assembly areas for potential deployment to exercises or to war. Messages were sent by code in early years giving the minimum possible information. Each unit then activated its portion of the Ground Defense Plan to meet the contents of the message. Calls to the homes of soldiers used a code word that no one abused or used lightly in any manner.

ALO: Authorized levels of organization are designed into the tables of authorization and equipment of Army units. ALO is the Army method of prioritization. ALO 1 means units are maintained at 100% of all authorizations, while ALO 2 & 3 units are maintained at 90 and 80 % respectively. The Army units closest to the enemy such as in Germany prior to 1993 and those in Korea and or those certain to be deployed first such as the 82d Airborne are all ALO 1 units. Soldiers in an ALO 3 unit often compare their supply status as one notch below the Red Chinese National Guard.

AOB: The Armor Officer Basic Course was of three months duration. Conducted at Fort Knox, KY, it was an indoctrination and skill development course for the Second Lieutenants of the Armor Force. The course was conducted by the Departments of Command and Staff, Maintenance and Weapons. These departments were commanded by a Colonel who was normally a former Armor Battalion or Cavalry Squadron Commander and a War College Graduate. The officers were responsible for the conduct and content of the course. Company grade officers and NCOs were in charge of its execution.

AOAC: The Armor Officer Advanced Course was a signature event for Captains either just after command as First Lieutenants or just before Command as Captains of Tank Companies or Cavalry Troops. The pendulum swung back and forth on the academic requirements for AOAC though in 1983 & 1984 it was a challenge for some.

ARCOM: The acronym for the Army Commendation Medal is ARCOM. The award of an impact ARCOM is within the purview of officers in the grade of Colonel. Impact awards were made to immediately reward positive behavior and to serve as an incentive.

Armorer: The individual soldier in charge of the Arms Room of a unit. Seldom did a unit have a school trained soldier for this important task. Armored units have a great many automatic weapons, rifles and pistols. An added task for Border Cavalry unit is the care and maintenance of foreign weapons provided for training and familiarization as well as cross border operations.

ASP: The term ASP refers to the Ammunition Supply Point or ammo dump. In a border cavalry unit, the first basic load of main gun ammunition was kept on the tanks while the machinegun bullets were stored in containers in the motor pool. The ammunition for mortars and howitzers being inherently more unstable as the propellant charge and the explosive shells were separate. TOW & Dragon missiles were also stored at the ASP. The Support Platoon Leader manages the basic load for the unit at the ASP.

ATGM: The acronym ATGM stands for Anti Tank Guided Missile and represented the poor man's answer to the military-industrial complex.

Article 32 Investigation: No charge or specification may be referred to a general court-martial for trial until a thorough and impartial investigation of all the matters set forth therein has been made. It is comparable to the Grand Jury of the civilian world.

Autobahn: The name of the interstate like system of roads in Germany first conceived and put into effect by Hitler to ease the movement of military forces. Superbly engineered, the system had speed limits posted as exceptions. Unless a speed limit was posted, the rule was "pedal to the metal" for the motorist.

481

Bad Kissingen: Bad Kissingen is a spa town in the Bavarian Region of Lower Franconia. It is located to the south of the Rhon Mountains on the Fraconian Saale River. It is one of the most famous spa towns in German due to the mineral springs which abound there. At the eastern edge of the town the US Army took over the former German Army Barracks and renamed it Daley Barracks. It was home to the Second Squadron of the 11th ACR. This unit was charged with the covering force mission for the Meiningen Gap, a prominent terrain feature and traditional invasion route guarded by a large number of Soviet Forces during the Cold War nearly 25 miles from Bad Kissingen.

BK: Army speak for the town of Bad Kissingen.

Basic Load: The prescribed amount of ammunition by type authorized for a given level of the Army. An individual rifleman was normally issued 210 rounds of M-16 ammunition as his basic load. Individual commanders designed the basic loads for their unit to fit the mission. Guards in garrison normally had one thirty round magazine for an M-16 and two seven round magazines of .45 for those armed with the pistol.

Bavarian: Each region of Germany had distinct customs, courtesies, food and speech patterns. Germany was not always a contiguous nation with common borders, customs and uniform political divisions. Accents in Germany are often like those of the USA in that a person from Maine and another from Georgia may both speak English but it does not sound the same.

Bavarian Motor Werk: The name of the factory or firm that makes the BMW is Bavarian Motor Werk.

BCGST: This is the acronym for the Bradley Crewman Gunnery Skills Test. The BCGST is a vehicle specific, comprehensive examination by crew position for each of the crewman on a Bradley or Cavalry Fighting Vehicle (CFV). Leaders must be able to do all of the tasks on the CFV. Tasks are graded to standards of completeness and most are timed. Failures are re-tested as often as necessary. Smart leaders use the test to establish a baseline of training for their crewmen. Good units have good BCGSTs and far less accidents and incidents than those who only pay it lip service. While it is a simple and basic test, it is difficult for the ignorant and impossible for the stupid to pass.

BDU: This is the acronym for Battle Dress Uniform. The uniform was a basic re-design of the former one of Olive Drab to one of a woodland makeup that facilitated camouflage. It was also much more comfortable and utilitarian given the multitude of pockets than the former uniform.

BEQ: The Bachelor Enlisted Quarters on Fort Knox were barracks set aside for use by bachelor NCOs either by virtue of being single, because of geography and being separated from ones family or by being on Temporary Duty at the Post.

BMP: A world wide first for Soviet designers, the BMP so named for the Russian language terms Boxevaya Marshina Pekhoty or fighting vehicle for Infantry. The BMP presented a nasty surprise for NATO and US forces with a 73 mm cannon with an effective range of 700 meters, a 7.62 turret mounted machinegun and an Anti-Tank Guided Missile, code named the SAGGER with a range of 3,000 meters. It was also amphibious and able to swim at a speed of 5 MPH with very little preparation required. The BMP was quick, making speeds of nearly 50 mph on paved roadways.

BOC: The Border Operations Center where a junior NCO worked at the direction of the Camp OIC, a First or Second Lieutenant and employed enlisted men to post maps, answer phones and radios and assist him on a twelve hour tour of duty. The BOC was located on the main street of the Border Camp and had a clear view of the Reaction Squad and the Front Gate.

Border Condition: During the Cold War different levels of manning in response to Soviet actions of threats were used. Border Condition One although adjustable, was an order for a Cavalry Troop to move to its wartime sector on the East West German Border. The amounts of supplies carried and the status of weapons as loaded or not loaded, were part of the Commander's order, reflected the situation and were obeyed to the letter. Units and their movement were used by the National Command Authority to send a message to the Soviets. Units did not determine the content or scope of the message, they just carried it out.

Border Jeeps: These vehicles were of suspicious parentage and in dubious condition as they were stripped down models of the M-151A1 Army Jeep. The vehicles were operated without canvas, and in some cases, windshields, in order to have an unhindered field of view of 360 degrees while on patrol. Reports from forces using them were entitled US Jeep. US soldiers joked that their jeeps were devoid of canvas to limit the defections of East Germans as only a lunatic would leave his warm heater in a canvas covered East German Command Car for one of their rag bag vehicles. The departing unit could not leave the Border at the end of their tour unless all of the Border Jeeps were fully functional.

Border Operations: The Cavalry never slept en masse while the East/West German Border was active. Each Squadron maintained a Border Camp under the Command of a Captain from a Troop, Battery or Company. Reports from the Camp were sent to the Regimental Border Operations cell. This cell was staffed by veteran troopers with experience on the Border so that they could effectively manage situations for the Regimental Staff during the duty day and the duty officer after duty hours. Their main task was to keep V Corps informed of events and patterns developing at the Border and to prevent the command from being surprised.

Border Resident Office: A fixture of military intelligence that saw its members stationed at or near the East West German border to provide on the spot advice and consent to Army forces. The BRO never slept as someone was always on duty.

BP: The English firm of British Petroleum had service stations throughout West Germany. They were the preferred firm to accept the gasoline coupons from American Forces in a theater wide strategy to prevent black marketing of gasoline and petroleum products. German fuel prices were artificially high and US Force gas prices were artificially low for many years. It was never fun for an American to be forced to buy fuel for a gas hog sedan on the economy particularly in a super high priced area such as Switzerland or Austria.

Bratwurst: A German sausage sold at roadside stands and windows of businesses as well as by mobile lunch wagons. A fixture of the 10 am workman's break time for the German populace it was also an excuse to have a beer. Sold with a hard roll termed a brochen and some spicy mustard it was/is a wonderful treat particularly in Germany's colder climate.

Bundesbahn: The DB was a state-owned company that, with few local exceptions, exercised a monopoly concerning rail transport throughout West Germany. The DB was placed under the control of the *Bundesverkehrsministerium* (Federal Transport Ministry). With its headquarters in Frankfurt in 1985 the DB was the third-largest employer in the FRG, with a strength of 322,383 employees. A special transit police provided security. Trains moved in excess of 80 mph so tanks or their parts perched on rail cars moving through narrow tunnels required accurate placement and were tightly tied down.

Bundesfehr: The Bundesfehr is the term for the West German Army. It is filled by an annual draft levy and has a small cadre of professional NCOs and Officers. It is a highly skilled, trained and capable force when units have peaked after their training cycle.

Bundesgruenzschutz (BGS): The BGS of the 1980's was a uniformed professional para-military organization charged with the maintenance of the integrity of German borders, riot control and customs regulation. The training is very long and demanding and discipline is very strict. The training process is spread out over several years with vetting and testing conducted in stages. Privates could not marry, slept, ate a prescribed diet and lived on base. Officers began training in high school and finished their schooling in the BGS. They were of the finest character and manly virtue with some Olympians among them. They were regarded by the Cavalry as the best soldiers and companions anyone in a tough spot could want. They did not brag, bluff or back up. Their enemies either went to jail or to the graveyard.

Bundespost: The West German version of the Post Office, the Deutsche Bundespost also was responsible for telephones, telecommunications and savings account banks. The Bundespost was the largest single employer with 543,200 employees in 1985.

CG: Commanding General of an Installation responsible for the leadership, life support, property management, public safety, training, administration, support of tenant activities and Military Justice. He was most often the most technically and tactically competent Major General of his respective branch of the Army not in active command of a Division or awaiting promotion to LTG for those Training and Doctrine Command installations with a troop training mission.

Charge of Quarters: The NCO placed in charge of the barracks of a unit during the absence of the commanding officer of a troop, battery or company. Accompanied by a runner, he was the commander's representative. As such, he had the complete backing of the First Sergeant and Commander to deal with miscreants, emergencies and anything not covered by his detailed and voluminous instructions. It was fertile ground for the positive growth of responsibility for junior NCOs and a duty filled with snares and booby traps for the weak and unprincipled leader.

Chip collector: The M1 tank turret system is hydraulically actuated. Shavings are hard to digest for pumps, lines and valves. The designers put a chip collector into the system flow. Located in an obscure spot, draining it invariably resulted in a soaking for the maintenance man. Few Sergeant First Class with a promotion series number to the next grade of Master Sergeant took the trouble to learn where it was and how to drain it as they considered that beneath the dignity of the office of a First Sergeant.

Chobham armor: Chobham armor is the name informally given to a composite armor developed in the 1960s at the British tank research centre on Chobham Common, Surrey, England. The name has since become the common generic term for ceramic vehicle armor. The American Army bought it in quantity first to bring the price down so that the British could afford it for their tank. Since the Americans steal their best ideas it seems only fair they be compensated.

CID: The Criminal Investigation Division of the Army is its investigative arm. Its members most often wear civilian clothes, carry their weapons concealed or in a briefcase and have broad powers of arrest and are generally incorruptible. The activities of the CID cross the entire gamut of Military Justice. The CID is noted for its ability to infiltrate units by finding "sweet faced" young Soldiers and placing them in units to act as informants. Even though the use of these informants is few and far between, the occasions of their appearance cause deep paranoia and fear in the hearts of miscreants, and that is a good thing.

Class B Dependent: A foreign national cohabiting with an American Service member, without benefit of clergy, is termed to be a Class B Dependent.

Classes of Supply: Class I – Subsistence; **Class II** – Clothing; individual equipment, tentage, organizational tool sets and kits, hand tools, unclassified maps, administrative and housekeeping supplies and equipment; **Class III** - Petroleum, Oil and Lubricants (POL) (package and bulk); **Class IV** - Construction materials; **Class V** - Ammunition of all types; **Class VI** - Personal demand items; **Class VII** - Major end items such as launchers, tanks, mobile machine shops, and vehicles; **Class VIII** - Medical material; **Class IX** - Repair parts and components; **Class X** - Material to support nonmilitary programs.

COHORT Unit: This is the acronym for Cohesion Operational Readiness and Training **(COHORT)** soldier replacement system. It was an attempt by the Army leadership to replicate the British regimental system. The idea was to reap the benefits of the cohesion, subliminal understanding and trust derived from long and fruitful association of the same group of soldiers in the same unit and the same time. In the end, the personnel geeks won the day and the individual replacement system remained. Thus the support tail continued to wag the Army dog, tough on the dog but the tail loves it.

Cold Start: The term Cold Start refers to the practice of starting the vehicles of the unit in very cold weather once during the hours before and once after midnight to ensure they will run if called.

Colors: The term Colors describes the US Flag, known as National Colors, the Army Flag, Brigade, Regimental, Battalion and Squadron Flags are known as Unit Colors. Colors are the responsibility of the senior NCO for maintenance, proper display, care, security and finally, for the training of the Soldiers of the Color Guard who carry them in ceremonies.

Combat Infantryman's Badge (CIB): Infantry soldiers and officers are awarded this badge based on their participation in combat against an armed foe in time of war. There were three kinds of soldiers after the Vietnam War ended in the Army, those who had one, those who wished they had one and those who were damn glad they did not have one. For each additional war one fought in as an Infantryman, a star over the wreath of the Badge was authorized. Though rare, those Infantrymen who wore a CIB with one star were highly respected. Those with two stars over their CIB were venerated.

Combat Integrity: The term combat integrity refers to a value demonstrated by an overt act or acts, of acting to assist fellow Soldiers regardless of the threat, personal risk, or loss in time of war. Those who have it rarely know it, and those who don't, can never find it.

Commissary: The commissary is an entity run for the benefit of Soldiers and their families beginning in 1867. It is identical in most every way to a local Kroger, Safeway or A & P store. It provides a place for authorized patrons to purchase goods at a price with a 5% markup for overhead. This is possible because a large part of the amortized expense of a grocery chain such as real estate acquisition, building construction and other expense such police and fire protection come with the Post. Commissaries are now under the control of DoD and the sub-agency, DeCA, or Defense Commissary Agency with some 264 stores worldwide.

Commo: The word commo is Army shorthand for communications. It can be used to describe the means for communication, describe the process of it or delineate the MOS of one responsible for the repair and service of equipment associated with the process such as, "commo puke". When it works it is wonderful and when it fails only those who outrank the one on the other end can use it for an excuse for failure. High ranking folk never have a "commo" failure and if they do, it is never their fault.

Contractor: Highly skilled and high ranking Soldiers are in great demand by defense contractors. They are well versed in their respective combat systems, speak the argot, have contacts, do not need health insurance, generally speak at least one foreign language and are highly motivated.

Control Measure: A provision in an order from a higher authority to a subordinate element that requires an action, a report, or a request to proceed by the subordinate such as a phase line of advance, is a control measure. A lack of stated control measures often results in an excess of initiative and enthusiasm in youthful and exuberant subordinates. Requiring a child to call home when school event has ended and to wait outside to be picked up by a parent is a control measure.

Coyote: A euphemism for a single, mature woman who for reasons best known to her, cohabits with a Sergeants Major Academy student living in bachelor quarters at Fort Bliss, Texas.

CSM: Command Sergeant Major. The highest enlisted rank for the Army except for the office of Sergeant Major of the Army. Approximately 2,000 CSM were authorized for the entire army of some 670,000 assigned soldiers. The CSM serves as the enlisted advisor and bellwether at every level from Battalion to Department of the Army. The CSM is the primary conduit for information from the Commanding Officer to the NCO support channel. The goal is for the CSM to be the most tactically and technically proficient NCO in the unit.

Cut Out: In the dope arena, the term used is by inference a chain cut out where the agent is only aware of only the person providing the information and the person receiving it. This arrangement increases security and maintains everyone's anonymity.

CV Boot: The CV boot is a rubber cover over the transaxle of a vehicle. If the boot is torn, missing or worn, dirt and foreign material ruins the ability of the transaxle to transfer power, thus disabling the vehicle. No transaxle ever failed an Army vehicle at a convenient moment.

CVC: This is acronym for Combat Vehicle Crewman Helmet. Consisting of a cloth liner under a hard shell of plastic, it contained two ear phones, a microphone and a connecting cord to tank's communication system.

DA: The Department of the Army. The senior service followed by the Navy, the Marines and the Air Force. DA is to be found in the Pentagon as well as in buildings in and about Washington, D.C.

Demerit: A written annotation used to denote a shortcoming in the performance of a trainee, candidate or cadet. At some academies, acquiring too many demerits was cause for dismissal.

DEROS: An acronym describing the date of earliest return from overseas for an individual assigned on permanent change of station orders to a locale outside of the Continental United States (CONUS).

DF2: Diesel Fuel grade 2, the fuel of the eighties for diesel powered vehicles of the Army.

DOL: The acronym for the Directorate of Logistics. The DOL is an entity of the Garrison Staff of an Installation charged to deliver logistics in form of goods and service to sustain and maintain the force. It provides parts, transport, buses, mechanics, moves household goods and coordinates unit movement. A workforce of 375 with a $200 million dollar budget is not unusual for a DOL although the size is dictated by the mission.

DRAGON: A wire guided missile with more faults than virtues as it required a level of proficiency unobtainable through practice or training for the average soldier. Fired in the open, inside the range band of the Soviet systems, the operator remained exposed during the flight of the missile. A good Dragon gunner was a treasure because they were rare.

Duece and a Half: The nickname for an Army truck rated at two and one half tons carry capacity is deuce and a half.

DWI: The classification of a driver operating a vehicle while impaired usually due to alcohol. It was the kiss of death to many a promising career for all ranks of service.

Eastie: Eastie was an obscure and seldom used nick name for an East German.

Earth Pig: The sarcastic nick name for Infantrymen awarded by non-Infantrymen, most of whom had never carried an 85 pound load on their back.

Echelons of Army Maintenance: *Operator:* Tasks performed by the assigned crew using assigned tools as prescribed by the vehicle technical manual. *Organization:* Maintenance performed by Company, Battery, or Troop level units under the direction of the Executive Officer. *Direct Support:* Team from Regiment is assigned to each squadron. *General Support:* Provided Regiment by Corps. *Depot:* Items deemed non-repairable by Direct Support/General Support that are sent to a Depot.

EER: The term EER is an acronym for an Enlisted Efficiency Report. The centralized promotion board system for Sergeant First Class raised the writing of the EER to an art form. Platitudes were not enough and some form of qualifying metric to meet a standard had to part of the narrative. EERs were almost always late. A late Officer Efficiency Report in the Cav was as rare as a crap shooting Chaplain.

EIB: The Expert Infantryman's Badge is awarded to Infantrymen who meet stringent prerequisites, are recommended by their leadership and who pass a grueling test regimen administered by a board from their Battalion. It is a mark of distinction to win this badge. It is not worn once the Combat Infantryman's Badge is won.

Eleven B (11B): The numerical designation of the Military Occupation Specialty for an Infantryman.

ETS: ETS is defined as the date one's term of service in the military ends, ergo the shorthand term ETS.

E-Type Target Silhouette: A paper or plastic target used to simulate the head and generic torso of a human being and used for target practice for pistols, rifles, sub-machine guns, and machineguns by the Army. Also used by creative soldiers to serve as a left and right unit limit marker by erecting one on flank elements. The target was then marked with a distinct brand using thermal tape which produced a heat signature when plugged into the auxiliary power outlet of the marked vehicle. It thus showed all with thermal sights and night vision goggles

487

where the unit was at a given moment. It was most useful when operating with helos armed with Hellfire Missiles.

FEBA: Forward Edge of the Battle Area. It is a place where reputations are made in peace time and people get killed in time of war.

Foosballer: This is the German term for a soccer player.

FTX: This is the acronym for Field Training Exercise and can and is used to describe events employing units sized from platoon to Division.

Fulda: Fulda is the name of a city located in the state of Hesse on the Fulda River. It lends its name to a traditional invasion route, the Fulda Gap, used by Napoleon and others. The Soviet Union stationed large forces near this gap to due to their perception of potential danger. It is the largest city closest to this historical terrain and was within 30 miles of the demarcation line between the Russian and American Armies in 1945. It was home to the headquarters of both the 14th and the 11th Cavalry who served as the covering force for V Corps of the American Army.

GAK: The acronym for an **East German** Grenzaufklärungszug **(GAK)** was GAK. GAKS were the elite version of the East German Border force. More highly trained and trusted than the conscripts, GAKs patrolled outside the fence on the narrow strip of land between it and the West German Border. Family members of the GAKs were often held hostage to ensure they did not defect.

Gasthaus: An establishment that served alcohol and most of the time, a full bill of fare of food, in Germany.

General Officer Preparatory Unit (GOPU): This course was given to General Officers slated for command of the Heavy Divisions. They were brought up to date on each type of equipment in their respective formations even if they had three different tank types. No effort was spared to put on this course.

GDP: The General Defense Plan for a maneuver unit was an extremely detailed document. While plans never survive contact intact, the GDP still served many good and cogent purposes. The least of these purposes was awareness and the greatest was focus. No document is of any use to those whose lips move when they read it.

General Support & Direct Support: Army maintenance was organized into categories/levels that emanated from each echelon. In the case of the Corps Cavalry, Regiment provided Direct Support to Squadrons while Corps provided General Support to the Regiment.

GS: GS is the shorthand for Government Service employee. Soldiers can be hired under the provisions for veteran's preference. They can in many instances begin work immediately as civilian employees if their skill and knowledge is critical. They are often the most valuable of employees as they are highly skilled, motivated and speak the argot of the military. They are well accepted by the Soldiers if they leave their rank behind when they get out and concentrate on their mission, not their ego.

Handicap Black Message: This term described a message format from higher headquarters was designed to test the ability of Border units to react to situations in a format of see, report, analyze, and act. Designed to be executed at the lowest level, it was a good test of the training, élan and esprit de corps of the Border Cavalry units. Good units did not fail it and bad ones could not pass it.

Headspace and Timing Gauge: The headspace and timing gauge is a metal instrument of two pieces connected by a lightweight chain. It is used in a sixteen step procedure to set up the M2 Heavy Barrel Browning Machinegun for firing. The basis of issue is one per machinegun. It is a vital piece of equipment for a machine gunner as the gun will not work without being correctly adjusted. While it is true field expedients can be used, the device is the best method.

HEP: The acronym for a round of ammunition name High Explosive Plastic was HEP. Service HEP was a dangerous round to use as it could become unstable over time and function in the gun tube before traveling the full distance to the mouth of the cannon. The round hit its target and the plastic explosive squashed against and blew thus causing metal of the turret wall to come apart in small pieces termed spalling and fatally wound the enemy. It was also used against bunkers. At longer ranges, the high parabola of the flight of the round all but guaranteed a hit on the most vulnerable part of any armored vehicle, the top.

HET: A HET is a Heavy Equipment Transporter capable of moving a tank over improved roads at a high rate of speed far cheaper and faster than it can be driven on its tracks. Anyone who wants to also say it is safer has obviously never traveled on the same road as Egyptian HET Drivers.

Inspector General Inspection (IG): The Inspector General Inspection in the era between 1948-1972 was conducted by personnel assigned to the IG Office. It often was a white glove affair with reality coming in a distant last place to functionality. Though farcical at times, it carried a very real threat for those who failed it. It was the baseline to grade performance without a war. After 1972, the IG was deemed assistance to the commander with inspections focusing on function rather than form. As the Brigade Commander was the Chief Inspector, he got a firsthand look at the abilities, or lack of them, of each Captain and First Sergeant under his command.

ITV: ITV is the acronym for the Improved Tow Vehicle. The addition of two TOW firing points on a raised launcher placed on a modified M-113 enabled the Army to mount a new weapons system, the TOW, on a tried and true chassis to give a robust anti-tank weapon to the Infantry and Scouts thus making it into the M-901-ITV. The capacity of the vehicle to carry ten additional missiles was well received by the soldiers facing the Russian hordes.

Kaserne: The German word for Army cantonment areas is kaserne. Years of living in Germany resulted in a mixed patois for the veteran soldiers where German and English were used interchangeably without conscious thought.

Kilometer: A kilometer is a unit of distance measurement of the metric system. It consists of 1,000 meters each 39 inches long. It also defines the size of a military map square also referred to as a "click". A distance of 10 kilometers would be said to be "ten clicks to the east." To find the estimated conversion of a metric number to the English derived American system multiply by .6, e.g.: 80 kilometers per hour is equal to 48 miles per hour.

Kilometer Zones: Borders are traditionally the flashpoints for wars. To preclude surprise, the erstwhile allies, the Russians negotiated with the forces that would become the North Atlantic Treaty Organization (NATO) to establish limits of advance of forces. These were further defined as one kilometer and ten kilometers in horizontal distance from the border. Sign posts in German and English warned visitors not to approach these zones. Border forces on both sides existed to watch the military forces on the other side and to prevent the unaware, the unlettered, or the unprincipled members of their respective societies from provoking an incident to cause a war. The border is a hunting ground for spies and provocateurs. The difficulty of separating the sheep and the goats from the wolves was simplified for the Border Cavalry. They simply detained everyone found in the wrong zone and let the Border Resident Office sort it out.

Kurheim: A German Hotel catering to vacationers granted paid leave from the stress of their work place by their employer with travel, lodging and a meal allowance as part of their due from a grateful government. It was also a term for a hotel or spa with curative mineral water, massage, mud baths and other esoteric cures available. Also referred to as a Kurheim District as many of the establishments were grouped together to use the same group of mineral springs. Kurheimers were an amusing lot as they formed partnerships with the opposite sex as they were there without their partner. Promptly at the witching hour of 930 pm they departed the local bar to make bed check at their lodgings.

Laser: An acronym depicting a device employing a Light Amplification Source of Emitted Radiation. Lasers are used to determine range, designate targets and in experiments to destroy targets, as an offensive weapons system.

Lay, Dump, Laze, and Blaze: This was the mantra for the M1 tank gunner. To kill a target the crew must LAY the gun tube on it, as the turret moves, sensors generate input to the sight automatically, if this input is not helpful, the gunner DUMPS it, he then presses a thumb button to fire his laser hence LAZE, in a millionth of a second the range to target shows up, if it is cogent, it is time to BLAZE and after announcing "On the Way" the gun is fired. If the crew misses a step in this intricate Kabuki Dance, their shit could be flaky against a worthwhile opponent. This little ditty was useful as a memory jogger.

Leatherman: A multifaceted tool carried by soldiers in a leather case on their belt underneath their BDUs or on their CTA-50 web harness.

Levy (ies): A requirement to furnish resources to a higher authority based on military or political authority by the command or order.

LLMF: Soldier slang for those who cannot find their way either in land navigation or in the problem solving process and is an acronym for Lost Like a Mother F__ker. Mother Nature makes it happen but character provides the ability to recovery, if there is any to draw from.

Local Training Area (LTA): An area of land set aside for the training of forces in squad and platoon maneuver techniques as well as the Tank and Bradley Crew Practice Course. It was also the area where the unit dispersed as part of its alert

LSD: LSD (lysergic acid diethylamide) is one of the major drugs making up the hallucinogen class. LSD was discovered in 1938 and is one of the most potent mood-changing chemicals. It is manufactured from lysergic acid, which is found in ergot, a fungus that grows on rye and other grains. LSD, commonly referred to as "acid," is sold on the street in tablets, capsules, and, occasionally, liquid form. It is odorless, colorless, and has a slightly bitter taste and is usually taken by mouth. Often LSD is added to absorbent paper, such as blotter paper, and divided into small decorated squares, with each square representing one dose. (Placed in the coffee urn at a Cavalry Border Camp, 60 plus doses of LSD would have produced a disaster.)

LFX: This is the acronym for a Live Fire Exercise. It is a universal term and when amended, described the size of the unit engaged. An example of this would be, Troop CALFEX or a Combined Arms Live Fire Exercise. This event places a number of combat multiplying weapons at the disposal of a commander. These multipliers for Troop Sized Events include A-10's, Cobra Attack Helicopters and a Battery of 155 Howitzers. When these fired in support of, and in concert with, the organic weapons of the Troop with 9 tank cannon tubes and 12 Cavalry fighting vehicles firing TOW Missiles and 25 mm Cannon, it was a concert dedicated to the War God Mars of the first order.

M-3 Bradley: The **M3 Bradley Cavalry Fighting Vehicle (CFV)** is a tracked armored reconnaissance vehicle manufactured by BAE Landsystem. The M3 CFV is used by heavy armored cavalry units. In the Persian Gulf War of 1991, the Bradley and the powerful 25mm cannon / TOW anti-tank missile combination accounted for more enemy tanks destroyed than that of the M1 Abrams. The rear of a Bradley and a NATO # 59 target are strikingly similar when viewed through a tank thermal sight at ranges over 800 meters. Scouts deploy in front of tanks and the US Army trains as it fights.

M-88: The model number of the largest tank recovery vehicle in the Army inventory is M-88. It is a radio equipped tracked vehicle capable of: Recovery of mired vehicles; Towing; fueling and de-fueling; lifting and replacement of engines; hosting hydraulic tools; and being a personnel carrier for a crew of mechanics. It mounted a .50 caliber machinegun for air defense and to destroy enemy equipment to include their web gear.

M-113: The model number of the largest production run of a personnel carrier since WW II was the M-113. It served as a personnel carrier, mini-command post, mortar carrier and scout vehicle as well as a TOW weapons carrier in the Cavalry. It was amphibious by design though it sank like a rock unless perfectly prepared and checked. It was a dependable, spacious, noisy, uncomfortable but lovable piece of gear. All variants in the Cavalry mounted a .50 machine gun.

M-577: The model number of the command post variant of the M-113 was the M-577. The modification allowed soldiers to stand upright inside the vehicle to work the maps and radios. There was also a canvas tent attached enabling the work area of the command post to be expanded to dimensions of a nearly ten feet wide and twenty foot long. The M-577 was included in the thermal training to ensure the tankers knew what it looked like in their sights at night.

Meinegen Gap: The Meinegen Gap was the smaller and the most southern invasion route running east and west within the 11th ACR covering force area.

Mad Minute: The Mad Minute in Vietnam was one in which the Armored Cavalry fired into the jungle or around its position with all weapons for one minute. In the peacetime Army serving in Germany, the exercise was useful to demonstrate to new Soldiers the relative power of the Cavalry Troop. It did not endear the US Army to its neighbors living near Wildflicken.

Marder: The Marder serves the German Army as an Armored Personnel Carrier. It is armed with a 20mm cannon, a 7.62 machinegun, can be outfitted with the Roland AntiTank Missile, and carries a crew of 3 with 7 passengers (who if they are not good friends will be after ten days together).

MILES: This acronym describes the Multiple Integrated Laser Engagement System. It is most easily explained as laser tag, or combat simulation without blood and death. Sensors on vehicles are affixed and connected to a yellow flashing light. When the vehicle is struck with a well aimed shot from a weapons system capable of killing it, the light illuminates and remains lit until an Umpire (later known as an Observer Controller), a game official, re-sets it. The individual soldier wears MILES gear on the torso and helmet that reacts to effective fire with an incessant tone when a killing or crippling shot is achieved. Casualties, vehicle or human, are assessed as killed, wounded or damaged. Each must be evacuated and the logistic system must engage to replace them. If the support system above his level of command is faulty due to sloth, stupidity or stock control, the commander must then continue his operations without the missing pieces. The Umpire has a device with which he can cause casualties pointing it and pulling the trigger. It is universally known as the "God Gun". Equipment can be re-set with a device known as the "green key. MILES exists to teach soldiers "If you can be seen you can be hit and if you can be hit you can be killed."

MG: This is an acronym depicting the Additional Skill Identifier for a Master Gunner. The MG designator reflected the skills and knowledge of an NCO selected by his unit who graduated from a 26 week long course at either Fort Knox for M-1 tanks or Fort Benning for M-3 Bradley. A grueling course, with a normal wash out rate of 50%, from which the survivors were recognized experts in all phases and requirements of Abrams and Bradley gunnery. One tank MG was authorized for each level of command and one Bradley MG was authorized for each platoon. It was/is a Darwinian affair where the elders ate the young who did not thrive.

Nam: The diminutive for the Republic of South Vietnam used as shorthand by soldiers.

National Guard Blues: National Guard blues is the derisive nickname for the Army Green Uniform when worn with a white shirt and a four in hand tie. Those who bought their own formal uniform of Dress Blues held those who did not own them either too cheap or too improvident to be an NCO.

NBC: An acronym meaning Nuclear, Biological, Radiological, and used to described or define attacks, activity, training, munitions, places, people and things associated with any of the words stated. Soldiers knew and always will know the utter desolation, horror and hopelessness that accompany the use of weapons of mass destruction. Soldiers serving where there will be little or no warning, hate WMD worse than any segment of society.

NCO: The term is shorthand for the term Non-Commissioned Officer. NCOs serve from the rank of Corporal thru Sergeant Major of the Army. Their primary task is to train, maintain, lead and sustain their units in peace and war.

NCO Club: A self supporting entity created to give Noncommissioned officers in the grade of Corporal through CSM a place for recreation and relaxation. The Clubs served alcohol, many had restaurants, and nearly all booked shows and bands and the bar had a large TV tuned the one station available, Armed Forces Television Network.

NET Team: An acronym for a New Equipment Training Team assembled by DA to meet the training requirements for the issue and equipping of units with the latest acquisitions by the service. NET Teams provide the first exposure and technical training for units to provide them with a baseline of knowledge. After NET is complete, the unit returns to home station or to field training sites to come to grips with the changes in techniques, tactics and procedures engendered by the new gear. Clever Commanders realize NET is a beginning and not an end. It is amusing to see the PhDs who invented the system look on in awe as the soldier makes it do something they never thought it would do. At some point many of the inventors realize it is not a contract for the GI, it is his ass on the line.

Nineteen Echo (19E): The numerical designation for the Military Occupational Specialty of an M60A1 or A3 armor crewman. (Known to Scouts & Infantry as a DAT, Dumb Ass Tanker)

Nineteen Kilo (19K): The numerical designation for the Military Occupational Specialty of M1 armor crewman. (Known to all as an EDAT, Electronic Dumb Ass Tanker)

492

Non-Resident Course for the Sergeants Major Academy (USASMA) : This course enabled Master Sergeants, Sergeants Major and Command Sergeants Major to attend the Sergeants Major Academy by correspondence course. 80% who began, failed it. Tests were multiple choice but retests were essay. Required monographs with recordings and graphics were graded by field grade officers. A finishing school held at Fort Bliss in June of each year ensured students were slim, trim fighting machines able to walk, talk and interact. Standards were strictly enforced.

NTC: At once: a location, a training event, a crucible, a desert, a proving ground for weapons, concepts and doctrine, a birthplace and a cemetery for careers, reputations and ambitions for Soldiers. The vision for the NTC is to: Provide tough, realistic joint and combined arms training; Focus at the battalion task force and brigade levels; Assist commanders in developing trained, competent leaders and soldiers; Identify unit training deficiencies, provide feedback to improve the force and prepare for success on the future joint battlefield; provide a venue for transformation. Once soldiers understand they are not there to win but to learn, they start to learn. Sometimes they even win a few battles. The NTC changes the behavior of soldiers so that lessons are truly learned. It is the only institution of its kind in the world today. It ensures the continued winning streak of the Army and keeps the volunteer Army in being and the draft a bad memory.

OCS: This is an acronym for Officer Candidate School. OCS provides a method for advancement for Soldiers from the ranks to become officers through training and winnowing processes while being held to a very high standard. It is a voluntary school and the source of some of the Army's most dedicated and decorated officers.

OP: The letters OP are used as Army shorthand to describe an observation post. An OP can be as small as one soldier placed in a location so that he can see, report and warn the main body of the approach of an enemy force. OPs along the East West German Border were quite comfortable facilities with large windows, fixed radio antennae, heaters, indoor plumbing and permanent telephone connections. They were a squad function and commanded by an Sergeant First Class or Staff Sergeant.

OPFOR: The term OPFOR is an acronym for Opposing Forces. The ideal manner to train soldiers is by using one force to either attack or assume the defense against a like sized force. Ideally, the OPFOR is composed of a force selected for their ability to fight and win consistently against heavy odds. The force is coached by the Commander to press the weakness of the organization being trained be it planning, organization, training or motivation, or all four. For a lesson to be learned it must change the behavior of the student. Pain teaches change as an alternative. The OPFOR hurts the unit's pride and instills determination. No soldier likes to play on the losing side.

OVM: The acronym OVM stands for On Vehicle Maintained and refers to equipment required in event of a breakdown or an emergency. It normally is considered to be: shovel; pick axe; warning triangle; first aid kit; jack; wheel nut wrench; operator's manual and other specified equipment. Ideally, it is always located on every vehicle. In ALO 1 units it is a truism but in ALO 3 units it is almost never so.

Parallel Bore Sight: An arcane technique used to align the sights of the M60A1 tank at the engineering offset distance they are placed from it. The further the distance to the target, the more accurate the fire of the tank becomes. The procedure allows M60A1 tankers to hit targets at 4,800 meters with 90% accuracy. Given a parallel bore sight target and a muzzle bore sight device, the process takes five minutes and can be performed on board ship or in a C5A on the way to war. Of course, test firing on board the C5A is not recommended.

PCC: The prospective commander's course was an update on tactics, techniques, equipment and procedures. It was conducted as required for one week periods by the three departments of the Armor Center, the purpose was to bring prospective Battalion and Brigade Commanders up to date on tactics, techniques and procedures for the weapons systems assigned to their units. The course was closely tailored to their wishes and requirements. It included both day and night range firing.

PCI: The acronym PCI describes the activity known as the Pre-Combat Inspection. It is cursory inspection of a unit prior to combat. The PCI uncovers deficiencies and reinforces orders.

Personnel Service Detachment (PSD): A group of Soldiers on detached service from a parent Personnel Services Battalion (PSB) commanded by a Captain located near combat units also detached from their parent unit by distance by virtue of their mission. The PSD provided all of the necessary service and support for personnel actions and was supposed to be a working partner for the units.

PH: PH is shorthand for Probability of Hit meaning the likelihood a round of ammunition will strike a target as expressed in percentage form from 01% to 100%.

PK: The logical extension of geek speak after PH is PK or the Probability of Kill as an expression of the chances a given round of ammunition will kill a given target as expressed in percentage form from 01% to 100%. (Note: Soldiers have to love geeks after the technological leaps made by the US Army and they do.)

Polish Labor Battalion: There were a number of Labor and Service Battalions still giving valuable service to the US Army in the 1980's. They were composed of Displaced Persons, many of whom were Polish nationals who were impressed as slave labor by the Nazis. These men wore fatigue uniforms, lived in barracks, and had separate canteens or clubs. They could, and did, work rings around anyone in the theater as guards, engineers and truck drivers. After surviving the Nazis, most obstacles were very minor to them. Many dreamed of a return to their native land but few never saw it again. Most of them lived out their remaining lives in Germany.

Pomme Fritz: The German term for French Fries was Pomme Fritz.

POV: The acronym for Privately Owned Vehicle.

Promotion Board: Army promotion boards in units are run by the CSM with authority delegated by the Battalion level commander. These boards convene monthly and serve to officially qualify soldiers in the rank of Specialist to Sergeant and Sergeants for Staff Sergeant (SSG). Soldiers are presented by their first line leader. Graded individually on appearance, élan, knowledge, bearing and potential, most are recommended for promotion and placed on an order of merit list based on points earned. Some Battalion commanders believe the standards of the CSM and 1SGs are too high and the conduct of the boards is too harsh.

PSNCO: A Personnel Services NCO, usually a Sergeant First Class in charge of the staff section S-1, the Army version of a Human Resources office at the local level.

494

PT Test: The US Army conducts a physical fitness test to assess the individual readiness of Soldiers for war. The test is conducted a minimum of twice per year in the units of the Army. The standing achieved by Soldiers on this test is used to measure them against the demands of combat. Various schools and branches of the Army conduct special physical testing due to the demands of their mission.

Push: Radio communication shorthand for "I am calling you on your primary assigned frequency" usually from a subordinate done deliberately to preclude misunderstanding. Used when sphincters are tight and lips should match. It is most helpful when there are several radios and auxiliary receivers blaring simultaneously in the vehicle.

PYE /WATSON device: The British firm Pye-Watson was the manufacturer of the Muzzle Bore sight Device (MBD) used in the 1980's. They are optical telescope-like devices that fit into the muzzle of a tank main gun. This allows the crew to align the tank's sights to the true center of the gun, normally at 1200 meters.

Quartering Party: A body of Soldiers made up from within a unit by selecting one trooper from each element of a unit conducting a movement to act as guides is known as the Quartering Party. The quartering party moves to the area where the unit will halt and prepare for future operations, known as an assembly area. The guides then select positions for the vehicles and activities of their element and proceed to guide them into position when they arrive from the march.

Rad: The diminutive for the German term for friend, Kamerade. Other words were often added satirically such as Ricky Rad. It was also used as sarcasm to poke fun at a newcomer to describe how much time before he could, or would, return to America such as - "Kamerade will rotate before you do."

Real World: The phrase "real world" defines the situation when a casual or an uninformed observer could not be expected to discern the difference between soldiers engaged in exercises with blanks fired and dead careers versus live rounds and dead soldiers on both sides.

REFORGER: This acronym is defined by the words Return of Forces to Germany. It represents an exercise of forces from the US that saw movements of entire divisions via an air bridge to Europe. Forces were bused to large and cloistered parking areas where they drew vehicles held in readiness for massive mobilization to fight WW III in Europe. A large maneuver of up to Corps sized elements was then conducted for 7-10 days which ranged across many miles of German terrain. While any Major who was a graduate of the Staff College could tell you the plan was fraught with dangers and a political deal, no one had a better one that pleased the civilian masters of the Defense Department.

R & R Area: Rest and Recreation locale for the restoration of commands and individual soldiers to rest and refit from war exigencies.

Scheduling Board: A Scheduling board was an arcane means of charting the events for a two year period. A plexiglass covered chart containing the events known to be scheduled were listed in a column on the left side of the chart. Known holidays and events directed by higher headquarters were the first entries on the chart. The weeks of the year were plotted across its top. The week the event was to take place was then indicated opposite the event. Thus, all known events or requirements were plotted in the year month and week they were planned to occur. This listing informed Soldiers, staff and family members and pointed out conflicts to those charged to plan future operations. By listing all events, conflict was easily seen and alternative solutions devised well in advance. Wheels on the bottom of the frame gave it mobility. Wives loved it, Soldiers used it and poor planners hated it.

SDAD: This is an acronym for Surface Danger Area Diagram. This is a drawing that depicts the area of a firing range layout. It prescribes firing points, direction of fire, left and right limits of fire as well as potential target locations. Each weapon has two known distances, maximum effective range and maximum range. Effective range is analogous to the second baseman throwing a runner out at home plate while maximum range is comparable to a contest in which the contestants throw a baseball as far as possible. The SDAD accounts for both and ensures the impact area of the training area or other features such as backstops, much like those at a baseball stadium built for foul tips and passed balls, contain the fired rounds.

SF: SF is Army shorthand for Special Forces, the wearers of the Green Beret of story and song whose difficult selection and training processes are but minor harbingers of the hardships the graduates will face worldwide. SF exists to operate on the dark side of military operations by teaching and training indigenous folks to fight their own battles against oppressors. They are among the most well prepared and thoroughly schooled soldiers in the world.

Shatzi: The term shatzi is a word from German patois meaning loved one, baby or lover.

SMA: Acronym for the Sergeant Major of the Army. This position supports the tradition that every commander above Battalion level has a CSM. It gives the enlisted force a voice at the last level of the chain of command. The incumbent wears two stars inside a field of six stripes. The SMA travels the world for his term. The SMA epitomizes the beau ideal for enlisted Soldiers.

Spot Report: A spot report is a message sent by a Soldier to his higher headquarters listing information using the five w's: <u>Who</u> is calling, <u>What</u> is being reported, <u>Where</u> is it, <u>What time</u> did it happen, <u>What were they doing, What are you doing</u> about it.

Spring Butt: A term applied to a student fond of asking self-serving questions, usually to serve an unhealthy ego.

SS: The Waffen SS was an armed force of the Third Reich. It constituted the armed wing of the Schutzstaffel or Protective Squadron and was an organ of the Nazi party. Its primary loyalty was to the Party and to Adolph Hitler. After the war the SS was condemned as a criminal organization because of its connection to Nazi Party and its involvement in War Crimes.

Staff Duty: NCOs in the grade of Sergeant First Class & Staff Sergeant were selected for duty by roster to serve as the Staff Duty NCO/Officer of Regiments Brigades, Battalions and Squadrons. In most units circa 1980's, the staff duty officer remained in his quarters on call leaving the NCO in practical command. Each headquarters published a list of things, places and items to be supervised and checked during a given tour of duty that began at 1600 hours or 4 pm on weekdays and ended at 0600 when the headquarters staff appeared.

Schwimmbad: An indoor swimming pool complete with spa, tanning rooms, a surf machine, a coed sauna, weight room, locker room with showers, sinks and commodes, canteen and gift shop found in most cities in West Germany above 25,000 in population. The locals could always pick out the American GI's in the coed sauna as they were the only men with erections.

T-34, T-55, T-62,T-64,T-72,T-80: These are model numbers assigned to Russian tanks by the Intelligence community and generally reflect the either the year of design or the first occasion they were seen, or photographed, or both, in the west. US Forces, memorized the characteristics and data associated with each model with paying particular attention to the effective range and rate of fire of their respective main gun weapons.

TA-50: The term TA-50 is Army shorthand for the Common Table of Allowances CTA-50-901 that prescribes, the issue quantity, items, serviceability criteria and manner of wear of the field gear used by a soldier.

TOW Missile: The term refers to a tubular fired missile as it was Tracked Optically and Wire guided. It had a minimum arming range and a maximum range or 3,000 meters with a very high probability of hit and of kill upon hitting the target

TCGST: This is the acronym for the Tank Crew gunnery Skills Test. The TCGST is a vehicle specific, comprehensive examination by crew position for each of the crewman on a tank. Leaders must be able to do all of the tasks on the tank. Tasks are graded and failures re-tested. Good units conducting thorough TCGSTs prosper.

Training Device: A piece of equipment designed to replicate conditions most often of weapons firing or its effect. Devices range from the laser dot to .50 caliber rounds for replicated tank firing. This equipment enables units to use their local training area, small ranges on their kaserne or post thus conserving resources such as fuel, ammunition and travel. New devices use shelters and computer simulation to replicate tank crew stations and can train maneuver forces up to Brigade size for command post exercises.

TO& E: This acronym refers to the table of organization and equipment published by the Department of the Army at direction of Congress under title 18, USC that prescribes the mission, organization, manning and equipment of the Army units slated to go in harm's way.
Top Off: The term top off is used to describe the act of completely filling a fuel tank. The Army baseline for fuel re-supply is predicated on the assumption all vehicle fuel tanks are as full as possible when at rest. Running a combat vehicle out of fuel by not topping it off at every opportunity is a deadly sin.
TRP: A Target Reference Point or TRP is an easily recognizable point on the ground either natural or manmade used to initiate, distribute and control fires.

TT V,VI,VII,VIII, IX, X : Tank firing tables are written standards established to provide a training progression from the most simple tasks to most complex required to develop crews and platoons to be able to close with and destroy the enemy. Each table prescribed tasks, allocated ammunition, and with specified and implied support requirements for execution.

Thermal Sight or Thermal: The thermal sighting systems of the Abrams work on the principal of a refrigeration unit cooling the vehicle sight surface to a temperature so cold as to require measurement by the Kelvin Scale. The contrast between the receiver on the sight and the temperature of the object being viewed is then converted to a visual picture by a cathode ray tube. The operator selects either a black hot or white hot display mode.

USARUER: The United States Army Europe was part of the NATO force in that its Seventh Army was a maneuver force for that entity. Headquartered in Heidelberg, West Germany, USARUR was commanded by a General responsible for the myriad of Army units, installations and support systems of the command.

USARUER Driver's License: As part of the Status of Forces Treaty with West Germany, the United States operated a driver's licensing program through the local Military Police at each Installation large enough to have an MP contingent. The test was notoriously difficult. The rules of the road, right of way and a bewildering set of International road signs all combined to be the nemesis of the unwary and unprepared.

UCOFT: The unit Conduct of Fire Trainer was built for the armor force to replicate the crew duties of the turret crew of an M1 tank. The device has an instructor station which replaces the Command and Control element of the Commander. A cartoon like picture of terrain presents a field of view to the tank commander and gunner. Scripted exercises performed against the pressure of elapsed time develop the skills of the crew far cheaper than moving and firing a tank. It is utilized 24X7X360 save for Christmas, New Years, Thanksgiving, 4th of July and unit organization day. To make unit commanders use the device, the Generals simply reduced the number of main gun rounds issued to crews for "real firing". It was either use the UCOFT or fail tank gunnery. In a short time, simulation gained a large following among the knuckle draggers though few learned to love it.

Urinalysis Testing: The process of gaining urine samples for testing while eliminating clerical error to detect the use of illegal drugs by Soldiers in the command. The process was conducted by three general methods: 100 % of a unit, designated selection by the Commander, and random selection by Social Security Number series. Soldiers in the rank of Specialist and below were offered treatment and rehabilitation while NCOs and Officers were discharged.

V Corps: One of two main maneuver headquarters composing Seventh Army which was under the overall command the United States Army Europe and NATO. Corps of the era were organized for maneuver with an Armored Cavalry Regiment, an Armored Division, and an Infantry Division stationed in the Corps area with other Divisions slated to augment them from the United States in time an all out European war. Commanded by a Lieutenant General and Headquartered in the IG Farben building in Frankfurt, West Germany, V Corps was in direct command of the 11th Armored Cavalry Regiment.

VHS: A VHS was a video recording and playback system filmed with a TV Camera and replayed in a device termed a video component recorder which in turn played a visual and audio recording on a television set. It was the precursor to the present DVD system. In the 1980's it was the latest technology available.

Volksmarch: The literal translation of the term is peoples' walk. Large numbers of people, some of whom belong to Volksmarching Clubs, converge on a city or locale and walk over a prescribed course of various lengths varying from 10 to 50 kilometers on a given day. A prize, usually a pin commemorating the event is given to each person completing the course after payment of a small entry fee. The routes wend their way through kiosks with all sorts of beverages and snacks.